EDGAR RICE BURROUGHS
Science Fiction Classics

EDGAR RICE BURROUGHS

Science Fiction
Classics

Pellucidar
Thuvia—Maid of Mars
Tanar of Pellucidar
The Chessmen of Mars
The Master Mind of Mars

CASTLE

TABLE OF CONTENTS

PELLUCIDAR

PROLOG

Several years had elapsed since I had found the opportunity to do any big-game hunting; but at last I had my plans almost perfected for a return to my old stamping-grounds in northern Africa, where in other days I had had excellent sport in pursuit of the king of beasts.

The date of my departure had been set; I was to leave in two weeks. No schoolboy counting the lagging hours that must pass before the beginning of "long vacation" released him to the delirious joys of the summer camp could have been filled with greater impatience or keener anticipation.

And then came a letter that started me for Africa twelve days ahead of my schedule.

Often am I in receipt of letters from strangers who have found something in a story of mine to commend or to condemn. My interest in this department of my correspondence is ever fresh. I opened this particular letter with all the zest of pleasurable anticipation with which I had opened so many others. The post-mark (Algiers) had aroused my interest and curiosity, especially at this time, since it was Algiers that was presently to witness the termination of my coming sea voyage in search of sport and adventure.

Before the reading of that letter was completed lions and lion-hunting had fled my thoughts, and I was in a state of excitement bordering upon frenzy.

It — well, read it yourself, and see if you, too, do not find food for frantic conjecture, for tantalizing doubts, and for a great hope.

Here it is:

DEAR SIR: I think that I have run across one of the most remarkable coincidences in modern literature. But let me start at the beginning:

I am, by profession, a wanderer upon the face of the earth. I have no trade — nor any other occupation.

My father bequeathed me a competency; some remoter ancestor — a lust to roam. I have combined the two and invested them carefully and without extravagance.

I became interested in your story, *At the Earth's Core*, not so much because of the probability of the tale as of a great and abiding wonder that people should be paid real money for writing such impossible trash. You will pardon my candor, but it is necessary that you understand my mental attitude toward this particular story — that you may credit that which follows.

Shortly thereafter I started for the Sahara in search of a rather rare species of antelope that is to be found only occasionally within a limited area at a certain season of the year. My chase led me far from the haunts of civilized man.

It was a fruitless search, however, in so far as antelope is concerned; but one night as I lay courting sleep at the edge of a little cluster of date-palms that surround an ancient well in the midst of the arid, shifting sands, I suddenly became conscious of a strange sound coming apparently from the earth beneath my head.

It was an intermittent ticking!

No reptile or insect with which I am familiar reproduces any such notes. I lay for an hour — listening intently.

At last my curiosity got the better of me. I arose, lighted my lamp and commenced to investigate.

My bedding lay upon a rug stretched directly upon the warm sand. The noise appeared to be coming from beneath the rug. I raised it, but found nothing — yet, at intervals, the sound continued.

I dug into the sand with the point of my hunting-knife. A few inches below the surface of the sand I encountered a solid substance that had the feel of wood beneath the sharp steel.

Excavating about it, I unearthed a small wooden box. From this receptacle issued the strange sound that I had heard.

How had it come here?

What did it contain?

In attempting to lift it from its burying place I discovered that it seemed to be held fast by means of a very small insulated cable running farther into the sand beneath it.

My first impulse was to drag the thing loose by main strength; but fortunately I thought better of this and fell to examining the box. I soon saw that it was covered by a hinged lid, which was held closed by a simple screw-hook and eye.

It took but a moment to loosen this and raise the cover, when, to my utter astonishment, I discovered an ordinary telegraph instrument clicking away within.

"What in the world," thought I, "is this thing doing here?"

That it was a French military instrument was my first guess; but really there didn't seem much likelihood that this was the correct explanation, when one took into account the loneliness and remoteness of the spot.

As I sat gazing at my remarkable find, which was ticking and clicking away there in the silence of the desert night, trying to convey some message which I was unable to interpret, my eyes fell upon a bit of paper lying in the bottom of the box beside the instrument. I picked it up and examined it. Upon it were written but two letters:

D. I.

They meant nothing to me then. I was baffled.

Once, in an interval of silence upon the part of the receiving instrument, I moved the sending-key up and down a few times. Instantly the receiving mechanism commenced to work frantically.

I tried to recall something of the Morse Code, with ahich I had played as a little boy — but time had obliterated it from my memory. I became almost frantic as I let my imagination run riot among the possibilities for which this clicking instrument might stand.

Some poor devil at the unknown other end might be in dire need of succor. The very franticness of the instrument's wild clashing betokened something of the kind.

And there sat I, powerless to interpret, and so powerless to help!

It was then that the inspiration came to me. In a flash there leaped to my mind the closing paragraphs of the story I had read in the club at Algiers:

Does the answer lie somewhere upon the bosom of the broad Sahara, at the ends of two tiny wires, hidden beneath a lost cairn?

The idea seemed preposterous. Experience and intelligence combined to assure me that there could be no slightest grain of truth or possibility in your wild tale — it was fiction pure and simple.

And yet where *were* the other ends of those wires?

What was this instrument — ticking away here in the great Sahara — but a travesty upon the possible!

Would I have believed in it had I not seen it with my own eyes?

And the initials — D. I. — upon the slip of paper! David's initials were these — David Innes.

I smiled at my imaginings. I ridiculed the assumption that there was an inner world and that these wires led downward through the earth's crust to the surface of Pellucidar. And yet

Well, I sat there all night, listening to that tantalizing clicking, now and then moving the sending-key just to let the other end know that the instrument had been discovered. In the morning, after carefully returning the box to its hole and covering it over with sand, I called my servants about me, snatched a hurried breakfast, mounted my horse, and started upon a forced march for Algiers.

I arrived here today. In writing you this letter I feel that I am making a fool of myself.

There is no David Innes.

There is no Dian the Beautiful.

There is no world within a world.

Pellucidar is but a realm of your imagination — nothing more.

But ——

The incident of the finding of that buried telegraph instrument upon the lonely Sahara is little short of uncanny, in view of your story of the adventures of David Innes.

I have called it one of the most remarkable coincidences in modern fiction. I called it literature before, but — again pardon my candor — your story is not.

And now — why am I writing you?

Heaven knows, unless it is that the persistent clicking of that unfathomable enigma out there in the vast silences of the Sahara has so wrought upon my nerves that reason refuses longer to function sanely.

I cannot hear it now, yet I know that far away to the south, all alone beneath the sands, it is still pounding out its vain, frantic appeal.

It is maddening!

It is your fault — I want you to release me from it.

Cable me at once, at my expense, that there was no basis of fact for your story, *At the Earth's Core.*

Very respectfully yours,
COGDON NESTOR,
—— and —— Club,
Algiers.

June 1st, ——.

Ten minutes after reading this letter I had cabled Mr. Nestor as follows:

Story true. Await me Algiers.

As fast as train and boat would carry me, I sped toward my destination. For all those dragging days my mind was a whirl of mad conjecture, of frantic hope, of numbing fear.

The finding of the telegraph-instrument practically assured me that David Innes had driven Perry's iron mole back through the earth's crust to the buried world of Pellucidar; but what adventures had befallen him since his return?

Had he found Dian the Beautiful, his half-savage mate, safe among his friends, or had Hooja the Sly One succeeded in his nefarious schemes to abduct her?

Did Abner Perry, the lovable old inventor and paleontologist, still live?

Had the federated tribes of Pellucidar succeeded in overthrowing the mighty Mahars, the dominant race of reptilian monsters, and their fierce, gorilla-like soldiery, the savage Sagoths?

I must admit that I was in a state bordering upon nervous prostration when I entered the —— and —— Club, in Algiers, and inquired for Mr. Nestor. A moment later I was ushered into his presence, to find myself clasping hands with the sort of chap that the world holds only too few of.

He was a tall, smooth-faced man of about thirty, clean-cut, straight, and strong, and weather-tanned to the hue of a desert Arab. I liked him immensely from the first, and I hope that after our three months together in the desert country — three months not entirely lacking in adventure — he found that a man may be a writer of "impossible trash" and yet have some redeeming qualities.

The day following my arrival at Algiers we left for the south, Nestor having made all arrangements in advance, guessing, as he naturally did, that I could be coming to Africa for but a single purpose — to hasten at once to the buried telegraph-instrument and wrest its secret from it.

In addition to our native servants, we took along an English telegraph-operator named Frank Downes. Nothing of interest enlivened our journey by rail and caravan till we came to the cluster of date-palms about the ancient well upon the rim of the Sahara.

It was the very spot at which I first had seen David Innes. If he had ever raised a cairn above the telegraph instrument no sign of it remained now. Had it not been for the chance that caused Cogden Nestor to throw down his sleeping rug directly over the hidden instrument, it might still be clicking there unheard — and this story still unwritten.

When we reached the spot and unearthed the little box the instrument was quiet, nor did repeated attempts upon the part of our telegrapher succeed in winning a response from the other end of the line. After several days of futile endeavor to raise Pellucidar, we had begun to despair. I was as positive that the other end of that little cable protruded through the surface of the inner world as I am that I sit here today in my study — when about midnight of the fourth day I was awakened by the sound of the instrument.

Leaping to my feet I grasped Downes roughly by the neck and dragged him out of his blankets. He didn't need to be told what caused my excitement, for the instant he was awake he, too, heard the long-hoped-for click, and with a whoop of delight pounced upon the instrument.

Nestor was on his feet almost as soon as I. The three of us huddled about that little box as if our lives depended upon the message it had for us.

Downes interrupted the clicking with his sending-key. The noise of the receiver stopped instantly.

"Ask who it is, Downes," I directed.

He did so, and while we awaited the Englishman's translation of the reply, I doubt if either Nestor or I breathed.

"He says he's David Innes," said Downes. "He wants to know who we are."

"Tell him," said I; "and that we want to know how he is — and all that has befallen him since I last saw him."

For two months I talked with David Innes almost every day, and as Downes translated, either Nestor or I took notes. From these, arranged in chronological order, I have set down the following account of the further adventures of David Innes at the earth's core, practically in his own words.

Chapter I

LOST ON PELLUCIDAR

The Arabs, of whom I wrote you at the end of my last letter (Innes began), and whom I thought to be enemies intent only upon murdering me, proved to be exceedingly friendly— they were searching for the very band of marauders that had threatened my existence. The huge rhamphor-hynchus-like reptile that I had brought back with me from the inner world — the ugly Mahar that Hooja the Sly One had substituted for my dear Dian at the moment of my departure — filled them with wonder and with awe.

Nor less so did the mighty subterranean prospector which had carried me to Pellucidar and back again, and which lay out in the desert about two miles from my camp.

With their help I managed to get the unwieldy tons of its great bulk into a vertical position — the nose deep in a hole we had dug in the sand and the rest of it supported by the trunks of date-palms cut for the purpose.

It was a mighty engineering job with only wild Arabs and their wilder mounts to do the work of an electric crane — but finally it was completed, and I was ready for departure.

For some time I hesitated to take the Mahar back with me. She had been docile and quiet ever since she had discovered herself virtually a prisoner aboard the "iron mole." It had been, of course, impossible for me to communicate with her since she had no auditory organs and I no knowledge of her fourth-dimension, sixth-sense method of communication.

Naturally I am kind-hearted, and so I found it beyond me to leave even this hateful and repulsive thing alone in a strange and hostile world. The result was that when I entered the iron mole I took her with me.

That she knew that we were about to return to Pellucidar was evident, for immediately her manner changed from that of habitual gloom that had pervaded her, to an almost human expression of contentment and delight.

Our trip through the earth's crust was but a repetition of my two former journeys between the inner and the outer worlds. This time, however, I imagine that we must have maintained a more nearly perpendicular course, for we accomplished the journey in a few minutes' less time than upon the occasion of my first journey through the five-hundred-mile crust. Just a trifle less than seventy-two hours after our departure into the sands of the Sahara, we broke through the surface of Pellucidar.

Fortune once again favored me by the slightest of margins, for when I opened the door in the prospector's outer jacket I saw that we had missed coming up through the bottom of an ocean by but a few hundred yards.

The aspect of the surrounding country was entirely unfamiliar to me — I had no conception of precisely where I was upon the one hundred and twenty-four million square miles of Pellucidar's vast land surface.

The perpetual midday sun poured down its torrid rays from zenith, as it had done since the beginning of Pellucidarian time — as it would continue to do to the end of it. Before me, across the wide sea, the weird, horizonless seascape folded gently upward to meet the sky until it lost itself to view in the azure depths of distance far above the level of my eyes.

How strange it looked! How vastly different from the flat and puny area of the circumscribed vision of the dweller upon the outer crust!

I was lost. Though I wandered ceaselessly throughout a lifetime, I might never discover the whereabouts of my former friends of this strange and savage world. Never again might I see dear old Perry, nor Ghak the Hairy One, nor Dacor the Strong One, nor that other infinitely precious one — my sweet and noble mate, Dian the Beautiful!

But even so I was glad to tread once more the surface of Pellucidar. Mysterious and terrible, grotesque and savage though she is in many of her aspects, I can not but love her. Her very savagery appealed to me, for it is the savagery of unspoiled Nature.

The magnificence of her tropic beauties enthralled me. Her mighty land areas breathed unfettered freedom.

Her untracked oceans, whispering of virgin wonders unsullied by the eye of man, beckoned me out upon their restless bosoms.

Not for an instant did I regret the world of my nativity. I was in Pellucidar. I was *home*. And I was content.

As I stood dreaming beside the giant thing that had brought me safely through the earth's crust, my traveling companion, the hideous Mahar, emerged from the interior of the prospector and stood beside me. For a long time she remained motionless.

What thoughts were passing through the convolutions of her reptilian brain?

I do not know.

She was a member of the dominant race of Pellucidar. By a strange freak of evolution her kind had first developed the power of reason in that world of anomalies.

To her, creatures such as I were of a lower order. As Perry had discovered among the writings of her kind in the buried city of Phutra, it was still an open question among the Mahars as to whether man possessed means of intelligent communication or the power of reason.

Her kind believed that in the center of all-pervading solidity there was a single, vast, spherical cavity, which was Pellucidar. This cavity had been left there for the sole purpose of providing a place for the creation and propagation of the Mahar race. Everything within it had been put there for the uses of the Mahar.

I wondered what this particular Mahar might think now. I found pleasure in speculating upon just what the effect had been upon her of passing through the earth's crust, and coming out into a world that one of even less intelligence than the great Mahars could easily see was a different world from her own Pellucidar.

What had she thought of the outer world's tiny sun?

What had been the effect upon her of the moon and myriad stars of the clear African nights?

How had she explained them?

With what sensations of awe must she first have watched the sun moving slowly across the heavens to disappear at last beneath the western horizon, leaving in his wake that which the Mahar had never before witnessed — the darkness of night? For upon Pellucidar there is no night. The stationary sun hangs forever in the center of the Pellucidarian sky — directly overhead.

Then, too, she must have been impressed by the wondrous mechanism of the prospector which had bored its way from world to world and back again. And that it had been driven by a rational being must also have occurred to her.

Too, she had seen me conversing with other men upon the earth's surface. She had seen the arrival of the caravan of books and arms, and ammunition, and the balance of the heterogeneous collection which I had crammed into the cabin of the iron mole for transportation to Pellucidar.

She had seen all these evidences of a civilization and brain-power transcending in scientific achievement anything that her race had produced; nor once had she seen a creature of her own kind.

There could have been but a single deduction in the mind of the Mahar — there were other worlds than Pellucidar, and the *gilak* was a rational being.

Now the creature at my side was creeping slowly toward the near-by sea. At my hip hung a long-barreled six-shooter — somehow I had been unable to find the same sensation of security in the new-fangled automatics that had been perfected since my first departure from the outer world — and in my hand was a heavy express rifle.

I could have shot the Mahar with ease, for I knew intuitively that she was escaping — but I did not.

I felt that if she could return to her own kind with the story of her adventures, the position of the human race within Pellucidar would be advanced immensely at a single stride, for at once man would take his proper place in the considerations of the reptilia.

At the edge of the sea the creature paused and looked back at me. Then she slid sinuously into the surf.

For several minutes I saw no more of her as she luxuriated in the cool depths.

Then a hundred yards from shore she rose and there for another short while she floated upon the surface.

Finally she spread her giant wings, flapped them vigorously a score of times and rose above the blue sea. A single time she circled far aloft — and then straight as an arrow she sped away.

I watched her until the distant haze enveloped her and she had disappeared. I was alone.

My first concern was to discover where within Pellucidar I might be — and in what direction lay the land of the Sarians where Ghak the Hairy One ruled.

But how was I to guess in which direction lay Sari?

And if I set out to search — what then?

Could I find my way back to the prospector with its priceless freight of books, firearms, ammunition, scientific instruments, and still more books — its great library of reference works upon every conceivable branch of applied sciences?

And if I could not, of what value was all this vast storehouse of potential civilization and progress to be to the world of my adoption?

Upon the other hand, if I remained here alone with it, what could I accomplish single-handed?

Nothing.

But where there was no east, no west, no north, no south, no stars, no moon, and only a stationary midday sun, how was I to find my way back to this spot should ever I get out of sight of it?

I didn't know.

For a long time I stood buried in deep thought, when it occurred to me to try out one of the compasses I had brought and ascertain if it remained steadily fixed upon

The Mahar spread her giant wings and sped away.

an unvarying pole. I reentered the prospector and fetched a compass without.

Moving a considerable distance from the prospector that the needle might not be influenced by its great bulk of iron and steel, I turned the delicate instrument about in every direction.

Always and steadily the needle remained rigidly fixed upon a point straight out to sea, apparently pointing toward a large island some ten or twenty miles distant. This then should be north.

I drew my note-book from my pocket and made a careful topographical sketch of the locality within the range of my vision. Due north lay the island, far out upon the shimmering sea.

The spot I had chosen for my observations was the top of a large, flat boulder which rose six or eight feet above the turf. This spot I called Greenwich. The boulder was the "Royal Observatory."

I had made a start! I cannot tell you what a sense of relief was imparted to me by the simple fact that there was at least one spot within Pellucidar with a familiar name and a place upon a map.

It was with almost childish joy that I made a little circle in my note-book and traced the word Greenwich beside it.

Now I felt I might start out upon my search with some assurance of finding my way back again to the prospector.

I decided that at first I would travel directly south in the hope that I might in that direction find some familiar landmark. It was as good a direction as any. This much at least might be said of it.

Among the many other things I had brought from the outer world were a number of pedometers. I slipped three of these into my pockets with the idea that I might arrive at a more or less accurate mean from the registrations of them all.

On my map I would register so many paces south, so many east, so many west, and so on. When I was ready to return I would then do so by any route that I might choose.

I also strapped a considerable quantity of ammunition across my shoulders, pocketed some matches, and hooked an aluminum frypan and a small stew-kettle of the same metal to my belt.

I was ready — ready to go forth and explore a world!

Ready to search a land area of 124,-110,000 square miles for my friends, my incomparable mate, and good old Perry!

And so, after locking the door in the outer shell of the prospector, I set out upon my quest. Due south I traveled, across lovely valleys thick-dotted with grazing herds.

Through dense primeval forests I forced my way and up the slopes of mighty mountains searching for a pass to their farther sides.

Ibex and musk-sheep fell before my good old revolver, so that I lacked not for food in the higher altitudes. The forests and the plains gave plentifully of fruits and wild birds, antelope, aurochsen, and elk.

Occasionally, for the larger game animals and the gigantic beasts of prey, I used my express rifle, but for the most part the revolver filled all my needs.

There were times, too, when faced by a mighty cave bear, a saber-toothed tiger, or huge *felis spelaea,* black-maned and terrible, even my powerful rifle seemed pitifully inadequate — but fortune favored me so that I passed unscathed through adventures that even the recollection of causes the short hairs to bristle at the nape of my neck.

How long I wandered toward the south I do not know, for shortly after I left the prospector something went wrong with my watch, and I was again at the mercy of the baffling timelessness of Pellucidar, forging steadily ahead beneath the great, motionless sun which hangs eternally at noon.

I ate many times, however, so that days must have elapsed, possibly months with no familiar landscape rewarding my eager eyes.

I saw no men nor signs of men. Nor is this strange, for Pellucidar, in its land area, is immense, while the human race there is very young and consequently far from numerous.

Doubtless upon that long search mine was the first human foot to touch the soil in many places — mine the first human eye to rest upon the gorgeous wonders of the landscape.

It was a staggering thought. I could not but dwell upon it often as I made my lonely way through this virgin world. Then, quite suddenly, one day I stepped out of the peace of manless primality into the presence of man — and peace was gone.

It happened thus:

I had been following a ravine downward out of a chain of lofty hills and had paused at its mouth to view the lovely little valley that lay before me. At one side was tangled wood, while straight ahead a river wound peacefully along parallel to the cliffs in which the hills terminated at the valley's edge.

Presently, as I stood enjoying the lovely scene, as insatiate for Nature's wonders as if I had not looked upon similar landscapes countless times, a sound of shouting broke from the direction of the woods. That the harsh, discordant notes rose from the throats of men I could not doubt.

I slipped behind a large boulder near the mouth of the ravine and waited. I could hear the crashing of underbrush in the forest, and I guessed that whoever came came quickly — pursued and pursuers, doubtless.

In a short time some hunted animal would break into view, and a moment later a score of half-naked savages would come leaping after with spears or clubs or great stone-knives.

I had seen the thing so many times during my life within Pellucidar that I felt that I could anticipate to a nicety precisely what I was about to witness. I hoped that the hunters would prove friendly and be able to direct me toward Sari.

Even as I was thinking these thoughts the quarry emerged from the forest. But it was no terrified four-footed beast. Instead, what I saw was an old man — a terrified old man!

Staggering feebly and hopelessly from what must have been some very terrible fate, if one could judge from the horrified expressions he continually cast behind him toward the wood, he came stumbling on in my direction.

He had covered but a short distance from the forest when I beheld the first of his pursuers — a Sagoth, one of those grim and terrible gorilla-men who guard the mighty amahars in their buried cities, faring forth from time to time upon slave-raiding or punitive expeditions against the human race of Pellucidar, of whom the dominant race of the inner world think as we think of the bison or the wild sheep of our own world.

Close behind the foremost Sagoth came others until a full dozen raced, shouting after the terror-stricken old man. They would be upon him shortly, that was plain.

One of them was rapidly overhauling him, his back-thrown spear-arm testifying to his purpose.

And then, quite with the suddenness of an unexpected blow, I realized a past familiarity with the gait and carriage of the fugitive.

Simultaneously there swept over me the staggering fact that the old man was — Perry! That he was about to die before my very eyes with no hope that I could reach him in time to avert the awful catastrophe — for to me it meant a real catastrophe!

Perry was my best friend.

Dian, of course, I looked upon as more than friend. She was my mate — a part of me.

I had entirely forgotten the rifle in my hand and the revolvers at my belt; one does not readily synchronize his thoughts with the stone age and the twentieth century simultaneously.

Now from past habit I still thought in the stone age, and in my thoughts of the stone age there were no thoughts of firearms.

The fellow was almost upon Perry when the feel of the gun in my hand awoke me from the lethargy of terror that had gripped me. From behind my boulder I threw up the heavy express rifle — a mighty engine of destruction that might bring down a cave bear or a mammoth at a single shot — and let drive at the Sagoth's broad, hairy breast.

At the sound of the shot he stopped stockstill. His spear dropped from his hand.

Then he lunged forward upon his face.

The effect upon the others was little less remarkable. Perry alone could have possibly guessed the meaning of the loud report or explained its connection with the sudden collapse of the Sagoth. The other gorilla-men halted for but an instant. Then with renewed shrieks of rage they sprang forward to finish Perry.

At the same time I stepped from behind my boulder, drawing one of my revolvers that I might conserve the more precious ammunition of the express rifle. Quickly I fired again with the lesser weapon.

Then it was that all eyes were directed toward me. Another Sagoth fell to the bullet from the revolver; but it did not stop his companions. They were out for revenge as

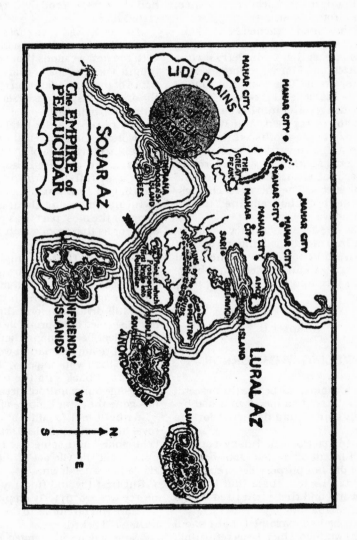

well as blood now, and they meant to have both.

As I ran forward toward Perry I fired four more shots, dropping three of our antagonists. Then at last the remaining seven wavered. It was too much for them, this roaring death that leaped, invisible, upon them from a great distance.

As they hesitated I reached Perry's side. I have never seen such an expression upon any man's face as that upon Perry's when he recognized me. I have no words wherewith to describe it. There was not time to talk then — scarce for a greeting. I thrust the full, loaded revolver into his hand, fired the last shot in my own, and reloaded. There were but six Sagoths left then.

They started toward us once more, though I could see that they were terrified probably as much by the noise of the guns as by their effects. They never reached us. Half-way the three that remained turned and fled, and we let them go.

The last we saw of them they were disappearing into the tangled undergrowth of the forest. And then Perry turned and threw his arms about my neck and, burying his old face upon my shoulder, wept like a child.

Chapter II

TRAVELING WITH TERROR

We made camp there beside the peaceful river. There Perry told me all that had befallen him since I had departed for the outer crust.

It seemed that Hooja had made it appear that I had intentionally left Dian behind, and that I did not purpose ever returning to Pellucidar. He told them that I was of another world and that I had tired of this and of its inhabitants.

To Dian he had explained that I had a mate in the world to which I was returning; that I had never intended taking Dian the Beautiful back with me; and that she had seen the last of me.

Shortly afterward Dian had disappeared from the camp, nor had Perry seen or heard aught of her since.

He had no conception of the time that had elapsed since I had departed, but guessed that many years had dragged their slow way into the past.

Hooja, too, had disappeared very soon after Dian had left. The Sarians, under Ghak the Hairy One, and the Amozites under Dacor the Strong One, Dian's brother, had fallen out over my supposed defection, for Ghak would not believe that I had thus treacherously deceived and deserted them.

The result had been that these two powerful tribes had fallen upon one another with the new weapons that Perry and I had taught them to make and to use. Other tribes of the new federation took sides with the original disputants or set up petty revolutions of their own.

The result was the total demolition of the work we had so well started.

Taking advantage of the tribal war, the Mahars had gathered their Sagoths in force and fallen upon one tribe after another in rapid succession, wreaking awful havoc among them and reducing them for the most part to as pitiable a state of terror as that from which we had raised them.

Alone of all the once-mighty federation the Sarians and the Amozites with a few other tribes continued to maintain their defiance of the Mahars; but these tribes were still divided among themselves, nor had it seemed at all probable to Perry when he had last been among them that any attempt at re-amalgamation would be made.

"And thus, your majesty," he concluded, "has faded back into the oblivion of the Stone Age our wondrous dream and with it has gone the First Empire of Pellucidar."

We both had to smile at the use of my royal title, yet I was indeed still "Emperor of Pellucidar," and some day I meant to rebuild what the vile act of the treacherous Hooja had torn down.

But first I would find my empress. To me she was worth forty empires.

"Have you no clue as to the whereabouts of Dian?" I asked.

"None whatever," replied Perry. "It was in search of her that I came to the pretty pass in which you discovered me, and from which, David, you saved me.

"I knew perfectly well that you had not intentionally deserted either Dian or Pellucidar. I guessed that in some way Hooja the Sly One was at the bottom of the matter, and I determined to go to Amoz, where I guessed that Dian might come to the protection of her brother, and do my utmost to convince her, and through her Dacor the Strong One, that we had all been victim of a treacherous plot to which you were no party.

"I came to Amoz after a most trying and terrible journey, only to find that Dian was not among her brother's people and that they knew naught of her whereabouts.

"Dacor, I am sure, wanted to be fair and just, but so great were his grief and anger over the disappearance of his sister that he could not listen to reason, but kept repeating time and again that only your return to Pellucidar could prove the honesty of your intentions.

"Then came a stranger from another tribe, sent I am sure at the instigation of Hooja. He so turned the Amozites against me that I was forced to flee their country to escape assassination.

"In attempting to return to Sari I became lost, and then the Sagoths discovered me. For a long time I eluded them, hiding in caves and wading in rivers to throw them off my trail.

"I lived on nuts and fruits and the edible roots that chance threw in my way.

"I traveled on and on, in what directions I could not even guess; and at last I could elude them no longer and the end came as I had long foreseen that it would come, except that I had not foreseen that you would be there to save me."

We rested in our camp until Perry had regained sufficient strength to travel again. We planned much, rebuilding all our shattered air-castles; but above all we planned most to find Dian.

I could not believe that she was dead, yet where she might be in this savage world, and under what frightful conditions she might be living, I could not guess.

When Perry was rested we returned to the prospector, where he fitted himself out fully like a civilized human being — underclothing, socks, shoes, khaki jacket and breeches and good, substantial puttees.

When I had come upon him he was clothed in rough *sadok* sandals, a gee-string and a tunic fashioned from the shaggy hide of a *thag*. Now he wore real clothing again for the first time since the ape-folk had stripped us of our apparel that long-gone day that had witnessed our advent within Pellucidar.

With a bandoleer of cartridges across his shoulder, two six-shooters at his hips, and a rifle in his hand he was a much rejuvenated Perry.

Indeed he was quite a different person altogether from the rather shaky old man who had entered the prospector with me ten or eleven years before, for the trial trip that had plunged us into such wondrous adventures and into such a strange and hitherto undreamed-of world.

Now he was straight and active. His muscles, almost atrophied from disuse in his former life, had filled out.

He was still an old man of course, but instead of appearing ten years older than he really was, as he had when we left the outer world, he now appeared about ten years younger. The wild, free life of Pellucidar had worked wonders for him.

Well, it must need have done so or killed him, for a man of Perry's former physical condition could not long have survived the dangers and rigors of the primitive life of the inner world.

Perry had been greatly interested in my map and in the "royal observatory" at Greenwich. By use of the pedometers we had retraced our way to the prospector with ease and accuracy.

Now that we were ready to set out again we decided to follow a different route on the chance that it might lead us into more familiar territory.

I shall not weary you with a repetition of the countless adventures of our long search. Encounters with wild beasts of gigantic size were of almost daily occurrence; but with our deadly express rifles we ran comparatively little risk when one recalls that previously we had both traversed this world of frightful dangers inadequately armed with crude, primitive weapons and all but naked.

We ate and slept many times — so many that we lost count — and so I do not know how long we roamed, though our map shows the distances and directions quite accurately. We must have covered a great many thousand square miles of territory, and yet we had seen nothing in the way of a familiar landmark, when from the heights of a mountain-range we were crossing I descried far in the distance great masses of billowing clouds.

Now clouds are practically unknown in the skies of Pellucidar. The moment that my eyes rested upon them my heart leaped. I seized Perry's arm and, pointing toward the horizonless distance, shouted:

"The Mountains of the Clouds!"

"They lie close to Phutra, and the country of our worst enemies, the Mahars," Perry remonstrated.

"I know it," I replied, "but they give us a starting-point from which to prosecute our search intelligently. They are at least a familiar landmark.

"They tell us that we are upon the right trail and not wandering far in the wrong direction.

"Furthermore, close to the Mountains of the Clouds dwells a good friend, Ja the Mezop. You did not know him, but you know all that he did for me and all that he will gladly do to aid me.

"At least he can direct us upon the right direction toward Sari."

"The Mountains of the Clouds constitute a mighty range," replied Perry. "They must cover an enormous territory. How are you to find your friend in all the great country that is visible from their rugged flanks?"

"Easily," I answered him, "for Ja gave me minute directions. I recall almost his exact words:

"'You need merely come to the foot of the highest peak of the Mountains of the Clouds. There you will find a river that flows into the Lural Az.

"'Directly opposite the mouth of the river you will see three large islands far out — so far that they are barely discernible. The one to the extreme left as you face them from the mouth of the river is Anoroc, where I rule the tribe of Anoroc.'"

And so we hastened onward toward the great cloud-mass that was to be our guide for several weary marches. At last we came close to the towering crags, Alp-like in their grandeur.

Rising nobly among its noble fellows, one stupendous peak reared its giant head thousands of feet above the others. It was he whom we sought; but at its foot no river wound down toward any sea.

"It must rise from the opposite side," suggested Perry, casting a rueful glance at the forbidding heights that barred our further progress. "We cannot endure the arctic cold of those high flung passes, and to traverse the endless miles about this interminable range might require a year or more. The land we seek must lie upon the opposite side of the mountains."

"Then we must cross them," I insisted.

Perry shrugged.

"We can't do it, David," he repeated. "We are dressed for the tropics. We should freeze to death among the snows and glaciers long before we had discovered a pass to the opposite side."

"We must cross them," I reiterated. "We will cross them."

I had a plan, and that plan we carried out. It took some time.

First we made a permanent camp part way up the slopes where there was good water. Then we set out in search of the great, shaggy cave bear of the higher altitudes.

He is a mighty animal — a terrible animal. He is but little larger than his cousin of the lesser, lower hills; but he makes up for it in the awfulness of his ferocity and in the length and thickness of his shaggy coat. It was his coat that we were after.

We came upon him quite unexpectedly. I was trudging in advance along a rocky trail worn smooth by the padded feet of countless ages of wild beasts. At a shoulder of the mountain around which the path ran I came face to face with the Titan.

I was going up for a fur coat. He was coming down for breakfast. Each realized that here was the very thing he sought.

With a horrid roar the beast charged me.

At my right the cliff rose straight upward for thousands of feet.

At my left it dropped into a dim, abysmal cañon.

In front of me was the bear.

Behind me was Perry.

I shouted to him in warning, and then I raised my rifle and fired into the broad breast of the creature. There was no time to take aim; the thing was too close upon me.

But that my bullet took effect was evident from the howl of rage and pain that broke from the frothing jowls. It didn't stop him, though.

I fired again, and then he was upon me. Down I went beneath his ton of maddened, clawing flesh and bone and sinew.

I thought my time had come. I remember feeling sorry for poor old Perry, left all alone in this inhospitable, savage world.

And then of a sudden I realized that the bear was gone and that I was quite unharmed. I leaped to my feet, my rifle still clutched in my hand, and looked about for my antagonist.

I thought that I should find him farther down the trail, probably finishing Perry, and so I leaped in the direction I supposed him to be, to find Perry perched upon a projecting rock several feet above the trail. My cry of warning had given him time to reach this point of safety.

There he squatted, his eyes wide and his mouth ajar, the picture of abject terror and consternation.

"Where is he?" he cried when he saw me. "Where is he?"

"Didn't he come this way?" I asked.

"Nothing came this way," replied the old man. "But I heard his roars — he must have been as large as an elephant."

"He was," I admitted; "but where in the world do you suppose he disappeared to?"

Then came a possible explanation to my mind. I returned to the point at which the bear had hurled me down and peered over the edge of the cliff into the abyss below.

Far, far down I saw a small brown blotch near the bottom of the cañon. It was the bear.

My second shot must have killed him, and so his dead body, after hurling me to the path, had toppled over into the abyss. I shivered at the thought of how close I, too, must have been to going over with him.

It took us a long time to reach the carcass, and arduous labor to remove the great pelt. But at last the thing was accomplished, and we returned to camp dragging the heavy trophy behind us.

Here we devoted another considerable period to scraping and curing it. When this was done to our satisfaction we made heavy boots, trousers, and coats of the shaggy skin, turning the fur in.

From the scraps we fashioned caps that came down around our ears, with flaps that fell about our shoulders and breasts. We were now fairly well equipped for our search for a pass to the opposite side of the Mountains of the Clouds.

Our first step now was to move our camp upward to the very edge of the perpetual snows which cap this lofty range. Here we built a snug, secure little hut, which we provisioned and stored with fuel for its diminutive fireplace.

With our hut as a base we sallied forth in search of a pass across the range.

Our every move was carefully noted upon our maps which we now kept in duplicate. By this means we were saved tedious and unnecessary retracing of ways already explored.

Systematically we worked upward in both directions from our base, and when we had at last discovered what seemed might prove a feasible pass we moved our belongings to a new hut farther up.

It was hard work — cold, bitter, cruel work. Not a step did we take in advance but the grim reaper strode silently in our tracks.

There were the great cave bears in the timber, and gaunt, lean wolves — huge creatures twice the size of our Canadian timber-wolves. Farther up we were assailed by enormous white bears — hungry, devilish fellows, who came roaring across the rough glacier tops at the first glimpse of us, or stalked us stealthily by scent when they had not yet seen us.

It is one of the peculiarities of life within Pellucidar that man is more often the hunted than the hunter. Myriad are the huge-bellied carnivora of this primitive world. Never, from birth to death, are those great bellies sufficiently filled, so always are their mighty owners prowling about in search of meat.

Terribly armed for battle as they are, man presents to them in his primal state an easy prey, slow of foot, puny of strength, ill-equipped by nature with natural weapons of defense.

The bears looked upon us as easy meat. Only our heavy rifles saved us from prompt extinction. Poor Perry never was a raging lion at heart, and I am convinced that the terrors of that awful period must have caused him poignant mental anguish.

When we were abroad pushing our trail farther and farther toward the distant break which, we assumed, marked a feasible way across the range, we never knew at what second some great engine of clawed and fanged destruction might rush upon us from behind, or lie in wait for us beyond an ice-hummock or a jutting shoulder of the craggy steeps.

The roar of our rifles was constantly shattering the world-old silence of stupendous cañons upon which they eye of man had never before gazed. And when in the comparative safety of our hut we lay down to sleep the great beasts roared and fought without the walls, clawed and battered at the door, or rushed their colossal frames

Face to face with the Titan.

headlong against the hut's sides until it rocked and trembled to the impact.

Yes, it was a gay life.

Perry had got to taking stock of our ammunition each time we returned to the hut. It became something of an obsession with him.

He'd count our cartridges one by one and then try to figure how long it would be before the last was expended and we must either remain in the hut until we starved to death or venture forth, empty, to fill the belly of some hungry bear.

I must admit that I, too, felt worried, for our progress was indeed snail-like, and our ammunition could not last forever. In discussing the problem, finally we came to the decision to burn our bridges behind us and make one last supreme effort to cross the divide.

It would mean that we must go without sleep for a long period, and with the further chance that when the time came that sleep could no longer be denied we might still be high in the frozen regions of perpetual snow and ice, where sleep would mean certain death, exposed as we would be to the attacks of wild beasts and without shelter from the hideous cold.

But we decided that we must take these chances, and so at last we set forth from our hut for the last time, carrying such necessities as we felt we could least afford to do without. The bears seemed unusually troublesome and determined that time, and as we clambered slowly upward beyond the highest point to which we had previously attained, the cold became infinitely more intense.

Presently, with two great bears dogging our footsteps we entered a dense fog.

We had reached the heights that are so often cloud-wrapped for long periods. We could see nothing a few paces beyond our noses.

We dared not turn back into the teeth of the bears which we could hear grunting behind us. To meet them in this bewildering fog would have been to court instant death.

Perry was almost overcome by the hopelessness of our situation. He flopped down on his knees and began to pray.

It was the first time I had heard him at his old habit since my return to Pellucidar, and I had thought that he had given up his little idiosyncrasy; but he hadn't. Far from it.

I let him pray for a short time undisturbed, and then as I was about to suggest that we had better be pushing along one of the bears in our rear let out a roar that made the earth fairly tremble beneath our feet.

It brought Perry to his feet as if he had been stung by a wasp, and sent him racing ahead through the blinding fog at a gait that I knew must soon end in disaster were it not checked.

Crevasses in the glacier-ice were far too frequent to permit of reckless speed even in a clear atmosphere, and then there were hideous precipices along the edges of which our way often led us. I shivered as I thought of the poor old fellow's peril.

At the top of my lungs I called to him to stop, but he did not answer me. And then I hurried on in the direction he had gone, faster by far than safety dictated.

For a while I thought I heard him ahead of me, but at last, though I paused often to listen and to call to him, I heard nothing more, not even the grunting of the bears that had been behind us. All was deathly silence — the silence of the tomb. About me lay the thick, impenetrable fog.

I was alone. Perry was gone — gone forever, I had not the slightest doubt.

Somewhere near by lay the mouth of a treacherous fissure, and far down at its icy bottom lay all that was mortal of my old friend, Abner Perry. There would his body lie preserved in its icy sepulcher for countless ages, until on some far distant day the slow-moving river of ice had wound its snail-like way down to the warmer level, there to disgorge its grisly evidence of grim tragedy, and what in that far future age, might mean baffling mystery.

Chapter III

SHOOTING THE CHUTES — AND AFTER

Through the fog I felt my way along by means of my compass. I no longer heard the bears, nor did I encounter one within the fog.

Experience has since taught me that these great beasts are as terror-stricken by this phenomenon as a landsman by a fog at sea, and that no sooner does a fog envelop them than they make the best of their way to lower levels and a clear atmosphere. It was well for me that this was true.

I felt very sad and lonely as I crawled along the difficult footing. My own predicament weighed less heavily upon me than the loss of Perry, for I loved the old fellow.

That I should ever win the opposite slopes of the range I began to doubt, for though I am naturally sanguine, I imagine that the bereavement which had befallen me had cast such a gloom over my spirits that I could see no slightest ray of hope for the future.

Then, too, the blighting, gray oblivion of the cold, damp clouds through which I wandered was depressing. Hope thrives best in sunlight, and I am sure that it does not thrive at all in a fog.

But the instinct of self-preservation is stronger than hope. It thrives, fortunately, upon nothing. It takes root upon the brink of the grave, and blossoms in the jaws of death. Now it flourished bravely upon the breast of dead hope, and urged me onward and upward in a stern endeavor to justify its existence.

As I advanced the fog became denser. I could see nothing beyond my nose. Even the snow and ice I trod were invisible.

I could not see below the breast of my bearskin coat. I seemed to be floating in a sea of vapor.

To go forward over a dangerous glacier under such conditions was little short of madness; but I could not have stopped going had I known positively that death lay two paces before my nose. In the first place, it was too cold to stop, and in the second, I should have gone mad but for the excitement of the perils that beset each forward step.

For some time the ground had been rougher and steeper, until I had been forced to scale a considerable height that had carried me from the glacier entirely. I was sure from my compass that I was following the right general direction, and so I kept on.

Once more the ground was level. From the wind that blew about me I guessed that I must be upon some exposed peak or ridge.

And then quite suddenly I stepped out into space. Wildly I turned and clutched at the ground that had slipped from beneath my feet.

Only a smooth, icy surface was there. I found nothing to clutch or stay my fall, and a moment later so great was my speed that nothing could have stayed me.

As suddenly as I had pitched into space, with equal suddenness did I emerge from the fog, out of which I shot like a projectile from a cannon into clear daylight. My speed was so great that I could see nothing about me but a blurred and indistinct sheet of smooth and frozen snow, that rushed past me with express-train velocity.

I must have slid downward thousands of feet before the steep incline curved gently on to a broad, smooth, snow-covered plateau. Across this I hurtled with slowly diminishing velocity, until at last objects about me began to take definite shape.

Far ahead, miles and miles away, I saw a great valley and mighty woods, and beyond these a broad expanse of water. In the nearer foreground I discerned a small, dark blob of color upon the shimmering whiteness of the snow.

"A bear," thought I, and thanked the instinct that had impelled me to cling tenaciously to my rifle during the moments of my awful tumble.

At the rate I was going it would be but a moment before I should be quite abreast the thing; nor was it long before I came to a sudden stop in soft snow, upon which the sun was shining, not twenty paces from the object of my most immediate apprehension.

It was standing upon its hind legs waiting for me. As I scrambled to my feet to meet it, I dropped my gun in the snow and doubled up with laughter.

It was Perry.

The expression upon his face, combined with the relief I felt at seeing him again safe and sound, was too much for my overwrought nerves.

"David!" he cried. "David, my boy! God has been good to an old man. He has answered my prayer."

It seems that Perry in his mad flight had plunged over the brink at about the same point as that at which I had stepped over it a short time later. Chance had done for us what long periods of rational labor had failed to accomplish.

We had crossed the divide. We were upon the side of the Mountains of the Clouds that we had for so long been attempting to reach.

We looked about. Below us were green trees and warm jungles. In the distance was a great sea.

"The Lural Az," I said, pointing toward its blue-green surface.

Somehow — the gods alone can explain it — Perry, too, had clung to his rifle during his mad descent of the icy slope. For that there was cause for great rejoicing.

Neither of us was worse for his experience, so after shaking the snow from our clothing, we set off at a great rate down toward the warmth and comfort of the forest and the jungle.

The going was easy by comparison with the awful obstacles we had had to encounter upon the opposite side of the divide. There were beasts, of course, but we came through safely.

Before we halted to eat or rest, we stood beside a little mountain brook beneath the wondrous trees of the primeval forest in an atmosphere of warmth and comfort. It reminded me of an early June day in the Maine woods.

We fell to work with our short axes and cut enough small trees to build a rude protection from the fiercer beasts. Then we lay down to sleep.

How long we slept I do not know. Perry says that inasmuch as there is no means of measuring time within Pellucidar, there can be no such thing as time here, and that we may have slept an outer earthly year, or we may have slept but a second.

But this I know. We had stuck the ends of some of the saplings into the ground in the building of our shelter, first stripping the leaves and branches from them, and when we awoke we found that many of them had thrust forth sprouts.

Personally, I think that we slept at least a month; but who may say? The sun marked midday when we closed our eyes; it was still in the same position when we opened them; nor had it varied a hair's breadth in the interim.

It is most baffling, this question of elapsed time within Pellucidar.

Anyhow, I was famished when we awoke. I think that it was the pangs of hunger that awoke me. Ptarmigan and wild boar fell before my revolver within a dozen moments of my awakening. Perry soon had a roaring fire blazing by the brink of the little stream.

It was a good and delicious meal we made. Though we did not eat the entire boar, we made a very large hole in him, while the ptarmigan was but a mouthful.

Having satisfied our hunger, we determined to set forth at once in search of Anoroc and my old friend, Ja the Mezop. We each thought that by following the little stream downward, we should come upon the large river which Ja had told me emptied into the Lural Az opposite his island.

We did so; nor were we disappointed, for at last after a pleasant journey — and what journey would not be pleasant after the hardships we had endured among the peaks of the Mountains of the Clouds — we came upon a broad flood that rushed majestically onward in the direction of the great sea we had seen from the snowy slopes of the mountains.

For three long marches we followed the left bank of the growing river, until at last we saw it roll its mighty volume into the vast waters of the sea. Far out across the rippling ocean we descried three islands. The one to the left must be Anoroc.

At last we had come close to a solution of our problem — the road to Sari.

But how to reach the islands was now the foremost question in our minds. We must build a canoe.

Perry is a most resourceful man. He has an axiom which carries the thought-kernel that what man has done, man can do, and it doesn't cut any figure with Perry whether a fellow knows how to do it or not.

He set out to make gunpowder once, shortly after our escape from Phutra and at the beginning of the confederation of the wild tribes of Pellucidar. He said that some one, without any knowledge of the fact that such a thing might be concocted, had once stumbled upon it by accident, and so he couldn't see why a fellow who knew all about powder except how to make it couldn't do as well.

He worked mighty hard mixing all sorts of things together, until finally he evolved a substance that looked like powder. He had been very proud of the stuff, and had gone about the village of the Sarians exhibiting it to every one who would listen to him, and explaining what its purpose was and what terrific havoc it would work, until finally the natives became so terrified at the stuff that they wouldn't come within a rod of Perry and his invention.

Finally, I suggested that we experiment with it and see what it would do, so Perry built a fire, after placing the powder at a safe distance, and then touched a glowing ember to a minute particle of the deadly explosive. It extinguished the ember.

Repeated experiments with it determined me that in searching for a high explosive, Perry had stumbled upon a fire-extinguisher that would have made his fortune for him back in our own world.

So now he set himself to work to build a scientific canoe. I had suggested that we construct a dugout, but Perry convinced me that we must build something more in keeping with our positions of supermen in this world of the Stone Age.

"We must impress these natives with our superiority," he explained. "You must not forget, David, that you are emperor of Pellucidar. As such you may not with dignity approach the shores of a foreign power in so crude a vessel as a dugout."

I pointed out to Perry that it wasn't much more incongruous for the emperor to cruise in a canoe, than it was for the prime minister to attempt to build one with his own hands.

He had to smile at that; but in extenuation of his act he assured me that it was quite customary for prime ministers to give their personal attention to the building of imperial navies; "and this," he said, "is the imperial navy of his Serene Highness, David I, Emperor of the Federated Kingdoms of Pellucidar."

I grinned; but Perry was quite serious about it. It had always seemed rather more or less of a joke to me that I should be addressed as majesty and all the rest of it. Yet my imperial power and dignity had been a very real thing during my brief reign.

Twenty tribes had joined the federation, and their chiefs had sworn eternal fealty to one another and to me. Among them were many powerful though savage nations. Their chiefs we had made kings; their tribal lands kingdoms.

We had armed them with bows and arrows and swords, in addition to their own more primitive weapons. I had trained them in military discipline and in so much of the art of war as I had gleaned from extensive reading of the campaigns of Napoleon, Von Moltke, Grant, and the ancients.

We had marked out as best we could natural boundaries dividing the various kingdoms. We had warned tribes beyond these boundaries that they must not trespass, and we had marched against and severely punished those who had.

We had met and defeated the Mahars and the Sagoths. In short, we had demonstrated our rights to empire, and very rapidly were we being recognized and heralded abroad when my departure for the outer world and Hooja's treachery had set us back.

But now I had returned. The work that fate had undone must be done again, and though I must need smile at my imperial honors, I none the less felt the weight of duty and obligation that rested upon my shoulders.

Slowly the imperial navy progressed toward completion. She was a wondrous craft, but I had my doubts about her. When I voiced them to Perry, he reminded me gently that my people for many generations had been mine-owners, not ship-builders, and consequently I couldn't be expected to know much about the matter.

I was minded to inquire into his hereditary fitness to design battleships; but inasmuch as I already knew that his father had been a minister in a backwoods village far from the coast, I hesitated lest I offend the dear old fellow.

He was immensely serious about his work, and I must admit that in so far as appearances went he did extremely well with the meager tools and assistance at his command. We had only two short axes and our hunting-knives; yet with these we hewed trees, split them into planks, surfaced and fitted them.

The "navy" was some forty feet in length by ten feet beam. Her sides were quite straight and fully ten feet high — "for the purpose," explained Perry, "of adding dignity to her appearance and rendering it less easy for an enemy to board her."

As a matter of fact, I knew that he had had in mind the safety of her crew under javelin-fire — the lofty sides made an admirable shelter. Inside she reminded me of nothing so much as a floating trench. There was also some slight analogy to a huge coffin.

Her prow sloped sharply backward from the water-line — quite like a line of battleship. Perry had designed her more for her moral effect upon an enemy, I think, than for any real harm she might inflict, and so

PELLUCIDAR

21

those parts which were to show were the most imposing.

Below the water-line she was practically non-existent. She should have had considerable draft; but, as the enemy couldn't have seen it, Perry decided to do away with it, and so made her flat-bottomed. It was this that caused my doubts about her.

There was another little idiosyncrasy of design that escaped us both until she was about ready to launch — there was no method of propulsion. Her sides were far too high to permit the use of sweeps, and when Perry suggested that we pole her, I remonstrated on the grounds that it would be a most undignified and awkward manner of sweeping down upon the foe, even if we could find or wield poles that would reach to the bottom of the ocean.

Finally I suggested that we convert her into a sailing vessel. When once the idea took hold Perry was most enthusiastic about it, and nothing would do but a four-masted, full-rigged ship.

Again I tried to dissuade him, but he was simply crazy over the psychological effect which the appearance of this strange and mighty craft would have upon the natives of Pellucidar. So we rigged her with thin hides for sails and dried gut for rope.

Neither of us knew much about sailing a full-rigged ship; but that didn't worry me a great deal, for I was confident that we should never be called upon to do so, and as the day of launching approached I was positive of it.

We had built her upon a low bank of the river close to where it emptied into the sea, and just above high tide. Her keel we had laid upon several rollers cut from small trees, the ends of the rollers in turn resting upon parallel tracks of long saplings. Her stern was toward the water.

A few hours before we were ready to launch her she made quite an imposing picture, for Perry had insisted upon setting every shred of "canvas." I told him that I didn't know much about it, but I was sure that at launching the hull only should have been completed, everything else being completed after she had floated safely.

At the last minute there was some delay while we sought a name for her. I wanted her christened the Perry in honor both of her designer and that other great naval genius of another world, Captain Oliver Hazard Perry, of the United States Navy.

But Perry was too modest; he wouldn't hear of it.

We finally decided to establish a system in the naming of the fleet. Battle-ships of the first class should bear the names of kingdoms of the federation; armored cruisers the names of kings; cruisers the names of cities, and so on down the line. Therefore, we decided to name the first battle-ship Sari, after the first of the federated kingdoms.

The launching of the Sari proved easier than I contemplated. Perry wanted me to get in and break something over the bow as she floated out upon the bosom of the river, but I told him that I should feel safer on dry land until I saw which side up the Sari would float.

I could see by the expression of the old man's face that my words had hurt him; but I noticed that he didn't offer to get in himself, and so I felt less contrition than I might otherwise.

When we cut the ropes and removed the blocks that held the Sari in place she started for the water with a lunge. Before she hit it she was going at a reckless speed, for we had laid our tracks quite down to the water, greased them, and at intervals placed rollers all ready to receive the ship as she moved forward with stately dignity. But there was no dignity in the Sari.

When she touched the surface of the river she must have been going twenty or thirty miles an hour. Her momentum carried her well out into the stream, until she came to a sudden halt at the end of the long line which we had had the foresight to attach to her bow and fasten to a large tree upon the bank.

The moment her progress was checked she promptly capsized. Perry was overwhelmed. I didn't upbraid him, nor remind him that I had "told him so."

His grief was so genuine and so apparent that I didn't have the heart to reproach him, even were I inclined to that particular sort of meanness.

"Come, come, old man!" I cried. "It's not as bad as it looks. Give me a hand with this rope, and we'll drag her up as far as we can; and then when the tide goes out we'll try another scheme. I think we can make a go of her yet."

Well, we managed to get her up into shallow water. When the tide receded she lay there on her side in the mud, quite a pitiable object for the premier battle-ship of a world — "the terror of the seas" was the way Perry had occasionally described her.

We had to work fast; but before the tide came in again we had stripped her of her sails and masts, righted her, and filled her about a quarter full of rock ballast. If she didn't stick too fast in the mud I was sure that she would float this time right side up.

I can tell you that it was with palpitating hearts that we sat upon the river-bank and watched that tide come slowly in. The tides of Pellucidar don't amount to much by comparison with our higher tides of the outer world, but I knew that it ought to prove ample to float the Sari.

Nor was I mistaken. Finally we had the satisfaction of seeing the vessel rise out of the mud and float slowly up-stream with the tide. As the water rose we pulled her in quite close to the bank and clambered aboard.

She rested safely now upon an even keel; nor did she leak, for she was well calked with fiber and tarry pitch. We rigged up a single short mast and light sail, fastened planking down over the ballast to form a deck, worked her out into midstream with a couple of sweeps, and dropped our primitive stone anchor to await the turn of the tide that would bear us out to sea.

While we waited we devoted the time to the construction of an upper deck, since the one immediately above the ballast was some seven feet from the gunwale. The second deck was four feet above this. In it was a large, commodious hatch, leading to the lower deck. The sides of the ship rose three feet above the upper deck, forming an excellent breastwork, which we loopholed at intervals that we might lie prone and fire upon an enemy.

Though we were sailing out upon a peaceful mission in search of my friend Ja, we knew that we might meet with people of some other island who would prove unfriendly.

At last the tide turned. We weighed anchor. Slowly we drifted down the great river toward the sea.

About us swarmed the mighty denizens of the primeval deep — plesiosauri and ichthyosauria with all their horrid, slimy cousins whose names were as the names of aunts and uncles to Perry, but which I have never been able to recall an hour after having heard them.

At last we were safely launched upon the journey to which we had looked forward for so long, and the results of which meant so much to me.

Chapter IV

FRIENDSHIP AND TREACHERY

The Sari proved a most erratic craft. She might have done well enough upon a park lagoon if safely anchored, but upon the bosom of a mighty ocean she left much to be desired.

Sailing with the wind she did her best; but in quartering or when close-hauled she drifted terribly, as a nautical man might have guessed she would. We couldn't keep within miles of our course, and our progress was pitifully slow.

Instead of making for the island of Anoroc, we bore far to the right, until it became evident that we should have to pass between the two right-hand islands and attempt to return toward Anoroc from the opposite side.

As we neared the islands Perry was quite overcome by their beauty. When we were directly between two of them he fairly went into raptures; nor could I blame him.

The tropical luxuriance of the foliage that dipped almost to the water's edge and the vivid colors of the blooms that shot the green made a most gorgeous spectacle.

Perry was right in the midst of a flowery panegyric on the wonders of the peaceful beauty of the scene when a canoe shot out from the nearest island. There were a dozen warriors in it; it was quickly followed by a second and third.

Of course we couldn't know the intentions of the strangers, but we could pretty well guess them.

Perry wanted to man the sweeps and try to get away from them, but I soon convinced him that any speed of which the Sari was capable would be far too slow to outdistance the swift, though awkward, dugouts of the Mezops.

I waited until they were quite close enough to hear me, and then I hailed them. I told them that we were friends of the Mezops, and that we were upon a visit to Ja of Anoroc, to which they replied that they were at war with Ja, and that if we would wait a minute they'd board us and throw our corpses to the azdyryths.

I warned them that they would get the worst of it if they didn't leave us alone, but they only shouted in derision and paddled swiftly toward us. It was evident that they were considerably impressed by the appearance and dimensions of our craft, but as these fellows know no fear they were not at all awed.

Seeing that they were determined to give battle, I leaned over the rail of the *Sari* and brought the imperial battle-squadron of the Emperor of Pellucidar into action for the first time in the history of a world. In other and simpler words, I fired my revolver at the nearest canoe.

The effect was magical. A warrior rose from his knees, threw his paddle aloft, stiffened into rigidity for an instant, and then toppled overboard.

The others ceased paddling, and, with wide eyes, looked first at me and then at the battling sea-things which fought for the corpse of their comrade. To them it must have seemed a miracle that I should be able to stand at thrice the range of the most powerful javelin-thrower and with a loud noise and a smudge of smoke slay one of their number with an invisible missile.

But only for an instant were they paralyzed with wonder. Then, with savage shouts, they fell once more to their paddles and forged rapidly toward us.

Again and again I fired. At each shot a warrior sank to the bottom of the canoe or tumbled overboard.

When the prow of the first craft touched the side of the *Sari* it contained only dead and dying men. The other two dugouts were approaching rapidly, so I turned my attention toward them.

I think that they must have been commencing to have some doubts — those wild, naked, red warriors — for when the first man fell in the second boat the others stopped paddling and commenced to jabber among themselves.

The third boat pulled up alongside the second and its crews joined in the conference. Taking advantage of the lull in the battle, I called out to the survivors to return to their shore.

"I have no fight with you," I cried, and then I told them who I was and added that if they would live in peace they must sooner or later join forces with me.

"Go back now to your people," I counseled them, "and tell them that you have seen David I, Emperor of the Federated Kingdoms of Pellucidar, and that single-handed he has overcome you, just as he intends overcoming the Mahars and the Sagoths and any other peoples of Pellucidar who threaten the peace and welfare of his empire."

Slowly they turned the noses of their canoes toward land. It was evident that they were impressed; yet that they were loath to give up without further contesting my claim to naval supremacy was also apparent, for some of their number seemed to be exhorting the others to a renewal of the conflict.

However, at last they drew slowly away, and the *Sari*, which had not decreased her snail-like speed during this, her first engagement, continued upon her slow, uneven way.

Presently Perry stuck his head up through the hatch and hailed me.

"Have the scoundrels departed?" he asked. "Have you killed them all?"

"Those whom I failed to kill have departed, Perry," I replied.

He came out on deck and, peering over the side, descried the lone canoe floating a short distance astern with its grim and grisly freight. Farther his eyes wandered to the retreating boats.

"David," said he at last, "this is a notable occasion. It is a great day in the annals of Pellucidar. We have won a glorious victory.

"Your majesty's navy has routed a fleet of the enemy thrice its own size, manned by ten times as many men. Let us give thanks."

I could scarce restrain a smile at Perry's use of the pronoun "we," yet I was glad to share the rejoicing with him as I shall always be glad to share everything with the dear old fellow.

Perry is the only male coward I have ever known whom I could respect and love. He was not created for fighting; but I think that if the occasion should ever arise where it became necessary he would give his life cheerfully for me — yes, I *know* it.

It took us a long time to work around the islands and draw in close to Anoroc. In the leisure afforded we took turns working on our map, and by means of the compass and a little guesswork we set down the shore-line we had left and the three islands with fair accuracy.

Crossed sabers marked the spot where the first great naval engagement of a world had taken place. In a note-book we jotted down, as had been our custom, details that would be of historical value later.

Opposite Anoroc we came to anchor quite close to shore. I knew from my previous experience with the tortuous trails of the island that I could never find my way inland to the hidden tree-village of the Mezop chieftain, Ja; so we remained aboard the *Sari*, firing our express rifles at intervals to attract the attention of the natives.

After some ten shots had been fired at considerable intervals a body of copper-colored warriors appeared upon the shore. They watched us for a moment and then I hailed them, asking the whereabouts of my old friend Ja.

They did not reply at once, but stood with their heads together in serious and animated discussion. Continually they turned their eyes toward our strange craft. It was evident that they were greatly puzzled by our appearance as well as unable to explain the source of the loud noises that had attracted their attention to us. At last one of the warriors addressed us.

"Who are you who seek Ja?" he asked. "What would you of our chief?"

"We are friends," I replied. "I am David. Tell Ja that David, whose life he once saved from a *sithic*, has come again to visit him.

"If you will send out a canoe we will come ashore. We cannot bring our great warship closer in."

Again they talked for a considerable time. Then two of them entered a canoe that several dragged from its hiding-place in the jungle and paddled swiftly toward us.

They were magnificent specimens of manhood. Perry had never seen a member of this red race close to before. In fact, the dead men in the canoe we had left astern after the battle and the survivors who were paddling rapidly toward their shore were the first he ever had seen. He had been greatly impressed by their physical beauty and the promise of superior intelligence which their well-shaped skulls gave.

The two who now paddled out received us into their canoe with dignified courtesy. To my inquiries relative to Ja they explained that he had not been in the village when our signals were heard, but that runners had been sent out after him and that doubtless he was already upon his way to the coast.

One of the men remembered me from the occasion of my former visit to the island; he was extremely agreeable the moment that he came close enough to recognize me. He said that Ja would be delighted to welcome me, and that all the tribe of Anoroc knew of me by repute, and had received explicit instructions from their chieftain that if any of them should ever come upon me to show me every kindness and attention.

Upon shore we were received with equal honor. While we stood conversing with our bronze friends a tall warrior leaped suddenly from the jungle.

It was Ja. As his eyes fell upon me his face lighted with pleasure. He came quickly forward to greet me after the manner of his tribe.

Toward Perry he was equally hospitable. The old man fell in love with the savage giant as completely as had I. Ja conducted us along the maze-like trail to his strange village, where he gave over one of the tree-houses for our exclusive use.

Perry was much interested in the unique habitation, which resembled nothing so much as a huge wasp's nest built around the bole of a tree well above the ground.

After we had eaten and rested Ja came to see us with a number of his head men. They listened attentively to my story, which included a narrative of the events leading to the formation of the federated kingdoms, the battle with the Mahars, my journey to the outer world, and my return to Pellucidar and search for Sari and my mate.

Ja told me that the Mezops had heard something of the federation and had been much interested in it. He had even gone so far as to send a party of warriors toward Sari to investigate the reports, and to arrange for the entrance of Anoroc into the empire in case it appeared that there was any truth in the rumors that one of the aims of the federation was the overthrow of the Mahars.

The delegation had met with a party of Sagoths. As there had been a truce between the Mahars and the Mezops for many generations, they camped with these warriors of the reptiles, from whom they learned that the federation had gone to pieces. So the party returned to Anoroc.

When I showed Ja our map and explained its purpose to him, he was much interested. The location of Anoroc, the Mountains of the Clouds, the river, and the strip of sea-coast were all familiar to him.

He quickly indicated the position of the inland sea and, close beside it, the city of Phutra, where one of the powerful Mahar nations had its seat. He likewise showed us where Sari should be and carried his own coast-line as far north and south as it was known to him.

His additions to the map convinced us that Greenwich lay upon the verge of this same sea, and that it might be reached by water more easily than by the arduous crossing of the mountains or the dangerous approach through Phutra, which lay almost directly in line between Anoroc and Greenwich to the northwest.

If Sari lay upon the same water then the shore-line must bend far back toward the southwest of Greenwich — an assumption which, by the way, we found later to be true. Also, Sari was upon a lofty plateau at the southern end of a mighty gulf of the Great Ocean.

The location which Ja gave to distant Amoz puzzled us, for it placed it due north of Greenwich, apparently in mid-ocean. As Ja had never been so far and knew only of Amoz through hearsay, we thought that he must be mistaken; but he was not. Amoz lies directly north of Greenwich across the mouth of the same gulf as that upon which Sari is.

The sense of direction and location of these primitive Pellucidarians is little short of uncanny, as I have had occasion to remark in the past. You may take one of them to the uttermost ends of his world, to places of which he has never even heard, yet without sun or moon or stars to guide him, without map or compass, he will travel straight for home in the shortest direction.

Mountains, rivers, and seas may have to be gone around, but never once does his sense of direction fail him — the homing instinct is supreme.

In the same remarkable way they never forget the location of any place to which they have ever been, and know that of many of which they have only heard from others who have visited them.

In short, each Pellucidarian is a walking geography of his own district and of much of the country contiguous thereto. It al-

ways proved of the greatest aid to Perry and me; nevertheless we were anxious to enlarge our map, for we at least were not endowed with the homing instinct.

After several long councils it was decided that, in order to expedite matters, Perry should return to the prospector with a strong party of Mezops and fetch the freight I had brought from the outer world. Ja and his warriors were much impressed by our firearms, and were also anxious to build boats with sails.

As we had arms at the prospector and also books on boat-building we thought that it might prove an excellent idea to start these naturally maritime people upon the construction of a well built navy of stanch sailing-vessels. I was sure that with definite plans to go by Perry could oversee the construction of an adequate flotilla.

I warned him, however, not to be too ambitious, and to forget about dreadnoughts and armored cruisers for a while and build instead a few small sailing-boats that could be manned by four or five men.

I was to proceed to Sari, and while prosecuting my search for Dian attempt at the same time the rehabilitation of the federation. Perry was going as far as possible by water, with the chances that the entire trip might be made in that manner, which proved to be the fact.

With a couple of Mezops as companions I started for Sari. In order to avoid crossing the principal range of the Mountains of the Clouds we took a route that passed a little way south of Phutra. We had eaten four times and slept once, and were, as my companions told me, not far from the great Mahar city, when we were suddenly confronted by a considerable band of Sagoths.

They did not attack us, owing to the peace which exists between the Mahars and the Mezops, but I could see that they looked upon me with considerable suspicion. My friends told them that I was a stranger from a remote country, and as we had previously planned against such a contingency I pretended ignorance of the language which the human beings of Pellucidar employ in conversing with the gorilla-like soldiery of the Mahars.

I noticed, and not without misgivings, that the leader of the Sagoths eyed me with an expression that betokened partial recognition. I was sure that he had seen me before during the period of my incarceration in Phutra and that he was trying to recall my identity.

It worried me not a little. I was extremely thankful when we bade them adieu and continued upon our journey.

Several times during the next few marches I became acutely conscious of the sensation of being watched by unseen eyes, but I did not speak of my suspicions to my companions. Later I had reason to regret my reticence, for ——

Well, this is how it happened:

We had killed an antelope and after eating our fill I had lain down to sleep. The Pellucidarians, who seem seldom if ever to require sleep, joined me in this instance, for we had had a very trying march along the northern foothills of the Mountains of the Clouds, and now with their bellies filled with meat they seemed ready for slumber.

When I awoke it was with a start to find a couple of huge Sagoths astride me. They pinioned my arms and legs, and later chained my wrists behind my back. Then they let me up.

I saw my companions; the brave fellows lay dead where they had slept, javelined to death without a chance at self-defense.

I was furious. I threatened the Sagoth leader with all sorts of dire reprisals; but when he heard me speak the hybrid language that is the medium of communication between his kind and the human race of the inner world he only grinned, as much as to say, "I thought so!"

They had not taken my revolvers or ammunition away from me because they did not know what they were; but my heavy rifle I had lost. They simply left it where it had lain beside me.

So low in the scale of intelligence are they, that they had not sufficient interest in this strange object even to fetch it along with them.

I knew from the direction of our march that they were taking me to Phutra. Once there I did not need much of an imagination to picture what my fate would be. It was the arena and a wild thag or fierce tarag for me — unless the Mahars elected to take me to the pits.

In that case my end would be no more certain, though infinitely more horrible and painful, for in the pits I should be subjected to cruel vivisection. From what I had once seen of their methods in the pits of Phutra I knew them to be the opposite of

merciful, whereas in the arena I should be quickly despatched by some savage beast.

Arrived at the underground city, I was taken immediately before a slimy Mahar. When the creature had received the report of the Sagoth its cold eyes glistened with malice and hatred as they were turned balefully upon me.

I knew then that my identity had been guessed. With a show of excitement that I had never before seen evinced by a member of the dominant race of Pellucidar, the Mahar hustled me away, heavily guarded, through the main avenue of the city to one of the principal buildings.

Here we were ushered into a great hall where presently many Mahars gathered.

In utter silence they conversed, for they have no oral speech since they are without auditory nerves. Their method of communication Perry has likened to the projection of a sixth sense into a fourth dimension, where it becomes cognizable to the sixth sense of their audience.

Be that as it may, however, it was evident that I was the subject of discussion, and from the hateful looks bestowed upon me not a particularly pleasant subject.

How long I waited for their decision I do not know, but it must have been a very long time. Finally one of the Sagoths addressed me. He was acting as interpreter for his masters.

"The Mahars will spare your life," he said, "and release you on one condition."

"And what is that condition?" I asked, though I could guess its terms.

"That you return to them that which you stole from the pits of Phutra when you killed the four Mahars and escaped," he replied.

I had thought that that would be it. The great secret upon which depended the continuance of the Mahar race was safely hid where only Dian and I knew.

I ventured to imagine that they would have given me much more than my liberty to have it safely in their keeping again; but after that — what?

Would they keep their promises?

I doubted it. With the secret of artificial propagation once more in their hands their numbers would soon be made so to overrun the world of Pellucidar that there could be no hope for the eventual supremacy of the human race, the cause for which I so devoutly hoped, for which I had consecrated my life, and for which I was now willing to give my life.

Yes! In that moment as I stood before the heartless tribunal I felt that my life would be a very little thing to give could it save to the human race of Pellucidar the chance to come into its own by insuring the eventual extinction of the hated, powerful Mahars.

"Come!" exclaimed the Sagoths. "The mighty Mahars await your reply."

"You may say to them," I answered, "that I shall not tell them where the great secret is hid."

When this had been translated to them there was a great beating of reptilian wings, gaping of sharp-fanged jaws, and hideous hissing. I thought that they were about to fall upon me on the spot, and so I laid my hands upon my revolvers; but at length they became more quiet and presently transmitted some command to my Sagoth guard, the chief of which laid a heavy hand upon my arm and pushed me roughly before him from the audience-chamber.

They took me to the pits, where I lay carefully guarded. I was sure that I was to be taken to the vivisection laboratory, and it required all my courage to fortify myself against the terrors of so fearful a death. In Pellucidar, where there is no time, death-agonies may endure for eternities.

Accordingly, I had to steel myself against an endless doom, which now stared me in the face!

Chapter V

SURPRISES

But at last the allotted moment arrived — the moment for which I had been trying to prepare myself, for how long I could not even guess. A great Sagoth came and spoke some words of command to those who watched over me. I was jerked roughly to my feet and with little consideration hustled upward toward the higher levels.

Out into the broad avenue they conducted me, where, amid huge throngs of Mahars, Sagoths, and heavily guarded slaves, I was led, or, rather, pushed and shoved roughly, along in the same direction that the mob moved. I had seen such a concourse of people once before in the buried city of Phutra; I guessed, and

rightly, that we were bound for the great arena where slaves who are condemned to death meet their end.

Into the vast amphitheater they took me, stationing me at the extreme end of the arena. The queen came, with her slimy, sickening retinue. The seats were filled. The show was about to commence.

Then, from a little doorway in the opposite end of the structure, a girl was led into the arena. She was at a considerable distance from me. I could not see her features.

I wondered what fate awaited this other poor victim and myself, and why they had chosen to have us die together. My own fate, or rather, my thought of it, was submerged in the natural pity I felt for this lone girl, doomed to die horribly beneath the cold, cruel eyes of her awful captors. Of what crime could she be guilty that she must expiate it in the dreaded arena?

As I stood thus thinking, another door, this time at one of the long sides of the arena, was thrown open, and into the theater of death slunk a mighty tarag, the huge cave tiger of the Stone Age. At my sides were my revolvers. My captors had not taken them from me, because they did not yet realize their nature. Doubtless they thought them some strange manner of war-club, and as those who are condemned to the arena are permitted weapons of defense, they let me keep them.

The girl they had armed with a javelin. A brass pin would have been almost as effective against the ferocious monster they had loosed upon her.

The tarag stood for a moment looking about him — first up at the vast audience and then about the arena. He did not seem to see me at all, but his eyes fell presently upon the girl. A hideous roar broke from his titanic lungs — a roar which ended in a long-drawn scream that is more human than the death-cry of a tortured woman — more human but more awesome. I could scarce restrain a shudder.

Slowly the beast turned and moved toward the girl. Then it was that I came to myself and to a realization of my duty. Quickly and as noiselessly as possible I ran down the arena in pursuit of the grim creature. As I ran I drew one of my pitifully futile weapons. Ah! Could I but have had my lost express-gun in my hands at that moment! A single well-placed shot would have crumpled even this great monster.

*With a hideous roar the beast turned and slunk
toward the girl.*

The best I could hope to accomplish was to divert the thing from the girl to myself and then to place as many bullets as possible in it before it reached and mauled me into insensibility and death.

There is a certain unwritten law of the arena that vouchsafes freedom and immunity to the victor, be he beast or human being — both of whom, by the way, are all the same to the Mahar. That is, they were accustomed to look upon man as a lower animal before Perry and I broke through the Pellucidarian crust, but I imagine that they were beginning to alter their views a trifle and to realize that in the *gilak* — their word for human being — they had a highly organized, reasoning being to contend with.

Be that as it may, the chances were that the tarag alone would profit by the law of the arena. A few more of his long strides, a prodigious leap, and he would be upon the girl. I raised a revolver and fired. The bullet struck him in the left hind leg. It couldn't have damaged him much; but the report of the shot brought him around, facing me.

I think the snarling visage of a huge, enraged, saber-toothed tiger is one of the most terrible sights in the world. Especially if he be snarling at you and there be nothing between the two of you but bare sand.

Even as he faced me a little cry from the girl carried my eyes beyond the brute to her face. Hers was fastened upon me with an expression of incredulity that baffles description. There was both hope and horror in them, too.

"Dian!" I cried. "My Heavens, Dian!"

I saw her lips form the name David, as with raised javelin she rushed forward upon the tarag. She was a tigress then — a primitive savage female defending her loved one. Before she could reach the beast with her puny weapon, I fired again at the point where the tarag's neck met his left shoulder. If I could get a bullet through there it might reach his heart. The bullet didn't reach his heart, but it stopped him for an instant.

It was then that a strange thing happened. I heard a great hissing from the stands occupied by the Mahars, and as I glanced toward them I saw three mighty *thipdars* — the winged dragons that guard the queen, or, as Perry calls them, pterodactyls — rise swiftly from their rocks

and dart lightning-like, toward the center of the arena. They are huge, powerful reptiles. One of them, with the advantage which his wings might give him, would easily be a match for a cave bear or a tarag.

These three, to my consternation, swooped down upon the tarag as he was gathering himself for a final charge upon me. They buried their talons in his back and lifted him bodily from the arena as if he had been a chicken in the clutches of a hawk.

What could it mean?

I was baffled for an explanation; but with the tarag gone I lost no time in hastening to Dian's side. With a little cry of delight she threw herself into my arms. So lost were we in the ecstasy of reunion that neither of us — to this day — can tell what became of the tarag.

The first thing we were aware of was the presence of a body of Sagoths about us. Gruffly they commanded us to follow them. They led us from the arena and back through the streets of Phutra to the audience chamber in which I had been tried and sentenced. Here we found ourselves facing the same cold, cruel tribunal.

Again a Sagoth acted as interpreter. He explained that our lives had been spared because at the last moment Tu-al-sa had returned to Phutra, and seeing me in the arena had prevailed upon the queen to spare my life.

"Who is Tu-al-sa?" I asked.

"A Mahar whose last male ancestor was — ages ago — the last of the male rulers among the Mahars," he replied.

"Why should she wish to have my life spared?"

He shrugged his shoulders and then repeated my question to the Mahar spokesman. When the latter had explained in the strange sign-language that passes for speech between the Mahars and their fighting men the Sagoth turned again to me:

"For a long time you had Tu-al-sa in your power," he explained. "You might easily have killed her or abandoned her in a strange world — but you did neither. You did not harm her, and you brought her back with you to Pellucidar and set her free to return to Phutra. This is your reward."

Now I understood. The Mahar who had been my involuntary companion upon my return to the outer world was Tu-al-sa.

This was the first time that I had learned the lady's name. I thanked fate that I had not left her upon the sands of the Sahara — or put a bullet in her, as I had been tempted to do. I was surprised to discover the gratitude was a characteristic of the dominant race of Pellucidar. I could never think of them as aught but cold-blooded, brainless reptiles, though Perry had devoted much time in explaining to me that owing to a strange freak of evolution among all the genera of the inner world, this species of the reptilia had advanced to a position quite analogous to that which man holds upon the outer crust.

He had often told me that there was every reason to believe from their writings, which he had learned to read while we were incarcerated in Phutra, that they were a just race, and that in certain branches of science and arts they were quite well advanced, especially in genetics and metaphysics, engineering and architecture.

While it had always been difficult for me to look upon these things as other than slimy, winged crocodiles — which, by the way, they do not at all resemble — I was now forced to a realization of the fact that I was in the hands of enlightened creatures — for justice and gratitude are certain hallmarks of rationality and culture.

But what they purposed for us further was of most imminent interest to me. They might save us from the tarag and yet not free us. They looked upon us yet, to some extent, I knew, as creatures of a lower order, and so as we are unable to place ourselves in the position of the brutes we enslave — thinking that they are happier in bondage than in the free fulfilment of the purposes for which nature intended them — the Mahars, too, might consider our welfare better conserved in captivity than among the dangers of the savage freedom we craved. Naturally, I was next impelled to inquire their further intent.

To my question, put through the Sagoth interpreter, I received the reply that having spared my life they considered that Tu-al-sa's debt of gratitude was canceled. They still had against me, however, the crime of which I had been guilty — the unforgivable crime of stealing the great secret. They, therefore, intended holding Dian and me prisoners until the manuscript was returned to them.

They would, they said, send an escort of Sagoths with me to fetch the precious document from its hiding-place, keeping Dian at Phutra as a hostage and releasing us both the moment that the document was safely restored to their queen.

There was no doubt but that they had the upper hand. However, there was so much more at stake than the liberty or even the lives of Dian and myself, that I did not deem it expedient to accept their offer without giving the matter careful thought.

Without the great secret this maleless race must eventually become extinct. For ages they had fertilized their eggs by an artificial process, the secret of which lay hidden in the little cave of a far-off valley where Dian and I had spent our honeymoon. I was none too sure that I could find the valley again, nor that I cared to. So long as the powerful reptilian race of Pellucidar continued to propagate, just so long would the position of man within the inner world be jeopardized. There could not be two dominant races.

I said as much to Dian.

"You used to tell me," she replied, "of the wonderful things you could accomplish with the inventions of your own world. Now you have returned with all that is necessary to place this great power in the hands of the men of Pellucidar.

"You told me of great engines of destruction which would cast a bursting ball of metal among our enemies, killing hundreds of them at one time.

"You told me of mighty fortresses of stone which a thousand men armed with big and little engines such as these could hold forever against a million Sagoths.

"You told me of great canoes which moved across the water without paddles, and which spat death from holes in their sides.

"All these may now belong to the men of Pellucidar. Why should we fear the Mahars?

"Let them breed! Let their numbers increase by thousands. They will be helpless before the power of the Emperor of Pellucidar.

"But if you remain a prisoner in Phutra, what may we accomplish?

"What could the men of Pellucidar do without you to lead them?

"They would fight among themselves, and while they fought the Mahars would fall upon them, and even though the

Mahar race should die out, of what value would the emancipation of the human race be to them without the knowledge, which you alone may wield, to guide them toward the wonderful civilization of which you have told me so much that I long for its comforts and luxuries as I never before longed for anything.

"No, David; the Mahars cannot harm us if you are at liberty. Let them have their secret that you and I may return to our people, and lead them to the conquest of all Pellucidar."

It was plain that Dian was ambitious, and that her ambition had not dulled her reasoning faculties. She was right. Nothing could be gained by remaining bottled up in Phutra for the rest of our lives.

It was true that Perry might do much with the contents of the prospector, or iron mole, in which I had brought down the implements of outer-world civilization; but Perry was a man of peace. He could never weld the warring factions of the disrupted federation. He could never win new tribes to the empire. He would fiddle around manufacturing gunpowder and trying to improve upon it until some one blew him up with his own invention. He wasn't practical. He never would get anywhere without a balance-wheel — without some one to direct his energies.

Perry needed me and I needed him. If we were going to do anything for Pellucidar we must be free to do it together.

The outcome of it all was that I agreed to the Mahars' proposition. They promised that Dian would be well treated and protected from every indignity during my absence. So I set out with a hundred Sagoths in search of the little valley which I had stumbled upon by accident, and which I might and might not find again.

We traveled directly toward Sari. Stopping at the camp where I had been captured I recovered my express rifle, for which I was very thankful. I found it lying where I had left it when I had been overpowered in my sleep by the Sagoths who had captured me and slain my Mezop companions.

On the way I added materially to my map, an occupation which did not elicit from the Sagoths even a shadow of interest. I felt that the human race of Pellucidar had little to fear from these gorilla-men. They were fighters — that was all. We might even use them later ourselves in this same capacity. They had not sufficient brain power to constitute a menace to the advancement of the human race.

As we neared the spot where I hoped to find the little valley I became more and more confident of success. Every landmark was familiar to me, and I was sure now that I knew the exact location of the cave.

It was at about this time that I sighted a number of the half-naked warriors of the human race of Pellucidar. They were marching across our front. At sight of us they halted; that there would be a fight I could not doubt. These Sagoths would never permit an opportunity for the capture of slaves for their Mahar masters to escape them.

I saw that the men were armed with bows and arrows, long lances and swords, so I guessed that they must have been members of the federation, for only my people had been thus equipped. Before Perry and I came the men of Pellucidar had only the crudest weapons wherewith to slay one another.

The Sagoths, too, were evidently expecting battle. With savage shouts they rushed forward toward the human warriors.

Then a strange thing happened. The leader of the human beings stepped forward with upraised hands. The Sagoths ceased their war-cries and advanced slowly to meet him. There was a long parley during which I could see that I was often the subject of their discourse. The Sagoths' leader pointed in the direction in which I had told him the valley lay. Evidently he was explaining the nature of our expedition to the leader of the warriors. It was all a puzzle to me.

What human being could be upon such excellent terms with the gorilla-men?

I couldn't imagine. I tried to get a good look at the fellow, but the Sagoths had left me in the rear with a guard when they had advanced to battle, and the distance was too great for me to recognize the features of any of the human beings.

Finally the parley was concluded and the men continued on their way while the Sagoths returned to where I stood with my guard. It was time for eating, so we stopped where we were and made our meal. The Sagoths didn't tell me who it was they had met, and I did not ask, though I must confess that I was quite curious.

They permitted me to sleep at this halt. Afterward we took up the last leg of our journey. I found the valley without difficulty and led my guard directly to the cave. At its mouth the Sagoths halted and I entered alone.

I noticed as I felt about the floor in the dim light that there was a pile of fresh-turned rubble there. Presently my hands came to the spot where the great secret had been buried. There was a cavity where I had carefully smoothed the earth over the hiding-place of the document — the manuscript was gone!

Frantically I searched the whole interior of the cave several times over, but without other result than a complete confirmation of my worst fears. Someone had been here ahead of me and stolen the great secret.

The one thing within Pellucidar which might free Dian and me was gone, nor was it likely that I should ever learn its whereabouts. If a Mahar had found it, which was quite improbable, the chances were that the dominant race would never divulge the fact that they had recovered the precious document. If a cave man had happened upon it he would have no conception of its meaning or value, and as a consequence it would be lost or destroyed in short order.

With bowed head and broken hopes I came out of the cave and told the Sagoth chieftain what I had discovered. It didn't mean much to the fellow, who doubtless had but little better idea of the contents of the document I had been sent to fetch to his masters than would the cave man who in all probability had discovered it.

The Sagoth knew only that I had failed in my mission, so he took advantage of the fact to make the return journey to Phutra as disagreeable as possible. I did not rebel, though I had with me the means to destroy them all. I did not dare rebel because of the consequences to Dian. I intended demanding her release on the grounds that she was in no way guilty of the theft, and that my failure to recover the document had not lessened the value of the good faith I had had in offering to do so. The Mahars might keep me in slavery if they chose, but Dian should be returned safely to her people.

I was full of my scheme when we entered Phutra and I was conducted directly to the great audience-chamber. The Mahars listened to the report of the Sagoth chieftain, and so difficult is it to judge their emotions from their almost expressionless countenances, that I was at a loss to know how terrible might be their wrath as they learned that their great secret, upon which rested the fate of their race, might now be irretrievably lost.

Presently I could see that she who presided was communicating something to the Sagoth interpreter — doubtless something to be transmitted to me which might give me a forewarning of the fate which lay in store for me. One thing I had decided definitely: If they would not free Dian I should turn loose upon Phutra with my little arsenal. Alone I might even win to freedom, and if I could learn where Dian was imprisoned it would be worth the attempt to free her. My thoughts were interrupted by the interpreter.

"The mighty Mahars," he said, "are unable to reconcile your statement that the document is lost with your action in sending it to them by a special messenger. They wish to know if you have so soon forgotten the truth or if you are merely ignoring it."

"I sent them no document," I cried. "Ask them what they mean."

"They say," he went on after conversing with the Mahar for a moment, "that just before you returned to Phutra, Hooja the Sly One came, bringing the great secret with him. He said that you had sent him ahead with it, asking him to deliver it and return to Sari where you would await him, bringing the girl with him."

"Dian?" I gasped. "The Mahars have given over Dian into the keeping of Hooja."

"Surely," he replied. "What of it? She is only a gilak," as you or I would say, "She is only a cow."

Chapter VI

A PENDENT WORLD

The Mahars set me free as they had promised, but with strict injunctions never to approach Phutra or any other Mahar city. They also made it perfectly plain that they considered me a dangerous creature, and that having wiped the slate clean in so far as they were under obligations to me, they now considered me fair prey. Should I again fall into their hands, they intimated it would go ill with me.

They would not tell me in which direction Hooja had set forth with Dian, so I departed from Phutra, filled with bitterness against the Mahars, and rage toward the Sly One who had once again robbed me of my greatest treasure.

At first I was minded to go directly back to Anoroc; but upon second thought turned my face toward Sari, as I felt that somewhere in that direction Hooja would travel, his own country lying in that general direction.

Of my journey to Sari it is only necessary to say that it was fraught with the usual excitement and adventure, incident to all travel across the face of savage Pellucidar. The dangers, however, were greatly reduced through the medium of my armament. I often wondered how it had happened that I had ever survived the first ten years of my life within the inner world, when, naked and primitively armed, I had traversed great areas of her beast-ridden surface.

With the aid of my map, which I had kept with great care during my march with the Sagoths in search of the great secret, I arrived at Sari at last. As I topped the lofty plateau in whose rocky cliffs the principal tribe of Sarians find their cave-homes, a great hue and cry arose from those who first discovered me.

Like wasps from their nests the hairy warriors poured from their caves. The bows with their poison-tipped arrows, which I had taught them to fashion and to use, were raised against me. Swords of hammered iron — another of my innovations — menaced me, as with lusty shouts the horde charged down.

It was a critical moment. Before I should be recognized I might be dead. It was evident that all semblance of intertribal relationship had ceased with my going, and that my people had reverted to their former savage, suspicious hatred of all strangers. My garb must have puzzled them, too, for never before of course had they seen a man clothed in khaki and puttees.

Leaning my express rifle against my body I raised both hands aloft. It was the peace-sign that is recognized everywhere upon the surface of Pellucidar. The charging warriors paused and surveyed me. I looked for my friend Ghak, the Hairy One, king of Sari, and presently I saw him coming from a distance. Ah, but it was good to see his mighty, hairy form once more! A friend was Ghak — a friend well worth the having; and it had been some time since I had seen a friend.

Shouldering his way through the throng of warriors, the mighty chieftain advanced toward me. There was an expression of puzzlement upon his fine features. He crossed the space between the warriors and myself, halting before me.

I did not speak. I did not even smile. I wanted to see if Ghak, my principal lieutenant, would recognize me. For some time he stood there looking me over carefully. His eyes took in my large pith helmet, my khaki jacket, and bandoleers of cartridges, the two revolvers swinging at my hips, the large rifle resting against my body. Still I stood with my hands above my head. He examined my puttees and my strong tan shoes — a little the worse for wear now. Then he glanced up once more to my face. As his gaze rested there quite steadily for some moments I saw recognition tinged with awe creep across his countenance.

Presently without a word he took one of my hands in his and dropping to one knee raised my fingers to his lips. Perry had taught them this trick, nor ever did the most polished courtier of all the grand courts of Europe perform the little act of homage with greater grace and dignity.

Quickly I raised Ghak to his feet, clasping both his hands in mine. I think there must have been tears in my eyes then — I know I felt too full for words. The king of Sari turned toward his warriors.

"Our emperor has come back," he announced. "Come hither and ——"

But he got no further, for the shouts that broke from those savage throats would have drowned the voice of heaven itself. I had never guessed how much they thought of me. As they clustered around, almost fighting for the chance to kiss my hand, I saw again the vision of empire which I had thought faded forever.

With such as these I could conquer a world. With such as these I *would* conquer one! If the Sarians had remained loyal, so too would the Amozites be loyal still, and the Kalians, and the Suvians, and all the great tribes who had formed the federation that was to emancipate the human race of Pellucidar.

Perry was safe with the Mezops; I was safe with the Sarians; now if Dian were but safe with me the future would look bright indeed.

It did not take long to outline to Ghak all that had befallen me since I had departed from Pellucidar, and to get down to the business of finding Dian, which to me at that moment was of even greater importance than the very empire itself.

When I told him that Hooja had stolen her, he stamped his foot in rage.

"It is always the Sly One!" he cried. "It was Hooja who caused the first trouble between you and the Beautiful One.

"It was Hooja who betrayed our trust, and all but caused our recapture by the Sagoths that time we escaped from Phutra.

"It was Hooja who tricked you and substituted a Mahar for Dian when you started upon your return journey to your own world.

"It was Hooja who schemed and lied until he had turned the kingdoms one against another and destroyed the federation.

"When we had him in our power we were foolish to let him live. Next time ——"

Ghak did not need to finish his sentence.

"He has become a very powerful enemy now," I replied. "That he is allied in some way with the Mahars is evidenced by the familiarity of his relations with the Sagoths who were accompanying me in search of the great secret, for it must have been Hooja whom I saw conversing with them just before we reached the valley. Doubtless they told him of our quest and he hastened on ahead of us, discovered the cave and stole the document. Well does he deserve his appellation of the Sly One."

With Ghak and his head men I held a number of consultations. The upshot of them was a decision to combine our search for Dian with an attempt to rebuild the crumbled federation. To this end twenty warriors were despatched in pairs to ten of the leading kingdoms, with instructions to make every effort to discover the whereabouts of Hooja and Dian, while prosecuting their missions to the chieftains to whom they were sent.

Ghak was to remain at home to receive the various delegations which we invited to come to Sari on the business of the federation. Four hundred warriors were started for Anoroc to fetch Perry and the contents of the prospector, to the capitol of the empire, which was also the principal settlements of the Sarians.

At first it was intended that I remain at Sari, that I might be in readiness to hasten forth at the first report of the discovery of Dian; but I found the inaction in the face of my deep solicitude for the welfare of my mate so galling that scarce had the several units departed upon their missions before I, too, chafed to be actively engaged upon the search.

It was after my second sleep, subsequent to the departure of the warriors, as I recall, that I at last went to Ghak with the admission that I could no longer support the intolerable longing to be personally upon the trail of my lost love.

Ghak tried to dissuade me, though I could tell that his heart was with me in my wish to be away and really doing something. It was while we were arguing upon the subject that a stranger, with hands above his head, entered the village. He was immediately surrounded by warriors and conducted to Ghak's presence.

The fellow was a typical cave man — squat, muscular, and hairy, and of a type I had not seen before. His features, like those of all the primeval men of Pellucidar, were regular and fine. His weapons consisted of a stone ax and knife and a heavy knobbed bludgeon of wood. His skin was very white.

"Who are you?" asked Ghak. "And whence come you?"

"I am Kolk, son of Goork, who is chief of the Thurians," replied the stranger. "From Thuria I have come in search of the land of Amoz, where dwells Dacor, the Strong One, who stole my sister, Canda, the Graceful One, to be his mate.

"We of Thuria have heard of a great chieftain who has bound together many tribes, and my father has sent me to Dacor to learn if there be truth in these stories, and if so to offer the services of Thuria to him whom we have heard called emperor."

"The stories are true," replied Ghak, "and here is the emperor of whom you have heard. You need travel no farther."

Kolk was delighted. He told us much of the wonderful resources of Thuria, the Land of Awful Shadow, and of his long journey in search of Amoz.

"And why," I asked, "does Goork, your father, desire to join his kingdom to the empire?"

"There are two reasons," replied the young man. "Forever have the Mahars, who dwell beyond the Sidi Plains which lie at the farther rim of the Land of Awful Shadow, taken heavy toll of our people, whom they either force into life-long slavery or fatten for their feasts. We have heard that the great emperor makes successful war upon the Mahars, against whom we should be glad to fight.

"Recently has another reason come. Upon a great island which lies in the Sojar Az, but a short distance from our shores, a wicked man has collected a great band of outcast warriors of all tribes. Even are there many Sagoths among them, sent by the Mahars to aid the Wicked One.

"This band makes raids upon our villages, and it is constantly growing in size and strength, for the Mahars give liberty to any of their male prisoners who will promise to fight with this band against the enemies of the Mahars. It is the purpose of the Mahars thus to raise a force of our own kind to combat the growth and menace of the new empire of which I have come to seek information. All this we learned from one of our own warriors who had pretended to sympathize with this band and had then escaped at the first opportunity."

"Who could this man be," I asked Ghak, "who leads so vile a movement against his own kind?"

"His name is Hooja," spoke up Kolk, answering my question.

Ghak and I looked at each other. Relief was written upon his countenance and I know that it was beating strongly in my heart. At last we had discovered a tangible clue to the whereabouts of Hooja — and with the clue a guide!

But when I broached the subject to Kolk he demurred. He had come a long way, he explained, to see his sister and to confer with Dacor. Moreover, he had instructions from his father which he could not ignore lightly. But even so he would return with me and show me the way to the island of the Thurian shore if by doing so we might accomplish anything.

"But we cannot," he urged. "Hooja is powerful. He has thousands of warriors. He has only to call upon his Mahar allies to receive a countless horde of Sagoths to do his bidding against his human enemies.

"Let us wait until you may gather an equal horde from the kingdoms of your empire. Then we may march against Hooja with some show of success.

"But first must you lure him to the mainland, for who among you knows how to construct the strange things that carry Hooja and his band back and forth across the water?

"We are not island people. We do not go upon the water. We know nothing of such things."

I couldn't persuade him to do more than direct me upon the way. I showed him my map, which now included a great area of country extending from Anoroc upon the east to Sari upon the west, and from the river south of the Mountains of the Clouds north to Amoz. As soon as I had explained it to him he drew a line with his finger, showing a sea-coast far to the west and south of Sari, and a great circle which he said marked the extent of the Land of Awful Shadow in which lay Thuria.

The shadow extended southeast of the coast out into the sea half-way to a large island, which he said was the seat of Hooja's traitorous government. The island itself lay in the light of the noonday sun. Northwest of the coast and embracing a part of Thuria lay the Lidi Plains, upon the northwestern verge of which was situated the Mahar city which took such heavy toll of the Thurians.

Thus were the unhappy people now between two fires, with Hooja upon one side and the Mahars upon the other. I did not wonder that they sent out an appeal for succor.

Though Ghak and Kolk both attempted to dissuade me, I was determined to set out at once, nor did I delay longer than to make a copy of my map to be given to Perry that he might add to his that which I had set down since we parted. I left a letter for him as well, in which among other things I advanced the theory that the Sojar Az, or Great Sea, which Kolk mentioned as stretching eastward from Thuria, might indeed be the same mighty ocean as that which, swinging around the southern end of a continent, ran northward along the shore opposite Phutra, mingling its waters with the huge gulf upon which lay Sari, Amoz, and Greenwich.

Against this possibility I urged him to hasten the building of a fleet of small sailing-vessels, which we might utilize should I find it impossible to entice Hooja's horde to the mainland.

I told Ghak what I had written, and suggested that as soon as he could he should make new treaties with the various kingdoms of the empire, collect an army and march toward Thuria — this of course against the possibility of my detention through some cause or other.

Kolk gave me a sign to his father — a *lidi*, or beast of burden, crudely scratched upon a bit of bone, and beneath the lidi a man and a flower; all very rudely done perhaps, but none the less effective as I well knew from my long years among the primitive men of Pellucidar.

The lidi is the tribal beast of the Thurians; the man and the flower in the combination in which they appeared bore a double significance, as they constituted not only a message to the effect that the bearer came in peace, but were also Kolk's signature.

And so, armed with my credentials and my small arsenal, I set out alone upon my quest for the dearest girl in this world or yours.

Kolk gave me explicit directions, though with my map I do not believe that I could have gone wrong. As a matter of fact I did not need the map at all, since the principal landmark of the first half of my journey, a gigantic mountain-peak, was plainly visible from Sari, though a good hundred miles away.

At the southern base of this mountain a river rose and ran in a westerly direction, finally turning south and emptying into the Sojar Az some forty miles northeast of Thuria. All that I had to do was follow this river to the sea and then follow the coast to Thuria.

Two hundred and forty miles of wild mountain and primeval jungle, of untracked plain, of nameless rivers, of deadly swamps and savage forests lay ahead of me, yet never had I been more eager for an adventure than now, for never had more depended upon haste and success.

I do not know how long a time that journey required, and only half did I appreciate the varied wonders that each new march unfolded before me, for my mind and heart were filled with but a single image — that of a perfect girl whose great, dark eyes looked bravely forth from a frame of raven hair.

It was not until I had passed the high peak and found the river that my eyes first discovered the pendent world, the tiny satellite which hangs low over the surface of Pellucidar casting its perpetual shadow always upon the same spot — the area that is known here as the Land of Awful Shadow, in which dwells the tribe of Thuria.

From the distance and the elevation of the highlands where I stood the Pellucidarian noonday moon showed half in sunshine and half in shadow, while directly beneath it was plainly visible the round dark spot upon the surface of Pellucidar where the sun has never shone. From where I stood the moon appeared to hang so low above the ground as almost to touch it; but later I was to learn that it floats a mile above the surface — which seems indeed quite close for a moon.

Following the river downward I soon lost sight of the tiny planet as I entered the mazes of a lofty forest. Nor did I catch another glimpse of it for some time — several marches at least. However, when the river led me to the sea, or rather just before it reached the sea, of a sudden the sky became overcast and the size and luxuriance of the vegetation diminished as by magic — as if an omnipotent hand had drawn a line upon the earth, and said:

"Upon this side shall the trees and the shrubs, the grasses and the flowers, riot in profusion of rich colors, gigantic size and bewildering abundance; and upon that side shall they be dwarfed and pale and scant."

Instantly I looked above, for clouds are so uncommon in the skies of Pellucidar — they are practically unknown except above the mightiest mountain ranges — that it had given me something of a start to discover the sun obliterated. But I was not long in coming to a realization of the cause of the shadow.

Above me hung another world. I could see its mountains and valleys, oceans, lakes, and rivers, its broad, grassy plains and dense forests. But too great was the distance and too deep the shadow of its under side for me to distinguish any movement as of animal life.

Instantly a great curiosity was awakened within me. The questions which the sight of this planet, so tantalizingly close, raised in my mind were numerous and unanswerable.

Was it inhabited?

If so, by what manner and form of creature?

Were its people as relatively diminutive as their little world, or were they as disproportionately huge as the lesser attraction of gravity upon the surface of their globe would permit of their being?

As I watched it, I saw that it was revolving upon an axis that lay parallel to the surface of Pellucidar, so that during each revolution its entire surface was once exposed to the world below and once bathed in the heat of the great sun above. The little world had that which Pellucidar could not have — a day and night, and — greatest of boons to one outer-earthly born — time.

Here I saw a chance to give time to Pellucidar, using this mighty clock, revolving perpetually in the heavens, to record the passage of the hours for the earth below. Here should be located an observatory, from which might be flashed by wireless to every corner of the empire the correct time once each day. That this time would be easily measured I had no doubt, since so plain were the landmarks upon the under surface of the satellite that it would be but necessary to erect a simple instrument and mark the instant of passage of a given landmark across the instrument.

But then was not the time for dreaming; I must devote my mind to the purpose of my journey. So I hastened onward beneath the great shadow. As I advanced I could not but note the changing nature of the vegetation and the paling of its hues.

The river led me a short distance within the shadow before it emptied into the Sojar Az. Then I continued in a southerly direction along the coast toward the village of Thuria, where I hoped to find Goork and deliver to him my credentials.

I had progressed no great distance from the mouth of the river when I discerned, lying some distance at sea, a great island. This I assumed to be the stronghold of Hooja, nor did I doubt that upon it even now was Dian.

The way was most difficult, since shortly after leaving the river I encountered lofty cliffs split by numerous long, narrow fiords, each of which necessitated a considerable detour. As the crow flies it is about twenty miles from the mouth of the river to Thuria, but before I had covered half of it I was fagged. There was no familiar fruit or vegetable growing upon the rocky soil of the cliff-tops, and I would have fared ill for food had not a hare broken cover almost beneath my nose.

I carried bow and arrows to conserve my ammunition-supply, but so quick was the little animal that I had no time to draw and fit a shaft. In fact my dinner was a hundred yards away and going like the proverbial bat when I dropped my six-shooter on it. It was a pretty shot and when coupled with a good dinner made me quite contented with myself.

After eating I lay down and slept. When I awoke I was scarcely so self-satisfied, for I had not more than opened my eyes before I became aware of the presence, barely a hundred yards from me, of a pack of some twenty huge wolf-dogs — the things which Perry insisted upon calling hyaenodons — and almost simultaneously I discovered that while I slept my revolvers, rifle, bow, arrows, and knife had been stolen from me.

And the wolf-dog pack was preparing to rush me.

Chapter VII

FROM PLIGHT TO PLIGHT

I have never been much of a runner; I hate running. But if ever a sprinter broke into smithereens all world's records it was I that day when I fled before those hideous beasts along the narrow spit of rocky cliff between two narrow fiords toward the Sojar Az. Just as I reached the verge of the cliff the foremost of the brutes was upon me. He leaped and closed his massive jaws upon my shoulder.

The momentum of his flying body, added to that of my own, carried the two of us over the cliff. It was a hideous fall. The cliff was almost perpendicular. At its foot broke the sea against a solid wall of rock.

We struck the cliff-face once in our descent and then plunged into the salt sea. With the impact with the water the hyaenodon released his hold upon my shoulder.

As I came sputtering to the surface I looked about for some tiny foot or hand-hold where I might cling for a moment of rest and recuperation. The cliff itself offered me nothing, so I swam toward the mouth of the fiord.

At the far end I could see that erosion from above had washed down sufficient rubble to form a narrow ribbon of beach. Toward this I swam with all my strength. Not once did I look behind me, since every unnecessary movement in swimming detracts so much from one's endurance and speed. Not until I had drawn myself safely out upon the beach did I turn my eyes back toward the sea for the hyaenodon. He was swimming slowly and apparently painfully toward the beach upon which I stood.

I watched him for a long time, wondering why it was that such a doglike animal was not a better swimmer. As he neared me I realized that he was weakening rapidly. I had gathered a handful of stones to be ready for his assault when he landed, but in a moment I let them fall from my hands. It was evident that the brute either was no swimmer or else was severely injured, for by now he was making practically no headway. Indeed, it was with quite apparent difficulty that he kept his nose above the surface of the sea.

He was not more than fifty yards from shore when he went under. I watched the spot where he had disappeared, and in a moment I saw his head reappear. The look of dumb misery in his eyes struck a chord in my breast, for I love dogs. I forgot that he was a vicious, primordial wolf-thing — a man-eater, a scourge, and a terror. I saw only the sad eyes that looked like the eyes of Raja, my dead collie of the outer world.

I did not stop to weigh and consider. In other words, I did not stop to think, which I believe must be the way of men who do things — in contradistinction to those who think much and do nothing. Instead, I leaped back into the water and swam out toward the drowning beast. At first he showed his teeth at my approach, but just before I reached him he went under for the second time, so that I had to dive to get him.

I grabbed him by the scruff of the neck, and though he weighed as much as a Shetland pony, I managed to drag him to shore and well up upon the beach. Here I found that one of his forelegs was broken — the crash against the cliff-face must have done it.

By this time all the fight was out of him, so that when I had gathered a few tiny branches from some of the stunted trees that grew in the crevices of the cliff, and returned to him he permitted me to set his broken leg and bind it in splints. I had to tear part of my shirt into bits to obtain a bandage, but at last the job was done. Then I sat stroking the savage head and talking to the beast in the man-dog talk with which you are familiar, if you ever owned and loved a dog.

When he is well, I thought, he probably will turn upon me and attempt to devour me, and against that eventuality I gathered together a pile of rocks and set to work to fashion a stone-knife. We were bottled up at the head of that fiord as completely as if we had been behind prison bars. Before us spread the Sojar Az, and elsewhere about us rose unscalable cliffs.

Fortunately a little rivulet trickled down the side of the rocky wall, giving us ample supply of fresh water — some of which I kept constantly beside the hyaenodon in a huge, bowl-shaped shell, of which there were countless numbers among the rubble of the beach.

For food we subsisted upon shell-fish and an occasional bird that I succeeded in knocking over with a rock, for long practice as a pitcher on prep-school and varsity nines had made me an excellent shot with a hand-thrown missile.

It was not long before the hyaenodon's leg was sufficiently mended to permit him to rise and hobble about on three legs. I shall never forget with what intent interest I watched his first attempt. Close at my hand lay my pile of rocks. Slowly the beast came to his three good feet. He stretched himself, lowered his head, and lapped water from the drinking-shell at his side, turned and looked at me, and then hobbled off toward the cliffs.

Thrice he traversed the entire extent of our prison, seeking, I imagine, a loop-hole for escape, but finding none he returned in my direction. Slowly he came quite close to me, sniffed at my shoes, my puttees, my hands, and then limped off a few feet and lay down again.

Now that he was able to get around, I was a little uncertain as to the wisdom of my impulsive mercy.

How could I sleep with that ferocious thing prowling about the narrow confines of our prison?

Should I close my eyes it might be to open them again to the feel of those mighty jaws at my throat. To say the least, I was uncomfortable.

I have had too much experience with dumb animals to bank very strongly on any sense of gratitude which may be attributed to them by inexperienced sentimentalists. I believe that some animals love their masters, but I doubt very much if their affection is the outcome of gratitude — a characteristic that is so rare as to be only occasionally traceable in the seemingly unselfish acts of man himself.

But finally I was forced to sleep. Tired nature would be put off no longer. I simply fell asleep, willy nilly, as I sat looking out to sea. I had been very uncomfortable since my ducking in the ocean, for though I could see the sunlight on the water halfway out toward the island and upon the island itself, no ray of it fell upon us. We were well within the Land of Awful Shadow. A perpetual half-warmth pervaded the atmosphere, but clothing was slow in drying, and so from loss of sleep and great physical discomfort, I at last gave way to nature's demands and sank into profound slumber.

When I awoke it was with a start, for a heavy body was upon me. My first thought was that the hyaenodon had at last attacked me, but as my eyes opened and I struggled to rise, I saw that a man was astride me and three others bending close above him.

I am no weakling — and never have been. My experience in the hard life of the inner world has turned my thews to steel. Even such giants as Ghak the Hairy One have praised my strength; but to it is added another quality which they lack — science.

The man upon me held me down awkwardly, leaving me many openings — one of which I was not slow in taking advantage of, so that almost before the fellow knew that I was awake I was upon my feet with my arms over his shoulders and about his waist and hard hurled him heavily over my head to the hard rubble of the beach, where he lay quite still.

In the instant that I arose I had seen the hyaenodon lying asleep beside a boulder a few yards away. So nearly was he the color of the rock that he was scarcely discernible. Evidently the newcomers had not seen him.

I had not more than freed myself from one of my antagonists before the other three were upon me. They did not work silently now, but charged me with savage cries — a mistake upon their part. The fact that they did not draw their weapons against me convinced me that they desired to take me alive; but I fought as desperately as if death loomed immediate and sure.

The battle was short, for scarce had their first wild whoop reverberated through the rocky fiord, and they had closed upon me, than a hairy mass of demoniacal rage hurtled among us.

It was the hyaenodon!

In an instant he had pulled down one of the men, and with a single shake, terrier-like, had broken his neck. Then he was upon another. In their efforts to vanquish the wolf-dog the savages forgot all about me, thus giving me an instant in which to snatch a knife from the loin-string of him who had first fallen and account for another of them. Almost simultaneously the hyaendon pulled down the remaining enemy, crushing his skull with a single bite of those fearsome jaws.

The battle was over — unless the beast considered me fair prey, too. I waited, ready for him with knife and bludgeon — also filched from a dead foeman; but he paid no attention to me, falling to work instead to devour one of the corpses.

The beast had been handicapped but little by his splinted leg; but having eaten he lay down and commenced to gnaw at the bandage. I was sitting some little distance away devouring shellfish, of which, by the way, I was becoming exceedingly tired.

Presently the hyaenodon arose and came toward me. I did not move. He stopped in front of me and deliberately raised his bandaged leg and pawed my knee. His act was as intelligible as words — he wished the bandage removed.

I took the great paw in one hand and with the other untied and unwound the bandage, removed the splints and felt of the injured member. As far as I could judge the bone was completely knit. The joint was stiff; when I bent it a little the brute winced — but he neither growled nor tried to pull away. Very slowly and gently I rubbed the joint and applied pressure to it for a few moments.

Then I set it down upon the ground. The hyaenodon walked around me a few times, and then lay down at my side, his body touching mine. I laid my hand upon his head. He did not move. Slowly I scratched about his ears and neck and down beneath the fierce jaws. The only sign he gave was to raise his chin a trifle that I might better caress him.

That was enough! From that moment I have never again felt suspicion of Raja, as I immediately named him. Somehow all sense of loneliness vanished, too — I had a dog! I had never guessed precisely what it was that was lacking to life in Pellucidar, but now I knew that it was the total absence of domestic animals.

Man here had not yet reached the point where he might take the time from slaughter and escaping slaughter to make friends with any of the brute creation. I must qualify this statement a trifle and say that this was true of those tribes with which I was most familiar. The Thurians do domesticate the colossal lidi, traversing the great Lidi Plains upon the backs of these grotesque and stupendous monsters, and possibly there may also be other, far-distant peoples within this great world, who have tamed others of the wild things of jungle, plain or mountain.

The Thurians practice agriculture in a crude sort of way. It is my opinion that this is one of the earliest steps from savagery to civilization. The taming of wild beasts and their domestication follows.

Perry argues that wild dogs were first domesticated for hunting purposes; but I do not agree with him. I believe that if their domestication were not purely the result of an accident, as, for example, my taming of the hyaenodon, it came about through the desire of tribes who had previously domesticated flocks and herds to have some strong, ferocious beast to guard their roaming property. However, I lean rather more strongly to the theory of accident.

As I sat there upon the beach of the little fiord eating my unpalatable shell-fish, I commenced to wonder how it had been that the four savages had been able to reach me, though I had been unable to escape from my natural prison. I glanced about in all directions, searching for an explanation. At last my eyes fell upon the bow of a small dugout protruding scarce a foot from behind a large boulder lying half in the water at the edge of the beach.

At my discovery I leaped to my feet so suddenly that it brought Raja, growling and bristling, upon all fours in an instant. For the moment I had forgotten him. But his savage rumbling did not cause me any uneasiness. He glanced quickly about in all directions as if searching for the cause of my excitement. Then, as I walked rapidly down toward the dugout, he slunk silently after me.

The dugout was similar in many respects to those which I had seen in use by the Mezops. In it were four paddles. I was much delighted, as it promptly offered me the escape I had been craving.

I pushed it out into water that would float it, stepped in and called to Raja to enter. At first he did not seem to understand what I wished of him, but after I had paddled out a few yards he plunged through the surf and swam after me. When he had come alongside I grasped the scruff of his neck, and after a considerable struggle, in which I several times came near to overturning the canoe, I managed to drag him aboard, where he shook himself vigorously and squatted down before me.

After emerging from the fiord, I paddled southward along the coast, where presently the lofty cliffs gave way to lower and more level country. It was here somewhere that I should come upon the principal village of the Thurians. When, after a time, I saw in the distance what I took to be huts in a clearing near the shore, I drew quickly into land, for though I had been furnished with credentials by Kolk, I was not sufficiently familiar with the tribal characteristics of these people to know whether I should receive a friendly welcome or not; and in case I should not, I wanted to be sure of having a canoe hidden safely away so that I might undertake the trip to the island, in any event — provided, of course, that I escaped the Thurians should they prove belligerent.

At the point where I landed the shore was quite low. A forest of pale, scrubby ferns ran down almost to the beach. Here I dragged up the dugout, hiding it well within the vegetation, and with some loose rocks built a cairn upon the beach to mark my cache. Then I turned my steps toward the Thurian village.

As I proceeded I began to speculate upon the possible actions of Raja when we should enter the presence of other men than myself. The brute was padding softly at my side, his sensitive nose constantly atwitch and his fierce eyes moving restlessly from side to side — nothing would ever take Raja unawares!

The more I thought upon the matter the greater became my perturbation. I did not want Raja to attack any of the people upon whose friendship I so greatly depended, nor did I want him injured or slain by them.

I wondered if Raja would stand for a leash. His head as he paced beside me was level with my hip. I laid my hand upon it caressingly. As I did so he turned and looked up into my face, his jaws parting and his red tongue lolling as you have seen your own dog's beneath a love pat.

"Just been waiting all your life to be tamed and loved, haven't you, old man?" I asked. "You're nothing but a good old pup, and the man who put the hyaeno in your name ought to be sued for libel."

Raja bared his mighty fangs with up-curled, snarling lips and licked my hand.

"You're grinning, you old fraud, you!" I cried. "If you're not, I'll eat you. I'll bet a doughnut you're nothing but some kid's poor old Fido, masquerading around as a real, live man-eater."

Raja whined. And so we walked on to-gether toward Thuria — I talking to the beast at my side, and he seeming to enjoy my company no less than I enjoyed his. If you don't think it's lonesome wandering all by yourself through savage, unknown Pel-lucidar, why, just try it, and you will not wonder that I was glad of the company of this first dog — this living replica of the fierce and now extinct hyaenodon of the outer crust that hunted in savage packs the great elk across the snows of southern France, in the days when the mastodon roamed at will over the broad continent of which the British Isles were then a part, and perchance left his footprints and his bones in the sands of Atlantis as well.

Thus I dreamed as we moved on toward Thuria. My dreaming was rudely shattered by a savage growl from Raja. I looked down at him. He had stopped in his tracks as one turned to stone. A thin ridge of stiff hair bristled along the entire length of his spine. His yellow-green eyes were fastened upon the scrubby jungle at our right.

I fastened my fingers in the bristles at his neck and turned my eyes in the direc-tion that his pointed. At first I saw noth-ing. Then a slight movement of the bushes riveted my attention. I thought it must be some wild beast, and was glad of the primi-tive weapons I had taken from the bodies of the warriors who had attacked me.

Presently I distinguished two eyes peer-ing at us from the vegetation. I took a step in their direction, and as I did so a youth arose and fled precipitately in the direction we had been going. Raja struggled to be after him, but I held tightly to his neck, an act which he did not seem to relish, for he turned on me with bared fangs.

I determined that now was as good a time as any to discover just how deep was Raja's affection for me. One of us must be master, and logically I was the one. He growled at me. I cuffed him sharply across the nose. He looked at me for a moment in surprised bewilderment, and then he growled again. I made another feint at him, expecting that it would bring him at my throat; but instead he winced and crouched down.

Raja was subdued!

I stooped and patted him. Then I took a piece of the rope that constituted a part of my equipment and made a leash for him.

Thus we resumed our journey toward Thuria. The youth who had seen us was evidently of the Thurians. That he had lost no time in racing homeward and spread-ing the word of my coming was evidenced when we had come within sight of the clearing, and the village — the first real vil-lage, by the way, that I had ever seen con-structed by human Pellucidarians. There was a rude rectangle walled with logs and boulders, in which were a hundred or more thatched huts of similar construction. There was no gate. Ladders that could be removed by night led over the palisade.

Before the village were assembled a great concourse of warriors. Inside I could see the heads of women and children peer-ing over the top of the wall; and also, farther back, the long necks of lidi, topped by their tiny heads. Lidi, by the way, is both the singular and plural form of the noun that describes the huge beasts of burden of the Thurians. They are enormous quad-rupeds, eighty or a hundred feet long, with very small heads perched at the top of very long, slender necks. Their heads are quite forty feet from the ground. Their gait is slow and deliberate, but so enormous are their strides that, as a matter of fact, they cover the ground quite rapidly.

Perry has told me that they are almost identical with the fossilized remains of the diplodocus of the outer crust's Jurassic age. I have to take his word for it — and I guess you will, unless you know more of such matters than I.

As we came in sight of the warriors the men set up a great jabbering. Their eyes were wide in astonishment — not only, I presume, because of my strange garmen-ture, but as well from the fact that I came in company with a jalok, which is the Pel-lucidarian name of the hyaenodon.

Raja tugged at his leash, growling and

showing his long white fangs. He would have liked nothing better than to be at the throats of the whole aggregation; but I held him in with the leash, though it took all my strength to do it. My free hand I held above my head, palm out, in token of the peacefulness of my mission.

In the foreground I saw the youth who had discovered us, and I could tell from the way he carried himself that he was quite overcome by his own importance. The warriors about him were all fine looking fellows, though shorter and squatter than the Sarians or the Amozites. Their color, too, was a bit lighter, owing, no doubt, to the fact that much of their lives is spent within the shadow of the world that hangs forever above their country.

A little in advance of the others was a bearded fellow tricked out in many ornaments. I didn't need to ask to know that he was the chieftain — doubtless Goork, father of Kolk. Now to him I addressed myself.

"I am David," I said, "Emperor of the Federated Kingdoms of Pellucidar. Doubtless you have heard of me?"

He nodded his head affirmatively.

"I come from Sari," I continued, "where I just met Kolk, the son of Goork. I bear a token from Kolk to his father, which will prove that I am a friend."

Again the warrior nodded. "I am Goork," he said. "Where is the token?"

"Here," I replied, and fished into the game-bag where I had placed it.

Goork and his people waited in silence. My hand searched the inside of the bag.

It was empty!

The token had been stolen with my arms!

Chapter VIII

CAPTIVE

When Goork and his people saw that I had no token they commenced to taunt me.

"You do not come from Kolk, but from the Sly One!" they cried. "He has sent you from the island to spy upon us. Go away, or we will set upon you and kill you."

I explained that all my belongings had been stolen from me, and that the robber must have taken the token, too; but they didn't believe me. As proof that I was one of Hooja's people, they pointed to my weapons, which they said were ornamented like those of the island clan. Further, they said that no good man went in company with a jalok — and that by this line of reasoning I certainly was a bad man.

I saw that they were not naturally a warlike tribe, for they preferred that I leave in peace rather than force them to attack me, whereas the Sarians would have killed a suspicious stranger first and inquired into his purposes later.

I think Raja sensed their antagonism, for he kept tugging at his leash and growling ominously. They were a bit in awe of him, and kept at a safe distance. It was evident that they could not comprehend why it was that this savage brute did not turn upon me and rend me.

I wasted a long time there trying to persuade Goork to accept me at my own valuation, but he was too canny. The best he would do was to give us food, which he did, and direct me as to the safest portion of the island upon which to attempt a landing, though even as he told me I am sure that he thought my request for information but a blind to deceive him as to my true knowledge of the insular stronghold.

At last I turned away from them — rather disheartened, for I had hoped to be able to enlist a considerable force of them in an attempt to rush Hooja's horde and rescue Dian. Back along the beach toward the hidden canoe we made our way.

By the time we came to the cairn I was dog-tired. Throwing myself upon the sand I soon slept, and with Raja stretched out beside me I felt a far greater security than I had enjoyed for a long time.

I awoke much refreshed to find Raja's eyes glued upon me. The moment I opened mine he rose, stretched himself, and without a backward glance plunged into the jungle. For several minutes I could hear him crashing through the brush. Then all was silent.

I wondered if he had left me to return to his fierce pack. A feeling of loneliness overwhelmed me. With a sigh I turned to the work of dragging the canoe down to the sea. As I entered the jungle where the dugout lay a hare darted from beneath the boat's side, and a well-aimed cast of my javelin brought it down. I was hungry — I had not realized it before — so I sat upon the edge of the canoe and devoured my repast. The last remnants gone, I again busied myself with preparations for my expedition to the island.

I did not know for certain that Dian was there; but I surmised as much. Nor could I guess what obstacles might confront me in an effort to rescue her. For a time I loitered about after I had the canoe at the water's edge, hoping against hope that Raja would return; but he did not, so I shoved the awkward craft through the surf and leaped into it.

I was still a little downcast by the desertion of my new-found friend, though I tried to assure myself that it was nothing but what I might have expected.

The savage brute had served me well in the short time that we had been together, and had repaid his debt of gratitude to me, since he had saved my life, or at least my liberty, no less certainly than I had saved his life when he was injured and drowning.

The trip across the water to the island was uneventful. I was mighty glad to be in the sunshine again when I passed out of the shadow of the dead world about halfway between the mainland and the island. The hot rays of the noonday sun did a great deal toward raising my spirits, and dispelling the mental gloom in which I had been shrouded almost continually since entering the Land of Awful Shadow. There is nothing more dispiriting to me than absence of sunshine.

I had paddled to the southwestern point, which Goork said he believed to be the least frequented portion of the island, as he had never seen boats put off from there. I found a shallow reef running far out into the sea and rather precipitous cliffs running almost to the surf. It was a nasty place to land, and I realized now why it was not used by the natives; but at last I managed, after a good wetting, to beach my canoe and scale the cliffs.

The country beyond them appeared more open and parklike than I had anticipated, since from the mainland the entire coast that is visible seems densely clothed with tropical jungle. This jungle, as I could see from the vantage-point of the cliff-top, formed but a relatively narrow strip between the sea and the more open forest and meadow of the interior. Farther back there was a range of low but apparently very rocky hills, and here and there all about were visible flat-topped masses of rock — small mountains, in fact — which reminded me of pictures I had seen of landscapes in New Mexico. Altogether, the country was very much broken and very beautiful. From where I stood I counted no less than a dozen streams winding down from among the table-buttes and emptying into a pretty river which flowed away in a northeasterly direction toward the opposite end of the island.

As I let my eyes roam over the scene I suddenly became aware of figures moving upon the flat top of a far-distant butte. Whether they were beast or human, though, I could not make out; but at least they were alive, so I determined to prosecute my search for Hooja's stronghold in the general direction of this butte.

To descend to the valley required no great effort. As I swung along through the lush grass and the fragrant flowers, my cudgel swinging in my hand and my javelin looped across my shoulders with its aurochs-hide strap, I felt equal to any emergency, ready for any danger.

I had covered quite a little distance, and I was passing through a strip of wood which lay at the foot of one of the flat-topped hills, when I became conscious of the sensation of being watched. My life within Pellucidar has rather quickened my senses of sight, hearing, and smell, and, too, certain primitive intuitive or instinctive qualities that seem blunted in civilized man. But, though I was positive that eyes were upon me, I could see no sign of any living thing within the wood other than the many, gay-plumaged birds and little monkeys which filled the trees with life, color, and action.

To you it may seem that my conviction was the result of an overwrought imagination, or to the actual reality of the prying eyes of the little monkeys or the curious ones of the birds; but there is a difference which I cannot explain between the sensation of casual observation and studied espionage. A sheep might gaze at you without transmitting a warning through your subjective mind, because you are in no danger from a sheep. But let a tiger gaze fixedly at you from ambush, and unless your primitive instincts are completely calloused you will presently commence to glance furtively about and be filled with vague, unreasoning terror.

Thus was it with me then. I grasped my

cudgel more firmly and unslung my javelin, carrying it in my left hand. I peered to left and right, but I saw nothing. Then, all quite suddenly, there fell about my neck and shoulders, around my arms and body, a number of pliant fiber ropes.

In a jiffy I was trussed up as neatly as you might wish. One of the nooses dropped to my ankles and was jerked up with a suddenness that brought me to my face upon the ground. Then something heavy and hairy sprang upon my back. I fought to draw my knife, but hairy hands grasped my wrists and, dragging them behind my back, bound them securely.

Next my feet were bound. Then I was turned over upon my back to look up into the faces of my captors.

And what faces! Imagine if you can a cross between a sheep and a gorilla, and you will have some conception of the physiognomy of the creature that bent close above me, and of those of the half-dozen others that clustered about. There was the facial length and great eyes of the sheep, and the bull-neck and hideous fangs of the gorilla. The bodies and limbs were both man and gorilla-like.

As they bent over me they conversed in a monosyllabic tongue that was perfectly intelligible to me. It was something of a simplified language that had no need for aught but nouns and verbs, but such words as it included were the same as those of the human beings of Pellucidar. It was amplified by many gestures which filled in the speech-gaps.

I asked them what they intended doing with me; but, like our own North American Indians when questioned by a white man, they pretended not to understand me. One of them swung me to his shoulder as lightly as if I had been a shoat. He was a huge creature, as were his fellows, standing fully seven feet upon his short legs and weighing considerably more than a quarter of a ton.

Two went ahead of my bearer and three behind. In this order we cut to the right through the forest to the foot of the hill where precipitous cliffs appeared to bar our farther progress in this direction. But my escort never paused. Like ants upon a wall, they scaled that seemingly unscalable barrier, clinging, Heaven knows how, to its ragged, perpendicular face. During most of the short journey to the summit I must

admit that my hair stood on end. Presently, however, we topped the thing and stood upon the level mesa which crowned it.

Immediately from all about, out of burrows and rough, rocky lairs, poured a perfect torrent of beasts similar to my captors. They clustered about, jabbering at my guards and attempting to get their hands upon me, whether from curiosity or a desire to do me bodily harm I did not know, since my escort with bared fangs and heavy blows kept them off.

Across the mesa we went, to stop at last before a large pile of rocks in which an opening appeared. Here my guards set me upon my feet and called out a word which sounded like "Gr-gr-gr!" and which I later learned was the name of their king.

Presently there emerged from the cavernous depths of the lair a monstrous creature, scarred from a hundred battles, almost hairless and with an empty socket where one eye had been. The other eye, sheeplike in its mildness, gave the most startling appearance to the beast, which but for that single timid orb was the most fearsome thing that one could imagine.

I had encountered the black, hairless, long-tailed ape-things of the mainland — the creatures which Perry thought might constitute the link between the higher orders of apes and man — but these brutemen of Gr-gr-gr seemed to set that theory back to zero, for there was less similarity between the black ape-men and these crea tures than there was between the latter and man, while both had many human attributes, some of which were better developed in one species and some in the other.

The black apes were hairless and built thatched huts in their arboreal retreats; they kept domesticated dogs and ruminants, in which respect they were farther advanced than the human beings of Pellucidar; but they appeared to have only a meager language, and sported long, apelike tails.

On the other hand, Gr-gr-gr's people were, for the most part, quite hairy, but they were tailless and had a language similar to that of the human race of Pellucidar; nor were they arboreal. Their skins, where skin showed, were white.

From the foregoing facts and others that I have noted during my long life within Pellucidar, which is now passing through an age analogous to some preglacial age of the outer crust, I am constrained to the belief that evolution is not so much a gradual transition from one form to another as it is an accident of breeding, either by crossing or the hazards of birth. In other words, it is my belief that the first man was a freak of nature — nor would one have to draw over-strongly upon his credulity to be convinced that Gr-gr-gr and his tribe were also freaks.

The great man-brute seated himself upon a flat rock — his throne, I imagine — just before the entrance to his lair. With elbows on knees and chin in palms he regarded me intently through his lone sheep-eye while one of my captors told of my taking.

When all had been related Gr-gr-gr questioned me. I shall not attempt to quote these people in their own abbreviated tongue — you would have even greater difficulty in interpreting them than did I. Instead, I shall put the words into their mouths which will carry to you the ideas which they intended to convey.

"You are an enemy," was Gr-gr-gr's initial declaration. "You belong to the tribe of Hooja."

Ah! So they knew Hooja and he was their enemy! Good!

"I am an enemy of Hooja," I replied. "He has stolen my mate and I have come here to take her away from him and punish Hooja."

"How could you do that alone?"

"I do not know," I answered, "but I should have tried had you not captured me. What do you intend to do with me?"

"You shall work for us."

"You will not kill me?" I asked.

"We do not kill except in self-defense," he replied; "self-defense and punishment. Those who would kill us and those who do wrong we kill. If we knew that you were one of Hooja's people we might kill you, for all Hooja's people are bad people; but you say you are an enemy of Hooja. You may not speak the truth, but until we learn that you have lied we shall not kill you. You shall work."

"If you hate Hooja," I suggested, "why not let me, who hate him, too, go and punish him?"

For some time Gr-gr-gr sat in thought. Then he raised his head and addressed my guard.

"Take him to his work," he ordered.

His tone was final. As if to emphasize it he turned and entered his burrow. My guard conducted me farther into the mesa, where we came presently to a tiny depression or valley, at one end of which gushed a warm spring.

The view that opened before me was the most surprising that I have ever seen. In the hollow, which must have covered several hundred acres, were numerous fields of growing things, and working all about with crude implements or with no implements at all other than their bare hands were many of the brute-men engaged in the first agriculture that I had seen within Pellucidar.

They put me to work cultivating in a patch of melons. I never was a farmer nor particularly keen for this sort of work, and I am free to confess that time never had dragged so heavily as it did during the hour or the year I spent there at that work. How long it really was I do not know, of course; but it was all too long.

The creatures that worked about me were quite simple and friendly. One of them proved to be a son of Gr-gr-gr. He had broken some minor tribal law, and was working out his sentence in the fields. He told me that his tribe had lived upon this hilltop always, and that there were other tribes like them dwelling upon other hilltops. They had no wars and had always lived in peace and harmony, menaced only by the larger carnivora of the island, until my kind had come under a creature called Hooja, and attacked and killed them when they chanced to descend from their natural fortresses to visit their fellows upon other lofty mesas.

Now they were afraid; but some day they would go in a body and fall upon Hooja and his people and slay them all. I explained to him that I was Hooja's enemy, and asked, when they were ready to go, that I be allowed to go with them, or, better still, that they let me go ahead and learn all that I could about the village where Hooja dwelt so that they might attack it with the best chance of success.

Gr-gr-gr's son seemed much impressed by my suggestion. He said that when he was through in the fields he would speak to his father about the matter.

Some time after this Gr-gr-gr came through the fields where we were, and his son spoke to him upon the subject, but the old gentleman was evidently in anything but a good humor, for he cuffed the youngster and, turning upon me, informed me that he was convinced that I had lied to him, and that I was one of Hooja's people.

"Wherefore," he concluded, "we shall slay you as soon as the melons are cultivated. Hasten, therefore."

And hasten I did. I hastened to cultivate the weeds which grew among the melon-vines. Where there had been one sickly weed before, I nourished two healthy ones. When I found a particularly promising variety of weed growing elsewhere than among my melons, I forthwith dug it up and transplanted it among my charges.

My masters did not seem to realize my perfidy. They saw me always laboring diligently in the melon-patch, and as time enters not into the reckoning of Pellucidarians — even of human beings and much less of brutes and half brutes — I might have lived on indefinitely through this subterfuge had not that occurred which took me out of the melon-patch for good and all.

Chapter IX

HOOJA'S CUTTHROATS APPEAR

I had built a little shelter of rocks and brush where I might crawl in and sleep out of the perpetual light and heat of the noonday sun. When I was tired or hungry I retired to my humble cot.

My masters never interposed the slightest objection. As a matter of fact, they were very good to me, nor did I see aught while I was among them to indicate that they are ever else than a simple, kindly folk when left to themselves. Their awe-inspiring size, terrific strength, mighty fighting-fangs, and hideous appearance are but the attributes necessary to the successful waging of their constant battle for survival, and well do they employ them when the need arises. The only flesh they eat is that of herbivorous animals and birds. When they hunt the mighty thag, the prehistoric bos of the outer crust, a single male, with his fiber rope, will catch and kill the greatest of the bulls.

Well, as I was about to say, I had this little shelter at the edge of my melon-patch. Here I was resting from my labors on a certain occasion when I heard a great hubbub in the village, which lay about a quarter of a mile away.

Presently a male came racing toward the field, shouting excitedly. As he approached I came from my shelter to learn what all the commotion might be about, for the monotony of my existence in the melon-patch must have fostered that trait of curiosity from which it had always been my secret boast I am peculiarly free.

The other workers also ran forward to meet the messenger, who quickly unburdened himself of his information, and as quickly turned and scampered back toward the village. When running these beast-men often go upon all fours. Thus they leap over obstacles that would slow up a human being, and upon the level attain a speed that would make a thoroughbred look to his laurels. The result in this instance was that before I had more than assimilated the gist of the word which had been brought to the fields, I was alone, watching my erstwhile co-workers speeding villageward.

I was alone! It was the first time since my capture that no beast-man had been within sight of me. I was alone! And all my captors were in the village at the opposite edge of the mesa repelling an attack of Hooja's horde!

It seemed from the messenger's tale that two of Gr-gr-gr's great males had been set upon by a half-dozen of Hooja's cutthroats while the former were peaceably returning from the thag hunt. The two had returned to the village unscratched, while but a single one of Hooja's half-dozen had escaped to report the outcome of the battle to their leader. Now Hooja was coming to punish Gr-gr-gr's people. With his large force, armed with the bows and arrows that Hooja had learned from me to make, with long lances and sharp knives, I feared that even the mighty strength of the beast-men could avail them but little.

At last had come the opportunity for which I waited! I was free to make for the far end of the mesa, find my way to the valley below, and while the two forces were engaged in their struggle, continue my search for Hooja's village, which I had learned from the beast-men lay farther on down the river that I had been following when taken prisoner.

As I turned to make for the mesa's rim

the sounds of battle came plainly to my ears — the hoarse shouts of men mingled with the half-beastly roars and growls of the brute-folk.

Did I take advantage of my opportunity?

I did not. Instead, lured by the din of strife and by the desire to deliver a stroke, however feeble, against hated Hooja, I wheeled and ran directly toward the village.

When I reached the edge of the plateau such a scene met my astonished gaze as never before had startled it, for the unique battle-methods of the half-brutes were rather the most remarkable I had ever witnessed. Along the very edge of the cliff-top stood a thin line of mighty males — the best rope-throwers of the tribe. A few feet behind these the rest of the males, with the exception of about twenty, formed a second line. Still farther in the rear all the women and young children were clustered into a single group under the protection of the remaining twenty fighting males and all the old males.

But it was the work of the first two lines that interested me. The forces of Hooja — a great horde of savage Sagoths and primeval cave men — were working their way up the steep cliff-face, their agility but slightly less than that of my captors who had clambered so nimbly aloft — even he who was burdened by my weight.

As the attackers came on they paused occasionally wherever a projection gave them sufficient foothold and launched arrows and spears at the defenders above them. During the entire battle both sides hurled taunts and insults at one another — the human beings naturally excelling the brutes in the coarseness and vileness of their vilification and invective.

The "firing-line" of the brute-men wielded no weapon other than their long fiber nooses. When a foeman came within range of them a noose would settle unerringly about him and he would be dragged, fighting and yelling, to the cliff-top, unless, as occasionally occurred, he was quick enough to draw his knife and cut the rope above him, in which event he usually plunged downward to a no less certain death than that which awaited him above.

Those who were hauled up within reach of the powerful clutches of the defenders had the nooses snatched from them and were catapulted back through the first line to the second, where they were seized and killed by the simple expedient of a single powerful closing of mighty fangs upon the backs of their necks.

But the arrows of the invaders were taking a much heavier toll than the nooses of the defenders and I foresaw that it was but a matter of time before Hooja's forces must conquer unless the brute-men changed their tactics, or the cave men tired of the battle.

Gr-gr-gr was standing in the center of the first line. All about him were boulders and large fragments of broken rock. I approached him and without a word toppled a large mass of rock over the edge of the cliff. It fell directly upon the head of an archer, crushing him to instant death and carrying his mangled corpse with it to the bottom of the declivity, and on its way brushing three more of the attackers into the hereafter.

Gr-gr-gr turned toward me in surprise. For an instant he appeared to doubt the sincerity of my motives. I felt that perhaps my time had come when he reached for me with one of his giant paws; but I dodged him, and running a few paces to the right hurled down another missile. It, too, did its allotted work of destruction. Then I picked up smaller fragments and with all the control and accuracy for which I had earned justly deserved fame in my collegiate days I rained down a hail of death upon those beneath me.

Gr-gr-gr was coming toward me again. I pointed to the litter of rubble upon the cliff-top.

"Hurl these down upon the enemy!" I cried to him. "Tell your warriors to throw rocks down upon them!"

At my words the others of the first line, who had been interested spectators of my tactics, seized upon great boulders or bits of rock, whichever came first to their hands, and, without waiting for a command from Gr-gr-gr, deluged the terrified cave men with a perfect avalanche of stone. In less than no time the cliff-face was stripped of enemies and the village of Gr-gr-gr was saved.

Gr-gr-gr was standing beside me when the last of the cave men disappeared in rapid flight down the valley. He was looking at me intently.

"Those were your people," he said. "Why did you kill them?"

"They were not my people," I returned. "I have told you that before, but you would not believe me. Will you believe me now when I tell you that I hate Hooja and his tribe as much as you do? Will you believe me when I tell you that I wish to be the friend of Gr-gr-gr?"

For some time he stood there beside me, scratching his head. Evidently it was no less difficult for him to readjust his preconceived conclusions than it is for most human beings; but finally the idea percolated — which it might never have done had he been a man, or I might qualify that statement by saying had he been some men. Finally he spoke.

"Gilak," he said, "you have made Gr-gr-gr ashamed. He would have killed you. How can he reward you?"

"Set me free," I replied quickly.

"You are free," he said. "You may go down when you wish, or you may stay with us. If you go you may always return. We are your friends."

Naturally, I elected to go. I explained all over again to Gr-gr-gr the nature of my mission. He listened attentively; after I had done he offered to send some of his people with me to guide me to Hooja's village. I was not slow in accepting his offer.

First, however, we must eat. The hunters upon whom Hooja's men had fallen had brought back the meat of a great thag. There would be a feast to commemorate the victory — a feast and dancing.

I had never witnessed a tribal function of the brute-folk, though I had often heard strange sounds coming from the village, where I had not been allowed since my capture. Now I took part in one of their orgies.

It will live forever in my memory. The combination of bestiality and humanity was oftentimes pathetic, and again grotesque or horrible. Beneath the glaring noonday sun, in the sweltering heat of the mesa-top, the huge, hairy creatures leaped in a great circle. They coiled and threw their fiber-ropes; they hurled taunts and insults at an imaginary foe; they fell upon the carcass of the thag and literally tore it to pieces; and they ceased only when, gorged, they could no longer move.

I had to wait until the processes of digestion had released my escort from its torpor. Some had eaten until their abdomens were so distended that I thought they must burst, for beside the thag there had

been fully a hundred antelopes of various sizes and varied degrees of decomposition, which they had unearthed from burial beneath the floors of their lairs to grace the banquet-board.

But at last we were started — six great males and myself. Gr-gr-gr had returned my weapons to me, and at last I was once more upon my oft-interrupted way toward my goal. Whether I should find Dian at the end of my journey or no I could not even surmise; but I was none the less impatient to be off, for if only the worst lay in store for me I wished to know even the worst at once.

I could scarce believe that my proud mate would still be alive in the power of Hooja; but time upon Pellucidar is so strange a thing that I realized that to her or to him only a few minutes might have elapsed since his subtle trickery had enabled him to steal her away from Phutra. Or she might have found the means either to repel his advances or escape him.

As we descended the cliff we disturbed a great pack of large hyena-like beasts — *hyaena spelaeus*, Perry calls them — who were busy among the corpses of the cave men fallen in battle. The ugly creatures were far from the cowardly things that our own hyenas are reputed to be; they stood their ground with bared fangs as we approached them. But, as I was later to learn, so formidable are the brute-folk that there are few even of the larger carnivora that will not make way for them when they go abroad. So the hyenas moved a little from our line of march, closing in again upon their feasts when we had passed.

We made our way steadily down the rim of the beautiful river which flows the length of the island, coming at last to a wood rather denser than any that I had before encountered in this country. Well within this forest my escort halted.

"There!" they said, and pointed ahead. "We are to go no further."

Thus having guided me to my destination they left me. Ahead of me, through the trees, I could see what appeared to be the foot of a steep hill. Toward this I made my way. The forest ran to the very base of a cliff, in the face of which were the mouths of many caves. They appeared untenanted; but I decided to watch for a while before venturing farther. A large tree, densely foliaged, offered a splendid vantage-point from which to spy upon the cliff, so I clambered among its branches where, securely hidden, I could watch what transpired about the caves.

It seemed that I had scarcely settled myself in a comfortable position before a party of cave men emerged from one of the smaller apertures in the cliff-face, about fifty feet from the base. They descended into the forest and disappeared. Soon after came several others from the same cave, and after them, at a short interval, a score of women and children, who came into the wood to gather fruit. There were several warriors with them — a guard, I presume.

After this came other parties, and two or three groups who passed out of the forest and up the cliff-face to enter the same cave. I could not understand it. All who had come out had emerged from the same cave. All who returned re-entered it. No other cave gave evidence of habitation, and no cave but one of extraordinary size could have accommodated all the people whom I had seen pass in and out of its mouth.

For a long time I sat and watched the coming and going of great numbers of the cave-folk. Not once did one leave the cliff by any other opening save that from which I had seen the first party come, nor did any re-enter the cliff through another aperture.

What a cave it must be, I thought, that houses an entire tribe! But dissatisfied of the truth of my surmise, I climbed higher among the branches of the tree that I might get a better view of other portions of the cliff. High above the ground I reached a point whence I could see the summit of the hill. Evidently it was a flat-topped butte similar to that on which dwelt the tribe of Gr-gr-gr.

As I sat gazing at it a figure appeared at the very edge. It was that of a young girl in whose hair was a gorgeous bloom plucked from some flowering tree of the forest. I had seen her pass beneath me but a short while before and enter the small cave that had swallowed all of the returning tribesmen.

The mystery was solved. The cave was but the mouth of a passage that led upward through the cliff to the summit of the hill. It served merely as an avenue from their lofty citadel to the valley below.

No sooner had the truth flashed upon me than the realization came that I must seek some other means of reaching the village, for to pass unobserved through this well-traveled thoroughfare would be impossible. At the moment there was no one in sight below me, so I slid quickly from my arboreal watch-tower to the ground and moved rapidly away to the right with the intention of circling the hill if necessary until I had found an unwatched spot where I might have some slight chance of scaling the heights and reaching the top unseen.

I kept close to the edge of the forest, in the very midst of which the hill seemed to rise. Though I carefully scanned the cliff as I traversed its base, I saw no sign of any other entrance than that to which my guides had led me.

After some little time the roar of the sea broke upon my ears. Shortly after I came upon the broad ocean which breaks at this point at the very foot of the great hill where Hooja had found safe refuge for himself and his villains.

I was just about to clamber along the jagged rocks which lie at the base of the cliff next to the sea, in search of some foothold to the top, when I chanced to see a canoe rounding the end of the island. I threw myself down behind a large boulder where I could watch the dugout and its occupants without myself being seen.

They paddled toward me for a while and then, about a hundred yards from me, they turned straight in toward the foot of the frowning cliffs. From where I was it seemed that they were bent upon self-destruction, since the roar of the breakers beating upon the perpendicular rock-face appeared to offer only death to any one who might venture within their relentless clutch.

A mass of rock would soon hide them from my view; but so keen was the excitement of the instant that I could not refrain from crawling forward to a point whence I could watch the dashing of the small craft to pieces on the jagged rocks that loomed before her, although I risked discovery from above to accomplish my design.

When I had reached a point where I could again see the dugout, I was just in time to see it glide unharmed between two needle-pointed sentinels of granite and floated quietly upon the unruffled bosom of a tiny cove.

Again I crouched behind a boulder to observe what would next transpire; nor did I have long to wait. The dugout, which contained but two men, was drawn close to the rocky wall. A fiber rope, one end of which was tied to the boat, was made fast about a projection of the cliff face.

Then the two men commenced the ascent of the almost perpendicular wall toward the summit several hundred feet above. I looked on in amazement, for, splendid climbers though the cave men of Pellucidar are, I never before had seen so remarkable a feat performed. Upward they moved without a pause, to disappear at last over the summit.

When I felt reasonably sure that they had gone for a while at least I crawled from my hiding-place and at the risk of a broken neck leaped and scrambled to the spot where their canoe was moored.

If they had scaled that cliff I could, and if I couldn't I should die in the attempt.

But when I turned to the accomplishment of the task I found it easier than I had imagined it would be, since I immediately discovered that shallow hand and footholds had been scooped in the cliff's rocky face, forming a crude ladder from the base to the summit.

At last I reached the top, and very glad I was, too. Cautiously I raised my head until my eyes were above the cliff-crest. Before me spread a rough mesa, liberally sprinkled with large boulders. There was no village in sight nor any living creature.

I drew myself to level ground and stood erect. A few trees grew among the boulders. Very carefully I advanced from tree to tree and boulder to boulder toward the inland end of the mesa. I stopped often to listen and look cautiously about me in every direction.

How I wished that I had my revolvers and rifle! I would not have to worm my way like a scared cat toward Hooja's village, nor did I relish doing so now; but Dian's life might hinge upon the success of my venture, and so I could not afford to take chances. To have met suddenly with discovery and had a score or more of armed warriors upon me might have been very grand and heroic; but it would have immediately put an end to all my earthly activities, nor have accomplished aught in the service of Dian.

Well, I must have traveled nearly a mile across that mesa without seeing a sign of anyone, when all of a sudden, as I crept around the edge of a boulder, I ran plump into a man, down on all fours like myself, crawling toward me.

Chapter X

THE RAID ON THE CAVE-PRISON

His head was turned over his shoulder as I first saw him — he was looking back toward the village. As I leaped for him his eyes fell upon me. Never in my life have I seen a more surprised mortal than this poor cave man. Before he could utter a single scream of warning or alarm I had my fingers on his throat and had dragged him behind the boulder, where I proceeded to sit upon him, while I figured out what I had best do with him.

He struggled a little at first, but finally lay still, and so I released the pressure of my fingers at his windpipe, for which I imagine he was quite thankful — I know that I should have been.

I hated to kill him in cold blood; but what else I was to do with him I could not see, for to turn him loose would have been merely to have the entire village aroused and down upon me in a moment. The fellow lay looking up at me with the surprise still deeply written on his countenance. At last, all of a sudden, a look of recognition entered his eyes.

"I have seen you before," he said. "I saw you in the arena at the Mahars' city of Phutra when the thipdars dragged the tarag from you and your mate. I never understood that. Afterward they put me in the arena with two warriors from Gombul."

He smiled in recollection.

"It would have been the same had there been ten warriors from Gombul. I slew them, winning my freedom. Look!"

He half turned his left shoulder toward me, exhibiting the newly healed scar of the Mahars' branded mark.

"Then," he continued, "as I was returning to my people I met some of them fleeing. They told me that one called Hooja the Sly One had come and seized our village, putting our people into slavery. So I hurried hither to learn the truth, and, sure enough, here I found Hooja and his wicked men living in my village, and my father's people but slaves among them.

"I was discovered and captured, but Hooja did not kill me. I am the chief's son, and through me he hoped to win my father's warriors back to the village to help him in a great war he says that he will soon commence.

"Among his prisoners is Dian the Beautiful One, whose brother, Dacor the Strong One, chief of Amoz, once saved my life when he came to Thuria to steal a mate. I helped him capture her, and we are good friends. So when I learned that Dian the Beautiful One was Hooja's prisoner, I told him that I would not aid him if he harmed her.

"Recently one of Hooja's warriors overheard me talking with another prisoner. We were planning to combine all the prisoners, seize weapons, and when most of Hooja's warriors were away, slay the rest and retake our hilltop. Had we done so we could have held it, for there are only two entrances — the narrow tunnel at one end and the steep path up the cliffs at the other.

"But when Hooja heard what we had planned he was very angry, and ordered that I die. They bound me hand and foot and placed me in a cave until all the warriors should return to witness my death; but while they were away I heard someone calling me in a muffled voice which seemed to come from the wall of the cave. When I replied the voice, which was a woman's, told me that she had overheard all that had passed between me and those who had brought me thither, and that she was Dacor's sister and would find a way to help me.

"Presently a little hole appeared in the wall at the point from which the voice had come. After a time I saw a woman's hand digging with a bit of stone. Dacor's sister made a hole in the wall between the cave where I lay bound and that in which she had been confined, and soon she was by my side and had cut my bonds.

"We talked then, and I offered to make the attempt to take her away and back to the land of Sari, where she told me she would be able to learn the whereabouts of her mate. Just now I was going to the other end of the island to see if a boat lay there, and if the way was clear for our escape. Most of the boats are always away now, for a great many of Hooja's men and nearly all the slaves are upon the Island of Trees, where Hooja is having many boats built to carry his warriors across the water to the mouth of a great river which he discovered while he was returning from Phutra — a vast river that empties into the sea there."

The speaker pointed toward the northeast.

"It is wide and smooth and slow-running almost to the land of Sari," he added.

"And where is Dian the Beautiful One now?" I asked.

I had released my prisoner as soon as I found that he was Hooja's enemy, and now the pair of us were squatting beside the boulder while he told his story.

"She returned to the cave where she had been imprisoned," he replied, "and is awaiting me there."

"There is no danger that Hooja will come while you are away?"

"Hooja is upon the Island of Trees," he replied.

"Can you direct me to the cave so that I can find it alone?" I asked.

He said he could, and in the strange yet explicit fashion of the Pellucidarians he explained minutely how I might reach the cave where he had been imprisoned, and through the hole in its wall reach Dian.

I thought it best for but one of us to return, since two could accomplish but little more than one and would double the risk of discovery. In the meantime he could make his way to the sea and guard the boat, which I told him lay there at the foot of the cliff.

I told him to await us at the cliff-top, and if Dian came alone to do his best to get away with her and take her to Sari, as I thought it quite possible that, in case of detection and pursuit, it might be necessary for me to hold off Hooja's people while Dian made her way alone to where my new friend was to await her. I impressed upon him the fact that he might have to resort to trickery or even to force to get Dian to leave me; but I made him promise that he would sacrifice everything, even his life, in an attempt to rescue Dacor's sister.

Then we parted — he to take up his position where he could watch the boat and await Dian, I to crawl cautiously on toward the caves. I had no difficulty in following the directions given me by Juag, the name by which Dacor's friend said he was called. There was the leaning tree, my first point he told me to look for after rounding the boulder where we had met. After that I crawled to the balanced rock, a huge boulder resting upon a tiny base no larger than the palm of your hand.

From here I had my first view of the village of caves. A low bluff ran diagonally across one end of the mesa, and in the face of this bluff were the mouths of many caves. Zig-zag trails led up to them, and narrow ledges scooped from the face of the soft rock connected those upon the same level.

The cave in which Juag had been confined was at the extreme end of the cliff nearest me. By taking advantage of the bluff itself, I could approach within a few feet of the aperture without being visible from any other cave. There were few people about at the time; most of these were congregated at the foot of the far end of the bluff, where they were so engrossed in excited conversation that I felt but little fear of detection. However I exercised the greatest care in approaching the cliff. After watching for a while until I caught an instant when every head was turned away from me, I darted, rabbitlike, into the cave.

Like many of the man-made caves of Pellucidar, this one consisted of three chambers, one behind another, and all unlit except for what sunlight filtered in through the external opening. The result was gradually increasing darkness as one passed into each succeeding chamber.

In the last of the three I could just distinguish objects, and that was all. As I was groping around the walls for the hole that should lead into the cave where Dian was imprisoned, I heard a man's voice quite close to me.

The speaker had evidently but just entered, for he spoke in a loud tone, demanding the whereabouts of one whom he had come in search of.

"Where are you, woman?" he cried. "Hooja has sent for you."

And then a woman's voice answered him:

"And what does Hooja want of me?"

The voice was Dian's. I groped in the direction of the sounds, feeling for the hole.

"He wishes you brought to the Island of Trees," replied the man; "for he is ready to take you as his mate."

"I will not go," said Dian. "I will die first."

"I am sent to bring you, and bring you I shall."

I could hear him crossing the cave toward her.

Frantically I clawed the wall of the cave in which I was in an effort to find the elusive aperture that would lead me to Dian's side.

I heard the sound of a scuffle in the next

cave. Then my fingers sank into loose rock and earth in the side of the cave. In an instant I realized why I had been unable to find the opening while I had been lightly feeling the surface of the walls — Dian had blocked up the hole she had made lest it arouse suspicion and lead to an early discovery of Juag's escape.

Plunging my weight against the crumbling mass, I sent it crashing into the adjoining cavern. With it came I, David, Emperor of Pellucidar. I doubt if any other potentate in a world's history ever made a more undignified entrance. I landed head first on all fours, but I came quickly and was on my feet before the man in the dark guessed what had happened.

He saw me, though, when I arose and, sensing that no friend came thus precipitately, turned to meet me even as I charged him. I had my stone knife in my hand, and he had his. In the darkness of the cave there was little opportunity for a display of science, though even at that I venture to say that we fought a very pretty duel.

Before I came to Pellucidar I do not recall that I ever had seen a stone knife, and I am sure that I never fought with a knife of any description; but now I do not have to take my hat off to any of them when it comes to wielding that primitive yet wicked weapon.

I could just see Dian in the darkness, but I knew that she could not see my features or recognize me; and I enjoyed in anticipation, even while I was fighting for her life and mine, her dear joy when she should discover that it was I who was her deliverer.

My opponent was large, but he also was active and no mean knife-man. He caught me once fairly in the shoulder — I carry the scar yet, and shall carry it to the grave. And then he did a foolish thing, for as I leaped back to gain a second in which to calm the shock of the wound he rushed after me and tried to clinch. He rather neglected his knife for the moment in his greater desire to get his hands on me. Seeing the opening, I swung my left fist fairly to the point of his jaw.

Down he went. Before ever he could scramble up again I was on him and had buried my knife in his heart. Then I stood up — and there was Dian facing me and peering at me through the dense gloom.

"You are not Juag!" she exlaimed. "Who are you?"

I took a step toward her, my arms outstretched.

"It is I, Dian," I said. "It is David."

At the sound of my voice she gave a little cry in which tears were mingled — a pathetic little cry that told me all without words how far hope had gone from her — and then she ran forward and threw herself in my arms. I covered her perfect lips and her beautiful face with kisses, and stroked her thick black hair, and told her again and again what she already knew — what she had known for years — that I loved her better than all else which two worlds had to offer. We couldn't devote much time, though, to the happiness of love-making, for we were in the midst of enemies who might discover us at any moment.

I drew her into the adjoining cave. Thence we made our way to the mouth of the cave that had given me entrance to the cliff. Here I reconnoitered for a moment, and seeing the coast clear, ran swiftly forth with Dian at my side. We dodged around the cliff-end, then paused for an instant, listening. No sound reached our ears to indicate that any had seen us, and we moved cautiously onward along the way by which I had come.

As we went Dian told me that her captors had informed her how close I had come in search of her — even to the Land of Awful Shadow — and how one of Hooja's men who knew me had discovered me asleep and robbed me of all my possessions. And then how Hooja had sent four others to find me and take me prisoner. But these men, she said, had not yet returned, or at least she had not heard of their return.

"Nor will you ever," I responded, "for they have gone to that place whence none ever returns." I then related my adventure with these four.

We had come almost to the cliff-edge where Juag should be awaiting us when we saw two men walking rapidly toward the same spot from another direction. They did not see us, nor did they see Juag, whom I now discovered hiding behind a low bush close to the verge of the precipice which drops into the sea at this point. As quickly as possible, without exposing ourselves too much to the enemy, we hastened forward that we might reach Juag as quickly as they.

But they noticed him first and immediately charged him, for one of them had been his guard, and they had both been sent to search for him, his escape having been discovered between the time he left the cave and the time when I reached it. Evidently they had wasted precious moments looking for him in other portions of the mesa.

When I saw that the two of them were rushing him, I called out to attract their attention to the fact that they had more than a single man to cope with. They paused at the sound of my voice and looked about.

When they discovered Dian and me they exchanged a few words, and one of them continued toward Juag while the other turned upon us. As he came nearer I saw that he carried in his hand one of my six-shooters, but he was holding it by the barrel, evidently mistaking it for some sort of war-club or tomahawk.

I could scarce refrain a grin when I thought of the wasted possibilities of that deadly revolver in the hands of an untutored warrior of the stone age. Had he but reversed it and pulled the trigger he might still be alive; maybe he is for all I know, since I did not kill him then. When he was about twenty feet from me I flung my javelin with a quick movement that I had learned from Ghak. He ducked to avoid it, and instead of receiving it in his heart, for which it was intended, he got it on the side of the head.

Down he went all in a heap. Then I glanced toward Juag. He was having a most exciting time. The fellow pitted against Juag was a veritable giant; he was hacking and hewing away at the poor slave with a villainous-looking knife that might have been designed for butchering mastodons. Step by step, he was forcing Juag back toward the edge of the cliff with a fiendish cunning that permitted his adversary no chance to side-step the terrible consequences of retreat in this direction. I saw quickly that in another moment Juag must deliberately hurl himself to death over the precipice or be pushed over by his foeman.

And as I saw Juag's predicament I saw, too, in the same instant, a way to relieve him. Leaping quickly to the side of the fellow I had just felled, I snatched up my fallen revolver. It was a desperate chance to take, and I realized it in the instant that I threw the gun up from my hip and pulled the trigger. There was no time to aim. Juag was upon the very brink of the chasm. His relentless foe was pushing him hard, beating at him furiously with the heavy knife.

And then the revolver spoke — loud and sharp. The giant threw his hands above his head, whirled about like a huge top, and lunged forward over the precipice.

And Juag?

He cast a single affrighted glance in my direction — never before, of course, had he heard the report of a firearm — and with a howl of dismay he, too, turned and plunged headforemost from sight. Horror-struck, I hastened to the brink of the abyss just in time to see two splashes upon the surface of the little cove below.

For an instant I stood there watching with Dian at my side. Then, to my utter amazement, I saw Juag rise to the surface and swim strongly toward the boat.

The fellow had dived that incredible distance and come up unharmed!

I called to him to await us below, assuring him that he need have no fear of my weapon, since it would harm only my enemies. He shook his head and muttered something which I could not hear at so great a distance; but when I pushed him he promised to wait for us. At the same instant Dian caught my arm and pointed toward the village. My shot had brought a crowd of natives on the run toward us.

The fellow whom I had stunned with my javelin had regained consciousness and scrambled to his feet. He was now racing as fast as he could go back toward his people. It looked mighty dark for Dian and me with that ghastly descent between us and even the beginnings of liberty, and a horde of savage enemies advancing at a rapid run.

There was but one hope. That was to get Dian started for the bottom without delay. I took her in my arms just for an instant — I felt, somehow, that it might be for the last time. For the life of me I couldn't see how both of us could escape.

I asked her if she could make the descent alone — if she were not afraid. She smiled up at me bravely and shrugged her shoulders. She afraid! So beautiful is she that I am always having difficulty in remembering that she is a primitive, half-savage cave girl of the stone age, and often find myself mentally limiting her capacities to those of the effete and over-civilized beauties of the outer crust.

"And you?" she asked as she swung over the edge of the cliff.

"I shall follow you after I take a shot or two at our friends," I replied. "I just want to give them a taste of this new medicine which is going to cure Pellucidar of all its ills. That will stop them long enough for me to join you. Now hurry, and tell Juag to be ready to shove off the moment I reach the boat, or the instant that it becomes apparent that I cannot reach it.

"You, Dian, must return to Sari if anything happens to me, that you may devote your life to carrying out with Perry the hopes and plans for Pellucidar that are so dear to my heart. Promise me, dear."

She hated to promise to desert me, nor would she; only shaking her head and making no move to descend. The tribesmen were nearing us. Juag was shouting up to us from below. It was evident that he realized from my actions that I was attempting to persuade Dian to descend, and that grave danger threatened us from above.

"Dive!" he cried. "Dive!"

I looked at Dian and then down at the abyss below us. The cove appeared no larger than a saucer. How Juag ever had hit it I could not guess.

"Dive!" cried Juag. "It is the only way — there is no time to climb down."

Chapter XI

ESCAPE

Dian glanced downward and shuddered. Her tribe were hill people — they were not accustomed to swimming other than in quiet rivers and placid lakelets. It was not the steep that appalled her. It was the ocean — vast, mysterious, terrible.

To dive into it from this great height was beyond her. I couldn't wonder, either. To have attempted it myself seemed too preposterous even for thought. Only one consideration could have prompted me to leap headforemost from that giddy height — suicide; or at least so I thought at the moment.

"Quick!" I urged Dian. "You cannot dive; but I can hold them until you reach safety."

"And you?" she asked once more. "Can you dive when they come too close? Otherwise you could not escape them if you waited here until I reached the bottom."

I saw that she would not leave me unless she thought that I could make that frightful dive as we had seen Juag make it. I glanced once downward; then with a mental shrug I assured her that I would dive the moment that she reached the boat. Satisfied, she began the descent carefully, yet swiftly. I watched her for a moment, my heart in my mouth lest some slight misstep or the slipping of a finger-hold should pitch her to a frightful death upon the rocks below.

Then I turned toward the advancing Hoojans — "Hoosiers," Perry dubbed them — even going so far as to christen this island where Hooja held sway Indiana; it is so marked now upon our maps. They were coming on at a great rate. I raised my revolver, took deliberate aim at the foremost warrior, and pulled the trigger. With the bark of the gun the fellow lunged forward. He head doubled beneath him. He rolled over and over two or three times before he came to a stop, to lie very quietly in the thick grass among the brilliant wild flowers.

Those behind him halted. One of them hurled a javelin toward me, but it fell short — they were just beyond javelin-range. There were two armed with bows and arrows; these I kept my eyes on. All of them appeared awe-struck and frightened by the sound and effect of the firearm. They kept looking from the corpse to me and jabbering among themselves.

I took advantage of the lull in hostilities to throw a quick glance over the edge toward Dian. She was half-way down the cliff and progressing finely. Then I turned back toward the enemy. One of the bowmen was fitting an arrow to his bow. I raised my hand.

"Stop!" I cried. "Whoever shoots at me or advances toward me I shall kill as I killed him!"

I pointed at the dead man. The fellow lowered his bow. Again there was animated discussion. I could see that those who were not armed with bows were urging something upon the two who were.

At last the majority appeared to prevail, for simultaneously the two archers raised their weapons. At the same instant I fired at one of them, dropping him in his tracks. The other, however, launched his missile, but the report of my gun had given him such a start that the arrow flew wild above my head. A second after and he, too, was sprawled upon the sward with a round hole between his eyes. It had been a rather good shot.

I glanced over the edge again. Dian was almost at the bottom. I could see Juag standing just beneath her with his hands up-stretched to assist her.

A sullen roar from the warriors recalled my attention toward them. They stood shaking their fists at me and yelling insults. From the direction of the village I saw a single warrior coming to join them. He was a huge fellow, and when he strode among them I could tell by his bearing and their deference toward him that he was a chieftain. He listened to all they had to tell of the happenings of the last few minutes; then with a command and a roar he started for me with the whole pack at his heels. All they had needed had arrived — namely, a brave leader.

I had two unfired cartridges in the chambers of my gun. I let the big warrior have one of them, thinking that his death would stop them all. But I guess they were worked up to such a frenzy of rage by this time that nothing would have stopped them. At any rate, they only yelled the louder as he fell and increased their speed toward me. I dropped another with my remaining cartridge.

Then they were upon me — or almost. I thought of my promise to Dian — the awful abyss was behind me — a big devil with a huge bludgeon in front of me. I grasped my six-shooter by the barrel and hurled it squarely in his face with all my strength.

Then, without waiting to learn the effect of my throw, I wheeled, ran the few steps to the edge, and leaped as far out over that frightful chasm as I could. I know something of diving, and all that I know I put into that dive, which I was positive would be my last.

For a couple of hundred feet I fell in a horizontal position. The momentum I gained was terrific. I could feel the air almost as a solid body, so swiftly I hurtled through it. Then my position gradually changed to the vertical, and with hands outstretched I slipped through the air, cleaving it like a flying arrow. Just before I struck the water a perfect shower of javelins fell all about. My enemies had rushed to the brink and hurled their weapons after me. By a miracle I was untouched.

In the final instant I saw that I had cleared the rocks and was going to strike the water fairly. Then I was in and plumbing the depths. I suppose I didn't really go very far down, but it seemed to me that I should never stop. When at last I dared curve my hands upward and divert my progress toward the surface, I thought that I should explode for air before I ever saw the sun again except through a swirl of water. But at last my head popped above the waves, and I filled my lungs with air.

Before me was the boat, from which Juag and Dian were clambering. I couldn't understand why they were deserting it now, when we were about to set out for the mainland in it; but when I reached its side I understood. Two heavy javelins, missing Dian and Juag by but a hair's breadth, had sunk deep into the bottom of the dugout in a straight line with the grain of the wood, and split her almost in two from stem to stern. She was useless.

Juag was leaning over a near-by rock, his hand outstretched to aid me in clambering to his side; nor did I lose any time in availing myself of his preferred assistance. An occasional javelin was still dropping perilously close to us, so we hastened to draw as close as possible to the cliffside, where we were comparatively safe from the missiles.

Here we held a brief conference, in which it was decided that our only hope now lay in making for the opposite end of the island as quickly as we could, and utilizing the boat that I had hidden there to continue our journey to the mainland.

Gathering up three of the least damaged javelins that had fallen about us, we set out upon our journey, keeping well toward the south side of the island, which Juag said was less frequented by the Hoojans than the central portion where the river ran. I think that this ruse must have thrown our pursuers off our track, since we saw nothing of them nor heard any sound of pursuit during the greater portion of our march the length of the island.

But the way Juag had chosen was rough and roundabout, so that we consumed one or two more marches in covering the distance than if we had followed the river. This it was which proved our undoing.

Those who sought us must have sent a party up the river immediately after we escaped; for when we came at last onto the river-trail not far from our destination, there can be no doubt but that we were seen by Hoojans who were just ahead of us on the stream. The result was that as we were passing through a clump of bush a score of warriors leaped out upon us, and before we could scarce strike a blow in defense, had disarmed and bound us.

For a time thereafter I seemed to be entirely bereft of hope. I could see no ray of promise in the future — only immediate death for Juag and me, which didn't concern me much in the face of what lay in store for Dian.

Poor child! What an awful life she had led! From the moment that I had first seen her chained in the slave caravan of the Mahars until now, a prisoner of a no less cruel creature, I could recall but a few brief intervals of peace and quiet in her tempestuous existence. Before I had known her, Jubal the Ugly One had pursued her across a savage world to make her his mate. She had eluded him, and finally I had slain him; but terror and privations, and exposure to fierce beasts had haunted her footsteps during all her lonely flight from him. And when I had returned to the outer world the old trials had recommenced with Hooja in Jubal's role. I could almost have wished for death to vouchsafe her that peace which fate seemed to deny her in this life.

I spoke to her on the subject, suggesting that we expire together.

"Do not fear, David," she replied. "I shall end my life before ever Hooja can harm me; but first I shall see that Hooja dies."

She drew from her breast a little leathern thong, to the end of which was fastened a tiny pouch.

"What have you there?" I asked.

"Do you recall that time you stepped upon the thing you call viper in your world?" she asked.

I nodded.

"The accident gave you the idea for the poisoned arrows with which we fitted the warriors of the empire," she continued. "And, too, it gave me an idea. For a long time I have carried a viper's fang in my bosom. It has given me strength to endure many dangers, for it has always assured me immunity from the ultimate insult. I am not ready to die yet. First let Hooja embrace the viper's fang."

So we did not die together, and I am glad now that we did not. It is always a foolish thing to contemplate suicide; for no matter how dark the future may appear today, tomorrow may hold for us that which will alter our whole life in an instant, revealing to us nothing but sunshine and happiness. So, for my part, I shall always wait for tomorrow.

In Pellucidar, where it is always today, the wait may not be so long, and so it proved for us. As we were passing a lofty, flat-topped hill through a parklike wood a perfect network of fiber ropes fell suddenly about our guard, enmeshing them. A moment later a horde of our friends, the hairy gorilla-men, with the mild eyes and long faces of sheep leaped among them.

It was a very interesting fight. I was sorry that my bonds prevented me from taking part in it, but I urged on the brute-men with my voice, and cheered old Gr-gr-gr, their chief, each time that his mighty jaws crunched out the life of a Hoojan. When the battle was over we found that a few of our captors had escaped, but the majority of them lay dead about us. The gorilla-men paid no further attention to them. Gr-gr-gr turned to me.

"Gr-gr-gr and all his people are your friends," he said. "One saw the warriors of the Sly One and followed them. He saw them capture you, and then he flew to the village as fast as he could go and told me all that he had seen. The rest you know. You did much for Gr-gr-gr and Gr-gr-gr's people. We shall always do much for you."

I thanked him; and when I had told him of our escape and our destination, he insisted on accompanying us to the sea with a great number of his fierce males. Nor were we at all loath to accept his escort. We found the canoe where I had hidden it, and bidding Gr-gr-gr and his warriors farewell, the three of us embarked for the mainland.

I questioned Juag upon the feasibility of attempting to cross to the mouth of the great river of which he had told me, and up which he said we might paddle almost to Sari; but he urged me not to attempt it, since we had but a single paddle and no water or food. I had to admit the wisdom of his advice, but the desire to explore this great waterway was strong upon me, arousing in me at last a determination to make the attempt after first gaining the mainland and rectifying our deficiencies.

We landed several miles north of Thuria in a little cove that seemed to offer protection from the heavier seas which sometimes run, even upon these usually pacific oceans of Pellucidar. Here I outlined to Dian and Juag the plans I had in mind. They were to fit the canoe with a small sail, the purposes of which I had to explain to them both — since neither had ever seen or heard of such a contrivance before. Then they were to hunt for food which we could transport with us, and prepare a receptacle for water.

These two latter items were more in Juag's line, but he kept muttering about the sail and the wind for a long time. I could see that he was not even half convinced that any such ridiculous contraption could make a canoe move through the water.

We hunted near the coast for a while, but were not rewarded with any particular luck. Finally we decided to hide the canoe and strike inland in search of game. At Juag's suggestion we dug a hole in the sand at the upper edge of the beach and buried the craft, smoothing the surface over nicely and throwing aside the excess material we had excavated. Then we set out away from the sea. Traveling in Thuria is less arduous than under the midday sun which perpetually glares down on the rest of Pellucidar's surface; but it has its drawbacks, one of which is the depressing influence exerted by the everlasting shade of the Land of Awful Shadow.

The farther inland we went the darker it became, until we were moving at last through an endless twilight. The vegetation here was sparse and of a weird, colorless nature, though what did grow was wondrous in shape and form. Often we saw huge lidi, or beasts of burden, striding across the dim landscape, browsing upon the grotesque vegetation or drinking from the slow and sullen rivers that run down from the Lidi Plains to empty into the sea in Thuria.

What we sought was either thag — a sort of gigantic elk — or one of the larger species of antelope, the flesh of either of which dries nicely in the sun. The bladder of the thag would make a fine water-bottle, and its skin, I figured, would be a good sail. We traveled a considerable distance inland, entirely crossing the Land of Awful Shadow and emerging at last upon that portion of the Lidi Plains which lies in the pleasant sunlight. Above us the pendent world revolved upon its axis, filling me especially — and Dian to an almost equal state — with wonder and insatiable curiosity as to what strange forms of life existed among the hills and valleys and along the seas and rivers, which we could plainly see.

Before us stretched the horizonless expanses of vast Pellucidar, the Lidi Plains rolling up about us, while hanging high in the heavens to the northwest of us I thought I discerned the many towers which marked the entrances to the distant Mahar city, whose inhabitants preyed upon the Thurians.

Juag suggested that we travel to the northeast, where, he said, upon the verge of the plain we would find a wooded country in which game should be plentiful. Acting upon his advice, we came at last to a forest-jungle, through which wound innumerable game-paths. In the depths of this forbidding wood we came upon the fresh spoor of thag.

Shortly after, by careful stalking, we came within javelin-range of a small herd. Selecting a great bull, Juag and I hurled our weapons simultaneously, Dian reserving hers for an emergency. The beast staggered to his feet, bellowing. The rest of the herd was up and away in an instant, only the wounded bull remaining, with lowered head and roving eyes searching for the foe.

Then Juag exposed himself to the view of the bull — it is a part of the tactics of the hunt — while I stepped to one side behind a bush. The moment that the savage beast saw Juag he charged him. Juag ran straight away, that the bull might be lured past my hiding-place. On he came — tons of mighty bestial strength and rage.

Dian had slipped behind me. She, too, could fight a thag should emergency require. Ah, such a girl! A rightful empress of a stone age by every standard which two worlds might bring to measure her!

Crashing down toward us came the bull thag, bellowing and snorting, with the power of a hundred outer-earthly bulls. When he was opposite me I sprang for the heavy mane that covered his huge neck. To tangle my fingers in it was the work of but an instant. Then I was running along at the beast's shoulder.

Now, the theory upon which this hunting custom is based is one long ago discovered by experience, and that is that a thag cannot be turned from his charge once he has started toward the object of his wrath, so long as he can still see the thing he charges. He evidently believes that the man clinging to his mane is attempting to restrain him from overtaking his prey, and so he pays no attention to this enemy, who, of course, does not retard the mighty charge in the least.

Once in the gait of the plunging bull, it was but a slight matter to vault to his back, as cavalrymen mount their chargers upon the run. Juag was still running in plain sight ahead of the bull. His speed was but a trifle less than that of the monster that pursued him. These Pellucidarians are almost as fleet as deer; because I am not is one reason that I am always chosen for the close-in work of the thag-hunt. I could not keep in front of a charging thag long enough to give the killer time to do his work. I learned that the first — and last — time I tried it.

Once astride the bull's neck, I drew my long stone knife and, setting the point carefully over the brute's spine, drove it home with both hands. At the same instant I leaped clear of the stumbling animal. Now, no vertebrate can progress far with a knife through his spine, and the thag is no exception to the rule.

The fellow was down instantly. As he wallowed Juag returned, and the two of us leaped in when an opening afforded the opportunity and snatched our javelins from his side. Then we danced about him, more like two savages than anything else, until we got the opening we were looking for, when simultaneously, our javelins pierced his wild heart, stilling it forever.

The thag had covered considerable ground from the point at which I had leaped upon him. When, after despatching him, I looked back for Dian, I could see nothing of her. I called aloud, but receiving no reply, set out at a brisk trot to where I had left her. I had no difficulty in finding the self-same bush behind which we had hidden, but Dian was not there. Again and again I called, to be rewarded only by silence. Where could she be? What could have become of her in the brief interval since I had seen her standing just behind me?

I drew my long knife and drove it home with both hands.

Chapter XII

KIDNAPED!

I searched about the spot carefully. At last I was rewarded by the discovery of her javelin, a few yards from the bush that had concealed us from the charging thag — her javelin and the indications of a struggle revealed by the trampled vegetation and the overlapping footprints of a woman and a man. Filled with consternation and dismay, I followed these latter to where they suddenly disappeared a hundred yards from where the struggle had occurred. There I saw the huge imprints of a lidi's feet.

The story of the tragedy was all too plain. A Thurian had either been following us, or had accidentally espied Dian and taken a fancy to her. While Juag and I had been engaged with the thag, he had abducted her. I ran swiftly back to where Juag was working over the kill. As I approached him I saw that something was wrong in this quarter as well, for the islander was standing upon the carcass of the thag, his javelin poised for a throw.

When I had come nearer I saw the cause of his belligerent attitude. Just beyond him stood two large jaloks, or wolf-dogs, regarding him intently — a male and a female. Their behavior was rather peculiar, for they did not seem preparing to charge him. Rather, they were contemplating him in an attitude of questioning.

Juag heard me coming and turned toward me with a grin. These fellows love excitement. I could see by his expression that he was enjoying in anticipation the battle that seemed imminent. But he never hurled his javelin. A shout of warning from me stopped him, for I had seen the remnants of a rope dangling from the neck of the male jalok.

Juag again turned toward me, but this time in surprise. I was abreast him in a moment and, passing him, walked straight toward the two beasts. As I did so the female crouched with bared fangs. The male, however, leaped forward to meet me, not in deadly charge, but with every expression of delight and joy which the poor animal could exhibit.

It was Raja — the jalok whose life I had saved, and whom I then had tamed! There

was no doubt that he was glad to see me. I now think that his seeming desertion of me had been but due to a desire to search out his ferocious mate and bring her, too, to live with me.

When Juag saw me fondling the great beast he was filled with consternation, but I did not have much time to spare to Raja while my mind was filled with the grief of my new loss. I was glad to see the brute, and I lost no time in taking him to Juag and making him understand that Juag, too, was to be Raja's friend. With the female the matter was more difficult, but Raja helped us out by growling savagely at her whenever she bared her fangs against us.

I told Juag of the disappearance of' Dian, and of my suspicions as to the explanation of the catastrophe. He wanted to start right out after her, but I suggested that with Raja to help me it might be as well were he to remain and skin the thag, remove its bladder, and then return to where we had hidden the canoe on the beach. And so it was arranged that he was to do this and await me there for a reasonable time. I pointed to a great lake upon the surface of the pendent world above us, telling him that if after this lake had appeared four times I had not returned to go either by water or land to Sari and fetch Ghak with an army. Then, calling Raja after me, I set out after Dian and her abductor. First I took the wolf dog to the spot where the man had fought with Dian. A few paces behind us followed Raja's fierce mate. I pointed to the ground where the evidences of the struggle were plainest and where the scent must have been strong to Raja's nostrils.

Then I grasped the remnant of leash that hung about his neck and urged him forward upon the trail. He seemed to understand. With nose to ground he set out upon his task. Dragging me after him, he trotted straight out upon the Lidi Plains, turning his steps in the direction of the Thurian village. I could have guessed as much!

Behind us trailed the female. After a while she closed upon us, until she ran quite close to me and at Raja's side. It was not long before she seemed as easy in my company as did her lord and master.

We must have covered considerable distance at a very rapid pace, for we had reentered the great shadow, when we saw a huge lidi ahead of us, moving leisurely

across the level plain. Upon its back were
two human figures. If I could have known
that the jaloks would not harm Dian I
might have turned them loose upon the lidi
and its master; but I could not know, and
so dared take no chances.

However, the matter was taken out of
my hands presently when Raja raised his
head and caught sight of his quarry. With a
lunge that hurled me flat and jerked the
leash from my hand, he was gone with the
speed of the wind after the giant lidi and its
riders. At his side raced his shaggy mate,
only a trifle smaller than he and no whit
less savage.

They did not give tongue until the lidi
itself discovered them and broke into a
lumbering, awkward, but none the less
rapid gallop. Then the two hound-beasts
commenced to bay, starting with a low,
plaintive note that rose, weird and hideous, to terminate in a series of short, sharp
yelps. I feared that it might be the hunt-
ing-call of the pack; and if this were true,
there would be slight chance for either
Dian or her abductor — or myself, either,
as far as that was concerned. So I redoubled my efforts to keep pace with the hunt;
but I might as well have attempted to distance the bird upon the wing; as I have
often reminded you, I am no runner. In
that instance it was just as well that I am
not, for my very slowness of foot played into
my hands; while had I been fleeter, I might
have lost Dian that time forever.

The lidi, with the hounds running close
on either side, had almost disappeared in
the darkness that enveloped the surrounding landscape, when I noted that it was
bearing toward the right. This was accounted for by the fact that Raja ran upon
his left side, and unlike his mate, kept leaping for the great beast's shoulder. The man
on the lidi's back was prodding at the
hyaenodon with his long spear, but still
Raja kept springing up and snapping.

The effect of this was to turn the lidi toward the right, and the longer I watched
the procedure the more convinced I became that Raja and his mate were working
together with some end in view, for the
she-dog merely galloped steadily at the
lidi's right about opposite his rump.

I had seen jaloks hunting in packs, and
I recalled now what for the time I had not
thought of — the several that ran ahead
and turned the quarry back toward the

main body. This was precisely what Raja
and his mate were doing — they were turning the lidi back toward me, or at least Raja
was. Just why the female was keeping out
of it I did not understand, unless it was
that she was not entirely clear in her own
mind as to precisely what her mate was
attempting.

At any rate, I was sufficiently convinced
to stop where I was and await devel-
opments, for I could readily realize two
things. One was that I could never overhaul them before the damage was done if
they should pull the lidi down now. The
other thing was that if they did not pull it
down for a few minutes it would have completed its circle and returned close to where
I stood.

And this is just what happened. The lot
of them were almost swallowed up in the
twilight for a moment. Then they reappeared again, but this time far to the right
and circling back in my general direction. I
waited until I could get some clear idea of
the right spot to gain that I might intercept
the lidi; but even as I waited I saw the beast
attempt to turn still more to the right — a
move that would have carried him far to my
left in a much more circumscribed circle
than the hyaenodons had mapped out for
him. Then I saw the female leap forward
and head him; and when he would have
gone too far to the left, Raja sprang, snapping, at his shoulder and held him
straight.

Straight for me the two savage beasts
were driving their quarry! It was wonderful.

It was something else, too, as I realized
while the monstrous beast neared me. It
was like standing in the middle of the
tracks in front of an approaching express-
train. But I didn't dare waver; too much
depended upon my meeting that hurtling
mass of terrified flesh with a well-placed
javelin. So I stood there, waiting to be run
down and crushed by those gigantic feet,
but determined to drive home my weapon
in the broad breast before I fell.

The lidi was only about a hundred yards
from me when Raja gave a few barks in
a tone that differed materially from
his hunting-cry. Instantly both he and
his mate leaped for the long neck of the
ruminant.

Neither missed. Swinging in mid-air,
they hung tenaciously, their weight drag-

ging down the creature's head and so retarding its speed that before it had reached me it was almost stopped and devoting all its energies to attempting to scrape off its attackers with its forefeet.

Dian had seen and recognized me, and was trying to extricate herself from the grasp of her captor, who, handicapped by his strong and agile prisoner, was unable to wield his lance effectively upon the two jaloks. At the same time I was running swiftly toward them.

When the man discovered me he released his hold upon Dian and sprang to the ground, ready with his lance to meet me. My javelin was no match for his longer weapon, which was used more for stabbing than as a missile. Should I miss him at my first cast, as was quite probable, since he was prepared for me, I would have to face his formidable lance with nothing more than a stone knife. The outlook was scarcely entrancing. Evidently I was soon to be absolutely at his mercy.

Seeing my predicament, he ran toward me to get rid of one antagonist before he had to deal with the other two. He could not guess, of course, that the two jaloks were hunting with me; but he doubtless thought that after they had finished the lidi they would make after the human prey — the beasts are notorious killers, often slaying wantonly.

But as the Thurian came Raja loosened his hold upon the lidi and dashed for him, with the female close after. When the man saw them he yelled to me to help him, protesting that we should both be killed if we did not fight together. But I only laughed at him and ran toward Dian.

Both the fierce beasts were upon the Thurian simultaneously — he must have died almost before his body tumbled to the ground. Then the female wheeled toward Dian. I was standing by her side as the thing charged her, my javelin ready to receive her.

But again Raja was too quick for me. I imagined he thought she was making for me, for he couldn't have known anything of my relations toward Dian. At any rate he leaped full upon her back and dragged her down. There ensued forthwith as terrible a battle as one would wish to see if battles were gaged by volume of noise and riotousness of action. I thought that both the beasts would be torn to shreds. When finally the female ceased to strug-

gle and rolled over on her back, her forepaws limply folded, I was sure that she was dead. Raja stood over her, growling, his jaws close to her throat. Then I saw that neither of them bore a scratch. The male had simply administered a severe drubbing to his mate. It was his way of teaching her that I was sacred.

After a moment he moved away and let her rise, when she set about smoothing down her rumpled coat, while he came stalking toward Dian and me. I had an arm about Dian now. As Raja came close I caught him by the neck and pulled him up to me. There I stroked him and talked to him, bidding Dian do the same, until I think he pretty well understood that if I was his friend, so was Dian.

For a long time he was inclined to be shy of her, often baring his teeth at her approach, and it was a much longer time before the female made friends with us. But by careful kindness, by never eating without sharing our meat with them, and by feeding them from our hands, we finally won the confidence of both animals. However, that was a long time after.

With the two beasts trotting after us, we returned to where we had left Juag. Here I had the dickens' own time keeping the female from Juag's throat. Of all the venomous, wicked, cruel-hearted beasts on two worlds, I think a female hyaenodon takes the palm.

But eventually she tolerated Juag as she had Dian and me, and the five of us set out toward the coast, for Juag had just completed his labors on the thag when we arrived. We ate some of the meat before starting, and gave the hounds some. All that we could we carried upon our backs.

On the way to the canoe we met with no mishaps. Dian told me that the fellow who had stolen her had come upon her from behind while the roaring of the thag had drowned all other noises, and that the first she had known he had disarmed her and thrown her to the back of his lidi, which had been lying down close by waiting for him. By the time the thag had ceased bellowing the fellow had got well away upon his swift mount. By holding one palm over her mouth he had prevented her calling for help.

"I thought," she concluded, "that I should have to use the viper's tooth, after all."

We reached the beach at last and un-

earthed the canoe. Then we busied ourselves stepping a mast and rigging a small
sail — Juag and I, that is — while Dian cut
the thag meat into long strips for drying
when we should be out in the sunlight once
more.

At last all was done. We were ready to
embark. I had no difficulty in getting Raja
aboard the dugout; but Ranee — as we
christened her after I had explained to
Dian the meaning of Raja and its feminine
equivalent — positively refused for a time
to follow her mate aboard. In fact, we had to
shove off without her. After a moment,
however, she plunged into the water and
swam after us.

I let her come alongside, and then Juag
and I pulled her in, she snapping and
snarling at us as we did so; but, strange to
relate, she didn't offer to attack us after we
had ensconced her safely in the bottom
alongside Raja.

The canoe benaved much better under
sail than I had hoped — infinitely better
than the battle-ship *Sari* had — and we
made good progress almost due west
across the gulf, upon the opposite side of
which I hoped to find the mouth of the river
of which Juag had told me.

The islander was much interested and
impressed by the sail and its results. He
had not been able to understand exactly
what I hoped to accomplish with it while
we were fitting up the boat; but when he
saw the clumsy dugout move steadily
through the water without paddles, he was
as delighted as a child. We made splendid
headway on the trip, coming into sight of
land at last.

Juag had been terror-stricken when he
had learned that I intended crossing the
ocean, and when we passed out of sight of
land he was in a blue funk. He said that he
had never heard of such a thing before in
his life, and that always he had understood
that those who ventured far from land
never returned; for how could they find
their way when they could see no land to
steer for?

I tried to explain the compass to him;
and though he never really grasped the scientific explanation of it, yet he did learn to
steer by it quite as well as I. We passed several islands on the journey — islands
which Juag told me were entirely unknown
to his own island folk. Indeed, our eyes may
have been the first ever to rest upon them. I
should have liked to stop off and explore

them, but the business of empire would
brook no unnecessary delays.

I asked Juag how Hooja expected to
reach the mouth of the river which we were
in search of if he didn't cross the gulf, and
the islander explained that Hooja would
undoubtedly follow the coast around. For
some time we sailed up the coast searching
for the river, and at last we found it. So
great was it that I thought it must be a
mighty gulf until the mass of driftwood
that came out upon the first ebb tide convinced me that it was the mouth of a river.
There were the trunks of trees uprooted by
the undermining of the river banks, giant
creepers, flowers, grasses, and now and
then the body of some land animal or bird.

I was all excitement to commence our
upward journey when there occurred that
which I had never before seen within Pellucidar — a really terrific wind-storm. It
blew down the river upon us with a ferocity
and suddenness that took our breaths
away, and before we could get a chance to
make the shore it became too late. The best
that we could do was to hold the scudding
craft before the wind and race along in a
smother of white spume. Juag was terrified. If Dian was, she hid it; for was she
not the daughter of a once great chief, the
sister of a king, and the mate of an emperor?

Raja and Ranee were frightened. The
former crawled close to my side and buried
his nose against me. Finally even fierce
Ranee was moved to seek sympathy from a
human being. She slunk to Dian, pressing
close against her and whimpering, while
Dian stroked her shaggy neck and talked to
her as I talked to Raja.

There was nothing for us to do but try to
keep the canoe right side up and straight
before the wind. For what seemed an eternity the tempest neither increased nor
abated. I judged that we must have blown a
hundred miles before the wind and
straight out into an unknown sea!

As suddenly as the wind rose it died
again, and when it died it veered to blow at
right angles to its former course in a gentle
breeze. I asked Juag then what our course
was, for he had had the compass last. It
had been on a leather thong about his
neck. When he felt for it, the expression
that came into his eyes told me as plainly as
words what had happened — the compass
was lost! The compass was lost!

And we were out of sight of land without

a single celestial body to guide us! Even the pendent world was not visible from our position!

Our plight seemed hopeless to me, but I dared not let Dian and Juag guess how utterly dismayed I was; though, as I soon discovered, there was nothing to be gained by trying to keep the worst from Juag — he knew it quite as well as I. He had always known, from the legends of his people, the dangers of the open sea beyond the sight of land. The compass, since he had learned its uses from me, had been all that he had to buoy his hope of eventual salvation from the watery deep. He had seen how it had guided me across the water to the very coast that I desired to reach, and so he had implicit confidence in it. Now that it was gone, his confidence had departed, also.

There seemed but one thing to do; that was to keep on sailing straight before the wind — since we could travel most rapidly along that course — until we sighted land of some description. If it chanced to be the mainland, well and good; if an island — well, we might live upon an island. We certainly could not live long in this little boat, with only a few strips of dried thag and a few quarts of water left.

Quite suddenly a thought occurred to me. I was surprised that it had not come before as a solution to our problem. I turned toward Juag.

"You Pellucidarians are endowed with a wonderful instinct," I reminded him, "an instinct that points the way straight to your homes, no matter in what strange land you may find yourself. Now all we have to do is let Dian guide us toward Amoz, and we shall come in a short time to the same coast whence we just were blown."

As I spoke I looked at them with a smile of renewed hope; but there was no answering smile in their eyes. It was Dian who enlightened me.

"We could do all this upon land," she said. "But upon the water that power is denied us. I do not know why; but I have always heard that this is true — that only upon the water may a Pellucidarian be lost. This is, I think, why we all fear the great ocean so — even those who go upon its surfaces in canoes. Juag has told us that they never go beyond the sight of land."

We had lowered the sail after the blow while we were discussing the best course to pursue. Our little craft had been drifting idly, rising and falling with the great waves that were now diminishing. Sometimes we were upon the crest — again in the hollow. As Dian ceased speaking she let her eyes range across the limitless expanse of billowing waters. We rose to a great height upon the crest of a mighty wave. As we topped it Dian gave an exclamation and pointed astern.

"Boats!" she cried. "Boats! Many, many boats!"

Juag and I leaped to our feet; but our little craft had now dropped to the trough, and we could see nothing but walls of water close upon either hand. We waited for the next wave to lift us, and when it did we strained our eyes in the direction that Dian had indicated. Sure enough, scarce half a mile away were several boats, and scattered far and wide behind us as far as we could see were many others! We could not make them out in the distance or in the brief glimpse that we caught of them before we were plunged again into the next wave cañon; but they were boats.

And in them must be human beings likes ourselves.

Chapter XIII

RACING FOR LIFE

At last the sea subsided, and we were able to get a better view of the armada of small boats in our wake. There must have been two hundred of them. Juag said that he had never seen so many boats before in all his life. Where had they come from? Juag was first to hazard a guess.

"Hooja," he said, "was building many boats to carry his warriors to the great river and up it toward Sari. He was building them with almost all his warriors and many slaves upon the Island of Trees. No one else in all the history of Pellucidar has ever built so many boats as they told me Hooja was building. These must be Hooja's boats."

"And they were blown out to sea by the great storm just as we were," suggested Dian.

"There can be no better explanation of them," I agreed.

"What shall we do?" asked Juag.

"Suppose we make sure that they are really Hooja's people," suggested Dian. "It may be that they are not, and that if we run away from them before we learn definitely who they are, we shall be running away from a chance to live and find the mainland. They may be a people of whom we have never even heard, and if so we can ask them to help us — if they know the way to the mainland."

"Which they will not," interposed Juag.

"Well," I said, "it can't make our predicament any more trying to wait until we find out who they are. They are heading for us now. Evidently they have spied our sail, and guess that we do not belong to their fleet."

"They probably want to ask the way to the mainland themselves," said Juag, who was nothing if not a pessimist.

"If they want to catch us, they can do it if they can paddle faster than we can sail," I said. "If we let them come close enough to discover their identity, and can then sail faster than they can paddle, we can get away from them anyway, so we might as well wait."

And wait we did.

The sea calmed rapidly, so that by the time the foremost canoe had come within five hundred yards of us we could see them all plainly. Every one was headed for us. The dugouts, which were of unusual length, were manned by twenty paddlers, ten to a side. Besides the paddlers there were twenty-five or more warriors in each boat.

When the leader was a hundred yards from us Dian called our attention to the fact that several of her crew were Sagoths. That convinced us that the flotilla was indeed Hooja's. I told Juag to hail them and get what information he could, while I remained in the bottom of our canoe as much out of sight as possible. Dian lay down at full length in the bottom; I did not want them to see and recognize her if they were in truth Hooja's people.

"Who are you?" shouted Juag, standing up in the boat and making a megaphone of his palms.

A figure arose in the bow of the leading canoe — a figure that I was sure I recognized even before he spoke.

"I am Hooja!" cried the man, in answer to Juag.

For some reason he did not recognize his former prisoner and slave — possibly because he had so many of them.

"I come from the Island of Trees," he continued. "A hundred of my boats were lost in the great storm and all their crews drowned. Where is the land? What are you, and what strange thing is that which flutters from the little tree in the front of your canoe?"

He referred to our sail, flapping idly in the wind.

"We, too, are lost," replied Juag. "We know not where the land is. We are going back to look for it now."

So saying he commenced to scull the canoe's nose before the wind, while I made fast the primitive sheets that held our crude sail. We thought it time to be going.

There wasn't much wind at the time, and the heavy, lumbering dugout was slow in getting under way. I thought it never would gain any momentum. And all the while Hooja's canoe was drawing rapidly nearer, propelled by the strong arms of his twenty paddlers. Of course, their dugout was much larger than ours, and, consequently, infinitely heavier and more cumbersome; nevertheless, it was coming along at quite a clip, and ours was yet but barely moving. Dian and I remained out of sight as much as possible, for the two craft were now well within bow-shot of one another, and I knew that Hooja had archers.

Hooja called to Juag to stop when he saw that our craft was moving. He was much interested in the sail, and not a little awed, as I could tell by his shouted remarks and questions. Raising my head, I saw him plainly. He would have made an excellent target for one of my guns, and I had never been sorrier that I had lots them.

We were now picking up speed a trifle, and he was not gaining upon us so fast as at first. In consequence, his requests that we stop suddenly changed to commands as he became aware that we were trying to escape him.

"Come back!" he shouted. "Come back, or I'll fire!"

I use the word fire because it more nearly translates into English the Pellucidarian word *trag*, which covers the launching of any deadly missile.

But Juag only seized his paddle more tightly — the paddle that answered the purpose of rudder, and commenced to assist the wind by vigorous strokes. Then Hooja gave the command to some of his archers to fire upon us. I couldn't lie hidden in the bottom of the boat, leaving Juag alone exposed to the deadly shafts, so I arose and, seizing another paddle, set to work to help him. Dian joined me, though I did my best to persuade her to remain sheltered; but being a woman, she must have her own way.

The instant that Hooja saw us he recognized us. The whoop of triumph he raised indicated how certain he was that we were about to fall into his hands. A shower of arrows fell about us. Then Hooja caused his men to cease firing — he wanted us alive. None of the missiles struck us, for Hooja's archers were not nearly the marksmen that are my Sarians and Amozites.

We had now gained sufficient headway to hold our own on about even terms with Hooja's paddlers. We did not seem to be gaining, though; and neither did they. How long this nerve-racking experience lasted I cannot guess, though we had pretty nearly finished our meager supply of provisions when the wind picked up a bit and we commenced to draw away.

Not once yet had we sighted land, nor could I understand it, since so many of the seas I had seen before were thickly dotted with islands. Our plight was anything but pleasant, yet I think that Hooja and his forces were even worse off than we, for they had no food nor water at all.

Far out behind us in a long line that curved upward in the distance, to be lost in the haze, strung Hooja's two hundred boats. But one would have been enough to have taken us could it have come alongside. We had drawn some fifty yards ahead of Hooja — there had been times when we were scarce ten yards in advance — and were feeling considerably safer from capture. Hooja's men, working in relays, were commencing to show the effects of the strain under which they had been forced to work without food or water, and I think their weakening aided us almost as much as the slight freshening of the wind.

Hooja must have commenced to realize that he was going to lose us, for he again gave orders that we be fired upon. Volley after volley of arrows struck about us. The distance was so great by this time that most of the arrows fell short, while those that reached us were sufficiently spent to allow us to ward them off with our paddles. However, it was a most exciting ordeal.

Hooja stood in the bow of his boat, alternately urging his men to greater speed and shouting epithets at me. But we continued to draw away from him. At last the wind rose to a fair gale, and we simply raced away from our pursuers as if they were standing still. Juag was so tickled that he forgot all about his hunger and thirst. I think that he had never been entirely reconciled to the heathenish invention which I called a sail, and that down in the bottom of his heart he believed that the paddlers would eventually overhaul us; but now he couldn't praise it enough.

We had a strong gale for a considerable time, and eventually dropped Hooja's fleet so far astern that we could no longer discern them. And then — ah, I shall never forget that moment — Dian sprang to her feet with a cry of "Land!"

Sure enough, dead ahead, a long, low coast stretched across our bow. It was still a long way off, and we couldn't make out whether it was island or mainland; but at least it was land. If ever shipwrecked mariners were grateful, we were then. Raja and Ranee were commencing to suffer for lack of food, and I could swear that the latter often cast hungry glances upon us, though I am equally sure that no such hideous thoughts ever entered the head of her mate. We watched them both most closely, however. Once while stroking Ranee I managed to get a rope around her neck and make her fast to the side of the boat. Then I felt a bit safer for Dian. It was pretty close quarters in that little dugout for three human beings and two practically wild, man-eating dogs; but we had to make the best of it, since I would not listen to Juag's suggestion that we kill and eat Raja and Ranee.

We made good time to within a few miles of the shore. Then the wind died suddenly out. We were all of us keyed up to such a pitch of anticipation that the blow was doubly hard to bear. And it was a blow, too, since we could not tell in what quarter the wind might rise again; but Juag and I set to work to paddle the remaining distance.

Almost immediately the wind rose again from precisely the opposite direction from which it had formerly blown, so that it was mighty hard work making progress against it. Next it veered again so that we had to turn and run with it parallel to the coast to keep from being swamped in the trough of the seas.

And while we were suffering all these disappointments Hooja's fleet appeared in the distance!

They evidently had gone far to the left of our course, for they were now almost behind us as we ran parallel to the coast; but we were not much afraid of being overtaken in the wind that was blowing. The gale kept on increasing, but it was fitful, swooping down upon us in great gusts and then going almost calm for an instant. It was after one of these momentary calms that the catastrophe occurred. Our sail hung limp and our momentum decreased when of a sudden a particularly vicious squall caught us. Before I could cut the sheets the mast had snapped at the thwart in which it was stepped.

The worst had happened; Juag and I seized paddles and kept the canoe with the wind; but that squall was the parting shot of the gale, which died out immediately after, leaving us free to make for the shore, which we lost no time in attempting. But Hooja had drawn closer in toward shore than we, so it looked as if he might head us off before we could land. However, we did our best to distance him, Dian taking a paddle with us.

We were in a fair way to succeed when there appeared, pouring from among the trees beyond the beach, a horde of yelling, painted savages, brandishing all sorts of devilish-looking primitive weapons. So menacing was their attitude that we realized at once the folly of attempting to land among them.

Hooja was drawing closer to us. There was no wind. We could not hope to outpaddle him. And with our sail gone, no wind would help us, though, as if in derision at our plight, a steady breeze was now blowing. But we had no intention of sitting idle while our fate overtook us, so we bent to our paddles and, keeping parallel with the coast, did our best to pull away from our pursuers.

It was a grueling experience. We were weakened by lack of food. We were suffering the pangs of thirst. Capture and death were close at hand. Yet I think that we gave a good account of ourselves in our final effort to escape. Our boat was so much smaller and lighter than any of Hooja's that the three of us forced it ahead almost as rapidly as his larger craft could go under their twenty paddles.

As we raced along the coast for one of those seemingly interminable periods that may draw hours into eternities where the labor is soul-searing and there is no way to measure time, I saw what I took for the opening to a bay or the mouth of a great river a short distance ahead of us. I wished that we might make for it; but with the menace of Hooja close behind and the screaming natives who raced along the shore parallel to us, I dared not attempt it.

We were not far from shore in that mad flight from death. Even as I paddled I found opportunity to glance occasionally toward the natives. They were white, but hideously painted. From their gestures and weapons I took them to be a most ferocious race. I was rather glad that we had not succeeded in landing among them.

Hooja's fleet had been in much more compact formation when we sighted them this time than on the occasion following the tempest. Now they were moving rapidly in pursuit of us, all well within the radius of a mile. Five of them were leading, all abreast, and were scarce two hundred yards from us. When I glanced over my shoulder I could see that the archers had already fitted arrows to their bows in readiness to fire upon us the moment that they should draw within range.

Hope was low in my breast. I could not see the slightest chance of escaping them, for they were overhauling us rapidly now, since they were able to work their paddles in relays, while we three were rapidly wearying beneath the constant strain that had been put upon us.

It was then that Juag called my attention to the rift in the shore-line which I had thought either a bay or the mouth of a great river. There I saw moving slowly out into the sea that which filled my soul with wonder.

Chapter XIV

GORE AND DREAMS

It was a two-masted felucca with lateen sails! The craft was long and low. In it were more than fifty men, twenty or thirty of whom were at oars with which the craft was being propelled from the lee of the land. I was dumbfounded.

Could it be that the savage, painted natives I had seen on shore had so perfected the art of navigation that they were masters of such advanced building and rigging as this craft proclaimed? It seemed impossible! And as I looked I saw another of the same type swing into view and follow its sister through the narrow strait out into the ocean.

Nor were these all. One after another, following closely upon one another's heels, came fifty of the trim, graceful vessels. They were cutting in between Hooja's fleet and our little dugout.

When they came a bit closer my eyes fairly popped from head at what I saw, for in the eye of the leading felucca stood a man with a sea-glass leveled upon us. Who could they be? Was there a civilization within Pellucidar of such wondrous advancement as this? Were there far-distant lands of which none of my people had ever heard, where a race had so greatly outstripped all other races of this inner world?

The man with the glass had lowered it and was shouting to us. I could not make out his words, but presently I saw that he was pointing aloft. When I looked I saw a pennant fluttering from the peak of the forward lateen yard — a red, white, and blue pennant, with a single great white star in the field of blue.

Then I knew. My eyes went even wider than they had before. It was the navy! It was the navy of the empire of Pellucidar which I had instructed Perry to build in my absence. It was *my* navy!

I dropped my paddle and stood up and shouted and waved my hand. Juag and Dian looked at me as if I had gone suddenly mad. When I could stop shouting I told them, and they shared my joy and shouted with me.

But still Hooja was coming nearer, nor could the leading felucca overhaul him before he would be alongside or at least within bow-shot.

Hooja must have been as much mystified as we were as to the identity of the strange fleet; but when he saw me waving to them he evidently guessed that they were friendly to us, so he urged his men to redouble their efforts to reach us before the felucca cut him off.

He shouted word back to others of his fleet — word that was passed back until it had reached them all — directing them to run alongside the strangers and board

them, for with his two hundred craft and his eight or ten thousand warriors he evidently felt equal to overcoming the fifty vessels of the enemy, which did not seem to carry over three thousand men all told.

His own personal energies he bent to reaching Dian and me first, leaving the rest of the work to his other boats. I thought that there could be little doubt that he would be successful in so far as we were concerned, and I feared for the revenge that he might take upon us should the battle go against his force, as I was sure it would; for I knew that Perry and his Mezops must have brought with them all the arms and ammunition that had been contained in the prospector. But I was not prepared for what happened next.

As Hooja's canoe reached a point some twenty yards from us a great puff of smoke broke from the bow of the leading felucca, followed almost simultaneously by a terrific explosion, and a solid shot screamed close over the heads of the men in Hooja's craft, raising a great splash where it clove the water just beyond them.

Perry had perfected gunpowder and built cannon! It was marvelous! Dian and Juag, as much surprised as Hooja, turned wondering eyes toward me. Again the cannon spoke. I suppose that by comparison with the great guns of modern naval vessels of the outer world it was a pitifully small and inadequate thing; but here in Pellucidar, where it was the first of its kind, it was about as awe-inspiring as anything you might imagine.

With the report an iron cannon-ball about five inches in diameter struck Hooja's dugout just above the water-line, tore a great splintering hole in its side, turned it over, and dumped its occupants into the sea.

The four dugouts that had been abreast of Hooja had turned to intercept the leading felucca. Even now, in the face of what must have been a withering catastrophe to them, they kept bravely on toward the strange and terrible craft.

In them were fully two hundred men, while but fifty lined the gunwale of the felucca to repel them. The commander of the felucca, who proved to be Ja, let them come quite close and then turned loose upon them a volley of shots from small-arms.

The cave men and Sagoths in the dugouts seemed to wither before that blast of death like dry grass before a prairie fire. Those who were not hit dropped their bows and javelins and, seizing upon paddles, attempted to escape. But the felucca pursued them relentlessly, her crew firing at will.

At last I heard Ja shouting to the survivors in the dugouts — they were all quite close to us now — offering them their lives if they would surrender. Perry was standing close behind Ja, and I knew that this merciful action was prompted, perhaps commanded, by the old man; for no Pellucidarian would have thought of showing leniency to a defeated foe.

As there was no alternative save death, the survivors surrendered and a moment later were taken aboard the *Amoz*, the name that I could now see printed in large letters upon the felucca's bow, and which no one in that whole world could read except Perry and I.

When the prisoners were aboard, Ja brought the felucca alongside our dugout. Many were the willing hands that reached down to lift us to her decks. The bronze faces of the Mezops were broad with smiles, and Perry was fairly beside himself with joy.

Dian went aboard first and then Juag, as I wished to help Raja and Ranee aboard myself, well knowing that it would fare ill with any Mezop who touched them. We got them aboard at last, and a great commotion they caused among the crew, who had never seen a wild beast thus handled by man before.

Perry and Dian and I were so full of questions that we fairly burst, but we had to contain ourselves for a while, since the battle with the rest of Hooja's fleet had scarce commenced. From the small forward decks of the feluccas Perry's crude cannon were belching smoke, flame, thunder, and death. The air trembled to the roar of them. Hooja's horde, intrepid, savage fighters that they were, were closing in to grapple in a last death-struggle with the Mezops who manned our vessels.

The handling of our fleet by the red island warriors of Ja's clan was far from perfect. I could see that Perry had lost no time after the completion of the boats in setting out upon this cruise. What little the captains and crews had learned of handling feluccas they must have learned principally since they embarked upon this voyage, and

while experience is an excellent teacher and had done much for them, they still had a great deal to learn. In maneuvering for position they were continually fouling one another, and on two occasions shots from our batteries came near to striking our own ships.

No sooner, however, was I aboard the flagship than I attempted to rectify this trouble to some extend. By passing commands by word of mouth from one ship to another I managed to get the fifty feluccas into some sort of line, with the flag-ship in the lead. In this formation we commenced slowly to circle the position of the enemy. The dugouts came for us right along in an attempt to board us, but by keeping on the move in one direction and circling, we managed to avoid getting in each other's way, and were enabled to fire our cannon and our small arms with less danger to our own comrades.

When I had a moment to look about me, I took in the felucca on which I was. I am free to confess that I marveled at the excellent construction and stanch yet speedy lines of the little craft. That Perry had chosen this type of vessel seemed rather remarkable, for though I had warned him against turreted battle-ships, armor, and like useless show, I had fully expected that when I beheld his navy I should find considerable attempt at grim and terrible magnificence, for it was always Perry's idea to overawe these ignorant cave men when we had to contend with them in battle. But I had soon learned that while one might easily astonish them with some new engine of war, it was an utter impossibility to frighten them into surrender.

I learned later that Ja had gone carefully over the plans of various craft with Perry. The old man had explained in detail all that the text told him of them. The two had measured out dimensions upon the ground, that Ja might see the sizes of different boats. Perry had built models, and Ja had had him read carefully and explain all that they could find relative to the handling of sailing vessels. The result of this was that Ja was the one who had chosen the felucca. It was well that Perry had had so excellent a balance wheel, for he had been wild to build a huge frigate of the Nelsonian era — he told me so himself.

One thing that had inclined Ja particularly to the felucca was the fact that it included oars in its equipment. He realized the limitations of his people in the matter of sails, and while they had never used oars, the implement was so similar to a paddle that he was sure they quickly could master the art — and they did. As soon as one hull was completed Ja kept in on the water constantly, first with one crew and then with another, until two thousand red warriors had learned to row. Then they stepped their masts and a crew was told off for the first ship.

While the others were building they learned to handle theirs. As each succeeding boat was launched its crew took it out and practiced with it under the tutorage of those who had graduated from the first ship, and so on until a full complement of men had been trained for every boat.

Well, to get back to the battle: The Hoojans kept on coming at us, and as fast as they came we mowed them down. It was little else than slaughter. Time and time again I cried to them to surrender, promising them their lives if they would do so. At last there were but ten boatloads left. These turned in flight. They thought they could paddle away from us — it was pitiful! I passed the word from boat to boat to cease firing — not to kill another Hoojan unless they fired on us. Then we set out after them. There was a nice little breeze blowing and we bowled along after our quarry as gracefully and as lightly as swans upon a park lagoon. As we approached them I could see not only wonder but admiration in their eyes. I hailed the nearest dugout.

"Throw down your arms and come aboard us," I cried, "and you shall not be harmed. We will feed you and return you to the mainland. Then you shall go free upon your promise never to bear arms against the Emperor of Pellucidar again!"

I think it was the promise of food that interested them most. They could scarce believe that we would not kill them. But when I exhibited the prisoners we already had taken, and showed them that they were alive and unharmed, a great Sagoth in one of the boats asked me what guarantee I could give that I would keep my word.

"None other than my word," I replied. "That I do not break."

The Pelluciardians themselves are rather punctilious about this same matter, so the Sagoth could understand that I might possibly be speaking the truth. But he could not understand why we should not kill them unless we meant to enslave them, which I had as much as denied already when I had promised to set them free. Ja couldn't exactly see the wisdom of my plan, either. He thought that we ought to follow up the ten remaining dugouts and sink them all; but I insisted that we must free as many as possible of our enemies upon the mainland.

"You see," I explained, "these men will return at once to Hooja's Island, to the Mahar cities from which they come, or to the countries from which they were stolen by the Mahars. They are men of two races and of many countries. They will spread the story of our victory far and wide, and while they are with us, we will let them see and hear many other wonderful things which they may carry back to their friends and their chiefs. It's the finest chance for free publicity, Perry," I added to the old man, "that you or I have seen in many a day."

Perry agreed with me. As a matter of fact, he would have agreed to anything that would have restrained us from killing the poor devils who fell into our hands. He was a great fellow to invent gunpowder and firearms and cannon; but when it came to using these things to kill people, he was as tenderhearted as a chicken.

The Sagoth who had spoken was talking to other Sagoths in his boat. Evidently they were holding a council over the question of the wisdom of surrendering.

"What will become of you if you don't surrender to us?" I asked. "If we do not open up our batteries on you again and kill you all, you will simply drift about the sea helplessly until you die of thirst and starvation. You cannot return to the islands, for you have seen as well as we that the natives there are very numerous and warlike. They would kill you the moment you landed."

The upshot of it was that the boat of which the Sagoth speaker was in charge surrendered. The Sagoths threw down their weapons, and we took them aboard the ship next in line behind the *Amoz*. First Ja had to impress upon the captain and crew of the ship that the prisoners were not to be abused or killed. After that the remaining dugouts paddled up and surrendered. We distributed them among the entire fleet lest there be too many upon any one vessel. Thus ended the first real naval engagement that the Pellucidarian seas had ever witnessed — though Perry still insists that the action in which the *Sari* took part was a battle of the first magnitude.

The battle over and the prisoners disposed of and fed — and do not imagine that Dian, Juag, and I, as well as the two hounds were not fed also — I turned my attention to the fleet. We had the feluccas close in about the flag-ship, and with all the ceremony of a medieval potentate on parade I received the commanders of the forty-nine feluccas that accompanied the flag-ship — Dian and I together — the empress and the emperor of Pellucidar.

It was a great occasion. The savage, bronze warriors entered into the spirit of it, for as I learned later dear old Perry had left no opportunity neglected for impressing upon them that David was emperor of Pellucidar, and that all that they were accomplishing and all that he was accomplishing was due to the power, and redounded to the glory of David. The old man must have rubbed it in pretty strong, for those fierce warriors nearly came to blows in their efforts to be among the first of those to kneel before me and kiss my hand. When it came to kissing Dian's I think they enjoyed it more; I know I should have.

A happy thought occurred to me as I stood upon the little deck of the *Amoz* with the first of Perry's primitive cannon behind me. When Ja kneeled at my feet, the first to do me homage, I drew from its scabbard at his side the sword of hammered iron that Perry had taught him to fashion. Striking him lightly on the shoulder I created him king of Anoroc. Each captain of the forty-nine other feluccas I made a duke. I left it to Perry to enlighten them as to the value of the honors I had bestowed upon them.

During these ceremonies Raja and Ranee had stood beside Dian and me. Their bellies had been well filled, but still they had difficulty in permitting so much edible humanity to pass unchallenged. It was a good education for them though, and never after did they find it difficult to associate with the human race without arousing their appetites.

After the ceremonies were over we had a chance to talk with Perry and Ja. The former told me that Ghak, king of Sari, had sent my letter and map to him by a runner, and that he and Ja had at once decided to

set out on the completion of the fleet to ascertain the correctness of my theory that the Lural Az, in which the Anoroc Islands lay, was in reality the same ocean as that which lapped the shores of Thuria under the name of Sojar Az, or Great Sea.

Their destination had been the island retreat of Hooja, and they had sent word to Ghak of their plans that we might work in harmony with them. The tempest that had blown us off the coast of the continent had blown them far to the south also. Shortly before discovering us they had come into a great group of islands, from between the largest two of which they were sailing when they saw Hooja's fleet pursuing our dugout.

I asked Perry if he had any idea as to where we were, or in what direction lay Hooja's island or the continent. He replied by producing his map, on which he had carefully marked the newly discovered islands — there described as the Unfriendly Isles — which showed Hooja's island northwest of us about two points west.

He then explained that with compass, chronometer, log and reel, they had kept a fairly accurate record of their course from the time they had set out. Four of the feluccas were equipped with these instruments, and all of the captains had been instructed in their use.

I was very greatly surprised at the ease with which these savages had mastered the rather intricate detail of this unusual work, but Perry assured me that they were a wonderfully intelligent race, and had been quick to grasp all that he had tried to teach them.

Another thing that surprised me was the fact that so much had been accomplished in so short a time, for I could not believe that I had been gone from Anoroc for a sufficient period to permit of building a fleet of fifty feluccas and mining iron ore for the cannon and balls, to say nothing of manufacturing these guns and the crude mussle-loading rifles with which every Mezop was armed, as well as the gunpowder and ammunition they had in such ample quantities.

"Time!" exclaimed Perry. "Well, how long *were* you gone from Anoroc before we picked you up in the Sojar Az?"

That was a puzzler, and I had to admit it. I didn't know how much time had elapsed and neither did Perry, for time is nonexistent in Pellucidar.

"Then, you see, David," he continued, "I had almost unbelievable resources at my disposal. The Mezops inhabiting the Anoroc Islands, which stretch far out to sea beyond the three principal isles with which you are familiar, number well into the millions, and by far the greater part of them are friendly to Ja. Men, women, and children turned to and worked the moment Ja explained the nature of our enterprise.

"And not only were they anxious to do all in their power to hasten the day when the Mahars should be overthrown, but — and this counted for most of all — they are simply ravenous for greater knowledge and for better ways of doing things.

"The contents of the prospector set their imaginations to working overtime, so that they craved to own, themselves, the knowledge which had made it possible for other men to create and build the things which you brought back from the outer world.

"And then," continued the old man, "the element of time, or, rather, lack of time, operated to my advantage. There being no nights, there was no laying off from work — they labored incessantly stopping only to eat and, on rare occasions, to sleep. Once we had discovered iron ore we had enough mined in an incredibly short time to build a thousand cannon. I had only to show them once how a thing should be done, and they would fall to work by thousands to do it.

"Why, no sooner had we fashioned the first muzzle-loader and they had seen it work successfully, than fully three thousand Mezops fell to work to make rifles. Of course there was much confusion and lost motion at first, but eventually Ja got them in hand, detailing squads of them under competent chiefs to certain work.

"We now have a hundred expert gun-makers. On a little isolated isle we have a great powder-factory. Near the iron-mine, which is on the mainland, is a smelter, and on the eastern shore of Anoroc, a well equipped shipyard. All these industries are guarded by forts in which several cannon are mounted and where warriors are always on guard.

"You would be surprised now, David, at the aspect of Anoroc. I am surprised myself; it seems always to me as I compare it with the day that I first set foot upon it from the deck of the Sari that only a miracle could have worked the change that has taken place."

"It is a miracle," I said; "it is nothing short of a miracle to transplant all the wondrous possibilities of the twentieth century back to the Stone Age. It is a miracle to think that only five hundred miles of earth separate two epochs that are really ages and ages apart.

"It is stupendous, Perry! But still more stupendous is the power that you and I wield in this great world. These people look upon us as little less than supermen. We must show them that we are all of that.

"We must give them the best that we have, Perry."

"Yes," he agreed; "we must. I have been thinking a great deal lately that some kind of shrapnel shell or explosive bomb would be a most splendid innovation in their warfare. Then there are breech-loading rifles and those with magazines that I must hasten to study out and learn to reproduce as soon as we get settled down again; and ——"

"Hold on, Perry!" I cried. "I didn't mean these sorts of things at all. I said that we must give them the best we have. What we have given them so far has been the worst. We have given them war and the munitions of war. In a single day we have made their wars infinitely more terrible and bloody than in all their past ages they have been able o make them with their crude, primitive weapons.

"In a period that could scarcely have exceeded two outer earthly hours, our fleet practically annihilated the largest armada of native canoes that the Pellucidarians ever before had gathered together. We butchered some eight thousand warriors with the twentieth-century gifts we brought. Why, they wouldn't have killed that many warriors in the entire duration of a dozen of their wars with their own weapons! No, Perry; we've got to give them something better than scientific methods of killing one another."

The old man looked at me in amazement. There was reproach in his eyes, too.

"Why, David!" he said sorrowfully. "I thought that you would be pleased with what I had done. We planned these things together, and I am sure that it was you who suggested practically all of it. I have done only what I thought you wished done and I have done it the best that I know how."

I laid my hand on the old man's shoulder.

"Bless your heart, Perry!" I cried. "You've accomplished miracles. You have done precisely what I should have done, only you've done it better. I'm not finding fault; but I don't wish to lose sight myself, or let you lose sight, of the greater work which must grow out of this preliminary and necessary carnage. First we must place the empire upon a secure footing, and we can do so only by putting the fear of us in the hearts of our enemies; but after that ——

"Ah, Perry! That is the day I look forward to! When you and I can build sewing-machines instead of battleships, harvesters of crops instead of harvesters of men, plowshares and telephones, schools and colleges, printing-presses and paper! When our merchant marine shall ply the great Pellucidarian seas, and cargoes of silks and typewriters and books shall forge their ways where only hideous saurians have held sway since time began!"

"Amen!" said Perry.

And Dian, who was standing at my side, pressed my hand.

Chapter XV

CONQUEST AND PEACE

The fleet sailed directly for Hooja's island, coming to anchor at its northeastern extremity before the flat-topped hill that had been Hooja's stronghold. I sent one of the prisoners ashore to demand an immediate surrender; but as he told me afterward they wouldn't believe all that he told them, so they congregated on the cliff-top and shot futile arrows at us.

In reply I had five of the feluccas cannonade them. When they scampered away at the sound of the terrific explosions, and at sight of the smoke and the iron balls I landed a couple of hundred red warriors and led them to the opposite end of the hill into the tunnel that ran to its summit. Here we met a little resistance; but a volley from the muzzle-loaders turned back those who disputed our right of way, and presently we gained the mesa. Here again we met resistance, but at last the remnant of Hooja's horde surrendered.

Juag was with me, and I lost no time in returning to him and his tribe the hilltop that had been their ancestral home for ages until they were robbed of it by Hooja. I created a kingdom of the island, making Juag king there. Before we sailed I went to Gr-gr-gr, chief of the beast-men, taking Juag with me. There the three of us arranged a code of laws that would permit the brute-folk and the human beings of the island to live in peace and harmony. Gr-gr-gr sent his son with me back to Sari, capital of my empire, that he might learn the ways of the human beings. I have hopes of turning this race into the greatest agriculturists of Pellucidar.

When I returned to the fleet I found that one of the islanders of Juag's tribe, who had been absent when we arrived, had just returned from the mainland with the news that a great army was encamped in the Land of Awful Shadow, and that they were threatening Thuria. I lost no time in weighing anchors and setting out for the continent, which we reached after a short and easy voyage.

From the deck of the *Amoz* I scanned the shore through the glasses that Perry had brought with him. When we were close enough for the glasses to be of value I saw that there was indeed a vast concourse of warriors entirely encircling the walled village of Goork, chief of the Thurians. As we approached smaller objects became distinguishable. It was then that I discovered numerous flags and pennants floating above the army of the besiegers.

I called Perry and passed the glasses to him.

"Ghak of Sari," I said.

Perry looked through the lenses for a moment, and then turned to me with a smile.

"The red, white, and blue of the empire," he said. "It is indeed your majesty's army."

It soon became apparent that we had been sighted by those on shore, for a great multitude of warriors had congregated along the beach watching us. We came to anchor as close in as we dared, which with our light feluccas was within easy speaking distance of the shore. Ghak was there and his eyes were mighty wide, too; for, as he told us later, though he knew this must be Perry's fleet it was so wonderful to him that he could not believe the testimony of his own eyes even while he was watching it approach.

To give the proper effect to our meeting I commanded that each felucca fire twenty-one guns as a salute to His Majesty Ghak, King of Sari. Some of the gunners, in the exuberance of their enthusiasm, fired solid shot; but fortunately they had sufficient good judgment to train their pieces on the open sea, so no harm was done. After this we landed — an arduous task since each felucca carried but a single light dugout.

I learned from Ghak that the Thurian chieftain, Goork, had been inclined to haughtiness, and had told Ghak, the Hairy One, that he knew nothing of me and cared less; but I imagine that the sight of the fleet and the sound of the guns brought him to his senses, for it was not long before he sent a deputation to me, inviting me to visit him in his village. Here he apologized for the treatment he had accorded me, very gladly swore allegiance to the empire, and received in return the title of king.

We remained in Thuria only long enough to arrange the treaty with Goork, among the other details of which was his promise to furnish the imperial army with a thousand lidi, or Thurian beasts of burden, and drivers for them. These were to accompany Ghak's army back to Sari by land, while the fleet sailed to the mouth of the great river from which Dian, Juag, and I had been blown.

The voyage was uneventful. We found the river easily, and sailed up it for many miles through as rich and wonderful a plain as I have ever seen. At the head of navigation we disembarked, leaving a sufficient guard for the feluccas, and marched the remaining distance to Sari.

Ghak's army, which was composed of warriors of all the original tribes of the federation, showing how successful had been his efforts to rehabilitate the empire, marched into Sari some time after we arrived. With them were the thousand lidi from Thuria.

At a council of the kings it was decided that we should at once commence the great war against the Mahars, for these haughty reptiles presented the greatest obstacle to human progress within Pellucidar. I laid out a plan of campaign which met with the enthusiastic indorsement of the kings. Pursuant to it, I at once despatched fifty

lidi to the fleet with orders to fetch fifty cannon to Sari. I also ordered the fleet to proceed at once to Anoroc, where they were to take aboard all the rifles and ammunition that had been completed since their departure, and with a full complement of men to sail along the coast in an attempt to find a passage to the inland sea near which lay the Mahars' buried city of Phutra.

Ja was sure that a large and navigable river connected the sea of Phutra with the Lural Az, and that, barring accident, the fleet would be before Phutra as soon as the land forces were.

At last the great army started upon its march. There were warriors from every one of the federated kingdoms. All were armed either with bow and arrows or muzzle-loaders, for nearly the entire Mezop contingent had been enlisted for this march, only sufficient having been left aboard the feluccas to man them properly. I divided the forces into divisions, regiments, battalions, companies, and even to platoons and sections, appointing the full complement of officers and non-commissioned officers. On the long march I schooled them in their duties, and as fast as one learned I sent him among the others as a teacher.

Each regiment was made up of about a thousand bowmen, and to each was temporarily attached a company of Mezop musketeers and a battery of artillery — the latter, our naval guns, mounted upon the broad backs of the mighty lidi. There was also one full regiment of Mezop musketeers and a regiment of primitive spearmen. The rest of the lidi that we brought with us were used for baggage animals and to transport our women and children, for we had brought them with us, as it was our intention to march from one Mahar city to another until we had subdued every Mahar nation that menaced the safety of any kingdom of the empire.

Before we reached the plain of Phutra we were discovered by a company of Sagoths, who at first stood to give battle; but upon seeing the vast numbers of our army they turned and fled toward Phutra. The result of this was that when we came in sight of the hundred towers which mark the entrances to the buried city we found a great army of Sagoths and Mahars lined up to give us battle.

At a thousand yards we halted, and, placing our artillery upon a slight eminence at either flank, we commenced to drop solid shot among them. Ja, who was chief artillery officer, was in command of this branch of the service, and he did some excellent work, for his Mezop gunners had become rather proficient by this time. The Sagoths couldn't stand much of this sort of warfare, so they charged us, yelling like fiends. We let them come quite close, and then the musketeers who formed the first line opened up on them.

The slaughter was something frightful, but still the remnants of them kept on coming until it was a matter of hand-to-hand fighting. Here our spearmen were of value, as were also the crude iron swords with which most of the imperial warriors were armed.

We lost heavily in the encounter after the Sagoths reached us; but they were absolutely exterminated — not one remained even as a prisoner. The Mahars, seeing how the battle was going, had hastened to the safety of their buried city. When we had overcome their gorilla-men we followed after them.

But here we were doomed to defeat, at least temporarily; for no sooner had the first of our troops descended into the subterranean avenues than many of them came stumbling and fighting their way back to the surface, half-choked by the fumes of some deadly gas that the reptiles had liberated upon them. We lost a number of men here. Then I sent for Perry, who had remained discreetly in the rear, and had him construct a little affair that I had had in my mind against the possibility of our meeting with a check at the entrances to the underground city.

Under my direction he stuffed one of his cannon full of powder, small bullets, and pieces of stone, almost to the muzzle. Then he plugged the muzzle tight with a cone-shaped block of wood, hammered and jammed in as tight as it could be. Next he inserted a long fuse. A dozen men rolled the cannon to the top of the stairs leading down into the city, first removing it from its carriage. One of them then lit the fuse and the whole thing was given a smart shove down the stairway, while the detachment turned and scampered to a safe distance.

For what seemed a very long time nothing happened. We had commenced to think that the fuse had been put out while the piece was rolling down the stairway, or that the Mahars had guessed its purpose and extinguished it themselves, when the ground about the entrance rose suddenly into the air, to be followed by a terrific explosion and a burst of smoke and flame that shot high in company with dirt, stone, and fragments of cannon.

Perry had been working on two more of these giant bombs as soon as the first was completed. Presently we launched these into two of the other entrances. They were all that were required, for almost immediately after the third explosion a stream of Mahars broke from the exits furthest from us, rose upon their wings, and soared northward. A hundred men on lidi were despatched in pursuit, each lidi carrying two riflemen in addition to its driver. Guessing that the inland sea, which lay not far north of Phutra, was their destination, I took a couple of regiments and followed.

A low ridge intervenes between the Phutra plain where the city lies, and the inland sea where the Mahars were wont to disport themselves in the cool waters. Not until we had topped this ridge did we get a view of the sea.

Then we beheld a scene that I shall never forget so long as I may live.

Along the beach were lined up the troop of lidi, while a hundred yards from shore the surface of the water was black with the long snouts and cold, reptilian eyes of the Mahars. Our savage Mezop riflemen, and the shorter, squatter, white-skinned Thurian drivers, shading their eyes with their hands, were gazing seaward beyond the Mahars, whose eyes were fastened upon the same spot. My heart leaped when I discovered that which was chaining the attention of them all. Twenty graceful feluccas were moving smoothly across the waters of the sea toward the reptilian horde!

The sight must have filled the Mahars with awe and consternation, for never had they seen the like of these craft before. For a time they seemed unable to do aught but gaze at the approaching fleet; but when the Mezops opened on them with their muskets the reptiles swam rapidly in the direction of the feluccas, evidently thinking that these would prove the easier to overcome. The commander of the fleet permitted them to approach within a hundred yards Then he opened on them with all the cannon that could be brought to bear, as well as with the small arms of the sailors.

A great many of the reptiles were killed at the first volley. They wavered for a moment, then dived; nor did we see them again for a long time.

But finally they rose far out beyond the fleet, and when the feluccas came about and pursued them they left the water and flew away toward the north.

Following the fall of Phutra I visited Anoroc, where I found the people busy in the shipyards and the factories that Perry had established. I discovered something, too, that he had not told me of — something that seemed infinitely more promising than the powder-factory or the arsenal. It was a young man poring over one of the books I had brought back from the outer world! He was sitting in the log cabin that Perry had had built to serve as his sleeping quarters and office. So absorbed was he that he did not notice our entrance. Perry saw the look of astonishment in my eyes and smiled.

"I started teaching him the alphabet when we first reached the prospector, and were taking out its contents," he explained. "He was much mystified by the books and anxious to know of what use they were. When I explained he asked me to teach him to read, and so I worked with him whenever I could. He is very intelligent and learns quickly. Before I left he had made great progress, and as soon as he is qualified he is going to teach others to read. It was mighty hard work getting started, though, for everything had to be translated into Pellucidarian.

"It will take a long time to solve this problem, but I think that by teaching a number of them to read and write English we shall then be able more quickly to give them a written language of their own."

And this was the nucleus about which we were to build our great system of schools and colleges — this almost naked red warrior, sitting in Perry's little cabin upon the island of Anoroc, picking out words letter by letter from a work on intensive farming. Now we have ——

But I'll get to all that before I finish.

While we were at Anoroc I accompanied Ja in an expedition to South Island, the southernmost of the three largest which form the Anoroc group — Perry had given it its name — where we made peace with the tribe there that had for long been hostile toward Ja. They were now glad enough to make friends with him and come into the federation. From there we sailed with sixty-five feluccas for distant Luana, the main island of the group where dwell the hereditary enemies of Anoroc.

Twenty-five of the feluccas were of a new and larger type than those with which Ja and Perry had sailed on the occasion when they chanced to find and rescue Dian and me. They were longer, carried much larger sails, and were considerably swifter. Each carried four guns instead of two, and these were so arranged that one or more of them could be brought into action no matter where the enemy lay.

The Luana group lies just beyond the range of vision from the mainland. The largest island of it alone is visible from Anoroc; but when we neared it we found that it comprised many beautiful islands, and that they were thickly populated. The Luanians had not, of course, been ignorant of all that had been going on in the domains of their nearest and dearest enemies. They knew of our feluccas and our guns, for several of their raiding-parties had had a taste of both. But their principal chief, an old man, had never seen either. So, when he sighted us, he put out to overwhelm us, bringing with him a fleet of about a hundred large war-canoes, loaded to capacity with javelin-armed warriors. It was pitiful, and I told Ja as much. It seemed a shame to massacre these poor fellows if there was any way out of it.

To my surprise Ja felt much as I did. He said he had always hated to war with other Mezops when there were so many alien races to fight against. I suggested that we hail the chief and request a parley; but when Ja did so the old fool thought that we were afraid, and with loud cries of exultation urged his warriors upon us.

So we opened up on them, but at my suggestion centered our fire upon the chief's canoe. The result was that in about thirty seconds there was nothing left of that war dugout but a handful of splinters, while its crew — those who were not killed — were struggling in the water, battling with the myriad terrible creatures that had risen to devour them.

We saved some of them, but the majority died just as had Hooja and the crew of his canoe that time our second shot capsized them.

Again we called to the remaining warriors to enter into a parley with us; but the chief's son was there and he would not, now that he had seen his father killed. He was all for revenge. So we had to open up on the brave fellows with all our guns; but it didn't last long at that, for there chanced to be wiser heads among the Luanians than their chief or his son had possessed. Presently, an old warrior who commanded one of the dugouts surrendered. After that they came in one by one until all had laid their weapons upon our decks.

Then we called together upon the flagship all our captains, to give the affair greater weight and dignity, and all the principal men of Luana. We had conquered them, and they expected either death or slavery; but they deserved neither, and I told them so. It is always my habit here in Pellucidar to impress upon these savage people that mercy is as noble a quality as physical bravery, and that next to the men who fight shoulder to shoulder with one, we should honor the brave men who fight against us, and if we are victorious, award them both the mercy and honor that are their due.

By adhering to this policy I have won to the federation many great and noble peoples, who under the ancient traditions of the inner world would have been massacred or enslaved after we had conquered them; and thus I won the Luanians. I gave them their freedom, and returned their weapons to them after they had sworn loyalty to me and friendship and peace with Ja, and I made the old fellow, who had had the good sense to surrender, king of Luana, for both the old chief and his only son had died in the battle.

When I sailed away from Luana she was included among the kingdoms of the empire, whose boundaries were thus pushed eastward several hundred miles.

We now returned to Anoroc and thence to the mainland, where I again took up the campaign against the Mahars, marching from one great buried city to another until we had passed far north of Amoz into a country where I had never been. At each city we were victorious, killing or capturing the Sagoths and driving the Mahars further away.

I noticed that they always fled toward the north. The Sagoth prisoners we usually found quite ready to transfer their allegiance to us, for they are little more than brutes, and when they found that we could

fill their stomachs and give them plenty of fighting, they were nothing loath to march with us against the next Mahar city and battle with men of their own race.

Thus we proceeded, swinging in a great half-circle north and west and south again until we had come back to the edge of the Lidi Plains north of Thuria. Here we overcame the Mahar city that had ravaged the Land of Awful Shadow for so many ages. When we marched on to Thuria, Goork and his people went mad with joy at the tidings we brought them.

During this long march of conquest we had passed through seven countries, peopled by primitive human tribes who had not yet heard of the federation, and succeeded in joining them all to the empire. It was noticeable that each of these peoples had a Mahar city situated near by, which had drawn upon them for slaves and human food for so many ages that not even in legend had the population any folk-tale which did not in some degree reflect an inherent terror of the reptilians.

In each of these countries I left an officer and warriors to train them in military discipline, and prepare them to receive the arms that I intended furnishing them as rapidly as Perry's arsenal could turn them out, for we felt that it would be a long, long time before we should see the last of the Mahars. That they had flown north but temporarily until we should be gone with our great army and terrifying guns I was positive, and equally sure was I that they would presently return.

The task of ridding Pellucidar of these hideous creatures is one which in all probability will never be entirely completed, for their great cities must abound by the hundreds and thousands in the far-distant lands that no subject of the empire had ever laid eyes upon.

But within the present boundaries of my domain there are now none left that I know of, for I am sure we should have heard indirectly of any great Mahar city that had escaped us, although of course the imperial army has by no means covered the vast area which I now rule.

After leaving Thuria we returned to Sari, where the seat of government is located. Here, upon a vast, fertile plateau, overlooking the great gulf that runs into the continent from the Lural Az, we are building the great city of Sari. Here we are erecting mills and factories. Here we are teaching men and women the rudiments of agriculture. Here Perry has built the first printing-press, and a dozen young Sarians are teaching their fellows to read and write the language of Pellucidar.

We have just laws and only a few of them. Our people are happy because they are always working at something which they enjoy. There is no money, nor is any money value placed upon any commodity. Perry and I were as one in resolving that the root of all evil should not be introduced into Pellucidar while we lived.

A man may exchange that which he produces for something which he desires that another has produced; but he cannot dispose of the thing he thus acquires. In other words, a commodity ceases to have pecuniary value the instant that it passes out of the hands of its producer. All excess reverts to government; and, as this represents the production of the people as a government, government may dispose of it to other peoples in exchange for that which they produce. Thus we are establishing a trade between kingdoms, the profits from which go to the betterment of the people — to building factories for the manufacture of agricultural implements, and machinery for the various trades we are gradually teaching the people.

Already Anoroc and Luana are vying with one another in the excellence of the ships they build. Each has several large shipyards. Anoroc makes gunpowder and mines iron ore, and by means of their ships they carry on a very lucrative trade with Thuria, Sari, and Amoz. The Thurians breed lidi, which, having the strength and intelligence of an elephant, make excellent draft animals.

Around Sari and Amoz the men are domesticating the great striped antelope, the meat of which is most delicious. I am sure that it will not be long before they will have them broken to harness and saddle. The horses of Pellucidar are far too diminutive for such uses, some species of them being little larger than fox-terriers.

Dian and I live in a great palace overlooking the gulf. There is no glass in our windows, for we have no windows, the walls rising but a few feet above the floor-line, the rest of the space being open to the ceilings; but we have a roof to shade us from the perpetual noon-day sun. Perry and I decided to set a style in architecture that would not curse future generations with the white plague, so we have plenty of ventilation. Those of the people who prefer, still inhabit their caves, but many are building houses similar to ours.

At Greenwich we have located a town and an observatory — though there is nothing to observe but the stationary sun directly overhead. Upon the edge of the Land of Awful Shadow is another observatory, from which the time is flashed by wireless to every corner of the empire twenty-four times a day. In addition to the wireless, we have a small telephone system in Sari. Everything is yet in the early stages of development; but with the science of the outer-world twentieth century to draw upon we are making rapid progress, and with all the faults and errors of the outer world to guide us clear of dangers, I think that it will not be long before Pellucidar will become as nearly a Utopia as one may expect to find this side of heaven.

Perry is away just now, laying out a railway-line from Sari to Amoz. There are immense antracite coal-fields at the head of the gulf not far from Sari, and the railway will tape these. Some of his students are working on a locomotive now. It will be a strange sight to see an iron horse puffing through the primeval jungles of the stone age, while cave bears, saber-toothed tigers, mastodons and the countless other terrible creatures of the past look on from their tangled lairs in wide-eyed astonishment.

We are very happy, Dian and I, and I would not return to the outer world for all the riches of all its princes. I am content here. Even without my imperial powers and honors I should be content, for have I not that greatest of all treasures, the love of a good woman my wondrous empress, Dian the Beautiful?

THUVIA—MAID OF MARS

Chapter I

CARTHORIS AND THUVIA

Upon a massive bench of polished ersite beneath the gorgeous blooms of a giant pimalia a woman sat. Her shapely, sandaled foot tapped impatiently upon the jewel-strewn walk that wound beneath the stately sorapus trees across the scarlet sward of the royal gardens of Thuvan Dihn, Jeddak of Ptarth, as a dark-haired, red-skinned warrior bent low toward her, whispering heated words close to her ear.

"Ah, Thuvia of Ptarth," he cried, "you are cold even before the fiery blasts of my consuming love! No harder than your heart, nor colder is the hard, cold ersite of this thrice happy bench which supports your divine and fadeless form! Tell me, O Thuvia of Ptarth, that I may still hope — that though you do not love me now, yet some day, some day, my princess, I ——"

The girl sprang to her feet with an exclamation of surprise and displeasure. Her queenly head was poised haughtily upon her smooth red shoulders. Her dark eyes looked angrily into those of the man.

"You forget yourself, and the customs of Barsoom, Astok," she said. "I have given you no right thus to address the daughter of Thuvan Dihn, nor have you won such a right."

The man reached suddenly forth and grasped her by the arm.

"You shall be my princess!" he cried. "By the breast of Issus, thou shalt, nor shall any other come between Astok, Prince of Dusar, and his heart's desire. Tell me that there is another, and I shall cut out his foul heart and fling it to the wild calots of the dead sea-bottoms!"

At touch of the man's hand upon her flesh the girl went pallid beneath her coppery skin, for the persons of the royal women of the courts of Mars are held but little less than sacred. The act of Astok, Prince of Dusar, was profanation. There was no terror in the eyes of Thuvia of Ptarth — only horror for the thing the man had done and for its possible consequences.

"Release me." Her voice was level — frigid.

The man muttered incoherently and drew her roughly toward him.

"Release me!" she repeated sharply, "or I call the guard, and the Prince of Dusar knows what that will mean."

Quickly he threw his right arm about her shoulders and strove to draw her face to his lips. With a little cry she struck him full in the mouth with the massive bracelets that circled her free arm.

"Calot!" she exclaimed, and then: "The guard! The guard! Hasten in protection of the Princess of Ptarth!"

In answer to her call a dozen guardsmen came racing across the scarlet sward, their gleaming long-swords naked in the sun, the metal of their accouterments clanking against that of their leathern harness, and in their throats hoarse shouts of rage at the sight which met their eyes.

But before they had passed half across the royal garden to where Astok of Dusar still held the struggling girl in his grasp, another figure sprang from a cluster of dense foliage that half hid a golden fountain close at hand. A tall, straight youth he was, with black hair and keen gray eyes; broad of shoulder and narrow of hip; a clean-limbed fighting man. His skin was but faintly tinged with the copper color that marks the red men of Mars from the other races of the dying planet — he was like them, and yet there was a subtle difference greater even than that which lay in his lighter skin and his gray eyes.

There was a difference, too, in his movements. He came on in great leaps that carried him so swiftly over the ground that the speed of the guardsmen was as nothing by comparison.

Astok still clutched Thuvia's wrist as the young warrior confronted him. The newcomer wasted no time and he spoke but a single word.

"Calot!" he snapped, and then his clenched fist landed beneath the other's chin, lifting him high into the air and depositing him in a crumpled heap within the center of the pimalia bush beside the ersite bench.

Her champion turned toward the girl. "Kaor, Thuvia of Ptarth!" he cried. "It seems that fate timed my visit well."

"Kaor, Carthoris of Helium!" the princess returned the young man's greeting, "and what less could one expect of the son of such a sire?"

He bowed his acknowledgment of the compliment to his father, John Carter,

Another figure sprang from a cluster of dense foliage

Warlord of Mars. And then the guardsmen, panting from their charge, came up just as the Prince of Dusar, bleeding at the mouth, and with drawn sword, crawled from the entanglement of the pimalia.

Astok would have leaped to mortal combat with the son of Dejah Thoris, but the guardsmen pressed about him, preventing, though it was clearly evident that naught would have better pleased Carthoris of Helium.

"But say the word, Thuvia of Ptarth," he begged, "and naught will give me greater pleasure than meting to this fellow the punishment he has earned."

"It cannot be, Carthoris," she replied. "Even though he has forfeited all claim upon my consideration, yet is he the guest of the jeddak, my father, and to him alone may he account for the unpardonable act he has committed."

"As you say, Thuvia," replied the Heliumite. "But afterward he shall account to Carthoris, Prince of Helium, for this affront to the daughter of my father's friend." As he spoke, though, there burned in his eyes a fire that proclaimed a nearer, dearer cause for his championship of this glorious daughter of Barsoom.

The maid's cheek darkened beneath the satin of her transparent skin, and the eyes of Astok, Prince of Dusar, darkened, too, as he read that which passed unspoken between the two in the royal gardens of the jeddak.

"And thou to me," he snapped at Carthoris, answering the young man's challenge.

The guard still surrounded Astok. It was a difficult position for the young officer who commanded it. His prisoner was the son of a mighty jeddak; he was the guest of Thuvan Dihn — until but now an honored guest upon whom every royal dignity had been showered. To arrest him forcibly could mean naught else than war, and yet he had done that which in the eyes of the Ptarth warrior merited death.

The young man hesitated. He looked toward his princess. She, too, guessed all that hung upon the action of the coming moment. For many years Dusar and Ptarth had been at peace with each other. Their great merchant ships plied back and forth between the larger cities of the two nations. Even now, far above the gold-shot scarlet dome of the jeddak's palace, she could see the huge bulk of a giant freighter taking its majestic way through the thin Barsoomian air toward the west and Dusar.

By a word she might plunge these two mighty nations into a bloody conflict that would drain them of their bravest blood and their incalculable riches, leaving them all helpless against the inroads of their envious and less powerful neighbors, and at last a prey to the savage green hordes of the dead sea-bottoms.

No sense of fear influenced her decision, for fear is seldom known to the children of Mars. It was rather a sense of the responsibility that she, the daughter of their jeddak, felt for the welfare of her father's people.

"I called you, Padwar," she said to the lieutenant of the guard, "to protect the person of your princess, and to keep the peace that must not be violated within the royal gardens of the jeddak. That is all. You will escort me to the palace, and the Prince of Helium will accompany me."

Without another glance in the direction of Astok she turned, and taking Carthoris' proffered hand, moved slowly toward the massive marble pile that housed the ruler of Ptarth and his glittering court. On either side marched a file of guardsmen. Thus Thuvia of Ptarth found a way out of a dilemma, escaping the necessity of placing her father's royal guest under forcible restraint, and at the same time separating the two princes, who otherwise would have been at each other's throat the moment she and the guard had departed.

Beside the pimalia stood Astok, his dark eyes narrowed to mere slits of hate beneath his lowering brows as he watched the retreating forms of the woman who had aroused the fiercest passions of his nature and the man whom he now believed to be the one who stood between his love and its consummation.

As they disappeared within the structure Astok shrugged his shoulders and with a murmured oath crossed the gardens toward another wing of the building where he and his retinue were housed.

That night he took formal leave of Thuvan Dihn, and though no mention was made of the happening within the garden, it was plain to see through the cold mask of the jeddak's courtesy that only the customs of royal hospitality restrained him from voicing the contempt he felt for the Prince of Dusar.

Carthoris was not present at the leave-taking, nor was Thuvia. The ceremony was as stiff and formal as court etiquette could make it, and when the last of the Dusarians clambered over the rail of the battleship that had brought them upon this fateful visit to the court of Ptarth, and the mighty engine of destruction had risen slowly from the ways of the landing stage, a note of relief was apparent in the voice of Thuvan Dihn as he turned to one of his officers with a word of comment upon a subject foreign to that which had been uppermost in the minds of all for hours.

But, after all, was it so foreign?

"Inform Prince Sovan," he directed, "that it is our wish that the fleet which departed for Kaol this morning be recalled to cruise to the west of Ptarth."

As the warship, bearing Astok back to the court of his father, turned toward the west, Thuvia of Ptarth, sitting upon the same bench where the Prince of Dusar had affronted her, watched the twinkling lights of the craft growing smaller in the distance. Beside her, in the brilliant light of the nearer moon, sat Carthoris. His eyes were not upon the dim bulk of the battleship, but on the profile of the girl's upturned face.

"Thuvia," he whispered.

The girl turned her eyes toward his. His hand stole out to find hers, but she drew it gently away.

"Thuvia of Ptarth, I love you!" cried the young warrior. "Tell me that it does not offend."

She shook her head sadly. "The love of Carthoris of Helium," she said simply, "could be naught but an honor to any woman; but you must not speak, my friend, of bestowing upon me that which I may not reciprocate."

The young man got slowly to his feet. His eyes were wide in astonishment. It never had occurred to the Prince of Helium that Thuvia of Ptarth might love another.

"But at Kadabra!" he exclaimed. "And later here at your father's court, what did you do, Thuvia of Ptarth, that might have warned me that you could not return my love?"

"And what did I do, Carthoris of Helium," she returned, "that might lead you to believe that I *did* return it?"

He paused in thought, and then shook his head. "Nothing, Thuvia, that is true; yet I could have sworn you loved me. Indeed, you well knew how near to worship has been my love for you."

"And how might I know it, Carthoris?" she asked innocently. "Did you ever tell me as much? Ever before have words of love for me fallen from your lips?"

"But you *must* have known it!" he exclaimed. "I am like my father — witless in matters of the heart, and of a poor way with women; yet the jewels that strew these royal garden paths — the trees, the flowers, the sward — all must have read the love that has filled my heart since first my eyes were made new by imaging your perfect face and form; so how could you alone have been blind to it?"

"Do the maids of Helium pay court to their men?" asked Thuvia.

"You are playing with me!" exclaimed Carthoris, not, however, without appeal in his voice. "Say that you are but playing, and that after all you love me, Thuvia!"

"I cannot tell you that Carthoris, for I am promised to another."

Her tone was level, but was there not within it the hint of an infinite depth of sadness? Who may say?

"Promised to another?" Carthoris scarcely breathed the words. His face went almost white, and then his head came up as befitted him in whose veins flowed the blood of the overlord of a world.

"Carthoris of Helium wishes you every happiness with the man of your choice," he said. "With —" and then he hesitated, waiting for her to fill in the name.

"Kulan Tith, Jeddak of Kaol," she replied. "My father's friend and Ptarth's most puissant ally."

The young man looked at her intently for a moment before he spoke again.

"You love him, Thuvia of Ptarth?" he asked earnestly.

"I am promised to him," she replied simply.

He did not press her. "He is of Barsoom's noblest blood and mightiest fighters," mused Carthoris. "My father's friend and mine — would that it might have been another!" he muttered almost savagely. What the girl thought was hidden by the mask of her expression, which was tinged only by a little shadow of sadness that might have been for Carthoris, herself, or for them both.

Carthoris of Helium did not ask, though he noted it, for his loyalty to Kulan Tith was the loyalty of the blood of John Carter of Virginia for a friend, greater than which could be no loyalty.

He raised a jewel-encrusted bit of the girl's magnificent trappings to his lips.

"To the honor and happiness of Kulan Tith and the priceless jewel that has been bestowed upon him," he said, and though his voice was husky there was the true ring of sincerity in it. "I told you that I loved you, Thuvia, before I knew that you were promised to another. I may not tell you it again, but I am glad that you know it, for there is no dishonor in it either to you or to Kulan Tith or to myself. My love is such that it may embrace as well Kulan Tith — if you love him." There was almost a question in the statement.

"I am promised to him," she replied.

Carthoris backed slowly away. He laid one hand upon his heart, the other upon the pommel of his long-sword.

"These are yours — always," he said. A moment later he had entered the palace, and was gone from the girl's sight.

Had he returned at once he would have found her prone upon the ersite bench, her face buried in her arms. Was she weeping? There was none to see.

Carthoris of Helium had come all unannounced to the court of his father's friend that day. He had come alone in a small flier, sure of the same welcome that always awaited him at Ptarth. As there had been no formality in his coming there was no need of formality in his going.

To Thuvan Dihn he explained that he had been but testing an invention of his own with which his flier was equipped — a clever improvement of the ordinary Martian air compass, which when set for a certain destination, will remain constantly fixed thereon, making it only necessary to keep a vessel's prow always in the direction of the compass needle to reach any given point upon Barsoom by the shortest route.

Carthoris' improvement upon this consisted of an auxiliary device which steered the craft mechanically in the direction of the compass, and upon arrival directly over the point for which the compass was set, brought the craft to a stand-still and lowered it, also automatically, to the ground.

"You readily discern the advantages of this invention," he was saying to Thuvan Dihn, who had accompanied him to the landing stage upon the palace roof to inspect the compass and bid his young friend farewell.

A dozen officers of the court with several body servants were grouped behind the jeddak and his guest, eager listeners to the conversation — so eager on the part of one of the servants that he was twice rebuked by a noble for his forwardness in pushing himself ahead of his betters to view the intricate mechanism of the wonderful "controlling destination compass," as the thing was called.

"For example," continued Carthoris, "I have an all-night trip before me, as tonight. I set the pointer here upon the right-hand dial, which represents the eastern hemisphere of Barsoom, so that the point rests upon the exact latitude and longitude of Helium. Then I start the engine, roll up in my sleeping silks and furs, and with lights burning, race through the air toward Helium, confident that at the appointed hour I shall drop gently toward the landing stage upon my own palace, whether I am still asleep or no."

"Provided," suggested Thuvan Dihn, "you do not chance to collide with some other night wanderer in the meanwhile."

Carthoris smiled. "No danger of that," he replied. "See here," and he indicated a device at the right of the destination compass. "This is my 'obstruction evader,' as I call it. This visible device is the switch which throws the mechanism on or off. The instrument itself is below deck, geared both to the steering apparatus and the control levers.

"It is quite simple, being nothing more than a radium generator diffusing radio activity in all directions to a distance of a hundred yards or so from the flier. Should this enveloping force be interrupted in any direction a delicate instrument immediately apprehends the irregularity, at the same time imparting an impulse to a magnetic device which in turn actuates the steering mechanism, diverting the bow of the flier away from the obstacle until the craft's radio-activity sphere is no longer in contact with the obstruction, then she falls once more into her normal course. Should the disturbance approach from the rear, as in case of a faster-moving craft overhauling me, the mechanism actuates the speed control as well as the steering gear, and the flier shoots ahead and either up or down, as the oncoming vessel is upon a lower or higher plane than herself.

"In aggravated cases, that is when the obstructions are many, or of such a nature as to deflect the bow more than forty-five degrees in any direction, or when the craft has reached its destination and dropped to within a hundred yards of the ground, the mechanism brings her to a full stop, at the same time sounding a loud alarm which will instantly awaken the pilot. You see I have anticipated almost every contingency."

Thuvan Dihn smiled his appreciation of the marvelous device. The forward servant pushed almost to the flier's side. His eyes were narrowed to slits.

"All but one," he said.

The nobles looked at him in astonishment, and one of them grasped the fellow none too gently by the shoulder to push him back to his proper place. Carthoris raised his hand.

"Wait," he urged. "Let us hear what the man has to say — no creation of mortal mind is perfect. Perchance he has detected a weakness that it will be well to know at once. Come, my good fellow, and what may be the one contingency I have overlooked?"

As he spoke Carthoris observed the servant closely for the first time. He saw a man of giant stature and handsome, as are all those of the race of Martian red men; but the fellow's lips were thin and cruel, and across one cheek was the faint, white line of a sword-cut from the right temple to the corner of the mouth.

"Come," urged the Prince of Helium. "Speak!"

The man hesitated. It was evident that he regretted the temerity that had made him the center of interested observation. But at last, seeing no alternative, he spoke.

"It might be tampered with," he said, "by an enemy."

Carthoris drew a small key from his leathern pocket-pouch.

"Look at this," he said, handing it to the man. "If you know aught of locks, you will know that the mechanism which this unlooses is beyond the cunning of a picker of locks. It guards the vitals of the instrument from crafty tampering. Without it an enemy must half wreck the device to reach its heart, leaving his handiwork apparent to the most casual observer."

The servant took the key, glanced at it shrewdly, and then as he made to return it to Carthoris dropped it upon the marble flagging. Turning to look for it he planted the sole of his sandal full upon the glittering object. For an instant he bore all his weight upon the foot that covered the key, then he stepped back and with an exclamation as of pleasure that he had found it, stooped, recovered it, and returned it to the Heliumite. Then he dropped back to his station behind the nobles and was forgotten.

A moment later Carthoris had made his adieux to Thuvan Dihn and his nobles, and with lights twinkling had risen into the star-shot void of the Martian night.

Chapter II

SLAVERY

As the ruler of Ptarth, followed by his courtiers, descended from the landing stage above the palace, the servants dropped into their places in the rear of their royal or noble masters, and behind the others one lingered to the last. Then quickly stooping he snatched the sandal from his right foot, slipping it into his pocket-pouch.

When the party had come to the lower levels, and the jeddak had dispersed them by a sign, none noticed that the forward fellow who had drawn so much attention to himself before the Prince of Helium departed, was no longer among the other servants.

To whose retinue he had been attached none had thought to inquire, for the followers of a Martian noble are many, coming and going at the whim of their master, so that a new face is scarcely ever questioned, as the fact that a man has passed within the palace walls is considered proof positive that his loyalty to the jeddak is beyond question, so rigid is the examination of each who seeks service with the nobles of the court.

A good rule that, and only relaxed by courtesy in favor of the retinue of visiting royalty from a friendly foreign power.

It was late in the morning of the next day that a giant serving man in the harness of the house of a great Ptarth noble passed out into the city from the palace gates. Along one broad avenue and then another he strode briskly until he had passed beyond the district of the nobles and had come to the place of shops. Here he sought a pretentious building that rose spirelike toward the heavens, its outer walls elaborately wrought with delicate carvings and intricate mosaics.

It was the Palace of Peace in which were housed the representatives of the foreign powers, or rather in which were located their embassies; for the ministers themselves dwelt in gorgeous palaces within the district occupied by the nobles.

Here the man sought the embassy of Dusar. A clerk arose questioningly as he entered, and at his request to have a word with the minister asked his credentials. The visitor slipped a plain metal armlet from above his elbow, and pointing to an inscription upon its inner surface, whispered a word or two to the clerk.

The latter's eyes went wide, and his attitude turned at once to one of deference. He bowed the stranger to a seat, and hastened to an inner room with the armlet in his hand. A moment later he reappeared and conducted the caller into the presence of the minister.

For a long time the two were closeted together, and when at last the giant serving man emerged from the inner office his expression was cast in a smile of sinister satisfaction. From the Palace of Peace he hurried directly to the palace of the Dusarian minister.

That night two swift fliers left the same palace top. One sped its rapid course toward Helium; the other ——

Thuvia of Ptarth strolled in the gardens of her father's palace, as was her nightly custom before retiring. Her silks and furs were drawn about her, for the air of Mars is chill after the sun has taken his quick plunge beneath the planet's western verge.

The girl's thoughts wandered from her impending nuptials, that would make her empress of Kaol, to the person of the trim young Heliumite who had laid his heart at her feet the preceding day.

Whether it was pity or regret that saddened her expression as she gazed toward the southern heavens where she had watched the lights of his flier disappear the previous night, it would be difficult to say.

So, too, is it impossible to conjecture just what her emotions may have been as she discerned the lights of a flier speeding rapidly out of the distance from that very direction, as though impelled toward her garden by the very intensity of the princess' thoughts.

She saw it circle lower above the palace until she was positive that it but hovered in preparation for a landing.

Presently the powerful rays of its searchlight shot downward from the bow. They fell upon the landing stage for a brief instant, revealing the figures of the Ptarthian guard, picking into brilliant points of fire the gems upon their gorgeous harnesses.

Then the blazing eye swept onward across the burnished domes and graceful minarets, down into court and park and garden to pause at last upon the ersite bench and the girl standing there beside it, her face upturned full toward the flier.

For but an instant the searchlight halted upon Thuvia of Ptarth, then it was extinguished as suddenly as it had come to life. The flier passed on above her to disappear beyond a grove of lofty skeel trees that grew within the palace grounds.

The girl stood for some time as it had left her, except that her head was bent and her eyes downcast in thought.

Who but Carthoris could it have been? She tried to feel anger that he should have returned thus, spying upon her; but she found it difficult to be angry with the young prince of Helium.

What mad caprice could have induced him so to transgress the etiquette of nations? For lesser things great powers had gone to war.

The princess in her was shocked and angered — but what of the girl!

And the guard — what of them? Evidently they, too, had been so much surprised by the unprecedented action of the stranger that they had not even challenged; but that they had no thought to let the thing go unnoticed was quickly evidenced by the skirring of motors upon the landing stage and the quick shooting airward of a long-lined patrol boat.

Thuvia watched it dart swiftly eastward. So, too, did other eyes watch.

Within the dense shadows of the skeel grove, in a wide avenue beneath o'erspreading foliage, a flier hung a dozen feet above the ground. From its deck keen eyes watched the far-fanning searchlight of the patrol boat. No light shone from the enshadowed craft. Upon its deck was the silence of the tomb. Its crew of a half dozen red warriors watched the lights of the patrol boat diminishing in the distance.

"The intellects of our ancestors are with us tonight," said one in a low tone.

"No plan ever carried better," returned another. "They did precisely as the prince foretold."

He who had first spoken turned toward the man who squatted before the control board.

"Now!" he whispered. There was no other order given. Every man upon the craft had evidently been well schooled in each detail of that night's work. Silently the dark hull crept beneath the cathedral arches of the dark and silent grove.

Thuvia of Ptarth, gazing toward the east, saw the blacker blot against the blackness of the trees as the craft topped the buttressed garden wall. She saw the dim bulk incline gently downward toward the scarlet sward of the garden.

She knew that men came not thus with honorable intent. Yet she did not cry aloud to alarm the nearby guardsmen, nor did she flee to the safety of the palace.

Why?

I can see her shrug her shapely shoulders in reply as she voices the age-old, universal answer of the woman: Because!

Scarce had the flier touched the ground when four men leaped from its deck. They ran forward toward the girl.

Still she made no sign of alarm, standing as though hypnotized. Or could it have been as one who awaited a welcome visitor?

Not until they were quite close to her did she move. Then the nearer moon, rising above the surrounding foliage, touched their faces, lighting all with the brilliancy of her silver rays.

Thuvia of Ptarth saw only strangers — warriors in the harness of Dusar. Now she took fright, but too late!

Before she could voice but a single cry, rough hands seized her. A heavy silken scarf was wound about her head. She was lifted in strong arms and borne to the deck of the flier. There was the sudden whirl of propellers, the rushing of air against her body, and, from far beneath the shouting and the challenge from the guard.

Racing toward the south another flier sped toward Helium. In its cabin a tall red man bent over the soft sole of an upturned sandal. With delicate instruments he measured the faint imprint of a small object which appeared there. Upon a pad beside him was the outline of a key, and here he noted the results of his measurements.

A smile played upon his lips as he completed his task and turned to one who waited at the opposite side of the table.

"The man is a genius," he remarked, admiration in his voice.

"Only a genius could have evolved such a lock as this is designed to spring. Here, take the sketch, Larok, and give all thine own genius full and unfettered freedom in reproducing it in metal."

The warrior-artificer bowed. "Man builds naught," he said, "that man may not destroy." Then he left the cabin with the sketch.

As dawn broke upon the lofty towers which mark the twin cities of Helium — the scarlet tower of one and the yellow tower of its sister — a flier floated lazily out of the north.

Upon its bow was emblazoned the insignia of a lesser noble of a far city of the empire of Helium. Its leisurely approach and the evident confidence with which it moved across the city aroused no suspicion in the minds of the sleepy guard. Their round of duty nearly done, they had little thought beyond the coming of those who were to relieve them.

Peace reigned throughout Helium. Stagnant, emasculating peace. Helium had no enemies. There was naught to fear.

Without haste the nearest air patrol swung sluggishly about and approached the stranger. At easy speaking distance the officer upon her deck hailed the incoming craft.

The cheery "Kaor!" and the plausible explanation that the owner had come from distant parts for a few days of pleasure in gay Helium sufficed. The air-patrol boat sheered off, passing again upon its way. The stranger continued toward a public landing stage, where she dropped into the ways and came to rest.

At about the same time a warrior entered her cabin.

"It is done, Vas Kor," he said, handing a small metal key to the tall noble who had just risen from his sleeping silks and furs.

"Good!" exclaimed the latter. "You must have worked upon it all during the night, Larok."

The warrior nodded.

For but an instant the searchlight halted upon
Thuvia of Ptarth

"Now fetch me the Heliumetic metal you wrought some days since," commanded Vas Kor.

This done, the warrior assisted his master to replace the handsome jeweled metal of his harness with the plainer ornaments of an ordinary fighting man of Helium, and with the insignia of the same house that appeared upon the bow of the flier.

Vas Kor breakfasted on board. Then he emerged upon the aerial dock, entered an elevator, and was borne quickly to the street below, where he was soon engulfed by the early morning throng of workers hastening to their daily duties.

Among them his warrior trappings were no more remarkable than is a pair of trousers upon Broadway. All Martian men are warriors, save those physically unable to bear arms. The tradesman and his clerk clank with their martial trappings as they pursue their vocations. The schoolboy, coming into the world, as he does, almost adult from the snowy shell that has encompassed his development for five long years, knows so little of life without a sword at his hip that he would feel the same discomfiture at going abroad unarmed that an Earth boy would experience in walking the streets knickerbockerless.

Vas Kor's destination lay in Greater Helium, which lies some seventy-five miles across the level plain from Lesser Helium. He had landed at the latter city because the air patrol is less suspicious and alert than that above the larger metropolis, where lies the palace of the jeddak.

As he moved with the throng in the parklike canyon of the thoroughfare the life of an awakening Martian city was in evidence about him. Houses, raised high upon their slender metal columns for the night, were dropping gently toward the ground. Among the flowers upon the scarlet sward which lies about the buildings children were already playing, and comely women laughing and chatting with their neighbors as they culled gorgeous blossoms and graceful ferns for the vases within doors.

The pleasant "kaor" of the Barsoomian greeting fell continually upon the ears of the stranger as friends and neighbors took up the duties of a new day.

The district in which he had landed was residential — a district of merchants of the more prosperous sort. Everywhere were evidences of luxury and wealth. Slaves appeared upon every house top with gorgeous silks and costly furs, laying them in the sun for airing. Jewel-encrusted women lolled even thus early upon the carven balconies before their sleeping apartments. Later in the day they would repair to the roofs when the slaves had arranged couches and pitched silken canopies to shade them from the sun.

Strains of inspiring music broke agreeably from open windows, for the Martians have solved the problem of attuning the nerves pleasantly to the sudden transition from sleep to waking that proves so difficult a thing for most Earth folk.

Above him raced the long, light passenger fliers, plying, each in its proper plane, between the numerous landing stages for internal passenger traffic. Landing stages that tower high into the heavens are for the great international passenger liners. Freighters have other landing stages at various lower levels, to within a couple of hundred feet of the ground; nor dare any flier rise or drop from one plane to another except in certain restricted districts where horizontal traffic is forbidden.

Along the close-cropped sward which paves the avenue ground fliers were moving in continuous lines in opposite directions. For the greater part they skimmed along the surface of the sward, soaring gracefully into the air at times to pass over a slower-going driver ahead, or at intersections, where the north and south traffic has the right of way and that going east and west must rise above it.

From private hangers upon many a roof top, fliers were darting into the line of traffic. Gay farewells and parting admonitions mingled with the whirring of motors and the subdued noises of the city.

Yet with all the swift movement and the countless thousands rushing hither and thither, the predominant suggestion was that of luxurious ease and soft noiselessness.

Martians dislike harsh, discordant clamor. The only loud noises they can abide are the martial sounds of war, the clash of arms, the collision of two mighty dreadnaughts of the air. To them there is no sweeter music than this.

At the intersection of two broad avenues Vas Kor descended from the street level to one of the great pneumatic stations of the city. Here he paid before a little wicket the fare to his destination with a couple of the dull, oval coins of Helium.

Beyond the gatekeeper he came to a slowly moving line of what to Earthly eyes would have appeared to be conical-nosed, eight-foot projectiles for some giant gun. In slow procession the things moved in single file along a grooved track. A half dozen attendants assisted passengers to enter, or directed these carriers to their proper destination.

Vas Kor approached one that was empty. Upon its nose was a dial and a pointer. He set the pointer for a certain station in Greater Helium, raised the arched lid of the thing, stepped in and lay down upon the upholstered bottom. An attendant closed the lid, which locked with a little click, and the carrier continued its slow way.

Presently it switched itself automatically to another track, to enter, a moment later, one of a series of dark-mouthed tubes.

The instant that its entire length was within the black aperture it sprang forward with the speed of a rifle ball. There was an instant of whizzing — a soft, though sudden, stop, and slowly the carrier emerged upon another platform, another attendant raised the lid and Vas Kor stepped out at the station beneath the center of Greater Helium, seventy-five miles from the point at which he had embarked.

Here he sought the street level, stepping immediately into a waiting ground flier. He spoke no word to the slave sitting in the driver's seat. It was evident that he had been expected, and that the fellow had received his instructions before his coming.

Scarcely had Vas Kor taken his seat when the flier went quickly into the fast-moving procession, turning presently from the broad and crowded avenue into a less congested street. After a time it left the thronged district behind to enter a section of small shops, where it stopped before the entrance to one which bore the sign of a dealer in foreign silks.

Vas Kor entered the low-ceilinged room. A man at the far end motioned him toward an inner apartment, giving no further sign of recognition until he had passed in after the caller and closed the door.

Then he faced his visitor, saluting deferentially.

"Most noble —" he commenced, but Vas Kor silenced him with a gesture.

"No formalities," he said. "We must forget that I am aught other than your slave. If all has been as carefully carried out as it has been planned, we have no time to waste. Instead we should be upon our way to the slave market. Are you ready?"

The merchant nodded, and, turning to a great chest, produced the unemblazoned trappings of a slave. These Vas Kor immediately donned. Then the two passed from the shop through a rear door, traversed a winding alley to an avenue beyond, where they entered a swift flier which awaited them.

Five minutes later the merchant was leading his slave to the public market, where a great concourse of people filled the large open space in the center of which stood the slave block.

The crowds were enormous today, for Carthoris, Prince of Helium, was to be the principal bidder.

One by one the masters mounted the rostrum beside the slave block upon which stood their chattels. Briefly and clearly each recounted the virtues of his particular offering.

When all were done, the major-domo of the Prince of Helium recalled to the block such as had favorably impressed him. For such he made a fair offer.

There was little haggling as to price, and none at all when Vas Kor was placed upon the block. His merchant-master accepted the first offer that was made for him, and thus a Dusarian noble entered the household of Carthoris.

Chapter III

TREACHERY

The day following the coming of Vas Kor to the palace of the Prince of Helium great excitement reigned throughout the twin cities, reaching its climax in the palace of Carthoris. Word had come of the abduction of Thuvia of Ptarth from her father's court, and with it the veiled hint that the Prince of Helium might be suspected of considerable knowledge of the act and the whereabouts of the princess.

In the council chamber of John Carter, Warlord of Mars, was Tardos Mors, Jeddak of Helium; Mors Kajak, his son, Jed of Lesser Helium; Carthoris, and a score of the great nobles of the empire.

"There must be no war between Ptarth and Helium, my son," said John Carter. "That you are innocent of the charge that has been placed against you by insinuation, we well know; but Thuvan Dihn must know it well, too.

"There is but one who may convince him, and that one be you. You must hasten at once to the court of Ptarth, and by your presence there as well as by your words assure him that his suspicions are groundless. Bear with you the authority of the Warlord of Barsoom, and of the Jeddak of Helium to offer every resource of the allied powers to assist Thuvan Dihn to recover his daughter and punish her abductors, whomsoever they may be.

"Go! I know that I do not need to urge upon you the necessity for haste."

Carthoris left the council chamber, and hastened to his palace.

Here slaves were busy in a moment setting things to right for the departure of their master. Several worked about the swift flier that would bear the Prince of Helium rapidly toward Ptarth.

At last all was done. But two armed slaves remained on guard. The setting sun hung low above the horizon. In a moment darkness would envelop all.

One of the guardsmen, a giant of a fellow across whose right cheek there ran a thin scar from temple to mouth, approached his companion. His gaze was directed beyond and above his comrade. When he had come quite close he spoke.

"What strange craft is that?" he asked.

The other turned about quickly to gaze heavenward. Scarce was his back turned toward the giant than the short-sword of the latter was plunged beneath his left shoulder blade, straight through his heart.

Voiceless, the soldier sank in his tracks — stone dead. Quickly the murderer dragged the corpse into the black shadows within the hangar. Then he returned to the flier.

Drawing a cunningly wrought key from his pocket-pouch, he removed the cover of the right-hand dial of the controlling destination compass. For a moment he studied the construction of the mechanism beneath. Then he returned the dial to its place, set the pointer, and

removed it again to note the resultant change in the position of the parts affected by the act.

A smile crossed his lips. With a pair of cutters he snipped off the projection which extended through the dial from the external pointer — now the latter might be moved to any point upon the dial without affecting the mechanism below. The eastern hemisphere dial was useless.

Now he turned his attention to the western dial. This he set upon a certain point. Afterward he removed the cover of this dial also, and with keen tool cut the steel finger from the under side of the pointer.

As quickly as possible he replaced the second dial cover, and resumed his place on guard. To all intents and purposes the compass was as efficient as before; but, as a matter of fact, the moving of the pointers upon the dials resulted now in no corresponding shift of the mechanism beneath — and the device was set, immovably, upon a destination of the slave's own choosing.

Presently came Carthoris, accompanied by but a handful of his gentlemen. He cast but a casual glance upon the single slave who stood guard. The fellow's thin, cruel lips, and the sword cut that ran from temple to mouth aroused the suggestion of an unpleasant memory within him. He wondered where Saran Tal had found the man — then the matter faded from his thoughts, and in another moment the Prince of Helium was laughing and chatting with his companions, though below the surface his heart was cold with dread, for what contingencies confronted Thuvia of Ptarth he could not even guess.

First to his mind, naturally, had sprung the thought that Astok of Dusar had stolen the fair Ptarthian; but almost simultaneously with the report of the abduction had come news of the great fêtes at Dusar in honor of the return of the jeddak's son to the court of his father.

It could not have been he, thought Carthoris, for on the very night that Thuvia was taken Astok had been in Dusar, and yet ——

He entered the flier, exchanging casual remarks with his companions as he unlocked the mechanism of the compass and set the pointer upon the capital city of Ptarth.

With a word of farewell he touched the button which controlled the repulsive rays, and as the flier rose lightly into the air, the engine purred in answer to the touch of his finger upon a second button, the propellers whirred as his hand drew back the speed lever, and Carthoris, Prince of Helium, was off into the gorgeous Martian night beneath the hurtling moons and the million stars.

Scarce had the flier found its speed ere the man, wrapping his sleeping silks and furs about him, stretched at full length upon the narrow deck to sleep.

But sleep did not come at once at his bidding.

Instead, his thoughts ran riot in his brain, driving sleep away. He recalled the words of Thuvia of Ptarth, words that had half assured him that she loved him; for when he had asked her if she loved Kulan Tith, she had answered only that she was promised to him.

Now he saw that her reply was open to more than a single construction. It might, of course, mean that she did not love Kulan Tith; and so, by inference, be taken to mean that she loved another.

But what assurance was there that the other was Carthoris of Helium?

The more he thought upon it the more positive he became that not only was there no assurance in her words that she loved him, but none either in any act of hers. No, the fact was, she did not love him. She loved another. She had not been abducted — she had fled willingly with her lover.

With such pleasant thoughts filling him alternately with despair and rage, Carthoris at last dropped into the deep sleep of utter mental exhaustion.

The breaking of the sudden dawn found him still asleep. His flier was rushing swiftly above a barren, ochre plain — the world-old bottom of a long-dead Martian sea.

In the distance rose low hills. Toward these the craft was headed. As it approached them, a great promontory might have been seen from its deck, stretching out into what had once been a mighty ocean, and circling back once more to enclose the forgotten harbor of a forgotten city, which still stretched back from its deserted quays, an imposing pile of wondrous architecture of a long-dead past.

The countless dismal windows, vacant and forlorn, stared, sightless, from their marble walls; the whole sad city taking on the semblance of scattered mounds of dead men's sun-bleached skulls — the casements having the appearance of eyeless sockets, the portals, grinning jaws.

Closer came the flier, but now its speed was diminishing — yet this was not Ptarth.

Above the central plaza it stopped, slowly settling Marsward. Within a hundred yards of the ground it came to rest, floating gently in the light air, and at the same instant an alarm sounded at the sleeper's ear.

Carthoris sprang to his feet. Below him he looked to see the teeming metropolis of Ptarth. Beside him, already, there should have been an air patrol.

He gazed about in bewildered astonishment. There indeed was a great city, but it was not Ptarth. No multitudes surged through its broad avenues. No signs of life broke the dead monotony of its deserted roof tops. No gorgeous silks, no priceless furs lent life and color to the cold marble and the gleaming ersite.

No patrol boat lay ready with its familiar challenge. Silent and empty lay the great city — empty and silent the surrounding air.

What had happened?

Carthoris examined the dial of his compass. The pointer was set upon Ptarth. Could the creature of his genius have thus betrayed him? He would not believe it.

Quickly he unlocked the cover, turning it back upon its hinge. A single glance showed him the truth, or at least a part of it — the steel projection that communicated the movement of the pointer upon the dial to the heart of the mechanism beneath had been severed.

Who could have done the thing — and why?

Carthoris could not hazard even a faint guess. But the thing now was to learn in what portion of the world he was, and then take up his interrupted journey once more.

If it had been the purpose of some enemy to delay him, he had succeeded well, thought Carthoris, as he unlocked the cover of the second dial, the first having shown that its pointer had not been set at all.

Beneath the second dial he found the steel pin severed as in the other, but the controlling mechanism had first been set for a point upon the western hemisphere.

He had just time to judge his location

roughly at some place southwest of Helium, and at a considerable distance from the twin cities, when he was startled by a woman's scream beneath him.

Leaning over the side of the flier, he saw what appeared to be a red woman being dragged across the plaza by a huge, green warrior — one of those fierce, cruel denizens of the dead sea-bottoms and deserted cities of dying Mars.

Carthoris waited to see no more. Reaching for the control board, he sent his craft racing plummet-like toward the ground.

The green man was hurrying his captive toward a huge thoat that browsed upon the ochre vegetation of the once scarlet-gorgeous plaza. At the same instant a dozen red warriors leaped from the entrance of a nearby ersite palace, pursuing the abductor with naked swords and shouts of rageful warning.

Once the woman turned her face upward toward the falling flier, and in the single swift glance, Carthoris saw that it was Thuvia of Ptarth!

Chapter IV

A GREEN MAN'S CAPTIVE

When the light of day broke upon the little craft to whose deck the Princess of Ptarth had been snatched from her father's garden, Thuvia saw that the night had wrought a change in her abductors.

No longer did their trappings gleam with the metal of Dusar, but instead there was emblazoned there the insignia of the Prince of Helium.

The girl felt renewed hope, for she could not believe that in the heart of Carthoris could lie intent to harm her.

She spoke to the warrior squatting before the control board.

"Last night you wore the trappings of a Dusarian," she said. "Now your metal is that of Helium. What means it?"

The man looked at her with a grin.

"The Prince of Helium is no fool," he said.

Just then an officer emerged from the tiny cabin. He reprimanded the warrior for conversing with the prisoner, nor would he himself reply to any of her inquiries.

No harm was offered her during the journey, and so they came at last to their destination with the girl no wiser as to her abductors or their purpose than at first.

Here the flier settled slowly into the plaza of one of those mute monuments of Mars' dead and forgotten past — the deserted cities that fringe the sad ochre sea-bottoms where once rolled the mighty floods upon whose bosoms moved the maritime commerce of the peoples that are gone forever.

Thuvia of Ptarth was no stranger to such places. During her wanderings in search of the River Iss, that time she had set out upon what, for countless ages, had been the last, long pilgrimage of Martians, toward the Valley Dor, where lies the Lost Sea of Korus, she had encountered several of these sad reminders of the greatness and the glory of ancient Barsoom.

And again, during her flight from the temples of the Holy Therns with Tars Tarkas, Jeddak of Thark, she had seen them, with their weird and ghostly inmates, the great white apes of Barsoom.

She knew, too, that many of them were used now by the nomadic tribes of green men, but that among them all was no city that the red men did not shun, for without exception they stood amidst vast, waterless tracts, unsuited for the continued sustenance of the dominant race of Martians.

Why, then, should they be bringing her to such a place? There was but a single answer. Such was the nature of their work that they must needs seek the seclusion that a dead city afforded. The girl trembled at thought of her plight.

For two days her captors kept her within a huge palace that even in decay reflected the splendor of the age which its youth had known.

Just before dawn on the third day she had been aroused by the voices of two of her abductors.

"He should be here by dawn," one was saying. "Have her in readiness upon the plaza — else he will never land. The moment he finds that he is in a strange country he will turn about — methinks the prince's plan is weak in this one spot."

"There was no other way," replied the other. "It is wondrous work to get them both here at all, and even if we do not succeed in luring him to the ground, we shall have accomplished much."

Just then the speaker caught the eyes of

Thuvia upon him, revealed by the quick-moving patch of light cast by Thuria in her mad race through the heavens.

With a quick sign to the other, he ceased speaking, and advancing toward the girl, motioned her to rise. Then he led her out into the night toward the center of the great plaza.

"Stand here," he commanded, "until we come for you. We shall be watching, and should you attempt to escape it will go ill with you — much worse than death. Such are the prince's orders."

Then he turned and retraced his steps toward the palace, leaving her alone in the midst of the unseen terrors of the haunted city, for in truth these places are haunted in the belief of many Martians who still cling to an ancient superstition which teaches that the spirits of Holy Therns who die before their allotted one thousand years, pass, on occasions, into the bodies of the great white apes.

To Thuvia, however, the real danger of attack by one of these ferocious, manlike beasts was quite sufficient. She no longer believed in the weird soul transmigration that the therns had taught her before she was rescued from their clutches by John Carter; but she well knew the horrid fate that awaited her should one of the terrible beasts chance to spy her during its nocturnal prowlings.

What was that?

Surely she could not be mistaken. Something had moved, stealthily, in the shadow of one of the great monoliths that line the avenue where it entered the plaza opposite her!

Thar Ban, jed among the hordes of Torquas, rode swiftly across the ochre vegetation of the dead sea-bottom toward the ruins of ancient Aaanthor.

He had ridden far that night, and fast, for he had but come from the despoiling of the incubator of a neighboring green horde with which the hordes of Torquas were perpetually warring.

His giant thoat was far from jaded, yet it would be well, thought Thar Ban, to permit him to graze upon the ochre moss which grows to greater height within the protected courtyards of deserted cities, where the soil is richer than on the sea-bottoms, and the plants partly shaded from the sun during the cloudless Martian day.

Within the tiny stems of this dry-seeming plant is sufficient moisture for the needs of the huge bodies of the mighty thoats, which can exist for months without water, and for days without even the slight moisture which the ochre moss contains.

As Thar Ban rode noiselessly up the broad avenue which leads from the quays of Aaanthor to the great central plaza, he and his mount might have been mistaken for specters from a world of dreams, so grotesque the man and beast, so soundless the great thoat's padded, nailless feet upon the moss-grown flagging of the ancient pavement.

The man was a splendid specimen of his race. Fully fifteen feet towered his great height from sole to pate. The moonlight glistened against his glossy green hide, sparkling the jewels of his heavy harness and the ornaments that weighted his four muscular arms, while the upcurving tusks that protruded from his lower jaw gleamed white and terrible.

At the side of his thoat were slung his long radium rifle and his great, forty-foot, metal-shod spear, while from his own harness depended his long-sword and his short-sword, as well as his lesser weapons.

His protruding eyes and antennae-like ears were turning constantly hither and thither, for Thar Ban was yet in the country of the enemy, and, too, there was always the menace of the great white apes, which, John Carter was wont to say, are the only creatures that can arouse in the breasts of these fierce denizens of the dead sea-bottoms even the remotest semblance of fear.

As the rider neared the plaza, he reined suddenly in. His slender, tubular ears pointed rigidly forward. An unwonted sound had reached them. Voices! And where there were voices, outside of Torquas, there, too, were enemies. All the world of wide Barsoom contained naught but enemies for the fierce Torquasians.

Thar Ban dismounted. Keeping in the shadows of the great monoliths that line the Avenue of Quays of sleeping Aaanthor, he approached the plaza. Directly behind him, as a hound at heel, came the slate-gray thoat, his white belly shadowed by his barrel, his vivid yellow feet merging into the yellow of the moss beneath them.

In the center of the plaza Thar Ban saw

the figure of a red woman. A red warrior was conversing with her. Now the man turned and retraced his steps toward the palace at the opposite side of the plaza.

Thar Ban watched until he had disappeared within the yawning portal. Here was a captive worth having! Seldom did a female of their hereditary enemies fall to the lot of a green man. Thar Ban licked his thin lips.

Thuvia of Ptarth watched the shadow behind the monolith at the opening to the avenue opposite her. She hoped that it might be but the figment of an overwrought imagination.

But no! Now, clearly and distinctly, she saw it move. It came from behind the screening shelter of the ersite shaft.

The sudden light of the rising sun fell upon it. The girl trembled. The *thing* was a huge green warrior!

Swiftly he sprang toward her. She screamed and tried to flee; but she had scarce turned toward the palace when a giant hand fell upon her arm, she was whirled about, and half dragged, half carried toward a huge thoat that was slowly grazing out of the avenue's mouth onto the ochre moss of the plaza.

At the same instant she turned her face upward toward the whirring sound of something above her, and there she saw a swift flier dropping toward her, the head and shoulders of a man leaning far over the side; but the man's features were deeply shadowed, so that she did not recognize them.

Now from behind her came the shouts of her red abductors. They were racing madly after him who dared to steal what they already had stolen.

As Thar Ban reached the side of his mount he snatched his long radium rifle from its boot, and, wheeling, poured three shots into the oncoming red men.

Such is the uncanny marksmanship of these Martian savages that three red warriors dropped in their tracks as three projectiles exploded in their vitals.

The others halted, nor did they dare return the fire for fear of wounding the girl.

Then Thar Ban vaulted to the back of this thoat, Thuvia of Ptarth still in his arms, and with a savage cry of triumph disappeared down the black canyon of the Avenue of Quays between the sullen palaces of forgotten Aaanthor.

Carthoris' flier had not touched the ground before he had sprung from its deck to race after the swift thoat, whose eight long legs were sending it down the avenue at the rate of an express train; but the men of Dusar who still remained alive had no mind to permit so valuable a capture to escape them.

They had lost the girl. That would be a difficult thing to explain to Astok; but some leniency might be expected could they carry the Prince of Helium to their master instead.

So the three who remained set upon Carthoris with their long-swords, crying to him to surrender; but they might as successfully have cried aloud to Thuria to cease her mad hurtling through the Barsoomian sky, for Carthoris of Helium was a true son of the Warlord of Mars and his incomparable Dejah Thoris.

Carthoris' long-sword had been already in his hand as he leaped from the deck of the flier, so the instant that he realized the menace of the three red warriors, he wheeled to face them, meeting their onslaught as only John Carter himself might have done.

So swift his sword, so mighty and agile his half-earthly muscles, that one of his opponents was down, crimsoning the ochre moss with his life-blood, when he had scarce made a single pass at Carthoris.

Now the two remaining Dusarians rushed simultaneously upon the Heliumite. Three long-swords clashed and sparkled in the moonlight, until the great white apes, roused from their slumbers, crept to the lowering windows of the dead city to view the bloody scene beneath them.

Thrice was Carthoris touched, so that the red blood ran down his face, blinding him and dyeing his broad chest. With his free hand he wiped the gore from his eyes, and with the fighting smile of his father touching his lips, leaped upon his antagonists with renewed fury.

A single cut of his heavy sword severed the head of one of them, and then the other, backing away clear of that point of death, turned and fled toward the palace at his back.

Carthoris made no step to pursue. He had other concern than the meting of even well-deserved punishment to strange men who masqueraded in the metal of his own house, for he had seen that these men were

*With a savage cry of triumph, Thar Ban
disappeared down the black canyon of the
Avenue of Quays*

tricked out in the insignia that marked his personal followers.

Turning quickly toward his flier, he was soon rising from the plaza in pursuit of Thar Ban.

The red warrior whom he had put to flight turned in the entrance to the palace, and, seeing Carthoris' intent, snatched a rifle from those that he and his fellows had left leaning against the wall as they had rushed out with drawn swords to prevent the theft of their prisoner.

Few red men are good shots, for the sword is their chosen weapon; so now as the Dusarian drew bead upon the rising flier and touched the button upon his rifle's stock, it was more to chance than proficiency that he owed the partial success of his aim.

The projectile grazed the flier's side, the opaque coating breaking sufficiently to permit daylight to strike in upon the powder vial within the bullet's nose. There was a sharp explosion. Carthoris felt his craft reel drunkenly beneath him, and the engine stopped.

The momentum the air boat had gained carried her on over the city toward the sea-bottom beyond.

The red warrior in the plaza fired several more shots, none of which scored. Then a lofty minaret shut the drifting quarry from his view.

In the distance before him Carthoris could see the green warrior bearing Thuvia of Ptarth away upon his mighty thoat. The direction of his flight was toward the northwest of Aaanthor, where lay a vast mountainous country little known to red men.

The Heliumite now gave his attention to his injured craft. A close examination revealed the fact that one of the buoyancy tanks had been punctured, but the engine itself was uninjured.

A splinter from the projectile had damaged one of the control levers beyond the possibility of repair outside a machine shop; but after considerable tinkering, Carthoris was able to propel his wounded flier at low speed, a rate which could not approach the rapid gait of the thoat, whose eight long, powerful legs carried it over the ochre vegetation of the dead sea-bottom at terrific speed.

The Prince of Helium chafed and fretted at the slowness of his pursuit, yet he was thankful that the damage was no worse, for now he could at least move more rapidly than on foot.

But even this meager satisfaction was soon to be denied him, for presently the flier commenced to sag toward the port and by the bow. The damage to the buoyancy tanks had evidently been more grievous than he had at first believed.

All the balance of that long day Carthoris crawled erratically through the still air, the bow of the flier sinking lower and lower, and the list to port becoming more and more alarming, until at last, near dark, he was floating almost bow-down, his harness buckled to a heavy deck ring to keep him from being precipitated to the ground below.

His forward movement was now confined to a slow drifting with the gentle breeze that blew out of the southeast, and when this died down with the setting of the sun, he let the flier sink gently to the mossy carpet beneath.

Far before him loomed the mountains toward which the green man had been fleeing when last he had seen him, and with dogged resolution the son of John Carter, endowed with the indomitable will of his mighty sire, took up the pursuit on foot.

All that night he forged ahead until, with the dawning of a new day, he entered the low foothills that guard the approach to the fastness of the mountains of Torquas.

Rugged, granitic walls towered before him. Nowhere could he discern an opening through the formidable barrier; yet somewhere into this inhospitable world of stone the green warrior had borne the woman of the red man's heart's desire.

Across the yielding moss of the sea-bottom there had been no spoor to follow, for the soft pads of the thoat but pressed down in his swift passage the resilient vegetation, which sprang up again behind his fleeing feet, leaving no sign.

But here in the hills, where loose rock occasionally strewed the way; where black loam and wild flowers partially replaced the somber monotony of the waste places of the lowlands, Carthoris hoped to find some sign that would lead him in the right direction.

Yet, search as he would, the baffling mystery of the trail seemed likely to remain forever unsolved.

It was drawing toward the day's close

once more when the keen eyes of the Heliumite discerned the tawny yellow of a sleek hide moving among the boulders several hundred yards to his left.

Crouching quickly behind a large rock, Carthoris watched the thing before him. It was a huge banth, one of those savage Barsoomian lions that roam the desolate hills of the dying planet.

The creature's nose was close to the ground. It was evident that he was following the spoor of meat by scent.

As Carthoris watched him, a great hope leaped into the man's heart. Here, possibly, might lie the solution to the mystery he had been endeavoring to solve. This hungry carnivore, keen always for the flesh of man, might even now be trailing the two whom Carthoris sought!

Cautiously the youth crept out upon the trail of the man-eater. Along the foot of the perpendicular cliff the creature moved, sniffing at the invisible spoor, and now and then emitting the low moan of the hunting banth.

Carthoris had followed the creature for but a few minutes when it disappeared as suddenly and mysteriously as though dissolved into thin air.

The man leaped to his feet. Not again was he to be cheated as the man had cheated him. He sprang forward at a reckless pace to the spot at which he last had seen the great, skulking brute.

Before him loomed the sheer cliff, its face unbroken by any aperture into which the huge banth might have wormed its great carcass. Beside him was a small, flat boulder, not larger than the deck of a ten-man flier, nor standing to a greater height than twice his own stature.

Perhaps the banth was in hiding behind this? The brute might have discovered the man upon his trail, and even now be lying in wait for his easy prey.

Cautiously, with drawn long-sword, Carthoris crept around the corner of the rock. There was no banth there, but something which surprised him infinitely more than would the presence of twenty banths.

Before him yawned the mouth of a dark cave leading downward into the ground. Through this the banth must have disappeared. Was it his lair? Within its dark and forbidding interior might there not lurk not one but many of the fearsome creatures?

Carthoris did not know, nor, with the thought that had been spurring him onward upon the trail of the creature uppermost in his mind, did he much care; for into this gloomy cavern he was sure the banth had trailed the green man and his captive, and into it he, too, would follow, content to give his life in the service of the woman he loved.

Not an instant did he hesitate, nor yet did he advance rashly; but with ready sword and cautious steps, for the way was dark, he stole on. As he advanced, the obscurity became impenetrable blackness.

Chapter V

THE FAIR RACE

Downward along a smooth, broad floor led the strange tunnel, for such Carthoris was now convinced was the nature of the shaft he at first had thought but a cave.

Before him he could hear the occasional low moans of the banth, and presently from behind came a similar uncanny note. Another banth had entered the passageway on *his* trail!

His position was anything but pleasant. His eyes could not penetrate the darkness even to the distinguishing of his hand before his face, while the banths, he knew, could see quite well, though absence of light were utter.

No other sounds came to his ears than the dismal, bloodthirsty moanings of the beast ahead and the beast behind.

The tunnel had led straight, from where he had entered it beneath the side of the rock furtherest from the unscalable cliffs, toward the mighty barrier that had baffled him so long.

Now it was running almost level, and presently he noted a gradual ascent.

The beast behind him was gaining upon him, crowding him perilously close upon the heels of the beast in front. Presently he should have to do battle with one, or both. More firmly he gripped his weapon.

Now he could hear the breathing of the banth at his heels. Not for much longer could he delay the encounter.

Long since he had become assured that the tunnel led beneath the cliffs to the opposite side of the barrier, and he had hoped that he might reach the moonlit open before being compelled to grapple with either of the monsters.

The sun had been setting as he entered the tunnel, and the way had been sufficiently long to assure him that darkness now reigned upon the world without.

He glanced behind him. Blazing out of the darkness, seemingly not ten paces behind, glared two flaming points of fire. As the savage eyes met his, the beast emitted a frightful roar and then he charged.

To face that savage mountain of onrushing ferocity, to stand unshaken before the hideous fangs that he knew were bared in slavering blood-thirstiness, though he could not see them, required nerves of steel; but of such were the nerves of Carthoris of Helium.

He had the brute's eyes to guide his point, and, as true as the sword hand of his mighty sire, his guided the keen point to one of those blazing orbs, even as he leaped lightly to one side.

With a hideous scream of pain and rage, the wounded banth hurtled, clawing, past him. Then it turned to charge once more; but this time Carthoris saw but a single gleaming point of fiery hate directed upon him.

Again the needle point met its flashing target. Again the horrid cry of the stricken beast reverberated through the rocky tunnel, shocking in its torture-laden shrillness, deafening in its terrific volume.

But now, as it turned to charge again, the man had no guide whereby to direct his point. He heard the scraping of the padded feet upon the rocky floor. He knew the thing was charging down upon him once again, but he could see nothing.

Yet, if he could not see his antagonist, neither could his antagonist now see him.

Leaping, as he thought, to the exact center of the tunnel, he held his sword point ready on a line with the beast's chest. It was all that he could do, hoping that chance might send the point into the savage heart as he went down beneath the great body.

So quickly was the thing over that Carthoris could scarce believe his senses as the mighty body rushed madly past him. Either he had not placed himself in the center of the tunnel, or else the blinded banth had erred in its calculations.

However, the huge body missed him by a foot, and the creature continued on down the tunnel as though in pursuit of the prey that had eluded him.

Carthoris, too, followed the same direction, nor was it long before his heart was gladdened by the sight of the moonlit exit from the long, dark passage.

Before him lay a deep hollow, entirely surrounded by gigantic cliffs. The surface of the valley was dotted with enormous trees, a strange sight so far from a Martian waterway. The ground itself was clothed in brilliant scarlet sward, picked out with innumerable patches of gorgeous wild flowers.

Beneath the glorious effulgence of the two moons the scene was one of indescribable loveliness, tinged with the weirdness of strange enchantment.

For only an instant, however, did his gaze rest upon the natural beauties outspread before him. Almost immediately they were riveted upon the figure of a great banth standing across the carcass of a new-killed thoat.

The huge beast, his tawny mane bristling around his hideous head, kept his eyes fixed upon another banth that charged erratically hither and thither, with shrill screams of pain, and horrid roars of hate and rage.

Carthoris quickly guessed that the second brute was the one he had blinded during the fight in the tunnel, but it was the dead thoat that centered his interest more than either of the savage carnivora.

The harness was still upon the body of the huge Martian mount, and Carthoris could not doubt but that this was the very animal upon which the green warrior had borne away Thuvia of Ptarth.

But where were the rider and his prisoner? The Prince of Helium shuddered as he thought upon the probability of the fate that had overtaken them.

Human flesh is the food most craved by the fierce Barsoomian lion, whose great carcass and giant thews require enormous quantities of meat to sustain them.

Two human bodies would have but whetted the creature's appetite, and that he had killed and eaten the green man and the red girl seemed only too likely to Carthoris. He had left the carcass of the mighty thoat to be devoured after having consumed the more toothsome portion of his banquet.

Now the sightless banth, in its savage, aimless charging and counter-charging, had passed beyond the kill of its fellow, and there the light breeze that was blowing wafted the scent of new blood to its nostrils.

No longer were its movements erratic. With outstretched tail and foaming jaws it charged straight as an arrow, for the body of the thoat and the mighty creature of destruction that stood with forepaws upon the slate-gray side, waiting to defend its meat.

When the charging banth was twenty paces from the dead thoat the killer gave vent to its hideous challenge, and with a mighty spring leaped forward to meet it.

The battle that ensued awed even the warlike Barsoomian. The mad rending, the hideous and deafening roaring, the implacable savagery of the blood-stained beasts held him in the paralysis of fascination, and when it was over and the two creatures, their heads and shoulders torn to ribbons, lay with their dead jaws still buried in each other's bodies, Carthoris tore himself from the spell only by an effort of the will.

Hurrying to the side of the dead thoat he searched for traces of the girl he feared had shared the thoat's fate, but nowhere could he discover anything to confirm his fears.

With slightly lightened heart he started out to explore the valley, but scarce a dozen steps had he taken when the glistening of a jeweled bauble lying on the sward caught his eye.

As he picked it up his first glance showed him that it was a woman's hair ornament, and emblazoned upon it was the insignia of the royal house of Ptarth.

But, sinister discovery, blood, still wet, splotched the magnificent jewels of the setting.

Carthoris half choked as the dire possibilities which the thing suggested presented themselves to his imagination. Yet he could not, would not believe it.

It was impossible that that radiant creature could have met so hideous an end. It was incredible that the glorious Thuvia should ever cease to be.

Upon his already jewel-encrusted harness, to the strap that crossed his great chest beneath which beat his loyal heart, Carthoris, Prince of Helium, fastened the gleaming thing that Thuvia of Ptarth had worn, and wearing, had made holy to the Heliumite.

Then he proceeded upon his way into the heart of the unknown valley.

For the most part the giant trees shut off his view to any but the most limited distances. Occasionally he caught glimpses of the towering hills that bounded the valley upon every side, and though they stood out clear beneath the light of the two moons, he knew that they were far off, and that the extent of the valley was immense.

For half the night he continued his search, until presently he was brought to a sudden halt by the distant sound of squealing thoats.

Guided by the noise of these habitually angry beasts, he stole forward through the trees until at last he came upon a level, treeless plain, in the center of which a mighty city reared its burnished domes and vividly colored towers.

About the walled city the red man saw a huge encampment of the green warriors of the dead sea-bottoms, and as he let his eyes rove carefully over the city he realized that here was no deserted metropolis of a dead past.

But what city could it be? His studies had taught him that in this little-explored portion of Barsoom the fierce tribe of Torquasian green men ruled supreme, and that as yet no red man had succeeded in piercing to the heart of their domain to return again to the world of civilization.

The men of Torquas had perfected huge guns with which their uncanny marksmanship had permitted them to repulse the few determined efforts that nearby red nations had made to explore their country by means of battle fleets of airships.

That he was within the boundary of Torquas, Carthoris was sure, but that there existed there such a wondrous city he never had dreamed, nor had the chronicles of the past even hinted at such a possibility, for the Torquasians were known to live, as did the other green men of Mars, within the deserted cities that dotted the dying planet, nor ever had any green horde built so much as a single edifice, other than the low-walled incubators where their young are hatched by the sun's heat.

The encircling camp of green warriors lay about five hundred yards from the city's walls. Between it and the city was no semblance of breastwork or other protection against rifle or cannon fire; yet distinctly now in the light of the rising sun Carthoris could see many figures moving along the summit of the high wall, and upon the roof tops beyond.

That they were beings like himself he was sure, though they were at too great a distance from him for him to be positive that they were red men.

Almost immediately after sunrise the green warriors commenced firing upon the little figures upon the wall. To Carthoris' surprise the fire was not returned, but presently the last of the city's inhabitants had sought shelter from the weird marksmanship of the green men, and no further sign of life was visible beyond the wall.

Then Carthoris, keeping within the shelter of the trees that fringed the plain, began circling the rear of the besiegers' line, hoping against hope that somewhere he would obtain sight of Thuvia of Ptarth, for even now he could not believe that she was dead.

That he was not discovered was a miracle, for mounted warriors were constantly riding back and forth from the camp into the forest; but the long day wore on and still he continued his seemingly fruitless quest, until, near sunset, he came opposite a mighty gate in the city's western wall.

Here seemed to be the principal force of the attacking horde. Here a great platform had been erected whereon Carthoris could see squatting a huge green warrior, surrounded by others of his kind.

This, then, must be the notorious Hortan Gur, Jeddak of Torquas, the fierce old ogre of the southwestern hemisphere, as only for a jeddak are platforms raised in temporary camps or upon the march by the green hordes of Barsoom.

As the Heliumite watched he saw another green warrior push his way forward toward the rostrum. Beside him he dragged a captive, and as the surrounding warriors parted to let the two pass, Carthoris caught a fleeting glimpse of the prisoner. His heart leaped in rejoicing. Thuvia of Ptarth still lived!

It was with difficulty that Carthoris restrained the impulse to rush forward to the side of the Ptarthian princess; but in the end his better judgment prevailed, for in the face of such odds he knew that he should have been but throwing away, uselessly, any future opportunity he might have to succor her.

He saw her dragged to the foot of the rostrum. He saw Hortan Gur address her. He could not hear the creature's words, nor Thuvia's reply; but it must have angered the green monster, for Carthoris saw him leap toward the prisoner, striking her a cruel blow across the face with his metal-banded arm.

Then the son of John Carter, Jeddak of Jeddaks, Warlord of Barsoom, went mad. The old, blood-red haze through which his sire had glared at countless foes, floated before his eyes.

His half-Earthly muscles, responding quickly to his will, sent him in enormous leaps and bounds toward the green monster that had struck the woman he loved.

The Torquasians were not looking in the direction of the forest. All eyes had been upon the figures of the girl and their jeddak, and loud was the hideous laughter that rang out in appreciation of the wit of the green emperor's reply to his prisoner's appeal for liberty.

Carthoris had covered about half the distance between the forest and the green warriors, when a new factor succeeded in still further directing the attention of the latter from him.

Upon a high tower within the beleaguered city a man appeared. From his upturned mouth there issued a series of frightful shrieks; uncanny shrieks that swept, shrill and terrifying, across the city's walls, over the heads of the besiegers, and out across the forest to the uttermost confines of the valley.

Once, twice, thrice the fearsome sound smote upon the ears of the listening green men, and then far, far off across the broad woods came sharp and clear from the distance an answering shriek.

It was but the first. From every point rose similar savage cries, until the world seemed to tremble to their reverberations.

The green warriors looked nervously this way and that. They knew not fear, as Earth men may know it; but in the face of the unusual their wonted self-assurance deserted them.

And then the great gate in the city wall opposite the platform of Hortan Gur swung suddenly wide. From it issued as strange a sight as Carthoris ever had witnessed, though at the moment he had time to cast but a single fleeting glance at the tall bowmen emerging through the portal behind their long, oval shields; to note their flowing auburn hair; and to realize that the growling things at their side were fierce Barsoomian lions.

Then he was in the midst of the astonished Torquasians. With drawn longsword he was among them, and to Thuvia of Ptarth, whose startled eyes were the first to fall upon him, it seemed that she was looking upon John Carter himself, so strangely similar to the fighting of the father was that of the son.

Even to the famous fighting smile of the Virginian was the resemblance true. And the sword arm! Ah, the subtleness of it, and the speed!

All about was turmoil and confusion. Green warriors were leaping to the backs of their restive, squealing thoats. Calots were growling out their savage gutturals, whining to be at the throats of the oncoming foemen.

Thar Ban and another by the side of the rostrum had been the first to note the coming of Carthoris, and it was with them he battled for possession of the red girl, while the others hastened to meet the host advancing from the beleaguered city.

Carthoris sought both to defend Thuvia of Ptarth and reach the side of the hideous Hortan Gur that he might avenge the blow the creature had struck the girl.

He succeeded in reaching the rostrum, over the dead bodies of two warriors who had turned to join Thar Ben and his companion in repulsing this adventurous red man, just as Hortan Gur was about to leap from it to the back of his thoat.

The attention of the green warriors turned principally upon the bowmen advancing upon them from the city, and upon the savage banths that paced beside them — cruel beasts of war, infinitely more terrible than their own savage calots.

As Carthoris leaped to the rostrum he drew Thuvia up beside him, and then he turned upon the departing jeddak with an angry challenge and a sword thrust.

As the Heliumite's point pricked his green hide, Hortan Gur turned upon his adversary with a snarl, but at the same instant two of his chieftains called to him to hasten, for the charge of the fair-skinned inhabitants of the city was developing into a more serious matter than the Torquasians had anticipated.

Instead of remaining to battle with the red man, Hortan Gur promised him his attention after he had disposed of the presumptuous citizens of the walled city, and, leaping astride his thoat, galloped madly off to meet the rapidly advancing bowmen.

The other warriors quickly followed their jeddak, leaving Thuvia and Carthoris alone upon the platform.

Between them and the city raged a terrific battle. The fair-skinned warriors, armed only with their long bows and a kind of short-handled war-ax, were almost helpless beneath the savage mounted green men at close quarters; but at a distance their sharp arrows did fully as much execution as the radium projectiles of the green men.

But if the warriors themselves were outclassed, not so their savage companions, the fierce banths. Scarce had the two lines come together when hundreds of these appalling creatures had leaped among the Torquasians, dragging warriors from their thoats — dragging down the huge thoats themselves, and bringing consternation to all before them.

The numbers of the citizenry, too, was to their advantage, for it seemed that scarce a warrior fell but his place was taken by a score more, in such a constant stream did they pour from the city's great gate.

And so it came, what with the ferocity of the banths and the numbers of the bowmen, that at last the Torquasians fell back, until presently the platform upon which stood Carthoris and Thuvia lay directly in the center of the fight.

That neither was struck by a bullet or an arrow seemed a miracle to both; but at last the tide had rolled completely past them, so that they were alone between the fighters and the city, except for the dying and the dead, and a score or so of growling banths, less well trained than their fellows, who prowled among the corpses seeking meat.

To Carthoris the strangest part of the battle had been the terrific toll taken by the bowmen with their relatively puny weapons. Nowhere that he could see was there a single wounded green man, but the corpses of their dead lay thick upon the field of battle.

Death seemed to follow instantly the slightest pinprick of a bowman's arrow, nor apparently did one ever miss its goal. There could be but one explanation: the missiles were poison-tipped.

Presently the sounds of conflict died in the distant forest. Quiet reigned, broken only by the growling of the devouring banths. Carthoris turned toward Thuvia of

Between them and the city raged a terrific battle

Ptarth. As yet neither had spoken.

"Where are we, Thuvia?" he asked.

The girl looked at him questioningly. His very presence had seemed to proclaim a guilty knowledge of her abduction. How else might he have known the destination of the flier that brought her!

"Who should know better than the Prince of Helium?" she asked in return. "Did he not come hither of his own free will?"

"From Aaanthor I came voluntarily upon the trail of the green man who had stolen you, Thuvia," he replied; "but from the time I left Helium until I awoke above Aaanthor I thought myself bound for Ptarth.

"It had been intimated that I had guilty knowledge of your abduction," he explained simply, "and I was hastening to the jeddak, your father, to convince him of the falsity of the charge, and to give my service to your recovery. Before I left Helium someone tampered with my compass, so that it bore me to Aaanthor instead of to Ptarth. That is all. You believe me?"

"But the warriors who stole me from the garden!" she exclaimed. "After we arrived at Aaanthor they wore the metal of the Prince of Helium. When they took me they were trapped in Dusarian harness. There seemed but a single explanation. Whoever dared the outrage wished to put the onus upon another, should he be detected in the act; but once safely away from Ptarth he felt safe in having his minions return to their own harness."

"You believe that I did this thing, Thuvia?" he asked.

"Ah, Carthoris," she replied sadly, "I did not wish to believe it; but when everything pointed to you — even then I would not believe it."

"I did not do it, Thuvia," he said. "But let me be entirely honest with you. As much as I love your father, as much as I respect Kulan Tith, to whom you are betrothed, as well as I know the frightful consequences that must have followed such an act of mine, hurling into war, as it would, three of the greatest nations of Barsoom — yet, notwithstanding all this, I should not have hesitated to take you thus, Thuvia of Ptarth, had you even hinted that it would not have displeased *you*.

"But you did nothing of the kind, and so I am here, not in my own service, but in yours, and in the service of the man to whom you are promised, to save you for him, if it lies within the power of man to do so," he concluded, almost bitterly.

Thuvia of Ptarth looked into his face for several moments. Her breast was rising and falling as though to some resistless emotion. She half took a step toward him. Her lips parted as though to speak — swiftly and impetuously.

And then she conquered whatever had moved her.

"The future acts of the Prince of Helium," she said coldly, "must constitute the proof of his past honesty of purpose."

Carthoris was hurt by the girl's tone, as much as by the doubt as to his integrity which her words implied.

He had half hoped that she might hint that his love would be acceptable — certainly there was due him at least a little gratitude for his recent acts in her behalf; but the best he received was cold skepticism.

The Prince of Helium shrugged his broad shoulders. The girl noted it, and the little smile that touched his lips, so that it became her turn to be hurt.

Of course she had not meant to hurt him. He might have known that after what he had said she could not do anything to encourage him! But he need not have made his indifference quite so palpable. The men of Helium were noted for their gallantry — not for boorishness. Possibly it was the Earth blood that flowed in his veins.

How could she know that the shrug was but Carthoris' way of attempting, by physical effort, to cast blighting sorrow from his heart, or that the smile upon his lips was the fighting smile of his father with which the son gave outward evidence of the determination he had reached to submerge his own great love in his efforts to save Thuvia of Ptarth for another, because he believed that she loved this other!

He reverted to his original question.

"Where are we?" he asked. "I do not know."

"Nor I," replied the girl. "Those who stole me from Ptarth spoke among themselves of Aaanthor, so that I thought it possible that the ancient city to which they took me was that famous ruin; but where we may be now I have no idea."

"When the bowmen return we shall doubtless learn all that there is to know," said Carthoris. "Let us hope that they prove friendly. What race may they be? Only in the most ancient of our legends and in the mural paintings of the deserted cities of the dead sea-bottoms are depicted such a race of auburn-haired, fair-skinned people. Can it be that we have stumbled upon a surviving city of the past which all Barsoom believes buried beneath the ages?"

Thuvia was looking toward the forest into which the green men and the pursuing bowmen had disappeared. From a great distance came the hideous cries of banths, and an occasional shot.

"It is strange that they do not return," said the girl.

"One would expect to see the wounded limping or being carried back to the city," replied Carthoris, with a puzzled frown. "But how about the wounded nearer the city? Have they carried them within?"

Both turned their eyes toward the field between them and the walled city, where the fighting had been most furious.

There were the banths, still growling about their hideous feast.

Carthoris looked at Thuvia in astonishment. Then he pointed toward the field.

"Where are they?" he whispered. *"What has become of their dead and wounded?"*

Chapter VI

THE JEDDAK OF LOTHAR

The girl looked her incredulity.

"They lay in piles," she murmured. "There were thousands of them but a minute ago."

"And now," continued Carthoris, "there remain but the banths and the carcasses of the green men."

"They must have sent forth and carried the dead bowmen away while we were talking," said the girl.

"It is impossible!" replied Carthoris. "Thousands of dead lay there upon the field but a moment since. It would have required many hours to have removed them. The thing is uncanny."

"I had hoped," said Thuvia, "that we might find an asylum with these fair-skinned people. Notwithstanding their valor upon the field of battle, they did not strike me as a ferocious or warlike people. I

had been about to suggest that we seek entrance to the city, but now I scarce know if I care to venture among people whose dead vanish into thin air."

"Let us chance it," replied Carthoris. "We can be no worse off within their walls than without. Here we may fall prey to the banths or the no less fierce Torquasians. There, at least, we shall find beings molded after our own images.

"All that causes me to hesitate," he added, "is the danger of taking you past so many banths. A single sword would scarce prevail were even a couple of them to charge simultaneously."

"Do not fear on that score," replied the girl, smiling. "The banths will not harm us."

As she spoke she descended from the platform, and with Carthoris at her side stepped fearlessly out upon the bloody field in the direction of the walled city of mystery.

They had advanced but a short distance when a banth, looking up from its gory feast, descried them. With an angry roar the beast walked quickly in their direction, and at the sound of its voice a score of others followed its example.

Carthoris drew his long-sword. The girl stole a quick glance at his face. She saw the smile upon his lips, and it was as wine to sick nerves; for even upon warlike Barsoom where all men are brave, woman reacts quickly to quiet indifference to danger — to dare-deviltry that is without bombast.

"You may return your sword," she said. "I told you that the banths would not harm us. Look!" and as she spoke she stepped quickly toward the nearest animal.

Carthoris would have leaped after her to protect her, but with a gesture she motioned him back. He heard her calling to the banths in a low, singsong voice that was half purr.

Instantly the great heads went up and all the wicked eyes were riveted upon the figure of the girl. Then, stealthily, they commenced moving toward her. She had stopped now and was standing waiting them.

One, closer to her than the others, hesitated. She spoke to him imperiously, as a master might speak to a refractory hound.

The great carnivore let its head droop, and with tail between its legs came slinking to the girl's feet, and after it came the others until she was entirely surrounded by the savage man-eaters.

Turning she led them to where Carthoris stood. They growled a little as they neared the man, but a few sharp words of command put them in their places.

"How do you do it?" exclaimed Carthoris.

"Your father once asked me that same question in the galleries of the Golden Cliffs within the Otz Mountains, beneath the temples of the therns. I could not answer him, nor can I answer you. I do not know whence comes my power over them, but ever since the day that Sator Throg threw me among them in the banth pit of the Holy Therns, and the great creatures fawned upon instead of devouring me, I ever have had the same strange power over them. They come at my call and do my bidding, even as the faithful Woola does the bidding of your mighty sire."

With a word the girl dispersed the fierce pack. Roaring, they returned to their interrupted feast, while Carthoris and Thuvia passed among them toward the walled city.

As they advanced the man looked with wonder upon the dead bodies of those of the green men that had not been devoured or mauled by the banths.

He called the girl's attention to them. No arrows protruded from the great carcasses. Nowhere upon any of them was the sign of mortal wound, nor even slightest scratch or abrasion.

Before the bowmen's dead had disappeared the corpses of the Torquasians had bristled with the deadly arrows of their foes. Where had the slender messengers of death departed? What unseen hand had plucked them from the bodies of the slain?

Despite himself Carthoris could scarce repress a shudder of apprehension as he glanced toward the silent city before them. No longer was sign of life visible upon wall or roof top. All was quiet — brooding, ominous quiet.

Yet he was sure that eyes watched them from somewhere behind that blank wall.

He glanced at Thuvia. She was advancing with wide eyes fixed upon the city gate. He looked in the direction of her gaze, but saw nothing.

His gaze upon her seemed to arouse her as from a lethargy. She glanced up at him, a quick, brave smile touching her lips, and then, as though the act was involuntary, she came close to his side and placed one of her hands in his.

He guessed that something within her that was beyond her conscious control was appealing to him for protection. He threw an arm about her and thus they crossed the field. She did not draw away from him, so engrossed was she in the mystery of the strange city before them.

They stopped before the gate. It was a mighty thing. From its construction Carthoris could but dimly speculate upon its unthinkable antiquity.

It was circular, closing a circular aperture, and the Heliumite knew from his study of ancient Barsoomian architecture that it rolled to one side, like a huge wheel, into an aperture in the wall.

Even such world-old cities as ancient Aaanthor were as yet undreamed of when the races lived that built such gates as these.

As he stood speculating upon the identity of this forgotten city, a voice spoke from above. There, leaning over the high wall, was a man.

His hair was auburn, his skin fair — fairer even than that of John Carter, the Virginian. His forehead was high, his eyes large and intelligent.

The language that he used was intelligible to the two below, yet there was a marked difference between it and their Barsoomian tongue.

"Who are you?" he asked. "And what do you here before the gate of Lothar?"

"We are friends," replied Carthoris. "This be the princess, Thuvia of Ptarth, who was captured by the Torquasian horde. I am Carthoris of Helium, Prince of the house of Tardos Mors, Jeddak of Helium, and son of John Carter, Warlord of Mars, and of his wife, Dejah Thoris."

"'Ptarth'?" repeated the man. "'Helium'?" He shook his head. "I never have heard of these places, nor did I know that there dwelt upon Barsoom a race of thy strange color. Where may these cities lie? From our loftiest tower we have never seen another city than Lothar."

Carthoris pointed toward the northeast.

"In that direction lie Helium and Ptarth," he said. "Helium is over eight thousand haads from Lothar, while Ptarth lies nine thousand five hundred haads northeast of Helium."[1]

Still the man shook his head.

"I know of nothing beyond the Lotharian hills," he said. "Naught may live there beside the hideous green hordes of Torquas. They have conquered all Barsoom except this single valley and the city of Lothar. Here we have defied them for countless ages, though periodically they renew their attempts to destroy us. From whence you come I cannot guess unless you be descended from the slaves the Torquasians captured in early times when they reduced the outer world to their vassalage; but we had heard that they destroyed all other races but their own."

Carthoris tried to explain that the Torquasians ruled but a relatively tiny part of the surface of Barsoom, and even this only because their domain held nothing to attract the red race; but the Lotharian could not seem to conceive of anything beyond the valley of Lothar other than a trackless waste peopled by the ferocious green hordes of Torquas.

After considerable parleying he consented to admit them to the city, and a moment later the wheel-like gate rolled back within its niche, and Thuvia and Carthoris entered the city of Lothar.

All about them were evidences of fabulous wealth. The facades of the buildings fronting upon the avenue within the wall were richly carven, and about the windows and doors were ofttimes set foot-wide borders of precious stones, intricate mosaics, or tablets of beaten gold bearing bas-reliefs depicting what may have been bits of the history of this forgotten people.

He with whom they had conversed across the wall was in the avenue to receive them. About him were a hundred or more men of the same race. All were clothed in flowing robes and all were beardless.

Their attitude was more of fearful suspicion than antagonism. They followed the newcomers with their eyes; but spoke no word to them.

Carthoris could not but notice the fact that though the city had been but a short time before surrounded by a horde of bloodthirsty demons yet none of the citizens appeared to be armed, nor was there sign of soldiery about.

He wondered if all the fighting men had sallied forth in one supreme effort to rout the foe, leaving the city all unguarded. He asked their host.

The man smiled.

"No creature other than a score or so of our sacred banths has left Lothar today," he replied.

"But the soldiers — the bowmen!" exclaimed Carthoris. "We saw thousands emerge from this very gate, overwhelming the hordes of Torquas and putting them to rout with their deadly arrows and their fierce banths."

Still the man smiled his knowing smile.

"Look!" he cried, and pointed down a broad avenue before him.

Carthoris and Thuvia followed the direction indicated, and there, marching bravely in the sunlight, they saw advancing toward them a great army of bowmen.

"Ah!" exclaimed Thuvia. "They have returned through another gate, or perchance these be the troops that remained to defend the city?"

Again the fellow smiled his uncanny smile.

"There are no soldiers in Lothar," he said. "Look!"

Both Carthoris and Thuvia had turned toward him while he spoke, and now as they turned back again toward the advancing regiments their eyes went wide in astonishment, for the broad avenue before them was as deserted as the tomb.

"And those who marched out upon the hordes today?" whispered Carthoris. "They, too, were unreal?"

---

[1]On Barsoom the *ad* is the basis of linear measurement. It is the equivalent of an Earthly foot, measuring about 11.694 Earth inches. As has been my custom in the past, I have generally translated Barsoomian symbols of time, distance, etc., into their Earthly equivalents, as being more easily understood by Earth readers. For those of a more studious turn of mind it may be interesting to know the Martian table of linear measurement, and so I give it here:

10 sofads	=	1 ad.
200 ads	=	1 haad.
100 haads	=	1 karad.
360 karads	=	1 circumference of Mars at equator.

A haad, or Barsoomian mile, contains about 2,339 Earth feet. A karad is one degree. A sofad about 1.17 Earth inches.

The man nodded.

"But their arrows slew the green warriors," insisted Thuvia.

"Let us go before Tario," replied the Lotharian. "He will tell you that which he deems it best you know. I might tell you too much."

"Who is Tario?" asked Carthoris.

"Jeddak of Lothar," replied the guide, leading them up the broad avenue down which they had but a moment since seen the phantom army marching.

For half an hour they walked along lovely avenues between the most gorgeous buildings that the two had ever seen. Few people were in evidence. Carthoris could not but note the deserted appearance of the mighty city.

At last they came to the royal palace. Carthoris saw it from a distance, and guessing the nature of the magnificent pile wondered that even here there should be so little sign of activity and life.

Not even a single guard was visible before the great entrance gate, nor in the gardens beyond, into which he could see, was there sign of the myriad life that pulses within the precincts of the royal estates of the red jeddaks.

"Here," said their guide, "is the palace of Tario."

As he spoke Carthoris again let his gaze rest upon the wondrous palace. With a startled exclamation he rubbed his eyes and looked again. No! He could not be mistaken. Before the massive gate stood a score of sentries. Within, the avenue leading to the main building was lined on either side by ranks of bowmen. The gardens were dotted with officers and soldiers moving quickly to and fro, as though bent upon the duties of the minute.

What manner of people were these who could conjure an army out of thin air? He glanced toward Thuvia. She, too, evidently had witnessed the transformation as her brow was drawn in perplexing thought.

With a little shudder she pressed more closely toward him.

"What do you make of it?" she whispered. "It is most uncanny."

"I cannot account for it," replied Carthoris, "unless we have gone mad."

Carthoris turned quickly toward the Lotharian. The fellow was smiling broadly.

"I thought that you just said that there were no soldiers in Lothar," said the Heliumite, with a gesture toward the guardsmen. "What are these?"

"Ask Tario," replied the other. "We shall soon be before him."

Nor was it long before they entered a lofty chamber at one end of which a man reclined upon a luxurious, regal couch that stood upon a high dais.

As the trio approached, the man turned dreamy eyes sleepily upon them. Twenty feet from the dais their conductor halted, and, whispering to Thuvia and Carthoris to follow his example, threw himself headlong to the floor. Then rising to hands and knees, he commenced crawling toward the foot of the throne, swinging his head to and fro and wiggling his body as you have seen a hound do when approaching its master.

Thuvia glanced quickly toward Carthoris. He was standing erect, with high-held head and arms folded across his broad chest. A haughty smile curved his lips.

The man upon the dais was eying him intently, and Carthoris of Helium was looking straight into the other's face.

"Who be these, Jav?" asked the man of him who crawled upon his belly along the floor.

"O Tario, most glorious Jeddak," replied Jav, "these be strangers who came with the hordes of Torquas to our gates, saying that they were prisoners of the green men. They tell strange tales of cities far beyond Lothar."

"Arise, Jav," commanded Tario, "and ask these two why they show not to Tario the respect that is his due."

Jav arose and faced the strangers. At sight of their erect positions his face went livid. He leaped toward them.

"Creatures!" he screamed. "Down! Down upon your bellies before the last of the jeddaks of Barsoom!"

Chapter VII

THE PHANTOM BOWMEN

As Jav leaped toward him Carthoris laid his hand upon the hilt of his long-sword. The Lotharian halted. The great apartment was empty save for the four at the dais, yet as Jav stepped back from the menace of the Heliumite's threatening attitude the latter found himself surrounded by a score of bowmen.

The man turned dreamy eyes sleepily upon them

From whence had they sprung? Both Carthoris and Thuvia looked their astonishment.

Now the former's sword leaped from its scabbard, and at the same instant the bowmen drew back their slim shafts.

Tario had half raised himself upon one elbow. For the first time he saw the full figure of Thuvia, who had been concealed behind the person of Carthoris.

"Enough!" cried the jeddak, raising a protesting hand, but at that very instant the sword of the Heliumite cut viciously at its nearest antagonist.

As the keen edge reached its goal Carthoris let the point fall to the floor, as with wide eyes he stepped backward in consternation, throwing the back of his left hand across his brow. His steel had cut but empty air — his antagonist had vanished — there were no bowmen in the room!

"It is evident that these are strangers," said Tario to Jav. "Let us first determine that they knowingly affronted us before we take measures for punishment."

Then he turned to Carthoris, but ever his gaze wandered to the perfect lines of Thuvia's glorious figure, which the harness of a Barsoomian princess accentuated rather than concealed.

"Who are you," he asked, "who knows not the etiquette of the court of the last of the mighty jeddaks?"

"I am Carthoris, Prince of Helium," replied the Heliumite. "And this is Thuvia, Princess of Ptarth. In the courts of our fathers men do not prostrate themselves before royalty. Not since the First Born tore their immortal goddess limb from limb have men crawled upon their bellies to any throne upon Barsoom. Now think you that the daughter of one mighty jeddak and the son of another would so humiliate themselves?"

Tario looked at Carthoris for a long time. At last he spoke.

"There is no other jeddak upon Barsoom than Tario," he said. "There is no other race than that of Lothar, unless the hordes of Torquas may be dignified by such an appellation. Lotharians are white; your skins are red. There are no women left upon Barsoom. Your companion is a woman."

He half rose from the couch, leaning far forward and pointing a long accusing finger at Carthoris.

"You are a lie!" he shrieked. "You are both lies, and you dare to come before Tario, last and mightiest of the jeddaks of Barsoom, and assert your reality. Someone shall pay well for this, Jav, and unless I mistake it is yourself who has dared thus flippantly to trifle with the good nature of your jeddak.

"Remove the man. Leave the woman. We shall see if both be lies. And later, Jav, you shall suffer for your temerity. There be few of us left, but — Komal must be fed. Go!"

Carthoris could see that Jav trembled as he prostrated himself once more before his ruler, and then, rising, turned toward the Prince of Helium.

"Come!" he said.

"And leave the Princess of Ptarth here alone?" cried Carthoris.

Jav brushed closely past him, whispering:

"Follow me — he cannot harm her, except to kill; and that he can do whether you remain or not. We had best go now — trust me."

Carthoris did not understand, but something in the urgency of the other's tone assured him, and so he turned away, but not without a glance toward Thuvia in which he attempted to make her understand that it was in her own interest that he left her.

For answer she turned her back full upon him, but not without first throwing him such a look of utter contempt that brought the scarlet to his cheek.

Then he hesitated, but Jav seized him by the wrist.

"Come!" he whispered. "Or he will have the bowmen upon you, and this time there will be no escape. Did you not see how futile is your steel against thin air!"

Carthoris turned unwillingly to follow. As the two left the room he turned to his companion.

"If I may not kill thin air," he asked, "how, then, shall I fear that thin air may kill me?"

"You saw the Torquasians fall before the bowmen?" asked Jav.

Carthoris nodded.

"So would you fall before them, and without one single chance for self-defense or revenge."

As they talked Jav led Carthoris to a small room in one of the numerous towers of the palace. Here were couches, and Jav bid the Heliumite be seated.

For several minutes the Lotharian eyed his prisoner, for such Carthoris now realized himself to be.

"I am half convinced that you are real," he said at last.

Carthoris laughed.

"Of course I am real," he said. "What caused you to doubt it? Can you not see me, feel me?"

"So may I see and feel the bowmen," replied Jav, "and yet we all know that they, at least, are not real."

Carthoris showed by the expression of his face his puzzlement at each new reference to the mysterious bowmen — the vanishing soldiery of Lothar.

"What then may they be?" he asked.

"You really do not know?" asked Jav.

Carthoris shook his head negatively.

"I can almost believe that you have told us the truth and that you are really from another part of Barsoom, or from another world. But tell me, in your own country have you no bowmen to strike terror to the hearts of the green hordesmen as they slay in company with the fierce banths of war?"

"We have soldiers," replied Carthoris. "We of the red race are all soldiers, but we have no bowmen to defend us, such as yours. We defend ourselves."

"You go out and get killed by your enemies!" cried Jav incredulously.

"Certainly," replied Carthoris. "How do the Lotharians?"

"You have seen," replied the other. "We send out our deathless archers — deathless because they are lifeless, existing only in the imaginations of our enemies. It is really our giant minds that defend us, sending out legions of imaginary warriors to materialize before the mind's eye of the foe.

"They see them — they see their bows drawn back — they see their slender arrows speed with unerring precision toward their hearts. And they die — killed by the power of suggestion."

"But the archers that are slain?" exclaimed Carthoris. "You call them deathless, and yet I saw their dead bodies piled high upon the battlefield. How may that be?"

"It is but to lend reality to the scene," replied Jav. "We picture many of our own defenders killed that the Torquasians may not guess that there are really no flesh and blood creatures opposing them.

"Once that truth became implanted in their minds, it is the theory of many of us, no longer would they fall prey to the suggestion of the deadly arrows, for greater would be the suggestion of the truth, and the more powerful suggestion would prevail — it is law."

"And the banths?" questioned Carthoris. "They, too, were but creatures of suggestion?"

"Some of them were real," replied Jav. "Those that accompanied the archers in pursuit of the Torquasians were unreal. Like the archers, they never returned, but, having served their purpose, vanished with the bowmen when the rout of the enemy was assured.

"Those that remained about the field were real. Those we loosed as scavengers to devour the bodies of the dead of Torquas. This thing is demanded by the realists among us. I am a realist. Tario is an etherealist.

"The etherealists maintain that there is no such thing as matter — that all is mind. They say that none of us exists, except in the imagination of his fellows, other than as an intangible, invisible mentality.

"According to Tario, it is but necessary that we all unite in imagining that there are no dead Torquasians beneath our walls, and there will be none, nor any need of the fierce scavenging banths."

"You, then, do not hold Tario's beliefs?" asked Carthoris.

"In part only," replied the Lotharian. "I believe, in fact I know, that there are some truly ethereal creatures. Tario is one, I am convinced. He has no existence except in the imaginations of his people.

"Of course, it is the contention of all us realists that all etherealists are but figments of the imagination. They contend that no food is necessary, nor do they eat; but anyone of the most rudimentary intelligence must realize that food is a necessity to creatures having actual existence."

"Yes," agreed Carthoris, "not having eaten today I can readily agree with you."

"Ah, pardon me," exclaimed Jav. "Pray be seated and satisfy your hunger," and with a wave of his hand he indicated a bountifully laden table that had not been there an instant before he spoke. Of that Carthoris was positive, for he had searched the room diligently with his eyes several times.

"It is well," continued Jav, "that you did not fall into the hands of an etherealist. Then, indeed, would you have gone hungry."

"But," exclaimed Carthoris, "this is not real food — it was not here an instant since, and real food does not materialize out of thin air."

Jav looked hurt.

"There is no real food or water in Lothar," he said; "nor has there been for countless ages. Upon such as you now see before you have we existed since the dawn of history. Upon such, then, may you exist."

"But I thought you were a realist," exclaimed Carthoris

"Indeed," cried Jav, "what more realistic than this bounteous feast? It is just here that we differ most from the etherealists. They claim that it is unnecessary to imagine food; but we have found that for the maintenance of life we must thrice daily sit down to hearty meals.

"The food that one eats is supposed to undergo certain chemical changes during the process of digestion and assimilation, the result, of course, being the rebuilding of wasted tissue.

"Now we all know that mind is all, though we may differ in the interpretation of its various manifestations. Tario maintains that there is no such thing as substance, all being created from the substanceless matter of the brain.

"We realists, however, know better. We know that mind has the power to maintain substance even though it may not be able to create substance — the latter is still an open question. And so we know that in order to maintain our physical bodies we must cause all our organs properly to function.

"This we accomplish by materializing food-thoughts, and by partaking of the food thus created. We chew, we swallow, we digest. All our organs function precisely as if we had partaken of material food. And what is the result? What must be the result? The chemical changes take place through both direct and indirect suggestion, and we live and thrive."

Carthoris eyed the food before him. It seemed real enough. He lifted a morsel to his lips. There was substance indeed. And flavor as well. Yes, even his palate was deceived.

Jav watched him, smiling, as he ate.

"Is it not entirely satisfying?" he asked.

"I must admit that it is," replied Carthoris. "But tell me, how does Tario live, and the other etherealists who maintain that food is unnecessary?"

Jav scratched his head.

"That is a question we often discuss," he replied. "It is the strongest evidence we have of the nonexistence of the etherealists; but who may know other than Komal?"

"Who is Komal?" asked Carthoris. "I heard your jeddak speak of him."

Jav bent low toward the ear of the Heliumite, looking fearfully about before he spoke.

"Komal is the essence," he whispered. "Even the etherealists admit that mind itself must have substance in order to transmit to imaginings the appearance of substance. For if there really was no such thing as substance it could not be suggested — what never has been cannot be imagined. Do you follow me?"

"I am groping," replied Carthoris dryly.

"So the essence must be substance," continued Jav. "Komal is the essence of the All, as it were. He is maintained by substance. He eats. He eats the real. To be explicit, he eats the realists. That is Tario's work.

"He says that inasmuch as we maintain that we alone are real we should, to be consistent, admit that we alone are proper food for Komal. Sometimes, as today, we find other food for him. He is very fond of Torquasians."

"And Komal is a man?" asked Carthoris.

"He is All, I told you," replied Jav. "I know not how to explain him in words that you will understand. He is the beginning and the end. All life emanates from Komal, since the substance which feeds the brain with imaginings radiates from the body of Komal.

"Should Komal cease to eat, all life upon Barsoom would cease to be. He cannot die, but he might cease to eat, and, thus, to radiate."

"And he feeds upon the men and women of your belief?" cried Carthoris.

"Women!" exclaimed Jav. "There are no women in Lothar. The last of the Lotharian females perished ages since, upon that cruel and terrible journey across the muddy plains that fringed the half-dried seas, when the green hordes scourged us across the world to this our last hiding place — our impregnable fortress of Lothar.

"Scarce twenty thousand men of all the countless millions of our race lived to reach Lothar. Among us were no women and no children. All these had perished by the way.

"As time went on, we, too, were dying and the race fast approaching extinction, when the Great Truth was revealed to us, that mind is all. Many more died before we perfected our powers, but at last we were able to defy death when we fully understood that death was merely a state of mind.

"Then came the creation of mind-people, or rather the materialization of imaginings. We first put these to practical use when the Torquasians discovered our retreat, and fortunate for us it was that it required ages of search upon their part before they found the single tiny entrance to the valley of Lothar.

"That day we threw our first bowmen against them. The intention was purely to frighten them away by the vast numbers of bowmen which we could muster upon our walls. All Lothar bristled with the bows and arrows of our ethereal host.

"But the Torquasians did not frighten. They are lower than the beasts — they know no fear. They rushed upon our walls, and standing one upon the shoulders of others they built human approaches to the wall tops, and were on the very point of surging in upon us and overwhelming us.

"Not an arrow had been discharged by our bowmen — we did but cause them to run to and fro along the wall top, screaming taunts and threats at the enemy.

"Presently I thought to attempt the thing — *the great thing*. I centered all my mighty intellect upon the bowmen of my own creation — each of us produces and directs as many bowmen as his mentality and imagination is capable of conjuring up.

"I caused them to fit arrows to their bows for the first time. I made them take aim at the hearts of the green men. I made the green men see all this, and then I made them see the arrows fly, and I made them think that the points pierced their hearts.

"It was all that was necessary. By hundreds they toppled from our walls, and when my fellows saw what I had done they were quick to follow my example, so that presently the hordes of Torquas had retreated beyond the range of our arrows.

"We might have killed them at any distance, but one rule of war we have maintained from the first — the rule of realism. We do nothing, or rather we cause our bowmen to do nothing within sight of the enemy that is beyond the understanding of the foe. Otherwise they might guess the truth, and that would be the end of us.

"But after the Torquasians had retreated beyond bow-shot, they turned upon us with their terrible rifles, and by constant popping at us made life miserable within our walls.

"So then I bethought the scheme to hurl our bowmen through the gates upon them. You have seen this day how well it works. For ages they have come down upon us at intervals, but always with the same results."

"And all this is due to your intellect, Jav?" asked Carthoris. "I should think that you would be high in the councils of your people."

"I am," replied Jav, proudly. "I am next to Tario."

"But why then your cringing manner of approaching the throne?"

"Tario demands it. He is jealous of me. He only awaits the slightest excuse to feed me to Komal. He fears that I may some day usurp his power."

Carthoris suddenly sprang from the table.

"Jav!" he exclaimed. "I am a beast! Here I have been eating my fill, while the Princess of Ptarth may perchance be still without food. Let us return and find some means of furnishing her with nourishment."

The Lotharian shook his head.

"Tario would not permit it," he said. "He will, doubtless, make an etherealist of her."

"But I must go to her," insisted Carthoris. "You say that there are no women in Lothar. Then she must be among men, and if this be so I intend to be near where I may defend her if the need arises."

"Tario will have his way," insisted Jav. "He sent you away and you may not return until he sends for you."

"Then I shall go without waiting to be sent for."

"Do not forget the bowmen," cautioned Jav.

"I do not forget them," replied Carthoris, but he did not tell Jav that he remembered something else that the Lotharian had let drop — something that was but a conjecture, possibly, and yet one well worth pinning a forlorn hope to, should necessity arise.

Carthoris started to leave the room. Jav stepped before him, barring his way.

"I have learned to like you, red man," he said; "but do not forget that Tario is still my jeddak, and that Tario has commanded that you remain here."

Carthoris was about to reply, when there came faintly to the ears of both a woman's cry for help.

With a sweep of his arm the Prince of Helium brushed the Lotharian aside, and with drawn sword sprang into the corridor without.

Chapter VIII

THE HALL OF DOOM

As Thuvia of Ptarth saw Carthoris depart from the presence of Tario, leaving her alone with the man, a sudden qualm of terror seized her.

There was an air of mystery pervading the stately chamber. Its furnishings and appointments bespoke wealth and culture, and carried the suggestion that the room was often the scene of royal functions which filled it to its capacity.

And yet nowhere about her, in antechamber or corridor, was there sign of any other being than herself and the recumbent figure of Tario, the jeddak, who watched her through half-closed eyes from the gorgeous trappings of his regal couch.

For a time after the departure of Jav and Carthoris the man eyed her intently. Then he spoke.

"Come nearer," he said, and, as she approached; "Whose creature are you? Who has dared materialize his imaginings of woman? It is contrary to the customs and the royal edicts of Lothar. Tell me, woman, from whose brain have you sprung? Jav's? No, do not deny it. I know that it could be no other than that envious realist. He seeks to tempt me. He would see me fall beneath the spell of your charms, and then he, your master, would direct my destiny and — my end. I see it all! I see it all!"

The blood of indignation and anger had been rising to Thuvia's face. Her chin was up, a haughty curve upon her perfect lips.

"I know naught," she cried, "of what you are prating! I am Thuvia, Princess of Ptarth. I am no man's 'creature.' Never before today did I lay eyes upon him you call

Jav, nor upon your ridiculous city, of which even the greatest nations of Barsoom have never dreamed.

"My charms are not for you, nor such as you. They are not for sale or barter, even though the price were a real throne. And as for using them to win your worse than futile power —" She ended her sentence with a shrug of her shapely shoulders, and a little scornful laugh.

When she had finished Tario was sitting upon the edge of his couch, his feet upon the floor. He was leaning forward with eyes no longer half closed, but wide with a startled expression in them.

He did not seem to note the *lèse majesté* of her words and manner. There was evidently something more startling and compelling about her speech than that.

Slowly he came to his feet.

"By the fangs of Komal!" he muttered. "But you are *real!* A *real* woman! No dream! No vain and foolish figment of the mind!"

He took a step toward her, with hands outstretched.

"Come!" he whispered. "Come, woman! For countless ages have I dreamed that some day you would come. And now that you are here I can scarce believe the testimony of my eyes. Even now, knowing that you are real, I still half dread that you may be a lie."

Thuvia shrank back. She thought the man mad. Her hand stole to the jeweled hilt of her dagger. The man saw the move, and stopped. A cunning expression entered his eyes. Then they became at once dreamy and penetrating as they fairly bored into the girl's brain.

Thuvia suddenly felt a change coming over her. What the cause of it she did not guess; but somehow the man before her began to assume a new relationship within her heart.

No longer was he a strange and mysterious enemy, but an old and trusted friend. Her hand slipped from the dagger's hilt. Tario came closer. He spoke gentle, friendly words, and she answered him in a voice that seemed hers and yet another's.

He was beside her now. His hand was upon her shoulder. His eyes were downbent toward hers. She looked up into his face. His gaze seemed to bore straight through her to some hidden spring of sentiment within her.

Her lips parted in sudden awe and wonder at the strange revealment of her inner self that was being laid bare before her consciousness. She had known Tario forever. He was more than friend to her. She moved a little closer to him. In one swift flood of light she knew the truth. She loved Tario, Jeddak of Lothar! She had always loved him.

The man, seeing the success of his strategy, could not restrain a faint smile of satisfaction. Whether there was something in the expression of his face, or whether from Carthoris of Helium in a far chamber of the palace came a more powerful suggestion, who may say? But something there was that suddenly dispelled the strange, hypnotic influence of the man.

As though a mask had been torn from her eyes, Thuvia suddenly saw Tario as she had formerly seen him, and, accustomed as she was to the strange manifestations of highly developed mentality which are common upon Barsoom, she quickly guessed enough of the truth to know that she was in grave danger.

Quickly she took a step backward, tearing herself from his grasp. But the momentary contact had aroused within Tario all the long-buried passions of his loveless existence.

With a muffled cry he sprang upon her, throwing his arms about her and attempting to drag her lips to his.

"Woman!" he cried. "Lovely woman! Tario would make you queen of Lothar. Listen to me! Listen to the love of the last of the jeddaks of Barsoom."

Thuvia struggled to free herself from his embrace.

"Stop, creature!" she cried. "Stop! I do not love you. Stop, or I shall scream for help!"

Tario laughed in her face.

"'Scream for help,'" he mimicked. "And who within the halls of Lothar is there who might come in answer to your call? Who would dare enter the presence ofsTario, unsummoned?"

"There is one," she replied, "who would come, and, coming, dare to cut you down upon your own throne, if he thought that you had offered affront to Thuvia of Ptarth!"

"Who, Jav?" asked Tario.

"Not Jav, nor any other soft-skinned Lotharian," she replied; "but a real man, a real warrior — Carthoris of Helium!"

Again the man laughed at her.

"You forget the bowmen," he reminded her. "What could your red warrior accomplish against my fearless legions?"

Again he caught her roughly to him, dragging her towards his couch.

"If you will not be my queen," he said, "you shall be my slave."

"Neither!" cried the girl.

As she spoke the single word there was a quick move of her right hand, Tario, releasing her, staggered back, both hands pressed to his side. At the same instant the room filled with bowmen, and then the jeddak of Lothar sank senseless to the marble floor.

At the instant that he lost consciousness the bowmen were about to release their arrows into Thuvia's heart. Involuntarily she gave a single cry for help, though she knew that not even Carthoris of Helium could save her now.

Then she closed her eyes and waited for the end. No slender shafts pierced her tender side. She raised her lids to see what stayed the hand of her executioners.

The room was empty save for herself and the still form of the jeddak of Lothar lying at her feet, a little pool of crimson staining the white marble of the floor beside him. Tario was unconscious.

Thuvia was amazed. Where were the bowmen? Why had they not loosed their shafts? What could it all mean?

An instant before the room had been mysteriously filled with armed men, evidently called to protect their jeddak; yet now, with the evidence of her deed plain before them, they had vanished as mysteriously as they had come, leaving her alone with the body of their ruler, into whose side she had slipped her long, keen blade.

The girl glanced apprehensively about, first for signs of the return of the bowmen, and then for some means of escape.

The wall behind the dais was pierced by two small doorways, hidden by heavy hangings. Thuvia was running quickly toward one of these when she heard the clank of a warrior's metal at the end of the apartment behind her.

Ah, if she had but an instant more of time she could have reached that screening arras and, perchance, have found some avenue of escape behind it; but now it was too late — she had been discovered!

*The jeddak of Lothar sank senseless to the
marble floor*

With a feeling that was akin to apathy she turned to meet her fate, and there, before her, running swiftly across the broad chamber to her side, was Carthoris, his naked long-sword gleaming in his hand.

For days she had doubted the intentions of the Heliumite. She had thought him a party to her abduction. Since Fate had thrown them together she had scarce favored him with more than the most perfunctory replies to his remarks, unless at such times as the weird and uncanny happenings at Lothar had surprised her out of her reserve.

She knew that Carthoris of Helium would fight for her; but whether to save her for himself or another, she was in doubt.

He knew that she was promised to Kulan Tith, Jeddak of Kaol, but if he had been instrumental in her abduction, his motives could not be prompted by loyalty to his friend, or regard for his honor.

And yet, as she saw him coming across the marble floor of the audience chamber of Tario of Lothar, his fine eyes filled with apprehension for her safety, his splendid figure personifying all that is finest in the fighting men of martial Mars, she could not believe that any faintest trace of perfidy lurked beneath so glorious an exterior.

Never, she thought, in all her life had the sight of any man been so welcome to her. It was with difficulty that she refrained from rushing forward to meet him.

She knew that he loved her; but, in time, she recalled that she was promised to Kulan Tith. Not even might she trust herself to show too great gratitude to the Heliumite, lest he misunderstand.

Carthoris was by her side now. His quick glance had taken in the scene within the room — the still figure of the jeddak sprawled upon the floor — the girl hastening toward a shrouded exit.

"Did he harm you, Thuvia?" he asked.

She held up her crimsoned blade that he might see it.

"No," she said, "he did not harm me."

A grim smile lighted Carthoris' face.

"Praised be our first ancestor!" he murmured. "And now let us see if we may not make good our escape from this accursed city before the Lotharians discover that their jeddak is no more."

With the firm authority that sat so well upon him in whose veins flowed the blood of John Carter of Virginia and Dejah Thoris of Helium, he grasped her hand and, turning back across the hall, strode toward the great doorway through which Jav had brought them into the presence of the jeddak earlier in the day.

They had almost reached the threshold when a figure sprang into the apartment through another entrance. It was Jav. He, too, took in the scene within at a glance.

Carthoris turned to face him, his sword ready in his hand, and his great body shielding the slender figure of the girl.

"Come, Jav of Lothar!" he cried. "Let us face the issue at once, for only one of us may leave this chamber alive with Thuvia of Ptarth." Then, seeing that the man wore no sword, he exclaimed: "Bring on your bowmen, then, or come with us as my prisoner until we have safely passed the outer portals of thy ghostly city."

"You have killed Tario!" exclaimed Jav, ignoring the other's challenge. "You have killed Tario! I see his blood upon the floor — real blood — real death. Tario was, after all, as real as I. Yet he was an etherealist. He would not materialize his sustenance. Can it be that they are right? Well, we, too, are right. And all these ages we have been quarreling — each saying that the other was wrong!

"However, he is dead now. Of that I am glad. Now shall Jav come into his own. Now shall Jav be jeddak of Lothar!"

As he finished, Tario opened his eyes and then quickly sat up.

"Traitor! Assassin!" he screamed, and then: "Kadar! Kadar!" which is the Barsoomian for guard.

Jav went sickly white. He fell upon his belly, wriggling toward Tario.

"Oh, my Jeddak, my Jeddak!" he whimpered. "Jav had no hand in this. Jav, your faithful Jav, but just this instant entered the apartment to find you lying prone upon the floor and these two strangers about to leave. How it happened I know not. Believe me, most glorious Jeddak!"

"Cease, knave!" cried Tario. "I heard your words: 'However, he is dead now. Of that I am glad. Now shall Jav come into his own. Now shall Jav be jeddak of Lothar.'

"At last, traitor, I have found you out. Your own words have condemned you as surely as the acts of these red creatures have sealed their fates — unless —" He paused. "Unless the woman ——"

But he got no further. Carthoris

guessed what he would have said, and before the words could be uttered he had sprung forward and struck the man across the mouth with his open palm.

Tario frothed in rage and mortification.

"And should you again affront the Princess of Ptarth," warned the Heliumite, "I shall forget that you wear no sword—not forever may I control my itching sword hand."

Tario shrank back toward the little doorways behind the dais. He was trying to speak, but so hideously were the muscles of his face working that he could utter no word for several minutes. At last he managed to articulate intelligibly.

"Die!" he shrieked. "Die!" and then he turned toward the exit at his back.

Jav leaped forward, screaming in terror.

"Have pity, Tario! Have pity! Remember the long ages that I have served you faithfully. Remember all that I have done for Lothar. Do not condemn me now to the death hideous. Save me! Save me!"

But Tario only laughed a mocking laugh and continued to back toward the hangings that hid the little doorway.

Jav turned toward Carthoris.

"Stop him!" he screamed. "Stop him! If you love life, let him not leave this room," and as he spoke he leaped in pursuit of his jeddak.

Carthoris followed Jav's example, but the "last of the jeddaks of Barsoom" was too quick for them. By the time they reached the arras behind which he had disappeared, they found a heavy stone door blocking their further progress.

Jav sank to the floor in a spasm of terror.

"Come, man!" cried Carthoris. "We are not dead yet. Let us hasten to the avenues and make an attempt to leave the city. We are still alive, and while we live we may yet endeavor to direct our own destinies. Of what avail, to sink spineless to the floor? Come, be a man!"

Jav but shook his head.

"Did you not hear him call the guards?" he moaned. "Ah, if we could have but intercepted him! Then there might have been hope; but, alas, he was too quick for us."

"Well, well," exclaimed Carthoris impatiently. "What if he did call the guards? There will be time enough to worry about that after they come — at present I see no indication that they have any idea of over-exerting themselves to obey their jeddak's

summons."

Jav shook his head mournfully in utter dejection.

"You do not understand," he said. "The guards have already come — and gone. They have done their work and we are lost. Look to the various exits."

Carthoris and Thuvia turned their eyes in the direction of the several doorways which pierced the walls of the great chamber. Each was tightly closed by huge stone doors.

"Well?" asked Carthoris.

"We are to die the death," whispered Jav faintly.

Further than that he would not say. He just sat upon the edge of the jeddak's couch and waited.

Carthoris moved to Thuvia's side, and, standing there with naked sword, he let his brave eyes roam ceaselessly about the great chamber, that no foe might spring upon them unseen.

For what seemed hours no sound broke the silence of their living tomb. No sign gave their executioners of the time or manner of their death. The suspense was terrible. Even Carthoris of Helium began to feel the terrific strain upon his nerves. If he could but know how and whence the hand of death was to strike, he could meet it unafraid, but to suffer longer the hideous tension of this blighting ignorance of the plans of their assassins was telling upon him grievously.

Thuvia of Ptarth drew quite close to him. She felt safer with the feel of his arm against hers, and with the contact of her the man took a new grip upon himself. With his old-time smile he turned toward her.

"It would seem that they are trying to frighten us to death," he said, laughing; "and, shame be upon me that I should confess it, I think they were close to accomplishing their designs upon me."

She was about to make some reply when a fearful shriek broke from the lips of the Lotharian.

"The end is coming!" he cried. "The end is coming! The floor! The floor! Oh, Komal, be merciful!"

Thuvia and Carthoris did not need to look at the floor to be aware of the strange movement that was taking place.

Slowly the marble flagging was sinking in all directions toward the center. At first the movement, being gradual, was scarce noticeable; but presently the angle of the floor became such that one might stand easily only by bending one knee considerably.

Jav was shrieking still, and clawing at the royal couch that had already commenced to slide toward the center of the room, where both Thuvia and Carthoris suddenly noted a small orifice which grew in diameter as the floor assumed more closely a funnel-like contour.

Now it became more and more difficult to cling to the dizzy inclination of the smooth and polished marble. Carthoris tried to support Thuvia, but himself commenced to slide and slip toward the ever-enlarging aperture.

Better to cling to the smooth stone he kicked off his sandals of zitidar hide and with his bare feet braced himself against the sickening tilt, at the same time throwing his arms supportingly about the girl.

In her terror her own hands clasped about the man's neck. Her cheek was close to his. Death, unseen and of unknown form, seemed close upon them, and because unseen and unknowable infinitely more terrifying.

"Courage, my princess," he whispered cheeringly.

She looked up into his face to see smiling lips above hers and brave eyes, untouched by terror, drinking deeply of her own.

Then the floor sagged and tilted more swiftly. There was a sudden slipping rush as they were precipitated toward the aperture.

Jav's screams rose weird and horrible in their ears, and then the three found themselves piled upon the royal couch of Tario, which had stuck within the aperture at the base of the marble funnel.

For a moment they breathed more freely, but presently they discovered that the aperture was continuing to enlarge. The couch slipped downward. Jav shrieked again. There was a sickening sensation as they felt all let go beneath them, as they fell through darkness to an unknown death.

Chapter IX

THE BATTLE IN THE PLAIN

The distance from the bottom of the funnel to the floor of the chamber beneath it could not have been great, for all three of the victims of Tario's wrath alighted unscathed.

Carthoris, still clasping Thuvia tightly to his breast, came to the ground catlike, upon his feet, breaking the shock for the girl. Scarce had his feet touched the rough stone flagging of this new chamber than his sword flashed out ready for instant use. But though the room was lighted, there was no sign of enemy about.

Carthoris looked toward Jav. The man was pasty white with fear.

"What is to be our fate?" asked the Heliumite. "Tell me, man! Shake off your terror long enough to tell me, so I may be prepared to sell my life and that of the Princess of Ptarth as dearly as possible."

"Komal!" whispered Jav. "We are to be devoured by Komal."

"Your deity?" asked Carthoris.

The Lotharian nodded his head. Then he pointed toward a low doorway at one end of the chamber.

"From thence will he come upon us. Lay aside your puny sword, fool. It will but enrage him the more and make our sufferings the worse."

Carthoris smiled, gripping his long-sword the more firmly.

Presently Jav gave a horrified moan, at the same time pointing toward the door.

"He has come," he whimpered.

Carthoris and Thuvia looked in the direction the Lotharian had indicated, expecting to see some strange and fearful creature in human form; but to their astonishment they saw the broad head and great-maned shoulders of a huge banth, the largest that either ever had seen.

Slowly and with dignity the mighty beast advanced into the room. Jav had fallen to the floor, and was wriggling his body in the same servile manner that he had adopted toward Tario. He spoke to the fierce beast as he would have spoken to a human being, pleading with it for mercy.

Carthoris stepped between Thuvia and the banth, his sword ready to contest the beast's victory over them. Thuvia turned toward Jav.

"Is this Komal, your god?" she asked.

Jav nodded affirmatively. The girl smiled, and then, brushing past Carthoris, she stepped swiftly toward the growling carnivore.

In low, firm tones she spoke to it as she had spoken to the banths of the Golden

Cliffs and the scavengers before the walls of Lothar.

The beast ceased its growling. With lowered head and catlike purr, it came slinking to the girl's feet. Thuvia turned toward Carthoris.

"It is but a banth," she said. "We have nothing to fear from it."

Carthoris smiled.

"I did not fear it," he replied, "for I, too, believed it to be only a banth, and I have my long-sword."

Jav sat up and gazed at the spectacle before him — the slender girl weaving her fingers in the tawny mane of the huge creature that he had thought divine, while Komal rubbed his hideous snout against her side.

"So this is your god!" laughed Thuvia.

Jav look bewildered. He scarce knew whether he dare chance offending Komal or not, for so strong is the power of superstition that even though we know that we have been reverencing a sham, yet still we hesitate to admit the validity of our new-found convictions.

"Yes," he said, "this is Komal. For ages the enemies of Tario have been hurled to this pit to fill his maw, for Komal must be fed."

"Is there any way out of this chamber to the avenues of the city?" asked Carthoris.

Jav shrugged.

"I do not know," he replied. "Never have I been here before, nor ever have I cared to be."

"Come," suggested Thuvia, "let us explore. There must be a way out."

Together the three approached the doorway through which Komal had entered the apartment that was to have witnessed their deaths. Beyond was a low-roofed lair, with a small door at the far end.

This, to their delight, opened to the lifting of an ordinary latch, letting them into a circular arena, surrounded by tiers of seats.

"Here is where Komal is fed in public," explained Jav. "Had Tario dared it would have been here that our fates had been sealed; but he feared too much thy keen blade, red man, and so he hurled us all downward to the pit. I did not know how closely connected were the two chambers. Now we may easily reach the avenues and the city gates. Only the bowmen may dispute the right of way, and, knowing their secret, I doubt that they have power to

harm us."

Another door led to a flight of steps that rose from the arena level upward through the seats to an exit at the back of the hall. Beyond this was a straight, broad corridor, running directly through the palace to the gardens at the side.

No one appeared to question them as they advanced, mighty Komal pacing by the girl's side.

"Where are the people of the palace — the jeddak's retinue?" asked Carthoris. "Even in the city streets as we came through I scarce saw sign of a human being, yet all about are evidences of a mighty population."

Jav sighed.

"Poor Lothar," he said. "It is indeed a city of ghosts. There are scarce a thousand of us left, who once were numbered in the millions. Our great city is peopled by the creatures of our own imaginings. For our own needs we do not take the trouble to materialize these peoples of our brain, yet they are apparent to us.

"Even now I see great throngs lining the avenue, hastening to and fro in the round of their duties. I see women and children laughing on the balconies — these we are forbidden to materialize; but yet I see them — they are here.... But why not?" he mused. "No longer need I fear Tario — he has done his worst, and failed. Why not indeed?

"Stay, friends," he continued. "Would you see Lothar in all her glory?"

Carthoris and Thuvia nodded their assent, more out of courtesy than because they fully grasped the import of his mutterings.

Jav gazed at them penetratingly for an instant, then, with a wave of his hand, cried: "Look!"

The sight that met them was awe-inspiring. Where before there had been naught but deserted pavements and scarlet swards, yawning windows and tenantless doors, now swarmed a countless multitude of happy, laughing people.

"It is the past," said Jav in a low voice. "They do not see us — they but live the old dead past of ancient Lothar — the dead and crumbled Lothar of antiquity, which stood upon the shore of Throxus, mightiest of the five oceans.

"See those fine, upstanding men swinging along the broad avenue? See the young girls and the women smile upon them? See the men greet them with love and respect? Those be seafarers coming up from their ships which lie at the quays at the city's edge.

"Brave men, they — ah, but the glory of Lothar has faded! See their weapons. They alone bore arms, for they crossed the five seas to strange places where dangers were. With their passing passed the martial spirit of the Lotharians, leaving, as the ages rolled by, a race of spineless cowards.

"We hated war, and so we trained not our youth in warlike ways. Thus followed our undoing, for when the seas dried and the green hordes encroached upon us we could do naught but flee. But we remembered the seafaring bowmen of the days of our glory — it is the memory of these which we hurl upon our enemies."

As Jav ceased speaking, the picture faded, and once more the three took up their way toward the distant gates, along deserted avenues, uncanny in their sepulchral silence.

Twice they sighted Lotharians of flesh and blood. At sight of them and the huge banth which they must have recognized as Komal, the citizens turned and fled.

"They will carry word of our flight to Tario," cried Jav, "and soon he will send his bowmen after us. Let us hope that our theory is correct, and that their shafts are powerless against minds cognizant of their unreality. Otherwise we are doomed.

"Explain, red man, to the woman the truths that I have explained to you, that she may meet the arrows with a stronger counter-suggestion of immunity."

Carthoris did as Jav bid him; but they came to the great gates without sign of pursuit developing. Here Jav set in motion the mechanism that rolled the huge, wheel-like gate aside, and a moment later the three, accompanied by the banth, stepped out into the plain before Lothar.

Scarce had they covered a hundred yards when the sound of many men shouting arose behind them. As they turned they saw a company of bowmen debouching upon the plain from the gate through which they had but just passed.

Upon the wall above the gate were a number of Lotharians, among whom Jav recognized Tario. The jeddak stood glaring at them, evidently concentrating all the forces of his trained mind upon them. That he was making a supreme effort to render his imaginary creatures deadly was apparent.

Jav turned white, and commenced to tremble. At the crucial moment he appeared to lose the courage of his conviction. The great banth turned back toward the advancing bowmen and growled. Carthoris placed himself between Thuvia and the enemy and, facing them, awaited the outcome of their charge.

Suddenly an inspiration came to Carthoris.

"Hurl your own bowmen against Tario's!" he cried to Jav. "Let us see a materialized battle between two mentalities."

The suggestion seemed to hearten the Lotharian, and in another moment the three stood behind solid ranks of huge bowmen who hurled taunts and menaces at the advancing company emerging from the walled city.

Jav was a new man the moment his battalions stood between him and Tario. One could almost have sworn the man believed these creatures of his strange hypnotic power to be real flesh and blood.

With hoarse battle cries they charged the bowmen of Tario. Barbed shafts flew thick and fast. Men fell, and the ground was red with gore.

Carthoris and Thuvia had difficulty in reconciling the reality of it all with their knowledge of the truth. They saw utan after utan march from the gate in perfect step to reinforce the outnumbered company which Tario had first sent forth to arrest them.

They saw Jav's forces grow correspondingly until all about them rolled a sea of fighting, cursing warriors, and the dead lay in heaps about the field.

Jav and Tario seemed to have forgotten all else beside the struggling bowmen that surged to and fro, filling the broad field between the forest and the city.

The wood loomed close behind Thuvia and Carthoris. The latter cast a glance toward Jav.

"Come!" he whispered to the girl. "Let them fight out their empty battle — neither, evidently, has power to harm the other. They are like two controversialists hurling words at one another. While they are engaged we may as well be devoting our energies to an attempt to find the passage through the cliffs to the plain beyond."

As he spoke, Jav, turning from the battle for an instant, caught his words. He saw the girl move to accompany the Heliumite. A cunning look leaped to the Lotharian's eyes.

The thing that lay beyond that look had been deep in his heart since first he had laid eyes upon Thuvia of Ptarth. He had not recognized it, however, until now that she seemed about to pass out of his existence.

He centered his mind upon the Heliumite and the girl for an instant.

Carthoris saw Thuvia of Ptarth step forward with outstretched hand. He was surprised at this sudden softening toward him, and it was with a full heart that he let his fingers close upon hers, as together they turned away from forgotten Lothar, into the woods, and bent their steps toward the distant mountains.

As the Lotharian had turned toward them, Thuvia had been surprised to hear Carthoris suddenly voice a new plan.

"Remain here with Jav," she had heard him say, "while I go to search for the passage through the cliffs."

She had dropped back in surprise and disappointment, for she knew that there was no reason why she should not have accompanied him. Certainly she should have been safer with him than left here alone with the strange Lotharian she could not understand.

And Jav watched the two and smiled his cunning smile.

When Carthoris had disappeared within the wood, Thuvia seated herself apathetically upon the scarlet sward to watch the seemingly interminable struggles of the bowmen.

The long afternoon dragged its weary way toward darkness and still the imaginary legions charged and retreated. The sun was about to set when Tario commenced to withdraw his troops slowly toward the city.

His plan for cessation of hostilities through the night evidently met with Jav's entire approval, for he caused his forces to form themselves in orderly utans and march just within the edge of the wood, where they were soon busily engaged in preparing their evening meal, and spreading down their sleeping silks and furs for the night.

Thuvia could scarce repress a smile as she noted the scrupulous care with which Jav's imaginary men attended to each tiny detail of deportment as truly as if they had been real flesh and blood warriors.

Sentries were posted between the camp and the city. Officers clanked hither and thither issuing commands and seeing to it that they were properly carried out.

Thuvia turned toward Jav.

"Why is it," she asked, "that you observe such careful nicety in the regulation of your creatures when Tario knows quite as well as you that they are but figments of your brain? Why not permit them simply to dissolve into thin air until you again require their futile service?"

"You do not understand them," replied Jav. "While they exist they are real. I do but call them into being now, and in a way direct their general actions. But thereafter, until I dissolve them, they are as actual as you or I. Their officers command them, under my guidance. I am the general — that is all. And the psychological effect upon the enemy is far greater than were I to treat them merely as substanceless vagaries.

"Then, too," continued the Lotharian, "there is always the hope, which with us is little short of belief, that some day these materializations will merge into the real — that they will remain, some of them, after we have dissolved their fellows, and that thus we shall have discovered a means for perpetuating our dying race.

"Some there are who claim already to have accomplished the thing. It is generally supposed that the etherealists have quite a few among their number who are permanent materializations. It is even said that such is Tario, but that cannot be, for he existed before we had discovered the full possibilities of suggestion.

"There are others among us who insist that none of us is real. That we could not have existed all these ages without material food and water had we ourselves been material. Although I am a realist, I rather incline toward this belief myself.

"It seems well and sensibly based upon the belief that our ancient forebears developed before their extinction such wondrous mentalities that some of the stronger minds among them lived after the death of their bodies — that we are but the deathless minds of individuals long dead.

"It would appear possible, and yet in so far as I am concerned I have all the attributes of corporeal existence. I eat, I sleep

—" He paused, casting a meaning look upon the girl — "I love!"

Thuvia could not mistake the palpable meaning of his words and expression. She turned away with a little shrug of disgust that was not lost upon the Lotharian.

He came close to her and seized her arm.

"Why not Jav?" he cried. "Who more honorable than the second of the world's most ancient race? Your Heliumite? He has gone. He has deserted you to your fate to save himself. Come, be Jav's!"

Thuvia of Ptarth rose to her full height, her lifted shoulder turned toward the man, her haughty chin upraised, a scornful twist to her lips.

"You lie!" she said quietly. "The Heliumite knows less of disloyalty than he knows of fear, and of fear he is as ignorant as the unhatched young."

"Then where is he?" taunted the Lotharian. "I tell you he has fled the valley. He has left you to your fate. But Jav will see that it is a pleasant one. Tomorrow we shall return into Lothar at the head of my victorious army, and I shall be jeddak and you shall be my consort. Come!" And he attempted to crush her to his breast.

The girl struggled to free herself, striking at the man with her metal armlets. Yet still he drew her toward him, until both were suddenly startled by a hideous growl that rumbled from the dark wood close behind them.

Chapter X

KAR KOMAK, THE BOWMAN

As Carthoris moved through the forest toward the distant cliffs with Thuvia's hand still tight pressed in his, he wondered a little at the girl's continued silence, yet the contact of her cool palm against his was so pleasant that he feared to break the spell of her new-found reliance in him by speaking.

Onward through the dim wood they passed until the shadows of the quick coming Martian night commenced to close down upon them. Then it was that Carthoris turned to speak to the girl at his side.

They must plan together for the future. It was his idea to pass through the cliffs at once if they could locate the passage, and he was quite positive that they were now close to it; but he wanted her assent to the proposition.

As his eyes rested upon her, he was struck by her strangely ethereal appearance. She seemed suddenly to have dissolved into the tenuous substance of a dream, and as he continued to gaze upon her, she faded slowly from his sight.

For an instant he was dumfounded, and then the whole truth flashed suddenly upon him. Jav had caused him to believe that Thuvia was accompanying him through the wood while, as a matter of fact, he had detained the girl for himself!

Carthoris was horrified. He cursed himself for his stupidity, and yet he knew that the fiendish power which the Lotharian had invoked to confuse him might have deceived any.

Scarce had he realized the truth than he had started to retrace his steps toward Lothar, but now he moved at a trot, the Earthly thews that he had inherited from his father carrying him swiftly over the soft carpet of fallen leaves and rank grass.

Thuria's brilliant light flooded the plain before the walled city of Lothar as Carthoris broke from the wood opposite the great gate that had given the fugitives egress from the city earlier in the day.

At first he saw no indication that there was another than himself anywhere about. The plain was deserted. No myriad bowmen camped now beneath the overhanging verdure of the giant trees. No gory heaps of tortured dead defaced the beauty of the scarlet sward. All was silence. All was peace.

The Heliumite, scarce pausing at the forest's verge, pushed on across the plain toward the city, when presently he descried a huddled form in the grass at his feet.

It was the body of a man, lying prone. Carthoris turned the figure over upon its back. It was Jav, but torn and mangled almost beyond recognition.

The prince bent low to note if any spark of life remained, and as he did so the lids raised and dull, suffering eyes looked up into his.

"The Princess of Ptarth!" cried Carthoris. "Where is she? Answer me, man, or I complete the work that another has so well begun."

"Komal," muttered Jav. "He sprang upon me . . . . and would have devoured me but for the girl. Then they went away together into the wood—the girl and the great banth . . . . her fingers twined in his tawny mane."

"Which way went they?" asked Carthoris.

"There," replied Jav faintly, "toward the passage through the cliffs."

The Prince of Helium waited to hear no more, but springing to his feet, raced back again into the forest.

It was dawn when he reached the mouth of the dark tunnel that would lead him to the other world beyond this valley of ghostly memories and strange hypnotic influences and menaces.

Within the long, dark passages he met with no accident or obstacle, coming at last into the light of day beyond the mountains, and no great distance from the southern verge of the domains of the Torquasians, not more than one hundred and fifty haad at the most.

From the boundary of Torquas to the city of Aaanthor is a distance of some two hundred haads, so that the Heliumite had before him a journey of more than one hundred and fifty Earth miles between him and Aaanthor.

He could at best but hazard a chance guess that toward Aaanthor Thuvia would take her flight. There lay the nearest water, and there might be expected some day a rescuing party from her father's empire; for Carthoris knew Thuvan Dihn well enough to know that he would leave no stone unturned until he had tracked down the truth as to his daughter's abduction, and learned all that there might be to learn of her whereabouts.

He realized, of course, that the trick which had laid suspicion upon him would greatly delay the discovery of the truth, but little did he guess to what vast proportions had the results of the villainy of Astok of Dusar already grown.

Even as he emerged from the mouth of the passage to look across the foothills in the direction of Aaanthor, a Ptarth battle fleet was winging its majestic way slowly toward the twin cities of Helium, while from far distant Kaol raced another mighty armada to join forces with its ally.

He did not know that in the face of the circumstantial evidence against him even his own people had commenced to entertain suspicions that he might have stolen the Ptarthian princess.

He did not know of the lengths to which the Dusarians had gone to disrupt the friendship and alliance which existed between the three great powers of the eastern hemisphere—Helium, Ptarth, and Kaol.

How Dusarian emissaries had found employment in important posts in the foreign offices of the three great nations, and how, through these men, messages from one jeddak to another were altered and garbled until the patience and pride of the three rulers and former friends could no longer endure the humiliations and insults contained in these falsified papers—not any of this he knew.

Nor did he know how even to the last John Carter, Warlord of Mars, had refused to permit the jeddak of Helium to declare war against either Ptarth or Kaol, because of his implicit belief in his son, and that eventually all would be satisfactorily explained.

And now two great fleets were moving upon Helium, while the Dusarian spies at the court of Tardos Mors saw to it that the twin cities remained in ignorance of their danger.

War had been declared by Thuvan Dihn, but the messenger who had been dispatched with the proclamation had been a Dusarian who had seen to it that no word of warning reached the twin cities of the approach of a hostile fleet.

For several days diplomatic relations had been severed between Helium and her two most powerful neighbors, and with the departure of the ministers had come a total cessation of wireless communication between the disputants, as is usual upon Barsoom.

But of all this Carthoris was ignorant. All that interested him at present was the finding of Thuvia of Ptarth. Her trail beside that of the huge banth had been well marked to the tunnel, and was once more visible leading southward into the deep foothills.

As he followed rapidly downward toward the dead sea-bottom, where he knew he must lose the spoor in the resilient ochre vegetation, he was suddenly surprised to see a naked man approaching him from the northeast.

As the fellow drew closer, Carthoris halted to await his coming. He knew that the man was unarmed, and that he was apparently a Lotharian, for his skin was white and his hair auburn.

He approached the Heliumite without sign of fear, and when quite close called out the cheery Barsoomian "kaor" of greeting.

"Who are you?" asked Carthoris.

"I am Kar Komak, odwar of the bowmen," replied the other. "A strange thing has happened to me. For ages Tario has been bringing me into existence as he needed the services of the army of his mind. Of all the bowmen it has been Kar Komak who has been oftenest materialized.

"For a long time Tario has been concentrating his mind upon my permanent materialization. It has been an obsession with him that some day this thing could be accomplished and the future of Lothar assured. He asserted that matter was nonexistent except in the imagination of man—that all was mental, and so he believed that by persisting in his suggestion he could eventually make of me a permanent suggestion in the minds of all creatures.

"Yesterday he succeeded, but at such a time! It must have come all unknown to him, as it came to me without my knowledge, as, with my horde of yelling bowmen, I pursued the fleeing Torquasians back to their ochre plains.

"As darkness settled and the time came for us to fade once more into thin air, I suddenly found myself alone upon the edge of the great plain which lies yonder at the foot of the low hills.

"My men were gone back to the nothingness from which they had sprung, but I remained—naked and unarmed—a lone creature in this vast wilderness.

"At first I could not understand, but at last came a realization of what had occurred. Tario's long suggestions had at last prevailed, and Kar Komak had become a reality in the world of men; but my harness and my weapons had faded away with my fellows, leaving me naked and unarmed in a hostile country far from Lothar."

"You wish to return to Lothar?" asked Carthoris.

"No!" replied Kar Komak quickly. "I have no love for Tario. Being a creature of his mind, I know him too well. He is cruel and tyrannical—a master I have no desire to serve. Now that he has succeeded in accomplishing my permanent materialization, he will be unbearable, and he will go on until he has filled Lothar with his creatures. I wonder if he has succeeded as well with the maid of Lothar."

"I thought there were no women there," said Carthoris.

"In a hidden apartment in the palace of Tario," replied Kar Komak, "the jeddak has maintained the suggestion of a beautiful girl, hoping that some day she would become permanent. I have seen her there. She is wonderful! But for her sake I hope that Tario succeeds not so well with her as he has with me.

"Now, red man, I have told you of myself—what of you?"

Carthoris liked the face and manner of the bowman. There had been no sign of doubt or fear in his expression as he had approached the heavily armed Heliumite, and he had spoken directly and to the point.

So the Prince of Helium told the bowman of Lothar who he was and what adventure had brought him to this far country.

"Good!" exclaimed the other, when he had done. "Kar Komak will accompany you. Together we shall find the Princess of Ptarth, and with you Kar Komak will return to the world of men—such a world as he knew in the long-gone past when the ships of mighty Lothar plowed angry Throxus, and the roaring surf beat against the mighty barrier of these parched and dreary hills."

"What mean you?" asked Carthoris. "Had you really a former actual existence?"

"Most assuredly," replied Kar Komak. "In my day I commanded the fleets of Lothar—mightiest of all the fleets that sailed the five salt seas.

"Wherever men lived upon Barsoom there was the name of Kar Komak known and respected. Peaceful were the land races in those distant days—only the seafarers were warriors; but now has the glory of the past faded, nor did I think until I met you that there remained upon Barsoom a single person of our own mold who lived and loved and fought as did the ancient seafarers of my time.

"Ah, but it will seem good to see men once again—real men! Never had I much respect for the landsmen of my day. They remained in their walled cities wasting their time in play, depending for their protection entirely upon the sea race. And the poor creatures who remain, the Tarios and Javs of Lothar, are even worse than their ancient forebears."

Carthoris was a trifle skeptical as to the wisdom of permitting the stranger to attach himself to him. There was always the chance that he was but the essence of some hypnotic treachery which Tario or Jav was attempting to exert upon the Heliumite; and yet, so sincere had been the manner and the words of the bowman, so much the fighting man did he seem, that Carthoris could not find it in his heart to doubt him.

The outcome of the matter was that he gave the naked odwar leave to accompany him, and together they set out upon the spoor of Thuvia and Komal.

Down to the ochre sea-bottom the trail led. There it disappeared, as Carthoris had known that it would; but where it entered the plain its direction had been toward Aaanthor, and so toward Aaanthor the two turned their faces.

It was a long and tedious journey, fraught with many dangers. The bowman could not travel at the pace set by Carthoris, whose muscles carried him with great rapidity over the face of the small planet, the force of gravity of which exerts so much less retarding power than that of the Earth. Fifty miles a day is a fair average for a Barsoomian, but the son of John Carter might easily have covered a hundred or more miles had he cared to desert his newfound comrade.

All the way they were in constant danger of discovery by roving bands of Torquasians, and especially was this true before they reached the boundary of Torquas.

Good fortune was with them, however, and although they sighted two detachments of the savage green men, they were not themselves seen.

And so they came, upon the morning of the third day, within sight of the glistening domes of distant Aaanthor. Throughout the journey Carthoris had ever strained his eyes ahead in search of Thuvia and the great banth; but not till now had he seen aught to give him hope.

This morning, far ahead, halfway between themselves and Aaanthor, the men saw two tiny figures moving toward the city. For a moment they watched them intently. Then Carthoris, convinced, leaped forward at a rapid run, Kar Komak following as swiftly as he could.

The Heliumite shouted to attract the girl's attention, and presently he was rewarded by seeing her turn and stand looking toward him. At her side the great banth stood with up-pricked ears, watching the approaching man.

Not yet could Thuvia of Ptarth have recognized Carthoris, though that it was he she must have been convinced, for she waited there for him without sign of fear.

Presently he saw her point toward the northwest, beyond him. Without slackening his pace, he turned his eyes in the direction she indicated.

Racing silently over the thick vegetation, not half a mile behind, came a score of fierce green warriors, charging him upon their mighty thoats.

To their right was Kar Komak, naked and unarmed, yet running valiantly toward Carthoris and shouting warning as though he, too, had but just discovered the silent, menacing company that moved so swiftly forward with couched spears and ready long-swords.

Carthoris shouted to the Lotharian, warning him back, for he knew that he could but uselessly sacrifice his life by placing himself, all unarmed, in the path of the cruel and relentless savages.

But Kar Komak never hesitated. With shouts of encouragement to his new friend, he hurried onward toward the Prince of Helium. The red man's heart leaped in response to this exhibition of courage and self-sacrifice. He regretted now that he had not thought to give Kar Komak one of his swords; but it was too late to attempt it, for should he wait for the Lotharian to overtake him or return to meet him, the Torquasians would reach Thuvia of Ptarth before he could do so.

Even as it was, it would be nip and tuck as to who came first to her side.

Again he turned his face in her direction, and now, from Aaanthor way, he saw a new force hastening toward them—two medium-sized war craft—and even at the distance they still were from him he discerned the device of Dusar upon their bows.

Now, indeed, seemed little hope for Thuvia of Ptarth. With savage warriors of the hordes of Torquas charging toward her from one direction, and no less implacable enemies, in the form of the creatures of Astok, Prince of Dusar, bearing down upon her from another, while only a banth, a red warrior, and an unarmed bowman were near to defend her, her plight was quite hopeless and her cause already lost ere ever it was contested.

As Thuvia saw Carthoris approaching,

she felt again that unaccountable sensation of entire relief from responsibility and
fear that she had experienced upon a
former occasion. Nor could she account for
it while her mind still tried to convince her
heart that the Prince of Helium had been
instrumental in her abduction from her
father's court. She only knew that she was
glad when he was by her side, and that
with him there all things seemed possible
— even such impossible things as escape
from her present predicament.

Now had he stopped, panting, before
her. A brave smile of encouragement lit his
face.

"Courage, my princess," he whispered.

To the girl's memory flashed the occasion upon which he had used those same
words—in the throneroom of Tario of
Lothar as they had commenced to slip
down the sinking marble floor toward an
unknown fate.

Then she had not chidden him for the
use of that familiar salutation, nor did she
chide him now, though she was promised
to another. She wondered at herself—
flushing at her own turpitude; for upon
Barsoom it is a shameful thing for a woman to listen to those two words from another than her husband or her betrothed.

Carthoris saw her flush of mortification, and in an instant regretted his words.
There was but a moment before the green
warriors would be upon them.

"Forgive me!" said the man in a low
voice. "Let my great love be my excuse—
that, and the belief that I have but a moment more of life," and with the words he
turned to meet the foremost of the green
warriors.

The fellow was charging with couched
spear, but Carthoris leaped to one side, and
as the great thoat and its rider hurtled
harmlessly past him he swung his long-
sword in a mighty cut that clove the green
carcass in twain.

At the same moment Kar Komak leaped
with bare hands clawing at the leg of
another of the huge riders; the balance of
the horde raced in to close quarters, dis-
mounting the better to wield their favorite
long-swords; the Dusarian fliers touched
the soft carpet of the ochre-clad sea-
bottom, disgorging fifty fighting men from
their bowels; and into the swirling sea of
cutting, slashing swords sprang Komal,
the great banth.

Chapter XI

GREEN MEN AND WHITE APES

A Torquasian sword smote a glancing
blow across the forehead of Carthoris. He
had a fleeting vision of soft arms about his
neck, and warm lips close to his before he
lost consciousness.

How long he lay there senseless he could
not guess; but when he opened his eyes
again he was alone, except for the bodies of
the dead green men and Dusarians, and
the carcass of a great banth that lay half
across his own.

Thuvia was gone, nor was the body of
Kar Komak among the dead.

Weak from loss of blood, Carthoris made
his way slowly toward Aaanthor, reaching
its outskirts at dark.

He wanted water more than any other
thing, and so he kept on up a broad avenue
toward the great central plaza, where he
knew the precious fluid was to be found in
a half-ruined building opposite the great
palace of the ancient jeddak, who once had
ruled this mighty city.

Disheartened and discouraged by the
strange sequence of events that seemed
foreordained to thwart his every attempt to
serve the Princess of Ptarth, he paid little
or no attention to his surroundings, moving through the deserted city as though no
great white apes lurked in the black
shadows of the mystery-haunted piles that
flanked the broad avenues and the great
plaza.

But if Carthoris was careless of his surroundings, not so other eyes that watched
his entrance into the plaza, and followed
his slow footsteps toward the marble pile
that housed the tiny, half-choked spring
whose water one might gain only by
scratching a deep hole in the red sand that
covered it.

And as the Heliumite entered the small
building a dozen mighty, grotesque figures
emerged from the doorway of the palace to
speed noiselessly across the plaza toward
him.

For half an hour Carthoris remained in
the building, digging for water and gaining
the few much-needed drops which were the
fruits of his labor. Then he rose and slowly
left the structure. Scarce had he stepped
beyond the threshold than twelve Torquasian warriors leaped upon him.

As the great thoat and his rider hurtled past,
Carthoris swung his long-sword in a mighty cut

No time then to draw long-sword; but swift from his harness flew his long, slim dagger, and as he went down beneath them more than a single green heart ceased beating at the bite of that keen point.

Then they overpowered him and took his weapons away; but only nine of the twelve warriors who had crossed the plaza returned with their prize.

They dragged their prisoner roughly to the palace pits, where in utter darkness they chained him with rusty links to the solid masonry of the wall.

"Tomorrow Thar Ban will speak with you," they said. "Now he sleeps. But great will be his pleasure when he learns who has wandered amongst us—and great will be the pleasure of Hortan Gur when Thar Ban drags before him the mad fool who dared prick the great jeddak with his sword."

Then they left him to the silence and the darkness.

For what seemed hours Carthoris squatted upon the stone floor of his prison, his back against the wall in which was sunk the heavy eye-bolt that secured the chain which held him.

Then, from out the mysterious blackness before him, there came to his ears the sound of naked feet moving stealthily upon stone—approaching nearer and nearer to where he lay, unarmed and defenseless.

Minutes passed—minutes that seemed hours—during which time periods of sepulchral silence would be followed by a repetition of the uncanny scraping of naked feet slinking warily upon him.

At last he heard a sudden rush of unshod soles across the empty blackness, and at a little distance a scuffling sound, heavy breathing, and once what he thought the muttered imprecation of a man battling against great odds. Then the clanging of a chain, and a noise as of the snapping back against stone of a broken link.

Again came silence. But for a moment only. Now he heard once more the soft feet approaching him. He thought that he discerned wicked eyes gleaming fearfully at him through the darkness. He knew that he could hear the heavy breathing of powerful lungs.

Then came the rush of many feet toward him, and the *things* were upon him.

Hands terminating in manlike fingers clutched at his throat and arms and legs. Hairy bodies strained and struggled against his own smooth hide as he battled in grim silence against these horrid foemen in the darkness of the pits of ancient Aaanthor.

Thewed like some giant god was Carthoris of Helium, yet in the clutches of these unseen creatures of the pit's Stygian night he was helpless as a frail woman.

Yet he battled on, striking futile blows against great, hispid breasts he could not see; feeling thick, squat throats beneath his fingers; the drool of saliva upon his cheek, and hot, foul breath in his nostrils.

Fangs, too, mighty fangs, he knew were close, and why they did not sink into his flesh he could not guess.

At last he became aware of the mighty surging of a number of his antagonists back and forth upon the great chain that held him, and presently came the same sound that he had heard at a little distance from him a short time before he had been attacked—his chain had parted and the broken end snapped back against the stone wall.

Now he was seized upon either side and dragged at a rapid pace through the dark corridors—toward what fate he could not even guess.

At first he had thought his foes might be of the tribe of Torquas, but their hairy bodies belied that belief. Now he was at last quite sure of their identity, though why they had not killed and devoured him at once he could not imagine.

After half an hour or more of rapid racing through the underground passages that are a distinguishing feature of all Barsoomian cities, modern as well as ancient, his captors suddenly emerged into the moonlight of a courtyard, far from the central plaza.

Immediately Carthoris saw that he was in the power of a tribe of the great white apes of Barsoom. All that had caused him doubt before as to the identity of his attackers was the hairiness of their breasts, for the white apes are entirely hairless except for a great shock bristling from their heads.

Now he saw the cause of that which had deceived him—across the chest of each of them were strips of hairy hide, usually of banth, in imitation of the harness of the green warriors who so often camped at their deserted city.

Carthoris had read of the existence of tribes of apes that seemed to be progressing slowly toward higher standards of intelligence. Into the hands of such, he realized, he had fallen; but—what were their intentions toward him?

As he glanced about the courtyard, he saw fully fifty of the hideous beasts, squatting on their haunches, and at a little distance from him another human being, closely guarded.

As his eyes met those of his fellow-captive a smile lit the other's face, and: "Kaor, red man!" burst from his lips. It was Kar Komak, the bowman.

"Kaor!" cried Carthoris, in response. "How came you here, and what befell the princess?"

"Red men like yourself descended in mighty ships that sailed the air, even as the great ships of my distant day sailed the five seas," replied Kar Komak. "They fought with the green men of Torquas. They slew Komal, god of Lothar. I thought they were your friends, and I was glad when finally those of them who survived the battle carried the red girl to one of the ships and sailed away with her into the safety of the high air.

"Then the green men seized me, and carried me to a great, empty city, where they chained me to a wall in a black pit. Afterward came these and dragged me hither. And what of you, red man?"

Carthoris related all that had befallen him, and as the two men talked the great apes squatted about them watching them intently.

"What are we to do now?" asked the bowman.

"Our case looks rather hopeless," replied Carthoris ruefully. "These creatures are born man-eaters. Why they have not already devoured us I cannot imagine—there!" he whispered. "See? The end is coming."

Kar Komak looked in the direction Carthoris indicated to see a huge ape advancing with a mighty bludgeon.

"It is thus they like best to kill their prey," said Carthoris.

"Must we die without a struggle?" asked Kar Komak.

"Not I," replied Carthoris, "though I know how futile our best defense must be against these mighty brutes! Oh, for a long-sword!"

"Or a good bow," added Kar Komak, "and a utan of bowmen."

At the words Carthoris half sprang to his feet, only to be dragged roughly down by his guard.

"Kar Komak!" he cried. "Why cannot you do what Tario and Jav did? They had no bowmen other than those of their own creation. You must know the secret of their power. Call forth your own utan, Kar Komak!"

The Lotharian looked at Carthoris in wide-eyed astonishment as the full purport of the suggestion bore in upon his understanding.

"Why not?" he murmured.

The savage ape bearing the mighty bludgeon was slinking toward Carthoris. The Heliumite's fingers were working as he kept his eyes upon his executioner. Kar Komak bent his gaze penetratingly upon the apes. The effort of his mind was evidenced in the great beads of sweat upon his contracted brows.

The creature that was to slay the red man was almost within arm's reach of his prey when Carthoris heard a hoarse shout from the opposite side of the courtyard. In common with the squatting apes and the demon with the club he turned in the direction of the sound to see a company of sturdy bowmen rushing from the doorway of a nearby building.

With screams of rage the apes leaped to their feet to meet the charge. A volley of arrows met them halfway, sending a dozen rolling lifeless to the ground. Then the apes closed with their adversaries. All their attention was occupied by the attackers—even the guard had deserted the prisoners to join in the battle.

"Come!" whispered Kar Komak. "Now may we escape while their attention is diverted from us by my bowmen."

"And leave those brave fellows leaderless?" cried Carthoris, whose loyal nature revolted at the merest suggestion of such a thing.

Kar Komak laughed.

"You forget," he said, "that they are but thin air—figments of my brain. They will vanish, unscathed, when we have no further need for them. Praised be your first ancestor, red man, that you thought of this chance in time! It would never have occurred to me to imagine that I might wield the same power that brought me into existence."

"You are right," said Carthoris. "Still, I hate to leave them, though there is naught else to do," and so the two turned from the courtyard, and making their way into one of the broad avenues, crept stealthily in the shadows of the building toward the great central plaza upon which were the buildings occupied by the green warriors when they visited the deserted city.

When they had come to the plaza's edge Carthoris halted.

"Wait here," he whispered. "I go to fetch thoats, since on foot we may never hope to escape the clutches of these green fiends."

To reach the courtyard where the thoats were kept it was necessary for Carthoris to pass through one of the buildings which surrounded the square. Which were occupied and which not he could not even guess, so he was compelled to take considerable chances to gain the enclosure in which he could hear the restless beasts squealing and quarreling among themselves.

Chance carried him through a dark doorway into a large chamber in which lay a score or more green warriors wrapped in their sleeping silks and furs. Scarce had Carthoris passed through the short hallway that connected the door of the building and the great room beyond it than he became aware of the presence of something or someone in the hallway through which he had but just passed.

He heard a man yawn, and then, behind him, he saw the figure of a sentry rise from where the fellow had been dozing, and stretching himself resume his wakeful watchfulness.

Carthoris realized that he must have passed within a foot of the warrior, doubtless rousing him from his slumber. To retreat now would be impossible. Yet to cross through that roomful of sleeping warriors seemed almost equally beyond the pale of possibility. The crucial moment had come.

Carthoris shrugged his broad shoulders and chose the lesser evil. Warily he entered the room. At his right, against the wall, leaned several swords and rifles and spears—extra weapons which the warriors had stacked here ready to their hands should there be a night alarm calling them suddenly from slumber. Beside each sleeper lay his weapon—these were never far from their owners from childhood to death.

The sight of the swords made the young man's palm itch. He stepped quickly to them, selecting two short-swords—one for Kar Komak, the other for himself; also some trappings for his naked comrade.

Then he started directly across the center of the apartment among the sleeping Torquasians.

Not a man of them moved until Carthoris had completed more than half of the short though dangerous journey. Then a fellow directly in his path turned restlessly upon his sleeping silks and furs.

The Heliumite paused above him, one of the short-swords in readiness should the warrior awaken. For what seemed an eternity to the young prince the green man continued to move uneasily upon his couch, then, as though actuated by springs, he leaped to his feet and faced the red man.

Instantly Carthoris struck, but not before a savage grunt escaped the other's lips. In an instant the room was in turmoil. Warriors leaped to their feet, grasping their weapons as they rose, and shouting to one another for an explanation of the disturbance.

To Carthoris all within the room was plainly visible in the dim light reflected from without, for the further moon stood directly at zenith; but to the eyes of the newly awakened green men objects as yet had not taken on familiar forms—they but saw vaguely the figures of warriors moving about their apartment.

Now one stumbled against the corpse of him whom Carthoris had slain. The fellow stooped and his hand came in contact with the cleft skull. He saw about him the giant figures of other green men, and so he jumped to the only conclusion that was open to him.

"The Thurds!" he cried. "The Thurds are upon us! Rise, warriors of Torquas, and drive home your swords within the hearts of Torquas' ancient enemies!"

Instantly the green men began to fall upon one another with naked swords. Their savage lust of battle was aroused. To fight, to kill, to die with cold steel buried in their vitals! Ah, that to them was Nirvana.

Carthoris was quick to guess their error and take advantage of it. He knew that in the pleasure of killing they might fight on long after they had discovered their mistake, unless their attention was distracted by sight of the real cause of the altercation, and so he lost no time in continuing across the room to the doorway upon the opposite side, which opened into the inner court, where the savage thoats were squealing and fighting among themselves.

Once here he had no easy task before him. To catch and mount one of these habitually rageful and intractable beasts was no child's play under the best of conditions; but now, when silence and time were such important considerations, it might well have seemed quite hopeless to a less resourceful and optimistic man than the son of the great warlord.

From his father he had learned much concerning the traits of these mighty beasts, and from Tars Tarkas, also, when he had visited that great green jeddak among his horde at Thark. So now he centered upon the work in hand all that he had ever learned about them from others and from his own experience, for he, too, had ridden and handled them many times.

The temper of the thoats of Torquas appeared even shorter than their vicious cousins among the Tharks and Warhoons, and for a time it seemed unlikely that he should escape a savage charge on the part of a couple of old bulls that circled, squealing, about him; but at last he managed to get close enough to one of them to touch the beast. With the feel of his hand upon the sleek hide the creature quieted, and in answer to the telepathic command of the red man sank to its knees docile as a lamb.

In a moment Carthoris was upon its back, guiding it toward the great gate that leads from the courtyard through a large building at one end into an avenue beyond.

The other bull, still squealing and enraged, followed after his fellow. There was no bridle upon either, for these strange creatures are controlled entirely by suggestion—when they are controlled at all.

Even in the hands of the giant green men bridle reins would be hopelessly futile against the mad savagery and mastodonic strength of the thoat, and so they are guided by that strange telepathic power with which the men of Mars have learned to communicate in a crude way with the lower orders of their planet.

With difficulty Carthoris urged the two beasts to the gate, where, leaning down, he raised the latch. Then the thoat that he was riding placed his great shoulder to the skeel-wood planking, pushed through, and a moment later the man and the two beasts were swinging silently down the avenue to the edge of the plaza, where Kar Komak hid.

Here Carthoris found considerable difficulty in subduing the second thoat, and as Kar Komak had never before ridden one of the beasts, it seemed a most hopeless job; but at last the bowman managed to scramble to the sleek back, and again the two beasts fled softly down the moss-grown avenues toward the open sea-bottom beyond the city.

All that night and the following day and the second night they rode toward the northeast. No indication of pursuit developed, and at dawn of the second day Carthoris saw in the distance the waving ribbon of great trees that marked one of the long Barsoomian waterways.

Immediately they abandoned their thoats and approached the cultivated district on foot. Carthoris also discarded the metal from his harness, or such of it as might serve to identify him as a Heliumite, or of royal blood, for he did not know to what nation belonged this waterway, and upon Mars it is always well to assume every man and nation your enemy until you have learned the contrary.

It was mid-forenoon when the two at last entered one of the roads that cut through the cultivated districts at regular intervals, joining the arid wastes on either side with the great, white, central highway that follows through the center from end to end of the far-reaching, threadlike farm lands.

The high wall surrounding the fields served as a protection against surprise by raiding green hordes, as well as keeping the savage banths and other carnivora from the domestic animals and the human beings upon the farms.

Carthoris stopped before the first gate he came to, pounding for admission. The young man who answered his summons greeted the two hospitably, though he looked with considerable wonder upon the white skin and auburn hair of the bowman.

After he had listened for a moment to a partial narration of their escape from the Torquasians, he invited them within, took them to his house and bade the servants there prepare food for them.

As they waited in the low-ceiled, pleasant living-room of the farmhouse until the meal should be ready, Carthoris drew his host into conversation that he might learn his nationality, and thus the nation under whose dominion lay the waterway where circumstance had placed him.

"I am Hal Vas," said the young man, "son of Vas Kor of Dusar, a noble in the retinue of Astok, Prince of Dusar. At present I am Dwar of the Road for this district."

Carthoris was very glad that he had not disclosed his identity, for though he had no idea of anything that had transpired since he had left Helium, or that Astok was at the bottom of all his misfortunes, he well knew that the Dusarian had no love for him, and that he could hope for no assistance within the dominions of Dusar.

"And who are you?" asked Hal Vas. "By your appearance I take you for a fighting man, but I see no insignia upon your harness. Can it be that you are a panthan?"

Now, these wandering soldiers of fortune are common upon Barsoom, where most men love to fight. They sell their services wherever war exists, and in the occasional brief intervals when there is no organized warfare between the red nations, they join one of the numerous expeditions that are constantly being dispatched against the green men in protection of the waterways that traverse the wilder portions of the globe.

When their service is over they discard the metal of the nation they have been serving until they shall have found a new master. In the intervals they wear no insignia, their war-worn harness and grim weapons being sufficient to attest their calling.

The suggestion was a happy one, and Carthoris embraced the chance it afforded to account satisfactorily for himself. There was, however, a single drawback. In times of war such panthans as happened to be within the domain of a belligerent nation were compelled to don the insignia of that nation and fight with her warriors.

As far as Carthoris knew Dusar was not at war with any other nation, but there was never any telling when one red nation would be flying at the throat of a neighbor, even though the great and powerful alliance at the head of which was his father, John Carter, had managed to maintain a long peace upon the greater portion of Barsoom.

A pleasant smile lighted Hal Vas' face as Carthoris admitted his vocation.

"It is well," exclaimed the young man, "that you chanced to come hither, for here you will find the means of obtaining service in short order. My father, Vas Kor, is even now with me, having come hither to recruit a force for the new war against Helium."

Chapter XII

TO SAVE DUSAR

Thuvia of Ptarth, battling for more than life against the lust of Jav, cast a quick glance over her shoulder toward the forest from which had rumbled the fierce growl. Jav looked, too.

What they saw filled each with apprehension. It was Komal, the banth-god, rushing wide-jawed upon them!

Which had he chosen for his prey? Or was it to be both?

They had not long to wait, for though the Lotharian attempted to hold the girl between himself and the terrible fangs, the great beast found him at last.

Then, shrieking, he attempted to fly toward Lothar, after pushing Thuvia bodily into the face of the man-eater. But his flight was of short duration. In a moment Komal was upon him, rending his throat and chest with demoniacal fury.

The girl reached their side a moment later, but it was with difficulty that she tore the mad beast from its prey. Still growling and casting hungry glances back upon Jav, the banth at last permitted itself to be led away into the wood.

With her giant protector by her side Thuvia set forth to find the passage through the cliffs that she might attempt the seemingly impossible feat of reaching far-distant Ptarth across the more than seventeen thousand haads of savage Barsoom.

She could not believe that Carthoris had deliberately deserted her, and so she kept a constant watch for him; but as she bore too far to the north in her search for the tunnel she passed the Heliumite as he was returning to Lothar in search of her.

Thuvia of Ptarth was having difficulty in determining the exact status of the Prince of Helium in her heart. She could not admit even to herself that she loved him, and yet she had permitted him to apply to her that term of endearment and possession to which a Barsoomian maid should turn deaf ears when voiced by other lips than those of her husband or fiance—"my princess."

Kulan Tith, Jeddak of Kaol, to whom she was affianced, commanded her respect and admiration. Had it been that she had surrendered to her father's wishes because of pique that the handsome Heliumite had not taken advantage of his visits to her father's court to push the suit for her hand that she had been quite sure he had contemplated since that distant day the two had sat together upon the carved seat within the gorgeous Garden of the Jeddaks that graced the inner courtyard of the palace of Salensus Oll at Kadabra?

Did she love Kulan Tith? Bravely she tried to believe that she did; but all the while her eyes wandered through the coming darkness for the figure of a clean-limbed fighting man—black-haired and gray-eyed. Black was the hair of Kulan Tith; but his eyes were brown.

It was almost dark when she found the entrance to the tunnel. Safely she passed through to the hills beyond, and here, under the bright light of Mars' two moons, she halted to plan her future action.

Should she wait here in the hope that Carthoris would return in search of her? Or should she continue her way northeast toward Ptarth? Where, first, would Carthoris have gone after leaving the valley of Lothar?

Her parched throat and dry tongue gave her the answer—toward Aaanthor and water. Well, she, too, would go first to Aaanthor, where she might find more than the water she needed.

With Komal by her side she felt little fear, for he would protect her from all other savage beasts. Even the great white apes would flee the mighty banth in terror. Men only need she fear, but she must take this and many other chances before she could hope to reach her father's court again.

When at last Carthoris found her, only to be struck down by the long-sword of a green man, Thuvia prayed that the same fate might overtake her.

The sight of the red warriors leaping from their fliers had, for a moment, filled her with renewed hope—hope that Carthoris of Helium might be only stunned and that they would rescue him; but when she saw the Dusarian metal upon their harness, and that they sought only to escape with her alone from the charging Torquasians, she gave up.

Komal, too, was dead—dead across the body of the Heliumite. She was, indeed, alone now. There was none to protect her.

The Dusarian warriors dragged her to the deck of a flier. All about them the green warriors surged in an attempt to wrest her from the red.

At last those who had not died in the conflict gained the decks of the two craft. The engines throbbed and purred—the propellers whirred. Quickly the swift boats shot heavenward.

Thuvia of Ptarth glanced about her. A man stood near, smiling down into her face. With a gasp of recognition she looked full into his eyes, and then with a little moan of terror and understanding she buried her face in her hands and sank to the polished skeel-wood deck. It was Astok, Prince of Dusar, who bent above her.

Swift were the fliers of Astok of Dusar, and great the need for reaching his father's court as quickly as possible, for the fleets of war of Helium and Ptarth and Kaol were scattered far and wide above Barsoom. Nor would it go well with Astok or Dusar should any one of them discover Thuvia of Ptarth a prisoner upon his own vessel.

Aaanthor lies in fifty south latitude, and forty east of Horz, the deserted seat of ancient Barsoomian culture and learning, while Dusar lies fifteen degrees north of the equator and twenty degrees east from Horz.

Great though the distance is, the fliers covered it without a stop. Long before they had reached their destination Thuvia of Ptarth had learned several things that cleared up the doubts that had assailed her mind for many days. Scarce had they risen above Aaanthor then she recognized one of the crew as a member of the crew of that other flier that had borne her from her father's gardens to Aaanthor. The presence of Astok upon the craft settled the whole question. She had been stolen by emissaries of the Dusarian prince—Carthoris of Helium had had nothing to do with it.

Nor did Astok deny the charge when she accused him. He only smiled and pleaded his love for her.

"I would sooner mate with a white ape!" she cried, when he would have urged his suit.

Astok glowered sullenly upon her.

"You shall mate with me, Thuvia of Ptarth," he growled, "or, by your first ancestor, you shall have your preference—and mate with a white ape."

The girl made no reply, nor could he draw her into conversation during the balance of the journey.

As a matter of fact Astok was a trifle awed by the proportions of the conflict which his abduction of the Ptarthian princess had induced, nor was he over comfortable with the weight of responsibility which the possession of such a prisoner entailed.

His one thought was to get her to Dusar, and there let his father assume the responsibility. In the meantime he would be as careful as possible to do nothing to affront her, lest they all might be captured and he have to account for his treatment of the girl to one of the great jeddaks whose interest centered in her.

And so at last they came to Dusar, where Astok hid his prisoner in a secret room high in the east tower of his own palace. He had sworn his men to silence in the matter of the identity of the girl, for until he had seen his father, Nutus, Jeddak of Dusar, he dared not let anyone know whom he had brought with him from the south.

But when he appeared in the great audience chamber before the cruel-lipped man who was his sire, he found his courage oozing, and he dared not speak of the princess hid within his palace. It occurred to him to test his father's sentiments upon the subject, and so he told a tale of capturing one who claimed to know the whereabouts of Thuvia of Ptarth.

"And if you command it, Sire," he said, "I will go and capture her—fetching her here to Dusar."

Nutus frowned and shook his head.

"You have done enough already to set Ptarth and Kaol and Helium all three upon us at once should they learn your part in the theft of the Ptarth princess. That you succeeded in shifting the guilt upon the Prince of Helium was fortunate, and a masterly move of strategy; but were the girl to know the truth and ever return to her father's court, all Dusar would have to pay the penalty, and to have her here a prisoner amongst us would be an admission of guilt from the consequences of which naught could save us. It would cost me my throne, Astok, and that I have no mind to lose.

"If we had her here—" the elder man suddenly commenced to muse, repeating the phrase again and again. "If we had her here, Astok," he exclaimed fiercely. "Ah, if we but had her here and none knew that she was here! Can you not guess, man? The guilt of Dusar might be forever buried with her bones," he concluded in a low, savage whisper.

Astok, Prince of Dusar, shuddered.

Weak he was; yes, and wicked, too; but the suggestion that his father's words implied turned him cold with horror.

Cruel to their enemies are the men of Mars; but the word "enemies" is commonly interpreted to mean men only. Assassination runs riot in the great Barsoomian cities; yet to murder a woman is a crime so unthinkable that even the most hardened of the paid assassins would shrink from you in horror should you even dare to suggest such a thing to him.

Nutus was apparently oblivious to his son's all-too-patent terror at his suggestion. Presently he continued:

"You say that you know where the girl lies hid, since she was stolen from your people at Aaanthor. Should she be found by any one of the three powers her unsupported story would be sufficient to turn them all against us.

"There is but one way, Astok," cried the older man. "You must return at once to her hiding place and fetch her hither in all secrecy. And, look you here! Return not to Dusar without her, upon pain of death!"

Astok, Prince of Dusar, well knew his royal father's temper. He knew that in the tyrant's heart there pulsed no single throb of love for any creature.

Astok's mother had been a slave woman. Nutus had never loved her. He had never loved another. In youth he had tried to find a bride at the courts of several of his powerful neighbors, but their women would have none of him.

After a dozen daughters of his own nobility had sought self-destruction rather than wed him he had given up. And then it had been that he had legally wed one of his slaves that he might have a son to stand among the jeds when Nutus died and a new jeddak was chosen.

Slowly Astok withdrew from the presence of his father. With white face and shaking limbs he made his way to his own palace. As he crossed the courtyard his glance chanced to wander to the great east tower looming high against the azure of the sky.

At sight of it beads of sweat broke out upon his brow.

Issus! No other hand than his could be trusted to do the horrid thing. With his own fingers he must crush the life from that perfect throat, or plunge the silent blade into the red, red heart.

Her heart! The heart that he had hoped would brim with love for him!

But had it done so? He recalled the haughty contempt with which his protestations of love had been received. He went cold and then hot at the memory of it. His compunctions cooled as the self-satisfaction of a near revenge crowded out the finer instincts that had for a moment asserted themselves—the good that he had inherited from the slave woman was once again submerged in the bad blood that had come down to him from his royal sire; as, in the end, it always was.

A cold smile supplanted the terror that had dilated his eyes. He turned his steps toward the tower. He would see her before he set out upon the journey that was to blind his father to the fact that the girl was already in Dusar.

Quietly he passed in through the secret way, ascending a spiral runway to the apartment in which the Princess of Ptarth was immured.

As he entered the room he saw the girl leaning upon the sill of the east casement, gazing out across the roof tops of Dusar toward distant Ptarth. He hated Ptarth. The thought of it filled him with rage. Why not finish her now and have it done with?

At the sound of his step she turned quickly toward him. Ah, how beautiful she was! His sudden determination faded beneath the glorious light of her wondrous beauty. He would wait until he had returned from his little journey of deception—maybe there might be some other way then. Some other hand to strike the blow—with that face, with those eyes before him, he could never do it. Of that he was positive. He had always gloried in the cruelty of his nature, but, Issus! he was not that cruel. No, another must be found—one whom he could trust.

He was still looking at her as she stood there before him meeting his gaze steadily and unafraid. He felt the hot passion of his love mounting higher and higher.

Why not sue once more? If she would relent, all might yet be well. Even if his father could not be persuaded they could fly to Ptarth, laying all the blame of the knavery and intrigue that had thrown four great nations into war, upon the shoulders of Nutus. And who was there that would doubt the justice of the charge?

"Thuvia," he said, "I come once again,

for the last time, to lay my heart at your feet. Ptarth and Kaol and Dusar are battling with Helium because of you. Wed me, Thuvia, and all may yet be as it should be."

The girl shook her head.

"Wait!" he commanded, before she could speak. "Know the truth before you speak words that may seal not only your own fate but that of the thousands of warriors who battle because of you.

"Refuse to wed me willingly, and Dusar would be laid waste should ever the truth be known to Ptarth and Kaol and Helium. They would raze our cities, leaving not one stone upon another. They would scatter our peoples across the face of Barsoom from the frozen north to the frozen south, hunting them down and slaying them, until this great nation remained only as a hated memory in the minds of men.

"But while they are exterminating the Dusarians countless thousands of their own warriors must perish—and all because of the stubbornness of a single woman who would not wed the prince who loves her.

"Refuse, Thuvia of Ptarth, and there remains but a single alternative—no man must ever know your fate. Only a handful of loyal servitors besides my royal father and myself know that you were stolen from the gardens of Thuvan Dihn by Astok, Prince of Dusar, or that today you be imprisoned in my palace.

"Refuse, Thuvia of Ptarth, and you must die to save Dusar—there is no other way. Nutus, the jeddak, has so decreed. I have spoken."

For a long moment the girl let her level gaze rest full upon the face of Astok of Dusar. Then she spoke, and though the words were few, the unimpassioned tone carried unfathomable depths of cold contempt.

"Better all that you have threatened," she said, "than you."

Then she turned her back upon him and went to stand once more before the east window, gazing with sad eyes toward distant Ptarth.

Astok wheeled and left the room, returning after a short interval of time with food and drink.

"Here," he said, "is sustenance until I return again. The next to enter this apartment will be your executioner. Commend yourself to your ancestors, Thuvia of

Ptarth, for within a few days you shall be with them."

Then he was gone.

Half an hour later he was interviewing an officer high in the navy of Dusar.

"Whither went Vas Kor?" he asked. "He is not at his palace."

"South, to the great waterway that skirts Torquas," replied the other. "His son, Hal Vas, is Dwar of the Road there, and thither has Vas Kor gone to enlist recruits among the workers on the farms."

"Good," said Astok, and a half-hour more found him rising above Dusar in his swiftest flier.

Chapter XIII

TURJUN, THE PANTHAN

The face of Carthoris of Helium gave no token of the emotions that convulsed him inwardly as he heard from the lips of Hal Vas that Helium was at war with Dusar, and that fate had thrown him into the service of the enemy.

That he might utilize this opportunity to the good of Helium scarce sufficed to outweigh the chagrin he felt that he was not fighting in the open at the head of his own loyal troops.

To escape the Dusarians might prove an easy matter; and then again it might not. Should they suspect his loyalty (and the loyalty of an impressed panthan was always open to suspicion), he might not find an opportunity to elude their vigilance until after the termination of the war, which might occur within days, or, again, only after long and weary years of bloodshed.

He recalled that history recorded wars in which actual military operations had been carried on without cessation for five or six hundred years, and even now there were nations upon Barsoom with which Helium had made no peace within the history of man.

The outlook was not cheering. He could not guess that within a few hours he would be blessing the fate that had thrown him into the service of Dusar.

"Ah!" exclaimed Hal Vas. "Here is my father now. Kaor! Vas Kor. Here is one you will be glad to meet — a doughty panthan —" He hesitated.

"Turjun," interjected Carthoris, seizing upon the first appellation that occurred to him.

As he spoke his eyes crossed quickly to the tall warrior who was entering the room. Where before had he seen that giant figure, that taciturn countenance, and the livid sword cut from temple to mouth?

"Vas Kor," repeated Carthoris mentally. "Vas Kor!" Where had he seen the man before?

And then the noble spoke, and like a flash it all came back to Carthoris—the forward servant upon the landing stage at Ptarth that time that he had been explaining the intricacies of his new compass to Thuvan Dihn; the lone slave that had guarded his own hangar that night he had left upon his ill-fated journey for Ptarth— the journey that had brought him so mysteriously to far Aaanthor.

"Vas Kor," he repeated aloud, "blessed be your ancestors for this meeting," nor did the Dusarian guess the wealth of meaning that lay beneath that hackneyed phrase with which a Barsoomian acknowledges an introduction.

"And blessed be yours, Turjun," replied Vas Kor.

Now came the introduction of Kar Komak to Vas Kor, and as Carthoris went through the little ceremony there came to him the only explanation he might make to account for the white skin and auburn hair of the bowman; for he feared that the truth might not be believed and thus suspicion be cast upon them both from the beginning.

"Kar Komak," he explained, "is, as you can see, a thern. He has wandered far from his ice-bound southern temples in search of adventure. I came upon him in the pits of Aaanthor; but though I have known him so short a time, I can vouch for his bravery and loyalty."

Since the destruction of the fabric of their false religion by John Carter, the majority of the therns had gladly accepted the new order of things, so that it was now no longer uncommon to see them mingling with the multitudes of red men in any of the great cities of the outer world, so Vas Kor neither felt nor expressed any great astonishment and no alarm.

All during the interview Carthoris watched, catlike, for some indication that Vas Kor recognized in the battered panthan the erstwhile gorgeous Prince of

Helium; but the sleepless nights, the long days of marching and fighting, the wounds and the dried blood had evidently sufficed to obliterate the last remnant of his likeness to his former self; and then Vas Kor had seen him but twice in all his life. Little wonder that he did not know him.

During the evening Vas Kor announced that on the morrow they should depart north toward Dusar, picking up recruits at various stations along the way.

In a great field behind the house a flier lay—a fair-sized cruiser-transport that would accommodate many men, yet swift and well armed also. Here Carthoris slept, and Kar Komak, too, with the other recruits, under guard of the regular Dusarian warriors that manned the craft.

Toward midnight Vas Kor returned to the vessel from his son's house, repairing at once to his cabin. Carthoris, with one of the Dusarians, was on watch. It was with difficulty that the Heliumite repressed a cold smile as the noble passed within a foot of him—within a foot of the long, slim, Heliumitic blade that swung in his harness.

How easy it would have been! How easy to avenge the cowardly trick that had been played upon him—to avenge Helium and Ptarth and Thuvia!

But his hand moved not toward the dagger's hilt, for first Vas Kor must serve a better purpose—he might know where Thuvia of Ptarth lay hidden now, if it had truly been Dusarians that had spirited her away during the fight before Aaanthor.

And then, too, there was the instigator of the entire foul plot. *He* must pay the penalty; and who better than Vas Kor could lead the Prince of Helium to Astok of Dusar?

Faintly out of the night there came to Carthoris' ears the purring of a distant motor. He scanned the heavens.

Yes, there it was far in the north, dimly outlined against the dark void of space that stretched illimitably beyond it, the faint suggestion of a flier passing, unlighted, through the black Barsoomian night.

Carthoris, knowing not whether the craft might be friend or foe of Dusar, gave no sign that he had seen, but turned his eyes in another direction, leaving the matter to the Dusarian who stood watch with him.

Presently the fellow discovered the oncoming craft, and sounded the low alarm which brought the balance of the watch and an officer from their sleeping silks and furs upon the deck nearby.

The cruiser-transport lay without lights, and, resting as she was upon the ground, must have been entirely invisible to the oncoming flier, which all presently recognized as a small craft.

It soon became evident that the stranger intended making a landing, for she was now spiraling slowly above them, dropping lower and lower in each graceful curve.

"It is the *Thuria*," whispered one of the Dusarian warriors. "I would know her in the blackness of the pits among ten thousand other craft."

"Right you are!" exclaimed Vas Kor, who had come on deck. And then he hailed:

"Kaor, *Thuria!*"

"Kaor!" came presently from above after a brief silence. Then: "What ship?"

"Cruiser-transport *Kalksus,* Vas Kor of Dusar."

"Good!" came from above. "Is there safe landing alongside?"

"Yes, close in to starboard. Wait, we will show our lights," and a moment later the smaller craft settled close beside the *Kalksus,* and the lights of the latter were immediately extinguished once more.

Several figures could be seen slipping over the side of the *Thuria* and advancing toward the *Kalksus.* Ever suspicious, the Dusarians stood ready to receive the visitors as friends or foes as closer inspection might prove them.

Carthoris stood quite near the rail, ready to take sides with the newcomers should chance have it that they were Heliumites playing a bold stroke of strategy upon this lone Dusarian ship. He had led like parties himself, and knew that such a contingency was quite possible.

But the face of the first man to cross the rail undeceived him with a shock that was not at all unpleasurable—it was the face of Astok, Prince of Dusar.

Scarce noticing the others upon the deck of the *Kalksus,* Astok strode forward to accept Vas Kor's greeting, then he summoned the noble below. The warriors and officers returned to their sleeping silks and furs, and once more the deck was deserted except for the Dusarian warrior and Turjun, the panthan, who stood guard.

The latter walked quietly to and fro. The former leaned across the rail, wishing for the hour that would bring him relief. He did not see his companion approach the lights of the cabin of Vas Kor. He did not see him stoop with ear close pressed to a tiny ventilator.

"May the white apes take us all," cried Astok ruefully, "if we are not in as ugly a snarl as you have ever seen! Nutus thinks that we have her in hiding far away from Dusar. He has bidden me bring her there."

He paused. No man should have heard from his lips the thing he was trying to tell. It should have been forever the secret of Nutus and Astok, for upon it rested the safety of a throne. With that knowledge any man could wrest from the Jeddak of Dusar whatever he listed.

But Astok was afraid, and he wanted from this older man the suggestion of an alternative. He went on.

"I am to kill her," he whispered, looking fearfully around. "Nutus merely wishes to see the body that he may know his commands have been executed. I am now supposed to be gone to the spot where we have her hidden that I may fetch her in secrecy to Dusar. None is to know that she has ever been in the keeping of a Dusarian. I do not need to tell you what would befall Dusar should Ptarth and Helium and Kaol ever learn the truth."

The jaws of the listener at the ventilator clicked together with a vicious snap. Before he had but guessed at the identity of the subject of this conversation. Now he knew. And they were to kill her! His muscular fingers clenched until the nails bit into the palms.

"And you wish me to go with you while you fetch her to Dusar," Vas Kor was saying. "Where is she?"

Astok bent close and whispered into the other's ear. The suggestion of a smile crossed the cruel features of Vas Kor. He realized the power that lay within his grasp. He should be a jed at least.

"And how may I help you, my Prince?" asked the older man suavely.

"I cannot kill her," said Astok. "Issus! I cannot do it! When she turns those eyes upon me my heart becomes water."

Vas Kor's eyes narrowed.

"And you wish—" He paused, the interrogation unfinished, yet complete.

Astok nodded.

"*You* do not love her," he said.

"But I love my life—though I am only a lesser noble," he concluded meaningly.

"You shall be a greater noble—a noble of the first rank!" exclaimed Astok.

"I would be a jed," said Vas Kor bluntly.

Astok hesitated.

"A jed must die before there can be another jed," he pleaded.

"Jeds have died before," snapped Vas Kor. "It would doubtless be not difficult for you to find a jed you do not love, Astok—there are many who do not love you."

Already Vas Kor was commencing to presume upon his power over the young prince. Astok was quick to note and appreciate the subtle change in his lieutenant. A cunning scheme entered his weak and wicked brain.

"As you say, Vas Kor!" he exclaimed. "You shall be a jed when the thing is done," and then, to himself: "Nor will it then be difficult for me to find a jed I do not love."

"When shall we return to Dusar?" asked the noble.

"At once," replied Astok. "Let us get under way now—there is naught to keep you here?"

"I had intended sailing on the morrow, picking up such recruits as the various Dwars of the Roads might have collected for me, as we returned to Dusar."

"Let the recruits wait," said Astok. "Or, better still, come you to Dusar upon the *Thuria,* leaving the *Kalksus* to follow and pick up the recruits."

"Yes," acquiesced Vas Kor; "that is the better plan. Come; I am ready," and he rose to accompany Astok to the latter's flier.

The listener at the ventilator came to his feet slowly, like an old man. His face was drawn and pinched and very white beneath the light copper of his skin. She was to die! And he helpless to avert the tragedy. He did not even know where she was imprisoned.

The two men were ascending from the cabin to the deck. Turjun, the panthan, crept close to the companionway, his sinuous fingers closing tightly upon the hilt of his dagger. Could he despatch them both before he was overpowered? He smiled. He could slay an entire utan of her enemies in his present state of mind.

They were almost abreast of him now. Astok was speaking.

"Bring a couple of your men along, Vas Kor," he said. "We are short-handed upon the *Thuria,* so quickly did we depart."

The panthan's fingers dropped from the

dagger's hilt. His quick mind had grasped here a chance for succoring Thuvia of Ptarth. He might be chosen as one to accompany the assassins, and once he had learned where the captive lay he could despatch Astok and Vas Kor as well as now. To kill them before he knew where Thuvia was hid was simply to leave her to death at the hands of others; for sooner or later Nutus would learn her whereabouts, and Nutus, Jeddak of Dusar, could not afford to let her live.

Turjun put himself in the path of Vas Kor that he might not be overlooked. The noble aroused the men sleeping upon the deck, but always before him the strange panthan whom he had recruited that same day found means for keeping himself to the fore.

Vas Kor turned to his lieutenant, giving instruction for the bringing of the *Kalksus* to Dusar, and gathering up of the recruits; then he signed to two stalwart warriors who stood close behind the padwar.

"You two accompany us to the *Thuria*," he said, "and put yourselves at the disposal of her dwar."

It was dark upon the deck of the *Kalksus*, so Vas Kor had not a good look at the faces of the two he chose; but that was of no moment, for they were but common warriors to assist with the ordinary duties upon a flier, and to fight if need be.

One of the two was Kar Komak, the bowman. The other was not Carthoris.

The Heliumite was mad with disappointment. He snatched his dagger from his harness; but already Astok had left the deck of the *Kalksus*, and he knew that before he could overtake him, should he despatch Vas Kor, he would be killed by the Dusarian warriors, who now were thick upon the deck. With either one of the two alive Thuvia was in as great danger as though both lived—it must be both!

As Vas Kor descended to the ground Carthoris boldly followed him, nor did any attempt to halt him, thinking, doubtless, that he was one of the party.

After him came Kar Komak and the Dusarian warrior who had been detailed to duty upon the *Thuria*. Carthoris walked close to the left side of the latter. Now they came to the dense shadow under the side of the *Thuria*. It was very dark there, so that they had to grope to find the rope ladder.

Kar Komak preceded the Dusarian. The latter reached upward for the swinging

rounds, and as he did so steel fingers closed upon his windpipe and a steel blade pierced the very center of his heart.

Turjun, the panthan, was the last to clamber over the rail of the *Thuria*, drawing the rope ladder in after him.

A moment later the flier was rising rapidly, headed for the north.

At the rail Kar Komak turned to speak to the warrior who had been detailed to accompany him. His eyes went wide as they rested upon the face of the young man whom he had met beside the granite cliffs that guard mysterious Lothar. How had he come in place of the Dusarian?

A quick sign, and Kar Komak turned once more to find the *Thuria*'s dwar that he might report himself for duty. Behind him followed the panthan.

Carthoris blessed the chance that had caused Vas Kor to choose the bowman of all others, for had it been another Dusarian there would have been questions to answer as to the whereabouts of the warrior who lay so quietly in the field beyond the residence of Hal Vas, Dwar of the Southern Road; and Carthoris had no answer to that question other than his sword point, which alone was scarce adequate to convince the entire crew of the *Thuria*.

The journey to Dusar seemed interminable to the impatient Carthoris, though as a matter of fact it was quickly accomplished. Some time before they reached their destination they met and spoke with another Dusarian war flier. From it they learned that a great battle was soon to be fought southeast of Dusar.

The combined navies of Dusar, Ptarth, and Kaol had been intercepted in their advance toward Helium by the mighty Heliumitic navy—the most formidable upon Barsoom, not alone in numbers and armament, but in the training and courage of its officers and warriors, and the zitidaric proportions of many of its monster battleships.

Not for many a day had there been the promise of such a battle. Four jeddaks were in direct command of their own fleets— Kulan Tith of Kaol, Thuvan Dihn of Ptarth, and Nutus of Dusar upon one side; while upon the other was Tardos Mors, Jeddak of Helium. With the latter was John Carter, Warlord of Mars.

From the far north another force was moving south across the barrier cliffs—the new navy of Talu, Jeddak of Okar, coming

A steel blade pierced the very center of his heart

in response to the call from the warlord. Upon the decks of the sullen ships of war black-bearded yellow men looked over eagerly toward the south. Gorgeous were they in their splendid cloaks of orluk and apt. Fierce, formidable fighters from the hothouse cities of the frozen north.

And from the distant south, from the Sea of Omean and the cliffs of gold, from the temples of the therns and the gardens of Issus, other thousands sailed into the north at the call of the great man they all had learned to respect, and, respecting, love. Pacing the flagship of this mighty fleet, second only to the navy of Helium, was the ebon Xodar, Jeddak of the First Born, his heart beating strong in anticipation of the coming moment when he should hurl his savage crews and the weight of his mighty ships upon the enemies of the warlord.

But would these allies reach the theater of war in time to be of avail to Helium? Or, would Helium need them?

Carthoris, with the other members of the crew of the *Thuria*, heard the gossip and the rumors. None knew of the two fleets, the one from the south and the other from the north, that were coming to support the ships of Helium, and all of Dusar were convinced that nothing now could save the ancient power of Helium from being wiped forever from the upper air of Barsoom.

Carthoris, too, loyal son of Helium that he was, felt that even his beloved navy might not be able to cope successfully with the combined forces of three great powers.

Now the *Thuria* touched the landing stage above the palace of Astok. Hurriedly the prince and Vas Kor disembarked and entered the drop that would carry them to the lower levels of the palace.

Close beside it was another drop that was utilized by common warriors. Carthoris touched Kar Komak upon the arm.

"Come!" he whispered. "You are my only friend among a nation of enemies. Will you stand by me?"

"To the death," replied Kar Komak.

The two approached the drop. A slave operated it.

"Where are your passes?" he asked.

Carthoris fumbled in his pocket pouch as though in search of them, at the same time entering the cage. Kar Komak followed him, closing the door. The slave did not start the cage downward. Every second counted. They must reach the lower level as soon as possible after Astok and Vas Kor if they would know whither the two went.

Carthoris turned suddenly upon the slave, hurling him to the opposite side of the cage.

"Bind and gag him, Kar Komak!" he cried.

Then he grasped the control lever, and as the cage shot downward at sickening speed, the bowman grappled with the slave. Carthoris could not leave the control to assist his companion, for should they touch the lower level at the speed at which they were going, all would be dashed to instant death.

Below him he could now see the top of Astok's cage in the parallel shaft, and he reduced the speed of his to that of the other. The slave commenced to scream.

"Silence him!" cried Carthoris.

A moment later a limp form crumpled to the floor of the cage.

"He is silenced," said Kar Komak.

Carthoris brought the cage to a sudden stop at one of the higher levels of the palace. Opening the door, he grasped the still form of the slave and pushed it out upon the floor. Then he banged the gate and resumed the downward drop.

Once more he sighted the top of the cage that held Astok and Vas Kor. An instant later it had stopped, and as he brought his car to a halt, he saw the two men disappear through one of the exits of the corridor beyond.

Chapter XIV

KULAN TITH'S SACRIFICE

The morning of the second day of her incarceration in the east tower of the palace of Astok, Prince of Dusar, found Thuvia of Ptarth waiting in dull apathy the coming of the assassin.

She had exhausted every possibility of escape, going over and over again the door and the windows, the floor and the walls.

The solid ersite slabs she could not even scratch; the tough Barsoomian glass of the windows would have shattered to nothing less than a heavy sledge in the hands of a strong man. The door and the lock were impregnable. There was no escape. And they had stripped her of her weapons so that she could not even anticipate the hour of her doom, thus robbing them of the satisfaction of witnessing her last moments.

When would they come? Would Astok do the deed with his own hands? She doubted that he had the courage for it. At heart he was a coward—she had known it since first she had heard him brag as, a visitor at the court of her father, he had sought to impress her with his valor.

She could not help but compare him with another. And with whom would an affianced bride compare an unsuccessful suitor? With her betrothed? And did Thuvia of Ptarth now measure Astok of Dusar by the standards of Kulan Tith, Jeddak of Kaol?

She was about to die; her thoughts were her own to do with as she pleased; yet furthest from them was Kulan Tith. Instead the figure of the tall and comely Heliumite filled her mind, crowding therefrom all other images.

She dreamed of his noble face, the quiet dignity of his bearing, the smile that lit his eyes as he conversed with his friends, and the smile that touched his lips as he fought with his enemies—the fighting smile of his Virginian sire.

And Thuvia of Ptarth, true daughter of Barsoom, found her breath quickening and heart leaping to the memory of this other smile—the smile that she would never see again. With a little half-sob the girl sank to the pile of silks and furs that were tumbled in confusion beneath the east window, burying her face in her arms.

In the corridor outside her prison-room two men had paused in heated argument.

"I tell you again, Astok," one was saying, "that I shall not do this thing unless you be present in the room."

There was little of the respect due royalty in the tone of the speaker's voice. The other, noting it, flushed.

"Do not impose too far upon my friendship for you, Vas Kor," he snapped. "There is a limit to my patience."

"There is no question of royal prerogative here," returned Vas Kor. "You ask me to become an assassin in your stead, and against your jeddak's strict injunctions. You are in no position, Astok, to dictate to me; but rather should you be glad to accede to my reasonable request that you be present, thus sharing the guilt with me. Why should I bear it all?"

The younger man scowled, but he advanced toward the locked door, and as it swung in upon its hinges, he entered the room beyond at the side of Vas Kor.

Across the chamber the girl, hearing them enter, rose to her feet and faced them. Under the soft copper of her skin she blanched just a trifle; but her eyes were brave and level, and the haughty tilt of her firm little chin was eloquent of loathing and contempt.

"You still prefer death?" asked Astok.

"To you, yes," replied the girl coldly.

The Prince of Dusar turned to Vas Kor and nodded. The noble drew his short-sword and crossed the room toward Thuvia.

"Kneel!" he commanded.

"I prefer to die standing," she replied.

"As you will," said Vas Kor, feeling the point of his blade with his left thumb. "In the name of Nutus, Jeddak of Dusar!" he cried, and ran quickly toward her.

"In the name of Carthoris, Prince of Helium!" came in low tones from the doorway.

Vas Kor turned to see the panthan he had recruited at his son's house leaping across the floor toward him. The fellow brushed past Astok with an: "After him, you—calot!"

Vas Kor wheeled to meet the charging man.

"What means this treason?" he cried.

Astok, with bared sword, leaped to Vas Kor's assistance. The panthan's sword clashed against that of the noble, and in the first encounter Vas Kor knew that he faced a master swordsman in his antagonist.

Before he half realized the stranger's purpose he found the man between himself and Thuvia of Ptarth, at bay facing the two swords of the Dusarians. But he fought not like a man at bay. Ever was he the aggressor, and though always he kept his flashing blade between the girl and her enemies, yet he managed to force them hither and thither about the room, calling to the girl to follow close behind him.

Until it was too late neither Vas Kor nor Astok dreamed of that which lay in the panthan's mind; but at last as the fellow stood with his back toward the door both understood—they were penned in their own prison, and now the intruder could slay them at his will, for Thuvia of Ptarth was bolting the door at the man's direc-

"I prefer to die standing," she replied

tion, first taking the key from the opposite side, where Astok had left it when they had entered.

Astok, as was his way, finding that the enemy did not fall immediately before their swords, was leaving the brunt of the fighting to Vas Kor, and now as his eyes appraised the panthan carefully they presently went wider and wider, for slowly he had come to recognize the features of the Prince of Helium.

The Heliumite was pressing close upon Vas Kor. The noble was bleeding from a dozen wounds. Astok saw that he could not for long withstand the cunning craft of that terrible sword hand.

"Courage, Vas Kor!" he whispered in the other's ear. "I have a plan. Hold him but a moment longer and all will be well," but the balance of the sentence, "with Astok, Prince of Dusar," he did not voice aloud.

Vas Kor, dreaming no treachery, nodded his head, and for a moment succeeded in holding Carthoris at bay. Then the Heliumite and the girl saw the Dusarian prince run swiftly to the opposite side of the chamber, touch something in the wall that sent a great panel swinging inward, and disappear into the black vault beyond.

It was done so quickly that by no possibility could they have intercepted him. Carthoris, fearful lest Vas Kor might similarly elude him, or Astok return immediately with reinforcements, sprang viciously in upon his antagonist, and a moment later the headless body of the Dusarian noble rolled upon the ersite floor.

"Come!" cried Carthoris. "There is no time to be lost. Astok will be back in a moment with enough warriors to overpower me."

But Astok had no such plan in mind, for such a move would have meant the spreading of the fact among the palace gossips that the Ptarthian princess was a prisoner in the east tower. Quickly would the word have come to his father, and no amount of falsifying could have explained away the facts that the jeddak's investigation would have brought to light.

Instead Astok was racing madly through a long corridor to reach the door of the tower-room before Carthoris and Thuvia left the apartment. He had seen the girl remove the key and place it in her pocket-pouch, and he knew that a dagger point driven into the keyhole from the op-

posite side would imprison them in the secret chamber till eight dead worlds circled a cold, dead sun.

As fast as he could run Astok entered the main corridor that led to the tower chamber. Would he reach the door in time? What if the Heliumite should have already emerged and he should run upon him in the passageway? Astok felt a cold chill run up his spine. He had no stomach to face that uncanny blade.

He was almost at the door. Around the next turn of the corridor it stood. No, they had not left the apartment. Evidently Vas Kor was still holding the Heliumite!

Astok could scarce repress a grin at the clever manner in which he had outwitted the noble and disposed of him at the same time. And then he rounded the turn and came face to face with an auburn-haired, white giant.

The fellow did not wait to ask the reason for his coming; instead he leaped upon him with a long-sword, so that Astok had to parry a dozen vicious cuts before he could disengage himself and flee back down the runway.

A moment later Carthoris and Thuvia entered the corridor from the secret chamber.

"Well, Kar Komak?" asked the Heliumite.

"It is fortunate that you left me here, red man," said the bowman. "I but just now intercepted one who seemed overanxious to reach this door—it was he whom they call Astok, Prince of Dusar."

Carthoris smiled.

"Where is he now?" he asked.

"He escaped my blade, and ran down this corridor," replied Kar Komak.

"We must lose no time then!" exclaimed Carthoris. "He will have the guard upon us yet!"

Together the three hastened along the winding passages through which Carthoris and Kar Komak had tracked the Dusarians by the marks of the latter's sandals in the thin dust that overspread the floors of these seldom-used passageways.

They had come to the chamber at the entrances to the lifts before they met with opposition. Here they found a handful of guardsmen, and an officer, who, seeing that they were strangers, questioned their presence in the palace of Astok.

Once more Carthoris and Kar Komak

had recourse to their blades, and before they had won their way to one of the lifts the noise of the conflict must have aroused the entire palace, for they heard men shouting, and as they passed the many levels on their quick passage to the landing stage they saw armed men running hither and thither in search of the cause of the commotion.

Beside the stage lay the *Thuria*, with three warriors on guard. Again the Heliumite and the Lotharian fought shoulder to shoulder, but the battle was soon over, for the Prince of Helium alone would have been a match for any three that Dusar could produce.

Scarce had the *Thuria* risen from the ways ere a hundred or more fighting men leaped to view upon the landing stage. At their head was Astok of Dusar, and as he saw the two he had thought so safely in his power slipping from his grasp, he danced with rage and chagrin, shaking his fists and hurling abuse and vile insults at them.

With her bow inclined upward at a dizzy angle, the *Thuria* shot meteor-like into the sky. From a dozen points swift patrol boats darted after her, for the scene upon the landing stage above the palace of the Prince of Dusar had not gone unnoticed.

A dozen times shots grazed the *Thuria's* side, and as Carthoris could not leave the control levers, Thuvia of Ptarth turned the muzzles of the craft's rapid-fire guns upon the enemy as she clung to the steep and slippery surface of the deck.

It was a noble race and a noble fight. One against a score now, for other Dusarian craft had joined in the pursuit; but Astok, Prince of Dusar, had built well when he built the *Thuria*. None in the navy of his sire possessed a swifter flier; no other craft so well armored or so well armed.

One by one the pursuers were distanced, and as the last of them fell out of range behind, Carthoris dropped the *Thuria's* nose to a horizontal plane, as with lever drawn to the last notch, she tore through the thin air of dying Mars toward the east and Ptarth.

Thirteen and a half thousand haads away lay Ptarth—a stiff thirty-hour journey for the swiftest of fliers, and between Dusar and Ptarth might lie half the navy of Dusar, for in this direction was the reported seat of the great naval battle that even now might be in progress.

Could Carthoris have known precisely where the great fleets of the contending red nations lay, he would have hastened to them without delay, for in the return of Thuvia to her sire lay the greatest hope of peace.

Half the distance they covered without sighting a single warship, and then Kar Komak called Carthoris' attention to a distant craft that rested upon the ochre vegetation of the great dead sea-bottom, above which the *Thuria* was speeding.

About the vessel many figures could be seen swarming. With the aid of powerful glasses, the Heliumite saw that they were green warriors, and that they were repeatedly charging down upon the crew of the stranded airship. The nationality of the latter he could not make out at so great a distance.

It was not necessary to change the course of the *Thuria* to permit of passing directly above the scene of battle, but Carthoris dropped his craft a few hundred feet that he might have a better and closer view.

If the ship was of a friendly power, he could do no less than stop and direct his guns upon her enemies, though with the precious freight he carried he scarcely felt justified in landing, for he could offer but two swords in reinforcement—scarce enough to warrant jeopardizing the safety of the Princess of Ptarth.

As they came close above the stricken ship, they could see that it would be but a question of minutes before the green horde would swarm across the armored bulwarks to glut the ferocity of their bloodlust upon the defenders.

"It would be futile to descend," said Carthoris to Thuvia. "The craft may even be of Dusar—she shows no insignia. All that we may do is fire upon the hordesmen," and as he spoke he stepped to one of the guns and deflected its muzzle toward the green warriors at the ship's side.

At the first shot from the *Thuria* those upon the vessel below evidently discovered her for the first time. Immediately a device fluttered from the bow of the warship on the ground. Thuvia of Ptarth caught her breath quickly, glancing at Carthoris.

The device was that of Kulan Tith, Jeddak of Kaol—the man to whom the Princess of Ptarth was betrothed!

How easy for the Heliumite to pass on,

leaving his rival to the fate that could not for long be averted! No man could accuse him of cowardice or treachery, for Kulan Tith was in arms against Helium, and, further, upon the *Thuria* were not enough swords to delay even temporarily the outcome that already was a foregone conclusion in the minds of the watchers.

What would Carthoris, Prince of Helium, son of the illustrious warlord, do?

Scarce had the device broken to the faint breeze ere the bow of the *Thuria* dropped at a sharp angle toward the ground.

"Can you navigate her?" asked Carthoris of Thuvia.

The girl nodded.

"I am going to try to take the survivors aboard," he continued. "It will need both Kar Komak and myself to man the guns while the Kaolians take to the boarding tackle. Keep her bow depressed against the rifle fire. She can bear it better in her forward armor, and at the same time the propellers will be protected."

He hurried to the cabin as Thuvia took the control. A moment later the boarding tackle dropped from the keel of the *Thuria*, and from a dozen points along either side stout, knotted leathern lines trailed downward. At the same time a signal broke from her bow:

"Prepare to board us."

A shout arose from the deck of the Kaolian warship. Carthoris, who by this time had returned from the cabin, smiled sadly. He was about to snatch from the jaws of death the man who stood between himself and the woman he loved.

"Take the port bow gun, Kar Komak," he called to the bowman, and himself stepped to the gun upon the starboard bow.

They could now feel the sharp shock of the explosions of the green warriors' projectiles against the armored sides of the staunch *Thuria*.

It was a forlorn hope at best. At any moment the repulsive ray tanks might be pierced. The men upon the Kaolian ship were battling with renewed hope. In the bow stood Kulan Tith, a brave figure fighting beside his brave warriors, beating back the ferocious green men.

The *Thuria* came low above the other craft. The Kaolians were forming under their officers in readiness to board, and then a sudden fierce fusillade from the rifles of the green warriors vomited their hail of death and destruction into the side of the brave flier.

Like a wounded bird she dived suddenly Marsward, careening drunkenly. Thuvia turned the bow upward in an effort to avert the imminent tragedy, but she succeeded only in lessening the shock of the flier's impact as she struck the ground beside the Kaolian ship.

When the green men saw only two warriors and a woman upon the deck of the *Thuria*, a savage shout of triumph arose from their ranks, while an answering groan broke from the lips of the Kaolians.

The former now turned their attention upon the new arrival, for they saw her defenders could soon be overcome and that from her deck they could command the deck of the better-manned ship.

As they charged a shout of warning came from Kulan Tith, upon the bridge of his own ship, and with it an appreciation of the valor of the act that had put the smaller vessel in these sore straits.

"Who is it," he cried, "that offers his life in the service of Kulan Tith? Never was wrought a nobler deed of self-sacrifice upon Barsoom!"

The green horde was scrambling over the *Thuria's* side as there broke from the bow the device of Carthoris, Prince of Helium, in reply to the query of the jeddak of Kaol. None upon the smaller flier had opportunity to note the effect of this announcement upon the Kaolians, for their attention was claimed solely now by that which was transpiring upon their own deck.

Kar Komak stood behind the gun he had been operating, staring with wide eyes at the onrushing hideous green warriors. Carthoris, seeing him thus, felt a pang of regret that, after all, this man that he had thought so valorous should prove, in the hour of need, as spineless as Jav or Tario.

"Kar Komak—man!" he shouted. "Grip yourself! Remember the days of the glory of the seafarers of Lothar. Fight! Fight, man! Fight as never man fought before. All that remains to us is to die fighting."

Kar Komak turned toward the Heliumite, a grim smile upon his lips.

"Why should we fight," he asked, "against such fearful odds? There is another way—a better way. Look!" He pointed toward the companionway that led below deck.

The green men, a handful of them, had already reached the *Thuria's* deck, as

Carthoris glanced in the direction the Lotharian had indicated. The sight that met his eyes set his heart to thumping in joy and relief—Thuvia of Ptarth might yet be saved! For from far below there poured a stream of giant bowmen, grim and terrible. Not the bowmen of Tario or Jav, but the bowmen of an odwar of bowmen—savage fighting men, eager for the fray.

The green warriors paused in momentary surprise and consternation, but only for a moment. Then with horrid war-cries they leaped forward to meet these strange, new foemen.

A volley of arrows stopped them in their tracks. In a moment the only green warriors upon the deck of the *Thuria* were dead warriors, and the bowmen of Kar Komak were leaping over the vessel's sides to charge the hordesmen upon the ground.

Utan after utan tumbled from the bowels of the *Thuria* to launch themselves upon the unfortunate green men. Kulan Tith and his Kaolians stood wide-eyed and speechless with amazement as they saw thousands of these strange, fierce warriors emerge from the companionway of the small craft that could not comfortably have accommodated more than fifty.

At last the green men could withstand the onslaught of overwhelming numbers no longer. Slowly, at first, they fell back across the ochre plain. The bowmen pursued them. Kar Komak, standing upon the deck of the *Thuria*, trembled with excitement.

At the top of his lungs he voiced the savage warcry of his forgotten day. He roared encouragement and commands at his battling utans, and then, as they charged further and further from the *Thuria*, he could no longer withstand the lure of battle.

Leaping over the ship's side to the ground, he joined the last of his bowmen as they raced off over the dead sea-bottom in pursuit of the fleeing green horde.

Beyond a low promontory of what once had been an island the green men were disappearing toward the west. Close upon their heels raced the fleet bowmen of a bygone day, and forging steadily ahead among them Carthoris and Thuvia could see the mighty figure of Kar Komak, brandishing aloft the Torquasian short-sword with which he was armed, as he urged his creatures after the retreating enemy.

As the last of them disappeared behind the promontory, Carthoris turned toward Thuvia of Ptarth.

"They have taught me a lesson, these vanishing bowmen of Lothar," he said. "When they have served their purpose they remain not to embarrass their masters by their presence. Kulan Tith and his warriors are here to protect you. My acts have constituted the proof of my honesty of purpose. Good-by," and he knelt at her feet, raising a bit of her harness to his lips.

The girl reached out a hand and laid it upon the thick black hair of the head bent before her. Softly she asked:

"Where are you going, Carthoris?"

"With Kar Komak, the bowman," he replied. "There will be fighting and forgetfulness."

The girl put her hands before her eyes, as though to shut out some mighty temptation from her sight.

"May my ancestors have mercy upon me," she cried, "if I say the thing I have no right to say; but I cannot see you cast your life away, Carthoris, Prince of Helium! Stay, my chieftain. Stay—I love you!"

A cough behind them brought both about, and there they saw standing, not two paces from them, Kulan Tith, Jeddak of Kaol.

For a long moment none spoke. Then Kulan Tith cleared his throat.

"I could not help hearing all that passed," he said. "I am no fool, to be blind to the love that lies between you. Nor am I blind to the lofty honor that has caused you, Carthoris, to risk your life and hers to save mine, though you thought that that very act would rob you of the chance to keep her for your own.

"Nor can I fail to appreciate the virtue that has kept your lips sealed against words of love for this Heliumite, Thuvia, for I know that I have but just heard the first declaration of your passion for him. I do not condemn you. Rather should I have condemned you had you entered a loveless marriage with me.

"Take back your liberty, Thuvia of Ptarth," he cried, "and bestow it where your heart already lies enchained, and when the golden collars are clasped about your necks you will see that Kulan Tith's is the first sword to be raised in declaration of eternal friendship for the new Princess of Helium and her royal mate!"

"Stay, my chieftain. Stay—I love you!"

A GLOSSARY OF NAMES AND TERMS USED
IN THE MARTIAN BOOKS

Aaanthor.   A dead city of ancient Mars.

Aisle of Hope.   An aisle leading to the courtroom in Helium.

Apt.   An Arctic monster. A huge, white-furred creature with six limbs, four of which, short and heavy, carry it over the snow and ice; the other two, which grow forward from its shoulders on either side of its long, powerful neck, terminate in white, hairless hands with which it seizes and holds its prey. Its head and mouth are similar in appearance to those of a hippopotamus except that from the sides of the lower jawbone two mighty horns curve slightly downward toward the front. Its two huge eyes extend in two vast oval patches from the center of the top of the cranium down either side of the head to below the roots of the horns, so that these weapons really grow out from the lower part of the eyes, which are composed of several thousand ocelli each. Each ocellus is furnished with its own lid, and the apt can, at will, close as many of the facets of his huge eyes as he chooses. (See THE WARLORD OF MARS.)

Astok.   Prince of Dusar.

Avenue of Ancestors.   A street in Helium.

Banth.   Barsoomian lion. A fierce beast of prey that roams the low hills surrounding the dead seas of ancient Mars. It is almost hairless, having only a great, bristly mane about its thick neck. Its long, lithe body is supported by ten powerful legs, its enormous jaws are equipped with several rows of long needlelike fangs, and its mouth reaches to a point far back of its tiny ears. It has enormous protruding eyes of green.   (See THE GODS OF MARS.)

Bar Comas.   Jeddak of Warhoon.   (See A PRINCESS OF MARS.)

Barsoom.   Mars.

Black pirates of Barsoom.   Men six feet and over in height. Have clear-cut and handsome features; their eyes are well set and large, though a slight narrowness lends them a crafty appearance. The iris is extremely black while the eyeball itself is quite white and clear. Their skin has the appearance of polished ebony.   (See THE GODS OF MARS.)

Calot.   A dog. About the size of a Shetland pony and has ten short legs. The head bears a slight resemblance to that of a frog, except that the jaws are equipped with three rows of long, sharp tusks.   (See A PRINCESS OF MARS.)

Carter, John.   Warlord of Mars.

Carthoris of Helium.   Son of John Carter and Dejah Thoris.

Dak Kova.   Jed among the Warhoons (later jeddak).

Darseen.   Chameleon-like reptile.

Dator.   Chief or prince among the First Born.

Dejah Thoris.   Princess of Helium.

Djor Kantos.   Son of Kantos Kan; padwar of the Fifth Utan.

Dor.   Valley of Heaven.

Dotar Sojat.   John Carter's Martian name, from the surnames of the first two warrior chieftains he killed.

Dusar. A Martian kingdom.

Dwar. Captain.

Ersite. A kind of stone.

Father of Therns. High Priest of religious cult.

First Born. Black race; black pirates.

Gate of Jeddaks. A gate in Helium.

Gozava. Tars Tarkas' dead wife.

Gur Tus. Dwar of the Tenth Utan.

Haad. Martian mile.

Hal Vas. Son of Vas Kor, the Dusarian noble.

Hastor. A city of Helium.

Hekkador. Title of Father of Therns.

Helium. The empire of the grandfather of Dejah Thoris.

Holy Therns. A Martian religious cult.

Hortan Gur. Jeddak of Torquas.

Hor Vastus. Padwar in the navy of Helium.

Horz. Deserted city; Barsoomian Greenwich.

Illall. A city of Okar.

Iss. River of Death.   (See A PRINCESS OF MARS.)

Issus. Goddess of Death, whose abode is upon the banks of the Lost Sea of Korus.   (See THE GODS OF MARS.)

Jav. A Lotharian.

Jed. King.

Jeddak. Emperor.

Kab Kadja. Jeddak of the Warhoons of the south.

Kadabra. Capital of Okar.

Kadar. Guard.

Kalksus. Cruiser-transport under Vas Kor.

Kantos Kan. Padwar in the Helium navy.

Kaol. A Martian kingdom in the eastern hemisphere.

Kaor. Greeting.

Karad. Martian degree.

Kar Komak. Odwar of Lotharian bowmen.

Komal. The Lotharian god; a huge banth.

Korad. A dead city of ancient Mars.   (See A PRINCESS OF MARS.)

Korus. The Lost Sea of Dor.

Kulan Tith. Jeddak of Kaol.   (See THE WARLORD OF MARS.)

Lakor. A thern.

Larok. A Dusarian warrior; artificer.

Lorquas Ptomel. Jed among the Tharks.   (See A PRINCESS OF MARS.)

Lothar. The forgotten city.

Marentina. A principality of Okar.

Matai Shang. Father of Therns. (See THE GODS OF MARS.)

Mors Kajak. A jed of lesser Helium.

Notan. Royal psychologist of Zodanga.

Nutus. Jeddak of Dusar.

Od. Martian foot.

Odwar. A commander, or general.

Okar. Land of the yellow men.

Old Ben (or Uncle Ben). The writer's body-servant (colored).

Omad. Man with one name.

Omean. The buried sea.

Orluk. A black and yellow striped Artic monster.

Otz Mountains. Surrounding the Valley Dor and the Lost Sea of Korus.

Padwar. Lieutenant.

Panthan. A soldier of fortune.

Parthak. The Zodangan who brought food to John Carter in the pits of Zat Arrras. (See THE GODS OF MARS.)

Pedestal of Truth. Within the courtroom of Helium.

Phaidor. Daughter of Matai Shang. (See THE GODS OF MARS.)

Pimalia. Gorgeous flowering plant.

Plant men of Barsoom. A race inhabiting the Valley Dor. They are ten or twelve feet in height when standing erect; their arms are very short and fashioned after the manner of an elephant's trunk, being sinuous; the body is hairless and ghoulish blue except for a broad band of white which encircles the protruding, single eye, the pupil, iris, and ball of which are dead white. The nose is a ragged, inflamed, circular hole in the center of the blank face, resembling a fresh bullet wound which has not yet commenced to bleed. There is no mouth in the head. With the exception of the face, the head is covered by a tangled mass of jet-black hair some eight or ten inches in length. Each hair is about the thickness of a large angleworm. The body, legs, and feet are of human shape but of monstrous proportions, the feet being fully three feet long and very flat and broad. The method of feeding consists in running their odd hands over the surface of the turf, cropping off the tender vegetation with razorlike talons and sucking it up from two mouths, which lie one in the palm of each hand. They are equipped with a massive tail about six feet long, quite round where it joins the body, but tapering to a flat, thin blade toward the end, which trails at right angles to the ground. (See THE GODS OF MARS.)

Prince Soran. Overlord of the navy of Ptarth.

Ptarth. A Martian kingdom.

Ptor. Family name of three Zodangan brothers.

Sab Than. Prince of Zodanga. (See A PRINCESS OF MARS.)

Safad. A Martian inch.

Sak. Jump.

Salensus Oll.   Jeddak of Okar.   (See THE WARLORD OF MARS.)

Saran Tal.   Carthoris' major-domo.

Sarkoja.   A green Martian woman.   (See A PRINCESS OF MARS.)

Sator Throg.   A Holy Thern of the Tenth Cycle.

Shador.   Island in Omean used as a prison.

Silian.   Slimy reptiles inhabiting the Sea of Korus.

Sith.   Hornet-like monster. Bald-faced and about the size of a Hereford bull. Has frightful jaws in front and mighty poisoned sting behind. The eyes, of myriad facets, cover three-fourths of the head, permitting the creature to see in all directions at one and the same time.   (See THE WARLORD OF MARS.)

Skeel.   A Martian hardwood.

Sola.   A young green Martian woman.

Solan.   An official of the palace.

Sompus.   A kind of tree.

Sorak.   A little pet animal among the red Martian women, about the size of a cat.

Sorapus.   A Martian hardwood.

Sorav.   An officer of Salensus Oll.

Tal.   A Martian second.

Tal Hajus.   Jeddak of Thark.

Talu.   Rebel Prince of Marentina.

Tan Gama.   Warhoon warrior.

Tardos Mors.   Grandfather of Dejah Thoris and jeddak of Helium.

Tario.   Jeddak of Lothar.

Tars Tarkas.   A green man, chieftain of the Tharks.

Temple of Reward.   In Helium.

Tenth Cycle.   A sphere, or plane of eminence, among the Holy Therns.

Thabis.   Issus' chief.

Than Kosis.   Jeddak of Zodanga.   (See A PRINCESS OF MARS.)

Thar Ban.   Jed among the green men of Tarquas.

Thark.   City and name of a green Martian horde.

Thoat.   A green Martian horse. Ten feet high at the shoulder, with four legs on either side; a broad, flat tail, larger at the tip than at the root which it holds straight out behind while running; a mouth splitting its head from snout to the long, massive neck. It is entirely devoid of hair and is of a dark slate color and exceedingly smooth and glossy. It has a white belly and the legs are shaded from slate at the shoulders and hips to a vivid yellow at the feet. The feet are heavily padded and nailless.   (See A PRINCESS OF MARS.)

Thorian.   Chief of the lesser Therns.

Throne of Righteousness.   In the courtroom of Helium.

Throxus.   Mightiest of the five oceans.

Thurds.   A green horde inimical to Torquas.

Thuria.   The nearer moon. (Also airship under Astok.)

Thurid.   A black dator.

Thuvan Dihn.   Jeddak of Ptarth.

Thuvia.   Princess of Ptarth.

Torith.   Officer of the guards at submarine pool.

Torkar Bar.   Kaolian noble; dwar of the Kaolian Road.

Torquas.   A green horde.

Turjun.   Carthoris' alias.

Utan.   A company of one hundred men (military).

Vas Kor.   A Dusarian noble.

Warhoon.   A community of green men; enemy of Thark.

Woola.   A Barsoomian calot.

Xat.   A Martian minute.

Xavarian.   A Helium warship.

Xodar.   Dator among the First Born.

Yersted.   Commander of the submarine.

Zad.   Tharkian warrior.

Zat Arrras.   Jed of Zodanga.

Zithad.   Dator of the guards of Issus.   (See THE GODS OF MARS.)

Zitidars.   Mastodonian draught animals.

Zodanga.   Martian city of red men at war with Helium.

Zode.   A Martian hour.

TANAR OF PELLUCIDAR

PROLOGUE

Jason Gridley is a radio bug. Had he not been, this story never would have been written. Jason is twenty-three and scandalously good looking — too good looking to be a bug of any sort. As a matter of fact, he does not seem buggish at all — just a normal, sane, young American, who knows a great deal about many things in addition to radio; aeronautics, for example, and golf, and tennis, and polo.

But this is not Jason's story — he is only an incident — an important incident in my life that made this story possible, and so, with a few more words of explanation, we shall leave Jason to his tubes and waves and amplifiers, concerning which he knows everything and I nothing.

Jason is an orphan with an income, and after he graduated from Stanford, he came down and bought a couple of acres at Tarzana, and that is how and when I met him.

While he was building he made my office his headquarters and was often in my study and afterward I returned the compliment by visiting him in his new "lab," as he calls it — a quite large room at the rear of his home, a quiet, restful room in a quiet, restful house of the Spanish-American farm type — or we rode together in the Santa Monica Mountains in the cool air of early morning.

Jason is experimenting with some new principle of radio concerning which the less I say the better it will be for my reputation, since I know nothing whatsoever about it and am likely never to.

Perhaps I am too old, perhaps I am too dumb, perhaps I am just not interested — I prefer to ascribe my abysmal and persistent ignorance of all things pertaining to radio to the last state; that of disinterestedness; it salves my pride.

I do know this, however, because Jason has told me, that the idea he is playing with suggests an entirely new and unsuspected — well, let us call it wave.

He says the idea was suggested to him by the vagaries of static and in groping around in search of some device to eliminate this he discovered in the ether an undercurrent that operated according to no previously known scientific laws.

At his Tarzana home he has erected a station and a few miles away, at the back of my ranch, another. Between these stations we talk to one another through some strange, ethereal medium that seems to pass through all other waves and all other stations, unsuspected and entirely harmless — so harmless is it that it has not the slightest effect upon Jason's regular set, standing in the same room and receiving over the same aerial.

But this, which is not very interesting to any one except Jason, is all by the way of getting to the beginning of the amazing narrative of the adventures of Tanar of Pellucidar.

Jason and I were sitting in his "lab" one evening discussing, as we often did, innumerable subjects, from "cabbages to kings," and coming back, as Jason usually did, to the Gridley wave, which is what we have named it.

Much of the time Jason kept on his ear phones, than which there is no greater discourager of conversation. But this does not irk me as much as most of the conversations one has to listen to through life. I like long silences and my own thoughts.

Presently, Jason removed the headpiece. "It is enough to drive a fellow to drink!" he exclaimed.

"What?" I asked.

"I am getting that same stuff again," he said. "I can hear voices, very faintly, but, unmistakably, human voices. They are speaking a language unknown to man. It is maddening."

"Mars, perhaps," I suggested, "or Venus."

He knitted his brows and then suddenly smiled one of his quick smiles. "Or Pellucidar."

I shrugged.

"Do you know, Admiral," he said (he calls me Admiral because of a yachting cap I wear at the beach), "that when I was a kid I used to believe every word of those crazy stories of yours about Mars and Pellucidar. The inner world at the earth's core was as real to me as the High Sierras, the San Joaquin Valley, or the Golden Gate, and I felt that I knew the twin cities of Helium better than I did Los Angeles.

"I saw nothing improbable at all in that trip of David Innes and old man Perry through the earth's crust to Pellucidar. Yes, sir, that was all gospel to me when I was a kid."

"And now you are twenty-three and know that it can't be true," I said, with a smile.

"You are not trying to tell me it is true, are you?" he demanded, laughing.

"I never have told any one that it is true," I replied; "I let people think what they think, but I reserve the right to do likewise."

"Why, you know perfectly well that it would be impossible for that iron mole of Perry's to have penetrated five hundred miles of the earth's crust, you know there is no inner world peopled by strange reptiles and men of the stone age, you know there is no Emperor of Pellucidar." Jason was becoming excited, but his sense of humor came to our rescue and he laughed.

"I like to believe that there is a Dian the Beautiful," I said.

"Yes," he agreed, "but I am sorry you killed off Hooja the Sly One. He was a corking villain."

"There are always plenty of villains," I reminded him.

"They help the girls to keep their 'figgers' and their school girl complexions," he said.

"How?" I asked.

"The exercise they get from being pursued."

"You are making fun of me," I reproached him, "but remember, please, that I am but a simple historian. If damsels flee and villains pursue I must truthfully record the fact."

"Baloney!" he exclaimed in the pure university English of America.

Jason replaced his headpiece and I returned to the perusal of the narrative of an ancient liar, who should have made a fortune out of the credulity of book readers, but seems not to have. Thus we sat for some time.

Presently Jason removed his ear phones and turned toward me. "I was getting music," he said; "strange, weird music, and then suddenly there came loud shouts and it seemed that I could hear blows struck and there were screams and the sound of shots."

"Perry, you know, was experimenting with gunpowder down there below, in Pellucidar," I reminded Jason, with a grin; but he was inclined to be serious and did not respond in kind.

"You know, of course," he said, "that there really has been a theory of an inner world for many years."

"Yes," I replied, "I have read works expounding and defending such a theory."

"It supposes polar openings leading into the interior of the earth," said Jason.

"And it is substantiated by many seemingly irrefutable scientific facts," I reminded him — "open polar sea, warmer water farthest north, tropical vegetation floating southward from the polar regions, the northern lights, the magnetic pole, the persistent stories of the Eskimos that they are descended from a race that came from a warm country far to the north."

"I'd like to make a try for one of the polar openings," mused Jason as he replaced the ear phones.

Again there was a long silence, broken at last by a sharp exclamation from Jason. He pushed an extra headpiece toward me.

"Listen!" he exclaimed.

As I adjusted the ear phones I heard that which we had never before received on the Gridley wave — code! No wonder that Jason Gridley was excited, since there was no station on earth, other than his own, attuned to the Gridley wave.

Code! What could it mean? I was torn by conflicting emotions — to tear off the ear phones and discuss this amazing thing with Jason, and to keep them on and listen.

I am not what one might call an expert in the intricacies of code, but I had no difficulty in understanding the simple signal of two letters, repeated in groups of three, with a pause after each group: "D.I., D.I., D.I.," pause; "D.I., D.I., D.I.," pause.

I glanced up at Jason. His eyes, filled with puzzled questioning, met mine, as though to ask, what does it mean?

The signals ceased and Jason touched his own key, sending his initials, "J.G., J.G., J.G.," in the same grouping that we had received the D.I. signal. Almost instantly he was interrupted — you could feel the excitement of the sender.

"D.I., D.I., D.I., Pellucidar," rattled against our ear-drums like machine gun fire. Jason and I sat in dumb amazement, staring at one another.

"It is a hoax!" I exclaimed, and Jason, reading my lips, shook his head.

"How can it be a hoax?" he asked. "There is no other station on earth equipped to send or to receive over the

Gridley wave, so there can be no means of perpetrating such a hoax."

Our mysterious station was on the air again: "If you get this, repeat my signal," and he signed off with "D.I., D.I., D.I."

"That would be David Innes," mused Jason.

"Emperor of Pellucidar," I added.

Jason sent the message, "D.I., D.I., D.I.," followed by, "what station is this," and "who is sending?"

"This is the Imperial Observatory at Greenwich, Pellucidar; Abner Perry sending. Who are you?"

"This is the private experimental laboratory of Jason Gridley, Tarzana, California; Gridley sending," replied Jason.

"I want to get into communication with Edgar Rice Burroughs; do you know him?"

"He is sitting here, listening in with me," replied Jason.

"Thank God, if that is true, but how am I to know that it is true?" demanded Perry.

I hastily scribbled a note to Jason: "Ask him if he recalls the fire in his first gunpowder factory and that the building would have been destroyed had they not extinguished the fire by shoveling his gunpowder onto it?"

Jason grinned as he read the note, and sent it.

"It was unkind of David to tell of that," came back the reply, "but now I know that Burroughs is indeed there, as only he could have known of that incident. I have a long message for him. Are you ready?"

"Yes," replied Jason.

"Then stand by."

And this is the message that Abner Perry sent from the bowels of the earth; from The Empire of Pellucidar.

INTRODUCTION

It must be some fifteen years since David Innes and I broke through the inner surface of the earth's crust and emerged into savage Pellucidar, but when a stationary sun hangs eternally at high noon and there is no restless moon and there are no stars, time is measureless and so it may have been a hundred years ago or one. Who knows?

Of course, since David returned to earth and brought back many of the blessings of civilization we have had the means to measure time, but the people did not like it. They found that it put restrictions and limitations upon them that they never had felt before and they came to hate it and ignore it until David, in the goodness of his heart, issued an edict abolishing time in Pellucidar.

It seemed a backward step to me, but I am resigned now, and, perhaps, happier, for when all is said and done, time is a hard master, as you of the outer world, who are slaves of the sun, would be forced to admit were you to give the matter thought.

Here, in Pellucidar, we eat when we are hungry, we sleep when we are tired, we set out upon journeys when we leave and we arrive at our destinations when we get there; nor are we old because the earth has circled the sun seventy times since our birth, for we do not know that this has occurred.

Perhaps I have been here fifteen years, but what matter. When I came I knew nothing of radio — my researches and studies were along other lines — but when David came back from the outer world he brought many scientific works and from these I learned all that I know of radio, which has been enough to permit me to erect two successful stations; one here at Greenwich and one at the capital of The Empire of Pellucidar.

But, try as I would, I never could get anything from the outer world, and after a while I gave up trying, convinced that the earth's crust was impervious to radio.

In fact we used our stations but seldom, for, after all, Pellucidar is only commencing to emerge from the stone age, and in the economy of the stone age there seems to be no crying need for radio.

But sometimes I played with it and upon several occasions I thought that I heard voices and other sounds that were not of Pellucidar. They were too faint to be more than vague suggestions of intriguing possibilities, but yet they did suggest something most alluring, and so I set myself to making changes and adjustments until this wonderful thing that has happened but now was made possible.

And my delight in being able to talk with you is second only to my relief in being able to appeal to you for help. David is in trouble. He is a captive in the north, or what he and I call north, for there are no points of compass known to Pellucidarians.

I have heard from him, however. He has sent me a message and in it he suggests a startling theory that would make aid from the outer crust possible if — but first let me tell you the whole story; the story of the disaster that befell David Innes and what led up to it and then you will be in a better position to judge as to the practicability of sending succor to David from the outer crust.

The whole thing dates from our victories over the Mahars, the once dominant race of Pellucidar. When, with our well organized armies, equipped with firearms and other weapons unknown to the Mahars or their gorilla-like mercenaries, the Sagoths, we defeated the reptilian monsters and drove their slimy hordes from the confines of The Empire, the human race of the inner world for the first time in its history took its rightful place among the orders of creation.

But our victories laid the foundation for the disaster that has overwhelmed us.

For a while there was no Mahar within the boundaries of any of the kingdoms that constitute The Empire of Pellucidar; but presently we had word of them here and there — small parties living upon the shores of sea or lake far from the haunts of man.

They gave us no trouble — their old power had crumbled beyond recall; their Sagoths were now numbered among the regiments of The Empire; the Mahars had no longer the means to harm us; yet we did not want them among us. They are eaters of human flesh and we had no assurance that lone hunters would be safe from their voracious appetites.

We wanted them to be gone and so David sent a force against them, but with orders to treat with them first and attempt to persuade them to leave The Empire peacefully rather than embroil themselves in another war that might mean total extermination.

Sagoths accompanied the expedition, for they alone of all the creatures of Pellucidar can converse in the sixth sense, fourth dimension language of the Mahars.

The story that the expedition brought back was rather pitiful and aroused David's sympathies, as stories of persecution and unhappiness always do.

After the Mahars have been driven from The Empire they had sought a haven where they might live in peace. They assured us that they had accepted the inevitable in a spirit of philosophy and entertained no thoughts of renewing their warfare against the human race or in any way attempting to win back their lost ascendancy.

Far away upon the shores of a mighty ocean, where there were no signs of man, they settled in peace, but their peace was not for long.

A great ship came, reminding the Mahars of the first ships they had seen — the ships that David and I had built — the first ships, as far as we knew, that ever had sailed the silent seas of Pellucidar.

Naturally it was a surprise to us to learn that there was a race within the inner world sufficiently far advanced to be able to build ships, but there was another surprise in store for us. The Mahars assured us that these people possessed firearms and that because of their ships and their firearms they were fully as formidable as we and they were much more ferocious; killing for the pure sport of slaughter.

After the first ship had sailed away the Mahars thought they might be allowed to live in peace, but this dream was short lived, as presently the first ship returned and with it were many others manned by thousands of bloodthirsty enemies against whose weapons the great reptiles had little or no defense.

Seeking only escape from man, the Mahars left their new home and moved back a short distance toward The Empire, but now their enemies seemed bent only upon persecution; they hunted them, and when they found them the Mahars were again forced to fall back before the ferocity of their continued attacks.

Eventually they took refuge within the boundaries of The Empire, and scarcely had David's expedition to them returned with its report when we had definite proof of the veracity of their tale through messages from our northernmost frontier bearing stories of invasion by a strange, savage race of white men.

Frantic was the message from Goork, King of Thuria, whose far-flung frontier stretches beyond the Land of Awful Shadow.

Some of his hunters had been surprised

and all but a few killed or captured by the invaders.

He had sent warriors, then, against them, but these, too, had met a like fate, being greatly outnumbered, and so he sent a runner to David begging the Emperor to rush troops to his aid.

Scarcely had the first runner arrived when another came, bearing tidings of the capture and sack of the principal town of the Kingdom of Thuria; and then a third arrived from the commander of the invaders demanding that David come with tribute or they would destroy his country and slay the prisoners they held as hostages.

In reply David dispatched Tanar, son of Ghak, to demand the release of all prisoners and the departure of the invaders.

Immediately runners were sent to the nearest kingdoms of The Empire and ere Tanar had reached the Land of Awful Shadow, ten thousand warriors were marching along the same trail to enforce the demands of the Emperor and drive the savage foe from Pellucidar.

As David approached the Land of Awful Shadow that lies beneath Pellucidar's mysterious satellite, a great column of smoke was observable in the horizonless distance ahead.

It was not necessary to urge the tireless warriors to greater speed, for all who saw guessed that the invaders had taken another village and put it to the torch.

And then came the refugees — women and children only — and behind them a thin line of warriors striving to hold back swarthy, bearded strangers, armed with strange weapons that resembled ancient harquebuses with bell-shaped muzzles — huge, unwieldy things that belched smoke and flame and stones and bits of metal.

That the Pellucidarians, outnumbered ten to one, were able to hold back their savage foes at all was due to the more modern firearms that David and I had taught them to make and use.

Perhaps half the warriors of Thuria were armed with these and they were all that saved them from absolute rout, and, perhaps, total annihilation.

Loud were the shouts of joy when the first of the refugees discovered and recognized the force that had come to their delivery.

Goork and his people had been wavering in allegiance to The Empire, as were several other distant kingdoms, but I believe that this practical demonstration of the value of the Federation ended their doubts forever and left the people of the Land of Awful Shadow and their king the most loyal subjects that David possessed.

The effect upon the enemy of the appearance of ten thousand well-armed warriors was quickly apparent. They halted, and, as we advanced, they withdrew, but though they retreated they gave us a good fight.

David learned from Goork that Tanar had been retained as a hostage, but though he made several attempts to open negotiations with the enemy for the purpose of exchanging some prisoners that had fallen into our hands, for Tanar and other Pellucidarians, he never was able to do so.

Our forces drove the invaders far beyond the limits of The Empire to the shores of a distant sea, where, with difficulty and the loss of many men, they at last succeeded in embarking their depleted forces on ships that were as archaic in design as were their ancient harquebuses.

These ships rose to exaggerated heights at stern and bow, the sterns being built up in several stories, or housed decks, one atop another. There was much carving in seemingly intricate designs everywhere above the water line and each ship carried at her prow a figurehead painted, like the balance of the ship, in gaudy colors — usually a life size or a heroic figure of a naked woman or a mermaid.

The men themselves were equally bizarre and colorful, wearing gay cloths about their heads, wide sashes of bright colors and huge boots with flapping tops — those that were not half naked and barefoot.

Besides their harquebuses they carried huge pistols and knives stuck in their belts and at their hips were cutlasses. Altogether, with their bushy whiskers and fierce faces, they were at once a bad looking and a picturesque lot.

From some of the last prisoners he took during the fighting at the seashore, David learned that Tanar was still alive and that the chief of the invaders had determined to take him home with him in the hope that he could learn from Tanar the secrets of our superior weapons and gunpowder, for, notwithstanding my first failures, I had, and not without some pride, finally achieved a gunpowder that would not only burn, but that would ignite with such force as to be quite satisfactory. I am now perfecting a noiseless, smokeless powder, though honesty compels me to confess that my first experiments have not been entirely what I had hoped they might be, the first batch detonated having nearly broken my ear-drums and so filled my eyes with smoke that I thought I had been blinded.

When David saw the enemy ships sailing away with Tanar he was sick with grief, for Tanar always has been an especial favorite of the Emperor and his gracious Empress, Dian the Beautiful. He was like a son to them.

We had no ships upon this sea and David could not follow with his army; neither, being David, could he abandon the son of his best friend to a savage enemy before he had exhausted every resource at his command in an effort toward rescue.

In addition to the prisoners that had fallen into his hands David had captured one of the small boats that the enemy had used in embarking his forces, and this it was that suggested to David the mad scheme upon which he embarked.

The boat was about sixteen feet long and was equipped with both oars and a sail. It was broad of beam and had every appearance of being staunch and seaworthy, though pitifully small in which to face the dangers of an unknown sea, peopled, as are all the waters of Pellucidar, with huge monsters possessing short tempers and long appetites.

Standing upon the shore, gazing after the diminishing outlines of the departing ships, David reached his decision. Surrounding him were the captains and the kings of the Federated Kingdoms of Pellucidar and behind these ten thousand warriors, leaning upon their arms. To one side the sullen prisoners, heavily guarded, gazed after their departing comrades, with what sensations of hopelessness and envy one may guess.

David turned toward his people. "Those departing ships have borne away Tanar, the son of Ghak, and perhaps a score more of the young men of Pellucidar. It is beyond reason to expect that the enemy ever will bring our comrades back to us, but it is easy to imagine the treatment they will receive at the hands of this savage, bloodthirsty race.

"We may not abandon them while a single avenue of pursuit remains open to us. Here is that avenue." He waved his hand across the broad ocean. "And here the means of traversing it." He pointed to the small boat.

"It would carry scarce twenty men," cried one, who stood near the Emperor.

"It need carry but three," replied David, "for it will sail to rescue, not by force, but by strategy; or perhaps only to locate the stronghold of the enemy, that we may return and lead a sufficient force upon it to overwhelm it."

"I shall go," concluded the Emperor. "Who will accompany me?"

Instantly every man within hearing of his voice, saving the prisoners only, flashed a weapon above his head and pressed forward to offer his services. David smiled.

"I knew as much," he said, "but I cannot take you all. I shall need only one and that shall be Ja of Anoroc, the greatest sailor of Pellucidar."

A great shout arose, for Ja, the King of Anoroc, who is also the chief officer of the navy of Pellucidar, is vastly popular throughout The Empire, and, though all were disappointed in not being chosen, yet they appreciated the wisdom of David's selection.

"But two is too small a number to hope for success," argued Ghak, "and I, the father of Tanar, should be permitted to accompany you."

"Numbers, such as we might crowd in that little boat, would avail us nothing," replied David, "so why risk a single additional life? If twenty could pass through the unknown dangers that lie ahead of us, two may do the same, while with fewer men we can carry a far greater supply of food and water against the unguessed extent of the great sea that we face and the periods of calm and the long search."

"But two are too few to man the boat," expostulated another, "and Ghak is right — the father of Tanar should be among his rescuers."

"Ghak is needed by The Empire," replied David. "He must remain to command the armies for the Empress until I return, but there shall be a third who will embark with us."

"Who?" demanded Ghak.

"One of the prisoners," replied David. "For his freedom we should readily find one willing to guide us to the country of the enemy."

Nor was this difficult since every prisoner volunteered when the proposal was submitted to them.

David chose a young fellow who said his name was Fitt and who seemed to possess a more open and honest countenance than any of his companions.

And then came the provisioning of the boat. Bladders were filled with fresh water, and quantities of corn and dried fish and jerked meat, as well as vegetables and fruits, were packed into other bladders, and all were stored in the boat until it seemed that she might carry no more. For three men the supplies might have been adequate for a year's voyage upon the outer crust, where time enters into all calculations.

The prisoner, Fitt, who was to accompany David and Ja, assured David that one fourth the quantity of supplies would be ample and that there were points along the route they might take where their water supply could be replenished and where game abounded, as well as native fruits, nuts and vegetables, but David would not cut down by a single ounce the supplies that he had decided upon.

As the three were about to embark David had a last word with Ghak.

"You have seen the size and the armament of the enemy ships, Ghak," he said. "My last injunction to you is to build at once a fleet that can cope successfully with these great ships of the enemy and while the fleet is building — and it must be built upon the shores of this sea — send expeditions forth to search for a waterway from this ocean to our own. Can you find it, all of our ships can be utilized and the building of the greater navy accelerated by utilizing the shipyards of Anoroc.

"When you have completed and manned fifty ships set forth to our rescue if we have not returned by then. Do not destroy these prisoners, but preserve them well for they alone can guide you to their country."

And then David I, Emperor of Pellucidar, and Ja, King of Anoroc, with the prisoner, Fitt, boarded the tiny boat; friendly hands pushed them out upon the long, oily swells of a Pellucidarian sea; ten thousand throats cheered them upon their way and ten thousand pairs of eyes watched them until they had melted into the mist of the upcurving, horizonless distance of a Pel-lucidarian seascape.

David had departed upon a vain but glorious adventure, and, in the distant capital of The Empire, Dian the Beautiful would be weeping.

Chapter I

STELLARA

The great ship trembled to the recoil of the cannon; the rattle of musketry. The roar of the guns aboard her sister ships and the roar of her own were deafening. Below decks the air was acrid with the fumes of burnt powder.

Tanar of Pellucidar, chained below with other prisoners, heard these sounds and smelled the smoke. He heard the rattle of the anchor chain; he felt the straining of the mast to which his shackles were bent and the altered motion of the hull told him that the ship was under way.

Presently the firing ceased and the regular rising and falling of the ship betokened that it was on its course. In the darkness of the hold Tanar could see nothing. Sometimes the prisoners spoke to one another, but their thoughts were not happy ones, and so, for the most part, they remained silent — waiting. For what?

They grew very hungry and very thirsty. By this they knew that the ship was far at sea. They knew nothing of time. They only knew that they were hungry and thirsty and that the ship should be far at sea — far out upon an unknown sea, setting its course for an unknown port.

Presently a hatch was raised and men came with food and water — poor, rough food and water that smelled badly and tasted worse; but it was water and they were thirsty.

One of the men said: "Where is he who is called Tanar?"

"I am Tanar," replied the son of Ghak.

"You are wanted on deck," said the man, and with a huge key he unlocked the massive, handwrought lock that held Tanar chained to the mast. "Follow me!"

The bright light of Pellucidar's perpetual day blinded the Sarian as he clambered to the deck from the dark hole in which he had been confined and it was a full minute before his eyes could endure the light, but his guard hustled him roughly along and Tanar was already stumbling up the long stairs leading to the high deck at the ship's stern before he regained the use of his eyes.

As he mounted the highest deck he saw the chiefs of the Korsar horde assembled and with them were two women. One appeared elderly and ill favored, but the other was young and beautiful, but for neither did Tanar have any eyes — he was interested only in the enemy men, for these he could fight, these he might kill, which was the sole interest that an enemy could hold for Tanar, the Sarian, and being what he was Tanar could not fight women, not even enemy women; but he could ignore them, and did.

He was led before a huge fellow whose bushy whiskers almost hid his face — a great, blustering fellow with a scarlet scarf bound about his head. But for an embroidered, sleeveless jacket, open at the front, the man was naked above the waist, about which was wound another gaudy sash into which were stuck two pistols and as many long knives, while at his side dangled a cutlass, the hilt of which was richly ornamented with inlays of pearl and semiprecious stones.

A mighty man was The Cid, chief of the Korsars — a burly, blustering, bully of a man, whose position among the rough and quarrelsome Korsars might be maintained only by such as he.

Surrounding him upon the high poop of his ship was a company of beefy ruffians of similar mold, while far below, in the waist of the vessel, a throng of lesser cutthroats, the common sailors, escaped from the dangers and demands of an arduous campaign, relaxed according to their various whims.

Stark brutes were most of these, naked but for shorts and the inevitable gaudy sashes and head cloths — an unlovely company, yet picturesque.

At The Cid's side stood a younger man who well could boast as hideous a countenance as any sun ever shone upon, for across a face that might have taxed even a mother's love, ran a repulsive scar from above the left eye to below the right hand corner of the mouth, cleaving the nose with a deep, red gash. The left eye was lidless and gazed perpetually upward and outward, as a dead eye might, while the upper lip was permanently drawn upward at the right side in a sardonic sneer that exposed a single fang-like tooth. No, Bohar the Bloody was not beautiful.

Before these two, The Cid and The Bloody One, Tanar was roughly dragged.

"They call you Tanar?" bellowed The Cid.

Tanar nodded.

"And you are the son of a king!" and he laughed loudly. "With a ship's company I could destroy your father's entire kingdom and make a slave of him, as I have of his son."

"You and many ships' companies," replied Tanar; "but I did not see any of them destroying the kingdom of Sari. The army that chased them into the ocean was commanded by my father, under the Emperor."

The Cid scowled. "I have made men walk the plank for less than that," he growled.

"I do not know what you mean," said Tanar.

"You shall," barked The Cid; "and then, by the beard of the sea god, you'll keep a civil tongue in your head. Hey!" he shouted to one of his officers, "have a prisoner fetched and the plank run out. We'll show this son of a king who The Cid is and that he is among real men now."

"Why fetch another?" demanded Bohar the Bloody. "This fellow can walk and learn his lesson at the same time."

"But he could not profit by it," replied The Cid.

"Since when did The Cid become a dry nurse to an enemy?" demanded Bohar, with a sneer.

Without a word The Cid wheeled and swung an ugly blow to Bohar's chin, and as the man went down the chief whipped a great pistol from his sash and stood over him, the muzzle pointed at Bohar's head.

"Perhaps that will knock your crooked face straight or bump some brains into your thick head," roared The Cid.

Bohar lay on his back glaring up at his chief.

"Who is your master?" demanded The Cid.

"You are," growled Bohar.

"Then get up and keep a civil tongue in your head," ordered The Cid.

As Bohar rose he turned a scowling face upon Tanar. It was as though his one good eye had gathered all the hate and rage and venom in the wicked heart of the man and was concentrating them upon the Sarian, the indirect cause of his humiliation, and from that instant Tanar knew that Bohar the Bloody hated him with a personal hatred distinct from any natural antipathy that he might have felt for an alien and an enemy.

On the lower deck men were eagerly running a long plank out over the starboard rail and making the inboard end fast to cleats with stout lines.

From an opened hatch others were dragging a strapping prisoner from the kingdom of Thuria, who had been captured in the early fighting in the Land of Awful Shadow.

The primitive warrior held his head high and showed no terror in the presence of his rough captors. Tanar, looking down upon him from the upper deck, was proud of this fellow man of the Empire. The Cid was watching, too.

"That tribe needs taming," he said.

The younger of the two women, both of whom had stepped to the edge of the deck and were looking down upon the scene in the waist, turned to The Cid.

"They seem brave men; all of them," she said. "It is a pity to kill one needlessly."

"Poof! girl," exclaimed The Cid. "What do you know of such things? It is the blood of your mother that speaks. By the beards of the gods, I would that you had more of your father's blood in your veins."

"It is brave blood, the blood of my mother," replied the girl, "for it does not fear to be itself before all men. The blood of my father dares not reveal its good to the eyes of men because it fears ridicule. It boasts of its courage to hide its cowardice."

The Cid swore a mighty oath. "You take advantage of our relationship, Stellara," he said, "but do not forget that there is a limit beyond which even you may not go with The Cid, who brooks no insults."

The girl laughed. "Reserve that talk for those who fear you," she said.

During this conversation, Tanar, who was standing near, had an opportunity to observe the girl more closely and was prompted to do so by the nature of her remarks and the quiet courage of her demeanor. For the first time he noticed her hair, which was like gold in warm sunlight, and because the women of his own country were nearly all dark haired the color of her hair impressed him. He thought it very lovely and when he looked more closely at her features he realized that they, too, were lovely, with a sunny, golden loveliness that seemed to reflect like qualities of heart and character. There was a certain feminine softness about her that was sometimes

lacking in the sturdy, self-reliant, primitive women of his own race. It was not in any sense a weakness, however, as was evidenced by her fearless attitude toward The Cid and by the light of courage that shone from her brave eyes. Intelligent eyes they were, too — brave, intelligent and beautiful.

But there Tanar's interest ceased and he was repulsed by the thought that this woman belonged to the uncouth bully, who ruled with an iron hand the whiskered brutes of the great fleet, for The Cid's reference to their relationship left no doubt in the mind of the Sarian that the woman was his mate.

And now the attention of all was focused on the actors in the tragedy below. Men had bound the wrists of the prisoner together behind his back and placed a blindfold across his eyes.

"Watch below, son of a king," said The Cid to Tanar, "and you will know what it means to walk the plank."

"I am watching," said Tanar, "and I see that it takes many of your people to make one of mine do this thing, whatever it may be."

The girl laughed, but The Cid scowled more deeply, while Bohar cast a venomous glance at Tanar.

Now men with drawn knives and sharp pikes lined the plank on either side of the ship's rail and others lifted the prisoner to the inboard end so that he faced the opposite end of the plank that protruded far out over the sea, where great monsters of the deep cut the waves with giant backs as they paralleled the ship's course — giant saurians, long extinct upon the outer crust.

Prodding the defenseless man with knife and pike they goaded him forward along the narrow plank to the accompaniment of loud oaths and vulgar jests and hoarse laughter.

Erect and proud, the Thurian marched fearlessly to his doom. He made no complaint and when he reached the outer end of the plank and his foot found no new place beyond he made no outcry. Just for an instant he drew back his foot and hesitated and then, silently, he leaped far out, and, turning, dove head foremost into the sea.

Tanar turned his eyes away and it chanced that he turned them in the direction of the girl. To his surprise he saw that she, too, had refused to look at the last moment and in her face, turned toward his, he saw an expression of suffering.

Could it be that this woman of The Cid's brutal race felt sympathy and sorrow for a suffering enemy?

Tanar doubted it. More likely that something she had eaten that day had disagreed with her.

"Now," cried The Cid, "you have seen a man walk the plank and know what I may do with you, if I choose."

Tanar shrugged. "I hope I may be as indifferent to my fate as was my comrade," he said, "for you certainly got little enough sport out of him."

"If I turn you over to Bohar we shall have sport," replied The Cid. "He has other means of enlivening a dull day that far surpass the tame exercise on the plank."

The girl turned angrily upon The Cid. "You shall not do that!" she cried. "You promised me that you would not torture any prisoners while I was with the fleet."

"If he behaves I shall not," said The Cid, "but if he does not I shall turn him over to Bohar the Bloody. Do not forget that I am Chief of Korsar and that even you may be punished if you interfere."

Again the girl laughed. "You can frighten the others, Chief of Korsar," she said, "but not me."

"If she were mine," muttered Bohar threateningly, but the girl interrupted him.

"I am not, nor ever shall be," she said.

"Do not be too sure of that," growled The Cid. "I can give you to whom I please; let the matter drop." He turned to the Sarian prisoner. "What is your name, son of a king?" he asked.

"Tanar."

"Listen well, Tanar," said The Cid impressively. "Our prisoners do not live beyond the time that they be of service to us. Some of you will be kept to exhibit to the people of Korsar, after which they will be of little use to me, but you can purchase life and, perhaps, freedom."

"How?" demanded Tanar.

"Your people were armed with weapons far better than ours," explained The Cid; "your powder was more powerful and more dependable. Half the time ours fails to ignite at the first attempt."

"That must be embarrassing," remarked Tanar.

"It is fatal," said The Cid.

"But what has it to do with me?" asked the prisoner.

"If you will teach us how to make better weapons and such powder as your people have you shall be spared and shall have your freedom."

Tanar made no reply — he was thinking — thinking of the supremacy that their superior weapons gave his people — thinking of the fate that lay in store for him and for those poor devils in the dark, foul hole below deck.

"Well?" demanded The Cid.

"Will you spare the others, too?" he asked.

"Why should I?"

"I shall need their help," said Tanar. "I do not know all that is necessary to make the weapons and the powder."

As a matter of fact he knew nothing about the manufacture of either, but he saw here a chance to save his fellow prisoners, or at least to delay their destruction and gain time in which they might find means of escape, nor did he hesitate to deceive The Cid, for is not all fair in war?

"Very well," said the Korsar chief; "if you and they give me no trouble you shall all live — provided you teach us how to make weapons and powder like your own."

"We cannot live in the filthy hole in which we are penned," retorted the Sarian; "neither can we live without food. Soon we shall all sicken and die. We are people of the open air — we cannot be smothered in dark holes filled with vermin and be starved, and live."

"You shall not be returned to the hole," said The Cid. "There is no danger that you will escape."

"And the others?" demanded Tanar.

"They remain where they are!"

"They will all die, and without them I cannot make powder," Tanar reminded him.

The Cid scowled. "You would have my ship overrun with enemies," he growled.

"They are unarmed."

"Then they certainly would be killed," said The Cid. "No one would survive long among that pack an' he were not armed"; he waved a hand contemptuously toward the half naked throng below.

"Then leave the hatches off and give them decent air and more and better food."

"I'll do it," said The Cid. "Bohar, have the forward hatches removed, place a guard there with orders to kill any prisoner who attempts to come on deck and any of our men who attempts to go below; see, too, that the prisoners get the same rations as our own men."

It was with a feeling of relief that amounted almost to happiness that Tanar saw Bohar depart to carry out the orders of The Cid, for he knew well that his people could not long survive the hideous and unaccustomed confinement and the vile food that had been his lot and theirs since they had been brought aboard the Korsar ship.

Presently The Cid went to his cabin and Tanar, left to his own devices, walked to the stern and leaning on the rail gazed into the hazy upcurving distance where lay the land of the Sarians, his land, beyond the haze.

Far astern a small boat rose and fell with the great, long billows. Fierce denizens of the deep constantly threatened it, storms menaced it, but on it forged in the wake of the great fleet — a frail and tiny thing made strong and powerful by the wills of three men.

But this Tanar did not see, for the mist hid it. He would have been heartened to know that his Emperor was risking his life to save him.

As he gazed and dreamed he became conscious of a presence near him, but he did not turn, for who was there upon that ship who might have access to this upper deck, whom he might care to see or speak with?

Presently he heard a voice at his elbow, a low, golden voice that brought him around facing its owner. It was the girl.

"You are looking back toward your own country?" she said.

"Yes."

"You will never see it again," she said, a note of sadness in her voice, as though she understood his feelings and sympathized.

"Perhaps not, but why should you care? I am an enemy."

"I do not know why I should care," replied the girl. "What is your name?"

"Tanar."

"Is that all?"

"I am called Tanar the Fleet One."

"Why?"

"Because in all Sari none can outdistance me."

"Sari — is that the name of your country?"

"Yes."

"What is it like?"

"It is a high plateau among the mountains. It is a very lovely country, with leaping rivers and great trees. It is filled with game. We hunt the great ryth there and the tarag for meat and for sport and there are countless lesser animals that give us food and clothing."

"Have you no enemies? You are not a warlike people as are the Korsars."

"We defeated the warlike Korsars," he reminded her.

"I would not speak of that too often," she said. "The tempers of the Korsars are short and they love to kill."

"Why do you not kill me then?" he demanded. "You have a knife and a pistol in your sash, like the others."

The girl only smiled.

"Perhaps you are not a Korsar," he exclaimed. "You were captured as I was and are a prisoner."

"I am no prisoner," she replied.

"But you are not a Korsar," he insisted.

"Ask The Cid — he will doubtless cutlass you for your impertinence; but why do you think I am not a Korsar?"

"You are too beautiful and too fine," he replied. "You have shown sympathy and that is a finer sentiment far beyond their mental capability. They are ————"

"Be careful, enemy; perhaps I am a Korsar!"

"I do not believe it," said Tanar.

"Then keep your beliefs to yourself, prisoner," retorted the girl in a haughty tone.

"What is this?" demanded a rough voice behind Tanar. "What has this thing said to you, Stellara?"

Tanar wheeled to face Bohar the Bloody.

"I questioned that she was of the same race as you," snapped Tanar before the girl could reply. "It is inconceivable that one so beautiful could be tainted by the blood of Korsar."

His face flaming with rage, Bohar laid a hand upon one of his knives and stepped truculently toward the Sarian. "It is death to insult the daughter of The Cid," he cried, whipping the knife from his sash and striking a wicked blow at Tanar.

The Sarian, light of foot, trained from childhood in the defensive as well as offensive use of edged weapons, stepped quickly to one side and then as quickly in again and once more Bohar the Bloody sprawled upon the deck to a well delivered blow.

Bohar was fairly foaming at the mouth with rage as he jerked his heavy pistol from his gaudy sash and aiming it at Tanar's chest from where he lay upon the deck, pulled the trigger. At the same instant the girl sprang forward as though to prevent the slaying of the prisoner.

It all happened so quickly that Tanar scarcely knew the sequence of events, but what he did know was that the powder failed to ignite, and then he laughed.

"You had better wait until I have taught you how to make powder that will burn before you try to murder me, Bohar," he said.

The Bloody One scrambled to his feet and Tanar stood ready to receive the expected charge, but the girl stepped between them with an imperious gesture.

"Enough of this!" she cried. "It is The Cid's wish that this man live. Would you like to have The Cid know that you tried to pistol him, Bohar?"

The Bloody One stood glaring at Tanar for several seconds, then he wheeled and strode away without a word.

"It would seem that Bohar does not like me," said Tanar, smiling.

"He dislikes nearly every one," said Stellara, "but he hates you — now."

"Because I knocked him down, I suppose. I cannot blame him."

"That is not the real reason," said the girl.

"What is, then?"

She hesitated and then she laughed. "He is jealous. Bohar wants me for his mate."

"But why should he be jealous of me?"

Stellara looked Tanar up and down and then she laughed again. "I do not know," she said. "You are not much of a man beside our huge Korsars — with your beardless face and your small waist. It would take two of you to make one of them."

To Tanar her tone implied thinly veiled contempt and it piqued him, but why it should he did not know and that annoyed him, too. What was she but the savage daughter of a savage, boorish Korsar?

When he had first learned from Bohar's lips that she was the daughter and not the mate of The Cid he had felt an unaccountable relief, half unconsciously and without at all attempting to analyze his reaction.

Perhaps it was the girl's beauty that had made such a relationship with The Cid seem repulsive, perhaps it was her lesser ruthlessness, which seemed superlative gentleness by contrast with the brutality of Bohar and The Cid, but now she seemed capable of a refined cruelty, which was, after all, what he might have expected to find in one form or another in the daughter of the Chief of the Korsars.

As one will, when piqued, and just at random, Tanar loosed a bolt in the hope that it might annoy her. "Bohar knows you better than I," he said; "perhaps he knew that he had cause for jealousy."

"Perhaps," she replied, enigmatically, "but no one will ever know, for Bohar will kill you — I know *him* well enough to know that."

Chapter II

DISASTER

Upon the timeless seas of Pellucidar a voyage may last for an hour or a year — that depends not upon its duration, but upon the important occurrences which mark its course.

Curving upward along the inside of the arc of a great circle the Korsar fleet ploughed the restless sea. Favorable winds carried the ships onward. The noonday sun hung perpetually at zenith. Men ate when they were hungry, slept when they were tired, or slept against the time when sleep might be denied them, for the people of Pellucidar seem endowed with a faculty that permits them to store sleep, as it were, in times of ease, against the more strenuous periods of hunting and warfare when there is no opportunity for sleep. Similarly, they eat with unbelievable irregularity.

Tanar had slept and eaten several times since his encounter with Bohar, whom he had seen upon various occasions since without an actual meeting. The Bloody One seemed to be biding his time.

Stellara had kept to her cabin with the old woman, who Tanar surmised was her mother. He wondered if Stellara would look like the mother or The Cid when she was older, and he shuddered when he considered either eventuality.

As he stood thus musing, Tanar's attention was attracted by the actions of the men on the lower deck. He saw them looking across the port bow and upward and, following the direction of their eyes with his, he saw the rare phenomenon of a cloud in the brilliant sky.

Some one must have notified The Cid at about the same time, for he came from his cabin and looked long and searchingly at the heavens.

In his loud voice The Cid bellowed commands and his wild crew scrambled to their stations like monkeys, swarming aloft or standing by on deck ready to do his bidding.

Down came the great sails and reefed were the lesser ones, and throughout the fleet, scattered over the surface of the shining sea, the example of the Commander was followed.

The cloud was increasing in size and coming rapidly nearer. No longer was it the small white cloud that had first attracted their attention, but a great, bulging, ominous, black mass that frowned down upon the ocean, turning it a sullen gray where the shadow lay.

The wind that had been blowing gently ceased suddenly. The ship fell off and rolled in the trough of the sea. The silence that followed cast a spell of terror over the ship's company.

Tanar, watching, saw the change. If these rough seafaring men blenched before the threat of the great cloud the danger must be great indeed.

The Sarians were mountain people. Tanar knew little of the sea, but if Tanar feared anything on Pellucidar it was the sea. The sight, therefore, of these savage Korsar sailors cringing in terror was far from reassuring.

Some one had come to the rail and was standing at his side.

"When that has passed," said a voice, "there will be fewer ships in the fleet of Korsar and fewer men to go home to their women."

He turned and saw Stellara looking upward at the cloud.

"You do not seem afraid," he said.

"Nor you," replied the girl. "We seem the only people aboard who are not afraid."

"Look down at the prisoners," he told her. "They show no fear."

"Why?" she asked.

"They are Pellucidarians," he replied, proudly.

"We are all of Pellucidar," she reminded him.

"I refer to The Empire," he said.

"Why are you not afraid?" she asked. "Are you so much braver than the Korsars?" There was no sarcasm in her tone.

"I am very much afraid," replied Tanar. "Mine are mountain people — we know little of the sea or its ways."

"But you show no fear," insisted Stellara.

"That is the result of heredity and training," he replied.

"The Korsars show their fear," she mused. She spoke as one who was of different blood. "They boast much of their bravery," she continued as though speaking to herself, "but when the sky frowns they show fear." There seemed a little note of contempt in her voice. "See!" she cried. "It is coming!"

The cloud was tearing toward them now and beneath it the sea was lashed to fury. Shreds of cloud whirled and twisted at the edges of the great cloud mass. Shreds of spume whirled and twisted above the angry waves. And then the storm struck the ship, laying it over on its side.

What ensued was appalling to a mountaineer, unaccustomed to the sea — the chaos of watery mountains, tumbling, rolling, lashing at the wallowing ship; the shrieking wind; the driving, blinding spume; the terror-stricken crew, cowed, no longer swaggering bullies.

Reeling, staggering, clutching at the rail Bohar the Bloody passed Tanar where he clung with one arm about a stanchion and the other holding Stellara, who would have been hurled to the deck but for the quick action of the Sarian.

The face of Bohar was an ashen mask against which the red gash of his ugly scar stood out in startling contrast. He looked at Tanar and Stellara, but he passed them by, mumbling to himself.

Beyond them was The Cid, screaming orders that no one could hear. Toward him Bohar made his way. Above the storm Tanar heard The Bloody One screaming at his chief.

"Save me! Save me!" he cried. "The boats — lower the boats! The ship is lost."

It was apparent, even to a landsman, that no small boat could live in such a sea even if one could have been lowered. The Cid paid no attention to his lieutenant, but clung where he was, bawling commands.

A mighty sea rose suddenly above the

bow; it hung there for an instant and then rolled in upon the lower deck — tons of crushing, pitiless, insensate sea — rolled in upon the huddled, screaming seamen. Naught but the high prow and the lofty poop showed above the angry waves — just for an instant the great ship strained and shuddered, battling for life.

"It is the end!" cried Stellara.

Bohar screamed like a dumb brute in the agony of death. The Cid knelt on the deck, his face buried in his arms. Tanar stood watching, fascinated by the terrifying might of the elements. He saw man shrink to puny insignificance before a gust of wind, and a slow smile crossed his face.

The wave receded and the ship, floundering, staggered upward, groaning. The smile left Tanar's lips as his eyes gazed down upon the lower deck. It was almost empty now. A few broken forms lay huddled in the scuppers; a dozen men, clinging here and there, showed signs of life. The others, all but those who had reached safety below deck, were gone.

The girl clung tightly to the man. "I did not think she could live through that," she said.

"Nor I," said Tanar.

"But you were not afraid," she said. "You seemed the only one who was not afraid."

"Of what use was Bohar's screaming?" he asked. "Did it save him?"

"Then you were afraid, but you hid it?"

He shrugged. "Perhaps," he said. "I do not know what you mean by fear. I did not want to die, if that is what you mean."

"Here comes another!" cried Stellara, shuddering, and pressing closer to him.

Tanar's arm tightened about the slim figure of the girl. It was an unconscious gesture of the protective instinct of the male.

"Do not be afraid," he said.

"I am not — now," she replied.

At the instant that the mighty comber engulfed the ship the angry hurricane struck suddenly with renewed fury — struck at a new angle — and the masts, already straining even to the minimum of canvas that had been necessary to give the ship headway and keep its nose into the storm, snapped like dry bones and crashed by the board in a tangle of cordage. The ship's head fell away and she rolled in the trough of the great seas, a hopeless derelict.

Above the screaming of the wind rose Bohar's screams. "The boats! The boats!" he repeated like a trained parrot gone mad from terror.

As though sated for the moment and worn out by its own exertions the storm abated, the wind died, but the great seas rose and fell and the great ship rolled, helpless. At the bottom of each watery gorge it seemed that it must be engulfed by the gray green cliff toppling above it and at the crest of each liquid mountain certain destruction loomed inescapable.

Bohar, still screaming, scrambled to the lower deck. He found men, by some miracle still alive in the open, and others cringing in terror below deck. By dint of curses and blows and the threat of his pistol he gathered them together and though they whimpered in fright he forced them to make a boat ready.

There were twenty of them and their gods or their devils must have been with them, for they lowered a boat and got clear of the floundering bulk in safety and without the loss of a man.

The Cid, seeing what Bohar contemplated, had tried to prevent the seemingly suicidal act by bellowing orders at him from above, but they had no effect and at the last moment The Cid had descended to the lower deck to enforce his commands, but he had arrived too late.

Now he stood staring unbelievingly at the small boat riding the great seas in seeming security while the dismasted ship, pounded by the stumps of its masts, seemed doomed to destruction.

From corners where they had been hiding came the balance of the ship's company and when they saw Bohar's boat and the seemingly relative safety of the crew they clamored for escape by the other boats. With the idea once implanted in their minds there followed a mad panic as the half-brutes fought for places in the remaining boats.

"Come!" cried Stellara. "We must hurry or they will go without us." She started to move toward the companionway, but Tanar restrained her.

"Look at them," he said. "We are safer at the mercy of the sea and the storm."

Stellara shrank back close to him. She saw men knifing one another — those behind knifing those ahead. Men dragging others from the boats and killing them on deck or being killed. She saw The Cid pistol a seaman in the back and leap to his place in the first boat to be lowered. She saw men leaping from the rail in a mad effort to reach this boat and falling into the sea, or being thrown in if they succeeded in boarding the tossing shell.

She saw the other boats being lowered and men crushed between them and the ship's side — she saw the depths to which fear can plunge the braggart and the bully as the last of the ship's company, failing to win places in the last boat, deliberately leaped into the sea and were drowned.

Standing there upon the high poop of the rolling derelict, Tanar and Stellara watched the frantic efforts of the oarsmen in the overcrowded small boats. They saw one boat foul another and both founder. They watched the drowning men battling for survival. They heard their hoarse oaths and their screams above the roaring of the sea and the shriek of the wind as the storm returned as though fearing that some might escape its fury.

"We are alone," said Stellara. "They have all gone."

"Let them go," replied Tanar. "I would not exchange places with them."

"But there can be no hope for us," said the girl.

"There is no more for them," replied the Sarian, "and at least we are not crowded into a small boat filled with cutthroats."

"You are more afraid of the men than you are of the sea," she said.

"For you, yes," he replied.

"Why should you fear for me?" she demanded. "Am I not also your enemy?"

He turned his eyes quickly upon her and they were filled with surprise. "That is so," he said; "but, somehow, I had forgotten it — you do not seem like an enemy, as the others do. You do not seem like one of them, even."

Clinging to the rail and supporting the girl upon the lurching deck, Tanar's lips were close to Stellara's ear as he sought to make himself heard above the storm. He sensed the faint aroma of a delicate sachet that was ever after to be a part of his memory of Stellara.

A sea struck the staggering ship throwing Tanar forward so that his cheek touched the cheek of the girl and as she turned her head his lips brushed hers. Each realized that it was an accident, but the effect was none the less surprising. Tanar, for the first time, felt the girl's body

against his and consciousness of contact must have been reflected in his eyes for Stellara shrank back and there was an expression of fear in hers.

Tanar saw the fear in the eyes of an enemy, but it gave him no pleasure. He tried to think only of the treatment that would have been accorded a woman of his tribe had one been at the mercy of the Korsars, but that, too, failed to satisfy him as it only could if he were to admit that he was of the same ignoble clay as the men of Korsar.

But whatever thoughts were troubling the minds of Stellara and Tanar were temporarily submerged by the grim tragedy of the succeeding few moments as another tremendous sea, the most gigantic that had yet assailed the broken ship, hurled its countless tons upon her shivering deck.

To Tanar it seemed, indeed, that this must mark the end since it was inconceivable that the unmanageable hulk could rise again from the smother of water that surged completely over her almost to the very highest deck of the towering poop, where the two clung against the tearing wind and the frightful pitching of the derelict.

But, as the sea rolled on, the ship slowly, sluggishly struggled to the surface like an exhausted swimmer who, drowning, struggles weakly against the inevitability of fate and battles upward for one last gasp of air that will, at best, but prolong the agony of death.

As the main deck slowly emerged from the receding waters, Tanar was horrified by the discovery that the forward hatch had been stove in. That the ship must have taken in considerable water, and that each succeeding wave that broke over it would add to the quantity, affected the Sarian less than knowledge of the fact that it was beneath this hatch that his fellow prisoners were confined.

Through the black menace of his almost hopeless situation had shone a single bright ray of hope that, should the ship weather the storm, there would be aboard her a score of his fellow Pellucidarians and that together they might find the means to rig a makeshift sail and work their way back to the mainland from which they had embarked; but with the gaping hatch and the almost certain conclusion to be drawn from it he realized that it would, indeed, be a miracle if there remained alive aboard the derelict any other than Stellara and himself.

The girl was looking down at the havoc wrought below and now she turned her face toward his.

"They must all be drowned," she said, "and they were your people. I am sorry."

"Perhaps they would have chosen it in preference to what might have awaited them in Korsar," he said.

"And they have been released only a little sooner than we shall be," she continued. "Do you notice how low the ship rides now and how sluggish she is? The hold must be half filled with water — another such sea as the last one will founder her."

For some time they stood in silence, each occupied with his own thoughts. The hulk rolled in the trough and momentarily it seemed that she might not roll back in time to avert the disaster of the next menacing comber, yet each time she staggered drunkenly to oppose a high side to the hungry waters.

"I believe the storm has spent itself," said Tanar.

"The wind has died and there has been no sea like the great one that stove in the forward hatch," said Stellara, hopefully.

The noonday sun broke from behind the black cloud that had shrouded it and the sea burst into a blaze of blue and silver beauty. The storm had passed. The seas diminished. The derelict rolled heavily upon the great swells, low in the water, but temporarily relieved of the menace of immediate disaster.

Tanar descended the companionway to the lower deck and approached the forward hatch. A single glance below revealed only what he could have anticipated — floating corpses rolling with the roll of the derelict. All below were dead. With a sigh he turned away and returned to the upper deck.

The girl did not even question him for she could read in his demeanor the story of what his eyes had beheld.

"You and I are the only living creatures that remain aboard," he said.

She waved a hand in a broad gesture that took in the sea about them. "Doubtless we alone of the entire ship's company have survived," she said. "I see no other ship nor any of the small boats."

Tanar strained his eyes in all directions. "Nor I," said he; "but perhaps some of them have escaped."

She shook her head. "I doubt it."

"Yours has been a heavy loss," sympathized the Sarian. "Beside so many of your people, you have lost your father and your mother."

Stellara looked up quickly into his eyes. "They were not my people," she said.

"What?" exclaimed Tanar. "They were not your people? But your father, The Cid, was Chief of the Korsars."

"He was not my father," replied the girl.

"And the woman was not your mother?"

"May the gods forbid!" she exclaimed.

"But The Cid! He treated you like a daughter."

"He thought I was his daughter, but I am not."

"I do not understand," said Tanar; "yet I am glad that you are not. I could not understand how you, who are so different from them, could be a Korsar."

"My mother was a native of the island of Amiocap and there The Cid, raiding for women, seized her. She told me about it many times before she died.

"Her mate was absent upon a great tandor hunt and she never saw him again. When I was born The Cid thought that I was his daughter, but my mother knew better for I bore upon my left shoulder a small, red birthmark identical with one upon the left shoulder of the mate from whom she had been stolen — my father.

"My mother never told The Cid the truth, for fear that he would kill me in accordance with the custom the Korsars follow of destroying the children of their captives if a Korsar is not the father."

"And the woman who was with you on board was not your mother?"

"No, she was The Cid's mate, but not my mother, who is dead."

Tanar felt a distinct sense of relief that Stellara was not a Korsar, but why this should be so he did not know, nor, perhaps, did he attempt to analyze his feelings.

"I am glad," he said again.

"But why?" she asked.

"Now we do not have to be enemies," he replied.

"Were we before?"

He hesitated and then he laughed. "I was not your enemy," he said, "but you reminded me that you were mine."

"It has been the habit of a lifetime to think of myself as a Korsar," exclaimed Stellara, "although I knew that I was not. I felt no enmity toward you."

"Whatever we may have been we must of necessity be friends now," he told her.

"That will depend upon you," she replied.

Chapter III

AMIOCAP

The blue waters of the great sea known as Korsar Az wash the shores of a green island far from the mainland — a long, narrow island with verdure clad hills and plateaus, its coast line indented by coves and tiny bays — Amiocap, an island of mystery and romance.

At a distance, and when there is a haze upon the waters, it looks like two islands, rather than one, so low and narrow it is at one point, where coves run in on either side and the sea almost meets.

Thus it appeared to the two survivors from the deck of the Korsar derelict drifting helplessly with the sluggish run of an ocean current and at the whim of vagrant winds.

Time is not even a word to the people of Pellucidar, so Tanar had given no thought to that. They had eaten many times, but as there was still an ample supply of provisions, even for a large ship's company, he felt no concern upon that score, but he had been worried by the depletion of their supply of good water, for the contents of many casks that he had broached had been undrinkable.

They had slept much, which is the way of Pellucidarians when there is naught else to do, storing energy for possible future periods of long drawn exertion.

They had been sleeping thus, for how long who may say in the measureless present of Pellucidar. Stellara was the first to come on deck from the cabin she had occupied next to that of The Cid. She looked about for Tanar, but not seeing him she let her eyes wander out over the upcurving expanse of water that merged in every direction with the blue domed vault of the brilliant sky, in the exact center of which hung the great noonday sun.

But suddenly her gaze was caught and held by something beside the illimitable waters and the ceaseless sun. She voiced a surprised and joyous cry and, turning, ran across the deck toward the cabin in which Tanar slept.

"Tanar! Tanar!" she cried, pounding upon the paneled door. "Land, Tanar, land!"

The door swung open and the Sarian stepped out upon the deck where Stellara stood pointing across the starboard rail of the drifting derelict.

Close by rose the green hills of a long shore line that stretched away in both directions for many miles, but whether it was the mainland or an island they could not tell.

"Land!" breathed Tanar. "How good it looks!"

"The pleasant green of the soft foliage often hides terrible beasts and savage men," Stellara reminded him.

"But they are the dangers that I know — it is the unknown dangers of the sea that I do not like. I am not of the sea."

"You hate the sea?"

"No," he replied, "I do not hate it; I do not understand it — that is all. But there is something that I do understand," and he pointed toward the land.

There was that in Tanar's tone that caused Stellara to look quickly in the direction that he indicated.

"Men!" she exclaimed.

"Warriors," said Tanar.

"There must be twenty of them in that canoe," she said.

"And here comes another canoeful behind them."

From the mouth of a narrow cove the canoes were paddling out into the open sea.

"Look!" cried Stellara. "There are many more coming."

One after another twenty canoes moved in a long column out upon the quiet waters and as they drew steadily toward the ship the survivors saw that each was filled with almost naked warriors. Short, heavy spears, bone-tipped, bristled menacingly; stone knives protruded from every G-string and stone hatchets swung at every hip.

As the flotilla approached, Tanar went to a cabin and returned with two of the heavy pistols left behind by a fleeing Korsar when the ship had been abandoned.

"Do you expect to repulse four hundred warriors with those?" asked the girl.

Tanar shrugged. "If they have never

heard the report of a firearm a few shots may suffice to frighten them away, for a time at least," he explained, "and if we do not go on the shore the current will carry us away from them in time."

"But suppose they do not frighten so easily?" she demanded.

"Then I can do no more than my best with the crude weapons and the inferior powder of the Korsars," he said with the conscious superiority of one who had, with his people, so recently emerged from the stone age that he often instinctively grasped a pistol by the muzzle and used it as a war club in sudden emergencies when at close quarters.

"Perhaps they will not be unfriendly," suggested Stellara.

Tanar laughed. "Then they are not of Pellucidar," he said, "but of some wondrous country inhabited by what Perry calls angels."

"Who is Perry?" she demanded. "I never heard of him."

"He is a madman who says that Pellucidar is the inside of a hollow stone that is as round as the strange world that hangs forever above the Land of Awful Shadow, and that upon the outside are seas and mountains and plains and countless people and a great country from which he comes."

"He must be quite mad," said the girl.

"Yet he and David, our Emperor, have brought us many advantages that were before unknown in Pellucidar, so that now we can kill more warriors in a single battle than was possible before during the course of a whole war. Perry calls this civilization and it is indeed a very wonderful thing."

"Perhaps he came from the frozen world from which the ancestors of the Korsars came," suggested the girl. "They say that that country lies outside of Pellucidar."

"Here is the enemy," said Tanar. "Shall I fire at that big fellow standing in the bow of the first canoe?" Tanar raised one of the heavy pistols and took aim, but the girl laid a hand upon his arm.

"Wait," she begged. "They may be friendly. Do not fire unless you must — I hate killing."

"I can well believe that you are no Korsar," he said, lowering the muzzle of his weapon.

There came a hail from the leading canoe. "We are prepared for you, Korsars,"

shouted the tall warrior standing in the bow. "You are few in numbers. We are many. Your great canoe is a useless wreck; ours are manned by twenty warriors each. You are helpless. We are strong. It is not always thus and this time it is not we who shall be taken prisoners, but you, if you attempt to land.

"But we are not like you, Korsars. We do not want to kill or capture. Go away and we shall not harm you."

"We cannot go away," replied Tanar. "Our ship is helpless. We are only two and our food and water are nearly exhausted. Let us land and remain until we can prepare to return to our own countries."

The warrior turned and conversed with the others in his canoe. Presently he faced Tanar again.

"No," he said; "my people will not permit Korsars to come among us. They do not trust you. Neither do I. If you do not go away we shall take you as prisoners and your fate will be in the hands of the Council of the Chiefs."

"But we are not Korsars," explained Tanar.

The warrior laughed. "You speak a lie," he said. "Do you think that we do not know the ships of Korsar?"

"This is a Korsar ship," replied Tanar; "but we are not Korsars. We were prisoners and when they abandoned their ship in a great storm they left us aboard."

Again the warriors conferred and those in other canoes that had drawn alongside the first joined in the discussion.

"Who are you then?" demanded the spokesman.

"I am Tanar of Pellucidar. My father is King of Sari."

"We are all of Pellucidar," replied the warrior; "but we never heard of a country called Sari. And the woman — she is your mate?"

"No!" cried Stellara, haughtily. "I am not his mate."

"Who are you? Are you a Sarian, also?"

"I am no Sarian. My father and mother were of Amiocap."

Again the warriors talked among themselves, some seeming to favor one idea, some another.

"Do you know the name of this country?" finally demanded the leading warrior, addressing Stellara.

"No," she replied.

"We were about to ask you that very question," said Tanar.

"And the woman is from Amiocap!" demanded the warrior.

"No other blood flows in my veins," said Stellara, proudly.

"Then it is strange that you do not recognize your own land and your own people," cried the warrior. "This is the island of Amiocap!"

Stellara voiced a low cry of pleased astonishment. "Amiocap!" she breathed softly, as to herself. The tone was a caress, but the warriors in the canoes were too far away to hear her. They thought she was silent and embarrassed because they had discovered her deception.

"Go away!" they cried again.

"You will not send me away from the land of my parents!" cried Stellara, in astonishment.

"You have lied to us," replied the tall warrior. "You are not of Amiocap. You do not know us, nor do we know you."

"Listen!" cried Tanar. "I was a prisoner aboard this ship and, being no Korsar, the girl told me her story long before we sighted this land. She could not have known that we were near your island. I do not know that she ever knew its location, but nevertheless I believe that her story is true.

"She has never said that she was from Amiocap, but that her parents were. She has never seen the island before now. Her mother was stolen by the Korsars before she was born."

Again the warriors spoke together in low tones for a moment and then, once more, the spokesman addressed Stellara. "What was your mother's name?" he demanded. "Who was your father?"

"My mother was called Allara," replied the girl. "I never saw my father, but my mother said that he was a chief and a great tandor hunter, called Fedol."

At a word from the tall warrior in the bow of the leading canoe the warriors paddled slowly nearer the drifting hulk, and as they approached the ship's waist Tanar and Stellara descended to the main deck, which was now almost awash, so deep the ship rode because of the water in her hold, and as the canoe drifted alongside, the warriors, with the exception of a couple, laid down their paddles and stood ready with their bone-tipped spears.

Now the two upon the ship's deck and the tall warrior in the canoe stood almost upon the same level and face to face. The latter was a smooth-faced man with finely molded features and clear, gray eyes that bespoke intelligence and courage. He was gazing intently at Stellara, as though he would search her very soul for proof of the veracity or falsity of her statements. Presently he spoke.

"You might well be her daughter," he said; "the resemblance is apparent."

"You knew my mother?" exclaimed Stellara.

"I am Vulhan. You have heard her speak of me?"

"My mother's brother!" exclaimed Stellara, with deep emotion, but there was no answering emotion in the manner of the Amiocap warrior. "My father, where is he? Is he alive?"

"That is the question," said Vulhan, seriously. "Who is your father! Your mother was stolen by a Korsar. If the Korsar is your father, you are a Korsar."

"But he is not my father. Take me to my own father — although he has never seen me he will know me and I shall know him."

"It will do no harm," said a warrior who stood close to Vulhan. "If the girl is a Korsar we shall know what to do with her."

"If she is the spawn of the Korsar who stole Allara, Vulhan and Fedol will know how to treat her," said Vulhan savagely.

"I am not afraid," said Stellara.

"And this other," said Vulhan, nodding toward Tanar. "What of him?"

"He was a prisoner of war that the Korsars were taking back to Korsar. Let him come with you. His people are not sea people. He could not survive by the sea alone."

"You are sure that he is no Korsar?" demanded Vulhan.

"Look at him!" exclaimed the girl. "The men of Amiocap must know the people of Korsar well by sight. Does this one look like a Korsar?"

Vulhan was forced to admit that he did not. "Very well," he said, "he may come with us, but whatever your fate, he must share it."

"Gladly," agreed Tanar.

The two quit the deck of the derelict as places were made for them in the canoe and as the little craft was paddled rapidly toward shore neither felt any sorrow at parting from the drifting hulk that had been their home for so long. The last they saw of her, just as they were entering the cove, from which they had first seen the canoes emerge, she was drifting slowly with the ocean current parallel with the green shore of Amiocap.

At the upper end of the cove the canoes were beached and dragged beneath the concealing foliage of the luxuriant vegetation. Here they were turned bottom side up and left until occasion should again demand their use.

The warriors of Amiocap conducted their two prisoners into the jungle that grew almost to the water's edge. At first there was no sign of trail and the leading warriors forced their way through the lush vegetation, which fortunately was free from thorns and briers, but presently they came upon a little path which opened into a broad, well beaten trail along which the party moved in silence.

During the march Tanar had an opportunity to study the men of Amiocap more closely and he saw that almost without exception they were symmetrically built, with rounded, flowing muscles that suggested a combination of agility and strength. Their features were regular, and there was not among them one who might be termed ugly. On the whole their expressions were open rather than cunning and kindly rather than ferocious; yet the scars upon the bodies of many of them and their well worn and efficient looking, though crude, weapons suggested that they might be bold hunters and fierce warriors. There was a marked dignity in their carriage and demeanor which appealed to Tanar as did their taciturnity, for the Sarians themselves are not given to useless talk.

Stellara, walking at his side, appeared unusually happy and there was an expression of contentment upon her face that the Sarian had never seen there before. She had been watching him as well as the Amiocapians, and now she addressed him in a whisper.

"What do you think of my people?" she asked, proudly. "Are they not wonderful?"

"They are a fine race," he replied, "and I hope for your sake that they will believe that you are one of them."

"It is all just as I have dreamed it so many times," said the girl, with a happy sigh. "I have always known that some day I should come to Amiocap and that it would be just as my mother told me that it was — the great trees, the giant ferns, the gorgeous, flowering vines and bushes. There are fewer savage beasts here than in other parts of Pellucidar and the people seldom war among themselves, so that for the most part they live in peace and contentment, broken only by the raids of the Korsars or an occasional raid upon their fields and villages by the great tandors. Do you know what tandors are, Tanar? Do you have them in your country?"

Tanar nodded. "I have heard of them in Amoz," he said, "though they are rare in Sari."

"There are thousands of them upon the island of Amiocap," said the girl, "and my people are the greatest tandor hunters in Pellucidar."

Again they walked on in silence, Tanar wondering what the attitude of the Amiocapians would be towards them, and if friendly whether they would be able to assist him in making his way back to the distant mainland, where Sari lay. To this primitive mountaineer it seemed little short of hopeless even to dream of returning to his native land, for the sea appalled him, nor did he have any conception as to how he might set a course across its savage bosom, or navigate any craft that he might later find at his disposal; yet so powerful is the homing instinct in the Pellucidarians that there was no doubt in his mind that so long as he lived he would always be searching for a way back to Sari.

He was glad that he did not have to worry about Stellara, for if it was true that she was among her own people she could remain upon Amiocap and there would rest upon him no sense of responsibility for her return to Korsar; but if they did not accept her — that was another matter; then Tanar would have to seek for means of escape from an island peopled by enemies and he would have to take Stellara with him.

But this train of thought was interrupted by a sudden exclamation from Stellara. "Look!" she cried. "Here is a village; perhaps it is the very village of my mother."

"What did you say?" inquired a warrior, walking near them.

"I said that perhaps this is the village where my mother lived before she was stolen by the Korsars."

"And you say that your mother was Allara?" inquired the warrior.

"Yes."

"This was indeed the village in which Allara lived," said the warrior; "but do not hope, girl, that you will be received as one of them, for unless your father also was of Amiocap, you are not an Amiocapian. It will be hard to convince any one that you are not the daughter of a Korsar father, and as such you are a Korsar and no Amiocapian."

"But how can you know that my father was a Korsar?" demanded Stellara.

"We do not have to know," replied the warrior; "it is merely a matter of what we believe, but that is a question that will have to be settled by Zural, the chief of the village of Lar."

"Lar," repeated Stellara. "That is the village of my mother! I have heard her speak of it many times. This, then, must be Lar."

"It is," replied the warrior, "and presently you shall see Zural."

The village of Lar consisted of perhaps a hundred thatched huts, each of which was divided into two or more rooms, one of which was invariably an open sitting room without walls, in the center of which was a stone fireplace. The other rooms were ordinarily tightly walled and windowless, affording the necessary darkness for the Amiocapians when they wished to sleep.

The entire clearing was encircled by the most remarkable fence that Tanar had ever seen. The posts, instead of being set in the ground, were suspended from a heavy fiber rope that ran from tree to tree, the lower ends of the posts hanging at least four feet above the ground. Holes had been bored through the posts at intervals of twelve or eighteen inches and into these were inserted hardwood stakes, four or five feet in length and sharpened at either end. These stakes protruded from the posts in all directions, parallel with the ground, and the posts were hung at such a distance from one another that the points of the stakes, protruding from contiguous posts, left intervals of from two to four feet between. As a safeguard against an attacking enemy they seemed futile to Tanar, for in entering the village the party had passed through the open spaces between the posts without being hindered by the barrier.

But conjecture as to the purpose of this strange barrier was crowded from his thoughts by other more interesting occurrences, for no sooner had they entered the village than they were surrounded by a horde of men, women and children.

"Who are these?" demanded some.

"They say that they are friends," replied Vulhan, "but we believe that they are from Korsar."

"Korsars!" cried the villagers.

"I am no Korsar," cried Stellara, angrily. "I am the daughter of Allara, the sister of Vulhan."

"Let her tell that to Zural. It is his business to listen, not ours," cried one. "Zural will know what to do with Korsars. Did they not steal his daughter and kill his son?"

"Yes, take them to Zural," cried another.

"It is to Zural that I am taking them," replied Vulhan.

The villagers made way for the warriors and their prisoners and as the latter passed through the aisles thus formed many were the ugly looks cast upon them and many the expressions of hatred that they overheard, but no violence was offered them and presently they were conducted to a large hut near the center of the village.

Like the other dwellings of the village of Lar, the floors of the chief's house were raised a foot or eighteen inches above the ground. The thatched roof of the great, open living room, into which they were conducted, was supported by enormous ivory tusks of the giant tandors. The floor, which appeared to be constructed of unglazed tile, was almost entirely covered by the hides of wild animals. There were a number of low, wooden stools standing about the room, and one higher one that might almost have been said to have attained the dignity of a chair.

Upon this larger stool was seated a stern faced man, who scrutinized them closely and silently as they were halted before him. For several seconds no one spoke, and then the man upon the chair turned to Vulhan.

"Who are these," he demanded, "and what do they in the village of Lar?"

"We took them from a Korsar ship that was drifting helplessly with the ocean current," said Vulhan, "and we have brought them to Zural, chief of the village of Lar, that he may hear their story and judge whether they be the friends they claim to be, or the Korsar enemies that we believe them to be. This one," and Vulhan pointed to Stellara, "says that she is the daughter of Allara."

"I am the daughter of Allara," said Stellara.

"And who was your father?" demanded Zural.

"My father's name is Fedol," replied Stellara.

"How do you know?" asked Zural.

"My mother told me."

"Where were you born?" demanded Zural.

"In the Korsar city of Allaban," replied Stellara.

"Then you are a Korsar," stated Zural with finality. "And this one, what has he to say for himself?" asked Zural, indicating Tanar with a nod.

"He claims that he was a prisoner of the Korsars and that he comes from a distant kingdom called Sari."

"I have never heard of such a kingdom," said Zural. "Is there any warrior here who has ever heard of it?" he demanded. "If there is, let him in justice to the prisoner, speak." But the Amiocapians only shook their heads for there was none who had ever heard of the kingdom of Sari. "It is quite plain," continued Zural, "that they are enemies and that they are seeking by falsehood to gain our confidence. If there is a drop of Amiocapian blood in one of them, we are sorry for that drop. Take them away, Vulhan. Keep them under guard until we decide how they shall be destroyed."

"My mother told me that the Amiocapians were a just and kindly people," said Stellara; "but it is neither just nor kindly to destroy this man who is not an enemy simply because you have never heard of the country from which he comes. I tell you that he is no Korsar. I was on one of the ships of the fleet when the prisoners were brought aboard. I heard The Cid and Bohar the Bloody when they were questioning this man, and I know that he is no Korsar and that he comes from a kingdom known as Sari. They did not doubt his word, so why should you? If you are a just and kindly people how can you destroy me without giving me an opportunity to talk with Fedol, my father. He will believe me; he will know that I am his daughter."

"The gods frown upon us if we harbor enemies in our village," replied Zural. "We should have bad luck, as all Amiocapians know. Wild beasts would kill our hunters and the tandors would trample our fields and destroy our villages. But worst of all

the Korsars would come and rescue you from us. As for Fedol, no man knows where he is. He is not of this village and the people of his own village have slept and eaten many times since they saw Fedol. They have slept and eaten many times since Fedol set forth upon his last tandor hunt. Perhaps the tandors have avenged the killing of many of their fellows, or perhaps Fedol fell into the clutches of the Buried People. These things we do not know, but we do know that Fedol went away to hunt tandors and that he never came back and that we do not know where to find him. Take them away, Vulhan, and we shall hold a council of the chiefs and then we shall decide what shall be done with them."

"You are a cruel and wicked man, Zural," cried Stellara, "and no better than the Korsars themselves."

"It is useless, Stellara," said Tanar, laying a hand upon the girl's arm. "Let us go quietly with Vulhan"; and then in a low whisper, "do not anger them, for there is yet hope for us in the council of the chiefs if we do not antagonize them." And so without further word Stellara and Tanar were led from the house of Zural the chief surrounded by a dozen stalwart warriors.

Chapter IV

LETARI

Stellara and Tanar were conducted to a small hut in the outskirts of the village. The building consisted of but two rooms; the open living room with the fireplace and a small dark, sleeping apartment. Into the latter the prisoners were thrust and a single warrior was left on guard in the living room to prevent their escape.

In a world where the sun hangs perpetually at zenith there is no darkness and without darkness there is little opportunity to escape from the clutches of a watchful enemy. Yet never for a moment was the thought of escape absent from the mind of Tanar the Sarian. He studied the sentries and as each one was relieved he tried to enter into conversation with his successor, but all to no avail — the warriors would not talk to him. Sometimes the guards dozed, but the village and the clearing about it were always alive with people so that it appeared unlikely that any opportunity for escape might present itself.

The sentries were changed, food was brought to the prisoners and when they felt so inclined they slept. Thus only might they measure the lapse of time, if such a thing occurred to them, which doubtless it did not. They talked together and sometimes Stellara sang — sang the songs of Amiocap that her mother had taught her, and they were happy and contented, although each knew that the specter of death hovered constantly above them. Presently he would strike, but in the meantime they were happy.

"When I was a youth," said Tanar, "I was taken prisoner by the black people with tails. They build their villages among the high branches of lofty trees and at first they put me in a small hut as dark as this and much dirtier and I was very miserable and very unhappy for I have always been free and I love my freedom, but now I am again a prisoner in a dark hut and in addition I know that I am going to die and I do not want to die, yet I am not unhappy. Why is it, Stellara, do you know?"

"I have wondered about the same thing myself," replied the girl. "It seems to me that I have never been so happy before in my life, but I do not know the reason."

They were sitting close together upon a fiber mat that they had placed near the doorway that they might obtain as much light and air as possible. Stellara's soft eyes looked thoughtfully out upon the little world framed by the doorway of their prison cell. One hand rested listlessly on the mat between them. Tanar's eyes rested upon her profile, and slowly his hand went out and covered hers.

"Perhaps," he said, "I should not be happy if you were not here."

The girl turned half frightened eyes upon him and withdrew her hand. "Don't," she said.

"Why?" he asked.

"I do not know, only that it makes me afraid."

The man was about to speak again when a figure darkened the opening in the doorway. A girl had come bringing food. Heretofore it had been a man — a taciturn man who had replied to none of Tanar's questions. But there was no suggestion of taciturnity upon the beautiful, smiling countenance of the girl.

"Here is food," she said. "Are you hungry?"

"Where there is nothing else to do but eat I am always hungry," said Tanar. "But where is the man who brought our food before?"

"That was my father," replied the girl. "He has gone to hunt and I have brought the food in his stead."

"I hope that he never returns from the hunt," said Tanar.

"Why?" demanded the girl. "He is a good father. Why do you wish him harm?"

"I wish him no harm," replied Tanar, laughing. "I only wish that his daughter would continue to bring our food. She is far more agreeable and much better looking."

The girl flushed, but it was evident that she was pleased.

"I wanted to come before," she said, "but my father would not let me. I saw you when they brought you into the village and I have wanted to see you again. I never before saw a man who looked like you. You are different from the Amiocapians. Are all the men of Sari as good looking as you?"

Tanar laughed. "I am afraid I have never given much thought to that subject," he replied. "In Sari we judge our men by what they do and not by what they look like."

"But you must be a great hunter," said the girl. "You look like a great hunter."

"How do great hunters look?" demanded Stellara with some asperity.

"They look like this man," replied the girl. "Do you know," she continued, "I have dreamed about you many times."

"What is your name?" asked Tanar.

"Letari," replied the girl.

"Letari," repeated Tanar. "That is a pretty name. I hope, Letari, that you will bring our food to us often."

"I shall never bring it again," she said, sadly.

"And why?" demanded Tanar.

"Because no one will bring it again," she said.

"And why is that? Are they going to starve us to death?"

"No, the council of the chiefs has decided that you are both Korsars and that you must be destroyed."

"And when will that be?" asked Stellara.

"As soon as the hunters return with food. We are going to have a great feast and dance, but I shall not enjoy it. I shall be very unhappy for I do not wish to see Tanar die."

"How are they going to destroy us?"

asked the man.

"Look," said the girl, pointing through the open doorway. There, in the distance, the two prisoners saw men setting two stakes into the ground. "There were many who wanted to give you to the Buried People," said Letari, "but Zural said that it has been so long since we have had a feast and a dance that he thought that we should celebrate the killing of two Korsars rather than let the Buried People have all the pleasure, and so they are going to tie you to those two stakes and pile dry wood and brush around you and burn you to death."

Stellara shuddered. "And my mother taught me that you were a kindly people," she said.

"Oh, we do not mean to be unkind," said Letari, "but the Korsars have been verý cruel to us and Zural believes that the gods will take word to the Korsars that you were burned to death and that perhaps it will frighten them and keep them away from Amiocap."

Tanar arose to his feet and stood very straight and stiff. The horror of the situation almost overwhelmed him. He looked down at Stellara's golden head and shuddered. "You cannot mean," he said, "that the men of Amiocap intend to burn this girl alive?"

"Why, yes," said Letari. "It would do no good to kill her first for then her spirit could not tell the gods that she was burned and they could not tell the Korsars."

"It is hideous," cried Tanar; "and you, a girl yourself, have you no sympathy; have you no heart?"

"I am very sorry that they are going to burn you," said Letari, "but as for her, she is a Korsar and I feel nothing but hatred and loathing for her, but you are different. I know that you are not a Korsar and I wish that I could save you."

"Will you — would you, if you could?" demanded Tanar.

"Yes, but I cannot."

The conversation relative to escape had been carried on in low whispers, so that the guard would not overhear, but evidently it had aroused his suspicion for now he arose and came to the doorway of the hut. "What are you talking about?" he demanded. "Why do you stay in here so long, Letari, talking with these Korsars? I heard what you said and I believe that you are in love with this man."

"What if I am?" demanded the girl. "Do not our gods demand that we love? What else do we live for upon Amiocap but love?"

"The gods do not say that we should love our enemies."

"They do not say that we should not," retorted Letari. "If I choose to love Tanar it is my own affair."

"Clear out!" snapped the warrior. "There are plenty of men in Lar for you to love."

"Ah!" sighed the girl as she passed through the doorway, "but there is none like Tanar."

"The hateful little wanton," cried Stellara after the girl had left.

"She does not hesitate to reveal what is in her heart," said Tanar. "The girls of Sari are not like that. They would die rather than reveal their love before the man had declared his. But perhaps she is only a child and did not realize what she said."

"A child nothing," snapped Stellara. "She knew perfectly well what she was saying and it is quite apparent that you liked it. Very well, when she comes to save you, go with her."

"You do not think that I intended to go with her alone even though an opportunity for escape presented itself through her, do you?" demanded Tanar.

"She told you that she would not help me to escape," Stellara reminded him.

"I know that, but it would be only in the hope of helping you to escape that I would take advantage of her help."

"I would rather be burned alive a dozen times than to escape with her help."

There was a venom in the girl's voice that had never been there before and Tanar looked at her in surprise. "I do not understand you, Stellara," he said.

"I do not understand myself," said the girl, and burying her face in her hands she burst into tears.

Tanar knelt quickly beside her and put an arm about her. "Don't," he begged, "please don't."

She pushed him from her. "Go away," she cried. "Don't touch me. I hate you."

Tanar was about to speak again when he was interrupted by a great commotion at the far end of the village. There were shouts and yells from men, mingled with a thunderous noise that fairly shook the ground, and then the deep booming of drums.

Instantly the men setting the stakes in

the ground, where Tanar and Stellara were to be burned, stopped their work, seized their weapons and rushed in the direction from which the noise was coming.

The prisoners saw men, women and children running from their huts and all directed their steps toward the same point. The guard before their door leaped to his feet and stood for a moment looking at the running villagers. Then, without a word or backward glance, he dashed off after them.

Tanar, realizing that for the moment at least they were unguarded, stepped from the dark cell out into the open living apartment and looked in the direction toward which the villagers were running. There he saw the cause of the disturbance and also an explanation of the purpose for which the strange hanging barrier had been erected.

Just beyond the barrier loomed two gigantic mammoths — huge tandors, towering sixteen feet or more in height — their wicked eyes red with hate and rage; their great tusks gleaming in the sunlight; their long, powerful trunks seeking to drag down the barrier from the sharpened stakes of which their flesh recoiled. Facing the mammoths was a shouting horde of warriors, screaming women and children, and above all rose the thundering din of the drums.

Each time the tandors sought to force their way through the barrier, or brush aside its posts, these swung about so that the sharpened stakes threatened their eyes or pricked the tender flesh of their trunks, while bravely facing them the shouting warriors hurled their stone-tipped spears.

But however interesting or inspiring the sight might be, Tanar had no time to spare to follow the course of this strange encounter. Turning to Stellara, he seized her hand. "Come," he cried. "Now is our chance!" And while the villagers were engrossed with the tandors at the far end of the village, Tanar and Stellara ran swiftly across the clearing and entered the lush vegetation of the forest beyond.

There was no trail and it was with difficulty that they forced their way through the underbrush for a short distance before Tanar finally halted.

"We shall never escape them in this way," he said. "Our spoor is as plain as the spoor of a dyryth after a rain."

"How else then may we escape?" asked Stellara.

Tanar was looking upward into the trees examining them closely. "When I was a prisoner among the black people with long tails," he said, "I had to learn to travel through the trees and this knowledge and the ability have stood me in good stead many times since and I believe that they may prove our salvation now."

"You go then," said Stellara, "and save yourself, for certainly I cannot travel through the trees, and there is no reason why we should both be recaptured when one of us can escape."

Tanar smiled. "You know that I would not do that," he said.

"But what else may you do?" demanded Stellara. "They will follow the trail we are making and recapture us before we are out of hearing of the village."

"We shall leave no trail," said Tanar. "Come," and leaping lightly to a lower branch he swung himself into the tree that spread above them. "Give me your hand," he said, reaching down to Stellara, and a moment later he had drawn the girl to his side. Then he stood erect and steadied the girl while she arose to her feet. Before them a maze of branches stretched away to be lost in the foliage.

"We shall leave no spoor here," said Tanar.

"I am afraid," said Stellara. "Hold me tightly."

"You will soon become accustomed to it," said Tanar, "and then you will not be afraid. At first I was afraid, but later I could swing through the trees almost as rapidly as the black men themselves."

"I cannot even take a single step," said Stellara. "I know that I shall fall."

"You do not have to take a step," said Tanar. "Put your arms around my neck and hold on tightly," and then he stooped and lifted her with his left arm while she clung tightly to him, her soft white arms encircling his neck.

"How easily you lifted me!" she said; "how strong you are; but no man living could carry my weight through these trees and not fall."

Tanar did not reply, but instead he moved off among the branches seeking sure footing and secure handholds as he went. The girl's soft body was pressed close to his and in his nostrils was the delicate sachet that he had sensed in his first contact with Stellara aboard the Korsar ship and which now seemed a part of her.

As Tanar swung through the forest, the girl marveled at the strength of the man. She had always considered him a weakling by comparison with the beefy Korsars, but now she realized that in those smoothly rolling muscles was concealed the power of a superman.

She found a fascination in watching him. He moved so easily and he did not seem to tire. Once she let her lips fall until they touched his thick, black hair and then, just a little, almost imperceptibly, she tightened her arms about his neck.

Stellara was very happy and then, of a sudden, she recalled Letari and she straightened up and relaxed her hold. "The vile wanton," she said.

"Who?" demanded Tanar. "What are you talking about?"

"That creature, Letari," said Stellara.

"Why she is not vile," said Tanar. "I thought she was very nice and she is certainly beautiful."

"I believe you are in love with her," snapped Stellara.

"That would not be difficult," said Tanar. "She seemed very lovable."

"Do you love her?" demanded Stellara.

"Why shouldn't I?" asked Tanar.

"Do you?" insisted the girl.

"Would you care if I did?" asked Tanar, softly.

"Most certainly not," said Stellara.

"Then why do you ask?"

"I didn't ask," said Stellara. "I do not care."

"Oh," said Tanar. "I misunderstood," and he moved on in silence, for the men of Sari are not talkative, and Stellara did not know what was in his mind for his face did not reflect the fact that he was laughing inwardly, and, anyway, Stellara could not see his face.

Tanar moved always in one direction and his homing instinct assured him that the direction lay toward Sari. As far as the land went he could move unerringly toward the spot in Pellucidar where he was born. Every Pellucidarian can do that, but put them on the water, out of sight of land, and that instinct leaves them and they have no more conception of direction than would you or I if we were transported suddenly to a land where there are no points of compass since the sun hangs perpetually at zenith and there is no moon and no stars. Tanar's only wish at present was to put

them as far as possible from the village of Lar. He would travel until they reached the coast for, knowing that Amiocap was an island, he knew that eventually they must come to the ocean. What they should do then was rather vague in his mind. He had visions of building a boat and embarking upon the sea, although he knew perfectly well that this would be madness on the part of a hill dweller such as he.

Presently he felt hungry and he knew that they must have traveled a considerable distance.

Sometimes Tanar kept track of distance by computing the number of steps that he took, for by much practice he had learned to count them almost mechanically, leaving his mind free for other perceptions and thoughts, but here among the branches of the trees, where his steps were not of uniform length, he had thought it not worth the effort to count them and so he could only tell by the recurrence of hunger that they must have covered considerable distance since they left the village of Lar.

During their flight through the forest they had seen birds and monkeys and other animals and, on several occasions, they had paralleled or crossed game trails, but as the Amiocapians had stripped him of his weapons he had no means of obtaining meat until he could stop long enough to fashion a bow and some arrows and a spear.

How he missed his spear! From childhood it had been his constant companion and for a long time he had felt almost helpless without it. He had never become entirely accustomed or reconciled to carrying firearms, feeling in the bottom of his primitive and savage heart that there was nothing more dependable than a sturdy, stone shod spear.

He had rather liked the bow and arrows that Innes and Perry had taught him to make and use, as the arrows had seemed like little spears. At least one could see them, whereas with the strange and noisy weapons, which belched forth smoke and flame, one could not see the projectile at all. It was most unnatural and uncanny.

But Tanar's mind was not occupied with such thoughts at this time. Food was dominant.

Presently they came to a small, natural clearing beside a crystal brook and Tanar swung lightly to the ground.

"We shall stop here," he said, "until I can make weapons and get meat for us."

With the feel of the ground beneath her feet again Stellara felt more independent. "I am not hungry," she said.

"I am," said Tanar.

"There are berries and fruits and nuts in plenty," she insisted. "We should not wait here to be overtaken by the warriors from Lar."

"We shall wait here until I have made weapons," said Tanar, with finality, "and then I shall not only be in a position to make a kill for meat, but I shall be able better to defend you against Zural's warriors."

"I wish to go on," said Stellara. "I do not wish to stay here," and she stamped her little foot.

Tanar looked at her in surprise. "What is the matter with you, Stellara? You were never like this before."

"I do not know what is the matter with me," said the girl. "I only know that I wish I were back in Korsar, in the house of The Cid. There, at least, I should be among friends. Here I am surrounded only by enemies."

"Then you would have Bohar the Bloody One as a mate, if he survived the storm, or if not he another like him," Tanar reminded her.

"At least he loved me," said Stellara.

"And you loved him?" asked Tanar.

"Perhaps," said Stellara.

There was a peculiar look on Tanar's face as his eyes rested upon the girl. He did not understand her, but he seemed to be trying to. She was looking past him, a strange expression upon her face when suddenly she voiced an exclamation of dismay and pointed past him.

"Look!" she cried. "Oh, God, look!"

Chapter V

THE TANDOR HUNTER

So filled with fear was Stellara's tone that Tanar felt the hair rise upon his scalp as he wheeled about to face the thing that had so filled the girl with horror, but even had he had time to conjure in his imagination a picture worthy of her fright, he could not have imagined a more fearsome or repulsive thing than that which was advancing upon them.

In conformation it was primarily human, but there the similarity ended. It had arms and legs and it walked erect upon two feet; but such feet! They were huge, flat things with nailless toes — short, stubby toes with webs between them. Its arms were short and in lieu of fingers its hands were armed with three heavy claws. It stood somewhere in the neighborhood of five feet in height and there was not a vestige of hair upon its entire naked body, the skin of which was of the sickly pallor of a corpse.

But these attributes lent to it but a fraction of its repulsiveness — it was its head and face that were appalling. It had no external ears, there being only two small orifices on either side of its head where these organs are ordinarily located. Its mouth was large with loose, flabby lips that were drawn back now into a snarl that exposed two rows of heavy fangs. Two small openings above the center of the mouth marked the spot where a nose should have been and, to add further to the hideousness of its appearance, it was eyeless, unless bulging protuberances forcing out the skin where the eyes should have been might be called eyes. Here the skin upon the face moved as though great, round eyes were rolling beneath. The hideousness of that blank face without eyelids, lashes or eyebrows shocked even the calm and steady nerves of Tanar.

The creature carried no weapons, but what need had it for weapons, armed as it was with those formidable claws and fangs? Beneath its pallid skin surged great muscles that attested its giant strength and upon its otherwise blank face the mouth alone was sufficient to suggest its diabolical ferocity.

"Run, Tanar!" cried Stellara. "Take to the trees! It is one of the Buried People." But the thing was too close to him to admit of escape even if Tanar had been minded to desert Stellara, and so he stood there quietly awaiting the encounter and then suddenly, as though to add to the uncanny horror of the situation, the thing spoke. From its flabby, drooling lips issued sounds — mumbled, ghastly sounds that yet took on the semblance of speech until it became intelligible in a distorted way to Tanar and Stellara.

"It is the woman I want," mumbled the creature. "Give me the woman, and the man may go." To Tanar's shocked sensibilities it was as though a mutilated corpse had risen from the grave and spoken, and he fell back a step with a sensation as nearly akin to horror as he had ever experienced:

"You cannot have the woman," said Tanar. "Leave us alone, or I will kill you."

An uncanny scream that was a mixture of laugh and shriek broke from the lips of the thing. "Then die!" it cried, as it launched itself upon the Sarian.

As it closed it struck upward with its heavy claws in an attempt to disembowel its antagonist, but Tanar eluded its first rush by leaping lightly to one side and then, turning quickly, he hurled himself upon the loathsome body and circling its neck with one powerful arm Tanar turned suddenly and, bending his body forward and downward, hurled the creature over his head and heavily to the ground.

But instantly it was up again and at him. Screaming with rage and frothing at the mouth it struck wildly with its heavy claws, but Tanar had learned certain things from David Innes that men of the stone age ordinarily do not know, for David had taught him, as he had taught many another young Pellucidarian, the art of self-defense, including boxing, wrestling and jiu-jitsu, and now again they came into good stead as they had upon other occasions since he had mastered them and once more he gave thanks for the fortunate circumstance that had brought David Innes from the outer crust to Pellucidar to direct the destinies of its human race as first emperor.

Combined with his knowledge, training and agility was Tanar's great strength, without which these other accomplishments would have been of far lesser value, and so as the creature struck, Tanar parried the blows, fending the wicked talons from his flesh and with a strength that surprised his antagonist since it was fully as great as his own.

But what was still more surprising to the monster was the frequency with which Tanar was able to step in and deliver telling blows to the body and head that, in its awkwardness and lack of skill, it was unable to properly protect.

To one side, watching the battle for which she was the stake, stood Stellara. She might have run away and hidden; she might have made good her escape, but no such thoughts entered her courageous little head. It would have been as impossible for her to desert her companion in the hour of his need as it would have been for him to leave her to her fate and so she stood there, helpless, awaiting the outcome.

To and fro across the clearing the battlers moved, trampling down the lush vegetation that sometimes grew so thickly as to hamper their movements, and now it became apparent to both Stellara and Tanar from the labored breathing of the creature that it was being steadily worn down and that it lacked the endurance of the Sarian. However, probably sensing something of this itself, it now redoubled its efforts and the ferocity of its attack, and, at the same time, Tanar discovered a vulnerable spot at which to aim his blows.

Striking for the face he had accidentally touched one of the bulging protuberances that lay beneath the skin where the eyes should have been. At the impact of the blow, light as it was, the creature screamed and leaped backward, instinctively raising one of its claws to the injured organ and thereafter Tanar directed all his efforts toward placing further and heavier blows upon those two bulging spots.

He struck again and landed cleanly a heavy blow upon one of them. With a shriek of pain the creature stepped back and clamped both paws to its hurt.

They were fighting very close to where Stellara stood. The creature's back was toward her and she could have reached out and touched him, so near was he to her. She saw Tanar spring forward to strike again. The creature dropped back quite abreast of her and then suddenly lowering its head it gave vent to a horrid shriek and charged the Sarian with all the hideous ferocity that it could gather.

It seemed as though it had mustered all its remaining vitality and thrown it into this last, mad charge. Tanar, his mind and muscles coordinating perfectly, quick to see openings and take advantage of them and equally quick to realize the advantages of retreat, leaped backward to avoid the mad charge and the flailing claws, but as he did so one of his heels struck a low bush and he fell heavily to the ground upon his back.

For the moment he was helpless and in that brief moment the creature could be upon him with those horrid fangs and ripping claws.

Tanar knew it. The thing charging him knew it and Stellara, standing so close to them, knew it, and so quickly did she act that Tanar had scarcely struck the ground as she launched herself bodily upon the charging monster from behind.

As a football player hurls himself forward to tackle an opponent so Stellara hurled herself at the creature. Her arms encircled its knees and then slipped down, as he kicked and struggled to free himself, until finally she secured a hold upon one of his skinny ankles just above its huge foot. There she clung and the creature lunged forward just short of Tanar, but instantly, with a howl of rage, it turned to rend the girl. But that brief instant of delay had been sufficient to permit Tanar to regain his feet and ere ever the talons or fangs could sink into the soft flesh of Stellara, Tanar was upon the creature's back. Fingers of steel encircled its throat and though it struggled and struck out with its heavy claws it was at last helpless in the clutches of the Sarian.

Slowly, relentlessly, Tanar choked the life from the monster and then, with an expression of disgust, he cast the corpse aside and stepped quickly to where Stellara was staggering weakly to her feet.

He put his arm about her and for a moment she buried her face in his shoulder and sobbed. "Do not be afraid," he said; "the thing is dead."

She raised her face toward him. "Let us go away from here," she said. "I am afraid. There may be more of the Buried People about. There must be an entrance to their underworld near here, for they do not wander far from such openings."

"Yes," he said, "until I have weapons I wish to see no more of them."

"They are horrible creatures," said Stellara, "and if there had been two of them we should both have been lost."

"What are they?" asked Tanar. "You seem to know about them. Where had you ever seen one before?"

"I have never seen one until just now," said she, "but my mother told me about them. They are feared and hated by all Amiocapians. They are Coripies and they inhabit dark caverns and tunnels beneath the surface of the ground. That is why we call them the Buried People. They live on flesh and wandering about the jungle they gather up the remains of our kills and devour the bodies of wild beasts that have died in the forest, but being afraid of our spears they do not venture far from the openings that lead down into their dark world. Occasionally they waylay a lone hunter and less often they come to one of our villages and seize a woman or child. No one has ever entered their world and escaped to tell about it, so that what my mother has told me about them is only what our people have imagined as to the underworld where the Buried People dwell for there has never been any Amiocapian warrior brave enough to venture into the dark recesses of one of their tunnels, or if there has been such one he has not returned to tell of it."

"And if the kindly Amiocapians had not decided to burn us to death, they might have given us to the Buried People?" said Tanar.

"Yes, they would have taken us and bound us to trees close to one of the entrances to the underworld, but do not blame my mother's people for that as they would have been doing only that which they considered right and proper."

"Perhaps they are a kindly people," said Tanar, with a grin, "for it was certainly far more kindly to accord us death by burning at the stake than to have left us to the horrid attentions of the Coripies. But come, we will take to the trees again, for this spot does not look as beautiful to me now as it did when we first looked upon it."

Once more they took up their flight among the branches and just as they were commencing to feel the urge to sleep Tanar discovered a small deer in a game trail beneath them, and making his kill the two satisfied their hunger, and then with small branches and great leaves Tanar constructed a platform in a tree — a narrow couch, where Stellara lay down to sleep while he stood guard, and after she had slept he slept, and then once more they resumed their flight.

Strengthened and refreshed by food and sleep they renewed their journey in higher spirits and greater hopefulness. The village of Lar lay far behind and since they had left it they had seen no other village nor any sign of man.

While Stellara had slept Tanar had busied himself in fashioning crude weapons against the time when he might find proper materials for the making of better ones. A slender branch of hard wood, gnawed to a point by his strong, white teeth, must answer him for a spear. His bow was constructed of another branch and strung with tendons taken from the deer he had killed, while his arrows were slender shoots cut from a tough shrub that grew plentifully throughout the forest. He fashioned a second, lighter spear for Stellara, and thus armed each felt a sense of security that had been entirely wanting before.

On and on they went, three times they ate and once again they slept, and still they had not reached the seacoast.

The great sun hung overhead; a gentle, cooling breeze moved through the forest; birds of gorgeous plumage and little monkeys unknown to the outer world flew or scampered, sang or chattered as the man and the woman disturbed them in their passage. It was a peaceful world and to Tanar, accustomed to the savage, carnivorous beasts that overran the great mainland of his birth, it seemed a very safe and colorless world; yet he was content that nothing was interfering with their progress toward escape.

Stellara had said no more about desiring to return to Korsar and the plan that always hovered among his thoughts included taking Stellara back to Sari with him.

The peaceful trend of Tanar's thoughts was suddenly shattered by the sound of shrill trumpeting. So close it sounded that it might almost have been directly beneath him, and an instant later as he parted the foliage ahead of him he saw the cause of the disturbance.

The jungle ended here upon the edge of open meadowland that was dotted with small clumps of trees. In the foreground there were two figures — a warrior fleeing for his life and behind him a huge tandor, which, though going upon three legs, was sure soon to overtake the man.

Tanar took the entire scene in at a glance and was aware that here was a lone tandor hunter who had failed to hamstring his prey in both hind legs.

It is seldom that man hunts the great tandor single-handed and only the bravest or the most rash would essay to do so. Ordinarily there are several hunters, two of whom are armed with heavy, stone axes.

While the others make a noise to attract the attention of the tandor and hide the sound of the approach of the axe men, the latter creep cautiously through the underbrush from the rear of the great animal until each is within striking distance of a hind leg. Then simultaneously they hamstring the monster, which, lying helpless, they dispatch with heavy spears and arrows.

He who would alone hamstring a tandor must be endowed not only with great strength and courage, but must be able to strike two unerring blows with his axe in such rapid succession that the beast is crippled almost before it realizes that it has been attacked.

It was evident to Tanar that this hunter had failed to get in his second blow quickly enough and now he was at the mercy of the great beast.

Since they had started upon their flight through the trees Stellara had overcome her fear and was now able to travel alone with only occasional assistance from Tanar. She had been following the Sarian and now she stood at his side, watching the tragedy being enacted below them.

"He will be killed," she cried. "Can we not save him?"

This thought had not occurred to Tanar, for was the man not an Amiocapian and an enemy; but there was something in the girl's tone that spurred the Sarian to action. Perhaps it was the instinct in the male to exhibit his prowess before the female. Perhaps it was because at heart Tanar was brave and magnanimous, or perhaps it was because that among all the other women in the world it was Stellara who had spoken. Who may know? Perhaps Tanar did not know himself what prompted his next act.

Shouting a word that is familiar to all tandor hunters and which is most nearly translatable into English as "Reverse!" he leaped to the ground almost at the side of the charging tandor and simultaneously he carried his spear hand back and drove the heavy shaft deep into the beast's side, just behind its left shoulder. Then he leaped back into the forest expecting that the tandor would do precisely what it did do.

With a squeal of pain it turned upon its new tormentor.

The Amiocapian, who still clung to his heavy axe, had heard, as though it was a miracle from the gods, the familiar signal that had burst so suddenly from Tanar's lips. It had told him what the other would attempt and he was ready, with the result that he turned back toward the beast at the instant that it wheeled to charge after Tanar, and as it crashed into the undergrowth of the jungle in pursuit of the Sarian the Amiocapian overtook it. The great axe moved swiftly as lightning and the huge beast, trumpeting with rage, sank helplessly to the ground and rolled over on its side.

"Down!" shouted the Amiocapian, to advise Tanar that the attack had been successful.

The Sarian returned and together the two warriors dispatched the great beast, while above them Stellara remained among the concealing verdure of the trees, for the women of Pellucidar do not rashly expose themselves to view of enemy warriors. In this instance she knew that it would be safer to wait and discover the attitude of the Amiocapian toward Tanar. Perhaps he would be grateful and friendly, but there was the possibility that he might not.

The beast dispatched, the two men faced one another. "Who are you," demanded the Amiocapian, "who came so bravely to the rescue of a stranger? I do not recognize you. You are not of Amiocap."

"My name is Tanar and I am from the kingdom of Sari, that lies far away on the distant mainland. I was captured by the Korsars, who invaded the empire of which Sari is a part. They were taking me and other prisoners back to Korsar when the fleet was overtaken by a terrific storm and the ship upon which I was confined was so disabled that it was deserted by its crew. Drifting helplessly with the wind and current it finally bore us to the shores of Amiocap, where we were captured by warriors from the village of Lar. They did not believe our story, but thought that we were Korsars and they were about to destroy us when we succeeded in making our escape.

"If you do not believe me," continued the Sarian, "then one of us must die for under no circumstances will we return to Lar to be burned at the stake."

"Whether I believe you or not," replied the Amiocapian, "I should be beneath the contempt of all men were I to permit any harm to befall one who has just saved my life at the risk of his own."

"Very well," said Tanar. "We shall go our way in the knowledge that you will not reveal our whereabouts to the men of the village of Lar."

"You say 'we,' " said the Amiocapian. "You are not alone then?"

"No, there is another with me," replied Tanar.

"Perhaps I can help you," said the Amiocapian. "It is my duty to do so. In what direction are you going and how do you plan to escape from Amiocap?"

"We are seeking the coast where we hope to be able to build a craft and to cross the ocean to the mainland."

The Amiocapian shook his head. "That will be difficult," he said. "Nay, impossible."

"We may only make the attempt," said Tanar, "for it is evident that we cannot remain here among the people of Amiocap, who will not believe that we are not Korsars."

"You do not look at all like the Korsars," said the warrior. "Where is your companion? Does he look like one?"

"My companion is a woman," replied Tanar.

"If she looks no more like a Korsar than you, then it were easy to believe your story and, I, for one, am willing to believe it and willing to help you. There are other villages upon Amiocap than Lar and other chiefs than Zural. We are all bitter against the Korsars, but we are not all blinded by our hate as is Zural. Fetch your companion and if she does not appear to be a Korsar, I will take you to my own village and see that you are well treated. If I am in doubt I will permit you to go your way; nor shall I mention the fact to others that I have seen you."

"That is fair enough," said Tanar, and then, turning, he called to the girl. "Come, Stellara! Here is a warrior who would see if you are a Korsar."

The girl dropped lightly to the ground from the branches of the tree above the two men.

As the eyes of the Amiocapian fell upon her he stepped back with an exclamation of shock and surprise.

"Gods of Amiocap!" he cried. "Allara!"

The two looked at him in amazement. "No, not Allara," said Tanar, "but Stellara, her daughter. Who are you that you should so quickly recognize the likeness?"

"I am Fedol," said the man, "and Allara was my mate."

"Then this is your daughter, Fedol," said Tanar.

The warrior shook his head, sadly. "No," he said, "I can believe that she is the daughter of Allara, but her father must have been a Korsar for Allara was stolen from me by the men of Korsar. She is a Korsar and though my heart urges me to accept her as my daughter, the customs of Amiocap forbid. Go your way in peace. If I can protect you I shall, but I cannot accept you, or take you to my village."

Stellara came close to Fedol, her eyes searching the tan skin upon his left shoulder. "You are Fedol," she said, pointing to the red birthmark upon his skin, "and here is the proof that my mother gave me, transmitted to me through your blood, that I am the daughter of Fedol," and she turned her left shoulder to him, and there lay upon the white skin a small, round, red mark identical with that upon the left shoulder of the Amiocapian.

For a moment Fedol stood spellbound, his eyes fixed upon Stellara's shoulder and then he took her into his arms and held her closely.

"My daughter!" he murmured. "Allara come back to me in the blood of our blood and the flesh of our flesh!"

Chapter VI

THE ISLAND OF LOVE

The noonday sun of Pellucidar shone down upon a happy trio as Fedol guided Stellara and Tanar towards the village of Paraht, where he ruled as chief.

"Will they receive us there as friends," asked Stellara, "or will they wish to destroy us as did the men of Lar?"

"I am chief," said Fedol. "Even if they questioned you, they will do as I command, but there will be no question for the proof is beyond dispute and they will accept you as the daughter of Fedol and Allara, as I have accepted you."

"And Tanar?" asked Stellara, "will you protect him, too?"

"Your word is sufficient that he is not a Korsar," replied Fedol. "He may remain with us as long as he wishes."

"What will Zural think of this?" asked Tanar. "He has condemned us to die. Will he not insist that the sentence be carried out?"

"Seldom do the villagers of Amiocap war one against the other," replied Fedol; "but if Zural wishes war he shall have it ere ever I shall give up you or my daughter to the burning stake of Lar."

Great was the rejoicing when the people of Paraht saw their chief, whom they had thought lost to them forever, returning. They clustered about him with glad cries of welcome, which were suddenly stilled by loud shouts of "The Korsars! The Korsars!" as the eyes of some of the people alighted upon Tanar and Stellara.

"Who cried 'Korsars'?" demanded Fedol. "What know you of these people?"

"I know them," replied a tall warrior. "I am from Lar. There are six others with me and we have been searching for these Korsars, who escaped just before they were to have been burned at the stake. We will take them back with us and Zural will rejoice that you have captured them."

"You will take them nowhere," said Fedol. "They are not Korsars. This one," and he placed a hand upon Stellara's shoulder, "is my daughter, and the man is a warrior from distant Sari. He is the son of the king of that country, which lies far away upon a mainland unknown to us."

"They told that same story to Zural," said the warrior from Lar; "but he did not believe them. None of us believed them. I was with Vulhan and his party when we took them from the Korsar ship that brought them to Amiocap."

"At first I did not believe them," said Fedol, "but Stellara convinced me that she is my daughter, just as I can convince you of the truth of her statement."

"How?" demanded the warrior.

"By the birthmark on my left shoulder," replied Fedol. "Look at it, and then compare it with the one upon her left shoulder. No one who knew Allara can doubt that Stellara is her daughter, so closely does the girl resemble her mother, and being Allara's daughter how could she inherit the birthmark upon her left shoulder from any other sire than me?"

The warriors from Lar scratched their heads. "It would seem the best of proof," replied the warriors' spokesman.

"It is the best of proof," said Fedol. "It is all that I need. It is all the people of Paraht need. Take the word to Zural and the people of Lar and I believe that they will accept my daughter and Tanar as we are accepting them, and I believe that they will be willing to protect them as we intend to protect them from all enemies, whether from Amiocap or elsewhere."

"I shall take your message to Zural," replied the warrior, and shortly afterward they departed on the trail toward Lar.

Fedol prepared a room in his house for Stellara and assigned Tanar to a large building that was occupied solely by bachelors.

Plans were made for a great feast to celebrate the coming of Stellara and a hundred men were dispatched to fetch the ivory and the meat of the tandor that Fedol and Tanar had slain.

Fedol decked Stellara with ornaments of bone and ivory and gold. She wore the softest furs and the gorgeous plumage of rare birds. The people of Paraht loved her and Stellara was happy.

Tanar was accepted at first by the men of the tribe with some reservations, not untinged with suspicion. He was their guest by the order of their chief and they treated him as such, but presently, when they came to know him and particularly after he had hunted with them, they liked him for himself and made him one of them.

The Amiocapians were, at first, an enigma to Tanar. Their tribal life and all their customs were based primarily upon love and kindness. Harsh words, bickering and scolding were practically unknown among them. These attributes of the softer side of man appeared at first weak and effeminate to the Sarian, but when he found them combined with great strength and rare courage his admiration for the Amiocapians knew no bounds, and he soon recognized in their attitude toward one another and toward life a philosophy that he hoped he might make clear to his own Sarians.

The Amiocapians considered love the most sacred of the gifts of the gods, and the greatest power for good and they practiced liberty of love without license. So that while they were not held in slavery by senseless man-made laws that denied the laws of God and nature, yet they were pure and virtuous to a degree beyond that which he had known in any other people.

With hunting and dancing and feasting, with tests of skill and strength in which the men of Amiocap contended in friendly rivalry, life for Stellara and Tanar was ideally happy.

Less and less often did the Sarian think of Sari. Sometime he would build a boat and return to his native country, but there was no hurry; he would wait, and gradually even that thought faded almost entirely from his mind. He and Stellara were often together. They found a measure of happiness and contentment in one another's society that was lacking at other times or with other people. Tanar had never spoken of love. Perhaps he had not thought of love for it seemed that he was always engaged upon some enterprise of the hunt, or contending in some of the sports and games of the men. His body and his mind were occupied — a condition which sometimes excludes thoughts of love, but wherever he went or whatever he did the face and figure of Stellara hovered ever in the background of his thoughts.

Without realizing it, perhaps, his every thought, his every act was influenced by the sweet loveliness of the chief's daughter. Her friendship he took for granted and it gave him great happiness, but yet he did not speak of love. But Stellara was a woman, and women live on love.

In the village of Paraht she saw the girls openly avowing their love to men, but she was still bound by the customs of Korsar and it would have been impossible for her to bring herself to tell a man that she loved him until he had avowed his love. And so hearing no word of love from Tanar, she was content with his friendship. Perhaps she, too, had given no more thought to the matter of love than he.

But there was another who did harbor thoughts of love. It was Doval, the Adonis of Paraht. In all Amiocap there was no handsomer youth than Doval. Many were the girls who had avowed their love to him, but his heart had been unmoved until he looked upon Stellara.

Doval came often to the house of Fedol the chief. He brought presents of skin and ivory and bone to Stellara and they were much together. Tanar saw and he was troubled, but why he was troubled he did not know.

The people of Paraht had eaten and slept many times since the coming of Tanar and Stellara and as yet no word had come from Zural, or the village of Lar, in answer to the message that Fedol had sent, but now, at last, there entered the village a party of warriors from Lar, and Fedol, sitting upon the chief's chair, received them in the tiled living room of his home.

"Welcome, men of Lar," said the chief. "Fedol welcomes you to the village of Paraht and awaits with impatience the message that you bring him from his friend, Zural the chief."

"We come from Zural and the people of Lar," said the spokesman, "with a message of friendship for Fedol and Paraht. Zural, our chief, has commanded us to express to you his deep sorrow for the unintentional wrong that he did your daughter and the warrior from Sari. He is convinced that Stellara is your daughter and that the man is no Korsar if you are convinced of these facts, and he has sent presents to them and to you and with these presents an invitation for you to visit the village of Lar and bring Stellara and Tanar with you that Zural and his people may make amends for the wrong that they unwittingly did them."

Fedol and Tanar and Stellara accepted the proffered friendship of Zural and his people, and a feast was prepared in honor of the visitors.

While these preparations were in progress a girl entered the village from the jungle. She was a dark-haired girl of extraordinary beauty. Her soft skin was scratched and soiled as from a long journey. Her hair was disheveled, but her eyes were bright with happiness and her teeth gleamed from between lips that were parted in a smile of triumph and expectation.

She made her way directly through the village to the house of Fedol and when the warriors of Lar descried her they exclaimed with astonishment.

"Letari!" cried one of them. "Where did you come from? What are you doing in the village of Paraht?"

But Letari did not answer. Instead she walked directly to where Tanar stood and halted before him.

"I have come to you," she said. "I have died many a death from loneliness and sorrow since you ran away from the village of Lar, and when the warriors returned and said that you were safe in the village of Paraht I determined to come here. And so when Zural sent these warriors to bear his message to Fedol I followed them. The way

has been hard and though I kept close behind them there were many times when wild beasts menaced me and I feared that I should never reach you, but at last I am here."

"But why have you come?" demanded Tanar.

"Because I love you," replied Letari. "Before the men of Lar and all the people of Paraht I proclaim my love."

Tanar flushed. In all his life he had never been in so embarrassing a position. All eyes were turned upon him and among them were the eyes of Stellara.

"Well?" demanded Fedol, looking at Tanar.

"The girl is mad," said the Sarian. "She cannot love me for she scarcely knows me. She never spoke to me but once before and that was when she brought food to Stellara and me when we were prisoners in the village of Lar."

"I am not mad," said Letari. "I love you."

"Will you have her?" asked Fedol.

"I do not love her," said Tanar.

"We will take her back to the village of Lar with us when we go," said one of the warriors.

"I shall not go," cried Letari. "I love him and I shall stay here forever."

The girl's declaration of love for Tanar seemed not to surprise any one but the Sarian. It aroused little comment and no ridicule. The Amiocapians, with the possible exception of Stellara, took it as a matter of course. It was the most natural thing in the world for the people of this island of love to declare themselves publicly in matters pertaining to their hearts or to their passions.

That the general effect of such a policy was not nor never had been detrimental to the people as a race was evident by their high intelligence, the perfection of their physique, their great beauty and their unquestioned courage. Perhaps the opposite custom, which has prevailed among most of the people of the outer crust for so many ages, is responsible for the unnumbered millions of unhappy human beings who are warped or twisted mentally, morally or physically.

But with such matters the mind of Letari was not concerned. It was not troubled by any consideration of posterity. All she thought of was that she loved the handsome stranger from Sari and that she wanted to be near him. She came close to him and looked up into his face.

"Why do you not love me?" she asked. "Am I not beautiful?"

"Yes, you are very beautiful," he said; "but no one can explain love, least of all I. Perhaps there are qualities of mind and character — things that we can neither see nor feel nor hear — that draw one heart forever to another."

"But I am drawn to you," said the girl. "Why are not you attracted to me?"

Tanar shook his head for he did not know. He wished that the girl would go away and leave him alone for she made him feel uneasy and restless and entirely uncomfortable, but Letari had no idea of leaving him alone. She was near him and there she intended to stay until they dragged her away and took her back to Lar, if they were successful in so doing, but she had determined in her little head that she should run away from them at the first opportunity and hide in the jungle until she could return to Paraht and Tanar.

"Will you talk to me?" she asked. "Perhaps if you talk to me you will love me."

"I will talk to you," said Tanar, "but I shall not love you."

"Let us walk a little way from these people where we may talk," she said.

"Very well," said Tanar. He was only too anxious himself to get away where he might hide his embarrassment.

Letari led the way down the village street, her soft arm brushing his. "I should be a good mate," she said, "for I should love only you, and if, after a while, you did not like me you could send me away for that is one of the customs of Amiocap — that when one of two people ceases to love they shall no longer be mates."

"But they do not become mates unless they both love," insisted Tanar.

"That is true," admitted Letari, "but presently you shall love me. I know that, for all men love me. I could have for my mate any man in Lar that I choose."

"You do not feel unkindly towards yourself," said Tanar, with a grin.

"Why should I?" asked Letari. "Am I not beautiful and young?"

Stellara watched Tanar and Letari walking down the village street. She saw how close together they walked and it seemed that Tanar was very much interested in what Letari had to say to him. Doval was standing at her side. She turned to him.

"It is noisy here," she said. "There are too many people. Walk with me to the end of the village."

It was the first time that Stellara had ever indicated a desire to be alone with him and Doval felt a strange thrill of elation. "I will walk with you to the end of the village, Stellara, or to the end of Pellucidar, forever, because I love you," he said.

The girl sighed and shook her head. "Do not talk about love," she begged. "I merely wish to walk and there is no one else here to walk with me."

"Why will you not love me?" asked Doval, as they left the house of the chief and entered the main street of the village. "Is it because you love another?"

"No," cried Stellara, vehemently. "I love no one. I hate all men."

Doval shook his head in perplexity. "I cannot understand you," he said. "Many girls have told me that they loved me. I think that I could have almost any girl in Amiocap as my mate if I asked her; but you, the only one that I love, will not have me."

For a few moments Stellara was silent in thought. Then she turned to the handsome youth at her side. "You are very sure of yourself, Doval," she said, "but I do not believe that you are right. I would be willing to bet that I could name a girl who would not have you; who, no matter how hard you tried to make her, would not love you."

"If you mean yourself, then there is one," he said, "but there is no other."

"Oh, yes, there is," insisted Stellara.

"Who is she?" demanded Doval.

"Letari, the girl from Lar," said Stellara.

Doval laughed. "She throws her love at the first stranger that comes to Amiocap," he said. "She would be too easy."

"Nevertheless you cannot make her love you," insisted Stellara.

"I do not intend to try," said Doval. "I do not love her. I love only you, and if I made her love me of what good would that be toward making you love me? No, I shall spend my time trying to win you."

"You are afraid," said Stellara. "You know that you would fail."

"It would do me no good if I succeeded," insisted Doval.

"It would make me like you very much better than I do now," said Stellara.

"You mean that?" asked Doval.

"I most certainly do," said Stellara.

"Then I shall make the girl love me," said Doval. "And if I do you promise to be mine?"

"I said nothing of the kind," said Stellara. "I only said that I should like you very much better than I do now."

"Well, that is something," said Doval. "If you will like me very much better than you do now that is at least a step in the right direction."

"However, there is no danger of that," said Stellara, "for you cannot make her love you."

"Wait, and see," said Doval.

As Tanar and Letari turned to come back along the village street they passed Doval and Stellara, and Tanar saw that they were walking very close together and whispering in low tones. The Sarian scowled; and suddenly he discovered that he did not like Doval and he wondered why because always he had thought Doval a very fine fellow. Presently it occurred to him that the reason was that Doval was not good enough for Stellara, but then if Stellara loved him that was all there was to it and with the thought that perhaps Stellara loved him Tanar became angry with Stellara. What could she see in this Doval, he wondered, and what business had Doval to walk alone with her in the village streets? Had not he, Tanar, always had Stellara to himself? Never before had any one interfered, although all the men liked Stellara. Well, if Stellara liked Doval better than she did him, he would show her that he did not care. He, Tanar the Sarian, son of Ghak, king of Sari, would not let any woman make a fool of him and so he ostentatiously put his arm around the slim shoulders of Letari and walked thus slowly the length of the village street; nor did Stellara fail to see.

At the feast that was given in honor of the messengers sent by Zural, Stellara sat by Doval and Tanar had Letari at his side, and Doval and Letari were happy.

After the feast was over most of the villagers returned to their houses and slept, but Tanar was restless and unhappy and could not sleep so he took his weapons, his heavy spear shod with bone, his bow and his arrows, and his stone knife with the ivory handle, that Fedol the chief had given him, and went alone into the forest to hunt.

If the villagers slept an hour or a day is a matter of no moment, since there was no way of measuring the time. When they awoke — some sooner, some later — they went about the various duties of their life. Letari sought for Tanar, but she could not find him; instead she came upon Doval.

"You are very beautiful," said the man.

"I know it," replied Letari.

"You are the most beautiful girl that I have ever seen," insisted Doval.

Letari looked at him steadily for a few moments. "I never noticed you before," she said. "You are very handsome. You are quite the handsomest man that I ever saw."

"That is what every one says," replied Doval. "Many girls have told me that they loved me, but still I have no mate."

"A woman wants something beside a handsome face in her mate," said Letari.

"I am very brave," said Doval, "and I am a great hunter. I like you. Come, let us walk together," and Doval put his arm about the girl's shoulders and together they walked along the village street, while, from the doorway of her sleeping apartment in the home of her father, the chief, Stellara watched, and as she watched, a smile touched her lips.

Over the village of Paraht rested the peace of Amiocap and the calm of eternal noon. The children played at games beneath the shade of the trees that had been left dotting the village here and there when the clearing had been made. The women worked upon skins, strung beads or prepared food. The men looked to their weapons against the next hunt, or lolled idly on furs in their open living rooms — those who were not still sleeping off the effects of the heavy feast. Fedol, the chief, was bidding farewell to Zural's messengers and entrusting to them a gift for the ruler of Lar, when suddenly the peace and quiet was shattered by hoarse cries and a shattering burst of musketry.

Instantly all was pandemonium. Then women and warriors rushed from their homes; shouts, curses and screams filled the air.

"Korsars! Korsars!" rang through the village, as the bearded ruffians, taking advantage of the surprise and confusion of the villagers, rushed rapidly forward to profit by the advantage they had gained.

CHAPTER VII

"KORSARS!"

Tanar the Sarian hunted through the primeval forest of Amiocap. Already his repute as a hunter stood high among the men of Paraht, but it was not to add further luster to his fame that he hunted now. It was to quiet a restlessness that would not permit him to sleep — restlessness and a strange depression that was almost unhappiness, but his thoughts were not always upon the hunt. Visions of Stellara often walked in front of him, the golden sunlight on her golden hair, and then beside her he saw the handsome Doval with an arm about her shoulder. He closed his eyes and shook his head to dispel the vision, but it persisted and he tried thinking of Letari, the beautiful maiden from Lar. Yes, Letari was beautiful. What eyes she had; and she loved him. Perhaps, after all, it would be as well to mate with her and remain forever upon Amiocap, but presently he found himself comparing Letari with Stellara and he found himself wishing that Letari possessed more of the characteristics of Stellara. She had not the character nor the intelligence of the daughter of Fedol. She offered him none of the restful companionship that had made his association with Stellara so infinitely happy.

He wondered if Stellara loved Doval, and if Doval loved Stellara, and with the thoughts he halted in his tracks and his eyes went wide as a sudden realization burst for the first time upon his consciousness.

"God!" he exclaimed aloud. "What a fool I have been. I have loved her always and did not know it," and wheeling about he set off at a brisk trot in the direction of Paraht, all thoughts of his hunt erased from his mind.

Tanar had hunted far, much farther than he had thought, but at last he came to the village of Fedol the chief. As he passed through the hanging barrier of Paraht, the first people that he saw were Letari and Doval. They were walking side by side and very close and the man's arm was about the slim shoulders of the girl.

Letari looked at Tanar in astonishment as she recognized him. "We all thought the Korsars had taken you with them," she cried.

"Korsars!" exclaimed Tanar. "What Korsars?"

"They were here," said Doval. "They raided the village, but we drove them off with just a small loss. There were not many of them. Where were you?"

"After the feast I went into the forest to hunt," said Tanar. "I did not know that there was a Korsar upon the island of Amiocap."

"It is just as well that you were not here," said Letari, "for while you were away I have learned that I love Doval."

"Where is Stellara?" demanded Tanar.

"She was taken by the Korsars," said Doval. "Thank God that it was not you, Letari," and, stooping, he kissed the girl upon the lips.

With a cry of grief and rage Tanar ran swiftly to the house of Fedol the chief. "Where is Stellara?" he demanded, springing unceremoniously into the center of the living room.

An old woman looked up from where she sat with her face buried in her hands. She was the sole occupant of the room. "The Korsars took her," she said.

"Where is Fedol then?" demanded Tanar.

"He has gone with warriors to try to rescue her," said the old woman, "but it is useless. They, who are taken by the Korsars, never come back."

"Which way did they go?" asked Tanar.

Sobbing with grief, the old woman pointed in the direction taken by the Korsars, and again she buried her face in her hands, grieving for the misfortune that had overtaken the house of Fedol the chief.

Almost immediately Tanar picked up the trail of the Korsars, which he could identify by the imprints of their heeled boots, and he saw that Fedol and his warriors had not followed the same trail, evidencing the fact that they must have gone in the wrong direction to succor Stellara successfully.

Sick with anguish, maddened by hate, the Sarian plunged on through the forest. Plain to his eyes lay the spoor of his quarry. In his heart was a rage that gave him the strength of many men.

In a little glade, partially surrounded by limestone cliffs, a small company of ragged, bewhiskered men had halted to rest. Where they had halted a tiny spring broke from the base of the cliff and trickled along its winding channel for a short distance to empty into a natural, circular opening in the surface of the ground. From deep in the bottom of this natural well the water falling from the rim could be heard splashing upon the surface of the water far below. It was dark down there — dark and mysterious, but the bearded ruffians gave no heed either to the beauty or the mystery of the spot.

One huge, fierce-visaged fellow, his countenance disfigured by an ugly scar, confronted a slim girl, who sat upon the turf, her back against a tree, her face buried in her arms.

"You thought me dead, eh?" he exclaimed. "You thought Bohar the Bloody dead? Well he is not dead. Our boat weathered the storm and passing close to Amiocap we saw the wreck of The Cid's ship lying upon the sand. Knowing that you and the prisoners had been left aboard when we quit the ship, I guessed that perhaps you might be somewhere upon Amiocap; nor was I wrong, Stellara. Bohar the Bloody is seldom wrong.

"We hid close to a village which they call Lar and at the first opportunity we captured one of the villagers — a woman — and from her we learned that you had indeed come ashore, but that you were then in the village of your father and we made the woman guide us there. The rest you know and now be cheerful for at last you are to mate with Bohar the Bloody and return to Korsar."

"Rather than that I shall die," cried the girl.

"But how?" laughed Bohar. "You have no weapons. Perhaps, however, you will choke yourself to death," and he laughed uproariously at his own joke.

"There is a way," cried the girl, and before he could guess what she intended, or stay her, she dodged quickly around him and ran toward the natural well that lay a few hundred feet away.

"Quick!" shouted Bohar. "Stop her!" And instantly the entire twenty sprang in pursuit. But Stellara was swift and there was likelihood that they would not overtake her in the short distance that lay before her and the edge of the abyss.

Fortune, however, was with Bohar the Bloody that day and almost at her goal Stellara's foot caught in a tangle of grasses and she stumbled forward upon her face. Before she could recover her feet the nearest Korsar had seized her, and then Bohar the Bloody ran to her side and, taking her from the grasp of the other Korsar, shook her violently.

"You she tarag!" he cried. "For this I shall fix you so that never again will you run away. When we reach the sea I shall cut off one of your feet and then I shall know that you will not run away from me again,"

and he continued to shake her violently.

Breaking suddenly and unexpectedly from the dense jungle into the opening of the glade a warrior came upon the scene being enacted at the edge of the well. At the moment he thought that Stellara was being killed and he went mad with rage; nor was his rage any the less when he recognized Bohar the Bloody as the author of the assault.

With an angry shout he leaped forward, his heavy spear ready in his hand. What mattered it that twenty men with firearms opposed him? He saw only Stellara in the cruel grip of the bestial Bohar.

At the sound of his voice the Korsar looked up and instantly Bohar recognized the Sarian.

"Look, Stellara," he said, with a sneer. "Your lover has come. It is well, for with no lover and only one foot you will have no reason at all for running away."

A dozen harquebuses had already been raised in readiness and the men stood looking toward Bohar.

Tanar had reached the opposite edge of the well, only a few yards distant, when Bohar nodded and there was a roar of musketry and a flash of flame accompanied by so dense a pall of black smoke that for an instant the figure of the Sarian was entirely obliterated from view.

Stellara, wide-eyed and trembling with pain and horror, tried to penetrate the smoke cloud with her frightened eyes. Quickly it lifted, revealing no sign of Tanar.

"Well done," cried Bohar to his men. "Either you blew him all to pieces, or his body fell into the hole," and going to the edge of the opening he looked down, but it was very dark there and he saw nothing. "Wherever he is, at least he is dead," said Bohar. "I should like to have crushed his life out with my own hands, but at least he is dead by my command and the blow that he struck me is wiped out, as Bohar wipes out the blows of all his enemies."

As the Korsars resumed the march toward the ocean, Stellara walked among them with bent head and moist, unseeing eyes. Often she stumbled and each time she was jerked roughly to her feet and shaken, at the same time being admonished in hoarse tones to watch her footing.

By the time they reached the seashore Stellara was sick with a high fever and she lay in the camp of the Korsars for what may have been a day or a month, too sick to move, while Bohar and his men felled timbers, hewed planks and constructed a boat to carry them to the distant shores of Korsar.

Rushing forward to rescue Stellara from the clutches of Bohar, Tanar's mind and eyes had been fixed on nothing but the figure of the girl. He had not seen the opening in the ground and at the instant that the Korsars fired their harquebuses he had stepped unwittingly into the opening and plunged to the water far below.

The fall had not hurt him. It had not even stunned him and when he came to the surface he saw before him a quiet stream moving gently through an opening in the limestone wall about him. Beyond the opening was a luminous cavern and into this Tanar swam, clambering to its rocky floor the moment that he had found a low place in the bank of the stream. Looking about him he found himself in a large cavern, the walls of which shone luminously, so considerable was their content of phosphorus.

There was a great deal of rubbish on the floor of the cave — the bones of animals and men, broken weapons, bits of hide. It might have been the dumping ground of some grewsome charnal house.

The Sarian walked back to the opening through which the little stream had borne him into the grotto, but a careful investigation revealed no avenue of escape in this direction, although he reentered the stream and swam into the bottom of the well where he found the walls worn so smooth by the long continued action of falling water that they gave no slightest indication of handhold or foothold.

Then slowly he made a circuit of the outer walls of the grotto, but only where the stream passed out at its far end was there any opening — a rough archway that rose some six feet above the surface of the underground stream.

Along one side was a narrow ledge and looking through the opening he saw a dim corridor leading away into the distance and obscurity.

There being no other way in which to search for freedom Tanar passed along the narrow ledge beneath the archway to find himself in a tunnel that followed the windings of the stream.

Only here and there small patches of the rock that formed the walls and ceiling of the corridor threw out a luminosity that barely relieved the inky darkness of the place, yet relieve it it did so that at least one might be sure of his footing, though at points where the corridor widened its walls were often lost in darkness.

For what distance he followed the tunnel Tanar did not know, but presently he came to a low and narrow opening through which he could pass only upon his hands and knees. Beyond there seemed to be a much lighter chamber and as Tanar came into this, still upon all fours, a heavy body dropped upon his back from above and then another at each side of him and he felt cold, clammy claws seizing his arms and legs, and arms encircled his neck — arms that felt against his flesh like the arms of a corpse.

He struggled but there were too many for him and in a moment he was disarmed and his ankles and wrists securely bound with tough thongs of rawhide. Then he was rolled over on his side and lay looking up into the horrid faces of Coripies, the Buried People of Amiocap.

The blank faces, the corpse-like skin, the bulging protuberances where the eyes would have been, the hairless bodies, the claw-like hands combined to produce such a hideous aspect in the monsters as to make the stoutest of hearts quail.

And when they spoke! The mumbled mouthing revealing yellow fangs withered the heart in the breast of the Sarian. Here, indeed, was a hideous end, for he knew that it was the end, since never in all the many tales the Amiocapians had told him of the Buried People was there any record of a human being escaping from their clutches.

Now they were addressing him and presently, in their hollow mewing, he discerned words. "How did you get into the land of the Coripies?" demanded one.

"I fell into a hole in the ground," replied Tanar. "I did not seek to come here. Take me out and I will reward you."

"What have you to give the Coripies more than your flesh?" demanded another.

"Do not think to get out for you never shall," said a third.

Now two of them lifted him lightly and placed him upon the back of one of their companions. So easily the creature carried him that Tanar wondered that he had ever overcome the Coripi that he had met upon the surface of the ground.

Through long corridors, some very dark and others partially lighted by outcroppings of phosphorescent rock, the creature bore him. At times they passed through large grottoes, beautifully wrought in intricate designs by nature, or climbed long stairways carved in the limestone, probably by the Coripies themselves, only presently to descend other stairways and follow winding tunnels that seemed interminable.

But at last the journey ended in a huge cavern, the ceiling of which rose at least two hundred feet above them. This stupendous grotto was more brilliantly lighted than any other section of the subterranean world that Tanar had passed through. Into its limestone walls were cut pathways that zig-zagged back and forth upward toward the ceiling, and the entire surface of the surrounding walls was pierced by holes several feet in diameter that appeared to be the mouths of caves.

Squatting about on the floor of the cavern were hundreds of Coripies of all ages and both sexes.

At one end of the grotto, in a large opening, a few feet above the floor, squatted a single, large Coripi. His skin was mottled with a purplish hue that suggested a corpse in which mortification had progressed to a considerable degree. The protuberances that suggested huge eyeballs beneath the skin protruded much further and were much larger than those in any other of the Coripies that Tanar had examined. The creature was, by far, the most repulsive of all the repulsive horde.

On the floor of the grotto, directly before this creature, were gathered a number of male Coripies and toward this congregation Tanar's captors bore him.

Scarcely had they entered the grotto when it became apparent to Tanar that these creatures could see, a thing that he had commenced to suspect shortly after his capture, for now, at sight of him, they commenced to scream and make strange, whistling sounds, and from the openings of many of the high flung caves within the walls heads protruded and the hideous, eyeless faces seemed to be bending eyes upon him.

One cry seemed to rise above all others as he was borne across the grotto towards the creature sitting in the niche. It was "Flesh! Flesh!" and it sounded grewsome and horrible in its suggestiveness.

Flesh! Yes, he knew that they ate human flesh and it seemed now that they were but awaiting a signal to leap upon him and devour him alive, tearing pieces from him with their heavy claws. But when one did rush upon him there came a scream from the creature in the niche and the fellow desisted, even as one of his captors had turned to defend him.

The cavern crossed at last, Tanar was deposited upon his feet in front of the creature squatting in the niche. Tanar could see the great eyeballs revolving beneath the pulsing skin of the protuberances and though he could see no eyes, he knew that he was being examined coldly and calculatingly.

"Where did you get it?" finally demanded the creature, addressing Tanar's captors.

"He tumbled into the Well of Sounding Water," replied one.

"How do you know?"

"He told us so."

"Do you believe him?"

"There was no other way in which he could enter the land of the Coripies," replied one of the captors.

"Perhaps he was leading a party in to slay us," said the creature in the niche. "Go, many of you, and search the corridors and the tunnels about the Well of Sounding Water." Then the creature turned to Tanar's captors. "Take this and put it with the others; we have not yet enough."

Tanar was now again placed upon the back of a Coripi, who carried him across the grotto and up one of the pathways cut into the face of the limestone wall. Ascending this pathway a short distance the creature turned into one of the cave openings, and Tanar found himself again in a narrow, dark, winding tunnel.

The tunnels and corridors through which he had already been conducted had impressed upon Tanar the great antiquity of this underground labyrinthian world, since there was every evidence that the majority of these tunnels had been hewn from the limestone rock or natural passageways enlarged to accommodate the Coripies, and as these creatures appeared to have no implements other than their heavy, three-toed claws the construction of the tunnels must have represented the labor of countless thousands of individuals over a period of many ages.

Tanar, of course, had only a hazy conception of what we describe as the measurable aspect of duration. His consideration of the subject concerned itself with the countless millions of times that these creatures must have slept and eaten during the course of their stupendous labors.

But the mind of the captive was also occupied with other matters as the Coripi bore him through the long tunnel. He thought of the statement of the creature in the niche, as he had ordered Tanar taken into confinement, to the effect that there were not yet enough. What did he mean? Enough of what? Enough prisoners? And when there were enough to what purpose would they be devoted?

But perhaps, to a far greater extent, his mind was occupied with thoughts of Stellara; with fears for her safety and with vain regret that he had been unable to accomplish her rescue.

From the moment that he had been so unexpectedly precipitated into the underground world of the Buried People, his dominant thought, of course, had been that of escape; but the further into the bowels of the earth he was carried the more hopeless appeared the outcome of any venture in this direction, yet he never for once abandoned it though he realized that he must wait until they had reached the place of his final confinement before he could intelligently consider any plan at all.

How far the tireless Coripi bore Tanar the Sarian could not guess, but presently they emerged into a dimly lighted grotto, before the narrow entrance to which squatted a dozen Coripies. Within the chamber were a score more and one human being — a man with sandy hair, close-set eyes and a certain mean, crafty expression of countenance that repelled the Sarian immediately.

"Here is another," said the Coripi who had carried Tanar to the cavern, and with that he dumped the Sarian unceremoniously upon the stone floor at the feet of the dozen Coripies who stood guard at the entrance.

With teeth and claws they severed the bonds that secured his wrists and ankles.

"They come slowly," grumbled one of the guards. "How much longer must we wait?"

"Old Xax wishes to have the greatest number that has ever been collected," remarked another of the Coripies.

"But we grow impatient," said the first speaker. "If he makes us wait much longer he may be one of the number here himself."

"Be careful," cautioned one of his fellows. "If Xax heard that you had said such a thing as that the number of our prisoners would be increased by one."

As Tanar arose to his feet, after his bonds were severed, he was pushed roughly toward the other inmates of the room, who he soon was to discover were prisoners, like himself, and quite naturally the first to approach him was the other human captive.

"Another," said the stranger. "Our numbers increase but slowly, yet each one brings us closer to our inevitable doom and so I do not know whether I am sorry to see you here or glad because of the human company that I shall now have. I have eaten and slept many times since I was thrown into this accursed place and always nothing but these hideous, mumbling things for company. God, how I hate and loathe them, yet they are in the same predicament as we for they, too, are doomed to the same fate."

"And what may that be?" asked Tanar.

"You do not know?"

"I may only guess," replied the Sarian.

"These creatures seldom get flesh with warm blood in it. They subsist mostly upon the fish in their underground rivers and upon the toads and lizards that inhabit their caves. Their expeditions to the surface ordinarily yield nothing more than the carcasses of dead beasts, yet they crave flesh and warm blood. Heretofore they had killed their condemned prisoners one by one as they were available, but this plan gave only a mouthful of flesh to a very few Coripies. Recently Xax hit upon the plan of preserving his own condemned and the prisoners from the outer world until he had accumulated a sufficient number to feast the entire population of the cavern of which he is chief. I do not know how many that will be, but steadily the numbers grow and perhaps it will not be long now before there are enough of us to fill the bellies of Xax's tribe."

"Xax!" repeated Tanar. "Was he the creature sitting in the niche in the great cavern to which I was first taken?"

"That was Xax. He is ruler of that cavern. In the underground world of the Buried People there are many tribes, each of which occupies a large cavern similar to that in which you saw Xax. These tribes are not always friendly and the most of the prisoners that you see in this cavern are members of other tribes, though there are a few from the tribe of Xax who have been condemned to death for one reason or another."

"And there is no escape?" asked Tanar.

"None," replied the other. "Absolutely none; but tell me who are you and from what country? I cannot believe that you are a native of Amiocap, for what Amiocapian is there who would need ask questions about the Buried People?"

"I am not of Amiocap," replied Tanar. "I am from Sari, upon the far distant mainland."

"Sari! I never heard of such a country," said the other. "What is your name?"

"Tanar, and yours?"

"I am Jude of Hime," replied the man. "Hime is an island not far from Amiocap. Perhaps you have heard of it."

"No," said Tanar.

"I was fishing in my canoe, off the coast of Hime," continued Jude, "when a great storm arose which blew me across the waters and hurled me upon the coast of Amiocap. I had gone into the forest to hunt for food when three of these creatures fell upon me and dragged me into their underworld."

"And you think that there is no escape?" demanded Tanar.

"None — absolutely none," replied Jude.

Chapter VIII

MOW

Imprisonment in the dark, illy lighted, poorly ventilated cavern weighed heavily upon Tanar of Pellucidar, and he knew that it was long for he had eaten and slept many times and though other Coripi prisoners were brought from time to time there seemed not to be enough to satisfy Xax's bloody craving for flesh.

Tanar had been glad of the companionship of Jude, though he never thoroughly understood the man, whose sour and unhappy disposition was so unlike his own. Jude apparently hated and mistrusted everyone, for even in speaking of the people of his own island he mentioned no one except in terms of bitterness and hatred, but this attitude Tanar generously attributed to the effect upon the mind of the Himean of his long and terrible incarceration among the creatures of the underworld, an experience which he was fully convinced might easily affect and unbalance a weak mind.

Even in the breasts of some of the Coripi prisoners Tanar managed to arouse sentiments somewhat analogous to friendship.

Among the latter was a young Coripi named Mow from the grotto of Ictl, who hated all the Coripies from the grotto of Xax and seemed suspicious of those from other grottoes.

Though the creatures seemed endowed with few human attributes or characteristics, yet it was apparent to Tanar that they set a certain value upon companionship, and being denied this among the creatures of his own kind Mow gradually turned to Tanar, whose courageous and happy spirit had not been entirely dampened by his lot.

Jude would have nothing to do with Mow or any other of the Coripies and he reproached Tanar for treating them in a friendly manner.

"We are all prisoners together," Tanar reminded him, "and they will suffer the same fate as we. It will neither lessen our danger nor add to our peace of mind to quarrel with our fellow prisoners, and I, for my part, find it interesting to talk with them about this strange world which they inhabit."

And, indeed, Tanar had learned many interesting things about the Coripies. Through his association with Mow he had discovered that the creatures were color blind, seeing everything in blacks and whites and grays through the skin that covered their great eyeballs. He learned also that owing to the restricted amount of food at their command it had been necessary to restrict their number, and to this end it had become customary to destroy women who gave birth to too many children, the third child being equivalent to a death sentence for the mother.

He learned also that among these unhappy Coripies there were no diversions and no aim in life other than eating. So meager and unvaried was their diet of fish and toads and lizards that the promise of warm flesh was the only great event in the tiresome monotony of their deadly existence.

Although Mow had no words for love and no conception of its significance, Tanar was able to gather from his remarks that this sentiment did not exist among the Buried People. A mother looked upon each child as a threat to her existence and a prophecy of death, with the result that she loathed children from birth; nor is this strange when the fact is considered that the men chose as the mothers of their children the women whom they particularly loathed and hated, since the custom of destroying a woman who had borne three children deterred them from mating with any female for whom they might have entertained any degree of liking.

When not hunting or fishing the creatures squatted around upon their haunches staring stupidly and sullenly at the floor of their cavern.

"I should think," said Tanar to Mow, "that, confronted by such a life, you would welcome death in any form."

The Coripi shook his head. "I do not want to die," he said.

"Why?" demanded Tanar.

"I do not know," replied Mow. "I simply wish to live."

"Then I take it that you would like to escape from this cavern, if you could," suggested Tanar.

"Of course I should like to escape," said Mow, "but if I try to escape and they catch me they will kill me."

"They are going to kill you anyway," Tanar reminded him.

"Yes, I never thought of that," said Mow. "That is quite true; they are going to kill me anyhow."

"Could you escape?" asked Tanar.

"I could if I had someone to help me," said Mow.

"This cavern is filled with men who will help you," said Tanar.

"The Coripies from the grotto of Xax will not help me," said Mow, "because if they escape there is no place where they may go in safety. If Xax recaptures them they will be killed, and the same is true if the ruler of any other grotto captures them."

"But there are men from other grottoes here," insisted Tanar, "and there are Jude and I."

Mow shook his head. "I would not save any of the Coripies. I hate them. They are all enemies from other grottoes."

"But you do not hate me," said Tanar, "and I will help you, and so will Jude."

"I need but one," said Mow, "but he must be very strong, stronger than you, stronger than Jude."

"How strong?" asked Tanar.

"He must be able to lift my weight," replied the Coripi.

"Look then," said Tanar, and seizing Mow he held him high above his head.

When he had set him down upon the floor again the Coripi gazed at Tanar for some time. "You are, indeed, strong," he said.

"Then let us make our plans for escape," said Tanar.

"Just you and I," said the Coripi.

"We must take Jude with us," insisted Tanar.

Mow shrugged his shoulders. "It is all the same to me," he said. "He is not a Coripi, and if we become hungry and cannot find other food we can eat him."

Tanar made no reply as he felt that it would be unwise to voice his disgust at this proposal and he was sure that he and Jude together could prevent the Coripi from succumbing to his lust for flesh.

"You have noticed at the far end of the cavern, where the shadows are so dense, that one may scarcely see a figure moving there?" asked Mow.

"Yes," said Tanar.

"There the dim shadows hide the rough, rocky walls and the ceiling there is lost in total darkness, but in the ceiling is an opening that leads through a narrow shaft into a dark tunnel."

"How do you know this?" asked Tanar.

"I discovered it once when I was hunting. I came upon a strange tunnel leading from that along which I was making my way to the upper world. I followed it to see where it led and I came at last to the opening in the ceiling of this cavern, from whence one may see all that takes place below without being himself seen. When I was brought here as a prisoner I recognized the spot immediately. That is how I know that one may escape if he has proper help."

"Explain," said Tanar.

"The wall beneath the opening is, as I have discovered, inclined backward from the floor to a considerable height and so rough that it can easily be scaled to a little ledge beneath the opening in the ceiling, but just so far beneath that one may not reach it unaided. If, however, I could lift you into the opening you could, in turn, reach down and help me up."

"But how may we hope to climb the wall without being seen by the guards?" demanded Tanar.

"That is the only chance of capture that we shall have to take," replied Mow. "It is very dark there and if we wait until another prisoner is brought and their attention is diverted we may be able to succeed in reaching the opening in the ceiling before we are discovered, and once there they cannot capture us."

Tanar discussed the plan with Jude, who was so elated at the prospect of escape that he almost revealed a suggestion of happiness.

And now commenced an interminable wait for the moment when a new prisoner might be brought into the cavern. The three conspirators made it a practice to spend most of their time in the shadows at the far end of the cavern so that the guards might become accustomed to seeing them there, and as no one other than themselves was aware of the opening in the ceiling at this point no suspicions were aroused, as the spot where they elected to be was at the opposite end of the cavern from the entrance, which was, in so far as the guards knew, the only opening into the cavern.

Tanar, Jude and Mow ate and slept several times until it began to appear that no more prisoners ever would be brought to the cavern; but if no prisoners came, news trickled in and one item filled them with such alarm that they determined to risk all upon the hazard of a bold dash for freedom.

Some Coripies coming to relieve a part of the guard reported that it had been with difficulty that Xax had been able to suppress an uprising among his infuriated tribesmen, many of whom had conceived the conviction that Xax was saving all of the prisoners for himself.

The result had been that a demand had been made upon Xax for an immediate feast of flesh. Perhaps already other Coripies were on their way to conduct the unfortunate prisoners to the great cavern of Xax, where they would be torn limb from limb by the fierce, hunger-mad throng.

And, true enough, there had been time for but one hunger before the party arrived to conduct them back to the main grotto of the tribe.

"Now is the time," whispered Tanar to Mow and Jude, seeing that the guard was engaged in conversation with the newcomers, and in accordance with their previously made plan the three started without an instant's hesitation to scale the far wall of the cavern.

Upon a little ledge, twenty-five feet from the floor, Tanar halted, and an instant later Mow and Jude stood upon either side of him. Without a word the Coripi lifted Tanar to his shoulders and in the darkness above Tanar groped for a handhold.

He soon found the opening into the shaft leading into the tunnel above, and, too, he found splendid handholds there so that an instant later he had drawn himself up into the opening and was sitting upon a small ledge that entirely encircled it.

Bracing himself, he reached down and seized the hand of Jude, who was standing upon Mow's shoulders, and drew the Himean to the ledge beside him.

At that instant a great shouting arose below them, and glancing down Tanar saw that one of the guards had discovered them and that now a general rush of both guard and prisoners was being made in their direction.

Even as Tanar reached down to aid Mow to the safety of the shaft's mouth, some of the Coripies were already scaling the wall below them. Mow hesitated and turned to look at the enemies clambering rapidly toward him.

The ledge upon which Mow stood was narrow and the footing precarious. The surprise and shock of their discovery may have unnerved him, or, in turning to look downward he may have lost his balance, but whatever it was Tanar saw him reel, topple and then lunge downward upon the ascending Coripies, scraping three of them from the wall in his descent as he crashed to the stone floor below, where he lay motionless.

Tanar turned to Jude. "We cannot help him," he said. "Come, we had better get out of this as quickly as possible."

Feeling for each new handhold and foothold the two climbed slowly up the short shaft and presently found themselves in the tunnel, which Mow had described. Darkness was absolute.

"Do you know the way to the surface?"

asked Jude.

"No," said Tanar. "I was depending upon Mow to lead us."

"Then we might as well be back in the cavern," said Jude.

"Not I," said Tanar, "for at least I am satisfied now that the Coripies will not eat me alive, if they eat me at all."

Groping his way through the darkness and followed closely by Jude, Tanar crept slowly through the Stygian darkness. The tunnel seemed interminable. They became very hungry and there was no food, though they would have relished even the filthy fragments of decayed fish that the Coripies had hurled them while they were prisoners.

"Almost," said Tanar, "could I eat a toad."

They became exhausted and slept, and then again they crawled and stumbled onward. There seemed no end to the interminable, inky corridor.

For long distances the floor of the tunnel was quite level, but then again it would pitch downward, sometimes so steeply that they had difficulty in clinging to the sloping floor. It turned and twisted as though its original excavators had been seldom of the same mind as to the direction in which they wished to proceed.

On and on the two went; again they slept, but whether that meant that they had covered a great distance, or that they were becoming weak from hunger, neither knew.

When they awoke they went on again for a long time in silence, but the sleep did not seem to have refreshed them much, and Jude especially was soon exhausted again.

"I cannot go much further," he said. "Why did you lure me into this crazy escapade?"

"You need not have come," Tanar reminded him, "and if you had not you would by now be out of your misery since doubtless all the prisoners have long since been torn to pieces and devoured by the Coripies of the grotto of Xax."

Jude shuddered. "I should not mind being dead," he said, "but I should hate to be torn to pieces by those horrible creatures."

"This is a much nicer death," said Tanar, "for when we are sufficiently exhausted we shall simply sleep and awake no more."

"I do not wish to die," wailed Jude.

"You have never seemed very happy," said Tanar. "I should think one as unhappy as you would be glad to die."

"I enjoy being unhappy," said Jude. "I know that I should be more miserable were I happy and anyway I should much rather be alive and unhappy than dead and unable to know that I was unhappy."

"Take heart," said Tanar. "It cannot be much further to the end of this long corridor. Mow came through it and he did not say that it was so great a length that he became either exhausted or hungry and he not only traversed it from end to end in one direction, but he had to turn around and retrace his steps after he reached the opening into the cavern which we left."

"The Coripies do not eat much; they are accustomed to starving," said Jude, "and they sleep less than we."

"Perhaps you are right," said Tanar, "but I am sure that we are nearing the end."

"I am," said Jude, "but not the end that I had wished."

Even as they discussed the matter they were moving slowly along, when far ahead Tanar discerned a slight luminosity.

"Look," he said, "there is light. We are nearing the end."

The discovery instilled new strength into both the men and with quickened steps they hastened along the tunnel in the direction of the promised escape. As they advanced, the light became more apparent until finally they came to the point where the tunnel they had been traversing opened into a large corridor, which was filled with a subdued light from occasional patches of phosphorescent rock in walls and ceiling, but neither to the right nor the left could they see any sign of daylight.

"Which way now?" demanded Jude.

Tanar shook his head. "I do not know," he said.

"At least I shall not die in that awful blackness," wailed Jude, and perhaps that factor of their seemingly inevitable doom had weighed most heavily upon the two Pellucidarians, for, living as these people do beneath the brilliant rays of a perpetual noonday sun, darkness is a hideous and abhorrent thing to them, so unaccustomed are they to it.

"In this light, however slight it may be," said Tanar, "I can no longer be depressed. I am sure that we shall escape."

"But in which direction?" again demanded Jude.

"I shall turn to the right," said Tanar.

Jude shook his head. "That probably is the wrong direction," he said.

"If you know that the right direction lies to the left," said Tanar, "let us go to the left."

"I do not know," said Jude; "doubtless either direction is wrong."

"All right," said Tanar, with a laugh. "We shall go to the right," and, turning, he set off at a brisk walk along the large corridor.

"Do you notice anything, Jude?" asked Tanar.

"No. Why do you ask?" demanded the Himean.

"I smell fresh air from the upper world," said Tanar, "and if I am right we must be near the mouth of the tunnel."

Tanar was almost running now; exhaustion was forgotten in the unexpected hope of immediate deliverance. To be out in the fresh air and the light of day! To be free from the hideous darkness and the constant menace of recapture by the hideous monsters of the underworld! And across that bright hope, like a sinister shadow, came the numbing fear of disappointment.

What, if, after all, the breath of air which was now clear and fresh in their nostrils should prove to be entering the corridor through some unscalable shaft, such as the Well of Sounding Water into which he had fallen upon his entrance into the country of the Buried People, or what, if, at the moment of escape, they should meet a party of the Coripies?

So heavily did these thoughts weigh upon Tanar's mind that he slackened his speed until once again he moved in a slow walk.

"What is the matter?" demanded Jude. "A moment ago you were running and now you are barely crawling along. Do not tell me that you were mistaken and that, after all, we are not approaching the mouth of the corridor."

"I do not know," said Tanar. "We may be about to meet a terrible disappointment and if that is true I wish to delay it as long as possible. It would be a terrible thing to have hope crushed within our breasts now."

"I suppose it would," said Jude, "but

that is precisely what I have been expecting."

"You, I presume, would derive some satisfaction from disappointment," said Tanar.

"Yes," said Jude, "I suppose I would. It is my nature."

"Then prepare to be unhappy," cried Tanar, suddenly, "for here indeed is the mouth of the tunnel."

He had spoken just as he had rounded a turn in the corridor, and when Jude came to his side the latter saw daylight creeping into the corridor through an opening just in front of them — an opening beyond which he saw the foliage of growing things and the blue sky of Pellucidar.

Emerging again to the light of the sun after their long incarceration in the bowels of the earth, the two men were compelled to cover their eyes with their hands, while they slowly accustomed themselves again to the brilliant light of the noonday sun of Pellucidar.

When he was able to uncover his eyes and look about him, Tanar saw that the mouth of the tunnel was high upon the precipitous side of a lofty mountain. Below them wooded ravines ran down to a mighty forest, just beyond which lay the sparkling waters of a great ocean that, curving upward, merged in the haze of the distance.

Faintly discernible in the mid-distance an island raised its bulk out of the waters of the ocean.

"That," said Jude, pointing, "is the island of Hime."

"Ah, if I, too, could but see my home from here," sighed Tanar, "my happiness would be almost complete. I envy you, Jude."

"It gives me no happiness to see Hime," said Jude. "I hate the place."

"Then you are not going to try to go back to it?" demanded Tanar.

"Certainly, I shall," said Jude.

"But, why?" asked Tanar.

"There is no other place where I may go," grumbled Jude. "At least in Hime they will not kill me for no reason at all as strangers would do if I went elsewhere."

Jude's attention was suddenly attracted by something below them in a little glade that lay at the upper end of the ravine, which started a little distance below the mouth of the tunnel.

"Look," he cried, "there are people."

Tanar looked in the direction in which Jude was pointing, and when his eyes found the figures far below they first went wide with incredulity and then narrowed with rage.

"God!" he exclaimed, and as he voiced that single exclamation he leaped swiftly downward in the direction of the figures in the glade.

Chapter IX

LOVE AND TREACHERY

Stellara, lying upon a pallet of grasses beneath the shade of a large tree, above the beach where the Korsars were completing the boat in which they hoped to embark for Korsar, knew that the fever had left her and that her strength was rapidly returning, but having discovered that illness, whether real or feigned, protected her from the attentions of Bohar, she continued to permit the Korsars to believe that she was quite ill. In her mind there constantly revolved various plans for escape, but she wished to delay the attempt as long as possible, not only that she might have time to store up a greater amount of reserve strength, but also because she realized that if she waited until the Korsar boat was completed it would be unlikely that the majority of the men would brook delay in departure for the purpose of gratifying any desire that Bohar might express to pursue and recapture her.

Again, it was necessary to choose a time when none of the Korsars was in camp and as one of the two, who were detailed to prepare food and stand guard, was invariably on duty it appeared possible that she might never have the opportunity she hoped for, though she had determined that this fact would not prevent her from making an attempt at escape.

All of her hopes in this direction were centered upon one contingency, which her knowledge of nautical matters made to appear almost a certainty of the near future, and this was the fact that the launching of the boat would require the united efforts and strength of the entire party.

She knew from the discussions and conversations that she had overheard that it was Bohar's intention to launch the boat the moment that the hull was completed and to finish the balance of the work upon

it while it floated in the little cove upon the beach of which it was being constructed.

This work would require no great amount of time or effort, since the mast, spars, rigging and sail were ready and at hand; bladders and gourds already prepared to receive fresh water, and food provisions for the trip, accumulated by the hunters detailed for this purpose, were neatly sewn up in hides and stored away in a cool, earth-covered dugout.

And so from her couch of grasses beneath the great tree Stellara watched the work progressing upon the hull of the boat that was to carry Bohar and his men to Korsar, and, as she watched, she planned her method of escape.

Above the camp rose the forested slopes of the hills which she must cross in her return to Paraht. For some distance the trees were scattered and then commenced the dense forest. If she could reach this unobserved she felt that she might entertain high hope of successful escape, for once in the denser growth she could take advantage of the skill and experience she had acquired under Tanar's tutorage and prosecute her flight along the leafy pathways of the branches, leaving no spoor that Bohar might follow and at the same time safeguarding herself from the attacks of the larger and more dangerous beasts of the forest, for, though few, there were still dangerous beasts upon Amiocap. Perhaps the most fearsome was the tarag, the giant, saber-toothed tiger that once roamed the hills of the outer crust. For the tandor she felt less concern since they seldom attack an individual unless molested; but in the hills which she must cross the greatest danger lay in the presence of the tarag and the ryth, the gigantic cave bear or Ursus Stelaeus, long since extinct upon the outer crust. Of the men of Amiocap whom she might possibly encounter she entertained little fear, even though they might be members of tribes other than hers, though she shuddered at the thought that she might fall into the hands of the Coripies, as these grotesque monsters engendered within her far greater fear than any of the other dangers that might possibly beset her way.

The exhilaration of contemplated flight and the high hopes produced within her at prospects of successfully returning to her father and her friends were dampened by the realization that Tanar would not be there to greet her. The supposed death of the Sarian had cast a blight upon her happiness that naught ever could remove and her sorrow was the deeper, perhaps, because no words of love had passed between them, and, therefore, she had not the consolation of happy memories to relieve the gnawing anguish of her grief.

The work upon the hull of the boat was at last completed and the men, coming to camp to eat, spoke hopefully of early departure for Korsar. Bohar approached Stellara's couch and stood glaring down upon her, his repulsive face darkened by a malignant scowl.

"How much longer do you intend to lie here entirely useless to me?" he demanded. "You eat and sleep and the flush of fever has left your skin. I believe that you are feigning illness in order to escape fulfilling your duties as my mate and if that is true, you shall suffer for it. Get up!"

"I am too weak," said Stellara. "I cannot rise."

"That can be remedied," growled Bohar, and seizing her roughly by the hair, he dragged her from her couch and lifted her to her feet.

As Bohar released his hold upon her, Stellara staggered, her legs trembled, her knees gave beneath her and she fell back upon her couch, and so realistic was the manner in which she carried out the deception that even Bohar was fooled.

"She is sick and dying," growled one of the Korsars. "Why should we take her along in an overcrowded boat to eat the food and drink the water that some of us may be dying for before we reach Korsar?"

"Right," cried another. "Leave her behind."

"Stick a knife into her," said a third. "She is good for nothing."

"Shut up!" cried Bohar. "She is going to be my mate and she is going with us." He drew his two huge pistols. "Whoever objects will stay here with a bullet in his guts. Eat now, you filthy hounds, and be quick about it for I shall need all hands and all your strength to launch the hull when you have eaten."

So they were going to launch the hull! Stellara trembled with excitement as the moment for her break for liberty drew near. With impatience she watched the Korsars as they bolted their food like a pack of hungry wolf-dogs. She saw some of them throw themselves down to sleep after they had eaten, but Bohar the Bloody kicked them into wakefulness, and, at the point of his pistol, herded them to the beach, taking every available man and leaving Stellara alone and unguarded for the first time since he had seized her in the village of Fedol the chief.

She watched them as they descended to the hull and she waited until they seemed to be wholly engrossed in their efforts to shove the heavy boat into the sea; then she rose from her pallet and scurried like a frightened rabbit toward the forest on the slopes above the camp.

The hazards of fate, while beyond our control, are the factors in life which oftentimes make for the success or failure of our most important ventures. Upon them hang the fruition of our most cherished hope. They are, in truth, in the lap of the gods, where lies our future, and it was only by the merest hazard that Bohar the Bloody chanced to glance back toward the camp at the very moment that Stellara rose from her couch to make her bid for freedom.

With an oath he abandoned the work of launching the hull, and, calling his men to follow him, ran hurriedly up the steep slope in pursuit.

His fellows took in the situation at a glance and hesitated. "Let him chase his own woman," growled one. "What have we to do with it? Our business is to launch the boat and get her ready to sail to Korsar."

"Right," said another, "and if he is not back by the time that we are ready we shall sail without him."

"Good," cried a third. "Let us make haste then in the hope that we may be prepared to sail before he returns."

And so Bohar the Bloody, unaccompanied by his men, pursued Stellara alone. Perhaps it was as well for the girl that this was true for there were many fleeter among the Korsars than the beefy Bohar.

The girl was instantly aware that her attempt to escape had been discovered, for Bohar was shouting in stentorian tones demanding that she halt, but his words only made her run the faster until presently she had darted into the forest and was lost to his view.

Here she took to the trees, hoping thereby to elude him even though she knew that her speed would be reduced. She heard the sound of his advance as he crashed through the underbrush and she knew that he was gaining rapidly upon her, but this did not unnerve her since she was confident that he could have no suspicion that she was in the branches of the trees and just so long as she kept among thick foliage he might pass directly beneath her without being aware of her close presence, and that is precisely what he did, cursing and puffing as he made his bull-like way up the steep slope of the hillside.

Stellara heard him pass and go crashing on in pursuit, and then she resumed her flight, turning to the right away from the direction of Bohar's advance until presently the noise of his passing was lost in the distance; then she turned upward again toward the height she must cross on her journey to Paraht.

Bohar sweated upward until finally almost utter exhaustion forced him to rest. He found himself in a little glade and here he lay down beneath a shrub that not only protected him from the rays of the sun, but hid him from sight as well, for in savage Pellucidar it is always well to seek rest in concealment.

Bohar's mind was filled with angry thoughts. He cursed himself for leaving the girl alone in camp and he cursed the girl for escaping, and he cursed the fate that had forced him to clamber up this steep hillside upon his futile mission, and most of all he cursed his absent followers whom he now realized had failed to accompany him. He knew that he had lost the girl and that it would be like looking for a particular minnow in the ocean to continue his search for her, and so, having rested, he was determined to hasten back to his camp when his attention was suddenly attracted by a noise at the lower end of the glade. Instinctively he reached for one of his pistols and to his dismay he found that both were gone, evidently having slipped from his sash or been scraped from it as he wallowed upward through the underbrush.

Bohar, despite his bluster and braggadocio, was far from courageous. Without his weapons he was an arrant coward and so now he cringed in his concealment as he strained his eyes to discover the author of the noise he had heard, and as he watched a cunning leer of triumph curled his hideous mouth, for before him, at the far end of the glade, he saw Stellara drop from the lower branches of a tree and come upward across the glade toward him.

As the girl came abreast of his hiding place, Bohar the Bloody leaped to his feet and confronted her. With a stifled exclamation of dismay Stellara turned and sought to escape, but the Korsar was too close and too quick and reaching forth he seized her roughly by the hair.

"Will you never learn that you cannot escape Bohar the Bloody?" he demanded. "You are mine and for this I shall cut off both your feet at the ankles when I get you into the boat, so that there will be no chance whatever that you may again run away from me. But come, mate willingly with me and it will go less hard with you," and he drew her slim figure into his embrace.

"Never," cried Stellara, and she struck him in the face with her two clenched fists.

With an oath Bohar seized the girl by the throat and shook her. "You she-ryth," he cried, "if I did not want you so badly I should kill you, and by the god of Korsar if ever you strike me again I shall kill you."

"Then kill me," cried Stellara, "for I should rather die than mate with you," and again she struck him with all her strength full in the face.

Bohar frothed with rage as he closed his fingers more tightly upon the girl's soft neck. "Die, then, you———"

The words died upon his lips and he wheeled about as there fell upon his ears a man's loud voice raised in anger.

As he stood there hesitating and looking in the direction of the sound, the underbrush at the upper end of the glade parted and a warrior, leaping into the clearing, ran swiftly toward him.

Bohar blanched as though he had seen a ghost, and then, hurling the girl roughly to the ground, he faced the lone warrior.

Bohar would have fled had he not realized the futility of flight, for what chance had he in a race with this lithe man, who leaped toward him with the grace and speed of a deer.

"Go away," shouted Bohar. "Go away and leave us alone. This is my mate."

"You lie," growled Tanar of Pellucidar as he leaped upon the Korsar.

Down went the two men, the Sarian on top, and as they fell each sought a hold upon the other's throat, and, failing to secure it, they struck blindly at one another's face.

Tanar was mad with rage. He fought like a wild beast, forgetting all that David Innes had taught him. His one thought was to kill; it mattered not how just so long as he killed; and Bohar, on the defensive fighting for his life, battled like a cornered rat. To his advantage were his great weight and his longer reach, but in strength and agility as well as courage Tanar was his superior.

Stellara slowly opened her eyes as she recovered from the swoon into which she had passed beneath the choking fingers of Bohar the Bloody. At first she did not recognize Tanar, seeing only two warriors battling to the death on the sward of the glade and guessing that she would be the prey of him who was victorious. But presently, in the course of the duel, the face of the Sarian was turned toward her.

"Tanar!" she cried. "God is merciful. I thought you were dead and He has given you back to me."

At her words the Sarian redoubled his efforts to overcome his antagonist, but Bohar succeeded in getting his fingers upon Tanar's throat.

Horrified, Stellara looked about her for a rock or a stick with which to come to the succor of her champion, but before she had found one she realized that he needed no outside assistance. With a single Herculean movement he tore himself loose from Bohar and leaped to his feet.

Instantly the Korsar sprang to an upright position and lowering his head he charged the Sarian — charged like a mad bull.

Now Tanar was fighting with cool calculation. The blood-madness of the first moment following tne sight of Stellara in the choking murderous fingers of the Korsar had passed. He awaited Bohar's rush, and as they came together he clamped an arm around the Korsar's head, and, turning swiftly, hurled the man over his shoulder and heavily to the ground. Then he waited.

Once more Bohar, shaking his head, staggered to his feet. Once more he rushed the Sarian, and once more that deadly arm was locked about his head, and once more he was hurled heavily to the ground.

This time he did not arise so quickly nor so easily. He came up staggering and feeling of his head and neck.

"Prepare to die," growled Tanar. "For the suffering you have inflicted upon Stellara you are about to die."

With a shriek of mingled rage and fright Bohar, gone mad, charged the Sarian again, and for the third time his great body flew through the air, to alight heavily upon the hard ground, but this time it did not arise; it did not stir, for Bohar the Bloody lay dead with a broken neck.

For a moment Tanar of Pellucidar stood ready over the body of his fallen foe, but when he realized that Bohar was dead he turned away with a sneer of disgust.

Before him stood Stellara, her beautiful eyes filled with incredulity and with happiness.

"Tanar!" It was only a whisper, but it carried to him a world of meaning that sent thrill after thrill through his body.

"Stellara!" he cried, as he took the girl in his arms. "Stellara, I love you."

Her soft arms stole around his neck and drew his face to hers. His mouth covered her mouth in a long kiss, and, as he raised his face to look down into hers, from her parted lips burst a single exclamation, "Oh, God!" and from the depth of her half-closed eyes burned a love beyond all understanding.

"My mate," he cried, as he pressed her form to him.

"My mate," breathed Stellara, "while life remains in my body and after life, throughout death, forever!"

Suddenly she looked up and drew away.

"Who is that, Tanar?" she asked.

As Tanar turned to look in the direction indicated by the girl he saw Jude emerging from the forest at the upper end of the glade. "It is Jude," he said to Stellara, "who escaped with me from the country of the Buried People."

Jude approached them, his sullen countenance clouded by its habitual scowl.

"He frightens me," said Stellara, pressing closer to Tanar.

"You need not fear him," said the Sarian. "He is always scowling and unhappy; but he is my friend and even if he were not he is harmless."

"I do not like him," whispered Stellara.

Jude approached and stopped before them. His eyes wandered for a moment to the body of Bohar and then came back and fastened themselves in a steady gaze upon Stellara. appraising her from head to foot.

*Tanar clamped an arm around the Korsar's head
and turning swiftly, hurled the man heavily to
the ground.*

There was a crafty boldness in his gaze that disturbed Stellara even more than his sullen scowl.

"Who is the woman?" he demanded, without taking his eyes from her face.

"My mate," replied Tanar.

"Then she is going with us?" asked Jude.

"Of course," replied the Sarian.

"And where are we going?" demanded Jude.

"Stellara and I will return to Paraht, where her father, Fedol, is chief," replied Tanar. "You may come with us if you wish. We will see that you are received as a friend and treated well until you can find the means to return to Hime."

"Is he from Hime?" asked Stellara, and Tanar felt her shudder.

"I am from Hime," said Jude, "but I do not care if I never return there if your people will let me live with them."

"That," said Tanar, "is something that must be decided by Fedol and his people, but I can promise you that they will let you remain with them, if not permanently, at least until you can find the means of returning to Hime. And now, before we set out for Paraht, let us renew our strength with food and sleep."

Without weapons it was not easy to obtain game and they had traveled up the mountain slopes for some distance before the two men were able to bring down a brace of large birds, which they knocked over with well aimed stones. The birds closely resembled wild turkeys, whose prototypes were doubtless the progenitors of the wild turkeys of the outer crust. The hunt had brought them to a wide plateau, just below the summit of the hills. It was a rolling table-land, waist deep in lush grasses, with here and there a giant tree or a group of trees offering shade from the vertical rays of the noonday sun.

Beside a small stream, which rippled gayly downward toward the sea, they halted to eat and sleep.

Jude gathered firewood while Tanar made fire by the primitive method of rapidly revolving a sharpened stick in a tinder-filled hole in a larger piece of dry wood. As these preparations were going forward Stellara prepared the birds and it was not long before the turkeys were roasting over a hot fire.

Their hunger appeased, the urge to sleep took possession of them, and now Jude insisted that he stand the first watch, arguing that he had not been subjected to the fatigue of battle as had Tanar, and so Stellara and the Sarian lay down beneath the shade of the tree while the scowling Himean stood watch.

Even in the comparative safety of Amiocap danger might always be expected to lurk in the form of carnivorous beast or hunting man, but the watcher cast no solicitous glances beyond the camp. Instead, he squatted upon his haunches, devouring Stellara with his eyes. Not once did he remove them from the beautiful figure of the girl except occasionally to glance quickly at Tanar, where the regular rising and falling of his breast denoted undisturbed slumber.

Whatever thoughts the beauty of the sleeping girl engendered in the breast of the Himean, they were reflected only in the unremitting scowl that never lifted itself from the man's dark brows.

Presently he arose noiselessly and gathered a handful of soft grasses, which he rolled into a small ball. Then he crept stealthily to where Stellara lay and kneeled beside her.

Suddenly he leaned over her and grasped her by the throat, at the same time clamping his other hand, in the palm of which lay the ball of grass, over her mouth.

Thus rudely awakened from deep slumber, her first glance revealing the scowling features of the Himean, Stellara opened her mouth to scream for help, and, as she did so, Jude forced the ball of grass between her teeth and far into her mouth, dragged her to her feet, and throwing her across his shoulder, bore her swiftly downward across the table-land.

Stellara struggled and fought to free herself, but Jude was a powerful man and her efforts were of no avail against his strength. He held her in such a way that both her arms were confined. The ball of grass expanded in her mouth and she could not force it out with her tongue alone. A single scream she knew would awaken Tanar and bring him to her rescue, but she could not scream.

Down across the rolling table-land the Himean carried Stellara to the edge of a steep cliff that overhung the sea at the upper end of a deep cove which cut far into the island at this point. Here Jude lowered

Stellara to her feet, but he still clung tightly to one of her wrists.

"Listen, woman," he growled, "you are coming to Hime to be the mate of Jude. If you come peaceably, no harm will befall you and if you will promise to make no outcry I shall remove the gag from your mouth. Do you promise?"

Stellara shook her head determinedly in an unquestionable negative and at the same time struggled to free herself from Jude's grasp.

With an ugly growl the man struck her and as she fell unconscious he gathered long grasses and twisted them into a rope and bound her wrists and ankles; then he lifted her again to his shoulder and started down over the edge of the cliff, where a narrow trail now became discernible.

It was evident that Jude had had knowledge of this path since he had come to it so unerringly, and the ease and assurance with which he descended it strengthened this conviction.

The descent was not over a hundred feet to a little ledge almost at the water's edge.

It was here that Stellara gained consciousness, and, as she opened her eyes, she saw before her a water-worn cave that ran far back beneath the cliff.

Into this, along the narrow ledge, Jude carried her to the far end of the cavern, where, upon a narrow, pebbly beach, were drawn up a half dozen dugouts — the light, well-made canoes of the Himeans.

In one of these Jude placed the girl, and, pushing it off into the deep water of the cove, leaped into it himself, seized the paddle and directed its course out toward the open sea.

Chapter X

PURSUIT

Awakening from a deep and refreshing slumber, Tanar opened his eyes and lay gazing up into the foliage of the tree above him. Happy thoughts filled his mind, a smile touched his lip and then, following the trend of his thoughts, his eyes turned to feast upon the dear figure of his mate.

She was not there, where he had last seen her huddled snugly in her bed of grasses, but still he felt no concern, thinking merely that she had awakened before him and arisen.

Idly his gaze made a circuit of the little camp, and then with a startled exclamation he leaped to his feet for he realized that both Stellara and Jude had disappeared. Again he looked about him, this time extending the field of his enquiring gaze, but nowhere was there any sign of either the man or the woman that he sought.

He called their names aloud, but there was no response, and then he fell to examining the ground about the camp. He saw where Stellara had been sleeping and to his keen eyes were revealed the tracks of the Himean as he had approached her couch. He saw other tracks leading away, the tracks of Jude alone, but in the crushed grasses where the man had gone he read the true story, for they told him that more than the weight of a single man had bent and bruised them thus; they told him that Jude had carried Stellara off, and Tanar knew that it had been done by force.

Swiftly he followed the well marked spoor through the long grass, oblivious of all else save the prosecution of his search for Stellara and the punishment of Jude. And so he was unaware of the sinister figure that crept along the trail behind him.

Down across the table-land they went — the man and the great beast following silently in his tracks. Down to a cliff overhanging the sea the trail led, and here as Tanar paused an instant to look out across the ocean he saw hazily in the distance a canoe and in the canoe were two figures, but who they were he could only guess since they were too far away for him to recognize.

As he stood there thus, stunned for a moment, a slight noise behind him claimed his attention, recalled him momentarily from the obsession of his sorrow and his rage so that he turned a quick, scowling glance in the direction from which the interruption had come, and there, not ten paces from him, loomed the snarling face of a great tarag.

The fangs of the saber-tooth gleamed in the sunlight; the furry snout was wrinkled in a snarl of anger; the lashing tail came suddenly to rest, except for a slight convulsive twitching of its tip; the beast crouched and Tanar knew that it was about to charge.

Unarmed and single-handed as he was, the man seemed easy prey for the carnivore; nor to right nor to left was there any avenue of escape.

All these things passed swiftly through the mind of the Sarian, yet never did they totally obliterate the memory of the two figures in the canoe far out at sea behind him; nor of the cliff overhanging the waters of the cove beneath. And then the tarag charged.

A hideous scream broke from the savage throat as the great beast hurled itself forward with lightning-like rapidity. Two great bounds it took, and in mid-spring of the second Tanar turned and dove head foremost over the edge of the cliff, for the only alternative that remained to him was death beneath the rending fangs and talons of the saber-tooth.

For all he knew jagged rocks might lie just beneath the surface of the water, but there was one chance that the water was deep, while no chance for life remained to him upon the cliff top.

The momentum of the great cat's spring, unchecked by the body of his expected prey, carried him over the edge of the cliff also so that man and beast hurtled downward almost side by side to the water far below.

Tanar cut the water cleanly with extended hands and turning quickly upwards came to the surface scarcely a yard from where the great cat had alighted.

The two faced one another and at sight of the man the tarag burst again into hideous screams and struck out swiftly toward him.

Tanar knew that he might outdistance the tarag in the water, but at the moment that they reached the beach he would be at the mercy of the great carnivore. The snarling face was close to his; the great talons were reaching for him as Tanar of Pellucidar dove beneath the beast.

A few, swift strokes brought him up directly behind the cat and an instant later he had reached out and seized the furry hide. The tarag turned swiftly to strike at him, but already the man was upon his shoulders and his weight was carrying the snarling face below the surface.

Choking, struggling, the maddened animal sought to reach the soft flesh of the man with his raking talons, but in the liquid element that filled the sea its usual methods of offense and defense were worthless. Quickly realizing that death stared it in the face, unless it could im-

mediately overcome this handicap, the tarag now strained its every muscle to reach the solid footing of the land, while Tanar on his part sought to prevent it. Now his fingers had crept from their hold upon the furry shoulders down to the white furred throat and like claws of steel they sank into the straining muscles.

No longer did the beast attempt to scream and the man, for his part, fought in silence.

It was a grim duel; a terrible duel; a savage encounter that might be enacted only in a world that was very young and between primitive creatures who never give up the stern battle for life until the scythe of the Grim Reaper had cut them down.

Deep into the gloomy cavern beneath the cliff the tarag battled for the tiny strip of beach at the far end and grimly the man fought to hold it back and force its head beneath the water. He felt the efforts of the beast weakening and yet they were very close to the beach. At any instant the great claws might strike bottom and Tanar knew that there was still left within that giant carcass enough vitality to rend him to shreds if ever the tarag got four feet on solid ground and his head above the water.

With a last supreme effort he tightened his fingers upon the throat of the tarag and sliding from its back sought to drag it from its course, and the animal upon its part made one, last supreme effort for life. It reared up in the water and wheeling about struck at the man. The raking talons grazed his flesh, and then he was back upon the giant shoulders forcing the head once more beneath the surface of the sea. He felt a spasm pass through the great frame of the beast beneath him; the muscles relaxed and the tarag floated limp.

A moment later Tanar dragged himself to the pebbly beach, where he lay panting from exhaustion.

Recovered, nor did it take him long to recover, so urgent were the demands of the pursuit upon which he was engaged, Tanar rose and looked about him. Before him were canoes, such as he had never seen before, drawn up upon the narrow beach. Paddles lay in each of the canoes as though they but awaited the early return of their owners. Whence they had come and what they were doing here in this lonely cavern, Tanar could not guess. They were unlike the canoes of the Amiocapians, which fact convinced him that they belonged to a people from some other island, or possibly from the mainland itself. But these were questions which did not concern him greatly at the time. Here were canoes. Here was the means of pursuing the two that he had seen far out at sea and whom he was convinced were none other than Jude and Stellara.

Seizing one of the small craft he dragged it to the water's edge and launched it. Then, leaping into it, he paddled swiftly down the cove out towards the sea, and as he paddled he had an opportunity to examine the craft more closely.

It was evidently fashioned from a single log of very light wood and was all of one piece, except a bulkhead at each end of the cockpit, which was large enough to accommodate three men.

Rapping with his paddle upon the surface of the deck and upon the bulkheads convinced him that the log had been entirely hollowed out beneath the deck and as the bulkheads themselves gave every appearance of having been so neatly fitted as to be watertight, Tanar guessed that the canoe was unsinkable.

His attention was next attracted by a well-tanned and well-worn hide lying in the bottom of the cockpit. A rawhide lacing ran around the entire periphery of the hide and as he tried to determine the purpose to which the whole had been put his eyes fell upon a series of cleats extending entirely around the edge of the cockpit, and he guessed that the hide was intended as a covering for it. Examining it more closely he discovered an opening in it about the size of a man's body and immediately its purpose became apparent to him. With the covering in place and laced tightly around the cockpit and also laced around the man's body the canoe could ship no water and might prove a seaworthy craft, even in severe storms.

As the Sarian fully realized his limitations as a seafaring man, he lost no time in availing himself of this added protection against the elements, and when he had adjusted it and laced it tightly about the outside of the cockpit and secured the lacing which ran around the opening in the center of the hide about his own body, he experienced a feeling of security that he had never before felt when he had been forced to surrender himself to the unknown dangers of the sea.

Now he paddled rapidly in the direction in which he had last seen the canoe with its two occupants, and when he had passed out of the cove into the open sea he espied them again, but this time so far out that the craft and its passengers appeared only as a single dot upon the broad waters. But beyond them hazily loomed the bulk of the island that Jude had pointed out as Hime and this tended to crystallize Tanar's assurance that the canoe ahead of him was being guided by Jude toward the island of his own people.

The open seas of Pellucidar present obstacles to the navigation of a small canoe that would seem insurmountable to men of the outer crust, for their waters are ofttimes alive with saurian monsters of a long past geologic epoch and it was encounters with these that the Sarian mountaineer apprehended with more acute concern than consideration of adverse wind or tempest aroused within him.

He had noticed that one end of the long paddle he wielded was tipped with a piece of sharpened ivory from the end of a tandor's tusk, but the thing seemed an utterly futile weapon with which to combat a tandoraz or an azdyryth, two of the mightiest and most fearsome inhabitants of the deep, but as far as he could see ahead the long, oily swells of a calm ocean were unruffled by marine life of any description.

Well aware of his small experience and great deficiency as a paddler, Tanar held no expectation of being able to overhaul the canoe manned by the experienced Jude. The best that he could hope was that he might keep it in view until he could mark the spot upon Hime where it landed. And once upon solid ground again, even though it was an island peopled by enemies, the Sarian felt that he would be able to cope with any emergency that might arise.

Gradually the outlines of Hime took definite shape before him, while those of Amiocap became correspondingly vague behind.

And between him and the island of Hime the little dot upon the surface of the sea told him that his quarry had not as yet made land. The pursuit seemed interminable. Hime seemed to be receding almost as rapidly as he approached it. He became hungry and thirsty, but there was neither food nor water. There was naught but to bend his paddle ceaselessly through the monotonous grind of pursuit, but at length the details of the shore-line grew more distinct. He saw coves and inlets and wooded hills and then he saw the canoe that he was following disappear far ahead of him beyond the entrance of a cove. Tanar marked the spot well in his mind and redoubled his efforts to reach the shore. And then fate arose in her inexorable perversity and confounded all his hopes and plans.

A sudden flurry on the surface of the water far to his right gave him his first warning. And then, like the hand of a giant, the wind caught his frail craft and turned it at right angles to the course he wished to pursue. The waves rolled; the wind shrieked; the storm was upon him in great fury and there was naught to do but turn and flee before it.

Down the coast of Hime he raced, parallel to the shore, further and further from the spot where Jude had landed with Stellara, but all the time Tanar was striving to drive his craft closer and closer to the wooded slopes of Hime.

Ahead of him, and upon his right, he could see what appeared to be the end of the island. Should he be carried past this he realized that all would be lost, for doubtless the storm would carry him on out of sight of land and if it did he knew that he could never reach Hime nor return to Amiocap, since he had no means whatsoever of ascertaining direction once land slipped from view in the haze of the upcurving horizon.

Straining every muscle, continuously risking being capsized, Tanar strove to drive inward toward the shore, and though he saw that he was gaining he knew that it was too late, for already he was almost abreast of the island's extremity, and still he was a hundred yards off shore. But even so he did not despair, or if he did despair he did not cease to struggle for salvation.

He saw the island slip past him, but there was yet a chance for in its lee he saw calm water and if he could reach that he would be saved.

Straining every muscle the Sarian bent to his crude paddle. Suddenly the breeze stopped and he shot out into the smooth water in the lee of the island, but he did not cease his strenuous efforts until the bow of the canoe had touched the sand of Hime.

Tanar leaped out and dragged the craft ashore. That he should ever need it again he doubted, yet he hid it beneath the foliage of nearby bushes, and alone and unarmed set forth to face the dangers of an unknown country in what appeared even to Tanar as an almost hopeless quest for Stellara.

To the Sarian it seemed wisest to follow the coast-line back until he found the spot at which Jude had landed and then trace his trail inland, and this was the plan that he proceeded to follow.

Being in a strange land, and, therefore, in a land of enemies, and being unarmed, Tanar was forced to move with great caution; yet constantly he sacrificed caution to speed. Natural obstacles impeded his progress. A great cliff running far out into the sea barred his way and it was with extreme difficulty that he found a path up the face of the frowning escarpment and then only after traveling inland for a considerable distance.

Beyond the summit rolled a broad table-land dotted with trees. A herd of thags grazed quietly in the sunlight or dozed beneath the shadowy foliage of the trees.

At sight of the man passing among them these great horned cattle became restless. An old bull bellowed and pawed the ground, and Tanar measured the distance to the nearest tree. But on he went, avoiding the beasts as best he could and hoping against hope that he could pass them successfully without further arousing their short tempers. But the challenge of the old bull was being taken up by others of his sex until a score of heavy shouldered mountains of beef were converging slowly upon the lone man, stopping occasionally to paw or gore the ground, while they bellowed forth their displeasure.

There was still a chance that he might pass them in safety. There was an opening among them just ahead of him, and Tanar accelerated his speed, but just at that instant one of the bulls took it into his head to charge and then the whole twenty bore down upon the Sarian like a band of iron locomotives suddenly endowed with the venom of hornets.

There was naught to do but seek the safety of the nearest tree and towards this Tanar ran at full speed, while from all sides the angry bulls raced to head him off.

With scarcely more than inches to spare Tanar swung himself into the branches of the tree just as the leading bull passed beneath him. A moment later the bellowing herd congregated beneath his sanctuary and while some contented themselves with pawing and bellowing, others placed their heavy heads against the bole of the tree and sought to push it down, but fortunately for Tanar it was a young oak and it withstood their sturdiest efforts.

But now, having treed him, the thags showed no disposition to leave him. For a while they milled around beneath him and then several deliberately lay down beneath the tree as though to prevent his escape.

To one accustomed to the daily recurrence of the darkness of night, following the setting of the sun, escape from such a dilemma as that in which Tanar found himself would have seemed merely a matter of waiting for the coming of night, but where the sun does not set and there is no night, and time is immeasurable and unmeasured, and where one may not know whether a lifetime or a second has been encompassed by the duration of such an event, the enforced idleness and delay are maddening.

But in spite of these conditions, or perhaps because of them, the Sarian possessed a certain philosophic outlook upon life that permitted him to accept his fate with marked stoicism and to take advantage of the enforced delay by fashioning a bow, arrows and a spear from the material afforded by the tree in which he was confined.

The tree gave him everything that he needed except the cord for his bow, and this he cut from the rawhide belt that supported his loin cloth — a long, slender strip of rawhide which he inserted in his mouth and chewed thoroughly until it was entirely impregnated with saliva. Then he bent his bow and stretched the wet rawhide from tip to tip. While it dried, he pointed his arrows with his teeth.

In drying the rawhide shrunk, bending the bow still further and tightening the string until it hummed to the slightest touch.

The weapons were finished and yet the great bulls still stood on guard, and while Tanar remained helpless in the tree Jude was taking Stellara toward the interior of the island.

But all things must end. Impatient of delay, Tanar sought some plan whereby he might rid himself of the short tempered beasts beneath him. He hit upon the plan of yelling and throwing dead branches at them and this did have the effect of bringing them all to their feet. A few wandered away to graze with the balance of the herd, but enough remained to keep Tanar securely imprisoned.

A great bull stood directly beneath him. Tanar jumped up and down upon a small branch, making its leafy end whip through the air, and at the same time he hurled bits of wood at the great thags. And then, suddenly, to the surprise and consternation of both man and beast, the branch broke and precipitated Tanar full upon the broad shoulders of the bull. Instantly his fingers clutched its long hair as, with a bellow of surprise and terror, the beast leaped forward.

Instinct took the frightened animal toward the balance of the herd and when they saw him with a man sitting upon his back they, too, became terrified, with the result that a general stampede ensued, the herd attempting to escape their fellow, while the bull raced to be among them.

Stragglers, that had been grazing at a considerable distance from the balance of the herd, were stringing out to the rear and it was the presence of these that made it impossible for Tanar to slip to the ground and make his escape. Knowing that he would be trampled by those behind if he left the back of the bull, there was no alternative but to remain where he was as long as he could.

The thag, now thoroughly frightened because of his inability to dislodge the man-thing from his shoulders, was racing blindly forward, and presently Tanar found himself carried into the very midst of the lunging herd as it thundered across the table-land toward a distant forest.

The Sarian knew that once they reached the forest he would doubtless be scraped from the back of the thag almost immediately by some low hanging limb, and if he were not killed or injured by the blow he would be trampled to death by the thags behind. But as escape seemed hopeless he could only await the final outcome of this strange adventure.

When the leaders of the herd approached the forest hope was rekindled in Tanar's breast, for he saw that the growth was so thick and the trees so close together that it was impossible for the beasts to enter the woods at a rapid gait.

Immediately the leaders reached the edge of the forest their pace was slowed down and those behind them, pushing forward, were stopped by those in front. Some of them attempted to climb up, or were forced up, upon the backs of those ahead. But, for the most part, the herd slowed down and contented itself with pushing steadily onward toward the woods with the result that when the beast that Tanar was astride arrived at the edge of the dark shadows his gait had been reduced to a walk, and as he passed beneath the first tree Tanar swung lightly into its branches.

He had lost his spear, but his bow and arrows that he had strapped to his back remained with him, and as the herd passed beneath him and he saw the last of them disappear in the dark aisles of the forest, he breathed a deep sigh of relief and turned once more toward the far end of the island.

The thags had carried him inland a considerable distance, so now he cut back diagonally toward the coast to gain as much ground as possible.

Tanar had not yet emerged from the forest when he heard the excited growling of some wild beast directly ahead of him.

He thought that he recognized the voice of a codon, and fitting an arrow to his bow he crept warily forward. What wind was blowing came from the beast toward him and presently brought to his nostrils proof of the correctness of his guess, together with another familiar scent — that of man.

Knowing that the beast could not catch his scent from upwind, Tanar had only to be careful to advance silently, but there are few animals on earth that can move more silently than primitive man when he elects to do so, and so Tanar came in sight of the beast without being discovered by it.

It was, as he had thought, a huge wolf, a prehistoric but gigantic counterpart of our own timber wolf.

No need had the codon to run in packs, for in size, strength, ferocity and courage it was a match for any creature that it sought to bring down, with the possible exception of the mammoth, and this great beast alone it hunted in packs.

The codon stood snarling beneath a great tree, occasionally leaping high against the bole as though he sought to reach something hidden by the foliage above.

Tanar crept closer and presently he saw the figure of a youth crouching among the lower branches above the codon. It was evident that the boy was terror-stricken, but the thing that puzzled Tanar was that he cast affrighted glances upward into the tree more often than he did downward toward the codon, and presently this fact convinced the Sarian that the youth was menaced by something above him.

Tanar viewed the predicament of the boy and then considered the pitiful inadequacy of his own makeshift bow and arrow, which might only infuriate the beast and turn it upon himself. He doubted that the arrows were heavy enough, or strong enough, to pierce through the savage heart and thus only might he hope to bring down the codon.

Once more he crept to a new position, without attracting the attention either of the codon or the youth, and from this new vantage point he could look further up into the tree in which the boy crouched and then it was that he realized the hopelessness of the boy's position, for only a few feet above him and moving steadily closer appeared the head of a great snake, whose wide, distended jaws revealed formidable fangs.

Tanar's consideration of the boy's plight was influenced by a desire to save him from either of the two creatures that menaced him and also by the hope that if successful he might win sufficient gratitude to enlist the services of the youth as a guide, and especially as a go-between in the event that he should come in contact with natives of the island.

Tanar had now crept to within seven paces of the codon, from the sight of which he was concealed by a low shrub behind which he lay. Had the youth not been so occupied between the wolf and the snake he might have seen the Sarian, but so far he had not seen him.

Fitting an arrow to his crude bow and inserting four others between the fingers of his left hand, Tanar arose quietly and drove a shaft into the back of the codon, between its shoulders.

With a howl of pain and rage the beast

wheeled about, only to receive another arrow full in the chest. Then his glaring eyes alighted upon the Sarian and, with a hideous growl, he charged.

With such rapidity do events of this nature transpire that they are over in much less time than it takes to record them, for a wounded wolf, charging its antagonist, can cover seven paces in an incredibly short space of time; yet even in that brief interval three more arrows sank deeply into the white breast of the codon, and the momentum of its last stride sent it rolling against the Sarian's feet — dead.

The youth, freed from the menace of the codon, leaped to the ground and would have fled without a word of thanks had not Tanar covered him with another arrow and commanded him to halt.

The snake, seeing another man and realizing, perhaps, that the odds were now against him, hesitated a moment and then withdrew into the foliage of the tree, as Tanar advanced toward the trembling youth.

"Who are you?" demanded the Sarian.

"My name is Balal," replied the youth. "I am the son of Scurv, the chief."

"Where is your village?" asked Tanar.

"It is not far," replied Balal.

"Will you take me there?" asked Tanar.

"Yes," replied Balal.

"Will your father receive me well?" continued the Sarian.

"You saved my life," said Balal. "For that he will treat you well, though for the most part we kill strangers who come to Garb."

"Lead on," said the Sarian.

Chapter XI

GURA

Balal led Tanar through the forest until they came at last to the edge of a steep cliff, which the Sarian judged was the opposite side of the promontory that had barred his way along the beach.

Not far from the cliff's edge stood the stump of a great tree that seemed to have been blasted and burned by lightning. It reared its head some ten feet above the ground and from its charred surface protruded the stub end of several broken limbs.

"Follow me," said Balal, and leaping to the protruding stub, he climbed to the top of the stump and lowered himself into the interior.

Tanar followed and found an opening some three feet in diameter leading down into the bole of the dead tree. Set into the sides of this natural shaft were a series of heavy pegs, which answered the purpose of ladder rungs to the descending Balal.

The noonday sun lighted the interior of the tree for a short distance, but their own shadows, intervening, blotted out everything that lay at a depth greater than six or eight feet.

None too sure that he was not being led into a trap and, therefore, unwilling to permit his guide to get beyond his reach, Tanar hastily entered the hollow stump and followed Balal downward.

The Sarian was aware that the interior of the tree led into a shaft dug in the solid ground and a moment later he felt his feet touch the floor of a dark tunnel.

Along this tunnel Balal led him and presently they emerged into a cave that was dimly lighted through a small opening opposite them and near the floor.

Through this aperture, which was about two feet in diameter and beyond which Tanar could see daylight, Balal crawled, followed closely by the Sarian, who found himself upon a narrow ledge, high up on the face of an almost vertical cliff.

"This," said Balal, "is the village of Garb."

"I see no village nor any people," said Tanar.

"They are here though," said Balal. "Follow me," and he led the way a short distance along the ledge, which inclined downward and was in places so narrow and so shelving that the two men were compelled to flatten themselves against the side of the cliff and edge their way slowly, inch by inch, sideways.

Presently the ledge ended and here it was much wider so that Balal could lie down upon it, and, lowering his body over the edge, he clung a moment by his hands and then dropped.

Tanar looked over the edge and saw that Balal had alighted upon another narrow ledge about ten feet below. Even to a mountaineer, such as the Sarian was, the feat seemed difficult and fraught with danger, but there was no alternative and so, lying down, he lowered himself slowly over the edge of the ledge, clung an instant with his fingers, and then dropped.

As he alighted beside the youth he was about to remark upon the perilous approach to the village of Garb, but it was so apparent that Balal took it as a matter of course and thought nothing of it that Tanar desisted, realizing, in the instant, that among cliff dwellers, such as these, the little feat that they had just accomplished was as ordinary and everyday an occurrence as walking on level ground was to him.

As Tanar had an opportunity to look about him on this new level, he saw, and not without relief, that the ledge was much wider and that the mouths of several caves opened upon it. In places, and more especially in front of the cave entrances, the ledge widened to as much as six or eight feet, and here Tanar obtained his first view of any considerable number of Himeans.

"Is it not a wonderful village?" asked Balal, and without waiting for an answer, "Look!" and he pointed downward over the edge of the ledge.

Following the direction indicated by the youth, Tanar saw ledge after ledge scoring the face of a lofty cliff from summit to base, and upon every ledge there were men, women and children.

"Come," said Balal, "I will take you to my father," and forthwith he led the way along the ledge.

As the first people they encountered saw Tanar they leaped to their feet, the men seizing their weapons. "I am taking him to my father, the chief," said Balal. "Do not harm him," and with sullen looks the warriors let them pass.

A log into which wooden pegs were driven served as an easy means of descent from one ledge to the next, and after descending for a considerable distance to about midway between the summit and the ground Balal halted at the entrance to a cave, before which sat a man, a woman and two children, a girl about Balal's age and a boy much younger.

As had all the other villagers they had passed, these, too, leaped to their feet and seized weapons when they saw Tanar.

"Do not harm him," repeated Balal. "I have brought him to you, Scurv, my father, because he saved my life when it was threatened simultaneously by a snake and

a wolf and I promised him that you would receive him and treat him well."

Scurv eyed Tanar suspiciously and there was no softening of the lines upon his sullen countenance even when he heard that the stranger had saved the life of his son. "Who are you and what are you doing in our country?" he demanded.

"I am looking for one named Jude," replied Tanar.

"What do you know of Jude?" asked Scurv. "Is he your friend?"

There was something in the man's tone that made it questionable as to the advisability of claiming Jude as a friend. "I know him," he said. "We were prisoners together among the Coripies on the island of Amiocap."

"You are an Amiocapian?" demanded Scurv.

"No," replied Tanar, "I am a Sarian from a country on a far distant mainland."

"Then what were you doing on Amiocap?" asked Scurv.

"I was captured by the Korsars and the ship in which they were taking me to their country was wrecked on Amiocap. All that I ask of you is that you give me food and show me where I can find Jude."

"I do not know where you can find Jude," said Scurv. "His people and my people are always at war."

"Do you not know where their country or village is?" demanded Tanar.

"Yes, of course I know where it is, but I do not know that Jude is there."

"Are you going to give him food," asked Balal, "and treat him well as I promised you would?"

"Yes," said Scurv, but his tone was sullen and his shifty eyes looked neither at Balal nor Tanar as he replied.

In the center of the ledge, opposite the mouth of the cave, a small fire was burning beneath an earthen bowl, which was supported by three or four small pieces of stone. Squatting close to this was a female, who, in youth, might have been a fine looking girl, but now her face was lined by bitterness and hate as she glared sullenly into the caldron, the contents of which she was stirring with the rib of some large animal.

"Tanar is hungry, Sloo," said Balal, addressing the woman. "When will the food be cooked?"

"Have I not enough to do preparing hides and cooking food for all of you without having to cook for every enemy that you see fit to bring to the cave of your father?"

"This is the first time I ever brought any one, mother," said Balal.

"Let it be the last, then," snapped the woman.

"Shut up, woman," snapped Scurv, "and hasten with the food."

The woman leaped to her feet, brandishing the rib above her head. "Don't tell me what to do, Scurv," she shrilled. "I have had about enough of you anyway."

"Hit him, mother!" screamed a lad of about eleven, jumping to his feet and dancing about in evident joy and excitement.

Balal leaped across the cook fire and struck the lad heavily with his open palm across the face, sending him spinning up against the cliff wall. "Shut up, Dhung," he cried, "or I'll pitch you over the edge."

The remaining member of the family party, a girl, just ripening into womanhood, remained silent where she was seated, leaning against the face of the cliff, her large, dark eyes taking in the scene being enacted before her. Suddenly the woman turned upon her. "Why don't you do something, Gura?" she demanded. "You sit there and let them attack me and never raise a hand in my defense."

"But no one has attacked you, mother," said the girl, with a sigh.

"But I will," yelled Scurv, seizing a short club that lay beside him. "I'll knock her head off if she doesn't keep a still tongue in it and hurry with that food." At this instant a loud scream attracted the attention of all toward another family group before a cave, a little further along the ledge. Here, a man, grasping a woman by her hair, was beating her with a stick, while several children were throwing pieces of rock, first at their parents and then at one another.

"Hit her again!" yelled Scurv.

"Scratch out his eyes!" screamed Sloo, and for the moment the family of the chief forgot their own differences in the enjoyable spectacle of another family row.

Tanar looked on in consternation and surprise. Never had he witnessed such tumult and turmoil in the villages of the Sarians, and coming, as he just had, from Amiocap, the island of love, the contrast was even more appalling.

"Don't mind them," said Balal, who was watching the Sarian and had noticed the expression of surprise and disgust upon

his face. "If you stay with us long you will get used to it, for it is always like this. Come on, let's eat, the food is ready," and drawing his stone knife he fished into the pot and speared a piece of meat.

Tanar, having no knife, had recourse to one of his arrows, which answered the purpose quite as well, and then, one by one, the family gathered around as though nothing unusual had happened, and fell, too, upon the steaming stew with avidity.

During the meal they did not speak other than to call one another vile names, if two chanced to reach into the caldron simultaneously and one interfered with another.

The caldron emptied, Scurv and Sloo crawled into the dark interior of their cave to sleep, where they were presently followed by Balal.

Gura, the daughter, took the caldron and started down the cliff toward the brook to wash out the receptacle and return with it filled with water.

As she made her precarious way down rickety ladders and narrow ledges, little Dhung, her brother, amused himself by hurling stones at her.

"Stop that," commanded Tanar. "You might hit her."

"That is what I am trying to do," said the little imp. "Why else should I be throwing stones at her? To miss her?" He hurled another missile and with that Tanar grabbed him by the scuff of the neck.

Instantly Dhung let out a scream that might have been heard in Amiocap — a scream that brought Sloo rushing from the cave.

"He is killing me," shrieked Dhung, and at that the cave woman turned upon Tanar with flashing eyes and a face distorted with rage.

"Wait," said Tanar, in a calm voice. "I was not hurting the child. He was hurling rocks at his sister and I stopped him."

"What business have you to stop him?" demanded Sloo. "She is his sister, he has a right to hurl rocks at her if he chooses."

"But he might have struck her, and if he had she would have fallen to her death below."

"What if she did? That is none of your business," snapped Sloo, and grabbing Dhung by his long hair she cuffed his ears and dragged him into the interior of the cave, where for a long time Tanar could hear blows and screams, mingled with the sharp tongue of Sloo and the curses of Scurv.

But finally these died down to silence, permitting the sounds of other domestic brawls from various parts of the cliff village to reach the ears of the disgusted Sarian.

Far below him Tanar saw the girl, Gura, washing the earthenware vessel in a little stream, after which she filled it with fresh water and lifted the heavy burden to her head. He wondered at the ease with which she carried the great weight and was at a loss to know how she intended to scale the precipitous cliff and the rickety, makeshift ladders with her heavy load. Watching her progress with considerable interest he saw her ascend the lowest ladder, apparently with as great ease and agility as though she was unburdened. Up she came, balancing the receptacle with no evident effort.

As he watched her he saw a man ascending also, but several ledges higher than the girl. The fellow came swiftly and noiselessly to the very ledge where Tanar stood. Paying no attention to the Sarian, he slunk cautiously along the ledge to the mouth of the cave next to that of Scurv. Drawing his stone knife from his loin cloth he crept within, and a moment later Tanar heard the sounds of screams and curses and then two men rolled from the mouth of the cave, locked in a deadly embrace. One of them was the fellow whom Tanar had just seen enter the cave. The other was a younger man and smaller and less powerful than his antagonist. They were slashing desperately at one another with their stone knives, but the duel seemed to be resulting in more noise than damage.

At this juncture, a woman came running from the cave. She was armed with the leg bone of a thag and with this she sought to belabor the older man, striking vicious blows at his head and body.

This attack seemed to infuriate the fellow to the point of madness, and, rather than incapacitating him, urged him on to redoubled efforts.

Presently he succeeded in grasping the knife hand of his opponent and an instant later he had driven his own blade into the heart of his opponent.

With a scream of anguish the woman struck again at the older man's head, but she missed her target and her weapon was splintered on the stone of the ledge. The victor leaped to his feet and seizing the body of his opponent hurled it over the cliff, and then grabbing the woman by the hair he dragged her about, shrieking and cursing, as he sought for some missile wherewith to belabor her.

As Tanar stood watching the disgusting spectacle he became aware that someone was standing beside him and, turning, he saw that Gura had returned. She stood there straight as an arrow, balancing the water vessel upon her head.

"It is terrible," said Tanar, nodding toward the battling couple.

Gura shrugged indifferently. "It is nothing," she said. "Her mate returned unexpectedly. That is all."

"You mean," asked Tanar, "that this fellow is her mate and that the other was not?"

"Certainly," said Gura, "but they all do it. What can you expect where there is nothing but hate," and walking to the entrance to her father's cave she set the water vessel down within the shadows just inside the entrance. Then she sat down and leaned her back against the cliff, paying no more attention to the matrimonial difficulties of her neighbor.

Tanar, for the first time, noticed the girl particularly. He saw that she had neither the cunning expression that characterized Jude and all of the other Himeans he had seen; nor were there the lines of habitual irritation and malice upon her face; instead it reflected an innate sadness and he guessed that she looked much like her mother might have when she was Gura's age.

Tanar crossed the ledge and sat down beside her. "Do your people always quarrel thus?" he asked.

"Always," replied Gura.

"Why?" he asked.

"I do not know," she replied. "They take their mates for life and are permitted but one and though both men and women have a choice in the selection of their mates they never seem to be satisfied with one another and are always quarreling, usually because neither one nor the other is faithful. Do the men and women quarrel thus in the land from which you come?"

"No," replied Tanar. "They do not. If they did they would be thrown out of the tribe."

"But suppose that they find that they do not like one another?" insisted the girl.

"Then they do not live together," replied Tanar. "They separate and if they care to they find other mates."

"That is wicked," said Gura. "We would kill any of our people who did such a thing."

Tanar shrugged and laughed.

"At least we are all a very happy people," he said, "which is more than you can say for yourselves, and, after all, happiness, it seems to me, is everything."

The girl thought for some time, seemingly studying an idea that was new to her.

"Perhaps you are right," she said, presently. "Nothing could be worse than the life that we live. My mother tells me that it was not thus in her country, but now she is as bad as the rest."

"Your mother is not a Himean?" asked Tanar.

"No, she is from Amiocap. My father captured her there when she was young."

"That accounts for the difference," mused Tanar.

"What difference?" she asked. "What do you mean?"

"I mean that you are not like the others, Gura," he replied. "You neither look like them nor act like them — neither you nor your brother, Balal."

"Our mother is an Amiocapian," she replied. "Perhaps we inherited something from her and then again, and most important, we are young and, as yet, have no mates. When that time comes we shall grow to be like the others, just as our mother has grown to be like them."

"Do many of your men take their mates from Amiocap?" asked Tanar.

"Many try to, but few succeed for as a rule they are driven away or killed by the Amiocapian warriors. They have a landing place upon the coast of Amiocap in a dark cave beneath a high cliff and of ten Himean warriors who land there scarce one returns, and he not always with an Amiocapian mate. There is a tribe living along our coast that has grown rich by crossing to Amiocap and bringing back the canoes of the warriors, who have crossed for mates and have died at the hands of the Amiocapian warriors."

For a few moments she was silent, absorbed in thought. "I should like to go to Amiocap," she mused, presently.

"Why?" asked Tanar.

"Perhaps I should find there a mate with whom I might be happy," she said.

Tanar shook his head sadly. "That is impossible, Gura," he said.

"Why?" she demanded. "Am I not beautiful enough for the Amiocapian warriors?"

"Yes," he replied, "you are very beautiful, but if you went to Amiocap they would kill you."

"Why?" she demanded again.

"Because, although your mother is an Amiocapian, your father is not," explained Tanar.

"That is their law?" asked Gura, sadly.

"Yes," replied Tanar.

"Well," she said with a sign, "then I suppose I must remain here and seek a mate whom I shall learn to hate and bring children into the world who will hate us both."

"It is not a pleasant outlook, said Tanar.

"No," she said, and then after a pause, "unless————"

"Unless, what?" asked the Sarian.

"Nothing," said Gura.

For a time they sat in silence, each occupied with his own thoughts, Tanar's being filled to the exclusion of all else by the face and figure of Stellara.

Presently the girl looked up at him. "What are you going to do after you find Jude?" she asked.

"I am going to kill him," replied Tanar.

"And then?" she queried.

"I do not know," said the Sarian. "If I find the one whom I believe to be with Jude we shall try to return to Amiocap."

"Why do you not remain here?" asked Gura. "I wish that you would."

Tanar shuddered. "I would rather die," he said.

"I do not blame you much," said the girl, "but I believe there is a way in which you might be happy even in Hime."

"How?" asked Tanar.

Gura did not answer and he saw the tears come to her eyes. Then she arose hurriedly and entered the cave.

Tanar thought that Scurv would never be done with his sleep. He wanted to talk to him and arrange for a guide to the village of Jude, but it was Sloo who first emerged from the cave.

She eyed him sullenly. "You still here?" she demanded.

"I am waiting for Scurv to send a guide to direct me to the village of Jude," replied the Sarian. "I shall not remain here an instant longer than is necessary."

"That will be too long," growled Sloo, and turning on her heels she reentered the cave.

Presently Balal emerged, rubbing his eyes. "When will Scurv send me on my way?" demanded Tanar.

"I do not know," replied the youth. "He has just awakened. When he comes out you should speak to him about it. He has just sent me to fetch the skin of the codon you killed. He was very angry to think that I left it lying in the forest."

After Balal departed, Tanar sat with his own thoughts for a long while.

Presently Gura came from the cave. She appeared frightened and excited. She came close to Tanar, and, kneeling, placed her lips close to his ear. "You must escape at once," she said, in a low whisper. "Scurv is going to kill you. That is why he sent Balal away."

"But why does he want to kill me?" demanded Tanar. "I saved the life of his son and I have only asked that he direct me to the village of Jude."

"He thinks Sloo is in love with you," explained Gura, "for when he awakened she was not in the cave. She was out here upon the ledge with you."

Tanar laughed. "Sloo made it very plain to me that she did not like me," he said, "and wanted me to be gone."

"I believe you," said Gura, "but Scurv, filled with suspicion and hatred and a guilty conscience, is anxious to believe anything bad that he can of Sloo, and as he does not wish to be convinced that he is wrong it stands to reason that nothing can convince him, so that your only hope is in flight."

"Thank you, Gura," said Tanar. "I shall go at once."

"No, that will not do," said the girl. "Scurv is coming out here immediately. He would miss you, possibly before you could get out of sight, and in a moment he could muster a hundred warriors to pursue you, and furthermore you have no proper weapons with which to start out in search of Jude."

"Perhaps you have a better plan, then," said Tanar.

"I have," said the girl. "Listen! Do you see where the stream enters the jungle," and she pointed across the clearing at the foot of the cliff toward the edge of a dark forest.

"Yes," said Tanar, "I see."

"I shall descend now and hide there in a large tree beside the stream. When Scurv comes out, tell him that you saw a deer there and ask him to loan you weapons, so that you may go and kill it. Meat is always welcome and he will postpone his attack upon you until you have returned with the carcass of your kill, but you will not return. When you enter the forest I shall be there to direct you to the village of Jude."

"Why are you doing this, Gura?" demanded Tanar.

"Never mind about that," said the girl. "Only do as I say. There is no time to lose as Scurv may come out from the cave at any moment," and without further words she commenced the descent of the cliff face.

Tanar watched her as, with the agility and grace of a chamois, the girl, oftentimes disdaining ladders, leaped lightly from ledge to ledge. Almost before he could realize it she was at the bottom of the cliff and moving swiftly toward the forest beyond, the foliage of which had scarcely closed about her when Scurv emerged from the cave. Directly behind him were Sloo and Dhung, and Tanar saw that each carried a club.

"I am glad you came out now," said Tanar, losing no time, for he sensed that the three were bent upon immediate attack.

"Why?" growled Scurv.

"I just saw a deer at the edge of the forest. If you will let me take weapons, perhaps I can repay your hospitality by bringing you the carcass."

Scurv hesitated, his stupid mind requiring time to readjust itself and change from one line of thought to another, but Sloo was quick to see the advantage of utilizing the unwelcome guest and she was willing to delay his murder until he had brought back his kill. "Get weapons," she said to Dhung, "and let the stranger fetch the deer."

Scurv scratched his head, still in a quandary, and before he had made up his mind one way or the other, Dhung reappeared with a lance and a stone knife, which, instead of handing to Tanar, he threw at him, but the Sarian caught the weapons, and, without awaiting further permission, clambered down the ladder to the next ledge and from thence downward to the ground. Several of the villagers, recognizing him as a stranger, sought to interfere with him, but Scurv, standing upon the ledge high above watching his descent, bellowed commands that he be left alone, and presently the Sarian was crossing the open towards the jungle.

Just inside the concealing verdure of the forest he was accosted by Gura, who was perched upon the limb of a tree above him.

"Your warning came just in time, Gura," said the man, "for Scurv and Sloo and Dhung came out almost immediately, armed and ready to kill me."

"I knew that they would," she said, "and I am glad that they will be disappointed, especially Dhung — the little beast! He begged to be allowed to torture you."

"It does not seem possible that he can be your brother," said Tanar.

"He is just like Scurv's mother," said the girl. "I knew her before she was killed. She was a most terrible old woman, and Dhung had inherited all of her venom and none of the kindly blood of the Amiocapians, which flows in the veins of my mother, despite the change that her horrid life has brought over her."

"And now," said Tanar, "point the way to Jude's village and I shall be gone. Never, Gura, can I repay you for your kindness to me — a kindness which I can only explain on the strength of the Amiocapian blood which is in you. I shall never see you again, Gura, but I shall carry the recollection of your image and your kindness always in my heart."

"I am going with you," said Gura.

"You cannot do that," said Tanar.

"How else may I guide you to the village of Jude then?" she demanded.

"You do not have to guide me; only tell me the direction in which it lies and I shall find it," replied Tanar.

"I am going with you," said the girl, determinedly. "There is only hate and misery in the cave of my father. I would rather be with you."

"But that cannot be, Gura," said Tanar.

"If I went back now to the cave of Scurv he would suspect me of having aided your escape and they would all beat me. Come, we cannot waste time here for if you do not return quickly, Scurv will become suspicious and set out upon your trail." She had dropped to the ground beside him and now she started off into the forest.

"Have it as you wish, then, Gura," said Tanar, "but I am afraid that you are going to regret your act — I am afraid that we are both going to regret it."

"At least I shall have a little happiness in life," said the girl, "and if I have that I shall be willing to die."

"Wait," said Tanar, "in which direction does the village of Jude lie?" The girl pointed. "Very well," said Tanar, "instead of going on the ground and leaving our spoor plainly marked for Scurv to follow, we shall take to the trees, for after having watched you descend the cliff I know that you must be able to travel as rapidly among the branches as you do upon the ground."

"I have never done it," said the girl, "but wherever you go I shall follow."

Although Tanar had been loath to permit the girl to accompany him, nevertheless he found that her companionship made what would have been otherwise a lonely adventure far from unpleasant.

Chapter XII

"I HATE YOU!"

The companions of Bohar the Bloody had not waited long for him after he had set out in pursuit of Stellara and had not returned. They hastened the work upon their boat to early completion, and, storing provisions and water, sailed out of the cove on the shores of which they had constructed their craft and bore away for Korsar with no regret for Bohar, whom they all cordially hated.

The very storm that had come near to driving Tanar past the island of Hime bore the Korsars down upon the opposite end, carried away their rude sail and finally dashed their craft, a total wreck, upon the rocks at the upper end of Hime.

The loss of their boat, their provisions and one of their number, who was smashed against a rock and drowned, left the remaining Korsars in even a more savage mood than was customary among them, and the fact that the part of the island upon which they were wrecked afforded no timber suitable for the construction of a boat made it necessary for them to cross over land to the opposite shore.

They were faced now with the necessity of entering a land filled with enemies in search of food and material for a new craft, and, to cap the climax of their misfortune, they found themselves with wet powder and forced to defend themselves, if necessity arose, with daggers and cutlasses alone.

The majority of them being old sailors they were well aware of where they were and even knew a great deal concerning the geography of Hime and the manners and customs of its people, for most of them had accompanied raiding parties into the interior on many occasions when the Korsar ships had fallen upon the island to steal furs and hides, in the perfect curing and tanning of which the Himean women were adept with the result that Himean furs and skins brought high prices in Korsar.

A council of the older sailors decided then to set off across country toward a harbor on the far side of the island, where the timber of an adjoining forest would afford them the material for building another craft with the added possibility of the arrival of a Korsar raider.

As these disgruntled men plodded wearily across the island of Hime, Jude led the reluctant Stellara toward his village, and Gura guided Tanar in the same direction.

Jude had been compelled to make wide detours to avoid unfriendly villagers; nor had Stellara's unwilling feet greatly accelerated his pace, for she constantly hung back, and, though he no longer had to carry her, he had found it necessary to make a leather thong fast about her neck and lead her along in this fashion to prevent the numerous, sudden breaks for liberty that she had made before he had devised this scheme.

Often she pulled back, refusing to go further, saying that she was tired and insisting upon lying down to rest, for in her heart she knew that wherever Jude or another took her, Tanar would seek her out.

Already in her mind's eyes she could see him upon the trail behind them and she hoped to delay Jude's march sufficiently so that the Sarian would overtake them before they reached his village and the protection of his tribe.

Gura was happy. Never before in all her life had she been so happy, and she saw in the end of their journey a possible end to this happiness and so she did not lead Tanar in a direct line to Carn, the village of Jude, but led him hither and thither upon various excuses so that she might have him to herself for as long a time as possible. She found in his companionship a gentleness and an understanding that she had never known in all her life before.

It was not love that Gura felt for Tanar, but something that might have easily been translated into love had the Sarian's own passion been aroused toward the girl, but his love for Stellara precluded such a possibility and while he found pleasure in the company of Gura he was yet madly impatient to continue directly upon the trail of Jude that he might rescue Stellara and have her for himself once more.

The village of Carn is not a cliff village, as is Garb, the village of Scurv. It consists of houses built of stone and clay and, entirely surrounded by a high wall, it stands upon the top of a lofty mesa protected upon all sides by steep cliffs, and overlooking upon one hand the forests and hills of Hime, and upon the other the broad expanse of the Korsar Az, or Sea of Korsar.

Up the steep cliffs toward Carn climbed Jude, dragging Stellara behind him. It was a long and arduous climb and when they reached the summit Jude was glad to stop and rest. He also had some planning to do, since in the village upon the mesa Jude had left a mate, and now he was thinking of some plan whereby he might rid himself of her, but the only plan that Jude could devise was to sneak into the city and murder her. But what was he to do with Stellara in the meantime? And then a happy thought occurred to him.

He knew a cave that lay just below the summit of the cliff and not far distant and toward this he took Stellara, and when they had arrived at it he bound her ankles and her wrists.

"I shall not leave you here long," he said. "Presently I shall return and take you into the village of Carn as my mate. Do not be afraid. There are few wild beasts upon the mesa, and I shall return long before any one can find you."

"Do not hurry," said Stellara. "I shall welcome the wild beast that reaches me before you return."

"You will think differently after you have been the mate of Jude for a while," said the man, and then he left her and hurried toward the walled village of Carn.

Struggling to a sitting posture Stellara could look out across the country that lay at the foot of the cliff and presently, below her, she saw a man and a woman emerge from the forest.

For a moment her heart stood still, for the instant that her eyes alighted upon him she recognized the man as Tanar. A cry of welcome was upon her lips when a new thought stilled her tongue.

Who was the girl with Tanar? Stellara saw how close she walked to him and she saw her look up into his face and though she was too far away to see the girl's eyes or her expression, there was something in the attitude of the slim body that denoted worship, and Stellara turned her face and buried it against the cold wall of the cave and burst into tears.

Gura pointed upward toward the high mesa. "There," she said, "just beyond the summit of that cliff lies Carn, the village where Jude lives, but if we enter it you will be killed and perhaps I, too, if the women get me first."

Tanar, who was examining the ground at his feet, seemed not to hear the girl's words. "Someone has passed just ahead of us," he said; "a man and a woman. I can see the imprints of their feet. The grasses that were crushed beneath their sandals are still rising slowly — a man and a woman — and one of them was Stellara and the other Jude."

"Who is Stellara?" asked the girl.

"My mate," replied Tanar.

The habitual expression of sadness that had marked Gura's face since childhood, but which had been supplanted by a radiant happiness since she had left the village of Garb with Tanar, returned as with tear-filled eyes she choked back a sob, which went unnoticed by the Sarian as he eagerly searched the ground ahead of them. And in the cave above them warm tears bathed the unhappy cheeks of Stellara, but the urge of love soon drew her eyes back to Tanar just at the moment that he turned and called Gura's attention to the well marked spoor he was following.

The eyes of the Sarian noted the despair in the face of his companion and the tears in her eyes.

"Gura!" he cried. "What is the matter? Why do you cry?" and impulsively he stepped close to her and put a friendly arm about her shoulders, and Gura, unnerved by kindness, buried her face upon his breast and wept. And this was what Stellara saw — this scene was what love and jealousy put their own interpretation upon — and the eyes of the Amiocapian maiden flashed with hurt pride and anger.

"Why do you cry, Gura?" demanded Tanar.

"Do not ask me," begged the girl. "It is nothing. Perhaps I am tired; perhaps I am afraid. But now we may not think of either fatigue or fear, for if Jude is taking your mate toward the village of Carn we must hasten to rescue her before it is too late."

"You are right," exclaimed Tanar. "We must not delay," and, followed by Gura, he ran swiftly toward the base of the cliff, tracing the spoor of Jude and Stellara where it led to the precarious ascent of the cliffside. And as they hastened on, brutal eyes watched them from the edge of the jungle from which they had themselves so recently emerged.

Where the steep ascent topped the summit of the cliff bare rock gave back no clew to the direction that Jude had taken, but twenty yards further on where the soft ground commenced again Tanar picked up the tracks of the man to which he called Gura's attention.

"Jude's footprints are here alone," he said.

"Perhaps the woman refused to go further and he was forced to carry her," suggested Gura.

"That is doubtless the fact," said Tanar, and he hastened onward along the plain trail left by the Himean.

The way led now along a well marked trail, which ran through a considerable area of bushes that grew considerably higher than a man's head, so that nothing was visible upon either side and only for short distances ahead of them and behind them along the winding trail. But Tanar did not slacken his speed, his sole aim being to overhaul the Himean before he reached the village.

As Tanar and Gura had capped the summit of the cliff and disappeared from view, eighteen hairy men came into view from the forest and followed their trail toward the foot of the cliff.

They were bushy whiskered fellows with gay sashes around their waists and equally brilliant cloths about their heads. Huge pistols and knives bristled from their waist cloths, and cutlasses dangled from their hips — fate had brought these survivors of The Cid's ship to the foot of the cliffs below the village of Carn at almost the same moment that Tanar had arrived. With sensations of surprise, not unmingled with awe, they had recognized the Sarian who had been a prisoner upon the ship and whom they thought they had seen killed by their musket fire at the edge of the natural well upon the island of Amiocap.

The Korsars, prompted by the pernicious stubbornness of ignorance, were moved by a common impulse to recapture Tanar. And with this end in view they waited until Gura and the Sarian had disappeared beyond the summit of the cliff, when they started in pursuit.

The walls of Carn lie no great distance from the edge of the table-land upon which it stands. In timeless Pellucidar events, which are in reality far separated, seem to follow closely, one upon the heels of another, and for this reason one may not say how long Jude was in the village of Carn, or whether he had had time to carry out the horrid purpose which had taken him thither, but the fact remained that as Tanar and Gura reached the edge of the bushes and looked across the clearing toward the walls of Carn they saw Jude sneaking from the city. Could they have seen his face they might have noticed a malicious leer of triumph and could they have known the purpose that had taken him thus stealthily to his native village they might have reconstructed the scenes of the bloody episode which had just been enacted within the house of the Himean. But Tanar only saw that Jude, whom he sought, was coming toward him, and that Stellara was not with him.

The Sarian drew Gura back into the concealment of the bushes that lined the trail which Jude was approaching.

On came the Himean and while Tanar awaited his coming, the Korsars were making their clumsy ascent of the cliff, while Stellara, sick from jealousy and unhappiness, leaned disconsolately against the cold stone of her prison cave.

Jude, unconscious of danger, hastened back toward the spot where he had left Stellara and as he came opposite Tanar, the Sarian leaped upon him.

The Himean reached for his knife, but he was helpless in the grasp of Tanar, whose steel fingers closed about his wrists with such strength that Jude dropped his weapon with a cry of pain as he felt both of his arms crushed beneath the pressure of the Sarian's grip.

"What do you want?" he cried. "Why do you attack me?"

"Where is Stellara?" demanded Tanar.

"I do not know," replied Jude. "I have not seen her."

"You lie," said Tanar. "I have followed her tracks and yours to the summit of the cliff. Where is she?" He drew his knife. "Tell me, or die."

"I left her at the edge of the cliff while I went to Carn to arrange to have her received in a friendly manner. I did it all for her protection, Tanar. She wanted to go back to Korsar and I was but helping her."

"Again you lie," said the Sarian; "but lead me to her and we shall hear her version of the story."

The Himean held back until the point of Tanar's knife pressed against his ribs; then he gave in. "If I lead you to her will you promise not to kill me?" asked Jude. "Will you let me return in peace to my village?"

"I shall make no promises until I learn from her own lips how you have treated her," replied the Sarian.

"She has not been harmed," said Jude. "I swear it."

"Then lead me to her," insisted Tanar.

Sullenly the Himean guided them back along the path toward the cave where he had left Stellara, while at the other edge of the bushes eighteen Korsars, warned by the noise of their approach, halted, listening, and presently melted silently from view in the surrounding shrubbery.

They saw Jude and Gura and Tanar emerge from the bushes, but they did not attack them; they waited to see for what purpose they had returned. They saw them disappear over the edge of the cliff at a short distance from the summit of the trail that led down into the valley. And then they emerged from their hiding places and followed cautiously after them.

Jude led Tanar and Gura to the cave where Stellara lay and when Tanar saw her, her dear wrists and ankles bound with thongs and her cheeks still wet with tears, he sprang forward and gathered her into his arms.

"Stellara!" he cried. "My darling!" But the girl turned her face away from him.

"Do not touch me," she cried. "I hate you."

"Stellara!" he exclaimed in amazement. "What has happened?" But before she could reply they were startled by a hoarse command from behind them, and, turning, found themselves looking into the muzzles of the pistols of eighteen Korsars.

"Surrender, Sarian!" cried the leader of the Korsars.

Gazing into the muzzles of about thirty-six huge pistols, which equally menaced the lives of Stellara and Gura, Tanar saw no immediate alternative but to surrender.

"What do you intend to do with us if we do surrender?" he demanded.

"That we shall decide later," growled the spokesman for the Korsars.

"Do you expect ever to return to Korsar?" asked Tanar.

"What is that to you, Sarian?" demanded the Korsar.

"It has a considerable bearing upon whether or not we surrender," replied Tanar. "You have tried to kill me before and you have found that I am hard to kill. I know something about your weapons and your powder and I know that even at such close quarters I may be able to kill some of you before you can kill me. But if you answer my question fairly and honestly and if your answer is satisfactory I shall surrender."

At Tanar's mention of his knowledge of their powder the Korsars immediately assumed that he knew that it was wet, whereas he was only alluding to its uniformly poor quality and so the spokesman decided that it would be better to temporize for the time being at least. "As soon as we can build a boat we shall return to Korsar," he said, "unless in the meantime a Korsar ship anchors in the bay of Carn."

"Good," commented the Sarian. "If you will promise to return the daughter of The Cid safe and unharmed to her people in Korsar I will surrender. And you must also promise that no harm shall befall this other girl and that she shall be permitted to go with you in safety to Korsar or to remain here among her own people as she desires."

"How about the other man?" demanded the Korsar.

"You may kill him when you kill me," replied Tanar.

Stellara's eyes widened in fearful apprehension as she heard the words of the Sarian and she found that jealousy was no match for true love.

"Very well," said the Korsar. "We accept the condition. The women shall return to Korsar with us, and you two men shall die."

"Oh, no," begged Jude. "I do not wish to die. I am a Himean. Carn is my home. You Korsars come there often to trade. Spare me and I shall see that you are furnished with more hides than you can pack in your boat, after you have built it."

The leader of the band laughed in his face. "Eighteen of us can take what we choose from the village of Carn," he said. "We are not such fools as to spare you that you may go and warn your people."

"Then take me along as a prisoner," wailed Jude.

"And have to feed you and watch you all the time? No, you are worth more to us dead than alive."

As Jude spoke he had edged over into the mouth of the cave, where he stood half behind Stellara as though taking shelter at the expense of the girl.

With a gesture of disgust, Tanar turned toward the Korsars. "Come," he said, impatiently. "If the bargain is satisfactory there is no use in discussing it further. Kill us, and take the women in safety to Korsar. You have given your word."

At the instant that Tanar concluded his appeal to the Korsars, Jude turned before any one could prevent him and disappeared into the cave behind him. Instantly Korsars leaped in pursuit, while the others awaited impatiently their return with Jude. But when they emerged they were empty handed.

"He escaped us," said one of those who had gone after the Himean. "This cave is the mouth of a dark, long tunnel with many branches. We could see nothing and fearful that we should become lost, we returned to the opening. It would be useless to try to find the man within unless one was familiar with the tunnel which honeycombs the cliff beyond this cave. We had better kill this one immediately before he has an opportunity to escape too," and the fellow raised his pistol and aimed it at Tanar, possibly hoping that his powder had dried since they had set out from the beach upon the opposite side of the island.

"Stop!" cried Stellara, jumping in front of the man. "As you all know I am the daughter of The Cid. If you return me to him in safety you will be well rewarded. I will see to that. You all knew that The Cid was taking this man to Korsar, but possibly you did not know why."

"No," said one of the Korsars, who, being only common sailors, had had no knowledge of the plans of their commander.

"He knows how to make firearms and powder far superior to ours and The Cid was taking him back to Korsar that he might teach the Korsars the secrets of powder making and the manufacture of weapons, that we do not know. If you kill him The Cid will be furious with you, and you all know what it means to anger The Cid. But if you return him, also, to Korsar your reward will be much larger."

"How do we know that The Cid is alive?" demanded one of the Korsars; "and if he is not, who is there who will pay reward for your return, or for the return of this man?"

"The Cid is a better sailor than Bohar the Bloody — that you all know. And if Bohar the Bloody brought his boat safely through to Amiocap there is little doubt but that The Cid took his safely to Korsar. But even if he did not, even if The Cid perished, still will you receive your reward if you return me to Korsar."

"Who will pay it?" demanded one of the sailors.

"Bulf," replied Stellara.

"Why should Bulf pay a reward for your return?" asked the Korsar.

"Because I am to be his mate. It was The Cid's wish and his."

By no change of expression did the Sarian reveal the pain that these words inflicted like a knife thrust through his heart. He merely stood with his arms folded, looking straight ahead. Gura's eyes were wide in surprise as she looked, first at Stellara and then at Tanar, for she recalled that the latter had told her that Stellara was his mate, and she had known, with woman's intuition, how much the man loved this woman. Gura was mystified and, too, she was saddened because she guessed the pain that Stellara's words had inflicted upon Tanar, and so her kind heart prompted her to move close to Tanar's side and to lay her hand gently upon his arm in mute expression of sympathy.

For a time the Korsars discussed Stellara's proposition in low whispers and then the spokesman addressed her. "But if The Cid is dead there will be no one to reward us for returning the Sarian; therefore, we might as well kill him for there will be enough mouths to feed during the long journey to Korsar."

"You do not know that The Cid is dead," insisted Stellara; "but if he is, who is there better fitted to be chief of the Korsars than Bulf? And if he is chief he will reward you for returning this man when I explain to him the purpose for which he was brought back to Korsar."

"Well," said the Korsar, scratching his head, "perhaps you are right. He may be more valuable to us alive than dead. If he will promise to help us work the boat and not try to escape we shall take him with us. But how about the girl here?"

"Keep her until we are ready to sail," growled one of the other Korsars, "and then turn her loose."

"If you wish to receive any reward for my return you will do nothing of the sort," said Stellara with finality, and then to Gura, "What do you wish to do?" Her voice was cold and haughty.

"Where Tanar goes there I wish to go," replied Gura.

Stellara's eyes narrowed and for an instant they flashed fire, but immediately they resumed their natural, kindly expression, though tinged with sadness. "Very well, then," she said, turning sadly away, "the girl must return with us to Korsar."

The sailors discussed this question at some length and most of them were opposed to it, but when Stellara insisted and assured them of a still greater reward they finally consented, though with much grumbling.

The Korsars marched boldly across the mesa, past the walls of Carn, their harquebuses ready in their hands, knowing full well the fear of them that past raids had implanted in the breasts of the Himeans. But they did not seek to plunder or demand tribute for they still feared that their powder was useless.

As they reached the opposite side of the mesa, where they could look out across the bay of Carn, a hoarse shout of pleasure arose from the throats of the Korsars, for there, at anchor in the bay, lay a Korsar ship. Not knowing how soon the vessel might weigh anchor and depart, the Korsars fairly tumbled down the precipitous trail to the beach, while in their rear the puzzled villagers watched them over the top of the wall of Carn until the last man had disappeared beyond the summit of the cliff.

Rushing to the edge of the water the Korsars tried to discharge their harquebuses to attract attention from the vessel. A few of the charges had dried and the resulting explosion awakened signs of life upon the anchored ship. The sailors on the shore tore off sashes and handkerchiefs, which they waved frantically as signals of distress, and presently they were rewarded by the sight of the lowering of a boat from the vessel.

Within speaking distance of the shore the boat came to a stop and an officer hailed the men on shore.

"Who are you," he demanded, "and what do you want?"

"We are part of the crew of the ship of The Cid," replied the sailor's spokesman. "Our ship was wrecked in mid-ocean and we made our way to Amiocap and then to Hime, but here we lost the boat that we built upon Amiocap."

Assured that the men were Korsars the officer commanded that the boat move in closer to the shore and finally it was beached close to where the party stood awaiting its coming.

The brief greetings and explanations over, the officer took them all aboard and shortly afterward Tanar of Pellucidar found himself again upon a Korsar ship of war.

The commander of the ship knew Stellara, and after questioning them carefully he approved her plan and agreed to take Tanar and Gura back to Korsar with them.

Following their interview with the officer, Tanar found himself momentarily alone with Stellara.

"Stellara!" he said. "What change has come over you?"

She turned and looked at him coldly. "In Amiocap you were well enough," she said, "but in Korsar you would be only a naked barbarian," and, turning, she walked away from him without another word.

Chapter XIII

PRISONERS

The voyage to Korsar was uneventful and during its entire extent Tanar saw nothing of either Stellara or Gura for, although he was not confined in the dark hold, he was not permitted above the first deck, and although he often looked up at the higher deck at the stern of the ship he never caught a glimpse of either of the girls, from which he concluded that Gura was confined in one of the cabins and that Stellara deliberately avoided him or any sight of him.

As they approached the coast of Korsar Tanar saw a level country curving upward into the mist of the distance. He thought that far away he discerned the outlines of hills, but of that he could not be certain. He saw cultivated fields and patches of forest land and a river running down to the sea — a broad, winding river upon the shore of which a city lay, inland a little from the ocean. There was no harbor at this point upon the coast, but the ship made directly for the mouth of the river, up which it sailed toward the city, which, as he approached it, he saw far surpassed in size and the pretentiousness of its buildings any habitation of man that he had ever seen upon the surface of Pellucidar, not even excepting the new capital of the confederated kingdoms of Pellucidar that the Emperor David was building.

Most of the buildings were white with red-tiled roofs, and there were some with lofty minarets and domes of various colors — blue and red and gold, the last shining in the sunlight like the jewels in the diadem of Dian the Empress.

Where the river widened the town had been built and here there rode at anchor a great fleet of ships of war and many lesser craft — fishing boats and river boats and barges. The street along the riverfront was lined with shops and alive with people.

As their ship approached cannon boomed from the deck of the anchored warships, and the salute was returned by their own craft, which finally came to anchor in mid-stream, opposite the city.

Small boats put out from the shore and were paddled rapidly toward the warship, which also lowered some of her own boats, into one of which Tanar was ordered under charge of an officer and a couple of sailors. As he was taken to shore and marched along the street he excited considerable attention among the crowds through which they passed, for he was immediately recognized as a barbarian captive from some uncivilized quarter of Pellucidar.

During the debarkation Tanar had seen nothing of either Stellara or Gura and now he wondered if he was ever to see them again. His mind was filled with the same sad thoughts that had been his companions during the entire course of the long journey from Hime to Korsar and which had finally convinced him that he had never known the true Stellara until she had avowed herself upon the deck of the ship in the harbor of Carn. Yes, he was all right upon Amiocap, but in Korsar he was only a naked savage, and this fact was borne in upon him now by the convincing evidence of the haughty contempt with which the natives of Korsar stared at him or exchanged rude jokes at his expense.

It hurt the Sarian's pride to think that he had been so deceived by the woman to whom he had given all his love. He would have staked his life upon his belief that hers was the sweetest and purest and most loyal of characters, and to learn at last that she was shallow and insincere cut him to t e quick and his suffering was lightened by but a single thought — his unquestioned belief in the sweet and enduring friendship of Gura.

It was with such thoughts that his mind was occupied as he was led into a building along the waterfront, which seemed to be in the nature of a guardhouse.

Here he was turned over to an officer in charge, and, after a few brief questions, two soldiers conducted him into another room, raised a heavy trap door in the floor and bade him descend a rude ladder that led downward into darkness below.

No sooner had his head descended below the floor joists than the door was slammed down above him. He heard the grating of a heavy bolt as the soldiers shut it and then the thud of their footsteps as they left the room above.

Descending slowly for about ten feet Tanar came at last to the surface of a stone floor. His eyes becoming accustomed to the change, he realized that the apartment into which he had descended was not in total darkness, but that daylight filtered into it from a small, barred window near the ceiling. Looking about him he saw that he was the only occupant of the room.

In the wall, opposite the window, he discerned a doorway and crossing to it he saw that it opened into a narrow corridor, running parallel with the length of the room. Looking up and down the corridor he discerned faint patches of light, as though other open doorways lined one side of the hallway.

He was about to enter upon a tour of investigation when the noise of something scurrying along the floor of the corridor attracted his attention, and looking back to his left he saw a dark form creeping toward him. It stood about a foot in height and was, perhaps, three feet long, but in the shadows of the corridor it loomed too indistinctly for him to recognize its details. But presently he saw that it had two shining eyes that seemed to be directed upon him.

As it came boldly forward Tanar stepped back into the room he was about to quit, preferring to meet the thing in the lesser darkness of the apartment rather than in the gloomy corridor, if it was the creature's intent to attack him.

On the thing came and turning into the doorway it stopped and surveyed the Sarian. In his native country Tanar had been familiar with a species of wood rat, which the Sarian considered large, but never in all his life had he dreamed that a rat could grow to the enormous proportions of the hideous thing that confronted him with its bold, gleaming, beady eyes.

Tanar had been disarmed when he had been taken aboard the Korsar ship, but even so he had no fear of a rodent, even if the thing should elect to attack him, which he doubted. But the ferocious appearance of the rat gave him pause as he thought what the result might be if a number of them should attack a man simultaneously.

Presently the rat, still standing facing him, squealed. For a time there was silence and then the thing squealed again and, as from a great distance, Tanar heard an answering squeal, and then another and another, and presently they grew louder and greater in volume, and he knew that the rat of the Korsar dungeon was calling its fellows to the attack and the feast.

He looked about him for some weapon of defense, but there was nothing but the bare stone of the floor and the walls. He heard the rat pack coming, and still the scout that had discovered him stood in the doorway, waiting.

But why should he, the man, wait? If he must die, he would die fighting and if he could take the rats as they came, one by one, he might make them pay for their meal and pay dearly. And so, with the agility of a tiger, the man leaped for the rodent, and so sudden and unexpected was his spring that one hand fell upon the loathsome creature before it could escape. With loud squeals it sought to fasten its fangs in his flesh, but the Sarian was too quick and too powerful. His fingers closed once upon the creature's neck. He swung its body around a few times until the neck broke and then he hurled the corpse toward the advancing pack that he could already see in the distance through the dim light in the corridor, in the center of which Tanar now stood awaiting his inevitable doom, but he was prepared to fight until he was dragged down by the creatures.

As he waited he heard a noise behind him and he thought that another pack was taking him in the rear, but as he glanced over his shoulder he saw the figure of a man, standing in front of a doorway further down the corridor.

"Come," shouted the stranger. "You will find safety here." Nor did Tanar lose any time in racing down the corridor to where the man stood, the rats close at his heels.

"Quick, in here," cried his savior, and seizing Tanar by the arm he dragged him through the doorway into a large room in which there were a dozen or more men.

At the doorway the rat pack stopped, glaring in, but not one of them crossed the threshold.

The room in which he found himself was lighted by two larger windows than that in the room which he had just quitted and in the better light he had an opportunity to examine the man who had rescued him. The fellow was a copper-colored giant with fine features.

As the man turned his face a little more toward the light of the windows, Tanar gave an exclamation of surprise and delight. "Ja!" he cried, and before Ja could reply to the salutation, another man sprang forward from the far end of the room.

"Tanar!" exclaimed the second man. "Tanar, the son of Ghak!" As the Sarian wheeled he found himself standing face to face with David Innes, Emperor of Pellucidar.

"Ja of Anoroc and the Emperor!" cried Tanar. "What has happened? What brought you here?"

"It is well that we were here," said Ja, "and that I heard the rat pack squealing just when I did. These other fellows," and he nodded toward the remaining prisoners, "haven't brains enough to try to save the newcomers that are incarcerated here. David and I have been trying to pound it into their stupid heads that the more of us

there are the safer we shall be from the attacks of the rats, but all they think of is that they are safe now, and so they do not care what becomes of the other poor devils that are shoved down here; nor have they brains enough to look into the future and realize that when some of us are taken out or die there may not be enough left to repel the attacks of the hungry beasts. But tell us, Tanar, where you have been and how you came here at last."

"It is a long story," replied the Sarian, "and first I would hear the story of my Emperor."

"There is little of interest in the adventures that befell us," said David, "but there may be points of great value to us in what I have managed to learn from the Korsars concerning a number of problems that have been puzzling me.

"When we saw the Korsars' fleet sail away with you and others of our people, prisoners aboard them, we were filled with dismay and as we stood upon the shore of the great sea above The Land of Awful Shadow, we were depressed by the hopelessness of ever effecting your rescue. It was then that I determined to risk the venture which is responsible for our being here in the dungeon of the capital of Korsar.

"From all those who volunteered to accompany me I selected Ja, and we took with us to be our pilot a Korsar prisoner named Fitt. Our boat was one of those abandoned by the Korsars in their flight and in it we pursued our course toward Korsar without incident until we were overwhelmed by the most terrific storm that I have ever witnessed."

"Doubtless the same storm that wrecked the Korsars' fleet that was bearing us away," said Tanar.

"Unquestionably," said David, "as you will know in a moment. The storm carried away all our rigging, snapping the mast short off at the deck, and left us helpless except for two pairs of oars.

"As you may know, these great sweeps are so heavy that, as a rule, two or three men handle a single oar, and as there were only three of us we could do little more than paddle slowly along with one man paddling on either side while the third relieved first one and then the other at intervals, and even this could be accomplished only after we had cut the great sweeps down to a size that one man might handle without undue fatigue.

"Fitt had laid a course which my compass showed me to be almost due north and this we followed with little or no deviation after the storm had subsided.

"We slept and ate many times before Fitt announced that we were not far from the island of Amiocap, which he says is half way between the point at which we had embarked and the land of Korsar. We still had ample water and provisions to last us the balance of our journey if we had been equipped with a sail, but the slow progress of paddling threatened to find us facing starvation, or death by thirst, long before we could hope to reach Korsar. With this fate staring us in the face we decided to land on Amiocap and refit our craft, but before we could do so we were overtaken by a Korsar ship and being unable either to escape or defend ourselves, we were taken prisoners.

"The vessel was one of those that had formed the armada of The Cid, and was, as far as they knew, the only one that had survived the storm. Shortly before they had found us they had picked up a boat-load of the survivors of The Cid's ship, including The Cid himself, and from The Cid we learned that you and the other prisoners had doubtless been lost with his vessel, which he said was in a sinking condition at the time that he abandoned it. To my surprise I learned that The Cid had also abandoned his own daughter to her fate and I believe that this cowardly act weighed heavily upon his mind, for he was always taciturn and moody, avoiding the companionship of even his own officers."

"She did not die," said Tanar. "We escaped together, the sole survivors, as far as we knew, of The Cid's ship, though later we were captured by the members of another boat crew that had also made the island of Amiocap and with them we were brought to Korsar."

"In my conversation with The Cid and also with the officers and men of the Korsar ship I sought to sound them on their knowledge of the extent of this sea, which is known as the Korsar Az. Among other things I learned that they possess compasses and are conversant with their use and they told me that to the west they had never sailed to the extreme limits of the Korsar Az, which they state reaches on, a vast

body of water, for countless leagues beyond the knowledge of man. But to the east they have followed the shore-line from Korsar southward almost to the shore upon which they landed to attack the empire of Pellucidar.

"Now this suggests, in fact almost proves, that Korsar lies upon the same great continent as the empire of Pellucidar and if we can escape from prison, we may be able to make our way by land back to our own country."

"But there is that 'if,' " said Ja. "We have eaten and slept many times since they threw us into this dark hole, yet we are no nearer escape now than we were at the moment that they put us here; nor do we even know what fate lies in store for us."

"These other prisoners tell us," resumed David, "that the fact that we were not immediately killed, which is the customary fate of prisoners of war among the Korsars, indicates that they are saving us for some purpose; but what that purpose is I cannot conceive."

"I can," said Tanar. "In fact I am quite sure that I know."

"And what is it?" demanded Ja.

"They wish us to teach them how to make firearms and powder such as ours," replied the Sarian. "But where do you suppose they ever got firearms and powder in the first place?"

"Or the great ships they sail," added Ja; "ships that are even larger than those which we build? These things were unknown in Pellucidar before David and Perry came to us, yet the Korsars appear to have known of them and used them always."

"I have an idea," said David; "yet it is such a mad idea that I have almost hesitated to entertain it, much less to express it."

"What is it?" asked Tanar.

"It was suggested to me in my conversations with the Korsars themselves," replied the Emperor. "Without exception they have all assured me that their ancestors came from another world — a world above which the sun did not stand perpetually at zenith, but crossed the heavens regularly, leaving the world in darkness half the time. They say that a part of this world is very cold and that their ancestors, who were seafaring men, became caught with their ships in the frozen waters; that their compasses turned in all directions and became useless to them and that when finally they broke through the ice and sailed away in the direction that they thought was south, they came into Pellucidar, which they found inhabited only by naked savages and wild beasts. And here they set up their city and built new ships, their numbers being augmented from time to time by other seafaring men from this world from which they say they originally came.

"They intermarried with the natives, which in this part of Pellucidar seemed to have been of a very low order." David paused.

"Well," asked Tanar, "what does it all mean?"

"It means," said David, "that if their legend is true, or based upon fact, that their ancestors came from the same outer world from which Perry and I came, but by what avenue? — that is the astounding enigma."

Many times during their incarceration the three men discussed this subject, but never were they able to arrive at any definite solution of the mystery. Food was brought them many times and several times they slept before Korsar soldiers came and took them from the dungeon.

They were led to the palace of The Cid, the architecture of which but tended to increase the mystery of the origin of this strange race in the mind of David Innes, for the building seemed to show indisputable proof of Moorish influence.

Within the palace they were conducted to a large room, comfortably filled with bewhiskered Korsars decked out in their gaudiest raiment, which far surpassed in brilliancy of coloring and ornamentation the comparatively mean clothes they had worn aboard ship. Upon a dais, at one end of the room, a man was seated upon a large, ornately carved chair. It was The Cid, and as David's eyes fell upon him his mind suddenly grasped, for the first time, a significant suggestion in the title of the ruler of the Korsars.

Previously the name had been only a name to David. He had not considered it as a title; nor had it by association awakened any particular train of thought, but now, coupled with the Moorish palace and the carved throne, it did.

The Cid! Rodrigo Diaz de Bivar — El Campeador — a national hero of eleventh century Spain. What did it mean? His thoughts reverted to the ships of the Korsars — their motley crews with harquebuses and cutlasses — and he recalled the thrilling stories he had read as a boy of the pirates of the Spanish Main. Could it be merely coincidence? Could a nation of people have grown up within the inner world, who so closely resembled the buccaneers of the seventeenth century, or had their forebears in truth found their way hither from the outer crust? David Innes did not know. He was frankly puzzled. But now he was being led to the foot of The Cid's throne and there was no further opportunity for the delightful speculation that had absorbed his mind momentarily.

The cruel, cunning eyes of The Cid looked down upon the three prisoners from out his brutal face. "The Emperor of Pellucidar!" he sneered. "The King of Anoroc! The son of the King of Sari!" and then he laughed uproariously. He extended his hand, his fingers parted and curled in a clutching gesture. "Emperor! King! Prince!" he sneered again, "and yet here you all are in the clutches of The Cid. Emperor — bah! I, The Cid, am the Emperor of all Pellucidar! You and your naked savages!" He turned on David. "Who are you to take the title of Emperor? I could crush you all," and he closed his fingers in a gesture of rough cruelty. "But I shall not. The Cid is generous and he is grateful, too. You shall have your freedom for a small price that you may easily pay." He paused as though he expected them to question him, but no one of the three spoke. Suddenly he turned upon David. "Where did you get your firearms and your powder? Who made them for you?"

"We made them ourselves," replied David.

"Who taught you to make them?" insisted The Cid. "But never mind; it is enough that you know and we would know. You may win your liberty by teaching us."

David could make gunpowder, but whether he could make any better gunpowder than the Korsars he did not know. He had left that to Perry and his apprentices in The Empire, and he knew perfectly well that he could not reconstruct a modern rifle such as was being turned out in the arsenals at Sari, for he had neither the drawings to make the rifles, nor the machinery, nor the drawings to make the machinery, nor the shops in which to make steel. But nevertheless here was one opportunity for possible freedom that might pave the way to escape and he could not throw it away, either for himself or his companions, by admitting their inability to manufacture modern firearms or improve the powder of the Korsars.

"Well," demanded The Cid, impatiently, "what is your answer?"

"We cannot make powder and rifles while a man eats," replied David; "nor can we make them from the air or from conversation. We must have materials; we must have factories; we must have trained men. You will sleep many times before we are able to accomplish all this. Are you willing to wait?"

"How many times shall we sleep before you have taught our people to make these things?" demanded The Cid.

David shrugged. "I do not know," he said. "In the first place I must find the proper materials."

"We have all the materials," said The Cid. "We have iron and we have the ingredients for making powder. All that you have to do is to put them together in a better way than we have been able to."

"You may have the materials, but it is possible that they are not of sufficiently good quality to make the things that will alone satisfy the subjects of the Emperor of Pellucidar. Perhaps your niter is low grade; there may be impurities in your sulphur; or even the charcoal may not be properly prepared; and there are even more important matters to consider in the selection of material and its manufacture into steel suitable for making the firearms of the Pellucidarians."

"You shall not be hurried," said The Cid. He turned to a man standing near him. "See that an officer accompanies these men always," he said. "Let them go where they please and do what they please in the prosecution of my orders. Furnish them with laborers if they desire them, but do not let them delay and do not let them escape, upon pain of death." And thus ended their interview with The Cid of Korsar.

As it chanced, the man to be detailed to watch them was Fitt, the fellow whom David had chosen to accompany him and Ja in their pursuit of the Korsar fleet, and Fitt, having become well acquainted with David and Ja and having experienced nothing but considerate treatment from them, was far from unfriendly, though, like the majority of all other Korsars, he was in-

clined to be savage and cruel.

As they were passing out of the palace they caught a glimpse of a girl in a chamber that opened onto the corridor in which they were. Fitt, big with the importance of his new position and feeling somewhat like a showman revealing and explaining his wonders to the ignorant and uninitiated, had been describing the various objects of interest that they had passed as well as the personages of importance, and now he nodded in the direction of the room in which they had seen the girl, although they had gone along the corridor so far by this time that they could no longer see her. "That," he said, "is The Cid's daughter." Tanar stopped in his tracks and turned to Fitt.

"May I speak to her?" he asked.

"You!" cried Fitt. "You speak to the daughter of The Cid!"

"I know her," said Tanar. "We two were left alone on the abandoned ship when it was deserted by its officers and crew. Go and ask her if she will speak to me."

Fitt hesitated. "The Cid might not approve," he said.

"He gave you no orders other than to accompany us," said David. "How are we to carry on our work if we are to be prevented from speaking to anyone whom we choose? At least you will be safe in leading us to The Cid's daughter. If she wishes to speak to Tanar the responsibility will not be yours."

"Perhaps you are right," said Fitt. "I will ask her." He stepped to the doorway of the apartment in which were Stellara and Gura, and now, for the first time, he saw that a man was with them. It was Bulf. The three looked up as he entered.

"There is one here who wishes to speak to The Cid's daughter," he said, addressing Stellara.

"Who is he?" demanded Bulf.

"He is Tanar, a prisoner of war from Sari."

"Tell him," said Stellara, "that The Cid's daughter does not recall him and cannot grant him an interview."

As Fitt turned and quit the chamber, Gura's ordinarily sad eyes flashed a look of angry surprise at Stellara.

Chapter XIV

TWO SUNS

David, Ja, and Tanar were quartered in barracks inside the palace wall and immediately set to work to carry out a plan that David had suggested and which included an inspection, not only of the Korsars' powder factory and the arsenals in which their firearms were manufactured, but also visits to the niter beds, sulphur deposits, charcoal pits and iron mines.

These various excursions for the purpose of inspecting the sources of supply and the methods of obtaining it aroused no suspicion in the mind of the Korsar, though their true purpose was anything other than it appeared to be.

In the first place David had not the slightest intention of teaching the Korsars how to improve their powder, thereby transforming them into a far greater menace to the peace of his empire than they could ever become while handicapped by an inferior grade of gunpowder that failed to explode quite as often as it exploded. These tours of inspection, however, which often took them considerable distances from the city of Korsar, afforded an excuse for delaying the lesson in powder making, while David and his companions sought to concoct some plan of escape that might contain at least the seed of success. Also they gave the three men a better knowledge of the surrounding country, familiarized them with the various trails and acquainted them with the manners and customs of the primitive tribes that carried on the agriculture of Korsar and all of the labor of the mines, niter beds and charcoal burning.

It was not long before they had learned that all the Korsars lived in the city of Korsar and that they numbered about five hundred thousand souls, and, as all labor was performed by slaves, every male Korsar above the age of fifteen was free for military service, while those between ten and fifteen were virtually so since this included the period of their training, during which time they learned all that could be taught them of seamanship and the art of piracy and raiding. David soon came to realize that the ferocity of the Korsars, rather than their number, rendered them a menace to the peace of Pellucidar, but he was positive that with an equal number of ships and men he could overcome them and he was glad that he had taken upon himself this dangerous mission, for the longer the three reconnoitered the environs of Korsar the more convinced they became that escape was possible.

The primitive savages from whom the Korsars had wrested their country and whom they had forced into virtual slavery were of such a low order of intelligence that David felt confident that they could never be successfully utilized as soldiers or fighting men by the Korsars, whom they outnumbered ten to one; their villages, according to his Korsar informant, stretching away into the vast hinterland, to the farthest extremities of which no man had ever penetrated.

The natives themselves spoke of a cold country to the north, in the barren and desolate wastes of which no man could live, and of mountains and forests and plains stretching away into the east and southeast to, as they put it, "the very shores of Molop Az" — the flaming sea of Pellucidarian legend upon which the land of Pellucidar floats.

This belief of the natives of the uninterrupted extent of the land mass to the south and southeast corroborated David's belief that Korsar lay upon the same continent as Sari, and this belief was further carried out by the distinct sense of perfect orientation which the three men experienced the moment they set foot upon the shores of Korsar; or rather which the born Pellucidarians, Ja and Tanar, experienced, since David did not possess this inborn homing instinct. Had there been an ocean of any considerable extent separating them from the land of their birth, the two Pellucidarians felt confident that they could not have been so certain as to the direction of Sari as they now were.

As their excursions to various points outside the city of Korsar increased in number the watchfulness of Fitt relaxed, so that the three men occasionally found themselves alone together in some remote part of the back country.

Tanar, wounded by the repeated rebuffs of Stellara, sought to convince himself that he did not love her. He tried to make himself believe that she was cruel and hard and unfaithful, but all that he succeeded in accomplishing was to make himself more unhappy, though he hid this from his companions and devoted himself as assiduously as they to planning their escape. It filled his heart with agony to think of going away forever from the vicinity of the woman he loved, even though there was little or no hope that he might see her should he remain, for gossip of the approaching nuptials of Stellara and Bulf was current in the barracks where he was quartered.

The window of the room to which he had been assigned overlooked a portion of the garden of The Cid — a spot of great natural beauty in which trees and flowers and shrubs bordered gravelled pathways and a miniature lake and streamlet sparkled in the sunlight.

Tanar was seldom in his apartment and when he was he ordinarily gave no more than casual attention to the garden beyond the wall, but upon one occasion, after returning from an inspection of an iron mine, he had been left alone with his own sad thoughts, and, seating himself upon the sill of the window, he was gazing down upon the lovely scene below when his attention was attracted by the figure of a girl as she came into view almost directly before him along one of the gravelled paths. She was looking up toward his window and their eyes met simultaneously. It was Gura.

Placing her finger to her lips, cautioning him to silence, she came quickly forward until she reached a point as close to his window as it was possible for her to come.

"There is a gate in the garden wall at the far end of your barracks," she said in a low whisper attuned to reach his ears. "Come to it at once."

Tanar stopped to ask no questions. The girl's tone had been peremptory. Her whole manner bespoke urgency. Descending the stairway to the ground floor Tanar left the building and walked slowly toward its far end. Korsars were all about him, but they had been accustomed to seeing him, and now he held himself to a slow and careless pace that aroused no suspicion. Just beyond the end of the barracks he came to a small, heavily planked door set in the garden wall and as he arrived opposite this, it swung open and he stepped quickly within the garden, Gura instantly closing the gate behind him.

"At last I have succeeded," cried the girl, "but I thought that I never should. I have tried so hard to see you ever since Fitt took you from The Cid's palace. I learned from one of the slaves where your quarters were in the barracks and whenever I have been free I have been always beneath your window. Twice before I saw you, but I could not attract your attention and now that I have succeeded, perhaps it is too late."

"Too late! What do you mean? Too late for what?" demanded Tanar.

"Too late to save Stellara," said the girl.

"She is in danger?" asked Tanar.

"The preparations for her marriage to Bulf are complete. She cannot delay it much longer."

"Why should she wish to delay it?" demanded the Sarian. "Is she not content with the man she has chosen?"

"Like all men, you are a fool in matters pertaining to a woman's heart," cried Gura.

"I know what she told me," said Tanar.

"After all that you had been through together; after all that she had been to you, how could you have believed that she loved another?" demanded Gura.

"You mean that she does not love Bulf?" asked Tanar.

"Of course she does not love him. He is a horrid beast."

"And she still loves me?"

"She has never loved anyone else," replied the girl.

"Then why did she treat me as she did? Why did she say the things that she said?"

"She was jealous."

"Jealous! Jealous of whom?"

"Of me," said Gura, dropping her eyes.

The Sarian stood looking dumbly at the dark-haired Himean girl standing before him. He noted her slim body, her drooping shoulders, her attitude of dejection. "Gura," he asked, "did I ever speak words of love to you? Did I ever give Stellara or another the right to believe that I loved you?"

She shook her head. "No," she said, "and I told Stellara that when I found out what she thought. I told her that you did not love me and finally she was convinced and asked me to find you and tell you that she still loves you. But I have another message for you from myself. I know you, Sarian. I know that you are not planning to remain here contentedly a prisoner of the Korsars. I know that you will try to escape and I have come to beg you to take Stellara with you, for she will kill herself before she will become the mate of Bulf."

"Escape," mused Tanar. "How may it be accomplished from the heart of The Cid's palace?"

"That is the man's work," said Gura. "It is for you to plan the way."

"And you?" asked Tanar. "You wish to come away with us?"

"Do not think of me," said Gura. "If you and Stellara can escape, I do not matter."

"But you do matter," said the man, "and I am sure that you do not wish to stay in Korsar."

"No, I do not wish to remain in Korsar," replied the girl, "and particularly so now that The Cid seems to have taken a fancy to me."

"You wish to return to Hime?" asked Tanar.

"After the brief taste of happiness I have had," replied the girl, "I could not return to the quarrels, the hatred and the constant unhappiness that constitute life within the cave of Scurv and which would be but continued in some other cave were I to take a mate in Hime."

"Then come with us," said the Sarian.

"Oh, if I only might!" exclaimed Gura.

"Then that is settled," exclaimed Tanar. "You shall come with us and if we reach Sari I know that you can find peace and happiness for yourself always."

"It sounds like a dream," said the girl, wistfully, "from which I shall awaken in the cave of Scurv."

"We shall make the dream come true," said the Sarian, "and now let us plan on how best we can get you and Stellara out of the palace of The Cid."

"That will not be so easy," said Gura.

"No, it is the most difficult part of our escape," agreed the Sarian; "but it must be done and I believe that the bolder the plan the greater its assurance of success."

"And it must be done at once," said Gura, "for the wedding arrangements are completed and Bulf is impatient for his mate."

For a moment Tanar stood in thought, seeking to formulate some plan that might contain at least a semblance of feasibility. "Can you bring Stellara to this gate at once?" he asked Gura.

"If she is alone, yes," replied the girl.

"Then go and fetch her and wait here with her until I return. My signal will be a low whistle. When you hear it, unlatch the gate."

"I shall return as quickly as possible," said Gura, and, as Tanar stepped through the doorway into the barrack yards, he closed and latched the gate behind him.

The Sarian looked about him and was delighted to note that apparently no one had seen him emerge from the garden. Instead of returning along the front of the barracks the way he had come, he turned in the opposite direction and made his way

directly to one of the main gates of the palace. And this strategy was prompted also by another motive — he wished to ascertain if he could pass the guard at the main gate without being challenged.

Tanar had not adopted the garments of his captors and was still conspicuous by the scant attire and simple ornaments of a savage warrior and already his comings and goings had made him a familiar figure around the palace yard and in the Korsar streets beyond. But he had never passed through a palace gate alone before; nor without the ever present Fitt.

As he neared the gate he neither hastened nor loitered, but maintained a steady pace and an unconcerned demeanor. Others were passing in and out and as the former naturally received much closer scrutiny by the guards than the latter, Tanar soon found himself in a Korsar street outside the palace of The Cid.

Before him were the usual sights now grown familiar — the narrow, dusty street, the small open shops or bazaars lining the opposite side, the swaggering Korsars in their brilliant kerchiefs and sashes, and the slaves bearing great burdens to and fro — garden truck and the fruits of the chase coming in from the back country, while bales of tanned hides, salt and other commodities, craved by the simple tastes of the aborigines, were being borne out of the city toward the interior. Some of the bales were of considerable size and weight, requiring the services of four carriers, and were supported on two long poles, the ends of which rested on the shoulders of the men.

There were lines of slaves carrying provisions and ammunition to a fleet of ships that was outfitting for a new raid, and another line bearing plunder from the hold of another ship that had but recently come to anchor in the river before the city.

All this activity presented a scene of apparent confusion, which was increased by the voices of the merchants hawking their wares and the shrill bickering of prospective purchasers.

Through the motley throng the Sarian shouldered his way back toward another gate that gave entrance to the palace ground close to the far end of the long, rambling barracks. As this was the gate through which he passed most often he was accorded no more than a glance as he passed through, and once within he hastened immediately to the quarters assigned to David. Here he found both David and Ja, to whom he immediately unfolded a plan that he had been perfecting since he left the garden of The Cid.

"And now," he said, "before you have agreed to my plan, let me make it plain that I do not expect you to accompany me if you feel that the chances of success are too slight. It is my duty, as well as my desire, to save Stellara and Gura. But I cannot ask you to place your plans for escape in jeopardy."

"Your plan is a good one," replied David, "and even if it were not it is the best that has been suggested yet. And as for our deserting either you or Stellara or Gura, that, of course, is not even a question for discussion. We shall go with you and I know that I speak for Ja as well as myself."

"I knew that you would say that," said the Sarian, "and now let us start at once to put the plan to test."

"Good," said David. "You make your purchases and return to the garden and Ja and I will proceed at once to carry out our part."

The three proceeded at once toward the palace gate at the far end of the barracks, and as they were passing through the Korsar in charge stopped them.

"Where now?" he demanded.

"We are going into the city to make purchases for a long expedition that we are about to make in search of new iron deposits in the back country, further than we have ever been before."

"And where is Fitt?" demanded the captain of the gate.

"The Cid sent for him, and while he is gone we are making the necessary preparations."

"All right," said the man, apparently satisfied. "You may pass."

"We shall return presently with porters," said David, "for some of our personal belongings and then go out again to collect the balance of our outfit. Will you leave word that we are to be passed in the event that you are not here?"

"I shall be here," said the man. "But what are you going to carry into the back country?"

"We expect that we may have to travel even beyond the furthest boundaries of Korsar, where the natives know little or nothing of The Cid and his authority, and for this reason it is necessary for us to carry provisions and articles of trade that we may barter with them for what we want, since we shall not have sufficient numbers in our party to take these things by force."

"I see," said the man; "but it seems funny that The Cid does not send muskets and pistols to take what he wants rather than spoil these savages by trading with them."

"Yes," said David, "it does seem strange," and the three passed out into the street of Korsar.

Beyond the gate David and Ja turned to the right toward the market place, while Tanar crossed immediately to one of the shops on the opposite side of the street. Here he purchased two large bags, made of well tanned hide, with which he returned immediately to the palace grounds and presently he was before the garden gate where he voiced a low whistle that was to be the signal by which the girls were to know that he arrived.

Almost immediately the gate swung open and Tanar stepped quickly within. As Gura closed the gate behind him, Tanar found himself standing face to face with Stellara. Her eyes were moist with tears, her lips were trembling with suppressed emotion as the Sarian opened his arms and pressed her to him.

The market place of the city of Korsar is a large, open square where the natives from the interior barter their agricultural produce, raw hides and the flesh of the animals they have taken in the chase, for the simple necessities which they wish to take back to their homes with them.

The farmers bring in their vegetables in large hampers made of reed bound together with grasses. These hampers are ordinarily about four feet in each dimension and are borne on a single pole by two men if lightly loaded, or upon two poles and by four carriers if the load is heavy.

David and Ja approached a group of men whose hampers were empty and who were evidently preparing to depart from the market, and after questioning several of the group they found two who were returning to the same village, which lay at a considerable distance almost due north of Korsar.

By the order of The Cid, Fitt had furnished his three prisoners with ample funds in the money of Korsar that they might make necessary purchases in the prosecution of their investigations and their experiments.

The money, which consisted of gold coins of various sizes and weights, was crudely stamped upon one side with what purported to be a likeness of The Cid, and upon the other with a Korsar ship. For so long a time had gold coin been the medium of exchange in Korsar and the surrounding country that it was accepted by the natives of even remote villages and tribes, so that David had little difficulty in engaging the services of eight carriers and their two hampers to carry equipment at least as far as their village, which in reality was much further than David had any intention of utilizing the services of the natives.

Having concluded his arrangements with the men, David and Ja led the way back to the palace gate, where the officer passed them through with a nod.

As they proceeded along the front of the barracks toward its opposite end their only fear was that Fitt might have returned from his interview with The Cid. If he had and if he saw and questioned them, all was lost. They scarcely breathed as they approached the entrance to their quarters, which were also the quarters of Fitt. But they saw nothing of him as they passed the doorway and hastened on to the door in the garden wall. Here they halted, directing the bearers to place the baskets close to the doorway. David Innes whistled. The door swung in, and at a word from Tanar the eight carriers entered, picked up two bundles just inside the gate and deposited one of them in each of the hampers waiting beyond the wall. The lids were closed. The slaves resumed their burden, and the party turned about to retrace its steps to the palace gate through which the carriers had just entered with their empty hampers.

Once again apprehension had chilled the heart of David Innes for fear that Fitt might have returned, but they passed the barracks and reached the gate without seeing him, and here they were halted by the Korsar in charge.

"It did not take you long," he said. "What have you in the hampers?" and he raised the cover of one of them.

"Only our personal belongings," said David. "When we return again we shall have our full equipment. Would you like to inspect it all at the same time?"

The Korsar, looking down at the skin bag lying at the bottom of the hamper, hesitated for a moment before replying. "Very well," he said, "I will do it all at the same time," and he let the cover drop back into place.

The hearts of the three men had stood still, but David Innes's voice betrayed no unwonted emotion as he addressed the captain of the gate. "When Fitt returns," he said, "tell him that I am anxious to see him and ask him if he will wait in our quarters until we return."

The Korsar nodded a surly assent and motioned for them to pass on through the gate.

Turning to the right, David led the party down the narrow street toward the market place. There he turned abruptly to the left, through a winding alleyway and double-backed to the north upon another street that paralleled that upon which the palace fronted. Here were poorer shops and less traffic and the carriers were able to make good time until presently the party passed out of the city of Korsar into the open country beyond. And then, by dint of threats and promises of additional pieces of gold, the three men urged the carriers to accelerate their speed to a swinging trot, which they maintained until they were forced to stop from exhaustion. A brief rest with food and they were off again; nor did they slacken their pace until they reached the rolling, wooded country at the foothills of the mountains, far north of Korsar.

Here, well within the shelter of the woods, the carriers set down their burdens and threw themselves upon the ground to rest, while Tanar and David swung back the covers of the hampers and untying the stout thongs that closed the mouths of the bags revealed their contents. Half smothered and almost unable to move their cramped limbs, Stellara and Gura were lifted from the baskets and revealed to the gaze of the astounded carriers.

Tanar turned upon the men. "Do you know who this woman is?" he demanded.

"No," said one of their number.

"It is Stellara, the daughter of The Cid," said the Sarian. "You have helped to steal her from the palace of her father. Do you know what that will mean if you are caught?"

The men trembled in evident terror. "We did not know she was in the basket," said one of them. "We had nothing to do with it.

It is you who stole her."

"Will the Korsars believe you when we tell them of the great quantities of gold we paid you if we are captured?" asked Tanar. "No, they will not believe you and I do not have to tell you what your fate will be. But there is safety for you if you will do what I tell you to do."

"What is that?" demanded one of the natives.

"Take up your hampers and hasten on to your village and tell no one, as long as you live, what you have done, not even your mates. If you do not tell, no one will know for we shall not tell."

"We will never tell," cried the men in chorus.

"Do not even talk about it among yourselves," cautioned David, "for even the trees have ears, and if the Korsars come to your village and question you tell them that you saw three men and two women traveling toward the east just beyond the borders of the city of Korsar. Tell them that they were too far away for you to recognize them, but that they may have been The Cid's daughter and her companion with the three men who abducted them."

"We will do as you say," replied the carriers.

"Then be gone," demanded David, and the eight men hurriedly gathered up their hampers and disappeared into the forest toward the north.

When the two girls were sufficiently revived and rested to continue the journey, the party set out again, making their way to the east for a short distance and then turning north again, for it had been Tanar's plan to throw the Korsars off the trail by traveling north, rather than east or south. Later they would turn to the east, far north of the area which the Korsars might be expected to comb in search of them, and then again, after many marches, they would change their direction once more to the south. It was a circuitous route, but it seemed the safest.

The forest changed to pine and cedar and there were windswept wastes dotted with gnarled and stunted trees. The air was cooler than they had ever known it in their native land, and when the wind blew from the north they shivered around roaring camp fires. The animals they met were scarcer and bore heavier fur, and nowhere was there sign of man.

Upon one occasion when they stopped to camp Tanar pointed at the ground before him. "Look!" he cried to David. "My shadow is no longer beneath me," and then, looking up, "the sun is not above us."

"I have noticed that," replied David, "and I am trying to understand the reason for it, and perhaps I shall with the aid of the legends of the Korsars."

As they proceeded their shadows grew longer and longer and the light and heat of the sun diminished until they traveled in a semi-twilight that was always cold.

Long since they had been forced to fashion warmer garments from the pelts of the beasts they had killed. Tanar and Ja wanted to turn back toward the southeast, for their strange homing instinct drew them in that direction toward their own country, but David asked them to accompany him yet a little further for his mind had evolved a strange and wonderful theory and he wished to press on yet a little further to obtain still stronger proof of its correctness.

When they slept they rested beside roaring fires and once, when they awoke, they were covered by a light mantle of a cold, white substance that frightened the Pellucidarians, but that David knew was snow. And the air was full of whirling particles and the wind bit those portions of their faces that were exposed, for now they wore fur caps and hoods and their hands were covered with warm mittens.

"We cannot go much further in this direction," said Ja, "or we shall all perish."

"Perhaps you are right," said David. "You four turn back to the southeast and I will go yet a little further to the north and overtake you when I have satisfied myself that a thing that I believe is true."

"No," cried Tanar, "we shall remain together. Where you go we shall go."

"Yes," said Ja, "we shall not abandon you."

"Just a little further north, then," said David, "and I shall be ready to turn back with you," and so they forged ahead over snow covered ground into the deepening gloom that filled the souls of the Pellucidarians with terror. But after a while the wind changed and blew from the south and the snow melted and the air became balmy again, and still further on the twilight slowly lifted and the light increased, though the midday sun of Pellucidar was now scarcely visible behind them.

"I cannot understand it," said Ja. "Why should it become lighter again, although the sun is ever further away behind us?"

"I do not know," said Tanar. "Ask David."

"I can only guess," said David, "and my guess seems so preposterous that I dare not voice it."

"Look!" cried Stellara, pointing ahead. "It is the sea."

"Yes," said Gura, "a gray sea; it does not look like water."

"And what is that?" cried Tanar. "There is a great fire upon the sea."

"And the sea does not curve upward in the distance," cried Stellara. "Everything is wrong in this country and I am afraid."

David had stopped in his tracks and was staring at the deep red glow ahead. The others gathered around him and watched it, too. "What is it?" demanded Ja.

"As there is a God in heaven it can be but one thing," replied David; "and yet I know that it cannot be that thing. The very idea is ridiculous. It is impossible and outlandish."

"But what might it be?" demanded Stellara.

"The sun," replied David.

"But the sun is almost out of sight behind us," Gura reminded him.

"I do not mean the sun of Pellucidar," replied David; "but the sun of the outer world, the world from which I came."

The others stood in silent awe, watching the edge of a blood red disc that seemed to be floating upon a gray ocean across whose reddened surface a brilliant pathway of red and gold led from the shoreline to the blazing orb, where the sea and sky seemed to meet.

Chapter XV

MADNESS

Now," said Stellara, "we can go no further;" nor indeed could they for east and west and north stretched a great, sullen sea and along the shore-line at their feet great ice cakes rose and fell with sullen roars and loud reports as the sea ground the churning mass.

For a long time David Innes, Emperor of Pellucidar, stood staring out across that vast and desolate waste of water. "What lies beyond?" he murmured to himself, and then, shaking his head, he turned away. "Come," he said, "let us strike back for Sari."

His companions received his words with shouts of joy. Smiles replaced the half troubled expressions that had marked their drawn faces since the moment that they had discovered that their beloved noonday sun was being left behind them.

With light steps, with laughter and joking, they faced the long, arduous journey that lay ahead of them.

During the second march, after they had turned back from the northern sea, Gura discovered a strange object to the left of their line of march.

"It looks as though it might be some queer sort of native hut," she said.

"We shall have to investigate it," said David, and the five made their way to the side of the strange object.

It was a large, heavy, wicker basket that lay inverted upon the barren ground. All about it were the rotted remnants of cordage.

At David's suggestion the men turned the basket over upon its side. Beneath it they found well preserved remnants of oiled silk and a network of fine cord.

"What is it?" asked Stellara.

"It is the basket and all that remains of the gas bag of a balloon," said David.

"What is a balloon," asked the girl, "and how did it get here?"

"I can explain what a balloon is," said David; "but if I were positive that I was correct in my conjecture as to how it came here, I would hold the answer to a thousand questions that have puzzled the men of the outer crust for ages." For a long time he stood silently contemplating the weather-worn basket. His mind submerged in thought was oblivious to all else. "If I only knew," he mused. "If I only knew, and yet how else could it have come here? What else could that red disc upon the horizon of the sea have been other than the midnight sun of the arctic regions."

"What in the world are you talking about?" demanded Gura.

"The poor devils," mused David, apparently oblivious of the girl's presence. "They made a greater discovery than they could have hoped for in their wildest dreams. I wonder if they lived to realize it." Slowly he removed his fur cap and stood facing the basket with bowed head, and for some unaccountable reason, which they could not explain, his companions bared their heads and followed his example. And after they had resumed their journey it was a long time before David Innes could shake off the effects of that desolate reminder of one of the world's most pathetic tragedies.

So anxious were the members of the party to reach the cheering warmth of the beloved Pellucidar that they knew, that they pressed on toward the south with the briefest of rests; nor were they wholly content until once more their shadows lay directly beneath them.

Sari, lying slightly east of south, their return from the north took them over a different route from that which they had followed up from Korsar. Of course the Pellucidarians did not know these points of compass as north or south, and even David Innes carried them in his mind more in accordance with the Pellucidarian scheme than that with which he had been familiar upon the outer crust.

Naturally, with the sun always at zenith and with no stars and no moon and no planets, the Pellucidarians have been compelled to evolve a different system of indicating direction than that with which we are familiar. By instinct they know the direction in which their own country lies and each Pellucidarian reckons all directions from this base line, and he indicates other directions in a simple and ingenious manner.

Suppose you were from Sari and were traveling from the ice girt sea above Korsar to any point upon Pellucidar, you would set and maintain your course in this manner. Extend the fingers of your right hand and hold it in a horizontal position, palm down, directly in front of your body, your little finger pointing in the direction of Sari — a direction which you know by instinct — and your thumb pointing to the left directly at right angles to the line in which your little finger is pointing. Now spread your left hand in the same way and lower it on top of your right hand, so that the little finger of your left hand exactly covers the little finger of your right hand.

You will now see the fingers and thumbs of your two hands cover an arc of one hundred and eighty degrees.

Sari lies southeast of Korsar, while The Land of Awful Shadow lies due south.

Therefore a Sarian pointing in the direction toward The Land of Awful Shadow would say that he was traveling two left fingers from Sari, since the middle finger of the left hand would be pointing about due south toward The Land of Awful Shadow. If he were going in the opposite direction, or north, he would merely add the word "back," saying that he was traveling two left fingers back from Sari, so that by this plan every point of compass is roughly covered, and with sufficient accuracy for all the requirements of the primitive Pellucidarians. The fact that when one is traveling to the right of his established base line and indicates it by mentioning the fingers of his left hand might, at first, be deemed confusing, but, of course, having followed this system for ages, it is perfectly intelligible to the Pellucidarians.

When they reached a point at which the city of Korsar lay three right fingers back from Sari, they were, in reality, due east of the Korsar city. They were now in fertile, semi-tropical land teeming with animal life. The men were armed with pistols as well as spears, bows and arrows and knives; while Stellara and Gura carried light spears and knives, and seldom was there a march that did not witness an encounter with one or more of the savage beasts of the primeval forests, verdure clad hills or rolling plains across which their journey led them.

They long since had abandoned any apprehension of pursuit or capture by the Korsars and while they had skirted the distant hinterland claimed by Korsar and had encountered some of the natives upon one or two occasions, they had seen no member of the ruling class with the result that for the first time since they had fallen into the clutches of the enemy they felt a sense of unquestioned freedom. And though the other dangers that beset their way might appear appalling to one of the outer world, they had no such effect upon any one of the five, whose experiences of life had tended to make them wholly self-reliant, and, while constantly alert and watchful, unoppressed by the possibility of future calamity. When danger suddenly confronted them, they were ready to meet it. After it had passed they did not depress their spirits by anticipating the next encounter.

Ja and David were anxious to return to

their mates, but Tanar and Stellara were supremely happy because they were together, and Gura was content merely to be near Tanar. Sometimes she recalled Balal, her brother, for he had been kind to her, but Scurv and Sloo and Dhung she tried to forget.

Thus they were proceeding, a happy and contented party, when, with the suddenness and unexpectedness of lightning out of a clear sky, disaster overwhelmed them.

They had been passing through a range of low, rocky hills and were descending a narrow gorge on the Sari side of the range when, turning the shoulder of a hill, they came face to face with a large party of Korsars, fully a hundred strong. The leaders saw and recognized them instantly and a shout of savage triumph that broke from their lips was taken up by all their fellows.

David, who was in the lead, saw that resistance would be futile and in the instant his plan was formed. "We must separate," he said. "Tanar, you and Stellara go together. Ja, take Gura with you, and I shall go in a different direction, for we must not all be captured. One, at least, must escape to return to Sari. If it is not I, then let the one who wins through take this message to Ghak and Perry. Tell Perry that I am positive that I have discovered that there is a polar opening in the outer crust leading into Pellucidar and that if he ever gets in radio communication with the outer world, he must inform them of this fact. Tell Ghak to rush his forces by sea on Korsar, as well as by land. And now, good-bye, and each for himself."

Turning in their tracks the five fled up the gorge and being far more active and, agile that the Korsars, they outdistanced them, and though the rattle of musketry followed them and bits of iron and stone fell about them, or whizzed past them, no one was struck.

Tanar and Stellara found and followed a steep ravine that led upward to the right, and almost at the same time Ja and Gura diverged to the left up the course of a dry waterway, while David continued on back up the main gorge.

Almost at the summit and within the reach of safety, Tanar and Stellara found their way blocked by a sheer cliff, which, while not more than fifteen feet in height, was absolutely unscalable; nor could they find footing upon the steep ravine sides to

the right or left, and as they stood there in this cul-de-sac, their backs to the wall, a party of twenty or thirty Korsars, toiling laboriously up the ravine, cut off their retreat; nor was there any place in which they might hide, but instead were compelled to stand there in full view of the first of the enemy that came within sight of them, and thus with freedom already within their grasp they fell again into the hands of the Korsars. And Tanar had been compelled to surrender without resistance because he did not dare risk Stellara's life by drawing the fire of the enemy.

Many of the Korsars were for dispatching Tanar immediately, but the officer in command forbade them for it was The Cid's orders that any of the prisoners that might be recaptured were to be returned alive. "And furthermore," he added, "Bulf is particularly anxious to get this Sarian back alive."

During the long march back to Korsar, Tanar and Stellara learned that this was one of several parties that The Cid had dispatched in search of them with orders never to return until they had rescued his daughter and captured her abductors. They also had impressed upon them the fact that the only reason for The Cid's insistence that the prisoners be returned alive was because he and Bulf desired to mete out to them a death commensurate with their crime.

During the long march back to Korsar, Tanar and Stellara were kept apart as a rule, though on several occasions they were able to exchange a few words.

"My poor Sarian," said Stellara upon one of these. "I wish to God that you had never met me for only sorrow and pain and death can come of it."

"I do not care," replied Tanar, "if I die tomorrow, or if they torture me forever, for no price is too high to pay for the happiness that I have had with you, Stellara."

"Ah, but they will torture you — that is what wrings my heart," cried the girl. "Take your life yourself, Tanar. Do not let them get you. I know them and I know their methods and I would rather kill you with my own hands than see you fall into their clutches. The Cid is a beast, and Bulf is worse than Bohar the Bloody. I shall never be his mate; of that you may be sure, and if you die by your own hand I shall follow you shortly. And if there is a life after this, as the ancestors of the Korsars taught them, then we shall meet again where all is peace and beauty and love."

The Sarian shook his head. "I know what is here in this life," he said, "and I do not know what is there in the other. I shall cling to this, and you must cling to it until some other hand than ours takes it from us."

"But they will torture you so horribly," she moaned.

"No torture can kill the happiness of our love, Stellara," said the man, and then guards separated them and they plodded on across the weary, interminable miles. How different the country looked through eyes of despair and sorrow from the sunlit paradise that they had seen when they journeyed through it, hand in hand with freedom and love.

But at last the long, cruel journey was over, a fitting prelude to its cruel ending, for at the palace gate Stellara and Tanar were separated. She was escorted to her quarters by female attendants whom she recognized as being virtually her guards and keepers, while Tanar was conducted directly into the presence of The Cid.

As he entered the room he saw the glowering face of the Korsar chieftain, and standing below the dais, just in front of him, was Bulf, whom he had seen but once before, but whose face no man could ever forget. But there was another there whose presence brought a look of greater horror to Tanar's face than did the brutal countenances of The Cid or Bulf, for standing directly before the dais, toward which he was being led, the Sarian saw David I, Emperor of Pellucidar. Of all the calamities that could have befallen, this was the worst.

As the Sarian was led to David's side he tried to speak to him, but was roughly silenced by the Korsar guards; nor were they ever again to be allowed to communicate with one another.

The Cid eyed them savagely, as did Bulf. "For you, who betrayed my confidence and abducted my daughter, there is no punishment that can fit your crime; there is no death so terrible that its dying will expiate your sin. It is not within me to conceive of any form of torture the infliction of which upon you would give me adequate pleasure. I shall have to look for suggestions outside of my own mind," and his eyes ran questioningly among his officers surrounding him.

"Let me have that one," roared Bulf, pointing at Tanar, "and I can promise you that you will witness such tortures as the eyes of man never before beheld; nor the body of man ever before endured."

"Will it result in death?" asked a tall Korsar with cadaverous face.

"Of course," said Bulf, "but not too soon."

"Death is a welcome and longed for deliverance from torture," continued the other. "Would you give either one of these the satisfaction and pleasure of enjoying even death?"

"But what else is there?" demanded The Cid.

"There is a living death that is worse than death," said the cadaverous one.

"And if you can name a torture worse than that which I had in mind," exclaimed Bulf, "I shall gladly relinquish all my claims upon this Sarian."

"Explain," commanded The Cid.

"It is this," said the cadaverous one. "These men are accustomed to sunlight, to freedom, to cleanliness, to fresh air, to companionship. There are beneath this palace dark, damp dungeons into which no ray of light ever filters, whose thick walls are impervious to sound. The denizens of these horrid places, as you know, would have an effect opposite to that of human companionship and the only danger, the only weak spot in my plan, lies in the fact that their constant presence might deprive these criminals of their reason and thus defeat the very purpose to which I conceive their presence necessary. A lifetime of hideous loneliness and torture in silence and in darkness! What death, what torture, what punishment can you mete out to these men that would compare in hideousness with that which I have suggested?"

After he had ceased speaking the others remained in silent contemplation of his proposition for some time. It was The Cid who broke the silence.

"Bulf," he said, "I believe that he is right, for I know that as much as I love life I would rather die than be left alone in one of the palace dungeons."

Bulf nodded his head slowly. "I hate to give up my plan," he said, "for I should like to inflict that torture upon this Sarian myself. But," and he turned to the cadaverous one, "you are right. You have named a torture infinitely worse than any that I could conceive."

"Thus is it ordered," said The Cid, "to

separate palace dungeons for life."

In utter silence, unbroken by the Korsar assemblage, Tanar and David were blindfolded; Tanar felt himself being stripped of all his ornaments and of what meager raiment it was his custom to wear, with the exception of his loin cloth. Then he was pushed and dragged roughly along, first this way and then that. He knew when they were passing through narrow corridors by the muffled echoes and there was a different reverberation of the footsteps of his guards as they crossed large apartments. He was hustled down flights of stone steps and through other corridors and at last he felt himself lowered into an opening, a guard seizing him under each arm. The air felt damp and it smelled of mold and must and of something else that was disgusting, but unrecognizable to his nostrils. And then they let go of him and he dropped a short distance and landed upon a stone flagging that felt damp and slippery to his bare feet. He heard a sound above his head — a grating sound as though a stone slab had been pushed across a stone floor to close the trap through which he had been lowered. Then Tanar snatched the bandage from his eyes, but he might as well have left it there for he found himself surrounded by utter darkness. He listened intently, but there was no sound, not even the sounds of the retreating footsteps of his guards — darkness and silence — they had chosen the most terrible torture that they could inflict upon a Sarian — silence, darkness and solitude.

For a long time he stood there motionless and then, slowly, he commenced to grope his way forward. Four steps he took before he touched the wall and this he followed two steps to the end, and there he turned and took six steps to cross before he reached the wall on the opposite side, and thus he made the circuit of his dungeon and found that it was four by six paces — perhaps not small for a dungeon, but narrower than the grave for Tanar of Pellucidar.

He tried to think — to think how he could occupy his time until death released him. Death! Could he not hasten it? But how? Six paces was the length of his prison cell. Could he not dash at full speed from one end to the other, crushing his brains out by the impact? And then he recalled his promise to Stellara, even in the face of her appeal to him to take his own life — "I shall not die of my own hand."

Again he made the circuit of his dungeon. He wondered how they would feed him, for he knew that they would feed him because they wished him to live as long as possible, as only thus might they encompass his torture. He thought of the bright sun shining down upon the table-lands of Sari. He thought of the young men and the maidens there free and happy. He thought of Stellara, so close, up there above him somewhere, and yet so infinitely far away. If he were dead, they would be closer. "Not by my own hand," he muttered.

He tried to plan for the future — the blank, dark, silent future — the eternity of loneliness that confronted him, and he found that through the despair of utter hopelessness his own unconquerable spirit could still discern hope, for no matter what his plans they all looked forward to a day of freedom and he realized that nothing short of death ever could rob him of this solace, and so his plan finally developed.

He must in some way keep his mind from dwelling constantly upon the present. He must erase from it all consideration of the darkness, the silence and the solitude that surrounded him. And he must keep fit, mentally and physically, for the moment of release or escape. And so he planned to walk and to exercise his arms and the other muscles of his body systematically to the end that he might keep in good condition and at the same time induce sufficient fatigue to enable him to sleep as much as possible, and when he rested preparatory to sleep he concentrated his mind entirely upon pleasant memories. And when he put the plan into practice he found that it was all that he had hoped that it would be. He exercised until he was thoroughly fatigued and then he lay down to pleasant day dreams until sleep claimed him. Being accustomed from childhood to sleeping upon hard ground, the stone flagging gave him no particular discomfort and he was asleep in the midst of pleasant memories of happy hours with Stellara.

But his awakening! As consciousness slowly returned it was accompanied by a sense of horror, the cause of which gradually filtered to his awakening sensibilities. A cold, slimy body was crawling across his chest. Instinctively his hand seized it to thrust it away and his fingers closed upon a scaly thing that wriggled and writhed and struggled.

Tanar leaped to his feet, cold sweat bursting from every pore. He could feel the hairs upon his head rising in horror. He stepped back and his foot touched another of those horrid things. He slipped and fell, and, falling, his body encountered others — cold, clammy, wriggling. Scrambling to his feet he retreated to the opposite end of his dungeon, but everywhere the floor was covered with writhing, scaly bodies. And now the silence became a pandemonium of seething sounds, a black caldron of venomous hisses.

Long bodies curled themselves about his legs and writhed and wriggled upward toward his face. No sooner did he tear one from him and hurl it aside than another took its place.

This was no dream as he had at first hoped, but stark, horrible reality. These hideous serpents that filled his cell were but a part of his torture, but they would defeat their purpose. They would drive him mad. Already he felt his mind tottering and then into it crept the cunning scheme of a madman. With their own weapons he would defeat their ends. He would rob them quickly of the power to torture him further, and he burst into a shrill, mirthless laugh as he tore a snake from around his body and held it before him.

The reptile writhed and struggled and very slowly Tanar of Pellucidar worked his hand upward to its throat. It was not a large snake for Pellucidar, measuring perhaps five feet in length with a body about six inches in diameter.

Grasping the reptile about a foot below its head with one hand, Tanar slapped it repeatedly in the face with the other and then held it close to his breast. Laughing and screaming, he struck and struck again, and at last the snake struck back, burying its fangs deep in the flesh of the Sarian.

With a cry of triumph Tanar hurled the thing from him, and then slowly sank to the floor upon the writhing, wriggling forms that carpeted it.

"With your own weapons I have robbed you of your revenge," he shrieked, and then he lapsed into unconsciousness.

Who may say how long he lay thus in the darkness and silence of that buried dungeon in a timeless world. But at length he stirred; slowly his eyes opened and as consciousness returned he felt about him. The stone flagging was bare. He sat up. He was not dead and to his surprise he discovered that he had suffered neither pain nor swelling from the strike of the serpent.

He arose and moved cautiously about the dungeon. The snakes were gone. Sleep had restored his mental equilibrium, but he shuddered as he realized how close he had been to madness, and he smiled somewhat shamefacedly, as he reflected upon the futility of his needless terror. For the first time in his life Tanar of Pellucidar had understood the meaning of the word fear.

As he paced slowly around his dungeon one foot came in contact with something lying on the floor in a corner — something which had not been there before the snakes came. He stooped and felt cautiously with his hand and found an iron bowl fitted with a heavy cover. He lifted the cover. Here was food and without questioning what it was or whence it came, he ate.

Chapter XVI

THE DARKNESS BEYOND

The deadly monotony of his incarceration dragged on. He exercised; he ate; he slept. He never knew how the food was brought to his cell, nor when, and after a while he ceased to care.

The snakes came usually while he slept, but since that first experience they no longer filled him with horror. And after a dozen repetitions of their visit they not only ceased to annoy him, but he came to look forward to their coming as a break in the deadly monotony of his solitude. He found that by stroking them and talking to them in low tones he could quiet their restless writhing. And after repeated recurrences of their visits he was confident that one of them had become almost a pet.

Of course in the darkness he could not differentiate one snake from another, but always he was awakened by the nose of one pounding gently upon his chest, and when he took it in his hands and stroked it, it made no effort to escape; nor ever again did one of them strike him with its fangs after that first orgy of madness, during which he had thought and hoped that the reptiles were venomous.

It took him a long time to find the opening through which the reptiles found ingress to his cell, but at length, after diligent search, he discovered an aperture about eight inches in diameter, some three feet above the floor. Its sides were worn smooth by the countless passings of scaly bodies. He inserted his hand in the opening and feeling around discovered that the wall at this point was about a foot in thickness, and when he inserted his arm to the shoulder he could feel nothing in any direction beyond the wall. Perhaps there was another chamber there — another cell like his — or possibly the aperture opened into a deep pit that was filled with snakes. He thought of many explanations and the more he thought the more anxious he became to solve the riddle of the mysterious space beyond his cell. Thus did his mind occupy itself with trivial things, and the loneliness and the darkness and the silence exaggerated the importance of the matter beyond all reason until it became an obsession with him. During all his waking hours he thought about that hole in the wall and what lay beyond in the Stygian darkness which his eyes could not penetrate. He questioned the snake that rapped upon his chest, but it did not answer him and then he went to the hole in the wall and asked the hole. And he was on the point of becoming angry when it did not reply when his mind suddenly caught itself, and with a shudder he turned away, realizing that this way led to madness and that he must, above all else, remain master of his mind.

But still he did not abandon his speculation; only now he conducted it with reason and sanity, and at last he hit upon a shrewd plan.

When next his food was brought and he had devoured it he took the iron cover from the iron pot, which had contained it, and hurled it to the stone flagging of his cell, where it broke into several pieces. One of these was long and slender and had a sharp point, which was what he had hoped he would find in the debris of the broken cover. This piece he kept; the others he put back into the pot and then he went to the aperture in the wall and commenced to scratch, slowly, slowly, slowly at the hard mortar in which the stones around the hole were set.

He ate and slept many times before his labor was rewarded by the loosening of a single stone next to the hole. And again he

ate and slept many times before a second stone was removed.

How long he worked at this he did not know, but the time passed more quickly now and his mind was so engrossed with his labors that he was almost happy.

During this time he did not neglect his exercising, but he slept less often. When the snakes came he had to stop his work, for they were continually passing in and out through the hole.

He wished that he knew how the food was brought to his cell, that he might know if there was danger that those who brought it could hear him scraping at the mortar in the wall, but as he never heard the food brought he hoped that those who brought it could not hear him and he was quite sure that they could not see him.

And so he worked on unceasingly until at last he had scratched away an opening large enough to admit his body, and then for a long time he sat before it, seeking to assure himself that he was master of his mind, for in this eternal night of solitude that had been his existence for how long he could not even guess, he realized that this adventure which he was facing had assumed such momentous proportions that once more he felt himself upon the brink of madness. And now he wanted to make sure that no matter what lay beyond that aperture he could meet it with calm nerves and a serene and sane mind, for he could not help but realize that keen disappointment might be lying in wait for him, since during all the long periods of his scratching and scraping since he had discovered the hole through which the snakes came into his cell he had realized that a hope of escape was the foundation of the desire that prompted him to prosecute the work. And though he expected to be disappointed he knew how cruel would be the blow when it fell.

With a touch that was almost a caress he let his fingers run slowly over the rough edges of the enlarged aperture. He inserted his head and shoulders into it and reached far out upon the other side, groping with a hand that found nothing, searching with eyes that saw nothing, and then he drew himself back into his dungeon and walked to its far end and sat down upon the floor and leaned back against the wall and waited — waited because he did not dare to pass that aperture to face some new discouragement.

It took him a long time to master himself, and then he waited again. But this time, after reasoned consideration of the matter that filled his mind.

He would wait until they brought his food and had taken away the empty receptacle — that he might be given a longer interval before possible discovery of his absence, in the event he did not return to his cell. And though he went often to the corner where the food was ordinarily deposited, it seemed an eternity before he found it there. And after he had eaten it, another eternity before the receptacle was taken away; but at last it was removed. And once again he crossed his cell and stood before the opening that led he knew not where.

This time he did not hesitate. He was master of his mind and nerves.

One after the other he put his feet through the aperture until he sat with his legs both upon the far side of the wall. Then, turning on his stomach, he started to lower himself, because he did not know where the floor might be, but he found it immediately, on the same level as his own. And an instant later he stood erect and if not free, at least no longer a prisoner within his own cell.

Cautiously he groped about him in the darkness, feeling his way a few inches at a time. This cell, he discovered, was much narrower than his own, but it was very long. By extending his hands in both directions he could touch both walls, and thus he advanced, placing a foot cautiously to feel each step before he took it.

He had brought with him from his cell the iron sliver that he had broken from the cover of the pot and with which he had scratched himself thus far toward freedom. And the possession of this bit of iron imparted to him a certain sense of security, since it meant that he was not entirely unarmed.

Presently, as he advanced, he became convinced that he was in a long corridor. One foot came in contact with a rough substance directly in the center of the tunnel. He took his hands from the walls and groped in front of him.

It was a rough-coated cylinder about eight inches in diameter that rose directly upward from the center of the tunnel, and his fingers quickly told him that it was the trunk of a tree with the bark still on, though worn off in patches.

Passing this column, which he guessed to be a support for a weak section of the roof of the tunnel, he continued on, but he had taken but a couple of steps when he came to a blank wall — the tunnel had come to an abrupt end.

Tanar's heart sank within him. His hopes had been rising with each forward step and now they were suddenly dashed to despair. Again and again his fingers ran over the cold wall that had halted his advance toward hoped for freedom, but there was no sign of break or crevice, and slowly he turned back toward his cell, passing the wooden column and retracing his steps in utter dejection. But as he moved sadly along he mustered all his spiritual forces, determined not to let this expected disappointment crush him. He would go back to his cell, but he would still continue to use the tunnel. It would be a respite from the monotony of his own four walls. It would extend the distance that he might walk and after all he would make it worth the effort that had been necessary to gain ingress to it.

Back in his own cell again he lay down to sleep, for he had denied himself sleep a great deal of late that he might prosecute the work upon which he had been engaged. When he awoke the snakes were with him again and his friend was tapping gently on his chest, and once again he took up the dull monotony of his existence, altered only by regular excursions into his new found domain, the black interior of which he came to know as well as he did his own cell, so that he walked briskly from the hole he had made to the wooden column at the far end of the tunnel, passed around it and walked back again at a brisk gait and with as much assurance as though he could see plainly, for he had counted the paces from one end to the other so many times that he knew to an instant when he had covered the distance from one extremity to the other.

He ate; he slept; he exercised; he played with his slimy, reptilian companion; and he paced the narrow tunnel of his discovery. And often when he passed around the wooden column at its far end, he speculated upon the real purpose of it.

Once he went to sleep in his own cell thinking about it, and when he awoke to the gentle tapping of the snake's snout upon his breast he sat up so suddenly that the reptile fell hissing to the flagging, for clear and sharp upon the threshold of his awakening mind stood an idea — a wonderful idea — why had he not thought of it before?

Excitedly he hastened to the opening leading into the tunnel. Snakes were passing through it, but he fought for precedence with the reptilian horde and tumbled through head first upon a bed of hissing snakes. Scrambling to his feet he almost ran the length of the corridor until his outstretched hands came in contact with the rough bole of the tree. There he stood quite some time, trembling like a leaf, and then, encircling the column with his arms and legs, he started to climb slowly and deliberately aloft. This was the idea that had seized him in its compelling grip upon his awakening.

Upward through the darkness he went, and pausing now and then to grope about with his hands, he found that the tree trunk ran up the center of a narrow, circular shaft.

He climbed slowly upward and at a distance of about thirty feet above the floor of the tunnel, his head struck stone. Feeling upward with one hand he discovered that the tree was set in mortar in the ceiling above him.

This could not be the end! What reason could there be for a tunnel and a shaft that led nowhere? He groped through the darkness in all directions with his hand and he was rewarded by finding an opening in the side of the shaft about six feet below the ceiling. Quitting the bole of the tree he climbed into the opening in the wall of the shaft, and here he found himself in another tunnel, lower and narrower than that at the base of the shaft. It was still dark, so that he was compelled to advance as slowly and with as great caution as he had upon that occasion when he first explored his tunnel below.

He advanced but a short distance when the tunnel turned abruptly to the right, and ahead of him, beyond the turn, he saw a ray of light!

A condemned man snatched from the jaws of death could not have greeted salvation with more joyousness than Tanar of Pellucidar greeted this first slender ray of daylight that he had seen for a seeming

eternity. It shone dimly through a tiny crevice, but it was light, the light of heaven that he had never expected to again behold.

Enraptured, he walked slowly toward it, and as he reached it his hand came in contact with rough, unpainted boards that blocked his way. It was through a tiny crack between two of these boards that the light was filtering.

As dim as the light was it hurt his eyes, so long unaccustomed to light of any kind. But by turning them away so that the light did not shine directly into them, he finally became accustomed to it, and when he did he discovered that as small as the aperture was through which the light came it let in sufficient to dispel the utter darkness of the interior of the tunnel and he also discovered that he could discern objects. He could see the stone walls on either side of the tunnel, and by looking closely he could see the boards that formed the obstacle that barred his further progress. And as he examined them he discovered that at one side there was something that resembled a latch, an invention of which he had been entirely ignorant before he had come aboard the Korsar ship upon which he had been made prisoner, for in Sari there are no locks nor latches.

But he knew the thing for what it was and it told him that the boards before him formed a door, which opened into light and toward liberty, but what lay immediately beyond?

He clinched his ear to the door and listened, but he heard no sound. Then very carefully he examined the latch, experimenting with it until he discovered how to operate it. Steadying his nerves, he pushed gently upon the rough planks. As they swung away from him slowly a flood of light rushed into the first narrow crack, and Tanar covered his eyes with his hands and turned away, realizing that he must become accustomed to the light slowly and gradually, or he might be permanently blinded.

With closed eyes he listened at the crack, but could hear nothing. And then with utmost care he started to accustom his eyes to the light, but it was long before he could stand the full glare that came through even this tiny crack.

When he could stand the light without pain he opened the door a little further and looked out. Just beyond the door lay a fairly large room, in which wicker hampers, iron and earthen receptacles and bundles sewed up in hides littered the floor and were piled high against the walls. Everything seemed covered with dust and cobwebs and there was no sign of a human being about.

Pushing the door open still further Tanar stepped from the tunnel into the apartment and looked about him. Everywhere the room was a litter of bundles and packages with articles of clothing strewn about, together with various fittings for ships, bales of hide and numerous weapons.

The thick coating of dust upon everything suggested to the Sarian that the room had not been visited lately.

For a moment he stood with his hand still on the open door and as he started to step into the room his hand stuck for an instant where he had grasped the rough boards. Looking at his fingers to ascertain the cause he discovered that they were covered with sticky pitch. It was his left hand and when he tried to rub the pitch from it he found that it was almost impossible to do so.

As he moved around the room examining the contents everything that he touched with his left hand stuck to it — it was annoying, but unavoidable.

An inspection of the room revealed several windows along one side and a door at one end.

The door was equipped with a latch similar to that through which he had just passed and which was made to open from the outside with a key, but which could be operated by hand from the inside. It was a very crude and simple affair, and for that Tanar would have been grateful had he known how intricate locks may be made.

Lifting the catch Tanar pushed the door slightly ajar and before him he saw a long corridor, lighted by windows upon one side and with doors opening from it upon the other. As he looked a Korsar came from one of the doorways and, turning, walked down the corridor away from him and a moment later a woman emerged from another doorway, and then he saw other people at the far end of the corridor. Quickly Tanar of Pellucidar closed and latched the door.

Here was no avenue of escape. Were he back in his dark cell he could not have been

cut off more effectually from the outer world than he was in this apartment at the far end of a corridor constantly used by Korsars; for with his smooth face and his naked body, he would be recognized and seized the instant that he stepped from the room. But Tanar was far from being overwhelmed by discouragement. Already he had come much further on the road to escape than he had previously dreamed could be possible and not only this thought heartened him, but even more the effect of daylight, which had for so long been denied him. He had felt his spirit and his courage expand beneath the beneficent influence of the light of the noonday sun, so that he felt ready for any emergency that might confront him.

Turning back once more into the room he searched it carefully for some other avenue of escape. He went to the windows and found that they overlooked the garden of The Cid, but there were many people there, too, in that part of the garden close to the palace. The trees cut off his view of the far end from which he had helped Stellara and Gura to escape, but he guessed that there were few, if any, people there, though to reach it would be a difficult procedure from the windows of this storeroom.

To his left, near the opposite side of the garden, he could see that the trees grew closely together and extended thus apparently the full length of the enclosure.

If those trees had been upon this side of the garden he guessed that he might have found a way to escape; at least as far as the gate in the garden wall close to the barracks, but they were not and so he must abandon thought of them.

There seemed, therefore, no other avenue of escape than the corridor into which he had just looked; nor could he remain indefinitely in this chamber where there was neither food nor water and with a steadily increasing danger that his absence from the dungeon would be discovered when they found that he did not consume the food they brought him.

Seating himself upon a bale of hide Tanar gave himself over to contemplation of his predicament and as he studied the matter his eyes fell upon some of the loose clothing strewn about the room. There he saw the shorts and shirts of Korsar, the gay sashes and head handkerchiefs, the wide topped boots, and with a half smile upon his lips he gathered such of them as he required, shook the dust from them and clothed himself after the manner of a Korsar. He needed no mirror though to know that his smooth face would betray him.

He selected pistols, a dirk and a cutlass, but he could find neither powder nor balls for his firearms.

Thus arrayed and armed he surveyed himself as best he might without a mirror. "If I could keep my back toward all Korsar," he mused, "I might escape with ease for I warrant I look as much a Korsar as any of them from the rear, but unless I can grow bushy whiskers I shall not deceive anyone."

As he sat musing thus he became aware suddenly of voices raised in altercation just outside the door of the storeroom. One was a man's voice; the other a woman's.

"And if you won't have me," growled the man, "I'll take you."

Tanar could not hear the woman's reply, though he heard her speak and knew from her voice that it was a woman.

"What do I care for The Cid?" cried the man. "I am as powerful in Korsar as he. I could take the throne and be Cid myself, if I chose."

Again Tanar heard the woman speak.

"If you do I'll choke the wind out of you," threatened the man. "Come in here where we can talk better. Then you can yell all you want for no one can hear you."

Tanar heard the man insert a key in the lock and as he did so the Pellucidarian sought a hiding place behind a pile of wicker hampers.

"And after you get out of this room," continued the man, "there will be nothing left for you to yell about."

"I have told you right along," said the woman, "that I would rather kill myself than mate with you, but if you take me by force I shall still kill myself, but I shall kill you first."

The heart of Tanar of Pellucidar leaped in his breast when he heard that voice. His fingers closed upon the hilt of the cutlass at his side, and as Bulf voiced a sneering laugh in answer to the girl's threat, the Sarian leaped from his concealment, a naked blade shining in his right hand.

At the sound behind him Bulf wheeled about and for an instant he did not recognize the Sarian in the Korsar garb, but

Stellara did and she voiced a cry of mingled surprise and joy.

"Tanar!" she cried. "My Tanar!"

As the Sarian rushed him Bulf fell back, drawing his cutlass as he retreated. Tanar saw that he was making for the door leading into the corridor and he rushed at the man to engage him before he could escape, so that Bulf was forced to stand and defend himself.

"Stand back," cried Bulf, "or you shall die for this," but Tanar of Pellucidar only laughed in his face, as he swung a wicked blow at the man's head, which Bulf but barely parried, and then they were at one another like two wild beasts.

Tanar drew first blood from a slight gash in Bulf's shoulder and then the fellow yelled for help.

"You said that no one could hear Stellara's cries for help from this apartment," taunted Tanar, "so why do you think that they can hear yours?"

"Let me out of here," cried Bulf. "Let me out and I will give you your freedom." But Tanar rushed him into a corner and the sharp edge of his cutlass sheared an ear from Bulf's head.

"Help!" shrieked the Korsar. "Help! It is Bulf. The Sarian is killing me."

Fearful that his loud cries might reach the corridor beyond and attract attention, Tanar increased the fury of his assault. He beat down the Korsar's guard. He swung his cutlass in one terrible circle that clove Bulf's ugly skull to the bridge of his nose, and with a gurgling gasp the great brute lunged forward upon his face. And Tanar of Pellucidar turned and took Stellara in his arms.

"Thank God," he said, "that I was in time."

"It must have been God Himself who led you to this room," said the girl. "I thought you dead. They told me that you were dead."

"No," said Tanar. "They put me in a dark dungeon beneath the palace, where I was condemned to remain for life."

"And you have been so near me all this time," said Stellara, "and I thought that you were dead."

"For a long time I thought that I was worse than dead," replied the man. "Darkness, solitude and silence — God! That is worse than death."

"And yet you escaped!" The girl's voice

was filled with awe.

"It was because of you that I escaped," said Tanar. "Thoughts of you kept me from going mad — thought and hope urged me on to seek some avenue of escape. Never again as long as life is in me shall I feel that there can be any situation that is entirely hopeless after what I have passed through."

Stellara shook her head. "Your hope will have to be strong, dear heart, against the discouragement that you must face in seeking a way out of the palace of The Cid and the city of Korsar."

"I have come this far," replied Tanar. "Already have I achieved the impossible. Why should I doubt my ability to wrest freedom for you and for me from whatever fate holds in store for us?"

"You cannot pass them with that smooth face, Tanar," said the girl, sadly. "Ah, if you only had Bulf's whiskers," and she glanced down at the corpse of the fallen man.

Tanar turned, too, and looked down at Bulf, where he lay in a pool of blood upon the floor. And then quickly he faced Stellara. "Why not?" he cried. "Why not?"

Chapter XVII

DOWN TO THE SEA

"What do you mean?" demanded Stellara.

"Wait and you shall see," replied Tanar, and drawing his dirk he stooped and turned Bulf over upon his back. Then with the razor-sharp blade of his weapon he commenced to hack off the bushy, black beard of the dead Korsar, while Stellara looked on in questioning wonder.

Spreading Bulf's headcloth flat upon the floor, Tanar deposited upon it the hair that he cut from the man's face, and when he had completed his grewsome tonsorial effort he folded the hair into the handkerchief, and, rising, motioned for Stellara to follow him.

Going to the door that led into the tunnel through which he had escaped from the dungeon, Tanar opened it, and, smearing his fingers with the pitch that exuded from the boards upon the inside of the door, he smeared some of it upon the side of his face and then turned to Stellara.

"Put this hair upon my face in as natural a way as you can. You have lived among them all your life, so you should know well how a Korsar's beard should look."

Horrible as the plan seemed and though she shrank from touching the hair of the dead man, Stellara steeled herself and did as Tanar bid. Little by little, patch by patch, Tanar applied pitch to his face and Stellara placed the hair upon it until presently only the eyes and nose of the Sarian remained exposed. The expression of the former were altered by increasing the size and bushiness of the eyebrows with shreds of Bulf's beard that had been left over, and then Tanar smeared his nose with some of Bulf's blood, for many of the Korsars had large, red noses. Then Stellara stood away and surveyed him critically. "Your own mother would not know you," she said.

"Do you think I can pass as a Korsar?" he asked.

"No one will suspect, unless they question you closely as you leave the palace."

"We are going together," said Tanar.

"But how?" asked Stellara.

"I have been thinking of another plan," he said. "I noticed when I was living in the barracks that sailors going toward the river had no difficulty in passing through the gate leaving the palace. In fact, it is always much easier to leave the palace than to enter it. On many occasions I have heard them say merely that they were going to their ships. We can do the same."

"Do I look like a Korsar sailor?" demanded Stellara.

"You will when I get through with you," said Tanar, with a grin.

"What do you mean?"

"There is Korsar clothing here," said Tanar; "enough to outfit a dozen and there is still plenty of hair on Bulf's head."

The girl drew back with a shudder. "Oh, Tanar! You cannot mean that."

"What other way is there?" he demanded. "If we can escape together is it not worth any price that we might have to pay?"

"You are right," she said. "I will do it."

When Tanar completed his work upon her, Stellara had been transformed into a bearded Korsar, but the best that he could do in the way of disguise failed to entirely hide the contours of her hips and breasts.

"I am afraid they will suspect," he said. "Your figure is too feminine for shorts and a shirt to hide it."

"Wait," exclaimed Stellara. "Sometimes

the sailors, when they are going on long voyages, wear cloaks, which they use to sleep in if the nights are cool. Let us see if we can find such a one here."

"Yes, I saw one," replied Tanar, and crossing the room he returned with a cloak made of wide striped goods. "That will give you greater height," he said. But when they draped it about her, her hips were still too much in evidence.

"Build out my shoulders," suggested Stellara, and with scarfs and handkerchiefs the Sarian built the girl's shoulders out so that the cloak hung straight and she resembled a short, stocky man, more than a slender, well-formed girl.

"Now we are ready," said the Sarian. Stellara pointed to the body of Bulf.

"We cannot leave that lying there," she said. "Someone may come to this room and discover it and when they do every man in the palace — yes, even in the entire city — will be arrested and questioned."

Tanar looked about the room and then he seized the corpse of Bulf and dragged it into a far corner, after which he piled bundles of hides and baskets upon it until it was entirely concealed, and over the blood stains upon the floor he dragged other bales and baskets until all signs of the duel had been erased or hidden.

"And now," he said, "is as good a time as another to put our disguises to the test." Together they approached the door. "You know the least frequented passages to the garden," said Tanar. "Let us make our way from the palace through the garden to the gate that gave us escape before."

"Then follow me," replied Stellara, as Tanar opened the door and the two stepped out into the corridor beyond. It was empty. Tanar closed the door behind him, and Stellara led the way down the passage.

They had proceeded but a short distance when they heard a man's voice in an apartment to the left.

"Where is she?" he demanded.

"I do not know," replied a woman's voice. "She was here but a moment ago and Bulf was with her."

"Find them and lose no time about it," commanded the man, sternly. And he stepped from the apartment just as Tanar and Stellara were approaching.

It was The Cid. Stellara's heart stopped beating as the Korsar ruler looked into the faces of Tanar and herself.

"Who are you?" demanded The Cid.

"We are sailors," said Tanar, quickly, before Stellara could reply.

"What are you doing here in my palace?" demanded the Korsar ruler.

"We were sent here with packages to the storeroom," replied Tanar, "and we are but now returning to our ship."

"Well, be quick about it. I do not like your looks," growled The Cid as he stamped off down the corridor ahead of them.

Tanar saw Stellara sway and he stepped to her side and supported her, but she quickly gained possession of herself, and an instant later turned to the right and led Tanar through a doorway into the garden.

"God!" whispered the man, as they walked side by side after quitting the building. "If The Cid did not know you, then your disguise must be perfect."

Stellara shook her head for even as yet she could not control her voice to speak, following the terror induced by her encounter with The Cid.

There were a number of men and women in the garden close to the palace. Some of these scrutinized them casually, but they passed by in safety and a moment later the gravel walk they were following wound through dense shrubbery that hid them from view and then they were at the doorway in the garden wall.

Again fortune favored them here and they passed out into the barracks yards without being noticed.

Electing to try the main gate because of the greater number of people who passed to and fro through it, Tanar turned to the right, passed along the full length of the barracks past a dozen men and approached the gate with Stellara at his side.

They were almost through when a stupid looking Korsar soldier stopped them. "Who are you," he demanded, "and what business takes you from the palace?"

"We are sailors," replied Tanar. "We are going to our ship."

"What were you doing in the palace?" demanded the man.

"We took packages there from the captain of the ship to The Cid's storeroom," explained the Sarian.

"I do not like the looks of you," said the man. "I have never seen either one of you before."

"We have been away upon a long cruise," replied Tanar.

"Wait here until the captain of the gate

returns," said the man. "He will wish to question you."

The Sarian's heart sank. "If we are late in returning to our ship, we shall be punished," said he.

"That is nothing to me," replied the soldier.

Stellara reached inside her cloak and beneath the man's shorts that covered her own apparel and searched until she found a pouch that was attached to her girdle. From this she drew something which she slipped into Tanar's hands. He understood immediately, and stepping close to the soldier he pressed two pieces of gold into the fellow's palm. "It will go very hard with us if we are late," he said.

The man felt the cool gold within his palm. "Very well," he said, gruffly, "go on about your business, and be quick about it."

Without waiting for a second invitation Tanar and Stellara merged with the crowd upon the Korsar street. Nor did either speak, and it is possible that Stellara did not even breathe until they had left the palace gate well behind.

"And where now?" she asked at last.

"We are going to sea," replied the man.

"In a Korsar ship?" she demanded.

"In a Korsar boat," he replied. "We are going fishing."

Along the banks of the river were moored many craft, but when Tanar saw how many men were on or around them he realized that the plan he had chosen, which contemplated stealing a fishing boat, most probably would end disastrously, and he explained his doubts to Stellara.

"We could never do it," she said. "Stealing a boat is considered the most heinous crime that one can commit in Korsar, and if the owner of a boat is not aboard it you may rest assured that some of his friends are watching it for him, even though there is little likelihood that anyone will attempt to steal it since the penalty is death."

Tanar shook his head. "Then we shall have to risk passing through the entire city of Korsar," he said, "and going out into the open country without any reasonable excuse in the event that we are questioned."

"We might buy a boat," suggested Stellara.

"I have no money," said Tanar.

"I have," replied the girl. "The Cid has always kept me well supplied with gold."

Once more she reached into her pouch and drew forth a handful of gold pieces. "Here," she said, "take these. If they are not enough you can ask me for more, but I think that you can buy a boat for half that sum."

Questioning the first man that he approached at the river side, Tanar learned that there was a small fishing boat for sale a short way down the river, and it was not long before they had found its owner and consummated the purchase.

As they pushed off into the current and floated down stream, Tanar became conscious of a sudden conviction that his escape from Korsar had been effected too easily; that there must be something wrong, that either he was dreaming or else disaster and recapture lay just ahead.

Borne down toward the sea by the slow current of the river, Tanar wielded a single oar, paddlewise from the stern, to keep the boat out in the channel and its bow in the right direction, for he did not wish to make sail under the eyes of Korsar sailors and fishermen, as he was well aware that he could not do so without attracting attention by his bungling to his evident inexperience and thus casting suspicion upon them.

Slowly the boat drew away from the city and from the Korsar raiders anchored in mid-stream and then, at last, he felt that it would be safe to hoist the sail and take advantage of the land breeze that was blowing.

With Stellara's assistance the canvas was spread and as it bellied to the wind the craft bore forward with accelerated speed, and then behind them they heard shouts, and, turning, saw three boats speeding toward them.

Across the waters came commands for them to lay to.

The pursuing boats, which had set out under sail and had already acquired considerable momentum, appeared to be rapidly overhauling the smaller craft. But presently, as the speed of the latter increased, the distance between them seemed not to vary.

The shouts of the pursuers had attracted the attention of the sailors on board the anchored raiders, and presently Tanar and Stellara heard the deep boom of a cannon and a heavy shot struck the water just off their starboard bow.

Tanar shook his head. "That is too

close," he said. "I had better come about."

"Why?" demanded Stellara.

"I do not mind risking capture," he said, "because in that event no harm will befall you when they discover your identity, but I cannot risk the cannon shots for if one of them strikes us, you will be killed."

"Do not come about," cried the girl. "I would rather die here with you than be captured, for capture would mean death for you and then I should not care to live. Keep on, Tanar, we may outdistance them yet. And as for their cannon shots, a small, moving boat like this is a difficult target and their marksmanship is none too good."

Again the cannon boomed and this time the ball passed over them and struck the water just beyond.

"They are getting our range," said Tanar.

The girl moved close to his side, where he sat by the tiller. "Put your arm around me, Tanar," she said. "If we must die, let us die together."

The Sarian encircled her with his free arm and drew her close to him, and an instant later there was a terrific explosion from the direction of the raider that had been firing on them. Turning quickly toward the ship, they saw what had happened — an overcharged cannon had exploded.

"They were too anxious," said Tanar.

It was some time before another shot was fired and this one fell far astern, but the pursuing boats were clinging tenaciously to their wake.

"They are not gaining," said Stellara.

"No," said Tanar, "and neither are we."

"But I think we shall after we reach the open sea," said the girl. "We shall get more wind there and this boat is lighter and speedier than theirs. Fate smiled upon us when it led us to this boat rather than to a larger one."

As they approached the sea their pursuers, evidently fearing precisely what Stellara had suggested, opened fire upon them with harquebuses and pistols. Occasionally a missile would come dangerously close, but the range was just a little too great for their primitive weapons and poor powder.

On they sailed out into the open Korsar Az, which stretched onward and upward into the concealing mist of the distance. Upon their left the sea ran inward forming a great bay, while almost directly ahead of them, though at so great a distance that it was barely discernible, rose the dim outlines of a headland, and toward this Tanar held his course.

The chase had settled down into a dogged test of endurance. It was evident that the Korsars had no intention of giving up their prey even though the pursuit led to the opposite shore of the Korsar Az, and it was equally evident that Tanar entertained no thought of surrender.

On and on they sped, the pursued and the pursuers. Slowly the headland took shape before them, and later a great forest was visible to the left of it — a forest that ran down almost to the sea.

"You are making for land?" said Stellara.

"Yes," replied the Sarian. "We have neither food nor water and if we had I am not sufficiently a sailor to risk navigating this craft across the Korsar Az."

"But if we take to the land, they will be able to trail us," said the girl.

"You forget the trees, Stellara," the man reminded her.

"Yes, the trees," she cried. "I had forgotten. If we can reach the trees I believe that we shall be safe."

As they approached the shore inside the headland, they saw great combing rollers breaking among the rocks and the angry, sullen boom of the sea came back to their ears.

"No boat can live in that," said Stellara.

Tanar glanced up and down the shoreline as far as he could see and then he turned and let his eyes rest sadly upon his companion.

"It looks hopeless," he said. "If we had time to make the search we might find a safer landing place, but within sight of us one place seems to be as good as another."

"Or as bad," said Stellara.

"It cannot be helped," said the Sarian. "To beat back now around that promontory in an attempt to gain the open sea again, would so delay us that we should be overtaken and captured. We must take our chances in the surf, or turn about and give up."

Behind them their pursuers had come about and were waiting, rising and falling upon the great billows.

"They think that they have us," said Stellara. "They believe that we shall tack here and make a run for the open sea around the end of that promontory, and they are ready to head us off."

Tanar held the boat's nose straight for the shore-line. Beyond the angry surf he could see a sandy beach, but between lay a barrier of rock upon which the waves broke, hurling their spume far into the air.

"Look!" exclaimed Stellara, as the boat raced toward the smother of boiling water. "Look! There! Right ahead! There may be a way yet!"

"I have been watching that place," said Tanar. "I have been holding her straight for it, and if it is a break in the rocky wall we shall soon know it, and if it is not ———"

The Sarian glanced back in the direction of the Korsars' boats and saw that they were again in pursuit, for by this time it must have become evident to them that their quarry was throwing itself upon the rocky shore-line in desperation rather than to risk capture by turning again toward the open sea.

Every inch of sail was spread upon the little craft and the taut, bellowing canvas strained upon the cordage until it hummed, as the boat sped straight for the rocks dead ahead.

Tanar and Stellara crouched in the stern, the man's left arm pressing the girl protectingly to his side. With grim fascination they watched the bow-sprit rise and fall as it rushed straight toward what seemed must be inevitable disaster.

They were there! The sea lifted them high in the air and launched them forward upon the rocks. To the right a jagged finger of granite broke through the smother of spume. To the left the sleek, water-worn side of a huge boulder revealed itself for an instant as they sped past. The boat grated and rasped upon a sunken rock, slid over and raced toward the sandy beach.

Tanar whipped out his dirk and slashed the halyards, bringing the sail down as the boat's keel touched the sand. Then, seizing Stellara in his arms, he leaped into the shallow water and hastened up the shore.

Pausing, they looked back toward the pursuing Korsars and to their astonishment saw that all three boats were making swiftly toward the rocky shore.

"They dare not go back without us," said Stellara, "or they would never risk that surf."

"The Cid must have guessed our identity, then, when a search failed to reveal you," said Tanar.

"It may also be that they discovered your absence from the dungeon, and coupling this with the fact that I, too, was missing, someone guessed the identity of the two sailors who sought to pass through the gate and who paid gold for a small boat at the river," suggested Stellara.

"There goes one of them on the rocks," cried Tanar, as the leading boat disappeared in a smother of water.

The second boat shared the same fate as its predecessor, but the third rode through the same opening that had carried Tanar and Stellara to the safety of the beach and as it did the two fugitives turned and ran toward the forest.

Behind them raced a dozen Korsars and amidst the crack of pistols and harquebuses Tanar and Stellara disappeared within the dark shadows of the primeval forest.

The story of their long and arduous journey through unknown lands to the kingdom of Sari would be replete with interest, excitement and adventure, but it is no part of this story.

It is enough to say that they arrived at Sari shortly before Ja and Gura made their appearance, the latter having been delayed by adventures that had almost cost them their lives.

The people of Sari welcomed the Amiocapian mate that the son of Ghak had brought back to his own country. And Gura they accepted, too, because she had befriended Tanar, though the young men accepted her for herself and many were the trophies that were laid before the hut of the beautiful Himean maiden. But she repulsed them all for in her heart she held a secret love that she had never divulged, but which, perhaps, Stellara had guessed and which may have accounted for the tender solicitude which the Amiocapian maid revealed for her Himean sister.

CONCLUSION

As Perry neared the end of the story of Tanar of Pellucidar, the sending became weaker and weaker until it died out entirely, and Jason Gridley could hear no more.

He turned to me. "I think Perry had something more to say," he said. "He was trying to tell us something. He was trying to ask something."

"Jason," I said, reproachfully, "didn't you tell me that the story of the inner world is perfectly ridiculous; that there could be no such place peopled by strange reptiles and men of the stone age? Didn't you insist that there is no Emperor of Pellucidar?"

"Tut-tut," he said. "I apologize. I am sorry. But that is past. The question now is what can we do."

"About what?" I asked.

"Do you not realize that David Innes lies a prisoner in a dark dungeon beneath the palace of The Cid of Korsar?" he demanded with more excitement than I have ever known Jason Gridley to exhibit.

"Well, what of it?" I demanded. "I am sorry, of course; but what in the world can we do to help him?"

"We can do a lot," said Jason Gridley, determinedly.

I must confess that as I looked at him I felt considerable solicitude for the state of his mind for he was evidently laboring under great excitement.

"Think of it!" he cried. "Think of that poor devil buried there in utter darkness, silence, solitude — and with those snakes! God!" he shuddered. "Snakes crawling all over him, winding about his arms and his legs and his body, creeping across his face as he sleeps, and nothing else to break the monotony — no human voice, the song of no bird, no ray of sunlight. Something must be done. He must be saved."

"But who is going to do it?" I asked.

"I am!" replied Jason Gridley.

THE END

THE CHESSMEN OF MARS

Prelude
JOHN CARTER COMES TO EARTH

Shea had just beaten me at chess, as usual, and, also as usual, I had gleaned what questionable satisfaction I might by twitting him with this indication of failing mentality by calling his attention for the nth time to that theory, propounded by certain scientists, which is based upon the assertion that phenomenal chess players are always found to be from the ranks of children under twelve, adults over seventy-two or the mentally defective — a theory that is lightly ignored upon those rare occasions that I win. Shea had gone to bed and I should have followed suit, for we are always in the saddle here before sunrise; but instead I sat there before the chess table in the library, idly blowing smoke at the dishonored head of my defeated king.

While thus profitably employed I heard the east door of the living-room open and someone enter. I thought it was Shea returning to speak with me on some matter of tomorrow's work; but when I raised my eyes to the doorway that connects the two rooms I saw framed there the figure of a bronzed giant, his otherwise naked body trapped with jewel-encrusted harness from which there hung at one side an ornate short-sword and at the other a pistol of strange pattern. The black hair, the steel-gray eyes, brave and smiling, the noble features — I recognized them at once, and leaping to my feet I advanced with outstretched hand.

"John Carter!" I cried. "You?"

"None other, my son," he replied, taking my hand in one of his and placing the other upon my shoulder.

"And what are you doing here?" I asked. "It has been long years since you revisited Earth, and never before in the trappings of Mars. Lord! but it is good to see you — and not a day older in appearance than when you trotted me on your knee in my babyhood. How do you explain it, John Carter, Warlord of Mars, or do you try to explain it?"

"Why attempt to explain the inexplicable?" he replied. "As I have told you before, I am a very old man. I do not know how old I am. I recall no childhood; but recollect only having been always as you see me now and as you saw me first when you were five years old. You, yourself, have aged, though not as much as most men in a corresponding number of years, which may be accounted for by the fact that the same blood runs in our veins; but I have not aged at all. I have discussed the question with a noted Martian scientist, a friend of mine; but his theories are still only theories. However, I am content with the fact — I never age, and I love life and the vigor of youth.

"And now as to your natural question as to what brings me to Earth again and in this, to earthly eyes, strange habiliment. We may thank Kar Komak, the bowman of Lothar. It was he who gave me the idea upon which I have been experimenting until at last I have achieved success. As you know I have long possessed the power to cross the void in spirit, but never before have I been able to impart to inanimate things a similar power. Now, however, you see me for the first time precisely as my Martian fellows see me — you see the very short-sword that has tasted the blood of many a savage foeman; the harness with the devices of Helium and the insignia of my rank; the pistol that was presented to me by Tars Tarkas, Jeddak of Thark.

"Aside from seeing you, which is my principal reason for being here, and satisfying myself that I can transport inanimate things from Mars to Earth, and therefore animate things if I so desire, I have no purpose. Earth is not for me. My every interest is upon Barsoom — my wife, my children, my work; all are there. I will spend a quiet evening with you and then back to the world I love even better than I love life."

As he spoke he dropped into the chair upon the opposite side of the chess table.

"You spoke of children," I said. "Have you more than Carthoris?"

"A daughter," he replied, "only a little younger than Carthoris, and, barring one, the fairest thing that ever breathed the thin air of dying Mars. Only Dejah Thoris, her mother, could be more beautiful than Tara of Helium."

For a moment he fingered the chessmen idly. "We have a game on Mars similar to chess," he said, "very similar. And there is a race there that plays it grimly with men and naked swords. We call the game *jetan*. It is played on a board like yours, except that there are a hundred squares and we use twenty pieces on each side. I never see it played without thinking of Tara of Helium and what befell her among the chessmen of Barsoom. Would you like to hear her story?"

I said that I would and so he told it to me, and now I shall try to re-tell it for you as nearly in the words of The Warlord of Mars as I can recall them, but in the third person. If there be inconsistencies and errors, let the blame fall not upon John Carter, but rather upon my faulty memory, where it belongs. It is a strange tale and utterly Barsoomian.

Chapter I
TARA IN A TANTRUM

Tara of Helium rose from the pile of silks and soft furs upon which she had been reclining, stretched her lithe body lanquidly, and crossed toward the center of the room, where, above a large table a bronze disc depended from the low ceiling. Her carriage was that of health and physical perfection — the effortless harmony of faultless coordination. A scarf of silken gossamer crossing over one shoulder was wrapped about her body; her black hair was piled high upon her head. With a wooden stick she tapped upon the bronze disc, lightly, and presently the summons was answered by a slave girl, who entered, smiling, to be greeted similarly by her mistress.

"Are my father's guests arriving?" asked the princess.

"Yes, Tara of Helium, they come," replied the slave. "I have seen Kantos Kan, Overlord of the Navy, and Prince Soran of Ptarth, and Djor Kantos, son of Kantos Kan," she shot a roguish glance at her mistress as she mentioned Djor Kantos' name, "and — oh, there were others, many have come."

"The bath, then, Uthia," said her mistress. "And why, Uthia," she added, "do you look thus and smile when you mention the name of Djor Kantos?"

The slave girl laughed gaily. "It is so plain to all that he worships you," she replied.

"It is not plain to me," said Tara of Helium. "He is the friend of my brother, Carthoris, and so he is here much; but not to see me. It is his friendship for Carthoris that brings him thus often to the palace of my father."

"But Carthoris is hunting in the north with Talu, Jeddak of Okar," Uthia reminded her.

"My bath, Uthia!" cried Tara of Helium. "That tongue of yours will bring you to some misadventure yet."

"The bath is ready, Tara of Helium," the girl responded, her eyes still twinkling with merriment, for she well knew that in the heart of her mistress was no anger that could displace the love of the princess for her slave. Preceding the daughter of The Warlord she opened the door of an adjoining room where lay the bath — a gleaming pool of scented water in a marble basin. Golden stanchions supported a chain of gold encircling it and leading down into the water on either side of marble steps. A glass dome let in the sunlight, which flooded the interior, glancing from the polished white of the marble walls and the procession of bathers and fishes, which, in conventional design, were inlaid with gold in a broad band that circled the room.

Tara of Helium removed the scarf from about her and handed it to the slave. Slowly she descended the steps to the water, the temperature of which she tested with a symmetrical foot, undeformed by tight shoes and high heels — a lovely foot, as God intended that feet should be and seldom are. Finding the water to her liking, the girl swam leisurely to and fro about the pool. With the silken ease of the seal she swam, now at the surface now below, her smooth muscles rolling softly beneath her clear skin — a wordless song of health and happiness and grace. Presently she emerged and gave herself into the hands of the slave girl, who rubbed the body of her mistress with a sweet smelling semi-liquid substance contained in a golden urn, until the glowing skin was covered with a foamy lather, then a quick plunge into the pool, a drying with soft towels, and the bath was over. Typical of the life of the princess was the simple elegance of her bath — no retinue of useless slaves, no pomp, no idle waste of precious moments. In another half hour her hair was dried and built into the strange, but becoming, coiffure of her station; her leathern trappings, encrusted with gold and jewels, had been adjusted to her figure and she was ready to mingle with the guests that had been bidden to the midday function at the palace of The Warlord.

As she left her apartments to make her

way to the gardens where the guests were congregating, two warriors, the insignia of the House of the Prince of Helium upon their harness, followed a few paces behind her, grim reminders that the assassin's blade may never be ignored upon Barsoom, where, in a measure, it counterbalances the great natural span of human life, which is estimated at not less than a thousand years.

As they neared the entrance to the garden another woman, similarly guarded, approached them from another quarter of the great palace. As she neared them Tara of Helium turned toward her with a smile and a happy greeting, while her guards knelt with bowed heads in willing and voluntary adoration of the beloved of Helium. Thus always, solely at the command of their own hearts, did the warriors of Helium greet Dejah Thoris, whose deathless beauty had more than once brought them to bloody warfare with other nations of Barsoom. So great was the love of the people of Helium for the mate of John Carter is amounted practically to worship, as though she were indeed the goddess that she looked.

The mother and daughter exchanged the gentle, Barsoomian, "kaor" of greeting and kissed. Then together they entered the gardens where the guests were. A huge warrior drew his short-sword and struck his metal shield with the flat of it, the brazen sound ringing out above the laughter and the speech.

"The Princess comes!" he cried. "Dejah Thoris! Thy Princess comes! Tara of Helium!" Thus always is royalty announced. The guests arose; the two women inclined their heads; the guards fell back upon either side of the entrance-way; a number of nobles advanced to pay their respects; the laughing and the talking were resumed and Dejah Thoris and her daughter moved simply and naturally among their guests, no suggestion of differing rank apparent in the bearing of any who were there, though there was more than a single Jeddak and many common warriors whose only title lay in brave deeds, or noble patriotism. Thus it is upon Mars where men are judged upon their own merits rather than upon those of their grandsires, even though pride of lineage be great.

Tara of Helium let her slow gaze wander among the throng of guests until presently it halted upon one she sought. Was the faint shadow of a frown that crossed her brow an indication of displeasure at the sight that met her eyes, or did the brilliant rays of the noonday sun distress her? Who may say! She had been reared to believe that one day she should wed Djor Kantos, son of her father's best friend. It had been the dearest wish of Kantos Kan and The Warlord that this should be, and Tara of Helium had accepted it as a matter of all but accomplished fact. Djor Kantos had seemed to accept the matter in the same way. They had spoken of it casually as something that would, as a matter of course, take place in the indefinite future, as, for instance, his promotion in the navy, in which he was now a padwar; or the set functions of the court of her grandfather, Tardos Mors, Jeddak of Helium; or Death. They had never spoken of love and that had puzzled Tara of Helium upon the rare occasions she gave it thought, for she knew that people who were to wed were usually much occupied with the matter of love and she had all of a woman's curiosity — she wondered what love was like. She was very fond of Djor Kantos and she knew that he was very fond of her. They liked to be together, for they liked the same things and the same people and the same books and their dancing was a joy, not only to themselves but to those who watched them. She could not imagine wanting to marry anyone other than Djor Kantos.

So perhaps it was only the sun that made her brows contract just the tiniest bit at the same instant that she discovered Djor Kantos sitting in earnest conversation with Olvia Marthis, daughter of the Jed of Hastor. It was Djor Kantos' duty immediately to pay his respects to Dejah Thoris and Tara of Helium; but he did not do so and presently the daughter of The Warlord frowned indeed. She looked long at Olvia Marthis, and though she had seen her many times before and knew her well, she looked at her today through new eyes that saw, apparently for the first time, that the girl from Hastor was noticeably beautiful even among those other beautiful women of Helium. Tara of Helium was disturbed. She attempted to analyze her emotions; but found it difficult. Olvia Marthis was her friend — she was very fond of her and she felt no anger toward her. Was she angry with Djor Kantos? No, she finally de-

"The Princess Comes! Dejah Thoris!
The Princess Comes!"

cided that she was not. It was merely surprise, then, that she felt — surprise that Djor Kantos could be more interested in another than in herself. She was about to cross the garden and join them when she heard her father's voice directly behind her.

"Tara of Helium!" he called, and she turned to see him approaching with a strange warrior whose harness and metal bore devices with which she was unfamiliar. Even among the gorgeous trappings of the men of Helium and the visitors from distant empires those of the stranger were remarkable for their barbaric splendor. The leather of his harness was completely hidden beneath ornaments of platinum thickly set with brilliant diamonds, as were the scabbards of his swords and the ornate holster that held his long, Martian pistol. Moving through the sunlit garden at the side of the great Warlord, the scintillant rays of his countless gems enveloping him as in an aureole of light imparted to his noble figure a suggestion of godliness.

"Tara of Helium, I bring you Gahan, Jed of Gathol," said John Carter, after the simple Barsoomian custom of presentation.

"Kaor! Gahan, Jed of Gathol," returned Tara of Helium.

"My sword is at your feet, Tara of Helium," said the young chieftain.

The Warlord left them and the two seated themselves upon an ersite bench beneath a spreading sorapus tree.

"Far Gathol," mused the girl. "Ever in my mind has it been connected with mystery and romance and the half-forgotten lore of the ancients. I cannot think of Gathol as existing today, possibly because I have never before seen a Gatholian."

"And perhaps too because of the great distance that separates Helium and Gathol, as well as the comparative insignificance of my little free city, which might easily be lost in one corner of mighty Helium," added Gahan. "But what we lack in power we make up in pride," he continued, laughing. "We believe ours the oldest inhabited city upon Barsoom. It is one of the few that has retained its freedom, and this despite the fact that its ancient diamond mines are the richest known and, unlike practically all the other fields, are today apparently as inexhaustible as ever."

"Tell me of Gathol," urged the girl. "The very thought fills me with interest," nor was it likely that the handsome face of the young jed detracted anything from the glamour of far Gathol.

Nor did Gahan seem displeased with the excuse for further monopolizing the society of his fair companion. His eyes seemed chained to her exquisite features, from which they moved no further than to a rounded breast, part hid beneath its jeweled covering, a naked shoulder or the symmetry of a perfect arm, resplendent in bracelets of barbaric magnificence.

"Your ancient history has doubtless told you that Gathol was built upon an island in Throxeus, mightiest of the five oceans of old Barsoom. As the ocean receded Gathol crept down the sides of the mountain, the summit of which was the island upon which she had been built, until today she covers the slopes from summit to base, while the bowels of the great hill are honeycombed with the galleries of her mines. Entirely surrounding us is a great salt marsh, which protects us from invasion by land, while the rugged and ofttimes vertical topography of our mountain renders the land of hostile airships a precarious undertaking."

"That, and your brave warriors?" suggested the girl.

Gahan smiled. "We do not speak of that except to enemies," he said, "and then with tongues of steel rather than of flesh."

"But with practice in the art of war has a people which nature has thus protected from attack?" asked Tara of Helium, who had liked the young jed's answer to her previous question, but yet in whose mind persisted a vague conviction of the possible effeminacy of her companion, induced, doubtless, by the magnificence of his trappings and weapons which carried a suggestion of splendid show rather than grim utility.

"Our natural barriers, while they have doubtless saved us from defeat on countless occasions, have not by any means rendered us immune from attack," he explained, "for so great is the wealth of Gathol's diamond treasury that there yet may be found those who will risk almost certain defeat in an effort to loot our unconquered city; so thus we find occasional practice in the exercise of arms; but there is more to Gathol than the mountain city. My country extends from Polodona (Equator) north ten karads and from the tenth karad west of Horz to the twentieth west, including thus a million square haads, the greater proportion of which is fine grazing land where run our great herds of thoats and zitidars.

"Surrounded as we are by predatory enemies our herdsmen must indeed be warriors or we should have no herds, and you may be assured they get plenty of fighting. Then there is our constant need of workers in the mines. The Gatholians consider themselves a race of warriors and as such prefer not to labor in the mines. The law is, however, that each male Gatholian shall give an hour a day in labor to the government. That is practically the only tax that is levied upon them. They prefer however, to furnish a substitute to perform this labor, and as our own people will not hire out for labor in the mines it has been necessary to obtain slaves, and I do not need to tell you that slaves are not won without fighting. We sell these slaves in the public market, the proceeds going, half and half, to the government and the warriors who bring them in. The purchasers are credited with the amount of labor performed by their particular slaves. At the end of a year a good slave will have performed the labor tax of his master for six years, and if slaves are plentiful he is freed and permitted to return to his own people."

"You fight in platinum and diamonds?" asked Tara, indicating his gorgeous trappings with a quizzical smile.

Gahan laughed. "We are a vain people," he admitted, good-naturedly, "and it is possible that we place too much value on personal appearances. We vie with one another in the splendor of our accoutrements when trapped for the observance of the lighter duties of life, though when we take the field our leather is the plainest I ever have seen worn by fighting men of Barsoom. We pride ourselves, too, upon our physical beauty, and especially upon the beauty of our women. May I dare to say, Tara of Helium, that I am hoping for the day when you will visit Gathol that my people may see one who is really beautiful?"

"The women of Helium are taught to frown with displeasure upon the tongue of the flatterer," rejoined the girl, but Gahan, Jed of Gathol, observed that she smiled as she said it.

A bugle sounded, clear and sweet, above the laughter and the talk. "The Dance of Barsoom!" exclaimed the young warrior. "I claim you for it, Tara of Helium."

The girl glanced in the direction of the bench where she had last seen Djor Kantos. He was not in sight. She inclined her head in assent to the claim of the Gatholian. Slaves were passing among the guests, distributing small musical instruments of a single string. Upon each instrument were characters which indicated the pitch and length of its tone. The instruments were of skeel, the string of gut, and were shaped to fit the left forearm of the dancer, to which it was strapped. There was also a ring wound with gut which was worn between the first and second joints of the index finger of the right hand and which, when passed over the string of the instrument, elicited the single note required of the dancer.

The guests had risen and were slowly making their way toward the expanse of scarlet sward at the south end of the gardens where the dance was to be held, when Djor Kantos came hurriedly toward Tara of Helium. "I claim —" he exclaimed as he neared her; but she interrupted him with a gesture.

"You are too late, Djor Kantos," she cried in mock anger. "No laggard may claim Tara of Helium; but haste now lest thou lose also Olvia Marthis, whom I have never seen wait long to be claimed for this or any other dance."

"I have already lost her," admitted Djor Kantos ruefully.

"And you mean to say that you came for Tara of Helium only after having lost Olvia Marthis?" demanded the girl, still simulating displeasure.

"Oh, Tara of Helium, you know better than that," insisted the young man. "Was it not natural that I should assume that you would expect me, who alone has claimed you for the Dance of Barsoom for at least twelve times past?"

"And sit and play with my thumbs until you saw fit to come for me?" she questioned. "Ah, no, Djor Kantos; Tara of Helium is for no laggard," and she threw him a sweet smile and passed on toward the assembling dancers with Gahan, Jed of far Gathol.

The Dance of Barsoom bears a relation similar to the more formal dancing functions of Mars that The Grand March does to ours, though it is infinitely more intricate and more beautiful. Before a Martian youth of either sex may attend an important social function where there is dancing, he must have become proficient in at least three dances — The Dance of Barsoom, his national dance, and the dance of his city. In these three dances the dancers furnish their own music, which never varies; nor do the steps or figures vary, having been handed down from time immemorial. All Barsoomian dances are stately and beautiful, but The Dance of Barsoom is a wondrous epic of motion and harmony — there is no grotesque posturing, no vulgar or suggestive movements. It has been described as the interpretation of the highest ideals of a world that aspired to grace and beauty and chastity in woman, and strength and dignity and loyalty in man.

Today, John Carter, Warlord of Mars, with Dejah Thoris, his mate, led in the dancing, and if there was another couple that vied with them in possession of the silent admiration of the guests it was the resplendent Jed of Gathol and his beautiful partner. In the ever-changing figures of the dance the man found himself now with the girl's hand in his and again with an arm about the lithe body that the jeweled harness but inadequately covered, and the girl, though she had danced a thousand dances in the past, realized for the first time the personal contact of a man's arm against her naked flesh. It troubled her that she should notice it, and she looked up questioningly and almost with displeasure at the man as though it was his fault. Their eyes met and she saw in his that which she had never seen in the eyes of Djor Kantos. It was at the very end of the dance and they both stopped suddenly with the music and stood there looking straight into each other's eyes. It was Gahan of Gathol who spoke first.

"Tara of Helium, I love you!" he said.

The girl drew herself to her full height. "The Jed of Gathol forgets himself," she exclaimed haughtily.

"The Jed of Gathol would forget everything but you, Tara of Helium," he replied. Fiercely he pressed the soft hand that he still retained from the last position of the dance. "I love you, Tara of Helium," he repeated. "Why should your ears refuse to hear what your eyes but just now did not refuse to see — and answer?"

"What meanest thou?" she cried. "Are the men of Gathol such boors, then?"

"They are neither boors nor fools," he replied, quietly. "They know when they love a woman — and when she loves them."

Tara of Helium stamped her little foot in anger. "Go!" she said, "before it is necessary to acquaint my father with the dishonor of his guest."

She turned and walked away. "Wait!" cried the man. "Just another word."

"Of apology?" she asked.

"Of prophecy," he said.

"I do not care to hear it," replied Tara of Helium, and left him standing there. She was strangely unstrung and shortly thereafter returned to her own quarter of the palace, where she stood for a long time by a window looking out beyond the scarlet tower of Greater Helium toward the northwest.

Presently she turned angrily away. "I hate him!" she exclaimed aloud.

"Whom?" inquired the privileged Uthia.

Tara of Helium stamped her foot. "That ill-mannered boor, the Jed of Gathol," she replied.

Uthia raised her slim brows.

At the stamping of the little foot, a great beast rose from the corner of the room and crossed to Tara of Helium where it stood looking up into her face. She placed her hand upon the ugly head. "Dear old Woola," she said; "no love could be deeper than yours, yet it never offends. Would that men might pattern themselves after you!"

Chapter II
AT THE GALE'S MERCY

Tara of Helium did not return to her father's guests, but awaited in her own apartments the word from Djor Kantos which she knew must come, begging her to return to the gardens. She would then refuse, haughtily. But no appeal came from Djor Kantos. At first Tara of Helium was angry, then she was hurt, and always she was puzzled. She could not understand. Occasionally she thought of the Jed of Gathol and then she would stamp her foot, for she was very angry indeed with Gahan. The presumption of the man! He had insinuated that he read love for him in her eyes. Never had she been so insulted and humiliated. Never had she so thoroughly hated a man. Suddenly she turned toward Uthia.

"My flying leather!" she commanded.

"But the guests!" exclaimed the slave girl. "Your father, The Warlord, will expect you to return."

"He will be disappointed," snapped Tara of Helium.

The slave hesitated. "He does not approve of your flying alone," she reminded her mistress.

The young princess sprang to her feet and seized the unhappy slave by the shoulders, "You are becoming unbearable, Uthia," she cried. "Soon there will be no alternative than to send you to the public slave-market. Then possibly you will find a master to your liking."

Tears came to the soft eyes of the slave girl. "It is because I love you, my princess," she said softly. Instantly Tara of Helium melted. She took the slave in her arms and kissed her.

"I have the disposition of a thoat, Uthia," she said. "Forgive me! I love you and there is nothing that I would not do for you and nothing would I do to harm you. Again, as I have so often in the past, I offer you your freedom."

"I do not wish my freedom if it will separate me from you, Tara of Helium," replied Uthia. "I am happy here with you — I think that I should die without you."

Again the girls kissed. "And you will not fly alone, then?" questioned the slave.

Tara of Helium laughed and pinched her companion. "You persistent little pest," she cried. "Of course I shall fly — does not Tara of Helium always do that which pleases her?"

Uthia shook her head sorrowfully. "Alas! she does," she admitted. "Iron is the Warlord of Barsoom to the influences of all but two. In the hands of Dejah Thoris and Tara of Helium he is as potters' clay."

"Then run and fetch my flying leather like the sweet slave you are," directed the mistress.

Far out across the ochre sea-bottoms beyond the twin cities of Helium raced the swift flier of Tara of Helium. Thrilling to the speed and the buoyancy and the obedience of the little craft the girl drove toward the northwest. Why she should choose that direction she did not pause to consider. Perhaps because in that direction lay the least known areas of Barsoom, and, *ergo*, Romance, Mystery, and Adventure. In that direction also lay far Gathol; but to that fact she gave no conscious thought.

She did, however, think occasionally of the jed of that distant kingdom, but the reaction to these thoughts was scarcely pleasurable. They still brought a flush of shame to her cheeks and a surge of angry blood to her heart. She was very angry with the Jed of Gathol, and though she should never see him again she was quite sure that hate of him would remain fresh in her memory forever. Mostly her thoughts revolved about another — Djor Kantos. And when she thought of him she thought also of Olvia Marthis of Hastor. Tara of Helium thought that she was jealous of the fair Olvia and it made her very angry to think that. She was angry with Djor Kantos and herself, but she was not angry at all with Olvia Marthis, whom she loved, and so of course she was not jealous really. The trouble was, that Tara of Helium had failed for once to have her own way. Djor Kantos had not come running like a willing slave when she had expected him, and, ah, here was the nub of the whole thing! Gahan, Jed of Gathol, a stranger, had been a witness to her humiliation. He had seen her unclaimed at the beginning of a great function and he had had to come to her rescue, as he doubtless thought, from the inglorious fate of a wallflower. At the recurring thought, Tara of Helium could feel her whole body burning with scarlet shame and then she went suddenly white and cold with rage; whereupon she turned her flier about so abruptly that she was all but torn from her lashings upon the flat, narrow deck. She reached home just before dark. The guests had departed. Quiet had descended upon the palace. An hour later she joined her father and mother at the evening meal.

"You deserted us, Tara of Helium," said John Carter. "It is not what the guests of John Carter should expect."

"They did not come to see me," replied Tara of Helium. "I did not ask them."

"They were no less your guests," replied her father.

The girl rose, and came and stood beside him and put her arms about his neck.

"My proper old Virginian," she cried, rumpling his shock of black hair.

"In Virginia you would be turned over your father's knee and spanked," said the man, smiling.

She crept into his lap and kissed him. "You do not love me any more," she announced. "No one loves me," but she could not compose her features into a pout because bubbling laughter insisted upon breaking through.

"The trouble is there are too many who love you," he said. "And now there is another."

"Indeed!" she cried. "What do you mean?"

"Gahan of Gathol has asked permission to woo you."

The girl sat up very straight and tilted her chin in the air. "I would not wed with a walking diamond-mine," she said. "I will not have him."

"I told him as much," replied her father, "and that you were as good as betrothed to another. He was very courteous about it; but at the same time he gave me to understand that he was accustomed to getting what he wanted and that he wanted you very much. I suppose it will mean another war. Your mother's beauty kept Helium at war for many years, and — well, Tara of Helium, if I were a young man I should doubtless be willing to set all Barsoom afire to win you, as I still would to keep your divine mother," and he smiled across the sorapus table and its golden service at the undimmed beauty of Mars' most beautiful woman.

"Our little girl should not yet be troubled with such matters," said Dejah Thoris. "Remember, John Carter, that you are not dealing with an Earth child, whose span of life would be more than half completed before a daughter of Barsoom reached actual maturity."

"But do not the daughters of Barsoom sometimes marry as early as twenty?" he insisted.

"Yes, but they may still be desirable in the eyes of men after forty generations of Earth folk have returned to dust — there is no hurry, at least, upon Barsoom. We do not fade and decay here as you tell me those of your planet do, though you, yourself, belie your own words. When the time seems proper Tara of Helium shall wed with Djor Kantos, and until then let us give the matter no further thought."

"No," said the girl, "the subject irks me, and I shall not marry Djor Kantos, or another — I do not intend to wed."

Her father and mother looked at her and smiled. "When Gahan of Gathol returns he may carry you off," said the former.

"He has gone?" asked the girl.

"His flier departs for Gathol in the morning," John Carter replied.

"I have seen the last of him then," remarked Tara of Helium with a sigh of relief.

"He says not," returned John Carter.

The girl dismissed the subject with a shrug and the conversation passed to other topics. A letter had arrived from Thuvia of Ptarth, who was visiting at her father's court while Carthoris, her mate, hunted in Okar. Word had been received that the Tharks and Warhoons were again at war, or rather that there had been an engagement, for war was their habitual state. In the memory of man there had been no peace between these two savage green hordes — and only a single temporary truce. Two new battleships had been launched at Hastor. A little band of holy therns was attempting to revive the ancient and discredited religion of Issus, who they claimed still lived in spirit and had communicated with them. There were rumors of war from Dusar. A scientist claimed to have discovered human life on the further moon. A madman had attempted to destroy the atmosphere plant. Seven people had been assassinated in Greater Helium during the last ten zodes (the equivalent of an Earth day).

Following the meal Dejah Thoris and The Warlord played at jetan, the Barsoomian game of chess, which is played upon a board of a hundred alternate black and orange squares. One player has twenty black pieces, the other, twenty orange pieces. A brief description of the game may interest those Earth readers who care for chess, and will not be lost upon those who pursue this narrative to its conclusion, since before they are done they will find that a knowledge of jetan will add to the interest and the thrills that are in store for them.

The men are placed upon the board as in chess upon the first two rows next the players. In order from left to right on the line of squares nearest the players, the jetan pieces are Warrior, Padwar, Dwar, Flier, Chief, Princess, Flier, Dwar, Padwar, Warrior. In the next line all are Panthans except the end pieces, which are called Thoats, and represent mounted warriors.

The Panthans, which are represented as warriors with one feather, may move one space in any direction except backward; the Thoats, mounted warriors with three feathers, may move one straight and one diagonal, and may jump intervening pieces; Warriors, foot soldiers with two feathers, straight in any direction, or diagonally, two spaces; Padwars, lieutenants wearing two feathers, two diagonal in any direction, or combination; Dwars, captains wearing three feathers, three spaces straight in any direction, or combination; Fliers, represented by a propellor with three blades, three spaces in any direction, or combination, diagonally, and may jump intervening pieces; the Chief, indicated by a diadem with ten jewels, three spaces in any direction, straight, or diagonal; Princess, diadem with a single jewel, same as Chief, and can jump intervening pieces.

The game is won when a player places any of his pieces on the same square with his opponent's Princess, or when a Chief takes a Chief. It is drawn when a Chief is taken by any opposing piece other than the opposing Chief; or when both sides have been reduced to three pieces, or less, of equal value, and the game is not terminated in the following ten moves, five apiece. This is but a general outline of the game, briefly stated.

It was this game that Dejah Thoris and John Carter were playing when Tara of Helium bid them good night, retiring to her own quarters and her sleeping silks and furs. "Until morning, my beloved," she called back to them as she passed from the apartment, nor little did she guess, nor her parents, that this might indeed be the last time that they would ever set eyes upon her.

The morning broke dull and gray. Ominous clouds billowed restlessly and low. Beneath them torn fragments scudded toward the northwest. From her window Tara of Helium looked out upon this unusual scene. Dense clouds seldom overcast the Barsoomian sky. At this hour of the day it was her custom to ride one of those small thoats that are the saddle animals of the red Martians, but the sight of the billowing clouds lured her to a new adventure. Uthia still slept and the girl did not disturb her. Instead, she dressed quietly and went to the hangar upon the roof of the palace directly above her quarters where her own swift flier was housed. She had never driven through the clouds. It was an adventure that always she had longed to experience. The wind was strong and it was with difficulty that she maneu-

vered the craft from the hangar without accident, but once away it raced swiftly out above the twin cities. The buffeting winds caught and tossed it, and the girl laughed aloud in sheer joy of the resultant thrills. She handled the little ship like a veteran, though few veterans would have faced the menace of such a storm in so light a craft. Swiftly she rose toward the clouds, racing with the scudding streamers of the storm-swept fragments, and a moment later she was swallowed by the dense masses billowing above. Here was a new world, a world of chaos unpeopled except for herself; but it was a cold, damp, lonely world and she found it depressing after the novelty of it had been dissipated, by an overpowering sense of the magnitude of the forces surging about her. Suddenly she felt very lonely and very cold and very little. Hurriedly, therefore, she rose until presently her craft broke through into the glorious sunlight that transformed the upper surface of the somber element into rolling masses of burnished silver. Here it was still cold, but without the dampness of the clouds, and in the eye of the brilliant sun her spirits rose with the mounting needle of her altimeter. Gazing at the clouds, now far beneath, the girl experienced the sensation of hanging stationary in mid-heaven; but the whirring of her propellor, the wind beating upon her, the high figures that rose and fell beneath the glass of her speedometer, these told her that her speed was terrific. It was then that she determined to turn back.

The first attempt she made above the clouds, but it was unsuccessful. To her surprise she discovered that she could not even turn against the high wind, which rocked and buffeted the frail craft. Then she dropped swiftly to the dark and wind-swept zone between the hurtling clouds and the gloomy surface of the shadowed ground. Here she tried again to force the nose of the flier back toward Helium, but the tempest seized the frail thing and hurled it remorselessly about, rolling it over and over and tossing it as it were a cork in a cataract. At last the girl succeeded in righting the flier, perilously close to the ground. Never before had she been so close to death, yet she was not terrified. Her coolness had saved her, that and the strength of the deck lashings that held her. Traveling with the storm she was safe, but where was it bearing her? She pictured the apprehension of her father and mother when she failed to appear at the morning meal. They would find her flier missing and they would guess that somewhere in the path of the storm it lay a wrecked and tangled mass upon her dead body, and then brave men would go out in search of her, risking their lives; and that lives would be lost in the search, she knew, for she realized now that never in her lifetime had such a tempest raged upon Barsoom.

She must turn back! She must reach Helium before her mad lust for thrills had cost the sacrifice of a single courageous life! She determined that greater safety and likelihood of success lay above the clouds, and once again she rose through the chilling, wind-tossed vapor. Her speed again was terrific, for the wind seemed to have increased rather than to have lessened. She sought gradually to check the swift flight of her craft, but though she finally succeeded in reversing her motor the wind but carried her on as it would. Then it was that Tara of Helium lost her temper. Had her world not always bowed in acquiescence to her every wish? What were these elements that they dared to thwart her? She would demonstrate to them that the daughter of The Warlord was not to be denied! They would learn that Tara of Helium might not be ruled even by the forces of nature!

And so she drove her motor forward again and then with her firm, white teeth set in grim determination she drove the steering lever far down to port with the intention of forcing the nose of her craft straight into the teeth of the wind, and the wind seized the frail thing and toppled it over upon its back, and twisted and turned it and hurled it over and over; the propellor raced for an instant in an air pocket and then the tempest seized it again and twisted it from its shaft, leaving the girl helpless upon an unmanageable atom that rose and fell, and rolled and tumbled — the sport of the elements she had defied. Tara of Helium's first sensation was one of surprise — that she had failed to have her own way. Then she commenced to feel concern — not for her own safety but for the anxiety of her parents and the dangers that the inevitable searchers must face. She reproached herself for the thoughtless selfishness that had jeopardized the peace and

safety of others. She realized her own grave danger, too; but she was still unterrified, as befitted the daughter of Dejah Thoris and John Carter. She knew that her buoyancy tanks might keep her afloat indefinitely, but she had neither food nor water, and she was being borne toward the least-known area of Barsoom. Perhaps it would be better to land immediately and await the coming of the searchers, rather than to allow herself to be carried still further from Helium, thus greatly reducing the chances of early discovery; but when she dropped toward the ground she discovered that the violence of the wind rendered an attempt to land tantamount to destruction and she rose again, rapidly.

Carried along a few hundred feet above the ground she was better able to appreciate the Titanic proportions of the storm thn when she had flown in the comparative serenity of the zone above the clouds, for now she could distinctly see the effect of the wind upon the surface of Barsoom. The air was filled with dust and flying bits of vegetation and when the storm carried her across an irrigated area of farm land she saw great trees and stone walls and buildings lifted high in air and scattered broadcast over the devastated country; and then she was carried swiftly on to other sights that forced in upon her consciousness a rapidly growing conviction that after all Tara of Helium was a very small and insignificant and helpless person. It was quite a shock to her self-pride while it lasted, and toward evening she was ready to believe that it was going to last forever. There had been no abatement in the ferocity of the tempest, nor was there indication of any. She could only guess at the distance she had been carried for she could not believe in the correctness of the high figures that had been piled upon the record of her odometer. They seemed unbelievable and yet, had she known it, they were quite true — in twelve hours she had flown and been carried by the storm full seven thousand haads. Just before dark she was carried over one of the deserted cities of ancient Mars. It was Torquas, but she did not know it. Had she, she might readily have been forgiven for abandoning the last vestige of hope, for to the people of Helium Torquas seems as remote as do the South Sea Islands to us. And still the tempest, its fury unabated, bore her on.

All that night she hurtled through the dark beneath the clouds, or rose to race through the moonlit void beneath the glory of Barsoom's two satellites. She was cold and hungry and altogether miserable, but her brave little spirit refused to admit that her plight was hopeless even though reason proclaimed the truth. Her reply to reason, sometimes spoken aloud in sudden defiance, recalled the Spartan stubbornness of her sire in the face of certain annihilation: "I still live!"

That morning there had been an early visitor at the palace of The Warlord. It was Gahan, Jed of Gathol. He had arrived shortly after the absence of Tara of Helium had been noted, and in the excitement he had remained unannounced until John Carter had happened upon him in the great reception corridor of the palace as The Warlord was hurrying out to arrange for the dispatch of ships in search of his daughter.

Gahan read the concern upon the face of The Warlord. "Forgive me if I intrude, John Carter," he said. "I but came to ask the indulgence of another day since it would be foolhardy to attempt to navigate a ship in such a storm."

"Remain, Gahan, a welcome guest until you choose to leave us," replied The Warlord; "but you must forgive any seeming inattention upon the part of Helium until my daughter is restored to us."

"Your daughter! Restored! What do you mean?" exclaimed the Gatholian. "I do not understand."

"She is gone, together with her light flier. That is all we know. We can only assume that she decided to fly before the morning meal and was caught in the clutches of the tempest. You will pardon me, Gahan, if I leave you abruptly — I am arranging to send ships in search of her;" but Gahan, Jed of Gathol, was already speeding in the direction of the palace gate. There he leaped upon a waiting thoat and followed by two warriors in the metal of Gathol, he dashed through the avenues of Helium toward the palace that had been set aside for his entertainment.

Chapter III
THE HEADLESS HUMANS

Above the roof of the palace that housed the Jed of Gathol and his entourage, the cruiser *Vanator* tore at her stout moorings.

The groaning tackle bespoke the mad fury of the gale, while the worried faces of those members of the crew whose duties demanded their presence on the straining craft gave corroborative evidence of the gravity of the situation. Only stout lashings prevented these men from being swept from the deck, while those upon the roof below were constantly compelled to cling to rails and stanchions to save themselves from being carried away by each new burst of meteoric fury. Upon the prow of the *Vanator* was painted the device of Gathol, but no pennants were displayed in the upper works since the storm had carried away several in rapid succession, just as it seemed to the watching men that it must carry away the ship itself. They could not believe that any tackle could withstand for long this Titanic force. To each of the twelve lashings clung a brawny warrior with drawn short-sword. Had but a single mooring given to the power of the tempest eleven short-swords would have cut the others; since, partially moored, the ship was doomed, while free in the tempest it stood at least some slight chance for life.

"By the blood of Issus, I believe they will hold!" screamed one warrior to another.

"And they do not hold may the spirits of our ancestors reward the brave warriors upon the *Vanator*," replied another of those upon the roof of the palace, "for it will not be long from the moment her cables part before her crew dons the leather of the dead; but yet, Tanus, I believe they will hold. Give thanks at least that we did not sail before the tempest fell, since now each of us has a chance to live."

"Yes," replied Tanus, "I should hate to be abroad today upon the stoutest ship that sails the Barsoomian sky."

It was then that Gahan the Jed appeared upon the roof. With him where the balance of his own party and a dozen warriors of Helium. The young chief turned to his followers.

"I sail at once upon the *Vanator*," he said, "in search of Tara of Helium who is thought to have been carried away upon a one-man flier by the storm. I do not need to explain to you the slender chances the *Vanator* has to withstand the fury of the tempest, nor will I order you to your deaths. Let those who wish remain behind without dishonor. The others will follow me," and he leaped for the rope ladder that lashed wildly in the gale.

The first man to follow him was Tanus and when the last reached the deck of the cruiser there remained upon the palace roof only the twelve warriors of Helium, who, with naked swords, had taken the posts of the Gatholians at the moorings.

Not a single warrior who had remained aboard the *Vanator* would leave her now.

"I expected no less," said Gahan, as with the help of those already on the deck he and the others found secure lashings. The commander of the *Vanator* shook his head. He loved his trim craft, the pride of her class in the little navy of Gathol. It was of her he thought — not of himself. He saw her lying torn and twisted upon the ochre vegetation of some distant sea-bottom, to be presently overrun and looted by some savage, green horde. He looked at Gahan.

"Are you ready, San Tothis?" asked the jed.

"All is ready."

"Then cut away!"

Word was passed across the deck and over the side to the Heliumetic warriors below that at the third gun they were to cut away. Twelve keen swords must strike simultaneously and with equal power, and each must sever completely and instantly three strands of heavy cable that no loose end fouling a block bring immediate disaster upon the *Vanator*.

Boom! The voice of the signal gun rolled down through the screaming wind to the twelve warriors upon the roof. *Boom!* Twelve swords were raised above twelve brawny shoulders. *Boom!* Twelve keen edges severed twelve complaining moorings, clean and as one.

The *Vanator*, her propellors whirling, shot forward with the storm. The tempest struck her in the stern as with a mailed fist and stood the great ship upon her nose, and then it caught her and spun her as a child's top spins; and upon the palace roof the twelve men looked on in silent helplessness and prayed for the souls of the brave warriors who were going to their death. And others saw, from Helium's lofty landing stages and from a thousand hangars upon a thousand roofs; but only for an instant did the preparations stop that would send other brave men into the frightful maelstrom of that apparently hopeless search, for such is the courage of the warriors of Barsoom.

But the *Vanator* did not fall to the ground, within sight of the city at least, though as long as the watchers could see her never for an instant did she rest upon an even keel. Sometime she lay upon one side or the other, or again she hurtled along keel up, or rolled over and over, or stood upon her nose or her tail at the caprice of the great force that carried her along. And the watchers saw that this great ship was merely being blown away with the other bits of debris great and small that filled the sky. Never in the memory of man or the annals of recorded history had such a storm raged across the face of Barsoom.

And in another instant was the *Vanator* forgotten as the lofty, scarlet tower that had marked Lesser Helium for ages crashed to ground, carrying death and demolition upon the city beneath. Panic reigned. A fire broke out in the ruins. The city's every force seemed crippled, and it was then that The Warlord ordered the men that were about to set forth in search of Tara of Helium to devote their energies to the salvation of the city, for he too had witnessed the start of the *Vanator* and realized the futility of wasting men who were needed sorely if Lesser Helium was to be saved from utter destruction.

Shortly after noon of the second day the storm commenced to abate, and before the sun went down, the little craft upon which Tara of Helium had hovered between life and death these many hours drifted slowly before a gentle breeze above a landscape of rolling hills that once had been lofty mountains upon a Martian continent. The girl was exhausted from loss of sleep, from lack of food and drink, and from the nervous reaction consequent to the terrifying experiences through which she had passed. In the near distance, just topping an intervening hill, she caught a momentary glimpse of what appeared to be a dome-capped tower. Quickly she dropped the flier until the hill shut it off from the view of the possible occupants of the structure she had seen. The tower meant to her the habitation of man, suggesting the presence of water and, perhaps, of food. If the tower was the deserted relic of a bygone age she would scarcely find food there, but there was still a chance that there might be water. If it was inhabited, then must her approach be cautious, for only enemies might be expected to abide in so far distant a land. Tara of Helium knew that she must be far from the twin cities of her grandfather's empire, but had she guessed within even a thousand haads of the reality, she had been stunned by realization of the utter hopelessness of her state.

Keeping the craft low, for the buoyancy tanks were still intact, the girl skimmed the ground until the gently-moving wind had carried her to the side of the last hill that intervened between her and the structure she had thought a man-built tower. Here she brought the flier to the ground among some stunted trees, and dragging it beneath one where it might be somewhat hidden from craft passing above, she made it fast and set forth to reconnoiter. Like most women of her class she was armed only with a single slender blade, so that in such an emergency as now confronted her she must depend almost solely upon her cleverness in remaining undiscovered by enemies. With utmost caution she crept warily toward the crest of the hill, taking advantage of every natural screen that the landscape afforded to conceal her approach from possible observers ahead, while momentarily she cast quick glances rearward lest she be taken by surprise from that quarter.

She came at last to the summit, where, from the concealment of low bush, she could see what lay beyond. Beneath her spread a beautiful valley surrounded by low hills. Dotting it were numerous circular towers, dome-capped, and surrounding each tower was a stone wall enclosing several acres of ground. The valley appeared to be in a high state of cultivation. Upon the opposite side of the hill and just beneath her was a tower and enclosure. It was the roof of the former that had first attracted her attention. In all respects it seemed identical in construction with those further out in the valley — a high, plastered wall of massive construction surrounding a similarly constructed tower, upon whose gray surface was painted in vivid colors a strange device. The towers were about forty sofads in diameter, approximately forty earth-feet, and sixty in height to the base of the dome. To an Earth man they would have immediately suggested the silos in which dairy farmers store ensilage for their herds; but closer scrutiny, revealing an occasional embrasured opening together with the strange construction of the domes, would have altered such a conclusion. Tara of Helium saw that the domes seemed to be faced with innumerable prisms of glass, those that were exposed to the declining sun scintillating so gorgeously as to remind her suddenly of the magnificent trappings of Gahan of Gathol. As she thought of the man she shook her head angrily, and moved cautiously forward a foot or two that she might get a less obstructed view of the nearer tower and its enclosure.

As Tara of Helium looked down into the enclosure surrounding the nearest tower, her brows contracted momentarily in frowning surprise, and then her eyes went wide in an expression of incredulity tinged with horror, for what she saw was a score or two of human bodies — naked and headless. For a long moment she watched, breathless; unable to believe the evidence of her own eyes — that these grewsome things moved and had life! She saw them crawling about on hands and knees over and across one another, searching about with their fingers. And she saw some of them at troughs, for which the others seemed to be searching, and those at the troughs were taking something from these receptacles and apparently putting it in a hole where their necks should have been. They were not far beneath her — she could see them distinctly and she saw that there were the bodies of both men and women, and that they were beautifully proportioned, and that their skin was similar to hers, but of a slightly lighter red. At first she had thought that she was looking upon a shambles and the bodies, but recently decapitated, were moving under the impulse of muscular reaction; but presently she realized that this was their normal condition. The horror of them fascinated her, so that she could scarce take her eyes from them. It was evident from their groping hands that they were eyeless, and their sluggish movements suggested a rudimentary nervous system and a correspondingly minute brain. The girl wondered how they subsisted for she could not, even by the wildest stretch of imagination, picture these imperfect creatures as intelligent tillers of the soil. Yet that the soil of the valley was tilled was evident and that these things had food was equally so. But who tilled the soil? Who kept and fed these unhappy things, and for what purpose? It was an enigma beyond her powers of deduction.

The sight of food aroused again a consciousness of her own gnawing hunger and the thirst that parched her throat. She could see both food and water within the enclosure; but would she dare enter even should she find means of ingress? She doubted it, since the very thought of possible contact with these grewsome creatures sent a shudder through her frame.

Then her eyes wandered again out across the valley until presently they picked out what appeared to be a tiny stream winding its way through the center of the farm lands — a strange sight upon Barsoom. Ah, if it were but water! Then might she hope with a real hope, for the fields would give her sustenance which she could gain by night, while by day she hid among the surrounding hills, and sometime, yes, sometime she knew, the searchers would come, for John Carter, Warlord of Barsoom, would never cease to search for his daughter until every square haad of the planet had been combed again and again. She knew him and she knew the warriors of Helium and so she knew that could she but manage to escape harm until they came, they would indeed come at last.

She would have to wait until dark before she dare venture into the valley, and in the meantime she thought it well to search out a place of safety nearby where she might be reasonably safe from savage beasts. It was possible that the district was free from carnivora, but one might never be sure in a strange land. As she was about to withdraw behind the brow of the hill her attention was again attracted to the enclosure below. Two figures had emerged from the tower. Their beautiful bodies seemed identical with those of the headless creatures among which they moved, but the newcomers were not headless. Upon their shoulders were heads that seemed human, yet which the girl intuitively sensed were not human. They were just a trifle too far away for her to see them distinctly in the waning light of the dying day, but she knew that they were too large, they were out of proportion to the perfectly proportioned bodies, and they were oblate in form. She could see that the men wore some manner of harness to which were slung the customary long-sword and short-sword of the Barsoomian warrior, and that about their short necks were massive leather collars cut to fit closely over the shoulders and

snugly to the lower part of the head. Their features were scarce discernible, but there was a suggestion of grotesqueness about them that carried to her a feeling of revulsion.

The two carried a long rope to which were fastened, at intervals of about two sofads, what she later guessed were light manacles, for she saw the warriors passing among the poor creatures in the enclosure and about the right wrist of each they fastened one of the manacles. When all had been thus fastened to the rope one of the warriors commenced to pull and tug at the loose end as though attempting to drag the headless company toward the tower, while the other went among them with a long, light whip with which he flicked them upon the naked skin. Slowly, dully, the creatures rose to their feet and between the tugging of the warrior in front and the lashing of him behind the hopeless band was finally herded within the tower. Tara of Helium shuddered as she turned away. What manner of creatures were these?

Suddenly it was night. The Barsoomian day had ended, and then the brief period of twilight that renders the transition from daylight to darkness almost as abrupt as the switching off of an electric light, and Tara of Helium had found no sanctuary. But perhaps there were no beasts to fear, or rather to avoid — Tara of Helium liked not the word fear. She would have been glad, however, had there been a cabin, even a very tiny cabin, upon her small flier; but there was no cabin. The interior of the hull was completely taken up by the buoyancy tanks. Ah, she had it! How stupid of her not to have thought of it before! She could moor the craft to the tree beneath which it rested and let it rise the length of the rope. Lashed to the deck rings she would then be safe from any roaming beast of prey that chanced along. In the morning she could drop to ground again before the craft was discovered.

As Tara of Helium crept over the brow of the hill down toward the valley, her presence was hidden by the darkness of the night from the sight of any chance observer who might be loitering by a window in the nearby tower. Cluros, the farther moon, was just rising above the horizon to commence his leisurely journey through the heavens. Eight zodes later he would set — a trifle over nineteen and a half Earth hours — and during that time Thuria, his vivacious mate, would have circled the planet twice and be more than half way around on her third trip. She had but just set. It would be more than three and a half hours before she shot above the opposite horizon to hurtle, swift and low, across the face of the dying planet. During this temporary absence of the mad moon Tara of Helium hoped to find both food and water, and gain again the safety of her flier's deck.

She groped her way through the darkness, giving the tower and its enclosure as wide a berth as possible. Sometimes she stumbled, for in the long shadows cast by the rising Cluros objects were grotesquely distorted, though the light from the moon was still not sufficient to be of much assistance to her. Nor, as a matter of fact, did she want light. She could find the stream in the dark, by the simple expedient of going down hill until she walked into it and she had seen that bearing trees and many crops grew throughout the valley, so that she would pass food in plenty ere she reached the stream. If the moon showed her the way more clearly and thus saved her from an occasinal fall, he would, too, show her more clearly to the strange denizens of the towers, and that, of course, must not be. Could she have waited until the following night conditions would have been better, since Cluros would not appear in the heavens at all and so, during Thuria's absence, utter darkness would reign; but the pangs of thirst and the gnawing of hunger could be endured no longer with food and drink both in sight, and so she had decided to risk discovery rather than suffer longer.

Safely past the nearest tower, she moved as rapidly as she felt consistent with safety, choosing her way wherever possible so that she might take advantage of the shadows of the trees that grew at intervals and at the same time discover those which bore fruit. In this latter she met with almost immediate success, for the very third tree beneath which she halted was heavy with ripe fruit. Never, thought Tara of Helium, had aught so delicious impinged upon her palate, and yet it was naught else than the almost tasteless usa, which is considered to be palatable only after having been cooked and highly spiced. It grows easily with little irrigation and the trees bear abundantly. The fruit, which ranks

high in food value, is one of the staple foods of the less well-to-do, and because of its cheapness and nutritive value forms one of the principal rations of both armies and navies upon Barsoom, a use which has won for it a Martian *sobriquet* which, freely translated into English, would be, The Fighting Potato. The girl was wise enough to eat but sparingly, but she filled her pocket-pouch with the fruit before she continued upon her way.

Two towers she passed before she came at last to the stream, and here again was she temperate, drinking but little and that very slowly, contenting herself with rinsing her mouth frequently and bathing her face, her hands, and her feet; and even though the night was cold, as Martian nights are, the sensation of refreshment more than compensated for the physical discomfort of the low temperature. Replacing her sandals she sought among the growing truck near the stream for whatever edible berries or tubers might be planted there, and found a couple of varieties that could be eaten raw. With these she replaced some of the usa in her pocket-pouch, not only to insure a variety but because she found them more palatable. Occasionally she returned to the stream to drink, but each time moderately. Always were her eyes and ears alert for the first signs of danger, but she had neither seen nor heard aught to disturb her. And presently the time approached when she felt she must return to her flier lest she be caught in the revealing light of low swinging Thuria. She dreaded leaving the water for she knew that she must become very thirsty before she could hope to come again to the stream. If she only had some little receptacle in which to carry water, even a small amount would tide her over until the following night; but she had nothing and so she must content herself as best she could with the juices of the fruit and tubers she had gathered.

After a last drink at the stream, the longest and deepest she had allowed herself, she rose to retrace her steps toward the hills; but even as she did so she became suddenly tense with apprehension. What was that? She could have sworn that she saw something move in the shadows beneath a tree not far away. For a long minute the girl did not move — she scarce breathed. Her eyes remained fixed upon the dense shadows below the tree, her ears strained through the silence of the night. A low moaning came down from the hills where her flier was hidden. She knew it well — the weird note of the hunting banth. And the great carnivore lay directly in her path. But he was not so close as this other thing, hiding there in the shadows just a little way off. What was it? It was the strain of uncertainty that weighed heaviest upon her. Had she known the nature of the creature lurking there half its menace would have vanished. She cast quickly about her in search of some haven of refuge should the thing prove dangerous.

Again arose the moaning from the hills, but this time closer. Almost immediately it was answered from the opposite side of the valley, behind her, and then from the distance to the right of her, and twice upon her left. Her eyes had found a tree, quite near. Slowly, and without taking her eyes from the shadows of that other tree, she moved toward the overhanging branches that might afford her sanctuary in the event of need, and at her first move a low growl rose from the spot she had been watching and she heard the sudden moving of a big body. Simultaneously the creature shot into the moonlight in full charge upon her, its tail erect, its tiny ears laid flat, its great mouth with its multiple rows of sharp and powerful fangs already yawning for its prey, its ten legs carrying it forward in great leaps, and now from the beast's throat issued the frightful roar with which it seeks to paralyze its prey. It was a banth — the great, maned lion of Barsoom. Tara of Helium saw it coming and leaped for the tree toward which she had been moving, and the banth realized her intention and redoubled his speed. As his hideous roar awakened the echoes in the hills, so too it awakened echoes in the valley; but these echoes came from the living throats of others of his kind, until it seemed to the girl that Fate had thrown her into the midst of a countless multitude of these savage beasts.

Almost incredibly swift is the speed of a charging banth, and fortunate it was that the girl had not been caught farther in the open. As it was, her margin of safety was next to negligible, for as she swung nimbly to the lower branches the creature in pursuit of her crashed among the foliage almost upon her as it sprang upward to seize her. It was only a combination of good fortune and agility that saved her. A stout branch deflected the raking talons of the carnivore, but so close was the call that a giant forearm brushed her flesh in the instant before she scrambled to the higher branches.

Baffled, the banth gave vent to his rage and disappointment in a series of frightful roars that caused the very ground to tremble, and to these were added the roarings and the growlings and the moanings of his fellows as they approached from every direction, in the hope of wresting from him whatever of his kill they could take by craft or prowess. And now he turned snarling upon them as they circled the tree, while the girl, huddled in a crotch above them, looked down upon the gaunt, yellow monsters padding on noiseless feet in a restless circle about her. She wondered now at the strange freak of fate that had permitted her to come down this far into the valley by night unharmed; but even more she wondered how she was to return to the hills. She knew that she would not dare venture it by night and she guessed, too, that by day she might be confronted by even graver perils. To depend upon this valley for sustenance she now saw to be beyond the pale of possibility because of the banths that would keep her from food and water by night, while the dwellers in the towers would doubtless make it equally impossible for her to forage by day. There was but one solution of her difficulty and that was to return to her flier and pray that the wind would waft her to some less terrorful land; but when might she return to the flier? The banths gave little evidence of relinquishing hope of her, and even if they wandered out of sight would she dare risk the attempt? She doubted it.

Hopeless indeed seemed her situation — hopeless it was.

Chapter IV
CAPTURED

As Thuria, swift racer of the night, shot again into the sky the scene changed. As by magic a new aspect fell athwart the face of Nature. It was as though in the instant one had been transported from one planet to another. It was the age-old miracle of the Martian nights that is always new, even to Martians — two moons resplendent in the heavens, where one had been but now;

conflicting, fast-changing shadows that altered the very hills themselves; far Cluros, stately, majestic, almost stationary, shedding his steady light upon the world below; Thuria, a great and glorious orb, swinging swift across the vaulted dome of the blue-black night, so low that she seemed to graze the hills, a gorgeous spectacle that held the girl now beneath the spell of its enchantment as it always had and always would.

"Ah, Thuria, mad queen of heaven!" murmured Tara of Helium. "The hills pass in stately procession, their bosoms rising and falling; the trees move in restless circles; the little grasses describe their little arcs; and all is movement, restless, mysterious movement without sound, while Thuria passes." The girl sighed and let her gaze fall again to the stern realities beneath. There was no mystery in the huge banths. He who had discovered her squatted there looking hungrily up at her. Most of the others had wandered away in search of other prey, but a few remained hoping yet to bury their fangs in that soft body.

The night wore on. Again Thuria left the heavens to her lord and master, hurrying on to keep her tryst with the Sun in other skies. But a single banth waited impatiently beneath the tree which harbored Tara of Helium. The others had left, but their roars, and growls, and moans thundered, or rumbled, or floated back to her from near and far. What prey found they in this little valley? There must be something that they were accustomed to find here that they should be drawn in so great numbers. The girl wondered what it could be.

How long the night! Numb, cold, and exhausted, Tara of Helium clung to the tree in growing desperation, for once she had dozed and almost fallen. Hope was low in her brave little heart. How much more could she endure? She asked herself the question and then, with a brave shake of her head, she squared her shoulders. "I still live!" she said aloud.

The banth looked up and growled.

Came Thuria again and after awhile the great Sun — a flaming lover, pursuing his heart's desire. And Cluros, the cold husband, continued his serene way, as placid as before his house had been violated by this hot Lothario. And now the Sun and both Moons rode together in the sky, lend-ing their far mysteries to make weird the Martian dawn. Tara of Helium looked out across the fair valley that spread upon all sides of her. It was rich and beautiful, but even as she looked upon it she shuddered, for to her mind came a picture of the headless things that the towers and the walls hid. Those by day and the banths by night! Ah, was it any wonder that she shuddered?

With the coming of the Sun the great Barsoomian lion rose to his feet. He turned angry eyes upon the girl above him, voiced a single ominous growl, and slunk away toward the hills. The girl watched him, and she saw that he gave the towers as wide a berth as possible and that he never took his eyes from one of them while he was passing it. Evidently the inmates had taught these savage creatures to respect them. Presently he passed from sight in a narrow defile, nor in any direction that she could see was there another. Momentarily at least the landscape was deserted. The girl wondered if she dared attempt to regain the hills and her flier. She dreaded the coming of the workmen to the fields as she was sure they would come. She shrank from again seeing the headless bodies, and found herself wondering if these things would come out into the fields and work. She looked toward the nearest tower. There was no sign of life there. The valley lay quiet now and deserted. She lowered herself stiffly to the ground. Her muscles were cramped and every move brought a twinge of pain. Pausing a moment to drink again at the stream she felt refreshed and then turned without more delay toward the hills. To cover the distance as quickly as possible seemed the only plan to pursue. The trees no longer offered concealment and so she did not go out of her way to be near them. The hills seemed very far away. She had not thought, the night before, that she had traveled so far. Really it had not been far, but now, with the three towers to pass in broad daylight, the distance seemed great indeed.

The second tower lay almost directly in her path. To make a detour would not lessen the chance of detection, it would only lengthen the period of her danger, and so she laid her course straight for the hill where her flier was, regardless of the tower. As she passed the first enclosure she thought that she heard the sound of movement within, but the gate did not open and she breathed more easily when it lay behind her. She came then to the second enclosure, the outer wall of which she must circle, as it lay across her route. As she passed close along it she distinctly heard not only movement within, but voices. In the world-language of Barsoom she heard a man issuing instructions — so many were to pick usa, so many were to irrigate this field, so many to cultivate that, and so on, as a foreman lays out the day's work for his crew.

Tara of Helium had just reached the gate in the outer wall. Without warning it swung open toward her. She saw that for a moment it would hide her from those within and in that moment she turned and ran, keeping close to the wall, until, passing out of sight beyond the curve of the structure, she came to the opposite side of the enclosure. Here, panting from her exertion and from the excitement of her narrow escape, she threw herself among some tall weeds that grew close to the foot of the wall. There she lay trembling for some time, not even daring to raise her head and look about. Never before had Tara of Helium felt the paralyzing effects of terror. She was shocked and angry at herself, that she, daughter of John Carter, Warlord of Barsoom, should exhibit fear. Not even the fact that there had been none there to witness it lessened her shame and anger, and the worst of it was she knew that under similar circumstances she would again be equally as craven. It was not the fear of death — she knew that. No, it was the thought of those headless bodies and that she might see them and that they might even touch her — lay hands upon her — seize her. She shuddered and trembled at the thought.

After a while she gained sufficient command of herself to raise her head and look about. To her horror she discovered that everywhere she looked she saw people working in the fields or preparing to do so. Workmen were coming from other towers. Little bands were passing to this field and that. There were even some already at work within thirty ads of her — about a hundred yards. There were ten, perhaps, in the party nearest her, both men and women, and all were beautiful of form and grotesque of face. So meager were their trappings that they were practically naked; a fact that was in no way remarkable among the tillers of the fields of Mars. Each wore the peculiar, high leather collar that completely hid the neck, and each wore sufficient other leather to support a single sword and a pocket-pouch. The leather was very old and worn, showing long, hard service, and was absolutely plain with the exception of a single device upon the left shoulder. The heads, however, were covered with ornaments of precious metals and jewels, so that little more than eyes, nose, and mouth were discernible. These were hideously inhuman and yet grotesquely human at the same time. The eyes were far apart and protruding, the nose scarce more than two small, parallel slits set vertically above a round hole that was the mouth. The heads were peculiarly repulsive — so much so that it seemed unbelievable to the girl that they formed an integral part of the beautiful bodies below them.

So fascinated was Tara of Helium that she could scarce take her eyes from the strange creatures — a fact that was to prove her undoing, for in order that she might see them she was forced to expose a part of her own head and presently, to her consternation, she saw that one of the creatures had stopped his work and was staring directly at her. She did not dare move, for it was still possible that the thing had not seen her, or at least was only suspicious that some creature lay hid among the weeds. If she could allay this suspicion by remaining motionless the creature might believe that he had been mistaken and return to his work; but, alas, such was not to be the case. She saw the thing call the attention of others to her and almost immediately four or five of them started to move in her direction.

It was impossible now to escape discovery. Her only hope lay in flight. If she could elude them and reach the hills and the flier ahead of them she might escape, and that could be accomplished in but one way — flight, immediate and swift. Leaping to her feet she darted along the base of the wall which she must skirt to the opposite side, beyond which lay the hill that was her goal. Her act was greeted by strange whistling sounds from the things behind her, and casting a glance over her shoulder she saw them all in rapid pursuit. There were also shrill commands that she halt, but to these she paid no attention. Before she had half circled the enclosure she discovered that her chances for successful escape were great, since it was evident to her that her pursuers were not so fleet as she. High indeed then were her hopes as she came in sight of the hill, but they were soon dashed by what lay before her, for there, in the fields that lay between, were fully a hundred creatures similar to those behind her and all were on the alert, evidently warned by the whistling of their fellows. Instructions and commands were shouted to and fro, with the result that those before her spread roughly into a great half circle to intercept her, and when she turned to the right, hoping to elude the net, she saw others coming from fields beyond, and to the left the same was true. But Tara of Helium would not admit defeat. Without once pausing she turned directly toward the center of the advancing semi-circle, beyond which lay her single chance of escape, and as she ran she drew her long, slim dagger. Like her valiant sire, if die she must, she would die fighting. There were gaps in the thin line confronting her and toward the widest of one of these she directed her course. The things on either side of the opening guessed her intent for they closed in to place themselves in her path. This widened the openings on either side of them and as the girl appeared almost to rush into their arms she turned suddenly at right angles, ran swiftly in the new direction for a few yards, and then dashed quickly toward the hill again. Now only a single warrior, with a wide gap on either side of him, barred her clear way to freedom, though all the others were speeding as rapidly as they could to intercept her. If she could pass this one without too much delay she could escape, of that she was certain. Her every hope hinged upon this. The creature before her realized it, too, for he moved cautiously, though swiftly, to intercept her, as a Rugby fullback might maneuver in the realization that he alone stood between the opposing team and a touchdown.

At first Tara of Helium had hoped that she might dodge him, for she could not but guess that she was not only more fleet but infinitely more agile than these strange creatures; but soon there came to her the realization that in the time consumed in an attempt to elude his grasp his nearer fellows would be upon her and escape then impossible, so she chose instead to charge straight for him, and when he guessed her decision he stood, half crouching and with outstretched arms, awaiting her. In one hand was his sword, but a voice arose, crying in tones of authority. "Take her alive! Do not harm her!" Instantly the fellow returned his sword to its scabbard and then Tara of Helium was upon him. Straight for that beautiful body she sprang and in the instant that the arms closed to seize her her sharp blade drove deep into the naked chest. The impact hurled them both to the ground and as Tara of Helium sprang to her feet again she saw, to her horror, that the loathsome head had rolled from the body and was now crawling away from her on six short, spider-like legs. The body struggled spasmodically and lay still. As brief as had been the delay caused by the encounter, it still had been of sufficient duration to undo her, for even as she rose two more of the things fell upon her and instantly thereafter she was surrounded. Her blade sank once more into naked flesh and once more a head rolled free and crawled away. Then they overpowered her and in another moment she was surrounded by fully a hundred of the creatures, all seeking to lay hands upon her. At first she thought that they wished to tear her to pieces in revenge for her having slain two of their fellows, but presently she realized that they were prompted more by curiosity than by any sinister motive.

"Come!" said one of her captors, both of whom had retained a hold upon her. As he spoke he tried to lead her away with him toward the nearest tower.

"She belongs to me," cried the other. "Did not I capture her? She will come with me to the tower of Moak."

"Never!" insisted the first. "She is Luud's. To Luud I will take her, and whosoever interferes may feel the keenness of my sword — in the head!" He almost shouted the last three words.

"Come! Enough of this," cried one who spoke with some show of authority. "She was captured in Luud's fields — she will go to Luud."

"She was discovered in Moak's fields, at the very foot of the tower of Moak," insisted he who had claimed her for Moak.

"You have heard the Nolach speak," cried the Luud. "It shall be as he says."

"Not while this Moak holds a sword," replied the other. "Rather will I cut her in twain and take my half to Moak than to relinquish her all to Luud," and he drew his sword, or rather he laid his hand upon its hilt in a threatening gesture; but before ever he could draw it the Luud had whipped his out and with a fearful blow cut deep into the head of his adversary. Instantly the big, round head collapsed, almost as a punctured balloon collapses, as a grayish semi-fluid matter spurted from it. The protruding eyes, apparently lidless, merely stared, the sphincter-like muscle of the mouth opened and closed, and then the head toppled from the body to the ground. The body stood dully for a moment and then slowly started to wander aimlessly about until one of the others seized it by the arm.

One of the two heads crawling about on the ground now approached. "This rykor belongs to Moak," it said. "I am a Moak, I will take it," and without further discussion it commenced to crawl up the front of the headless body, using its six short, spiderlike legs and two stout chelae which grew just in front of its legs and strongly resembled those of an Earthly lobster, except that they were both of the same size. The body in the meantime stood in passive indifference, its arms hanging idly at its sides. The head climbed to the shoulders and settled itself inside the leather collar that now hid its chelae and legs. Almost immediately the body gave evidence of intelligent animation. It raised its hands and adjusted the collar more comfortably, it took the head between its palms and settled it in place and when it moved around it did not wander aimlessly, but instead its steps were firm and to some purpose.

The girl watched all these things in growing wonder, and presently, no other of the Moaks seeming inclined to dispute the right of the Luud to her, she was led off by her captor toward the nearest tower. Several accompanied them, including one who carried the loose head under his arm. The head that was being carried conversed with the head upon the shoulders of the thing that carried it. Tara of Helium shivered. It was horrible! All that she had seen of these frightful creatures was horrible. And to be a prisoner, wholly in their power. Shadow of her first ancestor! What had she done to deserve so cruel a fate?

At the wall enclosing the tower they paused while one opened the gate and then they passed within the enclosure, which, to the girl's horror, she found filled with headless bodies. The creature who carried the bodiless head now set its burden upon the ground and the latter immediately crawled toward one of the bodies that was lying near by. Some wandered stupidly to and fro, but this one lay still. It was a female. The head crawled to it and made its way to the shoulders where it settled itself. At once the body sprang lightly erect. Another of those who had accompanied them from the fields approached with the harness and collar that had been taken from the dead body that the head had formerly topped. The new body now appropriated these and the hands deftly adjusted them. The creature was now as good as before Tara of Helium had struck down its former body with her slim blade. But there was a difference. Before it had been male — now it was female. That, however, seemed to make no difference to the head. In fact, Tara of Helium had noticed during the scramble and the fight about her that sex differences seemed of little moment to her captors. Males and females had taken equal part in her pursuit, both were identically harnessed and both carried swords, and she had seen as many females as males draw their weapons at the moment that a quarrel between the two factions seemed imminent.

The girl was given but brief opportunity for further observation of the pitiful creatures in the enclosure as her captor, after having directed the others to return to the fields, led her toward the tower, which they entered, passing into an apartment about ten feet wide and twenty long, in one end of which was a stairway leading to an upper level and in the other an opening to a similar stairway leading downward. The chamber, though on a level with the ground, was brilliantly lighted by windows in its inner wall, the light coming from a circular court in the center of the tower. The walls of this court appeared to be faced with what resembled glazed, white tile and the whole interior of it was flooded with dazzling light, a fact which immediately explained to the girl the purpose of the glass prisms of which the domes were constructed. The stairways themselves were sufficient to cause remark, since in nearly all Barsoomian architecture inclined runways are utilized for purposes of communication between different levels, and especially is this true of the more ancient forms and of those of remote districts where fewer changes have come to alter the customs of antiquity.

Down the stairway her captor led Tara of Helium. Down and down through chambers still lighted from the brilliant well. Occasionally they passed others going in the opposite direction and these always stopped to examine the girl and ask questions of her captor.

"I know nothing but that she was found in the fields and that I caught her after a fight in which she slew two rykors and in which I slew a Moak, and that I take her to Luud, to whom, of course, she belongs. If Luud wishes to question her that is for Luud to do — not for me." Thus always he answered the curious.

Presently they reached a room from which a circular tunnel led away from the tower, and into this the creature conducted her. The tunnel was some seven feet in diameter and flattened on the bottom to form a walk. For a hundred feet from the tower it was lined with the same tile-like material of the light well and amply illuminated by reflected light from that source. Beyond it was faced with stone of various shapes and sizes, neatly cut and fitted together — a very fine mosaic without a pattern. There were branches, too, and other tunnels which crossed this, and occasionally openings not more than a foot in diameter; these latter being usually close to the floor. Above each of these smaller openings was painted a different device, while upon the walls of the larger tunnels at all intersections and points of convergence hieroglyphics appeared. These the girl could not read though she guessed that they were the names of the tunnels, or notices indicating the points to which they led. She tried to study some of them out, but there was not a character that was familiar to her, which seemed strange, since, while the written languages of the various nations of Barsoom differ, it still is true that they have many characters and words in common.

She had tried to converse with her guard but he had not seemed inclined to talk with her and she had finally desisted. She could not but note that he had offered her no indignities, nor had he been either unnecessarily rough or in any way cruel.

The fact that she had slain two of the bodies with her dagger had apparently aroused no animosity or desire for revenge in the minds of the strange heads that surmounted the bodies — even those whose bodies had been killed. She did not try to understand it, since she could not approach the peculiar relationship between the heads and the bodies of these creatures from the basis of any past knowledge or experience of her own. So far their treatment of her seemed to augur naught that might arouse her fears. Perhaps, after all, she had been fortunate to fall into the hands of these strange people, who might not only protect her from harm, but even aid her in returning to Helium. That they were repulsive and uncanny she could not forget, but if they meant her no harm she could, at least, overlook their repulsiveness. Renewed hope aroused within her a spirit of greater cheerfulness, and it was almost blithely now that she moved at the side of her weird companion. She even caught herself humming a gay little tune that was then popular in Helium. The creature at her side turned its expressionless eyes upon her.

"What is that noise that you are making?" it asked.

"I was but humming an air," she replied.

"'Humming an air,'" he repeated. "I do not know what you mean; but do it again, I like it."

This time she sang the words, while her companion listened intently. His face gave no indication of what was passing in that strange head. It was as devoid of expression as that of a spider. It reminded her of a spider. When she had finished he turned toward her again.

"That was different," he said. "I liked that better, even, than the other. How do you do it?"

"Why," she said, "it is singing. Do you not know what song is?"

"No," he replied. "Tell me how you do it."

"It is difficult to explain," she told him, "since any explanation of it presupposes some knowledge of melody and of music, while your very question indicates that you have no knowledge of either."

"No," he said, "I do not know what you are talking about; but tell me how you do it."

"It is merely the melodious modulations

of my voice," she explained. "Listen!" and again she sang.

"I do not understand," he insisted; "but I like it. Could you teach me to do it?"

"I do not know, but I shall be glad to try."

"We will see what Luud does with you," he said. "If he does not want you I will keep you and you shall teach me to make sounds like that."

At his request she sang again as they continued their way along the winding tunnel, which was now lighted by occasional bulbs which appeared to be similar to the radium bulbs with which she was familiar and which were common to all the nations of Barsoom, insofar as she knew, having been perfected at so remote a period that their very origin was lost in antiquity. They consist, usually, of a hemispherica bowl of heavy glass in which is packed a compound containing what, according to John Carter, must be radium. The bowl is then cemented into a metal plate with a heavily insulated back and the whole affair set in the masonry of wall or ceiling as desired, where it gives off light of greater or less intensity, according to the composition of the filling material, for an almost incalculable period of time.

As they proceeded they met a greater number of the inhabitants of this underground world, and the girl noted that among many of these the metal and harness were more ornate than had been those of the workers in the fields above. The heads and bodies, however, were similar, even identical, she thought. No one offered her harm and she was now experiencing a feeling of relief almost akin to happiness, when her guide turned suddenly into an opening on the right side of the tunnel and she found herself in a large, well lighted chamber.

Chapter V
THE PERFECT BRAIN

The song that had been upon her lips as she entered died there — frozen by the sight of horror that met her eyes. In the center of the chamber a headless body lay upon the floor — a body that had been partially devoured — while over and upon it crawled a half a dozen heads upon their short, spider legs, and they tore at the flesh of the woman with their chelae and carried the bits to their awful mouths. They were eating human flesh — eating it raw!

Tara of Helium gasped in horror and turning away covered her eyes with her palms.

"Come!" said her captor. "What is the matter?"

"They are eating the flesh of the woman," she whispered in tones of horror.

"Why not?" he inquired. "Did you suppose that we kept the rykor for labor alone? Ah, no. They are delicious when kept and fattened. Fortunate, too, are those that are bred for food, since they are never called upon to do aught but eat."

"It is hideous!" she cried.

He looked at her steadily for a moment, but whether in surprise, in anger, or in pity his expressionless face did not reveal. Then he led her on across the room past the frightful thing, from which she turned away her eyes. Lying about the floor near the walls were half a dozen headless bodies in harness. These she guessed had been abandoned temporarily by the feasting heads until they again required their services. In the walls of this room there were many of the small, round openings she had noticed in various parts of the tunnels, the purpose of which she could not guess.

They passed through another corridor and then into a second chamber, larger than the first and more brilliantly illuminated. Within were several of the creatures with heads and bodies assembled, while many headless bodies lay about near the walls. Here her captor halted and spoke to one of the occupants of the chamber.

"I seek Luud," he said. "I bring to Luud a creature that I captured in the fields above."

The others crowded about to examine Tara of Helium. One of them whistled, whereupon the girl learned something of the smaller openings in the walls, for almost immediately there crawled from them, like giant spiders, a score or more of the hideous heads. Each sought one of the recumbent bodies and fastened itself in place. Immediately the bodies reacted to the intelligent direction of the heads. They arose, the hands adjusted the leather collars and put the balance of the harness in order, then the creatures crossed the room to where Tara of Helium stood. She noted that their leather was more highly ornamental than that worn by any of the others she had previously seen, and so she guessed that these must be higher in authority than the others. Nor was she mistaken. The demeanor of her captor indicated it. He addressed them as one who holds intercourse with superiors.

Several of those who examined her felt her flesh, pinching it gently between thumb and forefinger, a familiarity that the girl resented. She struck down their hands. "Do not touch me!" she cried, imperiously, for was she not a princess of Helium? The expressions on those terrible faces did not change. She could not tell whether they were angry or amused, whether her action had filled them with respect for her, or contempt. Only one of them spoke immediately.

"She will have to be fattened more," he said.

The girl's eyes went wide in horror. She turned upon her captor. "Do these frightful creatures intend to devour me?" she cried.

"That is for Luud to say," he replied, and then he leaned closer so that his mouth was near her ear. "That noise you made which you called song pleased me," he whispered, "and I will repay you by warning you not to antagonize these kaldanes. They are very powerful. Luud listens to them. Do not call them frightful. They are very handsome. Look at their wonderful trappings, their gold, their jewels."

"Thank you," she said. "You called them kaldanes — what does that mean?"

"We are all kaldanes," he replied.

"You, too?" and she pointed at him, her slim finger directed toward his chest.

"No, not this," he explained, touching his body; "this is a rykor; but this," and he touched his head, "is a kaldane. It is the brain, the intellect, the power that directs all things. The rykor," he indicated his body, "is nothing. It is not so much even as the jewels upon our harness; no, not so much as the harness itself. It carries us about. It is true that we would find difficulty getting along without it; but it has less value than harness or jewels because it is less difficult to reproduce." He turned again to the other kaldanes. "Will you notify Luud that I am here?" he asked.

"Sept has already gone to Luud. He will tell him," replied one. "Where did you find this rykor with the strange kaldane that cannot detach itself?"

The girl's captor narrated once more the story of her capture. He stated facts just as they had occurred, without embellish-

ment, his voice as expressionless as his face, and his story was received in the same manner that it was delivered. The creatures seemed totally lacking in emotion, or, at least, the capacity to express it. It was impossible to judge what impression the story made upon them, or even if they heard it. Their protruding eyes simply stared and occasionally the muscles of their mouths opened and closed. Familiarity did not lessen the horror the girl felt for them. The more she saw of them the more repulsive they seemed. Often her body was shaken by convulsive shudders as she looked at the kaldanes, but when her eyes wandered to the beautiful bodies and she could for a moment expunge the heads from her consciousness the effect was soothing and refreshing, though when the bodies lay, headless, upon the floor they were quite as shocking as the heads mounted on bodies. But by far the most grewsome and uncanny sight of all was that of the heads crawling about upon their spider legs. If one of these should approach and touch her Tara of Helium was positive that she should scream, while should one attempt to crawl up her person — ugh! the very idea induced a feeling of faintness.

Sept returned to the chamber. "Luud will see you and the captive. Come!" he said, and turned toward a door opposite that through which Tara of Helium had entered the chamber. "What is your name?" His question was directed to the girl's captor.

"I am Ghek, third foreman of the fields of Luud," he answered.

"And hers?"

"I do not know."

"It makes no difference. Come!"

The patrician brows of Tara of Helium went high. It made no difference, indeed! She, a princess of Helium; only daughter of The Warlord of Barsoom!

"Wait!" she cried. "It makes much difference who I am. If you are conducting me into the presence of your jed you may announce The Princess Tara of Helium, daughter of John Carter, The Warlord of Barsoom."

"Hold your peace!" commanded Sept. "Speak when you are spoken to. Come with me!"

The anger of Tara of Helium all but choked her. "Come," admonished Ghek, and took her by the arm, and Tara of Helium came. She was naught but a prisoner. Her rank and titles meant nothing to these inhuman monsters. They led her through a short, S-shaped passageway into a chamber entirely lined with the white tile-like material with which the interior of the light wall was faced. Close to the base of the walls were numerous smaller apertures, circular in shape, but larger than those of similar aspect that she had noted elsewhere. The majority of these apertures were sealed. Directly opposite the entrance was one framed in gold, and above it a peculiar device was inlaid in the same precious metal.

Sept and Ghek halted just within the room, the girl between them, and all three stood silently facing the opening in the opposite wall. On the floor beside the aperture lay a headless male body of almost heroic proportions, and on either side of this stood a heavily armed warrior, with drawn sword. For perhaps five minutes the three waited and then something appeared in the opening. It was a pair of large chelae and immediately thereafter there crawled forth a hideous kaldane of enormous proportions. He was half again as large as any that Tara of Helium had yet seen and his whole aspect infinitely more terrible. The skin of the others was a bluish gray — this one was of a little bluer tinge and the eyes were ringed with bands of white and scarlet, as was its mouth. From each nostril a band of white and one of scarlet extended outward horizontally the width of the face.

No one spoke or moved. The creature crawled to the prostrate body and affixed itself to the neck. Then the two rose as one and approached the girl. He looked at her and then he spoke to her captor.

"You are the third foreman of the fields of Luud?" he asked.

"Yes, Luud; I am called Ghek."

"Tell me what you know of this," and he nodded toward Tara of Helium.

Ghek did as he was bid and then Luud addressed the girl.

"What were you doing within the borders of Bantoom?" he asked.

"I was blown hither in a great storm that injured my flier and carried me I knew not where. I came down into the valley at night for food and drink. The banths came and drove me to the safety of a tree, and then your people caught me as I was trying to leave the valley. I do not know why they took me. I was doing no harm. All I ask is that you let me go my way in peace."

"None who enters Bantoom ever leaves," replied Luud.

"But my people are not at war with yours. I am a princess of Helium; my great-grandfather is a jeddak; my grandfather a jed; and my father is Warlord of all Barsoom. You have no right to keep me and I demand that you liberate me at once."

"None who enters Bantoom ever leaves," repeated the creature without expression. "I know nothing of the lesser creatures of Barsoom, of whom you speak. There is but one high race — the race of Bantoomians. All Nature exists to serve them. You shall do your share, but not yet — you are too skinny. We shall have to put some fat upon it, Sept. I tire of rykor. Perhaps this will have a different flavor. The banths are too rank and it is seldom that any other creature enters the valley. And you, Ghek; you shall be rewarded. I shall promote you from the fields to the burrows. Hereafter you shall remain underground as every Bantoomian longs to. No more shall you be forced to endure the hated sun, or look upon the hideous sky, or the hateful growing things that defile the surface. For the present you shall look after this thing that you have brought me, seeing that it sleeps and eats — and does nothing else. You understand me, Ghek; nothing else!"

"I understand, Luud," replied the other.

"Take it away!" commanded the creature.

Ghek turned and led Tara of Helium from the apartment. The girl was horrified by contemplation of the fate that awaited her — a fate from which it seemed, there was no escape. It was only too evident that these creatures possessed no gentle or chivalric sentiments to which she could appeal, and that she might escape from the labyrinthine mazes of their underground burrows appeared impossible.

Outside the audience chamber Sept overtook them and conversed with Ghek for a brief period, then her keeper led her through a confusing web of winding tunnels until they came to a small apartment.

"We are to remain here for a while. It may be that Luud will send for you again. If he does you will probably not be fattened — he will use you for another purpose." It was fortunate for the girl's peace of mind that she did not realize what he meant. "Sing for me," said Ghek, presently.

Tara of Helium did not feel at all like singing, but she sang, nevertheless, for there was always the hope that she might escape if given the opportunity and if she could win the friendship of one of the creatures, her chances would be increased proportionately. All during the ordeal, for such it was to the overwrought girl, Ghek stood with his eyes fixed upon her.

"It is wonderful," he said, when she had finished; "but I did not tell Luud — you noticed that I did not tell Luud about it. Had he known, he would have had you sing to him and that would have resulted in your being kept with him that he might hear you sing whenever he wished; but now I can have you all the time."

"How do you know he would like my singing?" she asked.

"He would have to," replied Ghek, "If I like a thing he has to like it, for are we not identical — all of us?"

"The people of my race do not all like the same things," said the girl.

"How strange!" commented Ghek. "All kaldanes like the same things and dislike the same things. If I discover something new and like it I know that all kaldanes will like it. That is how I know that Luud would like your singing. You see we are all exactly alike."

"But you do not look like Luud," said the girl.

"Luud is king. He is larger and more gorgeously marked; but otherwise he and I are identical, and why not? Did not Luud produce the egg from which I hatched?"

"What?" queried the girl; "I do not understand you."

"Yes," explained Ghek, "all of us are from Luud's eggs, just as all the swarm of Moak are from Moak's eggs."

"Oh!" exclaimed Tara of Helium understandingly; "you mean that Luud has many wives and that you are the offspring of one of them."

"No, not that at all," replied Ghek. "Luud has no wife. He lays the eggs himself. You do not understand."

Tara of Helium admitted that she did not.

"I will try to explain, then," said Ghek, "if you will promise to sing to me later."

"I promise," she said.

"We are not like the rykors," he began. "They are creatures of a low order, like yourself and the banths and such things. We have no sex — not one of us except our king, who is bi-sexual. He produces many eggs from which we, the workers and the warriors, are hatched; and one in every thousand eggs is another king egg, from which a king is hatched. Did you notice the sealed openings in the room where you saw Luud? Sealed in each of those is another king. If one of them escaped he would fall upon Luud and try to kill him and if he succeeded we should have a new king; but there would be no difference. His name would be Luud and all would go on as before, for are we not all alike? Luud has lived a long time and has produced many kings, so he lets only a few live that there may be a successor to him when he dies. The others he kills."

"Why does he keep more than one?" queried the girl.

"Sometimes accidents occur," replied Ghek, "and all the kings that a swarm has saved are killed. When this happens the swarm comes and obtains another king from a neighboring swarm."

"Are all of you the children of Luud?" she asked.

"All but a few, who are from the eggs of the preceding king, as was Luud; but Luud has lived a long time and not many of the others are left."

"You live a long time, or short?" Tara asked.

"A very long time."

"And the rykors, too; they live a long time?"

"No; the rykors live for ten years, perhaps," he said, "if they remain strong and useful. When they can no longer be of service to us, either through age or sickness, we leave them in the fields and the banths come at night and get them."

"How horrible!" she exclaimed.

"Horrible?" he repeated. "I see nothing horrible about that. The rykors are but brainless flesh. They neither see, nor feel, nor hear. They can scarce move but for us. If we did not bring them food they would starve to death. They are less deserving of thought than our leather. All that they can do for themselves is to take food from a trough and put it in their mouths, but with us — look at them!" and he proudly exhibited the noble figure that he surmounted, palpitant with life and energy and feeling.

"How do you do it?" asked Tara of Helium. "I do not understand it at all."

"I will show you," he said, and lay down upon the floor. Then he detached himself from the body, which lay as a thing dead. On his spider legs he walked toward the girl. "Now look," he admonished her. "Do you see this thing?" and he extended what appeared to be a bundle of tentacles from the posterior part of his head. "There is an aperture just back of the rykor's mouth and directly over the upper end of his spinal column. Into this aperture I insert my tenacles and seize the spinal cord. Immediately I control every muscle of the rykor's body — it becomes my own, just as you direct the movement of the muscles of your body. I feel what the rykor would feel if he had a head and brain. If he is hurt, I would suffer if I remained connected with him; but the instant one of them is injured or becomes sick we desert it for another. As we would suffer the pains of their physical injuries, similarly do we enjoy the physical pleasures of the rykors. When your body becomes fatigued you are comparatively useless; if it is sick, you are sick; if it is killed, you die. You are the slave of a mass of stupid flesh and bone and blood. There is nothing more wonderful about your carcass than there is about the carcass of a banth. It is only your brain that makes you superior to the anth, but your brain is bound by the limitations of your body. Not so, ours. With us brain is everything. Ninety per centum of our volume is brain. We have only the simplest of vital organs and they are very small for they do not have to assist in the support of a complicated system of nerves, muscles, flesh, and bone. We have no lungs, for we do not require air. Far below the levels to which we can take the rykors is a vast network of burrows where the real life of the kaldane is lived. There the air-breathing rykor would perish as you would perish. There we have stored vast quantities of food in hermetically sealed chambers. It will last forever. Far beneath the surface is water that will flow for countless ages after the surface water is exhausted. We are preparing for the time we know must come — the time when the last vestige of the Barsoomian atmosphere is spent — when the waters and the food are gone. For this purpose were we created, that there might not perish from the planet Nature's divinest creation — the perfect brain."

"But what purpose can you serve when that time comes?" asked the girl.

"You do not understand," he said. "It is too big for you to grasp, but I will try to explain it. Barsoom, the moons, the sun, the stars, were created for a single purpose. From the beginning of time Nature has labored arduously toward the consummation of this purpose. At the very beginning things existed with life, but with no brain. Gradually rudimentary nervous systems and minute brains evolved. Evolution proceeded. The brains became larger and more powerful. In us you see the highest development; but there are those of us who believe that there is yet another step — that some time in the far future our race shall develop into the super-thing — just brain. The incubus of legs and chelae and vital organs will be removed. The future kaldane will be nothing but a great brain. Deaf, dumb, and blind it will lie sealed in its buried vault far beneath the surface of Barsoom — just a great, wonderful, beautiful brain with nothing to distract it from eternal thought."

"You mean it will just lie there and think?" cried Tara of Helium.

"Just that!" he exclaimed. "Could aught be more wonderful?"

"Yes," replied the girl, "I can think of a number of things that would be infinitely more wonderful."

Chapter VI
IN THE TOILS OF HORROR

What the creature had told her gave Tara of Helium food for thought. She had been taught that every created thing fulfilled some useful purpose, and she tried conscientiously to discover just what was the rightful place of the kaldane in the universal scheme of things. She knew that it must have its place but what that place was it was beyond her to conceive. She had to give it up. They recalled to her mind a little group of people in Helium who had forsworn the pleasures of life in the pursuit of knowledge. They were rather patronizing in their relations with those whom they thought not so intellectual. They considered themselves quite superior. She smiled at recollection of a remark her father had once made concerning them, to the effect that if one of them ever dropped his egotism and broke it it would take a week to fumigate Helium. Her father liked normal people — people who knew too little and people who knew too much were equally a bore. Tara of Helium was like her father in this respect and like him, too, she was both sane and normal.

Outside of her personal danger there was much in this strange world that interested her. The rykors aroused her keenest pity, and vast conjecture. How and from what form had they evolved? She asked Ghek.

"Sing to me again and I will tell you," he said. "If Luud would let me have you, you should never die. I should keep you always to sing to me."

The girl marvelled at the effect her voice had upon the creature. Somewhere in that enormous brain there was a chord that was touched by melody. It was the sole link between herself and the brain when detached from the rykor. When it dominated the rykor it might have other human instincts; but these she dreaded even to think of. After she had sung she waited for Ghek to speak. For a long time he was silent, just looking at her through those awful eyes.

"I wonder," he said presently, "if it might not be pleasant to be of your race. Do you all sing?"

"Nearly all, a little," she said; "but we do many other interesting and enjoyable things. We dance and play and work and love and sometimes we fight, for we are a race of warriors."

"Love!" said the kaldane. "I think I know what you mean; but we, fortunately, are above sentiment — when we are detached. But when we dominate the rykor — ah, that is different, and when I hear you sing and look at your beautiful body I know what you mean by love. I could love you."

The girl shrank from him. "You promised to tell me the origin of the rykor," she reminded him.

"Ages ago," he commenced, "our bodies were larger and our heads smaller. Our legs were very weak and we could not travel fast or far. There was a stupid creature that went upon four legs. It lived in a hole in the ground, to which it brought its food, so we ran our burrows into this hole and ate the food it brought; but it did not bring enough for all — for itself and all the kaldanes that lived upon it, so we had also to go abroad and get food. This was hard work

for our weak legs. Then it was that we commenced to ride upon the backs of these primitive rykors. It took many ages, undoubtedly, but at last came the time when the kaldane had found means to guide the rykor, until presently the latter depended entirely upon the superior brain of his master to guide him to food. The brain of the rykor grew smaller as time went on. His ears went and his eyes, for he no longer had use for them — the kaldane saw and heard for him. By similar steps the rykor came to go upon its hind feet that the kaldane might be able to see farther. As the brain shrank, so did the head. The mouth was the only feature of the head that was used and so the mouth alone remains. Members of the red race fell into the hands of our ancestors from time to time. They saw the beauties and the advantages of the form that nature had given the red race over that which the rykor was developing into. By intelligent crossing the present rykor was achieved. He is really solely the product of the super-intelligence of the kaldane — he is our body, to do with as we see fit, just as you do what you see fit with your body, only we have the advantage of possessing an unlimited supply of bodies. Do you not wish that you were a kaldane?"

For how long they kept her in the subterranean chamber Tara of Helium did not know. It seemed a very long time. She ate and slept and watched the interminable lines of creatures that passed the entrance to her prison. There was a laden line passing from above carrying food, food, food. In the other line they returned empty handed. When she saw them she knew that it was daylight above. When they did not pass she knew it was night, and that the banths were about devouring the rykors that had been abandoned in the fields the previous day. She commenced to grow pale and thin. She did not like the food they gave her — it was not suited to her kind — nor would she have eaten overmuch palatable food, for the fear of becoming fat. The idea of plumpness had a new significance here — a horrible significance.

Ghek noted that she was growing thin and white. He spoke to her about it and she told him that she could not thrive thus beneath the ground — that she must have fresh air and sunshine, or she would wither and die. Evidently he carried her words to Luud, since it was not long after that he told her that the king had ordered that she be confined in the tower and to the tower she was taken. She had hoped against hope that this very thing might result from her conversation with Ghek. Even to see the sun again was something, but now there sprang to her breast a hope that she had not dared to nurse before, while she lay in the terrible labyrinth from which she knew she could never have found her way to the outer world; but now there was some slight reason to hope. At least she could see the hills and if she could see them might there not come also the opportunity to reach them? If she could have but ten minutes — just ten little minutes! The flier was still there — she knew that it must be. Just ten minutes and she would be free — free forever from this frightful place; but the days wore on and she was never alone, not even for half of ten minutes. Many times she planned her escape. Had it not been for the banths it had been easy of accomplishment by night. Ghek always detached his body then and sank into what seemed a semi-comatose condition. It could not be said that he slept, or at least it did not appear like sleep, since his lidless eyes were unchanged; but he lay quietly in a corner. Tara of Helium enacted a thousand times in her mind the scene of her escape. She would rush to the side of the rykor and seize the sword that hung in its harness. Before Ghek knew what she purposed, she would do this and then before he could give an alarm she would drive the blade through his hideous head. It would take but a moment to reach the enclosure. The rykors could not stop her, for they had no brains to tell them that she was escaping. She had watched from her window the opening and closing of the gate that led from the enclosure out into the fields and she knew how the great latch operated. She would pass through and make a quick dash for the hill. It was so near that they could not overtake her. It was so easy! Or it would have been but for the banths! The banths at night and the workers in the fields by day.

Confined to the tower and without proper exercise or food, the girl failed to show the improvement that her captors desired. Ghek questioned her in an effort to learn why it was that she did not grow round and plump; that she did not even look as well as when they had captured her.

His concern was prompted by repeated inquiries on the part of Luud and finally resulted in suggesting to Tara of Helium a plan whereby she might find a new opportunity of escape.

"I am accustomed to walking in the fresh air and the sunlight," she told Ghek. "I cannot become as I was before if I am to be always shut away in this one chamber, breathing poor air and getting no proper exercise. Permit me to go out in the fields every day and walk about while the sun is shining. Then, I am sure, I shall become nice and fat."

"You would run away," he said.

"But how could I if you were always with me?" she asked. "And even if I wished to run away, where could I go? I do not know even the direction of Helium. It must be very far. The very first night the banths would get me, would they not?"

"They would," said Ghek. "I will ask Luud about it."

The following day he told her that Luud had said that she was to be taken into the fields. He would try that for a time and see if she improved.

"If you do not grow fatter he will send for you anyway," said Ghek; "but he will not use you for food."

Tara of Helium shuddered.

That day and for many days thereafter she was taken from the tower, through the enclosure and out into the fields. Always was she alert for an opportunity to escape; but Ghek was always close by her side. It was not so much his presence that deterred her from making the attempt as the number of workers that were always between her and the hills where the flier lay. She could easily have eluded Ghek, but there were too many of the others. And then, one day, Ghek told her as he accompanied her into the open that this would be the last time.

"Tonight you go to Luud," he said. "I am sorry as I shall not hear you sing again."

"Tonight!" She scarce breathed the word, yet it was vibrant with horror.

She glanced quickly toward the hills. They were so close! Yet between were the inevitable workers — perhaps a score of them.

"Let us walk over there?" she said, indicating them. "I should like to see what they are doing."

"It is too far," said Ghek. "I hate the sun.

It is much pleasanter here where I can stand beneath the shade of this tree."

"All right," she agreed; "then you stay here and I will walk over. It will take me but a minute."

"No," he answered. "I will go with you. You want to escape; but you are not going to."

"I cannot escape," she said.

"I know it," agreed Ghek; "but you might try. I do not wish you to try. Possibly it will be better if we return to the tower at once. It would go hard with me should you escape."

Tara of Helium saw her last chance fading into oblivion. There would never be another after today. She cast about for some pretext to lure him even a little nearer to the hills.

"It is very little that I ask," she said. "Tonight you will want me to sing to you. It will be the last time. If you do not let me go and see what those kaldanes are doing I shall never sing to you again."

Ghek hesitated. "I will hold you by the arm all the time, then," he said.

"Why, of course, if you wish," she assented. "Come!"

The two moved toward the workers and the hills. The little party was digging tubers from the ground. She had noted this and that nearly always they were stooped low over their work, the hideous eyes bent upon the upturned soil. She led Ghek quite close to them, pretending that she wished to see exactly how they did the work, and all the time he held her tightly by her left wrist.

"It is very interesting," she said, with a sigh, and then, suddenly; "Look, Ghek!" and pointed quickly back in the direction of the tower. The kaldane, still holding her turned half away from her to look in the direction she had indicated and simultaneously, with the quickness of a banth, she struck him with her right fist, backed by every ounce of strength she possessed — struck the back of the pulpy head just above the collar. The blow was sufficient to accomplish her design, dislodging the kaldane from its rykor and tumbling it to the ground. Instantly the grasp upon her wrist relaxed as the body, no longer controlled by the brain of Ghek, stumbled aimlessly about for an instant before it sank to its knees and then rolled over on its back; but Tara of Helium waited not to note the full

results of her act. The instant the fingers loosened upon her wrist she broke away and dashed toward the hills. Simultaneously a warning whistle broke from Ghek's lips and in instant response the workers leaped to their feet, one almost in the girl's path. She dodged the outstretched arms and was away again toward the hills and freedom, when her foot caught in one of the hoe-like instruments with which the soil had been upturned and which had been left, half imbedded in the ground. For an instant she ran on, stumbling, in a mad effort to regain her equilibrium, but the upturned furrows caught at her feet — again she stumbled and this time went down, and as she scrambled to rise again a heavy body fell upon her and seized her arms. A moment later she was surrounded and dragged to her feet and as she looked around she saw Ghek crawling to his prostate rykor. A moment later he advanced to her side.

The hideous face, incapable of registering emotion, gave no clue to what was passing in the enormous brain. Was he nursing thoughts of anger, of hate, of revenge? Tara of Helium could not guess, nor did she care. The worst had happened. She had tried to escape and she had failed. There would never be another opportunity.

"Come!" said Ghek. "We will return to the tower." The deadly monotone of his voice was unbroken. It was worse than anger, for it revealed nothing of his intentions. It but increased her horror of these great brains that were beyond the possibility of human emotions.

And so she was dragged back to her prison in the tower and Ghek took up his vigil again, squatting by the doorway, but now he carried a naked sword in his hand and did not quit his rykor, only to change to another that he had brought to him when the first gave indication of weariness. The girl sat looking at him. He had not been unkind to her, but she felt no sense of gratitude, nor, on the other hand, any sense of hatred. The brains, incapable themselves of any of the finer sentiments, awoke none in her. She could not feel gratitude, or affection, or hatred of them. There was only the same unceasing sense of horror in their presence. She had heard great scientists discuss the future of the red race and she recalled that some had maintained that eventually the brain would entirely dominate the man. There would be no more instinctive acts or emotions, nothing would be done on impulse; but on the contrary reason would direct our every act. The propounder of the theory regretted that he might never enjoy the blessings of such a state, which, he argued, would result in the ideal life for mankind. Tara of Helium wished with all her heart that this learned scientist might be here to experience to the full the practical results of the fulfillment of his prophecy. Between the purely physical rykor and the purely mental kaldane there was little choice; but in the happy medium of normal, and imperfect, man, as she knew him, lay the most desirable state of existence. It would have been a splendid object lesson, she thought, to all those idealists who seek mass perfection in any phase of human endeavor, since here they might discover the truth that absolute perfection is as little to be desired as is its antithesis.

Gloomy were the thoughts that filled the mind of Tara of Helium as she awaited the summons from Luud — the summons that could mean for her but one thing; death. She guessed why he had sent for her and she knew that she must find the means for self-destruction before the night was over; but still she clung to hope and to life. She would not give up until there was no other way. She startled Ghek once by exclaiming aloud, almost fiercely: "I still live!"

"What do you mean?" asked the kaldane.

"I mean just what I say," she replied. "I still live and while I live I may still find a way. Dead, there is no hope."

"Find a way to what?" he asked.

"To life and liberty and mine own people," she responded.

"None who enters Bantoom ever leaves," he droned.

She did not reply and after a time he spoke again. "Sing to me," he said.

It was while she was singing that four warriors came to take her to Luud. They told Ghek that he was to remain where he was.

"Why?" asked Ghek.

"You have displeased Luud," replied one of the warriors.

"How?" demanded Ghek.

"You have demonstrated a lack of uncontaminable reasoning power. You have

permitted sentiment to influence you, thus demonstrating that you are a defective. You know the fate of defectives."

"I know the fate of defectives, but I am no defective," insisted Ghek.

"You permitted the strange noises which issue from her throat to please and soothe you, knowing well that their origin and purpose had nothing whatever to do with logic or the powers of reason. This in itself constitutes an unimpeachable indictment of weakness. Then, influenced doubtless by an illogical feeling of sentiment, you permitted her to walk abroad in the fields to a place where she was able to make an almost successful attempt to escape. Your own reasoning power, were it not defective, would convince you that you are unfit. The natural, and reasonable, consequence is destruction. Therefore you will be destroyed in such a way that the example will be beneficial to all other kaldanes of theswarm of Luud. In the meantime you will remain where you are.

"You are right," said Ghek. "I will remain here until Luud sees fit to destroy me in the most reasonable manner."

Tara of Helium shot a look of amazement at him as they led her from the chamber. Over her shoulder she called back to him: "Remember, Ghek, you still live!" Then they led her along the interminable tunnels to where Luud awaited her.

When she was conducted into his presence he was squatting in a corner of the chamber upon his six spidery legs. Near the opposite wall lay his rykor, its beautiful form trapped in gorgeous harness — a dead thing without a guiding kaldane. Luud dismissed the warriors who had accompanied the prisoner. Then he sat with his terrible eyes fixed upon her and without speaking for some time. Tara of Helium could but wait. What was to come she could only guess. When it came would be sufficiently the time to meet it. There was no necessity for anticipating the end. Presently Luud spoke.

"You think to escape," he said, in the deadly, expressionless monotone of his kind — the only possible result of orally expressing reason uninfluenced by sentiment. "You will not escape. You are merely the embodiment of two imperfect things — an imperfect brain and an imperfect body. The two cannot exist together in perfection. There you see a perfect body. He pointed toward the rykor. "It has no brain. Here," and he raised one of his chelae to his head, "is the perfect brain. It needs no body to function perfectly and properly as a brain. You would pit your feeble intellect against mine! Even now you are planning to slay me. If you are thwarted in that you expect to slay yourself. You will learn the power of mind over matter. I am the mind. You are the matter. What brain you have is too weak and ill-developed to deserve the name of brain. You have permitted it to be weakened by impulsive acts dictated by sentiment. It has no value. It has practically no control over your existence. You will not kill me. You will not kill yourself. When I am through with you you shall be killed f it seems the logical thing to do. You have no conception of the possibilities for power which lie in a perfectly developed brain. Look at that rykor. He has no brain. He can move but slightly of his own volition. An inherent mechanical instinct that we have permitted to remain in him allows him to carry food to his mouth; but he could not find food for himself. We have to place it within his reach and always in the same place. Should we put food at his feet and leave him alone he would starve to death. But now watch what a real brain may accomplish."

He turned his eyes upon the rykor and squatted there glaring at the insensate thing. Presently, to the girl's horror, the headless body moved. It rose slowly to its feet and crossed the room to Luud; it stooped and took the hideous head in its hands; it raised the head and set it on its shoulders.

"What chance have you against such power?" asked Luud. "As I did with the rykor so can I do with you."

Tara of Helium made no reply. Evidently no vocal reply was necessary.

"You doubt my ability!" stated Luud, which was precisely the fact, though the girl had only thought it — she had not said it.

Luud crossed the room and lay down. Then he detached himself from the body and crawled across the floor until he stood directly in front of the circular opening through which she had seen him emerge the day that she had first been brought to his presence. He stopped there and fastened his terrible eyes upon her. He did not speak, but his eyes seemed to be boring straight to the center of her brain. She felt an almost irresistible force urging her toward the kaldane. She fought to resist it; she tried to turn away her eyes, but she could not. They were held as in horrid fascination upon the glittering, lidless orbs of the great brain that faced her. Slowly, every step a painful struggle of resistance, she moved toward the horrific monster. She tried to cry aloud in an effort to awaken her numbing faculties, but no sound passed her lips. If those eyes would but turn away, just for an instant, she felt that she might regain the power to control her steps; but the eyes never left hers. They seemed but to burn deeper and deeper, gathering up every vestige of control of her entire nervous system.

As she approached the thing it backed slowly away upon its spider legs. She noticed that its chelae waved slowly to and fro before it as it backed, backed, backed, through the round aperture in the wall. Must she follow it there, too? What new and nameless horror lay concealed in that hidden chamber? No! she would not do it. Yet before she reached the wall she found herself down and crawling upon her hands and knees straight toward the hole from which the two eyes still clung to hers. At the very threshold of the opening she made a last, heroic stand, battling against the force that drew her on; but in the end she succumbed. With a gasp that ended in a sob Tara of Helium passed through the aperture into the chamber beyond.

The opening was but barely large enough to admit her. Upon the opposite, side she found herself in a small chamber. Before her squatted Luud. Against the opposite wall lay a large and beautiful male rykor. He was without harness or other trappings.

"You see now," said Luud, "the futility of revolt."

The words seemed to release her momentarily from the spell. Quickly she turned away her eyes.

"Look at me!" commanded Luud.

Tara of Helium kept her eyes averted. She felt a new strength, or at least a diminution of the creature's power over her. Had she stumbled upon the secret of its uncanny domination over her will? She dared not hope. With eyes averted she turned toward the aperture through which

To the girl's horror, the headless body moved

those baleful eyes had drawn her. Again Luud commanded her to stop, but the voice alone lacked all authority to influence her. It was not like the eyes. She heard the creature whistle and knew that it was summoning assistance; but because she did not dare look toward it she did not see it turn and concentrate its gaze upon the great, headless body lying by the further wall.

The girl was still slightly under the spell of the creature's influence — she had not regained full and independent domination of her powers. She moved as one in the throes of some hideous nightmare — slowly, painfully, as though each limb was hampered by a great weight, or as she were dragging her body through a viscous fluid. The aperture was close, ah, so close, yet, struggle as he would, she seemed to be making no appreciable progress toward it.

Behind her, urged on by the malevolent power of the great brain, the headless body crawled upon all-fours toward her. At last she had reached the aperture. Something seemed to tell her that once beyond it the domination of the kaldane would be broken. She was almost through into the adjoining chamber when she felt a heavy hand close upon her ankle. The rykor had reached forth and seized her, and though she struggled the thing dragged her back into the room with Luud. It held her tight and drew her close, and then, to her horror, it commenced to caress her.

"You see now," she heard Luud's dull voice, "the futility of revolt — and its punishment."

Tara of Helium fought to defend herself, but pitifully weak were her muscles against this brainless incarnation of brute power. Yet she fought, fought on in the face of hopeless odds for the honor of the proud name she bore — fought alone, she whom the fighting men of a mighty empire, the flower of Martian chivalry, would gladly have lain down their lives to save.

Chapter VII
A REPELLENT SIGHT

The cruiser Vanator careened through the tempest. That she had not been dashed to the ground, or twisted by the force of the elements into tangled wreckage, was due entirely to the caprice of Nature. For all the duration of the storm she rode, a helpless derelict, upon those storm-tossed waves of wind. But for all the dangers and vicissitudes they underwent, she and her crew might have borne charmed lives up to within an hour of the abating of the hurricane. It was then that the catastrophe occurred — a catastrophe indeed to the crew of the Vanator and the kingdom of Gathol.

The men had been without food or drink since leaving Helium, and they had been hurled about and buffeted in their lashings until all were worn to exhaustion. There was a brief lull in the storm during which one of the crew attempted to reach his quarters, after releasing the lashings which had held him to the precarious safety of the deck. The act in itself was a direct violation of orders and, in the eyes of the other members of the crew, the effect, which came with startling suddenness, took the form of a swift and terrible retribution. Scarce had the man released the safety snaps ere a swift arm of the storm-monster encircled the ship, rolling it over and over, with the result that the foolhardy warrior went overboard at the first turn.

Unloosed from their lashing by the constant turning and twisting of the ship and the force of the wind, the boarding and landing tackle had been trailing beneath the keel, a tangled mass of cordage and leather. Upon the occasions that the Vanator rolled completely over, these things would be wrapped about her until another revolution in the opposite direction, or the wind itself, carried them once again clear of the deck to trail, whipping in the storm, beneath the hurtling ship.

Into this fell the body of the warrior, and as a drowning man clutches at a straw so the fellow clutched at the tangled cordage that caught him and arrested his fall. With the strength of desperation he clung to the cordage, seeking frantically to entangle his legs and body in it. With each jerk of the ship his hand holds were all but torn loose, and though he knew that eventually they would be and that he must be dashed to the ground beneath, yet he fought with the madness that is born of hopelessness for the pitiful seconds which but prolonged his agony.

It was upon this sight then that Gahan of Gathol looked, over the edge of the careening deck of the Vanator, as he sought to learn the fate of his warrior. Lashed to the gunwale close at hand a single landing leather that had not fouled the tangled mass beneath whipped free from the ship's side, the hook snapping at its outer end. The Jed of Gathol grasped the situation in a single glance. Below him one of his people looked into the eyes of Death. To the jed's hand lay the means for succor.

There was no instant's hesitation. Casting off his deck lashings, he seized the landing leather and slipped over the ship's side. Swinging like a bob upon a mad pendulum he swung far out and back again, turning and twisting three thousand feet above the surface of Barsoom, and then, at last, the thing he had hoped for occurred. He was carried within reach of the cordage where the warrior still clung, though with rapidly diminishing strength. Catching one leg in a loop of the tangled strands Gahan pulled himself close enough to seize another quite near to the fellow. Clinging precariously to this new hold the jed slowly drew in the landing leather, down which he had clambered until he could grasp the hook at its end. This he fastened to a ring in the warrior's harness, just before the man's weakened fingers slipped from their hold upon the cordage.

Temporarily, at least, he had saved the life of his subject, and now he turned his attention toward insuring his own safety. Inextricably entangled in the mess to which he was clinging were numerous other landing hooks such as he had attached to the warrior's harness, and with one of these he sought to secure himself until the storm should abate sufficiently to permit him to climb to the deck, but even as he reached for one that swung near him the ship was caught in a renewed burst of the storm's fury, the thrashing cordage whipped and snapped to the lunging of the great craft and one of the heavy metal hooks, lashing through the air, struck the Jed of Gathol fair between the eyes.

Momentarily stunned, Gahan's fingers slipped from their hold upon the cordage and the man shot downward through the thin air of dying Mars toward the ground three thousand feet beneath, while upon the deck of the rolling *Vanator* his faithful warriors clung to their lashings all unconscious of the fate of their beloved leader; nor was it until more than an hour later, after the storm had materially subsided, that they realized he was lost, or knew the self-sacrificing heroism of the act that had sealed his doom. The *Vanator* now rested upon an even keel as she was carried along by a strong, though steady, wind. The warriors had cast off their deck lashings and the officers were taking account of losses and damage when a weak cry was heard from oversides, attracting their attention to the man hanging in the cordage beneath the keel. Strong arms hoisted him to the deck and then it was that the crew of the *Vanator* learned of the heroism of their jed and his end. How far they had traveled since his loss they could only vaguely guess, nor could they return in search of him in the disabled condition of the ship. It was a saddened company that drifted onward through the air toward whatever destination Fate was to choose for them.

And Gahan, Jed of Gathol — what of him? Plummet-like he fell for a thousand feet and then the storm seized him in its giant clutch and bore him far aloft again. As a bit of paper borne upon a gale he was tossed about in mid-air, the sport and plaything of the wind. Over and over it turned him and upward and downward it carried him, but after each new sally of the element he was brought nearer to the ground. The freaks of cyclonic storms are the rule of cyclonic storms, since such storms are in themselves freaks. They uproot and demolish giant trees, and in the same gust they transport frail infants for miles and deposit them unharmed in their wake.

And so it was with Gahan of Gathol. Expecting momentarily to be dashed to destruction he presently found himself deposited gently upon the soft, ochre moss of a dead sea-bottom, bodily no worse off for his harrowing adventure than in the possession of a slight swelling upon his forehead where the metal hook had struck him. Scarcely able to believe that Fate had dealt thus gently with him, the jed arose slowly, as though more than half convinced that he should discover crushed and splintered bones that would not support his weight. But he was intact. He looked about him in a vain effort at orientation. The air was filled with flying dust and debris. The Sun was obliterated. His vision was confined to a radius of a few hundred yards of ochre moss and dust-filled air. Five hundred yards away in any direction there might have arisen the walls of a great city and he not known it. It was useless to move from where he was until the air cleared, since he could not know in what direction he was moving, and so he stretched himself upon the moss and waited, pondering the fate of his warriors and his ship, but giving little thought to his own precarious situation.

Lashed to his harness were his swords, his pistols, and a dagger, and in his pocket-pouch a small quantity of the concentrated rations that form a part of the equipment of the fighting men of Barsoom. These things together with trained muscles, high courage, and an undaunted spirit sufficed him for whatever misadventures might lie between him and Gathol, which lay in what direction he knew not, nor at what distance.

The wind was falling rapidly and with it the dust that obscured the landscape. That the storm was over he was convinced, but he chafed at the inactivity the low visibility put upon him, nor did conditions better materially before night fell, so that he was forced to await the new day at the very spot at which the tempest had deposited him. Without his sleeping silks and furs he spent a far from comfortable night, and it was with feelings of unmixed relief that he saw the sudden dawn burst upon him. The air was now clear and in the light of the new day he saw an undulating plain stretching in all directions about him, while to the northwest there were barely discernible the outlines of low hills. Toward the southeast of Gathol was such a country, and as Gahan surmised the direction and the velocity of the storm to have carried him somewhere in the vicinity of the country he thought he recognized, he assumed that Gathol lay behind the hills he now saw, whereas, in reality, it lay far to the northeast.

It was two days before Gahan had crossed the plain and reached the summit of the hills from which he hoped to see his own country, only to meet at last with disappointment. Before him stretched another plain, of even greater proportions than that he had but just crossed, and beyond this other hills. In one material respect this plain differed from that behind him in that it was dotted with occasional isolated hills. Convinced, however, that Gathol lay somewhere in the direction of his search he descended into the valley and bent his steps toward the northwest.

For weeks Gahan of Gathol crossed valleys and hills in search of some familiar landmark that might point his way toward his native land, but the summit of each succeeding ridge revealed but another unfamiliar view. He saw few animals and no men, until he finally came to the belief that he had fallen upon that fabled area of ancient Barsoom which lay under the curse of her olden gods — the once rich and fertile country whose people in their pride and arrogance had denied the deities, and whose punishment had been extermination.

And then, one day, he scaled low hills and looked into an inhabited valley — a valley of trees and cultivated fields and plots of ground enclosed by stone walls surrounding strange towers. He saw people working in the fields, but he did not rush down to greet them. First he must know more of them and whether they might be assumed to be friends or enemies. Hidden by concealing shrubbery he crawled to a vantage point upon a hill that projected further into the valley, and here he lay upon his belly watching the workers closest to him. They were still quite a distance from him and he could not be quite sure of them, but there was something verging upon the unnatural about them. Their heads seemed out of proportion to their bodies — too large.

For a long time he lay watching them and ever more forcibly it was borne in upon his consciousness that they were not as he, and that it would be rash to trust himself among them. Presently he saw a couple appear from the nearest enclosure and slowly approach those who were working nearest to the hill where he lay in hiding. Immediately he was aware that one of these differed from all the others. Even at the greater distance he noted that the head was smaller and as they approached, he was confident that the harness of one of them was not as the harness of its companion or of that of any of those who tilled the fields.

The two stopped often, apparently in argument, as though one would proceed in the direction that they were going while the other demurred. But each time the smaller won reluctant consent from the other, and so they came closer and closer to the last line of workers toiling between the enclosure from which they had come and the hill where Gahan of Gathol lay watching, and then suddenly the smaller figure struck its companion full in the face. Gahan, horrified, saw the latter's head topple from its body, saw the body stagger and fall to the ground. The man half rose from his concealment the better to view the happenings in the valley below. The creature that had felled its companion was dashing madly in the direction of the hill upon which he was hidden, it dodged one of the workers that sought to seize it. Gahan hoped that it would gain its liberty, why he did not know, other than at closer range it had every appearance of being a creature of his own race. Then he saw it stumble and go down and instantly its pursuers were upon it. Then it was that Gahan's eyes chanced to return to the figure of the creature the fugitive had felled.

What horror was this that he was witnessing? Or were his eyes playing some ghastly joke upon him? No, impossible though it was — it was true — the head was moving slowly to the fallen body. It placed itself upon the shoulders, the body rose, and the creature, seemingly as good as new, ran quickly to where its fellows were dragging the hapless captive to its feet.

The watcher saw the creature take its prisoner by the arm and lead it back to the enclosure, and even across the distance that separated them from him he could note dejection and utter hopelessness in the bearing of the prisoner, and, too, he was half convinced that it was a woman, perhaps a red Martian of his own race. Could he be sure that this was true he must make some effort to rescue her even though the customs of his strange world required it only in case she was of his own country; but he was not sure; she might not be a red Martian at all, or, if she were, it was possible that she sprang from an enemy people as not. His first duty was to return to his own people with as little personal risk as possible, and though the thought of adventure stirred his blood he put the temptation aside with a sigh and turned away from the peaceful and beautiful valley that he longed to enter, for it was his intention to skirt its eastern edge and continue his search for Gathol beyond.

As Gahan of Gathol turned his steps along the southern slopes of the hills that bound Bantoom upon the south and east, his attention was attracted toward a small cluster of trees a short distance to his right. The low sun was casting long shadows. It would soon be night. The trees were off the path that he had chosen and he had little mind to be diverted from his way; but as he looked again he hesitated. There was something there besides boles of trees, and underbrush. There were suggestions of familiar lines of the handicraft of man. Gahan stopped and strained his eyes in the direction of the thing that had arrested his attention. No, he must be mistaken — the branches of the trees and a low bush had taken on an unnatural semblance in the horizontal rays of the setting sun. He turned and continued upon his way; but as he cast another side glance in the direction of the object of his interest, the sun's rays were shot back into his eyes from a glistening point of radiance among the trees.

Gahan shook his head and walked quickly toward the mystery, determined now to solve it. The shining object still lured him on and when he had come closer to it his eyes went wide in surprise, for the thing they saw was naught else than the jewel-encrusted emblem upon the prow of a small flier. Gahan, his hand upon his short-sword, moved silently forward, but as he neared the craft he saw that he had naught to fear, for it was deserted. Then he turned his attention toward the emblem. As its significance was flashed to his understanding his face paled and his heart went cold — it was the insignia of the house of The Warlord of Barsoom. Instantly he saw the dejected figure of the captive being led back to her prison in the valley just beyond the hills. Tara of Helium! And he had been so near to deserting her to her fate. The cold sweat stood in beads upon his brow.

A hasty examination of the deserted craft unfolded to the young jed the whole tragic story. The same tempest that had proved his undoing had borne Tara of Helium to this distant country. Here, doubtless, she had landed in hope of obtaining food and water since, without a propellor, she could not hope to reach her native city, or any other friendly port, other than by the merest caprice of Fate. The flier seemed intact except for the missing propellor and the fact that it had been carefully moored in the shelter of the clump of trees indicated that the girl had expected to return to it, while the dust and leaves upon its deck spoke of the long days, and even weeks, since she had landed. Mute yet eloquent proofs, these things, that Tara of Helium was a prisoner, and that she was the very prisoner whose bold dash for liberty he had so recently witnessed he now had not the slightest doubt.

The question now revolved solely about her rescue. He knew to which tower she had been taken — that much and no more. Of the number, the kind, or the disposition of her captors he knew nothing; nor did he care — for Tara of Helium he would face a hostile world alone. Rapidly he considered several plans for succoring her; but the one that appealed most strongly to him was that which offered the greatest chance of escape for the girl should he be successful in reaching her. His decision reached he turned his attention quickly toward the flier. Casting off its lashings he dragged it out from beneath the trees, and, mounting to the deck tested out the various controls. The motor started at a touch and purred sweetly, the buoyancy tanks were well stocked, and the ship answered pefectly to the controls which regulated her altitude. There was nothing needed but a propellor to make her fit for the long voyage to Helium. Gahan shrugged impatiently — there might not be a propellor within a thousand haads. But what mattered it? The craft even without a propellor would still answer the purpose his plan required of it — provided the captors of Tara of Helium were a people without ships, and he had seen nothing to suggest that they had ships. The architecture of their towers and enclosures assured him that they had not.

The sudden Barsoomian night had fallen. Cluros rode majestically the high heavens. The rumbling roar of a banth reverberated among the hills. Gahan of Gathol let the ship rise a few feet from the ground, then, seizing a bow rope, he dropped over the side. To tow the little craft was now a thing of ease, and as Gahan moved rapidly toward the brow of the hill above Bantoom the flier floated behind him as lightly as a swan upon a quiet lake. Now down the hill toward the tower dimly visible in the moonlight the Gatholian turned his steps. Closer behind him sounded the roar of the hunting banth. He wondered if the beast sought him or was following some other spoor. He could not be delayed now by any hungry beast of prey, for what might that very instant be befalling Tara of Helium he could not guess; and so he hastened his steps. But closer and closer came the horrid screams of the great carnivore, and now he heard the swift fall

of padded feet upon the hillside behind him. He glanced back just in time to see the beast break into a rapid charge. His hand leaped to the hilt of his long-sword, but he did not draw, for in the same instant he saw the futility of armed resistance, since behind the first banth came a herd of at least a dozen others. There was but a single alternative to a futile stand and that he grasped in the instant that he saw the overwhelming numbers of his antagonists.

Springing lightly from the ground he swarmed up the rope toward the bow of the flier. His weight drew the craft slightly lower and at the very instant that the man drew himself to the deck at the bow of the vessel, the leading banth sprang for the stern. Gahan leaped to his feet and rushed toward the great beast in the hope of dislodging it before it had succeeded in clambering aboard. At the same instant he saw that others of the banths were racing toward them with the quite evident intention of following their leader to the ship's deck. Should they reach it in any numbers he would be lost. There was but a single hope. Leaping for the altitude control Gahan pulled it wide. Simultaneously three banths leaped for the deck. The craft rose swiftly. Gahan felt the impact of a body against the keel, followed by the soft thuds of the great bodies as they struck the ground beneath. His act had not been an instant too soon. And now the leader had gained the deck and stood at the stern with glaring eyes and snarling jaws. Gahan drew his sword. The beast, possibly disconcerted by the novelty of its position, did not charge. Instead it crept slowly toward its intended prey. The craft was rising and Gahan placed a foot upon the control and stopped the ascent. He did not wish to chance rising to some higher air current that would bear him away. Already the craft was moving slowly toward the tower, carried thither by the impetus of the banth's heavy body leaping upon it from astern.

The man watched the slow approach of the monster, the slavering jowls, the malignant expression of the devilish face. The creature, finding the deck stable, appeared to be gaining confidence, and then the man leaped suddenly to one side of the deck and the tiny flier heeled as suddenly in response. The banth slipped and clutched frantically at the deck. Gahan leaped in with his naked sword; the great beast caught itself and reared upon its hind legs to reach forth and seize this presumptuous mortal that dared question its right to the flesh it craved; and then the man sprang to the opposite side of the deck. The banth toppled sideways at the same instant that it attempted to spring; a raking talon passed close to Gahan's head at the moment that his sword lunged through the savage heart, and as the warrior wrenched his blade from the carcass it slipped silently over the side of the ship.

A glance below showed that the vessel was drifting in the direction of the tower to which Gahan had seen the prisoner led. In another moment or two it would be directly over it. The man sprang to the control and let the craft drop quickly toward the ground were followed the banths, still hot for their prey. To land outside the enclosure spelled certain death, while inside he could see many forms huddled upon the ground as in sleep. The ship floated now but a few feet above the wall of the enclosure. There was nothing for it but to risk all on a bold bid for fortune, or drift helplessly past without hope of returning through the banth-infested valley, from many points of which he could now hear the roars and growls of these fierce Barsoomian lions.

Slipping over the side Gahan descended by the trailing anchor-rope until his feet touched the top of the wall, where he had no difficulty in arresting the slow drifting of the ship. Then he drew up the anchor and lowered it inside the enclosure. Still there was no movement upon the part of the sleepers beneath — they lay as dead men. Dull lights shone from openings in the tower; but there was no sign of guard or waking inmate. Clinging to the rope Gahan lowered himself within the enclosure, where he had his first close view of the creatures lying there in what he had thought sleep. With a half smothered exclamation of horror the man drew back from the headless bodies of the rykors. At first he thought them the corpses of decapitated humans like himself, which was quite bad enough; but when he saw them move and realized that they were endowed with life, his horror and disgust became even greater.

Here then was the explanation of the thing he had witnessed that afternoon,

when Tara of Helium had struck the head from her captor and Gahan had seen the head crawl back to its body. And to think that the pearl of Helium was in the power of such hideous things as these. Again the man shuddered, but he hastened to make fast the flier, clamber again to its deck and lower it to the floor of the enclosure. Then he strode toward a door in the base of the tower, stepping lightly over the recumbent forms of the unconscious rykors, and crossing the threshold disappeared within.

Chapter VIII
CLOSE WORK

Ghek, in his happier days third foreman of the fields of Luud, sat nursing his anger and his humiliation. Recently something had awakened within him the existence of which he had never before even dreamed. Had the influence of the strange captive woman aught to do with this unrest and dissatisfaction? He did not know. He missed the soothing influence of the noise she called singing. Could it be that there were other things more desirable than cold logic and undefiled brain power? Was well balanced imperfection more to be sought after then, than the high development of a single characteristic? He thought of the great, ultimate brain toward which all kaldanes were striving. It would be deaf, and dumb, and blind. A thousand beautiful strangers might sing and dance about it, but it could derive no pleasure from the singing or the dancing since it would possess no perceptive faculties. Already had the kaldanes shut themselves off from most of the gratifications of the senses. Ghek wondered if much was to be gained by denying themselves still further, and with the thought came a question as to the whole fabric of their theory. After all perhaps the girl was right; what purpose could a great brain serve sealed in the bowels of the earth?

And he, Ghek, was to die for this theory. Luud had decreed it. The injustice of it overwhelmed him with rage. But he was helpless. There was no escape. Beyond the enclosure the banths awaited him; within, his own kind, equally as merciless and ferocious. Among them there was no such thing as love, or loyalty, or friendship — they were just brains. He might kill Luud; but what would that profit him? Another king would be loosed from his sealed chamber and Ghek would be killed. He did not know it but he would not even have the poor satisfaction of satisfied revenge, since he was not capable of feeling so abstruse a sentiment.

Ghek, mounted upon his rykor, paced the floor of the tower chamber in which he had been ordered to remain. Ordinarily he would have accepted the sentence of Luud with perfect equanimity, since it was but the logical result of reason; but now it seemed different. The stranger woman had bewitched him. Life appeared a pleasant thing — there were great possibilities in it. The dream of the ultimate brain had receded into a tenuous haze far in the background of his thoughts.

At that moment there appeared in the doorway of the chamber a red warrior with naked sword. He was a male counterpart of the prisoner whose sweet voice had undermined the cold, calculating reason of the kaldane.

"Silence!" admonished the newcomer, his straight brows gathered in an ominous frown and the point of his long-sword playing menacingly before the eyes of the kaldane. "I seek the woman, Tara of Helium. Where is she? If you value your life speak quickly and speak the truth."

If he valued his life! It was a truth that Ghek had but just learned. He thought quickly. After all, a great brain is not without its uses. Perhaps here lay escape from the sentence of Luud.

"You are of her kind?" he asked. "You come to rescue her?"

"Yes."

"Listen, then. I have befriended her, and because of this I am to die. If I help you to liberate her, will you take me with you?"

Gahan of Gathol eyed the weird creature from crown to foot — the perfect body, the grotesque head, the expressionless face. Among such as these had the beautiful daughter of Helium been held captive for days and weeks.

"If she lives and is unharmed," he said, "I will take you with us."

"When they took her from me she was alive and unharmed," replied Ghek. "I cannot say what has befallen her since. Luud sent for her."

"Who is Luud? Where is he? Lead me to him." Gahan spoke quickly in tones vibrant with authority.

"Come, then," said Ghek, leading the way from the apartment and down a stairway toward the underground burrows of the kaldanes. "Luud is my king. I will take you to his chambers."

"Hasten!" urged Gahan.

"Sheathe your sword," warned Ghek, "so that should we pass others of my kind I may say to them that you are a new prisoner with some likelihood of winning their belief."

Gahan did as he was bid, but warning the kaldane that his hand was ever ready at his dagger's hilt.

"You need have no fear of treachery," said Ghek. "My only hope of life lies in you."

"And if you fail me," Gahan admonished him, "I can promise you as sure a death as even your king might guarantee you."

Ghek made no reply, but moved rapidly through the winding subterranean corridors until Gahan began to realize how truly was he in the hands of this strange monster. If the fellow should prove false it would profit Gahan nothing to slay him, since without his guidance the red man might never hope to retrace his way to the tower and freedom.

Twice they met and were accosted by other kaldanes; but in both instances Ghek's simple statement that he was taking a new prisoner to Luud appeared to allay all suspicion, and then at last they came to the ante-chamber of the king.

"Here, now, red man, thou must fight, if ever," whispered Ghek. "Enter there!" and he pointed to a doorway before them.

"And you?" asked Gahan, still fearful of treachery.

"My rykor is powerful," replied the kaldane. "I shall accompany you and fight at your side. As well die thus as in torture later at the will of Luud. Come!"

But Gahan had already crossed the room and entered the chamber beyond. Upon the opposite side of the room was a circular opening guarded by two warriors. Beyond this opening he could see two figures struggling upon the floor, and the fleeting glimpse he had of one of the faces suddenly endowed him with the strength of ten warriors and the ferocity of a wounded banth. It was Tara of Helium, fighting for her honor or her life.

The warriors, startled by the unexpected appearance of a red man, stood for a moment in dumb amazement, and in that moment Gahan of Gathol was upon them, and one was down, a sword-thrust through its heart.

"Strike at the heads," whispered the voice of Ghek in Gahan's ear. The latter saw the head of the fallen warrior crawl quickly within the aperture leading to the chamber where he had seen Tara of Helium in the clutches of a headless body. Then the sword of Ghek struck the kaldane of the remaining warrior from its rykor and Gahan ran his sword through the repulsive head.

Instantly the red warrior leaped for the aperture, while close behind him came Ghek.

"Look not upon the eyes of Luud," warned the kaldane, "or you are lost."

Within the chamber Gahan saw Tara of Helium in the clutches of a mighty body, while close to the wall upon the opposite side of the apartment crouched the hideous, spider-like Luud. Instantly the king realized the menace to himself and sought to fasten his eyes upon the eyes of Gahan, and in doing so he was forced to relax his concentration upon the rykor in whose embraces Tara struggled, so that almost immediately the girl found herself able to tear away from the awful, headless thing.

As she rose quickly to her feet she saw for the first time the cause of the interruption of Luud's plans. A red warrior! Her heart leaped in rejoicing and thanksgiving. What miracle of fate had sent him to her? She did not recognize him, though, this travel-worn warrior in the plain harness which showed no single jewel. How could she have guessed him the same as the scintillant creature of platinum and diamonds that she had seen for a brief hour under such different circumstances at the court of her august sire?

Luud saw Ghek following the strange warrior into the chamber. "Strike him down, Ghek!" commanded the king. "Strike down the stranger and your life shall be yours."

Gahan glanced at the hideous face of the king.

"Seek not his eyes," screamed Tara in warning; but it was too late. Already the horrid hypnotic gaze of the king kaldane had seized upon the eyes of Gahan. The red warrior hesitated in his stride. His sword point drooped slowly toward the floor. Tara glanced toward Ghek. She saw the creature

glaring with his expressionless eyes upon the broad back of the stranger. She saw the hand of the creature's rykor creeping stealthily toward the hilt of its dagger.

And then Tara of Helium raised her eyes aloft and poured forth the notes of Mars' most beautiful melody, *The Song of Love.*

Ghek drew his dagger from its sheath. His eyes turned toward the singing girl. Luud's glance wavered from the eyes of the man to the face of Tara, and the instant that the latter's song distracted his attention from his victim, Gahan of Gathol shook himself and as with a supreme effort of will forced his eyes to the wall above Luud's hideous head. Ghek raised his dagger above his right shoulder, took a single quick step forward, and struck. The girl's song ended in a stifled scream as she leaped forward with the evident intention of frustrating the kaldane's purpose; but she was too late, and well it was, for an instant later she realized the purpose of Ghek's act as she saw the dagger fly from his hand, pass Gahan's shoulder, and sink full to the guard in the soft face of Luud.

"Come!" cried the assassin, "we have no time to lose," and started for the aperture through which they had entered the chamber; but in his stride he paused as his glance was arrested by the form of the mighty rykor lying prone upon the floor — a king's rykor; the most beautiful, the most powerful, that the breeders of Bantoom could produce. Ghek realized that in his escape he could take with him but a single rykor, and there was none in Bantoom that could give him better service than this giant lying here. Quickly he transferred himself to the shoulders of the great, inert hulk. Instantly the latter was transformed to a sentient creature, filled with pulsing life and alert energy.

"Now," said the kaldane, "we are ready. Let whoso would revert to nothingness impede me." Even as he spoke he stooped and crawled into the chamber beyond, while Gahan, taking Tara by the arm, motioned her to follow. The girl looked him full in the eyes for the first time. "The Gods of my people have been kind," she said; "you came just in time. To the thanks of Tara of Helium shall be added those of The Warlord of Barsoom and his people. Thy reward shall surpass thy greatest desires."

Gahan of Gathol saw that she did not recognize him, and quickly he checked the warm greeting that had been upon his lips.

"Be thou Tara of Helium or another," he replied, "is immaterial, to serve thus a red woman of Barsoom is in itself sufficient reward."

As they spoke the girl was making her way through the aperture after Ghek, and presently all three had quitted the apartments of Luud and were moving rapidly along the winding corridors toward the tower. Ghek repeatedly urged them to greater speed, but the red men of Barsoom were never keen for retreat, and so the two that followed him moved all too slowly for the kaldane.

"There are none to impede our progress," urged Gahan, "so why tax the strength of the Princess by needless haste?"

"I fear not so much opposition ahead, for there are none there who know the thing that has been done in Luud's chambers this night; but the kaldane of one of the warriors who stood guard before Luud's apartment escaped, and you may count it a truth that he lost no time in seeking aid. That it did not come before we left is due solely to the rapidity with which events transpired in the king's[1] room. Long before we reach the tower they will be upon us from behind, and that they will come in numbers far superior to ours and with great and powerful rykors I well know."

Nor was Ghek's prophecy long in fulfilment. Presently the sounds of pursuit became audible in the distant clanking of accouterments and the whistling *call to arms* of the kaldanes.

"The tower is but a short distance now," cried Ghek. "Make haste while yet you may, and if we can barricade it until the sun rises we may yet escape."

"We shall need no barricades for we shall not linger in the tower," replied Gahan, moving more rapidly as he realized from the volume of sound behind them the great number of their pursuers.

"But we may not go further than the tower tonight," insisted Ghek. "Beyond the tower await the banths and certain death."

Gahan smiled. "Fear not the banths,"

he assured them. "Can we but reach the enclosure a little ahead of our pursuers we have naught to fear from any evil power within this accursed valley."

Ghek made no reply, nor did his expressionless face denote either belief or skepticism. The girl looked into the face of the man questioningly. She did not understand.

"Your flier," he said. "It is moored before the tower."

Her face lighted with pleasure and relief. "You found it!" she exclaimed. "What fortune!"

"It was fortune indeed," he replied. "Since it not only told that you were a prisoner here; but it saved me from the banths as I was crossing the valley from the hills to this tower into which I saw them take you this afternoon after your brave attempt at escape."

"How did you know it was I?" she asked, her puzzled brows scanning his face as though she sought to recall from past memories some scene in which he figured.

"Who is there but knows of the loss of the Princess Tara of Helium?" he replied. "And when I saw the device upon your flier I knew at once, though I had not known when I saw you among them in the fields a short time earlier. Too great was the distance for me to make certain whether their captive was man or woman. Had chance not divulged the hiding place of your flier I had gone my way, Tara of Helium. I shudder to think how close was the chance at that. But for the momentary shining of the sun upon the emblazoned device on the prow of your craft, I had passed on unknowing."

The girl shuddered. "The Gods sent you," she whispered reverently.

"The Gods sent me, Tara of Helium," he replied.

"But I do not recognize you," she said. "I have tried to recall you, but I have failed. Your name; what may it be?"

"It is not strange that so great a princess should not recall the face of every roving panthan of Barsoom," he replied with a smile.

"But your name?" insisted the girl.

"Call me Turan," replied the man, for it

[1] I have used the word *king* in describing the rulers or chiefs of the Bantoomian swarms, since the word itself is unpronounceable in English, nor does *jed* or *jeddak* of the red Martian tongue have quite the same meaning as the Bantoomian word, which has practically the same significance as the English word *queen* as applied to the leader of a swarm of bees.—J.C.

had come to him that if Tara of Helium rec-ognized him as the man whose impetuous avowal of love had angered her that day in the gardens of The Warlord, her situation might be rendered infinitely less bearable than were she to believe him a total stranger. Then, too, as a simple panthan[1] he might win a greater degree of her confi-dence by his loyalty and faithfulness and a place in her esteem that seemed to have been closed to the resplendent Jed of Gathol.

They had reached the tower now, and as they entered it from the subterranean cor-ridor a backward glance revealed the van of their pursuers — hideous kaldanes mounted upon swift and powerful rykors. As rapidly as might be the three ascended the stairways leading to the ground level, but after them, even more rapidly, came the minions of Luud. Ghek led the way, grasping one of Tara's hands the more eas-ily to guide and assist her, while Gahan of Gathol followed a few paces in their rear, his bared sword ready for the assault that all realized must come upon them now be-fore ever they reached the enclosure and the flier.

"Let Ghek drop behind to your side," said Tara, "and fight with you."

"There is but room for a single blade in these narrow corridors," replied the Gatho-lian. "Hasten on with Ghek and win to the deck of the flier. Have your hand upon the control, and if I come far enough ahead of these to reach the dangling cable you can rise at my word and I can clamber to the deck at my leisure; but if one of them emerges first into the enclosure you will know that I shall never come, and you will rise quickly and trust to the Gods of our ancestors to give you a fair breeze in the di-rection of a more hospitable people."

Tara of Helium shook her head. "We will not desert you, panthan," she said.

Gahan, ignoring her reply, spoke above her head to Ghek. "Take her to the craft moored within the enclosure," he com-manded. "It is our only hope. Alone, I may win to its deck; but have I to wait upon you two at the last moment the chances are that none of us will escape. Do as I bid." His tone was haughty and arrogant — the tone of a man who has commanded other men from birth, and whose will has been law. Tara of Helium was both angered and

[1] Soldier of Fortune; free-lance warrior.

vexed. She was not accustomed to being either commanded or ignored; but with all her royal pride she was no fool, and she knew the man was right; that he was risk-ing his life to save hers, so she hastened on with Ghek as she was bid, and after the first flush of anger she smiled, for the reali-zation came to her that this fellow was but a rough untutored warrior, skilled not in the finer usages of cultured courts. His heart was right, though; a brave and loyal heart, and gladly she forgave him the of-fense of his tone and manner. But what a tone! Recollection of it gave her sudden pause. Panthans were rough and ready men. Often they rose to positions of high-command, so it was not the note of author-ity in the fellow's voice that seemed re-markable; but something else — a quality that was indefinable, yet as distinct as it was familiar. She had heard it before when the voice of her great-grandsire, Tardos Mors, Jeddak of Helium, had risen in command; and in the voice of her grand-father, Mors Kajak, the jed; and in the ring-ing tones of her illustrious sire, John Carter, Warlord of Barsoom, when he addressed his warriors.

But now she had no time to speculate upon so trivial a thing, for behind her came the sudden clash of arms and she knew that Turan, the panthan, had crossed swords with the first of their pursuers. As she glanced back he was still visible beyond a turn in the stairway, so that she could see the quick swordplay that ensued. Daugh-ter of a world's greatest swordsman, she knew well the finest points of the art. She saw the clumsy attack of the kaldane and the quick, sure return of the panthan. As she looked down from above upon his al-most naked body, trapped only in the simplest of unadorned harness, and saw the play of the lithe muscles beneath the red-bronze skin, and witnessed the quick and delicate play of his sword point, to her sense of obligation was added a spontane-ous admission of admiration that was but the natural tribute of a woman to skill and bravery and, perchance, some trifle to manly symmetry and strength.

Three times the panthan's blade changed its position — once to fend a sav-age cut; once to feint; and once to thrust. And as he withdrew it from the last posi-tion the kaldane rolled lifeless from its stumbling rykor and Turan sprang quickly down the steps to engage the next behind, and then Ghek had drawn Tara upward and a turn in the stairway shut the battling panthan from her view; but still she heard the ring of steel on steel, the clank of accouterments and the shrill whistling of the kaldanes. Her heart moved her to turn back to the side of her brave defender; but her judgment told her that she could serve him best by being ready at the control of the flier at the moment he reached the enclosure.

Chapter IX

ADRIFT OVER STRANGE REGIONS

Presently Ghek pushed aside a door that opened from the stairway, and before them Tara saw the moonlight flooding the walled court where the headless rykors lay beside their feeding-troughs. She saw the perfect bodies, muscled as the best of her father's fighting men, and the females whose figures would have been the envy of many of Helium's most beautiful women. Ah, if she could but endow these with the power to act! Then indeed might the safety of the panthan be assured; but they were only poor lumps of clay, nor had she the power to quicken them to life. Ever must they lie thus until dominated by the cold, heartless brain of the kaldane. The girl sighed in pity even as she shuddered in disgust as she picked her way over and among the sprawled creatures toward the flier.

Quickly she and Ghek mounted to the deck after the latter had cast off the moorings. Tara tested the control, raising and lowering the ship a few feet within the walled space. It responded perfectly. Then she lowered it to the ground again and waited. From the open doorway came the sounds of conflict, now nearing them, now receding. The girl, having witnessed her champion's skill, had little fear of the outcome. Only a single antagonist could face him at a time upon the narrow stairway, he had the advantage of position and of the defensive, and he was a master of the sword while they were clumsy bunglers by comparison. Their sole advantage was in their numbers, unless they might find a way to come upon him from behind.

She paled at the thought. Could she have seen him she might have been further perturbed, for he took no advantage of many opportunities to win nearer the enclosure. He fought coolly, but with a savage persistence that bore little semblance to purely defensive action. Often he clambered over the body of a fallen foe to leap against the next behind, and once there lay five dead kaldanes behind him, so far had he pushed back his antagonists. They did not know it, these kaldanes that he fought, nor did the girl awaiting him upon the flier, but Gahan of Gathol was engaged in a more alluring sport than winning to freedom, for he was avenging the indignities that had been put upon the woman he loved; but presently he realized that he might be jeopardizing her safety uselessly, and so he struck down another before him and turning leaped quickly up the stairway, while the leading kaldanes slipped upon the brain-covered floor and stumbled in pursuit.

Gahan reached the enclosure twenty paces ahead of them and raced toward the flier. "Rise!" he shouted to the girl. "I will ascend the cable."

Slowly the small craft rose from the ground as Gahan leaped the inert bodies of the rykors lying in his path. The first of the pursuers sprang from the tower just as Gahan seized the trailing rope.

"Faster!" he shouted to the girl above, "or they will drag us down!" But the ship seemed scarcely to move, though in reality she was rising as rapidly as might have been expected of a one-man flier carrying a load of three. Gahan swung free above the top of the wall, but the end of the rope still dragged the ground as the kaldanes reached it. They were pouring in a steady stream from the tower into the enclosure. The leader seized the rope.

"Quick!" he cried. "Lay hold and we will drag them down."

It needed but the weight of a few to accomplish his design. The ship was stopped in its flight and then, to the horror of the girl, she felt it being dragged steadily downward. Gahan, too, realized the danger and the necessity for instant action. Clinging to the rope with his left hand, he had wound a leg about it, leaving his right hand free for his long-sword which he had not sheathed. A downward cut clove the soft head of a kaldane, and another severed the taut rope beneath the panthan's feet. The girl heard a sudden renewal of the shrill whistling of her foes, and at the same time she realized that the craft was rising again. Slowly it drifted upward, out of reach of the enemy, and a moment later she saw the figure of Turan clamber over the side. For the first time in many weeks her heart was filled with the joy of thanksgiving; but her first thought was of another.

"You are not wounded?" she asked.

"No, Tara of Helium," he replied. "They were scarce worth the effort of my blade, and never were they a menace to me because of their swords."

"They should have slain you easily," said Ghek. "So great and highly developed is the power of reason among us that they should have known before you struck just where, logically, you must seek to strike, and so they should have been able to parry your every thrust and easily find an opening to your heart."

"But they did not, Ghek," Gahan reminded him. "Their theory of development is wrong, for it does not tend toward a perfectly balanced whole. You have developed the brain and neglected the body and you can never do with the hands of another what you can do with your own hands. Mine are trained to the sword — every muscle responds instantly and accurately, and almost mechanically, to the need of the instant. I am scarcely objectively aware that I think when I fight, so quickly does my point take advantage of every opening, or spring to my defense if I am threatened that it is almost as though the cold steel had eyes and brains. You, with your kaldane brain and your rykor body, never could hope to achieve in the same degree of perfection those things that I can achieve. Development of the brain should not be the sum total of human endeavor. The richest and happiest peoples will be those who attain closest to well-balanced perfection of both mind and body, and even these must always be short of perfection. In absolute and general perfection lies stifling monotony and death. Nature must have contrasts; she must have shadows as well as high lights; sorrow with happiness; both wrong and right; and sin as well as virtue."

"Always have I been taught differently," replied Ghek; "but since I have known this woman and you, of another race, I have come to believe that there may be other standards fully as high and desirable as those of the kaldanes. At least I have had a glimpse of the thing you call happiness and I realize that it may be good even though I have no means of expressing it. I cannot laugh nor smile, and yet within me is a sense of contentment when this woman sings — a sense that seems to open before me wondrous vistas of beauty and unguessed pleasure that far transcend the cold joys of a perfectly functioning brain. I would that I had been born of thy race."

Caught by a gentle current of air the flier was drifting slowly toward the northeast across the valley of Bantoom. Below them lay the cultivated fields, and one after another they passed over the strange towers of Moak and Nolach and the other kings of the swarms that inhabited this weird and terrible land. Within each enclosure surrounding the towers grovelled the rykors, repellent, headless things, beautiful yet hideous.

"A lesson, those," remarked Gahan, indicating the rykors in an enclosure above which they were drifting at the time, "to that fortunately small minority of our race which worships the flesh and makes a god of appetite. You know them, Tara of Helium; they can tell you exactly what they had at the midday meal two weeks ago, and how the loin of the thoat should be prepared, and what drink should be served with the rump of the zitidar."

Tara of Helium laughed. "But not one of them could tell you the name of the man whose painting took the Jeddak's Award in The Temple of Beauty this year," she said. "Like the rykors, their development has not been balanced."

"Fortunate indeed are those in which there is combined a little good and a little bad, a little knowledge of many things outside their own callings, a capacity for love and a capacity for hate, for such as these can look with tolerance upon all, unbiased by the egotism of him whose head is so heavy on one side that all his brains run to that point."

As Gahan ceased speaking Ghek made a little noise in his throat as one does who would attract attention. "You speak as one who has thought much upon many subjects. Is it, then, possible that you of the red race have pleasure in thought? Do you know aught of the joys of introspection? Do reason and logic form any part of your lives?"

"Most assuredly," replied Gahan, "but

*Only a single antagonist could face him at a time
upon the narrow stairway*

not to the extent of occupying all our time
— at least not objectively. You, Ghek, are an
example of the egotism of which I spoke.
Because you and your kind devote your
lives to the worship of mind, you believe
that no other created beings think. And
possibly we do not in the sense that you do,
who think only of yourselves and your
great brains. We think of many things that
concern the welfare of a world. Had it not
been for the red men of Barsoom even the
kaldanes had perished from the planet, for
while you may live without air the things
upon which you depend for existence cannot, and there had been no air in sufficient
quantities upon Barsoom these many ages
had not a red man planned and built the
great atmosphere plant which gave new life
to a dying world.

"What have all the brains of all the kaldanes that have ever lived done to compare
with that single idea of a single red man?"

Ghek was stumped. Being a kaldane he
knew that brains spelled the sum total of
universal achievement, but it had never
occurred to him that they should be put to
use in practical and profitable ways. He
turned away and looked down upon the valley of his ancestors across which he was
slowly drifting, into what unknown world?
He should be a veritable god among the
underlings, he knew; but somehow a
doubt assailed him. It was evident that
these two from that other world were ready
to question his preeminence. Even
through *his* great egotism was filtering a
suspicion that they patronized him;
perhaps even pitied him. Then he began to
wonder what was to become of him. No
longer would he have many rykors to do his
bidding. Only this single one and when it
died there could not be another. When it
tired, Ghek must lie almost helpless while
it rested. He wished that he had never seen
this red woman. She had brought him only
discontent and dishonor and now exile.
Presently Tara of Helium commenced to
hum a tune and Ghek, the kaldane, was
content.

Gently they drifted beneath the hurtling moons above the mad shadows of a
Martian night. The roaring of the banths
came in diminishing volume to their ears
as their craft passed on beyond the boundaries of Bantoom, leaving behind the terrors of that unhappy land. But to what
were they being borne? The girl looked at
the man sitting cross-legged upon the deck
of the tiny flier, gazing off into the night
ahead, apparently absorbed in thought.

"Where are we?" she asked. "Toward
what are we drifting?"

Turan shrugged his broad shoulders.
"The stars tell me that we are drifting toward the northeast," he replied, "but
where we are, or what lies in our path I
cannot even guess. A week since I could
have sworn that I knew what lay behind
each succeeding ridge that I approached;
but now I admit in all humility that I have
no conception of what lies a mile in any direction. Tara of Helium, I am lost, and that
is all that I can tell you."

He was smiling and the girl smiled back
at him. There was a slightly puzzled expression on her face — there was something tantalizingly familiar about that
smile of his. She had met many a panthan
— they came and went, following the fighting of a world — but she could not place
this one.

"From what country are you, Turan?"
she asked suddenly.

"Know you not, Tara of Helium," he
countered, "that a panthan has no country? Today he fights beneath the banner of
one master, tomorrow beneath that of
another."

"But you must own allegiance to some
country when you are not fighting," she
insisted. "What banner, then, owns you
now?"

He rose and stood before her, then, bow-
ing low. "And I am acceptable," he said, "I
serve beneath the banner of the daughter
of The Warlord now — and forever."

She reached forth and touched his arm
with a slim brown hand. "Your services are
accepted," she said; "and if ever we reach
Helium I promise that your reward shall be
all that your heart could desire."

"I shall serve faithfully, hoping for that
reward," he said; but Tara of Helium did
not guess what was in his mind, thinking
rather that he was mercenary. For how
could the proud daughter of The Warlord
guess that a simple panthan aspired to her
hand and heart?

The dawn found them moving rapidly
over an unfamiliar landscape. The wind
had increased during the night and had
borne them far from Bantoom. The country below them was rough and inhospitable. No water was visible and the surface of

the ground was cut by deep gorges, while nowhere was any but the most meager vegetation discernible. They saw no life of any nature, nor was there any indication that the country could support life. For two days they drifted over this horrid wasteland. They were without food or water and suffered accordingly. Ghek had temporarily abandoned his rykor after enlisting Turan's assistance in lashing it safely to the deck. The less he used it the less would its vitality be spent. Already it was showing the effects of privation. Ghek crawled about the vessel like a great spider — over the side, down beneath the keel, and up over the opposite rail. He seemed equally at home one place as another. For his companions, however, the quarters were cramped, for the deck of a one-man flier is not intended for three.

Turan sought always ahead for signs of water. Water they must have, or that water-giving plant which makes life possible upon many of the seemingly arid areas of Mars; but there was neither the one nor the other for these two days and now the third night was upon them. The girl did not complain, but Turan knew that she must be suffering and his heart was heavy within him. Ghek suffered least of all, and he explained to them that his kind could exist for long periods without food or water. Turan almost cursed him as he saw the form of Tara of Helium slowly wasting away before his eyes, while the hideous kaldane seemed as full of vitality as ever.

"There are circumstances," remarked Ghek, "under which a gross and material body is less desirable than a highly developed brain."

Turan looked at him, but said nothing. Tara of Helium smiled faintly. "One cannot blame him," she said, "were we not a bit boastful in the pride of our superiority? When our stomachs were filled," she added.

"Perhaps there is something to be said for their system," Turan admitted. "If we could but lay aside our stomachs when they cried for food and water I have no doubt but that we should do so."

"I should never miss mine now," assented Tara; "It is mighty poor company."

A new day had dawned, revealing a less desolate country and renewing again the hope that had been low within them. Suddenly Turan leaned forward, pointing ahead.

"Look, Tara of Helium!" he cried. "A city! As I am Ga — as I am Turan the panthan, a city."

Far in the distance the domes and walls and slender towers of a city shone in the rising sun. Quickly the man seized the control and the ship dropped rapidly behind a low range of intervening hills, for well Turan knew that they must not be seen until they could discover whether friend or foe inhabited the strange city. Chances were that they were far from the abode of friends and so must the panthan move with the utmost caution; but there was a city and where a city was, was water, even though it were a deserted city, and food if it were inhabited.

To the red man food and water, even though it were a deserted city, and food if it were inhabited.

To the red man food and water, even in the citadel of an enemy, meant food and drink for Tara of Helium. He would accept it from friends or he would take it from enemies. Just so long as it was there he would have it — and there was shown the egotism of the fighting man, though Turan did not see it, nor Tara who came from a long line of fighting men; but Ghek might have smiled had he known how.

Turan permitted the flier to drift closer behind the screening hills, and then when he could advance no farther without fear of discovery, he dropped the craft gently to ground in a little ravine, and leaping over the side made her fast to a stout tree. For several moments they discussed their plans — whether it would be best to wait where they were until darkness hid their movements and then approach the city in search of food and water, or approach it now, taking advantage of what cover they could, until they could glean something of the nature of its inhabitants.

It was Turan's plan which finally prevailed. They would approach as close as safety dictated in the hope of finding water outside the city; food, too, perhaps. If they did not they could at least reconnoiter the ground by daylight, and then when night came Turan could quickly come close to the city and in comparative safety prosecute his search for food and drink.

Following the ravine upward they finally topped the summit of the ridge, from which they had an excellent view of that part of the city which lay nearest them, thoug themselves hidden by the brush behind which they crouched. Ghek had resumed his rykor, which had suffered less than either Tara or Turan through their enforced fast.

The first glance at the city, now much closer than when they had first discovered it, revealed the fact that it was inhabited. Banners and pennons broke from many a staff. People were moving about the gate before them. The high white walls were paced by sentinels at far intervals. Upon the roofs of higher buildings the women could be seen airing the sleeping silks and furs. Turan watched it all in silence for some time.

"I do not know them," he said at last. "I can not guess what city this may be. But it is an ancient city. Its people have no fliers and no firearms. It must be old indeed."

"How do you know they have not these things?" asked the girl.

"There are no landing-stages upon the roofs — not one that can be seen from here; while were we looking similarly at Helium we would see hundreds. And they have no firearms because their defenses are all built to withstand the attack of spear and arrow, with spear and arrow. They are an ancient people."

"If they are ancient perhaps they are friendly," suggested the girl. "Did we not learn as children in the history of our planet that it was once peopled by a friendly, peace-loving race?"

"But I fear they are not as ancient as that," replied Turan, laughing. "It has been long ages since the men of Barsoom loved peace."

"My father loves peace," returned the girl.

"And yet he is always at war," said the man.

She laughed. "But he *says* he likes peace."

"We all like peace," he rejoined; "peace with honor; but our neighbors will not let us have it, and so we must fight."

"And to fight well men must like to fight," she added.

"And to like to fight they must know how to fight," he said, "for no man likes to do the thing that he does not know how to do well."

"Or that some other man can do better than he."

"And so always there will be wars and men will fight," he concluded, "for always the men with hot blood in their veins will practice the art of war."

"We have settled a great question," said the girl, smiling; "but our stomachs are still empty."

"Your panthan is neglecting his duty," replied Turan; "and how can he with the great reward always before his eyes!"

She did not guess in what literal a sense he spoke.

"I go forthwith," he continued, "to wrest food and drink from the ancients."

"No," she cried, laying a hand upon his arm, "not yet. They would slay you or make you prisoner. You are a brave panthan and a mighty one, but you cannot overcome a city singlehanded."

She smiled up into his face and her hand still lay upon his arm. He felt the thrill of hot blood coursing through his veins. He could have seized her in his arms and crushed her to him. There was only Ghek the kaldane there, but there was something stronger within him that restrained his hand. Who may define it — that inherent chivalry that renders certain men the natural protectors of women?

From their vantage point they saw a body of armed warriors ride forth from the gate, and winding along a well-beaten road pass from sight about the foot of the hill from which they watched. The men were red, like themselves, and they rode the small saddle thoats of the red race. Their trappings were barbaric and magnificent, and in their head-dress were many feathers as had been the custom of ancients. They were armed with swords and long spears and they rode almost naked, their bodies being painted in ochre and blue and white. There were, perhaps, a score of them in the party as they galloped away on their tireless mounts they presented a picture at once savage and beautiful.

"They have the appearance of splendid warriors," said Turan. "I have a great mind to wall boldly into their city and seek service."

Tara shook her head. "Wait," she admonished. "What would I do without you, and if you were captured how could you collect your reward?"

"I should escape," he said. "At any rate I shall try it," and he started to rise.

"You shall not," said the girl, her tone all authority.

The man looked at her quickly — questioningly.

"You have entered my service," she said,

a trifle haughtily. "You have entered my service for hire and you shall do as I bid you."

Turan sank down beside her again with a half smile upon his lips. "It is yours to command, Princess," he said.

The day passed. Ghek, tiring of the sunlight, had deserted his rykor and crawled down a hole he had discovered close by. Tara and Turan reclined beneath the scant shade of a small tree. They watched the people coming and going through the gate. The party of horsemen did not return. A small herd of zitidars was driven into the city during the day, and once a caravan of broad-wheeled carts drawn by these huge animals wound out of the distant horizon and came down to the city. It, too, passed from their sight within the gateway. Then darkness came and Tara of Helium bid her parithan search for food and drink; but she cautioned him against attempting to enter the city. Before he left her he bent and kissed her hand as a warrior may kiss the hand of his queen.

Chapter X
ENTRAPPED

Turan the panthan approached the strange city under cover of the darkness. He entertained little hope of finding either food or water outside the wall, but he would try and then, if he failed, he would attempt to make his way into the city, for Tara of Helium must have sustenance and have it soon. He saw that the walls were poorly sentineled, but they were sufficiently high to render an attempt to scale them foredoomed to failure. Taking advantage of underbrush and trees, Turan managed to reach the base of the wall without detection. Silently he moved north past the gateway which was closed by a massive gate which effectively barred even the slightest glimpse within the city beyond. It was Turan's hope to find upon the north side of the city away from the hills a level plain where grew the crops of the inhabitants, and here too water from their irrigating system, but though he traveled far along that seemingly interminable wall he found no fields nor any water. He searched also for some means of ingress to the city, yet here, too, failure was his only reward, and now as he went keen eyes watched him from above and a silent stalker kept pace with him for a time upon the summit of the

wall; but presently the shadower descended to the pavement within and hurrying swiftly raced ahead of the stranger without.

He came presently to a small gate beside which was a low building and before the doorway of the building a warrior standing guard. He spoke a few quick words to the warrior and then entered the building only to return almost immediately to the street, followed by fully forty warriors. Cautiously opening the gate the fellow peered carefully along the wall upon the outside in the direction from which he had come. Evidently satisfied, he issued a few words of instruction to those behind him, whereupon half the warriors returned to the interior of the building, while the other half followed the man stealthily through the gateway where they crouched low among the shrubbery in a half circle just north of the gateway which they had left open. Here they waited in utter silence, nor had they long to wait before Turan the panthan came cautiously along the base of the wall. To the very gate he came and when he found it and that it was open he paused for a moment, listening; then he approached and looked within. Assured that there was none within sight to apprehend him he stepped through the gateway into the city.

He found himself in a narrow street that paralleled the wall. Upon the opposite side rose buildings of an architecture unknown to him, yet strangely beautiful. While the buildings were packed closely together there seemed to be no two alike and their fronts were of all shapes and heights and of many hues. The skyline was broken by spire and dome and minaret and tall, slender towers, while the walls supported many a balcony and in the soft light of Cluros, the farther moon, now low in the west, he saw, to his surprise and consternation, the figures of people upon the balconies. Directly opposite him were two women and a man. They sat leaning upon the rail of the balcony looking, apparently, directly at him; but if they saw him they gave no sign.

Turan hesitated a moment in the face of almost certain discovery and then, assured that they must take him for one of their own people, he moved boldly into the avenue. Having no idea of the direction in which he might best hope to find what he sought, and not wishing to arouse suspicion by further hesitation, he turned to the left and stepped briskly along the pavement with the intention of placing himself as quickly as possible beyond the observation of those nocturnal watchers. He knew that the night must be far spent; and so he could not but wonder why people should sit upon their balconies when they should have been asleep among their silks and furs. At first he had thought them the late guests of some convivial host; but the windows behind them were shrouded in darkness and utter quiet prevailed, quite upsetting such a theory. And as he proceeded he passed many another group sitting silently upon other balconies. They paid no attention to him, seeming not even to note his passing. Some leaned with a single elbow upon the rail, their chins resting in their palms; others leaned upon both arms across the balcony, looking down into the street, while several that he saw held musical instruments in their hands, but their fingers moved not upon the strings.

And then Turan came to a point where the avenue turned to the right, to skirt a building that jutted from the inside of the city wall, and as he rounded the corner he came full upon two warriors standing upon either side of the entrance to a building upon his right. It was impossible for them not to be aware of his presence, yet neither moved, nor gave other evidence that they had seen him. He stood there waiting, his hand upon the hilt of his long-sword but they neither challenged nor halted him. Could it be that these also thought him one of their own kind? Indeed upon no other grounds could he explain their inaction.

As Turan had passed through the gateway into the city and taken his unhindered way along the avenue, twenty warriors had entered the city and closed the gate behind them, and then one had taken to the wall and followed along its summit in the rear of Turan, and another had followed him along the avenue, while a third had crossed the street and entered one of the buildings upon the opposite side.

The balance of them, with the exception of a single sentinel beside the gate, had reentered the building from which they had been summoned. They were well built, strapping, painted fellows, their naked figures covered now by gorgeous robes against the chill of night. As they spoke of the stranger they laughed at the ease with which they had tricked him, and were still laughing as they threw themselves upon their sleeping silks and furs to resume their broken slumber. It was evident that they constituted a guard detailed for the gate beside which they slept, and it was equally evident that the gates were guarded and the city watched much more carefully than Turan had believed. Chagrined indeed had been the Jed of Gathol had he dreamed that he was being so neatly tricked.

As Turan proceeded along the avenue he passed other sentries beside other doors but now he gave them small heed, since they neither challenged nor otherwise outwardly noted his passing; but while at nearly every turn of the erratic avenue he passed one or more of these silent sentinels he could not guess that he had passed one of them many times and that his every move was watched by silent, clever stalkers. Scarce had he passed a certain one of these rigid guardsmen before the fellow awoke to sudden life, bounded across the avenue, entered a narrow opening in the outer wall where he swiftly followed a corridor built within the wall itself until presently he emerged a little distance ahead of Turan, where he assumed the stiff and silent attitude of a soldier upon guard. Nor did Turan know that a second followed in the shadows of the buildings behind him, nor of the third who hastened ahead of him upon some urgent mission.

And so the panthan moved through the silent streets of the strange city in search of food and drink for the woman he loved. Men and women looked down upon him from shadowy balconies, but spoke not; and sentinels saw him pass and did not challenge. Presently from along the avenue before him came the familiar sound of clanking accouterments, the herald of marching warriors, and almost simultaneously he saw upon his right an open doorway dimly lighted from within. It was the only available place where he might seek to hide from the approaching company, and while he had passed several sentries unquestioned he could scarce hope to escape scrutiny and questioning from a patrol, as he naturally assumed this body of men to be.

Inside the doorway he discovered a passage turning abruptly to the right and almost immediately thereafter to the left. There was none in sight within and so he stepped cautiously around the second turn the more effectually to be hidden from the street. Before him stretched a long corridor, dimly lighted like the entrance. Waiting there he heard the party approach the building, he heard someone at the entrance to his hiding place, and then he heard the door past which he had come slam to. He laid his hand upon his sword, expecting momentarily to hear footsteps approaching along the corridor; but none came. He approached the turn and looked around it; the corridor was empty to the closed door. Whoever had closed it had remained upon the outside.

Turan waited, listening. He heard no sound. Then he advanced to the door and placed an ear against it. All was silence in the street beyond. A sudden draft must have closed the door, or perhaps it was the duty of the patrol to see to such things. It was immaterial. They had evidently passed on and now he would return to the street and continue upon his way. Somewhere there would be a public fountain where he could obtain water, and the chance of food lay in the strings of dried vegetables and meat which hung before the doorways of nearly every Barsoomian home of the poorer classes that he had ever seen. It was this district he was seeking, and it was for this reason his search had lead him away from the main gate of the city which he knew would not be located in a poor district.

He attempted to open the door only to find that it resisted his every effort — it was locked upon the outside. Here indeed was a sorry contretemps. Turan the panthan scratched his head. "Fortune frowns upon me," he murmured; but beyond the door, Fate, in the form of a painted warrior, stood smiling. Neatly had he tricked the unwary stranger. The lighted doorway, the marching patrol — these had been planned and timed to a nicety by the third warrior who had sped ahead of Turan along another avenue, and the stranger had done precisely what the fellow had thought he would do — no wonder, then, that he smiled.

The exit barred to him Turan turned back into the corridor. He followed it cautiously and silently. Occasionally there was a door on one side or the other. These he tried only to find each securely locked.

The corridor wound more erratically the farther he advanced. A locked door barred his way at its end, but a door upon his right opened and he stepped into a dimly-lighted chamber, about the walls of which were three other doors, each of which he tried in turn. Two were locked; the other opened upon a runway leading downward. It was spiral and he could see no farther than the first turn. A door in the corridor he had quitted opened after he had passed, and the third warrior stepped out and followed after him. A faint smile still lingered upon the fellow's grim lips.

Turan drew his short-sword and cautiously descended. At the bottom was a short corridor with a closed door at the end. He approached the single heavy panel and listened. No sound came to him from beyond the mysterious portal. Gently he tried the door, which swung easily toward him at his touch. Before him was a low-ceiled chamber with a dirt floor. Set in its walls were several other doors and all were closed. As Turan stepped cautiously within, the third warrior descended the spiral runway behind him. The panthan crossed the room quickly and tried a door. It was locked. He heard a muffled click behind him and turned about with ready sword. He was alone; but the door through which he had entered was closed — it was the click of its lock that he had heard.

With a bound he crossed the room and attempted to open it; but to no avail. No longer did he seek silence, for he knew now that the thing had gone beyond the sphere of chance. He threw his weight against the wooden panel; but the thick skeel of which it was constructed would have withstood a battering ram. From beyond came a low laugh.

Rapidly Turan examined each of the other doors. They were all locked. A glance about the chamber revealed a wooden table and a bench. Set in the walls were several heavy rings to which rusty chains were attached — all too significant of the purpose to which the room was dedicated. In the dirt floor near the wall were two or three holes resembling the mouths of burrows — doubtless the habitat of the giant Martian rat. He had observed this much when suddenly the dim light was extinguished, leaving him in darkness utter and complete. Turan, groping about, sought the table and the bench. Placing the latter against the wall he drew the table in front of him and sat down upon the bench, his long-sword gripped in readiness before him. At least they should fight before they took him.

For some time he sat there waiting for he knew not what. No sound penetrated to his subterranean dungeon. He slowly revolved in his mind the incidents of the evening — the open, unguarded gate; the lighted doorway — the only one he had seen thus open and lighted along the avenue he had followed; the advance of the warriors at precisely the moment that he could find no other avenue of escape or concealment; the corridors and chambers that led past many locked doors to this underground prison leaving no other path for him to pursue.

"By my first ancestor!" he swore; "but it was simple and I a simpleton. They tricked me neatly and have taken me without exposing themselves to a scratch; but for what purpose?"

He wished that he might answer that question and then his thoughts turned to the girl waiting there on the hill beyond the city for him — and he would never come. He knew the ways of the more savage peoples of Barsoom. No, he would never come, now. He had disobeyed her. He smiled at the sweet recollection of those words of command that had fallen from her dear lips. He had disobeyed her and now he had lost the reward.

But what of her? What now would be her fate — starving before a hostile city with only an inhuman kaldane for company? Another thought — a horrid thought — obtruded itself upon him. She had told him of the hideous sights she had witnessed in the burrows of the kaldanes and he knew that they ate human flesh. Ghek was starving. Should he eat his rykor he would be helpless; but — there was sustenance there for them both, for the rykor and the kaldane. Turan cursed himself for a fool. Why had he left her? Far better to have remained and died with her, ready always to protect her, than to have left her at the mercy of the hideous Bantoomian.

Now Turan detected a heavy odor in the air. It oppressed him with a feeling of drowsiness. He would have risen to fight off the creeping lethargy, but his legs seemed weak, so that he sank again to the bench. Presently his sword slipped from his fingers and he sprawled forward upon the table, his head resting upon his arms.

Tara of Helium, as the night wore on and Turan did not return, became more and more uneasy, and when dawn broke with no sign of him she guessed that he had failed. Something more than her own unhappy predicament brought a feeling of sorrow to her heart — of sorrow and loneliness. She realized now how she had come to depend upon this panthan not only for protection but for companionship as well. She missed him, and in missing him realized suddenly that he had meant more to her than a mere hired warrior. It was as though a friend had been taken from her — an old and valued friend. She rose from her place of concealment that she might have a better view of the city.

U-Dor, dwar of the 8th Utan of O-Tar, Jeddak of Manator, rode back in the early dawn toward Manator from a brief excursion to a neighboring village. As he was rounding the hills south of the city, his keen eyes were attracted by a slight movement among the shrubbery close to the summit of the nearest hill. He halted his vicious mount and watched more closely. He saw a figure rise facing away from him and peer down toward Manator beyond the hill.

"Come!" He signalled to his followers, and with a word to his thoat turned the beast at a rapid gallop up the hillside. In his wake swept his twenty savage warriors, the padded feet of their mounts soundless upon the soft turf. It was the rattle of sidearms and harness that brought Tara of Helium suddenly about, facing them. She saw a score of warriors with couched lances bearing down upon her.

She glanced at Ghek. What would the spiderman do in this emergency? She saw him crawl to his rykor and attach himself. Then he arose, the beautiful body once again animated and alert. She thought that the creature was preparing for flight. Well, it made little difference to her. Against such as were streaming up the hill toward them a single mediocre swordsman such as Ghek was worse than no defense at all.

"Hurry, Ghek!" she admonished him. "Back into the hills! You may find there a hiding-place;" but the creature only stepped between her and the oncoming riders, drawing his long-sword.

"It is useless, Ghek," she said, when she saw that he intended to defend her. "What can a single sword accomplish against such odds?"

"I can die but once," replied the kaldane. "You and your panthan saved me from Luud and I but do what your panthan would do were he here to protect you."

"It is brave, but it is useless," she replied. "Sheathe your sword. They may not intend us harm."

Ghek let the point of his weapon drop to the ground, but he di not sheathe it, and thus the two stood waiting as U-Dor the dwar stopped his thoat before them while his twenty warriors formed a rough circle about. For a long minute U-Dor sat his mount in silence, looking searchingly first at Tara of Helium and then at her hideous companion.

"What manner of creature are you?" he asked presently. "And what do you before the gates of Manator?"

"We are from far countries," replied the girl, "and we are lost and starving. We ask only food and rest and the privilege to go our way seeking our own homes."

U-Dor smiled a grim smile. "Manator and the hills which guard it alone know the age of Manator," he said; "yet in all the ages that have rolled by since Manator first was, there be no record in the annals of Manator of a stranger departing from Manator."

"But I am a princess," cried the girl haughtily, "and my country is not at war with yours. You must give me and my companions aid and assist us to return to our own land. It is the law of Barsoom."

"Manator knows only the laws of Manator," replied U-Dor; "but come. You shall go with us to the city, where you, being beautiful, need have no fear. I, myself, will protect you if O-Tar so decrees. And as for your companion — but hold! You said 'companions' — there are others of your party then?"

"You see what you see," replied Tara haughtily.

"Be that as it may," said U-Dor. "If there be more they shall not escape Manator; but as I was saying, if your companion fights well he too may live, for O-Tar is just, and just are the laws of Manator. Come!"

Ghek demurred.

"It is useless," said the girl, seeing that he would have stood his ground and fought them. "Let us go with them. Why pit your puny blade against their mighty ones when there should lie in your great brain the means to outwit them?" She spoke in a low whisper, rapidly.

"You are right, Tara of Helium," he replied and sheathed his sword.

And so they moved down the hillside toward the gates of Manator — Tara, Princess of Helium, and Ghek, the kaldane of Bantoom — and surrounding them rode the savage, painted warriors of U-Dor, dwar of the 8th Utan of O-Tar, Jeddak of Manator.

Chapter XI

THE CHOICE OF TARA

The dazzling sunlight of Barsoom clothed Manator in an aureole of splendor as the girl and her captors rode into the city through The Gate of Enemies. Here the wall was some fifty feet thick, and the sides of the passageway within the gate were covered with parallel shelves of masonry from bottom to top. Within these shelves, or long, horizontal niches, stood row upon row of small figures, appearing like tiny, grotesque statuettes of men, their long, black hair falling below their feet and sometimes trailing to the shelf beneath. The figures were scarce a foot in height and but for their diminutive proportions might have been the mummified bodies of once living men. The girl noticed that as they passed, the warriors saluted the figures with their spears after the manner of Barsoomian fighting men in extending a military courtesy, and then they rode on into the avenue beyond, which ran, wide and stately, through the city toward the east.

On either side were great buildings wondrously wrought. Paintings of great beauty and antiquity covered many of the walls, their colors softened and blended by the suns of ages. Upon the pavement the life of the newly-awakened city was already afoot. Women in brilliant trappings, befeathered warriors, their bodies daubed with paint; artisans, armed but less gaily caparisoned, took their various ways upon the duties of the day. A giant zitidar, magnificent in rich harness, rumbled its broad-wheeled cart along the stone pavement toward The Gate of Enemies. Life and color and beauty wrought together a picture that filled the eyes of Tara of Helium with wonder and with admiration, for here was a scene out of the dead past of dying Mars. Such had been the cities of the founders of her race before Throxeus, mightiest of oceans, had disappeared from the face of a world. And from balconies on either side men and women looked down in silence upon the scene below.

The people in the street looked at the two prisoners, especially at the hideous Ghek, and called out in question or comment to their guard; but the watchers upon the balconies spoke not, nor did one so much as turn a head to note their passing. There were many balconies on each building and not a one that did not hold its silent party of richly trapped men and women, with here and there a child or two; but even the children maintained the uniform silence and immobility of their elders. As they approached the center of the city the girl saw that even the roofs bore companies of these idle watchers, harnessed and bejeweled as for some gala-day of laughter and music; but no laughter broke from those silent lips, nor any music from the strings of the instruments that many of them held in jeweled fingers.

And now the avenue widened into an immense square, at the far end of which rose a stately edifice gleaming white in virgin marble among the gaily painted buildings surrounding it and its scarlet sward and gaily-flowering, green-foliaged shrubbery. Toward this U-Dor led his prisoners and their guard to the great arched entrance before which a line of fifty mounted warriors barred the way. When the commander of the guard recognized U-Dor the guardsmen fell back to either side leaving a broad avenue through which the party passed. Directly inside the entrance were inclined runways leading upward on either side. U-Dor turned to the left and led them upward to the second floor and down a long corridor. Here they passed other mounted men and in chambers upon either side they saw more. Occasionally there was another runway leading either up or down. A warrior, his steed at full gallop, dashed into sight from one of these and raced swiftly past them upon some errand.

Nowhere as yet had Tara of Helium seen a man afoot in this great building; but when at a turn, U-Dor led them to the third floor she caught glimpses of chambers in which many riderless thoats were penned and others adjoining where dismounted

warriors lolled at ease or played games of skill or chance and many there were who played at jetan, and then the party passed into a long, wide hall of state, as magnificent an apartment as even a princess of mighty Helium ever had seen. The length of the room ran an arched ceiling ablaze with countless radium bulbs. The mighty spans extended from wall to wall leaving the vast floor unbroken by a single column. The arches were of white marble, apparently quarried in single, huge blocks from which each arch was cut complete. Between the arches, the ceiling was set solid about the radium bulbs with precious stones whose scintillant fire and color and beauty filled the whole apartment. The stones were carried down the walls in an irregular fringe for a few feet, where they appeared to hang like a beautiful and gorgeous drapery against the white marble of the wall. The marble ended some six or seven feet from the floor, the walls from that point down being wainscoted in solid gold. The floor itself was of marble richly inlaid with gold. In that single room was a vast treasure equal to the wealth of many a large city.

But what riveted the girl's attention even more than the fabulous treasure of decorations were the files of gorgeously harnessed warriors who sat their thoats in grim silence and immobility on either side of the central aisle, rank after rank of them to the farther walls, and as the party passed between them she could not note so much as the flicker of an eyelid, or the twitching of a thoat's ear.

"The Hall of Chiefs," whispered one of her guard, evidently noting her interest. There was a note of pride in the fellow's voice and something of hushed awe. Then they passed through a great doorway into the chamber beyond, a large, square room in which a dozen mounted warriors lolled in their saddles.

As U-Dor and his party entered the room, the warriors came quickly erect in their saddles and formed a line before another door upon the opposite side of the wall. The padwar commanding them saluted U-Dor who, with his party, had halted facing the guard.

"Send one to O-Tar announcing that U-Dor brings two prisoners worthy of the observation of the great jeddak," said U-Dor; "one because of her extreme beauty, the other because of his extreme ugliness."

"O-Tar sits in council with the lesser chiefs," replied the lieutenant; "but the words of U-Dor the dwar shall be carried to him," and he turned and gave instructions to one who sat his thoat behind him.

"What manner of creature is the male?" he asked of U-Dor. "It cannot be that both are of one race."

"They were together in the hills south of the city," explained U-Dor, "and they say that they are lost and starving."

"The woman is beautiful," said the padwar. "She will not long go begging in the city of Manator," and then they spoke of other matters — of the doings of the palace, of the expedition of U-Dor, until the messenger returned to say that O-Tar bade them bring the prisoners to him.

They passed then through a massive doorway, which, when opened, revealed the great council chamber of O-Tar, Jeddak of Manator, beyond. A central aisle led from the doorway the full length of the great hall, terminating at the steps of a marble dais upon which a man sat in a great throne-chair. Upon either side of the aisle were ranged rows of highly carved desks and chairs of skeel, a hard wood of great beauty. Only a few of the desks were occupied — those in the front row, just below the rostrum.

At the entrance U-Dor dismounted with four of his followers who formed a guard about the two prisoners who were then conducted toward the foot of the throne, following a few paces behind U-Dor. As they halted at the foot of the marble steps, the proud gaze of Tara of Helium rested upon the enthroned figure of the man above her. He sat erect without stiffness — a commanding presence trapped in the barbaric splendor that the Barsoomian chieftain loves. He was a large man, the perfection of whose handsome face was marred only by the hauteur of his cold eyes and the suggestion of cruelty imparted by too thin lips. It needed no second glance to assure the least observing that here indeed was a ruler of men — a fighting jeddak whose people might worship but not love, and for whose slightest favor warriors would vie with one another to go forth and die. This was O-Tar, Jeddak of Manator, and as Tara of Helium saw him for the first time she could not but acknowledge a certain admiration for this savage chieftain who so virily personified the ancient virtues of the God of War.

U-Dor and the jeddak interchanged the simple greetings of Barsoom, and then the former recounted the details of the discovery and capture of the prisoners. O-Tar scrutinized them both intently during U-Dor's narration of events, his expression revealing naught of what passed in the brain behind those inscrutable eyes. When the officer had finished the jeddak fastened his gaze upon Ghek.

"And you," he asked, "what manner of thing are you? From what country? Why are you in Manator?"

"I am a kaldane," replied Ghek; "the highest type of created creature upon the face of Barsoom; I am mind, you are matter. I come from Bantoom. I am here because we were lost and starving."

"And you!" O-Tar turned suddenly on Tara. "You, too, are a kaldane?"

"I am a princess of Helium," replied the girl. "I was a prisoner in Bantoom. This kaldane and a warrior of my own race rescued me. The warrior left us to search for food and water. He has doubtless fallen into the hands of your people. I ask you to free him and give us food and drink and let us go upon our way. I am a granddaughter of a jeddak, the daughter of a jeddak of jeddaks, The Warlord of Barsoom. I ask only the treatment that my people would accord you or yours."

"Helium," repeated O-Tar. "I know naught of Helium, nor does the Jeddak of Helium rule Manator. I, O-Tar, am Jeddak of Manator. I alone rule. I protect my own. You have never seen a woman or a warrior of Manator captive in Helium! Why should I protect the people of another jeddak? It is his duty to protect them. If he cannot, he is weak, and his people must fall into the hands of the strong. I, O-Tar, am strong. I will keep you. That —" he pointed at Ghek —"can it fight?"

"It is brave," replied Tara of Helium, "but it has not the skill at arms which my people possess."

"There is none then to fight for you?" asked O-Tar. We are a just people," he continued without waiting for a reply, "and had you one to fight for you he might win to freedom for himself and you as well."

"But U-Dor assured me that no stranger ever had departed from Manator," she answered.

O-Tar shrugged. "That does not disprove the justice of the laws of Manator," replied O-Tar, "but rather that the warriors of Manator are invincible. Had there come one who could defeat our warriors that one had won to liberty."

"And you fetch my warrior," cried Tara haughtily, "you shall see such swordplay as doubtless the crumbling walls of your decaying city never have witnessed, and if there be no trick in your offer we are already as good as free."

O-Tar smiled more broadly than before and U-Dor smiled, too, and the chiefs and warriors who looked on nudged one another and whispered, laughing. And Tara of Helium knew then that there was trickery in their justice; but though her situation seemed hopeless she did not cease to hope, for was she not the daughter of John Carter, Warlord of Barsoom, whose famous challenge to Fate, "I still live!" remained the one irreducible defense against despair? At thought of her noble sire the patrician chin of Tara of Helium rose a shade higher. Ah! if he but knew where she was there were little to fear then. The hosts of Helium would batter at the gates of Manator, the great green warriors of John Carter's savage allies would swarm up from the dead sea bottoms lusting for pillage and for loot, the stately ships of her beloved navy would soar above the unprotected towers and minarets of the doomed city which only capitulation and heavy tribute could then save.

But John Carter did not know! There was only one other to whom she might hope to look — Turan the panthan; but where was he? She had seen his sword in play and she knew that it had been wielded by a master hand, and who should know swordplay better than Tara of Helium, who had learned it well under the constant tutorage of John Carter himself. Tricks she knew that discounted even far greater physical prowess than her own, and a method of attack that might have been at once the envy and despair of the cleverest of warriors. And so it was that her thoughts turned to Turan the panthan, though not alone because of the protection he might afford her. She had realized, since he had left her in search of food, that there had grown between them a certain comradeship that she now missed. There had been that about him which seemed to have bridged the gulf between their stations in life. With him she had failed to consider that he was a panthan or that she was a princess — they had been comrades. Suddenly she realized that she missed him for himself more than for his sword. She turned toward O-Tar.

"Where is Turan, my warrior?" she demanded.

"You shall not lack for warriors," replied the jeddak. "One of your beauty will find plenty ready to fight for her. Possibly it shall not be necessary to look farther than the Jeddak of Manator. You please me, woman. What say you to such an honor?"

Through narrowed lids the Princess of Helium scrutinized the Jeddak of Manator, from feathered headdress to sandaled foot and back to feathered headdress.

"'Honor'!" she mimicked in tones of scorn. "I please thee, do I? Then know, swine, that thou pleaseth me not — that the daughter of John Carter is not for such as thou!"

A sudden, tense silence fell upon the assembled chiefs. Slowly the blood receded from the sinister face of O-Tar, Jeddak of Manator, leaving him a sickly purple in his wrath. His eyes narrowed to two thin slits, his lips were compressed to a bloodless line of malevolence. For a long moment there was no sound in the throne room of the palace at Manator. Then the jeddak turned toward U-Dor.

"Take her away," he said in a level voice that belied his appearance of rage. "Take her away, and at the next games let the prisoners and the common warriors play at jetan for her."

"And this?" asked U-Dor, pointing at Ghek.

"To the pits until the next games," replied O-Tar.

"So this is your vaunted justice!" cried Tara of Helium; "that two strangers who have not wronged you shall be sentenced without trial? And one of them is a woman. The swine of Manator are as just as they are brave."

"Away with her!" shouted O-Tar, and at a sign from U-Dor the guards formed about the two prisoners and conducted them from the chamber.

Outside the palace, Ghek and Tara of Helium were separated. The girl was led through long avenues toward the center of the city and finally into a low building, topped by lofty towers of massive construction. Here she was turned over to a warrior who wore the insignia of a dwar, or captain.

"It is O-Tar's wish," explained U-Dor to this one, "that she be kept until the next games, when the prisoners and the common warriors shall play for her. Had she not the tongue of a thoat she had been a worthy stake for our noblest steel," and U-Dor sighed. "Perhaps even yet I may win a pardon for her. It were too bad to see such beauty fall to the lot of some common fellow. I would have honored her myself."

"If I am to be imprisoned, imprison me," said the girl. "I do not recall that I was sentenced to listen to the insults of every low-born boor who chanced to admire me."

"You see, A-Kor," cried U-Dor, "the tongue that she has. Even so and worse spoke she to O-Tar the jeddak."

"I see," replied A-Kor, whom Tara saw was with difficulty restraining a smile. "Come, then, with me, woman," he said "and we shall find a safe place within The Towers of Jetan — but stay! what ails thee?"

The girl had staggered and would have fallen had not the man caught her in his arms. She seemed to gather herself then and bravely sought to stand erect without support. A-Kor glanced at U-Dor. "Knew you the woman was ill?" he asked.

"Possibly it is lack of food," replied the other. "She mentioned, I believe, that she and her companions had not eaten for several days."

"Brave are the warriors of O-Tar," sneered A-Kor; "lavish their hospitality. U-Dor, whose riches are uncounted, and the brave O-Tar, whose squealing thoats are stabled within marble halls and fed from troughs of gold, can spare no crust to feed a starving girl."

The black haired U-Dor scowled. "Thy tongue will yet pierce thy heart, son of a slave!" he cried. "Once too often mayst thou try the patience of the just O-Tar. Hereafter guard thy speech as well as thy towers."

"Think not to taunt me with my mother's state," said A-Kor. "'Tis the blood of the slave woman that fills my veins with pride, and my only shame is that I am also the son of thy jeddak."

"And O-Tar heard this?" queried U-Dor.

"O-Tar has already heard it from my own lips," replied A-Kor; "this, and more."

He turned upon his heel, a supporting arm still around the waist of Tara of Helium and thus he half led, half carried her into The Towers of Jetan, while U-Dor wheeled this thoat and galloped back in the direction of the palace.

Within the main entrance to The Towers of Jetan lolled a half-dozen warriors. To one of these spoke A-Kor, keeper of the towers. "Fetch Lan-O, the slave girl, and bid her bring food and drink to the upper level of the Thurian tower," then he lifted the half-fainting girl in his arms and bore her along the spiral, inclined runway that led upward within the tower.

Somewhere in the long ascent Tara lost consciousness. When it returned she found herself in a large, circular chamber, the stone walls of which were pierced by windows at regular intervals about the entire circumference of the room. She was lying upon a pile of sleeping silks and furs while there knelt above her a young woman who was forcing drops of some cooling beverage between her parched lips. Tara of Helium half rose upon an elbow and looked about. In the first moments of returning consciousness there were swept from the screen of recollection the happenings of many weeks. She thought that she awoke in the palace of The Warlord at Helium. Her brows knit as she scrutinized the strange face bending over her.

"Who are you?" she asked, and, "Where is Uthia?"

"I am Lan-O the slave girl," replied the other. "I know none by the name of Uthia."

Tara of Helium sat erect and looked about her. This rough stone was not the marble of her father's halls. "Where am I?" she asked.

"In The Thurian Tower," replied the girl, and then seeing that the other still did not understand she guessed the truth. "You are a prisoner in The Towers of Jetan in the city of Manator," she explained. "You were brought to this chamber, weak and fainting, by A-Kor, Dwar of The Towers of Jetan, who sent me to you with food and drink, for kind is the heart of A-Kor."

"I remember, now," said Tara, slowly. "I remember; but where is Turan, my warrior? Did they speak of him?"

"I heard naught of another," replied Lan-O; "you alone were brought to the towers. In that you are fortunate, for there be no nobler man in Manator than A-Kor. It is his mother's blood that makes him so. She was a slave girl from Gathol."

"Gathol!" exclaimed Tara of Helium.

"Lies Gathol close by Manator?"

"Nor close, yet still the nearest country," replied Lan-O. "About twenty-two degrees[1], it lies."

"Gathol!" murmured Tara, "Far Gathol!"

"But you are not from Gathol," said the slave girl; "your harness is not of Gathol."

"I am from Helium," said Tara.

"It is far from Helium to Gathol," said the slave girl, "but in our studies we learned much of the greatness of Helium, we of Gathol, so it seems not so far away."

"You, too, are from Gathol?" asked Tara.

"Many of us are from Gathol who are slaves in Manator," replied the girl. "It is to Gathol, nearest country, that the Manatorians look for slaves most often. They go in great numbers at intervals of three or seven years and haunt the roads that lead to Gathol, and thus they capture whole caravans leaving none to bear warning to Gathol of their fate. Nor do any ever escape from Manator to carry word of us back to Gahan our jed."

Tara of Helium ate slowly and in silence. The girl's words aroused memories of the last hours she had spent in her father's palace and the great midday function at which she had met Gahan of Gathol. Even now she flushed as she recalled his daring words.

Upon her reveries the door opened and a burly warrior appeared in the opening — a hulking fellow, with thick lips and an evil, leering face. The slave girl sprang to her feet, facing him.

"What does this mean, E-Med?" she cried; "was it not the will of A-Kor that this woman be not disturbed?"

"The will of A-Kor, indeed!" and the man sneered. "The will of A-Kor is without power inThe Towers of Jetan, or elsewhere, for A-Kor lies now in the pits of O-Tar, and E-Med is dwar of the Towers."

Tara of Helium saw the face of the slave girl pale and the terror in her eyes.

Chapter XII
GHEK PLAYS PRANKS

While Tara of Helium was being led to The Towers of Jetan, Ghek was escorted to the pits beneath the palace where he was imprisoned in a dimly-lighted chamber. Here he found a bench and a table standing upon the dirt floor near the wall, and set in the wall several rings from which depended short lengths of chain. At the base of the walls were several holes in the dirt floor. These, alone, of the several things he saw, interested him. Ghek sat down upon the bench and waited in silence, listening. Presently the lights were extinguished. If Ghek could have smiled he would have then, for Ghek could see as well in the dark as in the light — better, perhaps. He watched the dark openings of the holes in the floor and waited. Presently he detected a change in the air about him — it grew heavy with a strange odor, and once again might Ghek have smiled, could he have smiled.

Let them replace all the air in the chamber with their most deadly fumes; it would be all the same to Ghek, the kaldane, who, having no lungs, required no air. With the rykor it might be different. Deprived of air it would die; but if only a sufficient amount of the gas was introduced to stupefy an ordinary creature it would have no effect upon the rykor, who had no objective mind to overcome. So long as the excess of carbon dioxide in the blood was not sufficient to prevent heart action, the rykor would suffer only a diminution of vitality; but would still respond to the exciting agency of the kaldane's brain.

Ghek caused the rykor to assume a sitting position with its back against the wall where it might remain without direction from his brain. Then he released his contact with its spinal cord; but remained in position upon its shoulders, waiting and watching, for the kaldane's curiosity was aroused. He had not long to wait before the lights were flashed on and one of the locked doors opened to admit a half-dozen warriors. They approached him rapidly and worked quickly. First they removed all his weapons and then, snapping a fetter about one of the rykor's ankles, secured him to the end of one of the chains hanging from the walls. Next they dragged the long table to a new position and there bolted it to the floor so that an end, instead of the middle, was directly before the prisoner. On the table before him they set food and water and upon the opposite end of the table they laid the key to the fetter. Then they unlocked and opened all the doors and departed.

When Turan the panthan regained consciousness it was to the realization of a

[1] Approximately 814 Earth Miles.

sharp pain in one of his forearms. The effects of the gas departed as rapidly as they had overcome him so that as he opened his eyes he was in full possession of all his faculties. The lights were on again and in their glow there was revealed to the man the figure of a giant Martian rat crouching upon the table and gnawing upon his arm. Snatching his arm away he reached for his short-sword, while the rat, growling, sought to seize his arm again. It was then that Turan discovered that his weapons had been removed — short-sword, long-sword, dagger, and pistol. The rat charged him then and striking the creature away with his hand the man rose and backed off, searching for something with which to strike a harder blow. Again the rat charged and as Turan stepped quickly back to avoid the menacing jaws, something seemed to jerk suddenly upon his right ankle, and as he drew his left foot back to regain his equilibrium his heel caught upon a taut chain and he fell heavily backward to the floor just as the rat leaped upon his breast and sought his throat.

The Martian rat is a fierce and unlovely thing. It is many-legged and hairless, its hide resembling that of a new-born mouse in repulsiveness. In size and weight it is comparable to a large Airedale terrier. Its eyes are small and close-set, and almost hidden in deep, fleshly apertures. But its most ferocious and repulsive feature is its jaws, the entire bony structure of which protrudes several inches beyond the flesh, revealing five sharp, spadelike teeth in the upper jaw and the same number of similar teeth in the lower, the whole suggesting the appearance of a rotting face from which much of the flesh has sloughed away.

It was such a thing that leaped upon the breast of the panthan to tear at his jugular. Twice Turan struck it away as he sought to regain his feet, but both times it returned with increased ferocity to renew the attack. Its only weapons are its jaws since its broad, splay feet are armed with blunt talons. With its protruding jaws it excavates its winding burrows and with its broad feet it pushes the dirt behind it. To keep the jaws from his flesh then was Turan's only concern and this he succeeded in doing until chance gave him a hold upon the creature's throat. After that the end was but a matter of moments. Rising at last he flung the lifeless thing from him with a shudder of disgust.

Now he turned his attention to a hurried inventory of the new conditions which surrounded him since the moment of his incarceration. He realized vaguely what had happened. He had been anaesthetized and stripped of his weapons, and as he rose to his feet he saw that one ankle was fettered to a chain in the wall. He looked about the room. All the doors swung wide open! His captors would render his imprisonment the more cruel by leaving ever before him tempting glimpses of open aisles to the freedom he could not attain. Upon the end of the table and within easy reach was food and drink. This at least was attainable and at sight of it his starved stomach seemed almost to cry aloud for sustenance. It was with difficulty that he ate and drank in moderation.

As he devoured the food his eyes wandered about the confines of his prison until suddenly they seized upon a thing that lay on the table at the end farthest from him. It was a key. He raised his fettered ankle and examined the lock. There could be no doubt of it! The key that lay there on the table before him was the key to that very lock. A careless warrior had laid it there and departed, forgetting. Hope surged high in the breast of Gahan of Gathol, of Turan the panthan. Furtively his eyes sought the open doorways. There was no one in sight. Ah, if he could but gain his freedom! He would find some way from this odious city back to *her* side and never again would he leave her until he had won safety for her or death for himself.

He rose and moved cautiously toward the opposite end of the table where lay the coveted key. The fettered ankle halted his first step, but he stretched at full length along the table, extending eager fingers toward the prize. They almost laid hold upon it — a little more and they would touch it. He strained and stretched, but still the thing lay just beyond his reach. He hurled himself forward until the iron fetter bit deep into his flesh, but all futilely. He sat back upon the bench then and glared at the open doors and the key, realizing now that they were part of a well-laid scheme of refined torture, none the less demoralizing because it inflicted no physical suffering.

For just a moment the man gave way to useless regret and foreboding, then he gathered himself together, his brows cleared, and he returned to his unfinished meal. At least they should not have the

A giant Martian rat was gnawing upon his arm!

satisfaction of knowing how sorely they had hit him. As he ate it occurred to him that by dragging the table along the floor he could bring the key within his reach, but when he essayed to do so, he found that the table had been securely bolted to the floor during the period of his unconsciousness. Again Gahan smiled and shrugged and resumed his eating.

When the warriors had departed from the prison in which Ghek was confined, the kaldane crawled from the shoulders of the rykor to the table. Here he drank a little water and then directed the hands of the rykor to the balance of it and to the food, upon which the brainless thing fell with avidity. While it was thus engaged Ghek took his spider-like way along the table to the opposite end where lay the key to the fetter. Seizing it in a chela he leaped to the floor and scurried rapidly toward the mouth of one of the burrows against the wall, into which he disappeared. For long had the brain been contemplating these burrow entrances. They appealed to his kaldanean tastes, and further, they pointed a hiding place for the key and a lair for the only kind of food that the kaldane relished — flesh and blood.

Ghek had never seen an ulsio, since these great Martian rats had long ago disappeared from Bantoom, their flesh and blood having been greatly relished by the kaldanes; but Ghek had inherited, almost unimpaired, every memory of every ancestor, and so he knew that ulsio inhabited these lairs and that ulsio was good to eat, and he knew what ulsio looked like and what his habits were, though he had never seen him nor any picture of him. As we breed animals for the transmission of physical attributes, so the kaldanes breed themselves for the transmission of attributes of the mind, including memory and the power of recollection, and thus have they raised what we term instinct, above the level of the threshold of the objective mind where it may be commanded and utilized by recollection. Doubtless in our own subjective minds lie many of the impressions and experiences of our forebears. These may impinge upon our consciousness in dreams only, or in vague, haunting suggestions that we have before experienced some transient phase of our present existence. Ah, if we had but the power to recall them! Before us would unfold the forgotten story of the lost eons that have preceded us. We might even walk with God in the garden of His stars while man was still but a budding idea within His mind.

Ghek descended into the burrow at a steep incline for some ten feet, when he found himself in an elaborate and delightful network of burrows. The kaldane was elated. This indeed was life! He moved rapidly and fearlessly and he went as straight to his goal as you could to the kitchen of your own home. This goal lay at a low level in a spheroidal cavity about the size of a large barrel. Here, in a nest of torn bits of silk and fur lay six baby ulsios.

When the mother returned there were but five babies and a great spider-like creature, which she immediately sprang to attack only to be met by powerful chelae which seized and held her so that she could not move. Slowly they dragged her throat toward a hideous mouth and in a little moment she was dead.

Ghek might have remained in the nest for a long time, since there was ample food for many days; but he did not do so. Instead he explored the burrows. He followed them into many subterranean chambers of the city of Manator, and upward through walls to rooms above the ground. He found many ingeniously devised traps, and he found poisoned food and other signs of the constant battle that the inhabitants of Manator waged against these replusive creatures that dwelt beneath their homes and public buildings.

His exploration revealed not only the vast proportions of the network of runways that apparently traversed every portion of the city, but the great antiquity of the majority of them. Tons upon tons of dirt must have been removed, and for a long time he wondered where it had been deposited until in following downward a tunnel of great size and length he sensed before him the thunderous rush of subterranean waters, and presently came to the bank of a great, underground river, tumbling onward, no doubt, the length of a world to the buried sea of Omean. Into this torrential sewer had unthinkable generations of ulsios pushed their few handsful of dirt in the excavating of their vast labyrinth.

For only a moment did Ghek tarry by the river, for his seemingly aimless wanderings were in reality prompted by a definite purpose, and this he pursued with vigor and singleness of design. He followed such runways as appeared to terminate in the pits or other chambers of the inhabitants of the city, and these he explored, usually from the safety of a burrow's mouth, until satisfied that what he sought was not there. He moved swiftly upon his spider legs and covered remarkable distances in short periods of time.

His search not being rewarded with immediate success, he decided to return to the pit where his rykor lay chained and look to its wants. As he approached the end of the burrow that terminated in the pit he slackened his pace, stopping just within the entrance of the runway that he might scan the interior of the chamber before entering it. As he did so he saw the figure of a warrior appear suddenly in an opposite doorway. The rykor sprawled upon the table, his hands groping blindly for more food. Ghek saw the warrior pause and gaze in sudden astonishment at the rykor; he saw the fellow's eyes go wide and an ashen hue replace the copper bronze of his cheek. He stepped back as though someone had struck him in the face. For an instant only he stood thus as in a paralysis of fear, then he uttered a smothered shriek and turned and fled. Again was it a catastrophe that Ghek, the kaldane, could not smile.

Quickly entering the room he crawled to the table top and affixed himself to the shoulders of his rykor, and there he waited; and who may say that Ghek, though he could not smile, possessed not a sense of humor? For a half-hour he sat there, and then there came to him the sound of men approaching along corridors of stone. He could hear their arms clank against the rocky walls and he knew that they came at a rapid pace; but just before they reached the entrance to his prison they paused and advanced more slowly. In the lead was an officer, and just behind him, wide-eyed and perhaps still a little ashen, the warrior who had so recently departed in haste. At the doorway they halted and the officer turned sternly upon the warrior. With upraised finger he pointed at Ghek.

"There sits the creature! Didst thou dare lie, then, to thy dwar?"

"I swear," cried the warrior, "that I spoke the truth. But a moment since the thing groveled, headless, upon this very table! And may my first ancestor strike me

dead upon the spot if I speak other than a true word!"

The officer looked puzzled. The men of Mars seldom if ever lie. He scratched his head. Then he addressed Ghek. "How long have you been here?" he asked.

"Who knows better than those who placed me here and chained me to a wall?" he returned in reply.

"Saw you this warrior enter here a few minutes since?"

"I saw him," replied Ghek.

"And you sat there where you sit now?" continued the officer.

"Look thou to my chain and tell me then where else might I sit!" cried Ghek. "Art the people of thy city all fools?"

Three other warriors pressed behind the two in front, craning their necks to view the prisoner while they grinned at the discomfiture of their fellow. The officer scowled at Ghek.

"Thy tongue is as venomous as that of the she-banth O-Tar sent to The Towers of Jetan," he said.

"You speak of the young woman who was captured with me?" asked Ghek, his expressionless monotone and face revealing naught of the interest he felt.

"I speak of her," replied the dwar, and then turning to the warrior who had summoned him: "Return to thy quarters and remain there until the next games. Perhaps by that time thy eyes may have learned not to deceive thee."

The fellow cast a venomous glance at Ghek and turned away. The officer shook his head. "I do not understand it," he muttered. "Always has U-Van been a true and dependable warrior. Could it be —?" he glanced piercingly at Ghek. "Thou hast a strange head that misfits thy body, fellow," he cried. "Our legends tell us of those ancient creatures that placed hallucinations upon the minds of their fellows. If thou be such then maybe U-Van suffered from thy forbidden powers. If thou be such O-Tar will know well how to deal with thee." He wheeled about and motioned his warriors to follow him.

"Wait!" cried Ghek. "Unless I am to be starved, send me food."

"You have had food," replied the warrior.

"Am I to be fed but once a day?" asked Ghek. "I require food oftener than that. Send me food."

"You shall have food," replied the officer. "None may say that the prisoners of Manator are ill-fed. Just are the laws of Manator," and he departed.

No sooner had the sounds of their passing died away in the distance than Ghek clambered from the shoulders of his rykor, and scurried to the burrow where he had hidden the key. Fetching it he unlocked the fetter from about the creature's ankle, locked it empty and carried the key farther down into the burrow. Then he returned to his place upon his brainless servitor. After a while he heard footsteps approaching, whereupon he rose and passed into another corridor from that down which he knew the warrior was coming. Here he waited out of sight, listening. He heard the man enter the chamber and halt. He heard a muttered exclamation, followed by the jangle of metal dishes as a salver was slammed upon a table; then rapidly retreating footsteps, which quickly died away in the distance.

Ghek lost no time in returning to the chamber, recovering the key, relocking the rykor to his chain. Then he replaced the key in the burrow, and squatting on the table beside his headless body, directed its hands toward the food. While the rykor ate Ghek sat listening for the scraping sandals and clattering arms that he knew soon would come. Nor had he long to wait. Ghek scrambled to the shoulders of his rykor as he heard them coming. Again it was the officer who had been summoned by U-Van and with him were three warriors. The one directly behind him was evidently the same who had brought the food, for his eyes went wide when he saw Ghek sitting at the table and he looked very foolish as the dwar turned his stern glance upon him.

"It is even as I said," he cried. "He was not here when I brought his food."

"But he is here now," said the officer grimly, "and his fetter is locked about his ankle. Look! it has not been opened — but where is the key? It should be upon the table at the end opposite him. Where is the key, creature?" he shouted at Ghek.

"How should I, a prisoner, know better than my jailer the whereabouts of the key to my fetters?" he retorted.

"But it lay here," cried the officer, pointing to the other end of the table.

"Did you see it?" asked Ghek.

The officer hesitated. "No; but it must have been there," he parried.

"Did you see the key lying there?" asked Ghek, pointing to another warrior.

The fellow shook his head negatively. "And you? and you?" continued the kaldane addressing the others.

They both admitted that they never had seen the key. "And if it had been there how could I have reached it?" he continued.

"No, he could not have reached it," admitted the officer; "but there shall be no more of this! I-Zav, you will remain here on guard with this prisoner until you are relieved."

I-Zav looked anything but happy as this intelligence was transmitted to him, and he eyed Ghek suspiciously as the dwar and the other warriors turned and left him to his unhappy lot.

Chapter XIII
A DESPERATE DEED

E-Med crossed the tower chamber toward Tara of Helium and the slave girl, Lan-O. He seized the former roughly by a shoulder. "Stand!" he commanded. Tara struck his hand from her and rising, backed away.

"Lay not your hand upon the person of a princess of Helium, beast!" she warned.

E-Med laughed. "Think you that I play at jetan for you without first knowing something of the stake for which I play?" he demanded. "Come here!"

The girl drew herself to her full height, folding her arms across her breast, nor did E-Med note that the slim fingers of her right hand were inserted beneath the broad leather strap of her harness where it passed over her left shoulder.

"And O-Tar learns of this you shall rue it, E-Med," cried the slave girl; "there be no law in Manator that gives you this girl before you shall have won her fairly."

"What cares O-Tar for her fate?" replied E-Med. "Have I not heard? Did she not flout the great jeddak, heaping abuse upon him? By my first ancestor, I think O-Tar might make a jed of the man who subdued her," and again he advanced toward Tara.

"Wait!" said the girl in low, even tone. "Perhaps you know not what you do. Sacred to the people of Helium are the persons of the women of Helium. For the honor of the humblest of them would the great jeddak himself unsheathe his sword. The greatest nations of Barsoom have trembled to the thunders of war in defense of the person of Dejah Thoris, my mother.

We are but mortal and so may die; but we may not be defiled. You may play at jetan for a princess of Helium, but though you may win the match, never may you claim the reward. If thou wouldst possess a dead body press me too far, but know, man of Manator, that the blood of The Warlord flows not in the veins of Tara of Helium for naught. I have spoken."

"I know naught of Helium and O-Tar is *our* warlord," replied E-Med; "but I do know that I would examine more closely the prize that I shall play for and win. I would test the lips of her who is to be my slave after the next games; nor is it well, woman, to drive me too far to anger." His eyes narrowed as he spoke, his visage taking on the semblance of that of a snarling beast. "If you doubt the truth of my words ask Lan-O, the slave girl."

"He speaks truly, O woman of Helium," interjected Lan-O. "Try not the temper of E-Med, if you value your life."

But Tara of Helium made no reply. Already had she spoken. She stood in silence now facing the burly warrior who approached her. He came close and then quite suddenly he seized her and, bending, tried to draw her lips to his.

Lan-O saw the woman from Helium half turn, and with a quick movement jerk her right hand from where it had lain upon her breast. She saw the hand shoot from beneath the arm of E-Med and rise behind his shoulder and she saw in the hand a long, slim blade. The lips of the warrior were drawing closer to those of the woman, but they never touched them, for suddenly the man straightened, stiffly, a shriek upon his lips, and then he crumpled like an empty fur and lay, a shrunken heap, upon the floor. Tara of Helium stooped and wiped her blade upon his harness.

Lan-O, wide-eyed, looked with horror upon the corpse. "For this we shall both die," she cried.

"And who would live a slave in Manator?" asked Tara of Helium.

"I am not so brave as thou," said the slave girl, "and life is sweet and there is always hope."

"Life is sweet," agreed Tara of Helium, "but honor is sacred. But do not fear. When they come I shall tell them the truth — that you had no hand in this and no opportunity to prevent it."

For a moment the slave girl seemed to be thinking deeply. Suddenly her eyes lighted. "There is a way, perhaps," she said, "to turn suspicion from us. He has the key to this chamber upon him. Let us open the door and drag him out — maybe we shall find a place to hide him."

"Good!" exclaimed Tara of Helium, and the two immediately set about the matter Lan-O had suggested. Quickly they found the key and unlatched the door and then, between them, they half carried, half dragged, the corpse of E-Med from the room and down the stairway to the next level where Lan-O said there were vacant chambers. The first door they tried was unlatched, and through this the two bore their grisly burden into a small room lighted by a single window. The apartment bore evidence of having been utilized as a living-room rather than as a cell, being furnished with a degree of comfort and even luxury. The walls were paneled to a height of about seven feet from the floor, while the plaster above and the ceiling were decorated with faded paintings of another day.

As Tara's eyes ran quickly over the interior her attention was drawn to a section of paneling that seemed to be separated at one edge from the piece next adjoining it. Quickly she crossed to it, discovering that one vertical edge of an entire panel projected a half-inch beyond the others. There was a possible explanation which piqued her curiosity, and acting upon its suggestion she seized upon the projecting edge and pulled outward. Slowly the panel swung toward her, revealing a dark aperture in the wall behind.

"Look, Lan-O!" she cried. "See what I have found — a hole in which we may hide the thing upon the floor."

Lan-O joined her and together the two investigated the dark aperture, finding a small platform from which a narrow runway led downward into Stygian darkness. Thick dust covered the floor within the doorway, indicating that a great period of time had elapsed since human foot had trod it — a secret way, doubtless, unknown to living Manatorian. Here they dragged the corpse of E-Med, leaving it upon the platform, and as they left the dark and forbidden closet Lan-O would have slammed to the panel had not Tara prevented.

"Wait!" she said, and fell to examining the door frame and the stile.

"Hurry!" whispered the slave girl. "If they come we are lost."

"It may serve us well to know how to open this place again," replied Tara of Helium, and then suddenly she pressed a foot against a section of the carved base at the right of the open panel. "Ah!" she breathed, a note of satisfaction in her tone, and closed the panel until it fitted snugly in its place. "Come!" she said and turned toward the outer doorway of the chamber.

They reached their own cell without detection, and closing the door Tara locked it from the inside and placed the key in a secret pocket in her harness.

"Let them come," she said. "Let them question us! What could two poor prisoners know of the whereabouts of their noble jailer? I ask you, Lan-O, what could they?"

"Nothing," admitted Lan-O, smiling with her companion.

"Tell me of these men of Manator," said Tara presently. "Are they all like E-Med, or are some of them like A-Kor, who seemed a brave and chivalrous character?"

"They are not unlike the peoples of other countries," replied Lan-O. "There be among them both good and bad. They are brave warriors and mighty. Among themselves they are not without chivalry and honor, but in their dealings with strangers they know but one law — the law of might. The weak and unfortunate of other lands fill them with contempt and arouse all that is worst in their natures, which doubtless accounts for their treatment of us, their slaves."

"But why should they feel contempt for those who have suffered the misfortune of falling into their hands?" queried Tara.

"I do not know," said Lan-O; "A-Kor says that he believes that it is because their country has never been invaded by a victorious foe. In their stealthy raids never have they been defeated, because they have never waited to face a powerful force, and so they have come to believe themselves invincible, and the other peoples are held in contempt as inferior in valor and the practive of arms."

"Yet A-Kor is one of them," said Tara.

"He is a son of O-Tar, the jeddak," replied Lan-O; "but his mother was a high born Gatholian, captured and made slave by O-Tar, and A-Kor boasts that in his veins runs only the blood of his mother, and indeed is he different from the others. His chivalry is of a gentler form, though not

even his worst enemy has dared question his courage, while his skill with the sword, and the spear, and the thoat is famous throughout the length and breadth of Manator."

"What think you they will do with him?" asked Tara of Helium.

"Sentence him to the games," replied Lan-O. "If O-Tar be not greatly angered he may be sentenced to but a single game, in which case he may come out alive; but if O-Tar wishes really to dispose of him he will be sentenced to the entire series, and no warrior has ever survived the full ten, or rather none who was under a sentence from O-Tar."

"What are the games? I do not understand," said Tara. "I have heard them speak of playing at jetan, but surely no one can be killed at jetan. We play it often at home."

"But not as they play it in the arena at Manator," replied Lan-O. "Come to the window," and together the two approached an aperture facing toward the east. Below her Tara of Helium saw a great field entirely surrounded by the low building, and the lofty towers of which that in which she was imprisoned was but a unit. About the arena were tiers of seats; but the thing that caught her attention was a gigantic jetan board laid out upon the floor of the arena in great squares of alternate orange and black.

"Here they play at jetan with living pieces. They play for great stakes and usually for a woman — some slave of exceptional beauty. O-Tar himself might have played for you had you not angered him, but now you will be played for in an open game by slaves and criminals, and you will belong to the side that wins — not to a single warrior, but to all who survive the game."

The eyes of Tara of Helium flashed, but she made no comment.

"Those who direct the play do not necessarily take part in it," continued the slave girl, "but sit in those two great thrones which you see at either end of the board and direct their pieces from square to square."

"But where lies the danger?" asked Tara of Helium. "If a piece be taken it is merely removed from the board — this is a rule of jetan as old almost as the civilization of Barsoom."

"But here in Manator, when they play in the great arena with living men, that rule is altered," explained Lan-O. "When a warrior is moved to a square occupied by an opposing piece, the two battle to the death for possession of the square and the one that is successful advantages by the move. Each is caparisoned to simulate the piece he represents and in addition he wears that which indicates whether he be slave, a warrior serving a sentence, or a volunteer. If serving a sentence the number of games he must play is also indicated, and thus the one directing the moves knows which pieces to risk and which to conserve, and further than this, a man's chances are affected by the position that is assigned him for the game. Those who they wish to die are always Panthans in the game, for the Panthan has the least chance of surviving."

"Do those who direct the play ever actually take part in it?" asked Tara.

"Oh, yes," said Lan-O. "Often when two warriors, even of the highest class, hold a grievance against one another O-Tar compels them to settle it upon the arena. Then it is that they take active part and with drawn swords direct their own players from the position of Chief. They pick their own players, usually the best of their own warriors and slaves, if they be powerful men who possess such, or their friends may volunteer, or they may obtain prisoners from the pits. These are games indeed — the very best that are seen. Often the great chiefs themselves are slain."

"It is within this amphitheater that the justice of Manator is meted, then?" asked Tara.

"Very largely," replied Lan-O.

"How, then, through such justice, could a prisoner win his liberty?" continued the girl from Helium.

"If a man, and he survived ten games his liberty would be his," replied Lan-O.

"But none ever survives?" queried Tara. "And if a woman?"

"No stranger within the gates of Manator ever has survived ten games," replied the slave girl. "They are permitted to offer themselves into perpetual slavery if they prefer that to fighting at jetan. Of course they may be called upon, as any warrior, to take part in a game; but their chances then of surviving are increased, since they may never again have the chance of winning to liberty."

"But a woman," insisted Tara; "how may a woman win her freedom?"

Lan-O laughed. "Very simply," she cried, derisively. "She has but to find a warrior who will fight through ten consecutive games for her and survive."

"'Just are the laws of Manator,'" quoted Tara, scornfully.

Then it was that they heard footsteps outside their cell and a moment later a key turned in the lock and the door opened. A warrior faced them.

"Hast seen E-Med the dwar?" he asked.

"Yes," replied Tara, "he was here some time ago."

The man glanced quickly about the bare chamber and then searchingly first at Tara of Helium and then at the slave girl, Lan-O. The puzzled expression upon his face increased. He scratched his head. "It is strange," he said. "A score of men saw him ascend into this tower; and though there is but a single exit, and that well guarded, no man has seen him pass out."

Tara of Helium hid a yawn with the back of a shapely hand. "The Princess of Helium is hungry, fellow," she drawled; "tell your master that she would eat."

It was an hour later that food was brought, an officer and several warriors accompanying the bearer. The former examined the room carefully, but there was no sign that aught amiss had occurred there. The wound that had sent E-Med the dwar to his ancestors had not bled, fortunately for Tara of Helium.

"Woman," cried the officer, turning upon Tara, "you were the last to see E-Med the dwar. Answer me now and answer me truthfully. Did you see him leave this room?"

"I did," answered Tara of Helium.

"Where did he go from here?"

"How should I know? Think you that I can pass through a locked door of skeel?" the girl's tone was scornful.

"Of that we do not know," said the officer. "Strange things have happened in the cell of your companion in the pits of Manator. Perhaps you could pass through a locked door of skeel as easily as he performs seemingly more impossible feats."

"Whom do you mean," she cried; "Turan the panthan? He lives, then? Tell me, is he here in Manator unharmed?"

"I speak of that thing which calls itself

Ghek the kaldane," replied the officer.

"But Turan! Tell me, padwar, have you heard aught of him?" Tara's tone was insistent and she leaned a little forward toward the officer, her lips slightly parted in expectancy.

Into the eyes of the slave girl, Lan-O, who was watching her, there crept a soft light of understanding; but the officer ignored Tara's question — what was the fate of another slave to him? "Men do not disappear into thin air," he growled, "and if E-Med be not found soon O-Tar himself may take a hand in this. I warn you, woman, if you be one of those horrid Corphals that by commanding the spirits of the wicked dead gains evil mastery over the living, as many now believe the thing called Ghek to be, that lest you return E-Med, O-Tar will have no mercy on you."

"What foolishness is this?" cried the girl. "I am a princess of Helium, as I have told you all a score of times. Even if the fabled Corphals existed, as none but the most ignorant now believes, the lore of the ancients tells us that they entered only into the bodies of wicked criminals of the lowest class. Man of Manator, thou art a fool, and thy jeddak and all his people," and she turned her royal back upon the padwar, and gazed through the window across the Field of Jetan and the roofs of Manator toward the low hills and the rolling country and freedom.

"And you know so much of Corphals, then," he cried, "you know that while no common man dare harm them they may be slain by the hand of a jeddak with impunity!"

The girl did not reply, nor would she speak again, for all his threats and rage, for she knew now that none in all Manator dared harm her save O-Tar, the jeddak, and after a while the padwar left, taking his men with him. And after they had gone Tara stood for long looking out upon the city of Manator, and wondering what more of cruel wrongs Fate held in store for her. She was standing thus in silent meditation when there rose to her the strains of martial music from the city below — the deep, mellow tones of the long war trumpets of mounted troops, the clear, ringing notes of foot-soldiers' music. The girl raised her head and looked about, listening, and Lan-O, standing at an opposite window, looking toward the west,

motioned Tara to join her. Now they could see across roofs and avenues to The Gate of Enemies, through which troops were marching into the city.

"The Great Jed is coming," said Lan-O; "none other dares enter thus, with blaring trumpets, the cty of Manator. It is U-Thor, Jed of Manatos, second city of Manator. They call him The Great Jed the length and breadth of Manator, and because the people love him, O-Tar hates him. They say, who know, that it would need but slight provocation to inflame the two to war. How such a war would end no one could guess, for the people of Manator worship the great O-Tar, though they do not love him. U-Thor they love, but he is not the jeddak," and Tara understood, as only a Martian may, how much that simple statement encompassed.

The loyalty of a Martian to his jeddak is almost an instinct, and second not even to the instinct of self-preservation at that. Nor is this strange in a race whose religion includes ancestor worship, and where families trace their origin back into remote ages and a jeddak sits upon the same throne that his direct progenitors have occupied for, perhaps, hundreds of thousands of years, and rules the descendants of the same people that his forebears ruled. Wicked jeddaks have been dethroned, but seldom are they replaced by other than members of the imperial house, even though the law gives to the jeds the right to select whom they please.

"U-Thor is a just man and good, then?" asked Tara of Helium.

"There be none nobler," replied Lan-O. "In Manatos none but wicked criminals who deserve death are forced to play at jetan, and even then the play is fair and they have their chance for freedom. Volunteers may play, but the moves are not necessarily to the death — a wound, and even sometimes points in swordplay, deciding the issue. There they look upon jetan as a martial sport — here it is but butchery. And U-Thor is opposed to the ancient slave raids and to the policy that keeps Manator forever isolated from the other nations of Barsoom; but U-Thor is not jeddak and so there is no change."

The two girls watched the column moving up the broad avenue from The Gate of Enemies toward the palace of O-Tar. A gorgeous, barbaric procession of painted warriors in jewel-studded harness and waving feathers; vicious, squealing thoats caparisoned in rich trappings; far above their heads the long lances of their riders bore fluttering pennons; foot-soldiers swing easily along the stone pavement, their sandals of zitidar hide giving forth no sound; and at the rear of each utan a train of painted chariots, drawn by mammoth zitidars, carrying the equipment of the company to which they were attached. Utan after utan entered through the great gate, and even when the head of the column reached the palace of O-Tar they were not all within the city.

"I have been here many years," said the girl, Lan-O; "but never have I seen even The Great Jed bring so many fighting men into the city of Manator."

Through half-closed eyes Tara of Helium watched the warriors marching up the broad avenue, trying to imagine them the fighting men of her beloved Helium coming to the rescue of their princess. That splendid figure upon the great thoat might be John Carter, himself, Warlord of Barsoom, and behind him utan after utan of the veterans of the empire, and then the girl opened her eyes again and saw the host of painted, befeathered barbarians, and sighed. But yet she watched, fascinated by the martial scene, and now she noted again the groups of silent figures upon the balconies. No waving silks; no cries of welcome; no showers of flowers and jewels such as would have marked the entry of such a splendid, friendly pageant into the twin cities of her birth.

"The people do not seem friendly to the warriors of Manatos," she remarked to Lan-O; "I have not seen a single welcoming sign from the people on the balconies."

The slave girl looked at her in surprise. "It cannot be that you do not know!" she exclaimed. "Why, they are —" but she got no further. The door swung open and an officer stood before them.

"The slave girl, Tara, is summoned to the presence of O-Tar, the jeddak!" he announced.

Chapter XIV
AT GHEK'S COMMAND

Turan the panthan chafed in his chains. Time dragged; silence and monotony prolonged minutes into hours. Uncertainty of the fate of the woman he loved turned each hour into an eternity of hell. He listened impatiently for the sound of approaching footsteps that he might see and speak to some living creature and learn, perchance, some word of Tara of Helium. After torturing hours his ears were rewarded by the rattle of harness and arms. Men were coming! He waited breathlessly. Perhaps they were his executioners; but he would welcome them notwithstanding. He would question them. But if they knew naught of Tara he would not divulge the location of the hiding place in which he had left her.

Now they came — a half-dozen warriors and an officer, escorting an unarmed man; a prisoner, doubtless. Of this Turan was not left long in doubt, since they brought the newcomer and chained him to an adjoining ring. Immediately the panthan commenced to question the officer in charge of the guard.

"Tell me," he demanded, "why I have been made prisoner, and if other strangers were captured since I entered your city."

"What other prisoners?" asked the officer.

"A woman, and a man with a strange head," replied Turan.

"It is possible," said the officer; "but what were their names?"

"The woman was Tara, Princess of Helium, and the man was Ghek, a kaldane, of Bantoom."

"These were your friends?" asked the officer.

"Yes," replied Turan.

"It is what I would know," said the officer, and with a curt command to his men to follow him he turned and left the cell.

"Tell me of them!" cried Turan after him. "Tell me of Tara of Helium! Is she safe?" but the man did not answer and soon the sound of their departure died in the distance.

"Tara of Helium was safe but a short time since," said the prisoner chained at Turan's side.

The panthan turned toward the speaker, seeing a large man, handsome of face and with a manner both stately and dignified. "You have seen her?" he asked. "They captured her then? She is in danger?"

"She is being held in The Towers of Jetan as a prize for the next games," replied the stranger.

"And who are you?" asked Turan. "And why are you here, a prisoner?"

"I am A-Kor the dwar, keeper of The Towers of Jetan," replied the other. "I am here because I dared speak the truth of O-Tar the jeddak, to one of his officers."

"And your punishment?" asked Turan.

"I do not know. O-Tar has not yet spoken. Doubtless the games — perhaps the full ten, for O-Tar does not love A-Kor, his son."

"You are the jeddak's son," asked Turan.

"I am the son of O-Tar and of a slave, Haja of Gathol, who was a princess in her own land."

Turan looked searchingly at the speaker. A son of Haja of Gathol! A son of his mother's sister, this man, then, was his own cousin. Well did Gahan remember the mysterious disappearance of the Princess Haja and an entire utan of her personal troops. She had been upon a visit far from the city of Gathol and returning home had vanished with her whole escort from the sight of man. So this was the secret of the seeming mystery? Doubtless it explained many other similar disappearances that extended nearly as far back as the history of Gathol. Turan scrutinized his companion, discovering many evidences of resemblance to his mother's people. A-Kor might have been ten years younger than he, but such differences in age are scarce accounted among a people who seldom or never age outwardly after maturity and whose span of life may be a thousand years.

"And where lies Gathol?" asked Turan.

"Almost due east of Manator," replied A-Kor.

"And how far?"

"Some twenty-one degrees it is from the city of Manator to the city of Gathol," replied A-Kor; "but little more than ten degrees between the boundaries of the two countries. Between them, though, there lies a country of torn rocks and yawning chasms."

Well did Gahan know this country that bordered his upon the west — even the ships of the air avoided it because of the treacherous currents that rose from the deep chasms, and the almost total absence of safe landings. He knew now where Manator lay and for the first time in long weeks the way to his own Gathol, and here was a man, a fellow prisoner, in whose veins flowed the blood of his own ancestors — a man who knew Manator; its people, its customs and the country surrounding it — one who could aid him, with advice at least, to find a plan for the rescue of Tara of Helium and for escape. But would A-Kor — could he dare broach the subject? He could do no less than try.

"And O-Tar you think will sentence you to death?" he asked; "and why?"

"He would like to," replied A-Kor, "for the people chafe beneath his iron hand and their loyalty is but the loyalty of a people to the long line of illustrious jeddaks from which he has sprung. He is a jealous man and has found the means of disposing of most of those whose blood might entitle them to a claim upon the throne, and whose place in the affections of the people endowed them with any political significance. The fact that I was the son of a slave relegated me to a position of minor importance in the consideration of O-Tar, yet I am still the son of a jeddak and might sit upon the throne of Manator with as perfect congruity as O-Tar himself. Combined with this is the fact that of recent years the people, and especially many of the younger warriors, have evinced a growing affection for me, which I attribute to certain virtues of character and training derived from my mother, but which O-Tar assumes to be the result of an ambition upon my part to occupy the throne of Manator.

"And now, I am firmly convinced, he has seized upon my criticism of his treatment of the slave girl Tara as a pretext for ridding himself of me."

"But if you could escape and reach Gathol," suggested Turan.

"I have thought of that," mused A-Kor; "but how much better off would I be? In the eyes of the Gatholians I would be, not a Gatholian; but a stranger and doubtless they would accord me the same treatment that we of Manator accord strangers."

"Could you convince them that you are the son of the Princess Haja your welcome would be assured," said Turan; "while on the other hand you could purchase your freedom and citizenship with a brief period of labor in the diamond mines."

"How know you all these things?" asked A-Kor. "I thought you were from Helium."

"I am a panthan," replied Turan, "and I have served many countries, among them Gathol."

"It is what the slaves from Gathol have told me," said A-Kor, thoughtfully, "and my mother, before O-Tar sent her to live at Manatos. I think he must have feared her power and influence among the slaves from Gathol and their descendants, who number perhaps a million people throughout the land of Manator."

"Are these slaves organized?" asked Turan.

A-Kor looked straight into the eyes of the panthan for a long moment before he replied. "You are a man of honor," he said; "I read it in your face, and I am seldom mistaken in my estimate of a man; but —" and he leaned closer to the other —"even the walls have ears," he whispered, and Turan's question was answered.

It was later in the evening that warriors came and unlocked the fetter from Turan's ankle and led him away to appear before O-Tar, the jeddak. They conducted him toward the palace along narrow, winding streets and broad avenues; but always from the balconies there looked down upon them in endless ranks the silent people of the city. The palace itself was filled with life and activity. Mounted warriors galloped through the corridors and up and down the runways connecting adjacent floors. It seemed that no one walked within the palace other than a few slaves. Squealing, fighting thoats were stabled in magnificent halls while their riders, if not upon some duty of the palace, played at jetan with small figures carved from wood.

Turan noted the magnificence of the interior architecture of the palace, the lavish expenditure of precious jewels and metals, the gorgious mural decorations which depicted almost exclusively martial scenes, and principally duels which seemed to be fought upon jetan boards of heroic size. The capitals of many of the columns supporting the ceilings of the corridors and chambers through which they passed were wrought into formal likenesses of jetan pieces — everywhere there seemed a suggestion of the game. Along the same path that Tara of Helium had been led Turan was conducted toward the throne room of O-Tar the jeddak, and when he entered the Hall of Chiefs his interest turned to wonder and admiration as he viewed the ranks of statuesque thoatmen decked in their gorgeous, martial panoply. Never, he thought, had he seen upon Barsoom more soldierly figures or thoats so perfectly trained to perfection of immobility as these. Not a muscle quivered, not a tail lashed, and the riders were as motionless as their mounts — each warlike eye straight to the front, the great spears inclined at the same angle. It was a picture to fill the breast of a fighting man with awe and reverence. Nor did it fail in its effect upon Turan as they conducted him the length of the chamber, where he waited before great doors until he should be summoned into the presence of the ruler of Manator.

When Tara of Helium was ushered into the throne room of O-Tar she found the great hall filled with the chiefs and officers of O-Tar and U-Thor, the latter occupying the place of honor at the foot of the throne, as was his due. The girl was conducted to the foot of the aisle and halted before the jeddak, who looked down upon her from his high throne with scowling brows and fierce, cruel eyes.

"The laws of Manator are just," said O-Tar, addressing her; "thus is it that you have been summoned here again to be judged by the highest authority of Manator. Word has reached me that you are suspected of being a Corphal. What word have you to say in refutation of the charge?"

Tara of Helium could scarce restrain a sneer as she answered the ridiculous accusation of witchcraft. "So ancient is the culture of my people," she said, "that authentic history reveals no defense for that which we know existed only in the ignorant and superstitious minds of the most primitive peoples of the past. To those who are yet so untutored as to believe in the existence of Corphals, there can be no argument that will convince them of their error — only long ages of refinement and culture can accomplish their release from the bondage of ignorance. I have spoken."

"Yet you do not deny the accusation," said O-Tar.

"It is not worthy the dignity of a denial," she responded haughtily.

"And I were you, woman," said a deep voice at her side, "I should, nevertheless, deny it."

Tara of Helium turned to see the eyes of U-Thor, the great jed of Manatos, upon her. Brave eyes they were, but neither cold nor cruel. O-Tar rapped impatiently upon the arm of his throne. "U-Thor forgets," he cried, "that O-Tar is the jeddak."

"U-Thor remembers," replied the jed of Manatos, "that the laws of Manator permit any who may be accused to have advice and counsel before their judge."

Tara of Helium saw that for some reason this man would have assisted her, and so she acted upon his advice.

"I deny the charge," she said, "I am no Corphal."

"Of that we shall learn," snapped O-Tar. "U-Dor, where are those who have knowledge of the powers of this woman?"

And U-Dor brought several who recounted the little that was known of the disappearance of E-Med, and others who told of the capture of Ghek and Tara, suggesting by deduction that having been, found together they had sufficient in common to make it reasonably certain that one was as bad as the other, and that, therefore, it remained but to convict one of them of Corphalism to make certain the guilt of both. And then O-Tar called for Ghek, and immediately the hideous kaldane was dragged before him by warriors who could not conceal the fear in which they held this creature.

"And you!" said O-Tar in cold accusing tones. "Already have I been told enough of you to warrant me in passing through your heart the jeddak's steel — of how you stole the brains from the warrior U-Van so that he thought he saw your headless body still endowed with life; of how you caused another to believe that you had escaped, making him to see naught but an empty bench and a blank wall where you had been."

"Ah, O-Tar, but that is as nothing!" cried a young padwar who had come in command of the escort that brought Ghek. "The thing which he did to I-Zav, here, would prove his guilt alone."

"What did he to the warrior I-Zav?" demanded O-Tar. "Let I-Zav speak!"

The warrior I-Zav, a great fellow of bulging muscles and thick neck, advanced to the foot of the throne. He was pale and still trembling visibly as from a nervous shock.

"Let my first ancestor be my witness, O-Tar, that I speak the truth," he began. "I was left to guard this creature, who sat upon a bench, shackled to the wall. I stood by the open doorway at the opposite side of the chamber. He could not reach me, yet, O-Tar, may Iss engulf me if he did not drag me to him helpless as an unhatched egg. He dragged me to him, greatest of jeddaks, *with his eyes!* With his eyes he seized upon my eyes and dragged me to him and he made me lay my swords and dagger upon the table and back off into a corner, and still keeping his eyes upon my eyes his head quitted his body and crawling upon six short legs it descended to the floor and backed part way into the hole of an ulsio, but not so far that the eyes were not still upon me and then it returned with the key to its fetter and after resuming its place upon its own shoulders it unlocked the fetter and again dragged me across the room and made me to sit upon the bench where it had been and there it fastened the fetter about my ankle, and I could do naught for the power of its eyes and the fact that it wore my two swords and my dagger. And then the head disappeared down the hole of the ulsio with the key, and when it returned, it resumed its body and stood guard over me at the doorway until the padwar came to fetch it hither."

"It is enough!" said O-Tar, sternly. "Both shall receive the jeddak's steel," and rising from his throne he drew his long sword and descended the marble steps toward them, while two brawny warriors seized Tara by either arm and two seized Ghek, holding them facing the naked blade of the jeddak.

"Hold, just O-Tar!" cried U-Dor. "There be yet another to be judged. Let us confront him who calls himself Turan with these his fellows before they die."

"Good!" exclaimed O-Tar, pausing half way down the steps. "Fetch Turan, the slave!"

When Turan had been brought into the chamber he was placed a little to Tara's left and a step nearer the throne. O-Tar eyed him menacingly.

"You are Turan," he asked, "friend and companion of these?"

The panthan was about to reply when Tara of Helium spoke. "I know not this fellow," she said. "Who dares say that he be a friend and companion of the Princess Tara of Helium?"

Turan and Ghek looked at her in surprise, but at Turan she did not look, and to Ghek she passed a quick glance of warning, as to say: "Hold thy peace!"

The panthan tried not to fathom her

purpose for the head is useless when the heart usurps its functions, and Turan knew only that the woman he loved had denied him, and though he tried not even to think it his foolish heart urged but a single explanation — that she refused to recognize him lest she be involved in his difficulties.

O-Tar looked first at one and then at another of them; but none of them spoke. "Were they not captured together?" he asked of U-Dor.

"No," replied the dwar. "He who is called Turan was found seeking entrance to the city and was enticed to the pits. The following morning I discovered the other two upon the hill beyond The Gate of Enemies."

"But they are friends and companions," said a young padwar, "for this Turan inquired of me concerning these two, calling them by name and saying that they were his friends."

"It is enough," stated O-Tar, "all three shall die," and he took another step downward from the throne.

"For what shall we die?" asked Ghek. "Your people prate of the just laws of Manator, and yet you would slay three strangers without telling them of what crime they are accused."

"He is right," said a deep voice. It was the voice of U-Thor, the great jed of Manatos. O-Tar looked at him and scowled; but there came voices from other portions of the chamber seconding the demand for justice.

"Then know, though you shall die anyway," cried O-Tar, "that all three are convicted of Corphalism and that as only a jeddak may slay such as you in safety you are about to be honored with the steel of O-Tar."

"Fool!" cried Turan. "Know you not that in the veins of this woman flows the blood of ten thousand jeddaks — that greater than yours is her power in her own land? She is Tara, Princess of Helium, great-granddaughter of Tardos Mors, daughter of John Carter, Warlord of Barsoom. She cannot be a Corphal. Nor is this creature Ghek, nor am I. And you would know more, I can prove my right to be heard and to be believed if I may have word with the Princess Haja of Gathol, whose son is my fellow prisoner in the pits of O-Tar, his father."

At this U-Thor rose to his feet and faced O-Tar. "What means this?" he asked. "Speaks the man the truth? Is the son of Haja a prisoner in thy pits, O-Tar?"

"And what is it to the jed of Manatos who be the prisoners in the pits of his jeddak?" demanded O-Tar, angrily.

"It is this to the jed of Manatos," replied U-Thor in a voice so low as to be scarce more than a whisper and yet that was heard the whole length and breadth of the great throne room of O-Tar, Jeddak of Manator. "You gave me a slave woman, Haja, who had been a princess in Gathol, because you feared her influence among the slaves from Gathol. I have made of her a free woman, and I have married her and made her thus a princess of Manatos. Her son is my son, O-Tar, and though thou be my jeddak, I say to you that for any harm that befalls A-Kor you shall answer to U-Thor of Manatos."

O-Tar looked long at U-Thor, but he made no reply. Then he turned again to Turan. "If one be a Corphal," he said, "then all of you be Corphals, and we know well from the things that this creature has done," he pointed at Ghek, "that he is a Corphal, for no mortal has such powers as he. And as you are all Corphals you must all die." He took another step downward, when Ghek spoke.

"These two have no such powers as I," he said. "They are but ordinary, brainless things such as yourself. I have done all the things that your poor, ignorant warriors have told you; but this only demonstrates that I am of a higher order than yourselves, as is indeed the fact. I am a kaldane, not a Corphal. There is nothing supernatural or mysterious about me, other than that to the ignorant all things which they cannot understand are mysterious. Easily might I have eluded your warriors and escaped your pits; but I remained in the hope that I might help these two foolish creatures who have not the brains to escape without help. They befriended me and saved my life. I owe them this debt. Do not slay them — they are harmless. Slay me if you will. I offer my life if it will appease your ignorant wrath. I cannot return to Bantoom and so I might as well die, for there is no pleasure in intercourse with the feeble intellects that cumber the face of the world outside the valley of Bantoom."

"Hideous egotist," said O-Tar, "prepare

to die and assume not to dictate to O-Tar the jeddak. He has passed sentence and all three of you shall feel the jeddak's naked steel. I have spoken!"

He took another step downward and then a strange thing happened. He paused, his eyes fixed upon the eyes of Ghek. His sword slipped from nerveless fingers, and still he stood there swaying forward and back. A jed rose to rush to his side; but Ghek stopped him with a word.

"Wait!" he cried. "The life of your jeddak is in my hands. You believe me a Corphal and so you believe, too, that only the sword of a jeddak may slay me, therefore your blades are useless against me. Offer harm to any one of us, or seek to approach your jeddak until I have spoken, and he shall sink lifeless to the marble. Release the two prisoners and let them come to my side — I would speak to them, privately. Quick! do as I say; I would as lief as not slay O-Tar. I but let him live that I may gain freedom for my friends — obstruct me and he dies."

The guards fell back, releasing Tara and Turan, who came close to Ghek's side.

"Do as I tell you and do it quickly," whispered the kaldane. "I cannot hold this fellow long, nor could I kill him thus. There are many minds working against mine and presently mine will tire and O-Tar will be himself again. You must make the best of your opportunity while you may. Behind the arras that you see hanging in the rear of the throne above you is a secret opening. From it a corridor leads to the pits of the palace, where there are storerooms containing food and drink. Few people go there. From these pits lead others to all parts of the city. Follow one that runs due west and it will bring you to The Gate of Enemies. The rest will then lie with you. I can do no more; hurry before my waning powers fail me — I am not as Luud, who was a king. He could have held this creature forever. Make haste! Go!"

Chapter XV
THE OLD MAN OF THE PITS

"I shall not desert you, Ghek," said Tara of Helium, simply.

"Go! Go!" whispered the kaldane. "You can do me no good. Go, or all I have done is for naught."

Tara shook her head. "I cannot," she said.

"They will slay her," said Ghek to Turan, and the panthan, torn between loyalty to this strange creature who had offered its life for him, and love of the woman, hesitated but a moment, then he swept Tara from her feet and lifting her in his arms leaped up the steps that led to the throne of Manator. Behind the throne he parted the arras and found the secret opening. Into this he bore the girl and down a long, narrow corridor and winding runways that led to lower levels until they came to the pits of the palace of O-Tar. Here was a labyrinth of passages and chambers presenting a thousand hiding-places.

As Turan bore Tara up the steps toward the throne a score of warriors rose as though to rush forward to intercept them. "Stay!" cried Ghek, "or your jeddak dies," and they halted in their tracks, waiting the will of this strange, uncanny creature.

Presently Ghek took his eyes from the eyes of O-Tar and the jeddak shook himself as one who would be rid of a bad dream and straightened up, half dazed still.

"Look," said Ghek, then, "I have given your jeddak his life, nor have I harmed one of those whom I might easily have slain when they were in my power. No harm have I or my friends done in the city of Manator. Why then should you persecute us? Give us our lives. Give us our liberty."

O-Tar, now in command of his faculties, stooped and regained his sword. In the room was silence as all waited to hear the jeddak's answer.

"Just are the laws of Manator," he said at last. "Perhaps, after all, there is truth in the words of the stranger. Return him then to the pits and pursue the others and capture them. Through the mercy of O-Tar they shall be permitted to win their freedom upon the Field of Jetan, in the coming games."

Still ashen was the face of the jeddak as Ghek was led away and his appearance was that of a man who had been snatched from the brink of eternity into which he has gazed, not with the composure of great courage, but with fear. There were those in the throne room who knew that the execution of the three prisoners had but been delayed and the responsibility placed upon the shoulders of others, and one of those who knew was U-Thor, the great jed of Manatos. His curling lip betokened his scorn of the jeddak who had chosen

O-Tar's sword slipped from his nerveless fingers

humiliation rather than death. He knew that O-Tar had lost more of prestige in those few moments than he could regain in a lifetime, for the Martians are jealous of the courage of their chiefs — there can be no evasions of stern duty, no temporizing with honor. That there were others in the room who shared U-Thor's belief was evidenced by the silence and the grim scowls.

O-Tar glanced quickly around. He must have sensed the hostility and guessed its cause, for he went suddenly angry, and as one who seeks by the vehemence of his words to establish the courage of his heart he roared forth what could be considered as naught other than a challenge.

"The will of O-Tar, the jeddak, is the law of Manator," he cried, "and the laws of Manator are just — they cannot err. U-Dor, dispatch those who will search the palace, the pits, and the city, and return the fugitives to their cells.

"And now for you, U-Thor of Manatos! Think you with impunity to threaten your jeddak — to question his right to punish traitors and instigators of treason? What am I to think of your own loyalty, who takes to wife a woman I have banished from my court because of her intrigues against the authority of her jeddak and her master? But O-Tar is just. Make your explanations and your peace, then, before it is too late."

"U-Thor has nothing to explain," replied the jed of Manatos; "nor is he at war with his jeddak; but he has the right that every jed and every warrior enjoys, of demanding justice at the hands of the jeddak for whomsoever he believes to be persecuted. With increasing rigor has the jeddak of Manator persecuted the slaves from Gathol since he took to himself the unwilling Princess Haja. If the slaves from Gathol have harbored thoughts of vengeance and escape 'tis no more than might be expected from a proud and courageous people. Ever have I counselled greater fairness in our treatment of our slaves, many of whom, in their own lands, are people of great distinction and power; but always has O-Tar, the jeddak, flouted with arrogance my every suggestion. Though it has been through none of my seeking that the question has arisen now I am glad that it has, for the time was bound to come when the jeds of Manator would demand from O-Tar the respect and consideration that is their due from the man who holds his high office at

their pleasure. Know, then, O-Tar, that you must free A-Kor, the dwar, forthwith or bring him to fair trail before the assembled jeds of Manator. I have spoken."

"You have spoken well and to the point, U-Thor," cried O-Tar, "for you have revealed to your jeddak and your fellow jeds the depth of the disloyalty that I have long suspected. A-Kor already has been tried and sentenced by the supreme tribunal of Manator — O-Tar, the jeddak; and you too shall receive justice from the same unfailing source. In the meantime you are under arrest. To the pits with him! To the pits with U-Thor the false jed!" He clapped his hands to summon the surrounding warriors to do his bidding. A score leaped forward to seize U-Thor. They were warriors of the palace, mostly; but two score leaped to defend U-Thor, and with ringing steel they fought at the foot of the steps to the throne of Manator where stood O-Tar, the jeddak, with drawn sword ready to take his part in the mêlée.

At the clash of steel, palace guards rushed to the scene from other parts of the great building until those who would have defended U-Thor were outnumbered two to one, and then the jed of Manatos slowly withdrew with his forces, and fighting his way through the corridors and chambers of the palace came at last to the avenue. Here he was reinforced by the little army that had marched with him into Manator. Slowly they retreated toward The Gate of Enemies between the rows of silent people looking down upon them from the balconies and there, within the city walls, they made their stand.

In a dimly-lighted chamber beneath the palace of O-Tar the jeddak, Turan the panthan lowered Tara of Helium from his arms and faced her. "I am sorry, Princess," he said, "that I was forced to disobey your commands, or to abandon Ghek; but there was no other way. Could he have saved you I would have stayed in his place. Tell me that you forgive me."

"How could I do less?" she replied graciously. "But it seemed cowardly to abandon a friend."

"Had we been three fighting men it had been different," he said. "We could only have remained and died together, fighting; but you know, Tara of Helium, that we may not jeopardize a woman's safety even though we risk the loss of honor."

"I know that, Turan," she said; "but no one may say that you have risked honor, who knows the honor and bravery that are yours."

He heard her with surprise for these were the first words that she had spoken to him that did not savor of the attitude of a princess to a panthan — though it was more in her tone than the actual words that he apprehended the difference. How at variance were they to her recent repudiation of him! He could not fathom her, and so he blurted out the question that had been in his mind since she had told O-Tar that she did not know him.

"Tara of Helium," he said, "your words are balm to the wound you gave me in the throne room of O-Tar. Tell me, Princess, why you denied me."

She turned her great, deep eyes up to his and in them was a little of reproach.

"You did not guess," she asked, "that it was my lips alone and not my heart that denied you? O-Tar had ordered that I die, more because I was a companion of Ghek than because of any evidence against me, and so I knew that if I acknowledged you as one of us, you would be slain, too."

"It was to save me, then?" he cried, his face suddenly lighting.

"It was to save my brave panthan," she said in a low voice.

"Tara of Helium," said the warrior, dropping to one knee, "your words are as food to my hungry heart," and he took her fingers in his and pressed them to his lips.

Gently she raised him to his feet. "You need not tell me, kneeling," she said, softly.

Her hand was still in his as he rose and they were very close, and the man was still flushed with the contact of her body since he had carried her from the throne room of O-Tar. He felt his heart pounding in his breast and the hot blood surging through his veins as he looked at her beautiful face, with its downcast eyes and the half-parted lips that he would have given a kingdom to possess, and then he swept her to him and as he crushed her against his breast his lips smothered hers with kisses.

But only for an instant. Like a tigress the girl turned upon him, striking him, and thrusting him away. She stepped back, her head high and her eyes flashing fire. "You would dare?" she cried. "You would dare thus defile a princess of Helium?" she cried.

His eyes met hers squarely and there was no shame and no remorse in them.

"Yes, I would dare," he said. "I would dare love Tara of Helium; but I would not dare defile her or any woman with kisses that were not prompted by love of her alone." He stepped closer to her and laid his hands upon her shoulders. "Look into my eyes, daughter of The Warlord," he said, "and tell me that you do not wish the love of Turan, the panthan."

"I do not wish your love," she cried, pulling away. "I hate you!" and then turning away she bent her head into the hollow of her arm, and wept.

The man took a step toward her as though to comfort her when he was arrested by the sound of a cackling laugh behind him. Wheeling about, he discovered a strange figure of a man standing in a doorway. It was one of those rarities occasionally to be seen upon Barsoom — an old man with the signs of age upon him. Bent and wrinkled, he had more the appearance of a mummy than of a man.

"Love in the pits of O-Tar!" he cried, and again his thin laughter jarred upon the silence of the subterranean vaults. "A strange place to woo! A strange place to woo, indeed! When I was a young man we roamed in the gardens beneath giant pimalias and stole our kisses in the brief shadows of hurtling Thuria. We came not to the gloomy pits to speak of love; but times have changed and ways have changed, though I had never thought to live to see the time when the way of a man with a maid, or a maid with a man would change. Ah, but we kissed them then! And what if they objected, eh? What if they objected? Why, we kissed them more. Ey, ey, those were the days!" and he cackled again. "Ey, well do I recall the first of them I ever kissed, and I've kissed an army of them since; she was a fine girl, but she tried to slip a dagger into me while I was kissing her. Ey, ey, those were the days! But I kissed her. She's been dead over a thousand years now, but she was never kissed again like that while she lived, I'll swear, nor since she's been dead, either. And then there was that other —" but Turan, seeing a thousand or more years of osculatory memoirs portending, interrupted.

"Tell me, ancient one," he said, "not of thy loves but of thyself. Who are you? What do you here in the pits of O-Tar?"

"I might ask you the same, young man," replied the other. "Few there are who visit the pits other than the dead, except my pupils — ey! That is it — you are new pupils! Good! But never before have they sent a woman to learn the great art from the greatest artist. But times have changed. Now, in my day the women did no work — they were just for kissing and loving. Ey, those were the women. I mind the one we captured in the south —ey! she was a devil, but how she could love. She had breasts of marble and a heart of fire. Why, she —"

"Yes, yes," interrupted Turan; "we are pupils, and we are anxious to get to work. Lead on and we will follow."

"Ey, yes! Ey, yes! Come! All is rush and hurry as though there were not another countless myriad of ages ahead. Ey, yes! as many as lie behind. Two thousand years have passed since I broke my shell and always rush, rush, rush, yet I cannot see that aught has been accomplished. Manator is the same today as it was then — except the girls. We had the girls then. There was one that I gained upon The Fields of Jetan. Ey, but you should have seen —"

"Lead on!" cried Turan. "After we are at work you shall tell us of her."

"Ey, yes," said the old fellow and shuffled off down a dimly lighted passage. "Follow me!"

"You are going with him?" asked Tara.

"Why not?" replied Turan. "We know not where we are, or the way from these pits; for I know not east from west; but he doubtless knows and if we are shrewd we may learn from him that which we would know. At least we cannot afford to arouse his suspicions"; and so they followed him — followed along winding corridors and through many chambers, until they came at last to a room in which there were several marble slabs raised upon pedestals some three feet above the floor and upon each slab lay a human corpse.

"Here we are," exclaimed the old man. "These are fresh and we shall have to get to work upon them soon. I am working now on one for The Gate of Enemies. He slew many of our warriors. Truly is he entitled to a place in The Gate. Come, you shall see him."

He led them to an adjoining apartment. Upon the floor were many fresh, human bones and upon a marble slab a mass of shapeless flesh.

"You will learn this later," announced the old man; "but it will not harm you to watch me now, for there are not many thus prepared, and it may be long before you will have the opportunity to see another prepared for The Gate of Enemies. First, you see, I remove all the bones, carefully that the skin may be damaged as little as possible. The skull is the most difficult, but it can be removed by a skillful artist. You see, I have made but a single opening. This I now sew up, and that done, the body is hung so," and he fastened a piece of rope to the hair of the corpse and swung the horrid thing to a ring in the ceiling. Directly below it was a circular manhole in the floor from which he removed the cover revealing a well partially filled with a reddish liquid. "Now we lower it into this, the formula for which you shall learn in due time. We fasten it thus to the bottom of the cover, which we now replace. In a year it will be ready; but it must be examined often in the meantime and the liquid kept above the level of its crown. It will be a very beautiful piece, this one, when it is ready.

"And you are fortunate again, for there is one to come out today." He crossed to the opposite side of the room and raised another cover, reached in and dragged a grotesque looking figure from the hole. It was a human body, shrunk by the action of the chemical in which it had been immersed, to a little figure scarce a foot high.

"Ey! is it not fine?" cried the little old man. "Tomorrow it will take its place in The Gate of Enemies." He dried it off with cloths and packed it away carefully in a basket. "Perhaps you would like to see some of my *life* work," he suggested, and without waiting for their assent led them to another apartment, a large chamber in which were forty or fifty people. All were sitting or standing quietly about the walls, with the exception of one huge warrior who bestrode a great thoat in the very center of the room, and all were motionless. Instantly there sprang to the minds of Tara and Turan the rows of silent people upon the balconies that lined the avenues of the city, and the noble array of mounted warriors in The Hall of Chiefs, and the same explanation came to both but neither dared voice the question that was in his mind, for fear of revealing by his ignorance the fact that they were strangers in Manator and therefore impostors in the guise of pupils.

"It is very wonderful," said Turan. "It must require great skill and patience and time."

"That it does," replied the old man, "though having done it so long I am quicker than most; but mine are the most natural. Why, I would defy the wife of that warrior to say that insofar as appearances are concerned he does not live," and he pointed at the man upon the thoat. "Many of them, of course, are brought here wasted or badly wounded and these I have to repair. That is where great skill is required, for everyone wants his dead to look as they did at their best in life; but you shall learn — to mount them and paint them and repair them and sometimes to make an ugly one look beautiful. And it will be a great comfort to be able to mount your own. Why, for fifteen hundred years no one has mounted my own dead but myself.

"I have many, my balconies are crowded with them; but I keep a great room for my wives. I have them all, as far back as the first one, and many is the evening I spend with them — quiet evenings and very pleasant. And the the pleasure of preparing them and making them even more beautiful than in life partially recompenses one for their loss. I take my time with them, looking for a new one while I am working on the old. When I am not sure about a new one I bring her to the chamber where my wives are, and compare her charms with theirs, and there is always a great satisfaction at such times in knowing that they will not object. I love harmony."

"Did you prepare all the warriors in The Hall of Chiefs?" asked Turan.

"Yes, I prepare them and repair them," replied the old man. "O-Tar will trust no other. Even now I have two in another room who were damaged in some way and brought down to me. O-Tar does not like to have them gone long, since it leaves two riderless thoats in the Hall; but I shall have them ready presently. He wants them all there in the event any momentous question arises upon which the living jeds cannot agree, or do not agree with O-Tar. Such questions he carries to the jeds in The Hall of Chiefs. There he shuts himself up alone with the great chiefs who have attained wisdom through death. It is an excellent plan and there is never any friction or misunderstandings. O-Tar has said that it is the finest deliberative body upon Barsoom — much more intelligent than that com-

posed of the living jeds. But come, we must get to work; come into the next chamber and I will begin your instruction."

He led the way into the chamber in which lay the several corpses upon their marble slabs, and going to a cabinet he donned a pair of huge spectacles and commenced to select various tools from little compartments. This done he turned again toward his two pupils.

"Now let me have a look at you," he said. "My eyes are not what they once were, and I need these powerful lenses for my work, or to see distinctly the features of those around me."

He turned his eyes upon the two before him. Turan held his breath for he knew that now the man must discover that they wore not the harness or insignia of Manator. He had wondered before why the old fellow had not noticed it, for he had not known that he was half blind. The other examined their faces, his eyes lingering long upon the beauty of Tara of Helium, and then they drifted to the harness of the two. Turan thought that he noted an appreciable start of surprise on the part of the taxidermist, but if the old man noticed anything his next words did not reveal it.

"Come with I-Gos," he said to Turan, "I have materials in the next room that I would have you fetch hither. Remain here, woman, we shall be gone but a moment."

He led the way to one of the numerous doors opening into the chamber and entered ahead of Turan. Just inside the door he stopped, and pointing to a bundle of silks and furs upon the opposite side of the room directed Turan to fetch them. The latter had crossed the room and was stooping to raise the bundle when he heard the click of a lock behind him. Wheeling instantly he saw that he was alone in the room and that the single door was closed. Running rapidly to it he strove to open it, only to find that he was a prisoner.

I-Gos, stepping out and locking the door behind him, turned toward Tara.

"Your leather betrayed you," he said, laughing his cackling laugh. "You sought to deceive old I-Gos, but you found that though his eyes are weak his brain is not. But it shall not go ill with you. You are beautiful and I-Gos loves beautiful women. I might not have you elsewhere in Manator, but here there is none to deny old I-Gos. Few come to the pits of the dead — only those who bring the dead and they hasten away as fast as they can. No one will know that I-Gos has a beautiful woman locked with his dead. I shall ask you no questions and then I will not have to give you up, for I will not know to whom you belong, eh? And when you die I shall mount you beautifully and place you in the chamber with my other women. Will not that be fine, eh?" He had approached until he stood close beside the horrified girl. "Come!" he cried, seizing her by the wrist. "Come to I-Gos!"

Chapter XVI
ANOTHER CHANGE OF NAME

Turan dashed himself against the door of his prison in a vain effort to break through the solid skeel to the side of Tara whom he knew to be in grave danger, but the heavy panels held and he succeeded only in bruising his shoulders and his arms. At last he desisted and set about searching his prison for some other means of escape. He found no other opening in the stone walls, but his search revealed a heterogeneous collection of odds and ends of arms and apparel, of harness and ornaments and insignia, and sleeping silks and furs in great quantities. There were swords and spears and several large, two-bladed battle-axes, the heads of which bore a striking resemblance to the propellor of a small flier. Seizing one of these he attacked the door once more with great fury. He expected to hear something from I-Gos at this ruthless destruction, but no sound came to him from beyond the door, which was, he thought, too thick for the human voice to penetrate; but he would have wagered much that I-Gos heard him. Bits of the hard wood splintered at each impact of the heavy axe, but it was slow work and heavy. Presently he was compelled to rest, and so it went for what seemed hours — working almost to the verge of exhaustion and then resting for a few minutes; but ever the hole grew larger though he could see nothing of the interior of the room beyond because of the hanging that I-Gos had drawn across it after he had locked Turan within.

At last, however, the panthan had hewn an opening through which his body could pass, and seizing a long-sword that he had brought close to the door for the purpose he crawled through into the next room. Flinging aside the arras he stood ready,

sword in hand, to fight his way to the side of Tara of Helium — but she was not there. In the center of the room lay I-Gos, dead upon the floor; but Tara of Helium was nowhere to be seen.

Turan was nonplussed. It must have been her hand that had struck down the old man, yet she had made no effort to release Turan from his prison. And then he thought of those last words of hers: "I do not want your love! I hate you," and the truth dawned upon him — she had seized upon this first opportunity to escape him. With downcast heart Turan turned away. What should he do? There could be but one answer. While he lived and she lived he must still leave no stone unturned to effect her escape and safe return to the land of her people. But how? How was he even to find his way from this labyrinth? How was he to find her again? He walked to the nearest doorway. It chanced to be that which led into the room containing the mounted dead, awaiting transportation to balcony or grim room or whatever place was to receive them. His eyes travelled to the great, painted warrior on the thoat and as they ran over the splendid trappings and the serviceable arms a new light came into the pain-dulled eyes of the panthan. With a quick step he crossed to the side of the dead warrior and dragged him from his mount. With equal celerity he stripped him of his harness and his arms, and tearing off his own, donned the regalia of the dead man. Then he hastened back to the room in which he had been trapped, for there he had seen that which he needed to make his disguise complete. In a cabinet he found them — pots of paint that the old taxidermist had used to place the war-paint in its wide bands across the cold faces of dead warriors.

A few moments later Gahan of Gathol emerged from the room a warrior of Manator in every detail of harness, equipment, and ornamentation. He had removed from the leather of the dead man the insignia of his house and rank so that he might pass, with the least danger of arousing suspicion, as a common warrior.

To search for Tara of Helium in the vast, dim labyrinth of the pits of O-Tar seemed to the Gatholian a hopeless quest, foredoomed to failure. It would be wiser to seek the streets of Manator where he might hope to learn first if she had been recaptured and, if not, then he could return to the pits and pursue the hunt for her. To find egress from the maze he must perforce travel a considerable distance through the winding corridors and chambers, since he had no idea as to the location or direction of any exit. In fact, he could not have retraced his steps a hundred yards toward the point at which he and Tara had entered the gloomy caverns, and so he set out in the hope that he might find by accident either Tara of Helium or a way to the street level above.

For a time he passed room after room filled with the cunningly preserved dead of Manator, many of which were piled in tiers after the manner that firewood is corded, and as he moved through corridor and chamber he noticed hieroglyphics painted upon the walls above every opening and at each fork or crossing of corridors, until by observation he reached the conclusion that these indicated the designations of passageways, so that one who understood them might travel quickly and surely through the pits; but Turan did not understand them. Even could he have read the language of Manator they might not materially have aided one unfamiliar with the city; but he could not read them at all since, though there is but one spoken language upon Barsoom, there are as many different written languages as there are nations. One thing, however, soon became apparent to him — the hieroglyphic of a corridor remained the same until the corridor ended.

It was not long before Turan realized from the distance that he had traveled that the pits were part of a vast system undermining, possibly, the entire city. At least he was convinced that he had passed beyond the precincts of the palace. The corridors and chambers varied in appearance and architecture from time to time. All were lighted, though usually quite dimly, with radium bulbs. For a long time he saw no signs of life other than an occasional ulsio, then quite suddenly he came face to face with a warrior at one of the numerous crossings. The fellow looked at him, nodded, and passed on. Turan breathed a sigh of relief as he realized that his disguise was effective, but he was caught in the middle of it by a hail from the warrior who had stopped and turned toward him. The panthan was glad that a sword hung at his side, and glad too that they were buried in the dim recesses of the pits and that there would be but a single antagonist, for time was precious.

"Heard you any word of the other?" called the warrior to him.

"No," replied Turan, who had not the faintest idea to whom or what the fellow referred.

"He cannot escape," continued the warrior. "The woman ran directly into our arms, but she swore that she knew not where her companion might be found."

"They took her back to O-Tar?" asked Turan, for now he knew whom the other meant, and he would know more.

"They took her back to The Towers of Jetan," replied the warrior. "Tomorrow the games commence and doubtless she will be played for, though I doubt if any wants her, beautiful as she is. She fears not even O-Tar. By Cluros! but she would make a hard slave to subdue — a regular she-banth she is. Not for me," and he continued on his way shaking his head.

Turan hurried on searching for an avenue that led to the level of the streets above when suddenly he came to the open doorway of a small chamber in which sat a man who was chained to the wall. Turan voiced a low exclamation of surprise and pleasure as he recognized that the man was A-Kor, and that he had stumbled by accident upon the very cell in which he had been imprisoned. A-Kor looked at him questioningly. It was evident that he did not recognize his fellow prisoners. Turan crossed to the table and leaning close to the other whispered to him.

"I am Turan the panthan," he said, "who was chained beside you."

A-Kor looked at him closely. "Your own mother would never know you!" he said; "but tell me, what has transpired since they took you away?"

Turan recounted his experiences in the throne room of O-Tar and in the pits beneath, "and now," he continued, "I must find these Towers of Jeddak and see what may be done toward liberating the Princess of Helium."

A-Kor shook his head. "Long was I dwar of the Towers," he said, "and I can say to you, stranger, that you might as well attempt to reduce Manator, single handed, as to rescue a prisoner from The Towers of Jetan."

"But I must," replied Turan.

"Are you better than a good swordsman?" asked A-Kor presently.

"I am accounted so," replied Turan.

"Then there is a way — sst!" he was suddenly silent and pointing toward the base of the wall at the end of the room.

Turan looked in the direction the other's forefinger indicated, to see projecting from the mouth of an ulsio's burrow two large chelae and a pair of protruding eyes.

"Ghek!" he cried and immediately the hideous kaldane crawled out upon the floor and approached the table. A-Kor drew back with a half-stifled ejaculation of repulsion. "Do not fear," Turan reassured him. "It is my friend — he whom I told you held O-Tar while Tara and I escaped."

Ghek climbed to the table top and squatted between the two warriors. "You are safe in assuming," he said addressing A-Kor, "that Turan the panthan has no master in all Manator where the art of sword-play is concerned. I overheard your conversation — go on."

"You are his friend," continued A-Kor, "and so I may explain safely in your presence the only plan I know whereby he may hope to rescue the Princess of Helium. She is to be the stake of one of the games and it is O-Tar's desire that she be won by slaves and common warriors, since she repulsed him. Thus would he punish her. Not a single man, but all who survive upon the winning side are to possess her. With money, however, one may buy off the others before the game. That you could do, and if your side won and you survived she would become your slave."

"But how may a stranger and a hunted fugitive accomplish this?" asked Turan.

"No one will recognize you. You will go tomorrow to the keeper of the Towers and enlist in that game for which the girl is to be the stake, telling the keeper that you are from Manataj, the farthest city of Manator. If he questions you, you may say that you saw her when she was brought into the city after her capture. If you win her, you will find thoats stabled at my palace and you will carry from me a token that will place all that is mine at your disposal."

"But how can I buy off the others in the game without money?" asked Turan. "I have none — not even of my own country."

A-Kor opened his pocket-pouch and drew forth a packet of Manatorian money.

"Here is sufficient to buy them off twice over," he said, handing a portion of it to Turan.

"But why do you do this for a stranger?" asked the panthan.

"My mother was a captive princess here," replied A-Kor. "I but do for the Princess of Helium what my mother would have me do."

"Under the circumstances, then, Manatorian," replied Turan, "I cannot but accept your generosity on behalf of Tara of Helium and live in hope that some day I may do for you something in return."

"Now you must be gone," advised A-Kor. "At any minute a guard may come and discover you here. Go directly to the Avenue of Gates, which circles the city just within the outer wall. There you will find many places devoted to the lodging of strangers. You will know them by the thoat's head carved above the doors. Say that you are here from Manataj to witness the games. Take the name of U-Kal — it will arouse no suspicion, nor will you if you can avoid conversation. Early in the morning seek the keeper of The Towers of Jetan. May the strength and fortune of all your ancestors be with you!"

Bidding good-bye to Ghek and A-Kor, the panthan, following directions given him by A-Kor, set out to find his way to the Avenue of Gates, nor had he any great difficulty. On the way he met several warriors, but beyond a nod they gave him no heed. With ease he found a lodging place where there were many strangers from other cities of Manator. As he had had no sleep since the previous night he threw himself among the silks and furs of his couch to gain the rest which he must have, was he to give the best possible account of himself in the service of Tara of Helium the following day.

It was already morning when he awoke, and rising he paid for his lodgings, sought a place to eat, and a short time later was on his way toward The Towers of Jetan, which he had no difficulty in finding owing to the great crowds that were winding along the avenues toward the games. The new keeper of The Towers who had succeeded E-Med was too busy to scrutinize entries closely, for in addition to the many volunteer players there were scores of slaves and prisoners being forced into the games by their owners or the government. The name of each must be recorded as well as the position he was to play and the game or games in which he was to be entered, and then there were the substitutes for each that was entered in more than a single game — one for each additional game that an individual was entered for, that no succeeding game might be delayed by the death or disablement of a player.

"Your name?" asked a clerk as Turan presented himself.

"U-Kal," replied the panthan.

"Your city?"

"Manataj."

The keeper, who was standing beside the clerk, looked at Turan. "You have come a great way to play at jetan," he said. "It is seldom that the men of Manataj attend other than the decennial games. Tell me of O-Zar! Will he attend next year? Ah, but he was a noble fighter. If you be half the swordsman, U-Kal, the fame of Manataj will increase this day. But tell me, what of O-Zar?"

"He is well," replied Turan, glibly, "and he sent greetings to his friends in Manator."

"Good!" exclaimed the keeper, "and now in what game would you enter?"

"I would play for the Heliumetic princess, Tara," replied Turan.

"But man, she is to be the stake of a game for slaves and criminals," cried the keeper. "You would not volunteer for such a game!"

"But I would," replied Turan. "I saw her when she was brought into the city and even then I vowed to possess her."

"But you will have to share her with the survivors even if your color wins," objected the other.

"They may be brought to reason," insisted Turan.

"And you will chance incurring the wrath of O-Tar, who has no love for this savage barbarian," explained the keeper.

"And I win her O-Tar will be rid of her," said Turan.

The keeper of The Towers of Jetan shook his head. "You are rash," he said. "I would that I might dissuade the friend of my friend O-Zar from such madness."

"Would you favor the friend of O-Zar?" asked Turan.

"Gladly!" exclaimed the other. "What may I do for him?"

"Make me chief of the Black and give me for my pieces all slaves from Gathol, for I understand that these be excellent warriors," replied the panthan.

"It is a strange request," said the keeper, "but for my friend O-Zar I would do even more, though of course —" he hesitated — "it is customary for one who would be chief to make some slight payment."

"Certainly," Turan hastened to assure him; "I had not forgotten that. I was about to ask you what the customary amount is."

"For the friend of my friend it shall be nominal," replied the keeper, naming a figure that Gahan, accustomed to the high prices of wealthy Gathol, thought ridiculously low.

"Tell me," he said, handing the money to the keeper, "when the game for the Heliumite is to be played."

"It is the second in order of the day's games; and now if you will come with me you may select your pieces."

Turan followed the keeper to a large court which lay between the towers and the jetan field, where hundreds of warriors were assembled. Already chiefs for the games of the day were selecting their pieces and assigning them to positions, though for the principal games these matters had been arranged for weeks before. The keeper led Turan to a part of the courtyard where the majority of the slaves were assembled.

"Take your choice of those not assigned," said the keeper, "and when you have your quota conduct them to the field. Your place will be assigned you by an officer there, and there you will remain with your pieces until the second game is called. I wish you luck, U-Kal, though from what I have heard you will be more lucky to lose than to win the slave from Helium."

After the fellow had departed Turan approached the slaves. "I seek the best swordsmen for the second game," he announced. "Men from Gathol I wish, for I have heard that these be noble fighters."

A slave rose and approached him. "It is all the same in which game we die," he said. "I would fight for you as a panthan in the second game."

Another came. "I am not from Gathol," he said. "I am from Helium, and I would fight for the honor of a princess of Helium."

"Good!" exclaimed Turan. "Art a swordsman of repute in Helium?"

"I was a dwar under the great Warlord,

and I have fought at his side in a score of battles from The Golden Cliffs to The Carrion Caves. My name is Val Dor. Who knows Helium knows my prowess."

The name was well known to Gahan, who had heard the man spoken of on his last visit to Helium, and his mysterious disappearance discussed as well as his renown as a fighter.

"How could I know aught of Helium?" asked Turan; "but if you be such a fighter as you say no position could suit you better than that of Flier. What say you?"

The man's eyes denoted sudden surprise. He looked keenly at Turan, his eyes running quickly over the other's harness. Then he stepped quite close so that his words might not be overheard.

"Methinks you may know more of Helium than of Manator," he whispered.

"What mean you, fellow?" demanded Turan, seeking to cudgel his brains for the source of this man's knowledge, guess, or inspiration.

"I mean," replied Val Dor, "that you are not of Manator and that if you wish to hide the fact it is well that you speak not to a Manatorian as you did just speak to me of — Fliers! There be no Fliers in Manator and no piece in their game of Jetan bearing that name. Instead they call him who stands next to the Chief or Princess, Odwar. The piece has the same moves and power that the Flier has in the game as played outside Manator. Remember this then and remember, too, that if you have a secret it be safe in the keeping of Val Dor of Helium."

Turan made no reply but turned to the task of selecting the remainder of his pieces. Val Dor, the Heliumite, and Floran, the volunteer from Gathol, were of great assistance to him, since one or the other of them knew most of the slaves from whom his selection was to be made. The pieces all chosen, Turan led them to the place beside the playing field where they were to wait their turn, and here he passed the word around that they were to fight for more than the stake he offered for the princess should they win. This stake they accepted, so that Turan was sure of possessing Tara if his side was victorious, but he knew that these men would fight even more valorously for chivalry than for money, nor was it difficult to enlist the interest even of the Gatholians in the service of the princess.

And now he held out the possibility of a still further reward.

"I cannot promise you," he explained, "but I may say I have heard that this day which makes it possible that should we win this game we may even win your freedom!"

They leaped to their feet and crowded around him with many questions.

"It may not be spoken of aloud," he said; "but Floran and Val Dor know and they assure me that you may all be trusted. Listen! What I would tell you places my life in your hands, but you must know that every man will realize that he is fighting today the greatest battle of his life — for the honor and the freedom of Barsoom's most wondrous princess and for his own freedom as well — for the chance to return each to his own country and to the woman who awaits him there.

"First, then, is my secret. I am not of Manator. Like yourselves I am a slave, though for the moment disguised as a Manatorian from Manataj. My country and my identity must remain undisclosed for reasons that have no bearing upon our game today. I, then, am one of you. I fight for the same things that you will fight for.

"And now for that which I have but just learned. U-Thor the great led of Manatos, quarreled with O-Tar in the palace the day before yesterday and their warriors set upon one another. U-Thor was driven as far as The Gate of Enemies, where he now lies encamped. At any moment the fight may be renewed; but it is thought that U-Thor has sent to Manatos for reinforcements. Now, men of Gathol, here is the thing that interests you. U-Thor has recently taken to wife the Princess Haja of Gathol, who was slave to O-Tar and whose son, A-Kor, was dwar of The Towers of Jetan. Haja's heart is filled with loyalty for Gathol and compassion for her sons who are here enslaved, and this latter sentiment she has to some extent transmitted to U-Thor. Aid me, therefore, in freeing the Princess Tara of Helium and I believe that I can aid you and her and myself to escape the city. Bend close your ears, slaves of O-Tar, that no cruel enemy may hear my words," and Gahan of Gathol whispered in low tones the daring plan he had conceived. "And now," he demanded, when he had finished, "let him who does not dare, speak now." None replied. "And it would not betray you should I cast my sword at thy feet, it had been done ere this," said one in low tones pregnant with suppressed feeling.

"And I!" "And I!" "And I!" chorused the others in vibrant whispers.

Chapter XVII
A PLAY TO THE DEATH

Clear and sweet a trumpet spoke across The Fields of Jetan. From The High Tower its cool voice floated across the city of Manator and above the babel of human discords rising from the crowded mass that filled the seats of the stadium below. It called the players for the first game, and simultaneously there fluttered to the peaks of a thousand staffs on tower and battlement and the great wall of the stadium the rich, gay pennons of the fighting chiefs of Manator. Thus was marked the opening of The Jeddak's Games, the most important of the year and second only to the Grand Decennial Games.

Gahan of Gathol watched every play with eagle eye. The match was an unimportant one, being but to settle some petty dispute between two chiefs, and was played with professional jetan players for points only. No one was killed and there was but little blood spilled. It lasted about an hour and was terminated by the chief of the losing side deliberately permitting himself to be out-pointed, that the game might be called a draw.

Again the trumpet sounded, this time announcing the second and last game of the afternoon. While this was not considered an important match, those being reserved for the fourth and fifth days of the games, it promised to afford sufficient excitement since it was a game to the death. The vital difference between the game played with living men and that in which inanimate pieces are used, lies in the fact that while in the latter the mere placing of a piece upon a square occupied by an opponent piece terminates the move, in the former the two pieces thus brought together engage in a duel for possession of the square. Therefore there enters into the former game not only the strategy of jetan but the personal prowess and bravery of each individual piece, so that a knowledge not only of one's own men but of each player upon the opposing side is of vast value to a chief.

In this respect was Gahan handicapped, though the loyalty of his players did much to offset his ignorance of them, since they aided him in arranging the board to the best advantage and told him honestly the faults and virtues of each. One fought best in a losing game; another was too slow; another too impetuous; this one had fire and a heart of steel, but lacked endurance. Of the opponents, though, they knew little or nothing, and now as the two sides took their places upon the black and orange squares of the great jetan board Gahan obtained, for the first time, a close view of those who opposed him. The Orange Chief had not yet entered the field, but his men were all in place. Val Dor turned to Gahan. "They are all criminals from the pits of Manator," he said. "There is no slave among them. We shall not have to fight against a single fellow-countryman and every life we take will be the life of an enemy."

"It is well," replied Gahan; "but where is their Chief, and where the two Princesses?"

"They are coming now, see?" and he pointed across the field to where two women could be seen approaching under guard.

As they came nearer Gahan saw that one was indeed Tara of Helium, but the other he did not recognize, and then they were brought to the center of the field midway between the two sides and there waited until the Orange Chief arrived.

Floran voiced an exclamation of surprise when he recognized him. "By my first ancestor if it is not one of their great chiefs," he said, "and we were told that slaves and criminals were to play for the stake of this game."

His words were interrupted by the keeper of The Towers whose duty it was not only to announce the games and the stakes, but to act as referee as well.

"Of this, the second game of the first day of the Jeddak's Games in the four hundred and thirty-third year of O-Tar, Jeddak of Manator, the Princesses of each side shall be the sole stakes and to the survivors of the winning side shall belong both the Princesses, to do with as they shall see fit. The Orange Princess is the slave woman Lan-O of Gathol; the Black Princess is the slave woman Tara, a princess of Helium. The Black Chief is U-Kal of Manataj, a volunteer player; the Orange Chief is the dwar U-Dor of the 8th Utan of the jeddak of Manator, also a volunteer player. The squares shall be contested to the death. Just are the laws of Manator! I have spoken."

The initial move was won by U-Dor, following which the two Chiefs escorted their respective Princesses to the square each was to occupy. It was the first time Gahan had been alone with Tara since she had been brought upon the field. He saw her scrutinizing him closely as he approached to lead her to her place and wondered if she recognized him; but if she did she gave no sign of it. He could not but remember her last words — "I hate you!" and her desertion of him when he had been locked in the room beneath the palace by I-Gos, the taxidermist, and so he did not seek to enlighten her as to his identity. He meant to fight for her — to die for her, if necessary — and if he did not die to go on fighting to the end for her love. Gahan of Gathol was not easily to be discouraged, but he was compelled to admit that his chances of winning the love of Tara of Helium were remote. Already had she repulsed him twice. Once as jed of Gathol and again as Turan the panthan. Before his love, however, came her safety and the former must be relegated to the background until the latter had been achieved.

Passing among the players already at their stations the two took their places upon their respective squares. At Tara's left was the Black Chief, Gathan of Gathol; directly in front of her the Princess' Panthan, Floran of Gathol; and at her right the Princess' Odwar, Val Dor of Helium. And each of these knew the part that he was to play, win or lose, as did each of the other Black players. As Tara took her place Val Dor bowed low. "My sword is at your feet, Tara of Helium," he said.

She turned and looked at him, an expression of surprise and incredulity upon her face. "Val Dor, the dwar!" she exclaimed. "Val Dor of Helium — one of my father's trusted captains! Can it be possible that my eyes speak the truth?"

"It is Val Dor, Princess," the warrior replied, "and here to die for you if need be, as is every wearer of the Black upon this field of jetan today. Know Princess," he whispered, "that upon this side is no man of Manator, but each and every is an enemy of Manator."

She cast a quick, meaning glance toward Gahan. "But what of him?" she whispered, and then she caught her breath quickly in surprise. "Shade of the first jeddak!" she exclaimed. "I did but just recognize him through his disguise."

"And you trust him?" asked Val Dor. "I know him not; but he spoke fairly, as an honorable warrior, and we have taken him at his word."

"You have made no mistake," replied Tara of Helium. "I would trust him with my life — with my soul; and you, too, may trust him."

Happy indeed would have been Gahan of Gathol could he have heard those words; but Fate, who is usually unkind to the lover in such matters, ordained it otherwise, and then the game was on.

U-Dor moved his Princess' Odwar three squares diagonally to the right, which placed the piece upon the Black Chief's Odwar's seventh. The move was indicative of the game that U-Dor intended playing — a game of blood, rather than of science — and evidenced his contempt for his opponents.

Gahan followed with his Odwar's Panthan one square straight forward, a more scientific move, which opened up an avenue for himself through his line of Panthans, as well as announcing to the players and spectators that he intended having a hand in the fighting himself even before the exigencies of the game forced it upon him. The move elicited a ripple of applause from those sections of seats reserved for the common warriors and their women, showing perhaps that U-Dor was none too popular with these, and, too, it had its effect upon the morale of Gahan's pieces. A Chief may, and often does, play almost ;n entire game without leaving his own square, where, mounted upon a thoat, he may overlook the entire field and direct each move, nor may he be reproached for lack of courage should he elect thus to play the game since, by the rules, were he to be slain or so badly wounded as to be compelled to withdraw, a game that might otherwise have been won by the science of his play and the prowess of his men would be drawn. To invite personal combat, therefore, denotes confidence in his own swordsmanship, and great courage, two attributes that were calculated to fill the Black players with hope and valor when evinced by their Chief thus early in the game.

U-Dor's next move placed Lan-O's Odwar upon Tara's Odwar's fourth — within striking distance of the Black Princess. Another move and the game would be lost to Gahan unless the Orange Odwar was overthrown, or Tara moved to a position of safety; but to move his Princess now would be to admit his belief in the superiority of the Orange. In the three squares allowed him he could not place himself upon the square occupied by the Odwar of U-Dor's Princess. There was only one player upon the Black side that might dispute the square with the enemy and that was the Chief's Odwar, who stood upon Gahan's left. Gahan turned upon his thoat and looked at the man. He was a splendid looking fellow, resplendent in the gorgeous trappings of an Odwar, the five brilliant feathers which denoted his position rising defiantly erect from his thick, black hair. In common with every player upon the field and every spectator in the crowded stands he knew what was passing in his Chief's mind. He dared not speak, the ethics of the game forbade it, but what his lips might not voice his eyes expressed in martial fire, and eloquently: "The honor of the Black and the safety of our Princess are secure with me!"

Gahan hesitated no longer. "Chief's Odwar to Princess' Odwar's fourth!" he commanded. It was the courageous move of a leader who had taken up the gauntlet thrown down by his opponent.

The warrior sprang forward and leaped into the square occupied by U-Dor's piece. It was the first disputed square of the game. The eyes of the players were fastened upon the contestants, the spectators leaned forward in their seats after the first applause that had greeted the move, and silence fell upon the vast assemblage. If the Black went down to defeat, U-Dor could move his victorious piece on to the square occupied by Tara of Helium and the game would be over — over in four moves and lost to Gahan of Gathol. If the Orange lost U-Dor would have sacrificed one of his most important pieces and more than lost what advantage the first move might have given him.

Physically the two men appeared perfectly matched and each was fighting for his life, but from the first it was apparent that the Black Odwar was the better swordsman, and Gahan knew that he had

another and perhaps a greater advantage over his antagonist. The latter was fighting for his life only, without the spur of chivalry of loyalty. The Black Odwar had these to strengthen his arm, and besides these the knowledge of the thing that Gahan had whispered into the ears of his players before the game, and so he fought for what is more than life to the man of honor.

It was a duel that held those who witnessed it in spellbound silence. The weaving blades gleamed in the brilliant sunlight, ringing to the parries of cut and thrust. The barbaric harness of the duelists lent splendid color to the savage, martial scene. The Orange Odwar, forced upon the defensive, was fighting madly for his life. The Black, with cool and terrible efficiency, was forcing him steadily, step by step, into a corner of the square — a position from which there could be no escape. To abandon the square was to lose it to his opponent and win for himself ignoble and immediate death before the jeering populace. Spurred on by the seeming hopelessness of his plight, the Orange Odwar burst into a sudden fury of offense that forced the Black back a half dozen steps, and then the sword of U-Dor's piece leaped in and drew first blood, from the shoulder of his merciless opponent. An illy smothered cry of encouragement went up from U-Dor's men; the Orange Odwar, encouraged by his single success, sought to bear down the Black by the rapidity of his attack. There was a moment in which the swords moved with a rapidity that no man's eye might follow, and then the Black Odwar made a lightning parry of a vicious thrust, leaned quickly forward into the opening he had effected, and drove his sword through the heart of the Orange Odwar — to the hilt he drove it through the body of the Orange Odwar.

A shout arose from the stands, for wherever may have been the favor of the spectators, none there was who could say that it had not been a pretty fight, or that the better man had not won. And from the Black players came a sigh of relief as they relaxed from the tension of the past moments.

I shall not weary you with the details of the game — only the high features of it are necessary to your understanding of the outcome. The fourth move after the victory of the Black Odwar found Gahan upon U-Dor's fourth; an Orange Panthan was on the adjoining square diagonally to his right and the only opposing piece that could engage him other than U-Dor himself.

It had been apparent to both players and spectators for the past two moves, that Gahan was moving straight across the field into the enemy's country to seek personal combat with the Orange Chief—that he was staking all upon his belief in the superiority of his own swordsmanship, since if the two Chiefs engage, the outcome decides the game. U-Dor could move out and engage Gahan, or he could move his Princess' Panthan upon the square occupied by Gahan in the hope that the former would defeat the Black Chief and thus draw the game, which is the outcome if any other than a Chief slays the opposing Chief, or he could move away and escape, temporarily, the necessity for personal combat, or at least that is evidently what he had in mind as was obvious to all who saw him scanning the board about him; and his disappointment was apparent when he finally discovered that Gahan had so placed himself that there was no square to which U-Dor could move that it was not within Gahan's power to reach at his own next move.

U-Dor had placed his own Princess four squares east of Gahan when her position had been threatened, and he had hoped to lure the Black Chief after her and away from U-Dor; but in that he had failed. He now discovered that he might play his own Odwar into personal combat with Gahan; but he had already lost one Odwar and could ill spare the other. His position was a delicate one, since he did not wish to engage Gahan personally, while it appeared that there was little likelihood of his being able to escape. There was just one hope and that lay in his Princess' Panthan, so, without more deliberation he ordered the piece onto the square occupied by the Black Chief.

The sympathies of the spectators were all with Gahan now. If he lost, the game would be declared a draw, nor do they think better of drawn games upon Barsoom than do Earth men. If he won, it would doubtless mean a duel between the two Chiefs, a development for which they all were hoping. The game already bade fair to be a short one and it would be an angry crowd should it be decided to draw with only two

men slain. There were great, historic games on record where of the forty pieces on the field when the game opened only three survived — the two Princesses and the victorious Chief.

They blamed U-Dor, though in fact he was well within his rights in directing his play as he saw fit, nor was a refusal on his part to engage the Black Chief necessarily an imputation of cowardice. He was a great chief who had conceived a notion to possess the slave Tara. There was no honor that could accrue to him from engaging in combat with slaves and criminals, or an unknown warrior from Manataj, nor was the stake of sufficient import to warrant the risk.

But now the duel between Gahan and the Orange Panthan was on and the decision of the next move was no longer in other hands than theirs. It was the first time that these Manatorians had seen Gahan of Gathol fight, but Tara of Helium knew that he was master of his sword. Could he have seen the proud light in her eyes as he crossed blades with the wearer of the Orange, he might easily have wondered if they were the same eyes that had flashed fire and hatred at him that time he had covered her lips with mad kisses, in the pits of the palace of O-Tar. As she watched him she could not but compare his swordplay with that of the greatest swordsman of two worlds — her father, John Carter, of Virginia, Prince of Helium, Warlord of Barsoom — and she knew that the skill of the Black Chief suffered little by the comparison.

Short and to the point was the duel that decided possession of the Orange Chief's fourth. The spectators had settled themselves for an interesting engagement of at least average duration when they were brought almost standing by a brilliant flash of rapid swordplay that was over ere one could catch his breath. They saw the Black Chief step quickly back, his point upon the ground, while his opponent, his sword slipping from his fingers, clutched his breast, sank to his knees and then lunged forward upon his fae.

And then Gahan of Gathol turned his eyes directly upon U-Dor of Manator, three squares away. Three squares is a Chief's move — three squares in any direction or combination of directions, only provided that he does not cross the same square twice in a given move. The people saw and guessed Gahan's intention. They rose and roared forth their approval as he moved deliberately across the intervening squares toward the Orange Chief.

O-Tar, in the royal enclosure, sat frowning upon the scene. O-Tar was angry. He was angry with U-Dor for having entered this game for possession of a slave, for whom it had been his wish only slaves and criminals should strive. He was angry with the warrior from Manataj for having so far out-generaled and out-fought the men from Manator. He was angry with the populace because of their open hostility toward one who had basked in the sunshine of his favor for long years. O-Tar the jeddak had not enjoyed the afternoon. Those who surrounded him were equally glum — they, too, scowled upon the field, the players, and the people. Among them was a bent and wrinkled old man who gazed through weak and watery eyes upon the field and the players.

As Gahan entered his square, U-Dor leaped toward him with drawn sword with such fury as might have overborne a less skilled and powerful swordsman. For a minute the fighting was fast and furious and by comparison reducing to insignificance all that had gone before. Here indeed were two magnificent swordsmen, and here was to be a battle that bade fair to make up for whatever the people felt they had been defrauded of by the shortness of the game. Nor had it continued long before many there were who would have prophesied that they were witnessing a duel that was to become historic in the annals of jetan at Manator. Every trick, every subterfuge, know to the art of fence these men employed. Time and again each scored a point and brought blood to his opponent's copper hide until both were red with gore; but neither seemed able to administer the *coup de grace*.

From the position upon the opposite side of the field Tara of Helium watched the long-drawn battle. Always it seemed to her that the Black Chief fought upon the defensive, or when he assumed to push his opponent, he neglected a thousand openings that her practiced eye beheld. Never did he seem in real danger, nor never did he appear to exert himself to quite the pitch needful for victory. The duel already had been long contested and the day was draw-

ing to a close. Presently the sudden transition from daylight to darkness which, owing to the tenuity of the air upon Barsoom, occurs almost without the warning twilight of Earth, would occur. Would the fight never end? Would the game be called a draw after all? What ailed the Black Chief?

Tara wished that she might answer at least the last of these questions for she was sure that Turan the panthan, as she knew him, while fighting brilliantly, was not giving of himself all that he might. She could not believe that fear was restraining his hand, but that there was something beside inability to push U-Dor more fiercely she was confident. What it was, however, she could not guess.

Once she saw Gahan glance quickly up toward the sinking sun. In thirty minutes it would be dark. And then she saw and all those others saw a strange transition steal over the swordplay of the Black Chief. It was as though he had been playing with the great dwar, U-Dor, all these hours, and now he still played with him but there was a difference. He played with him terribly as a carnivore plays with its victim in the instant before the kill. The Orange Chief was helpless now in the hands of a swordsman so superior that there could be no comparison, and the people sat in open-mouthed wonder and awe as Gahan of Gathol cut his foe to ribbons and then struck him down with a blow that cleft him to the chin.

In twenty minutes the sun would set! But what of that?

Chapter XVIII

A TASK FOR LOYALTY

Long and loud was the applause that rose above the Field of Jetan at Manator, as The Keeper of the Towers summoned the two Princesses and the victorious Chief to the center of the field and presented to the latter the fruits of his prowess, and then, as custom demanded, the victorious players, headed by Gahan and the two Princesses, formed in procession behind The Keeper of the Towers and were conducted to the place of victory before the royal enclosure that they might receive the commendation of the jeddak. Those who were mounted gave up their thoats to slaves as all must be on foot for this ceremony. Directly beneath the royal enclosure are the gates to one of the tunnels that, passing beneath the seats, give ingress or egress to or from the Field. Before this gate the party halted while O-Tar looked down upon them from above. Val Dor and Floran, passing quietly ahead of the others, went directly to the gates, where they were hidden from those who occupied the enclosure with O-Tar. The Keeper of the Towers may have noticed them, but so occupied was he with the formality of presenting the victorious Chief to the jeddak that he paid no attention to them.

"I bring you, O-Tar, Jeddak of Manator, U-Kal of Manataj," he cried in a loud voice that might be heard by as many as possible, "victor over the Orange in the second of the Jeddak's Games of the four hundred and thirty-third year of O-Tar, and the slave woman Tara and the slave woman Lan-O that you may bestow these, the stakes, upon U-Kal."

As he spoke, a little, wrinkled, old man peered over the rail of the enclosure down upon the three who stood directly behind The Keeper, and strained his weak and watery eyes in an effort to satisfy the curiosity of old age in a matter of no particular import, for what were two slaves and a common warrior from Manataj to any who sat with O-Tar the jeddak?

"U-Kal of Manataj," said O-Tar, "you have deserved the stakes. Seldom have we looked upon more noble swordplay. And you tire of Manataj there be always here in the city of Manator a place for you in The Jeddak's Guard."

While the jeddak was speaking the little, old man, failing clearly to discern the features of the Black Chief, reached into his pocket-pouch and drew forth a pair of thick-lensed spectacles, which he placed upon his nose. For a moment he scrutinized Gahan closely, then he leaped to his feet and addressing O-Tar pointed a shaking finger at Gahan. As he rose Tara of Helium clutched the Black Chief's arm.

"Turan!" she whispered. "It is I-Gos, whom I thought to have slain in the pits of O-Tar. It is I-Gos and he recognizes you and will — "

But what I-Gos would do was already transpiring. In his falsetto voice he fairly screamed: "It is the slave Turan who stole the woman Tara from your throne room, O-Tar. He desecrated the dead chief I-Mal and wears his harness now!"

Instantly all was pandemonium. War-riors drew their swords and leaped to their feet. Gahan's victorious players rushed forward in a body, sweeping The Keeper of the Towers from his feet. Val Dor and Floran threw open the gates beneath the royal enclosure, opening the tunnel that led to the avenue in the city beyond the Towers. Gahan, surrounded by his men, drew Tara and Lan-O into the passageway, and at a rapid pace the party sought to reach the opposite end of the tunnel before their escape could be cut off. They were successful and when they emerged into the city the sun had set and darkness had come, relieved only by an antiquated and ineffective lighting system, which cast but a pale glow over the shadowy streets.

Now it was that Tara of Helium guessed why the Black Chief had drawn out his duel with U-Dor and realized that he might have slain his man at almost any moment he had elected. The whole plan that Gahan had whispered to his players before the game was thoroughly understood. They were to make their way to The Gate of Enemies and there offer their services to U-Thor, the great Jed of Manatos. The fact that most of them were Gatholians and that Gahan could lead rescuers to the pit where A-Kor, the son of U-Thor's wife, was confined, convinced the Jed of Gathol that they would meet with no rebuff at the hands of U-Thor. But even should he refuse them, still were they bound together to go on toward freedom, if necessary cutting their way through the forces of U-Thor at The Gate of Enemies — twenty men against a small army; but of such stuff are the warriors of Barsoom.

They had covered a considerable distance along the almost deserted avenue before signs of pursuit developed and then there came upon them suddenly from behind a dozen warriors mounted on thoats — a detachment, evidently, from The Jeddak's Guard. Instantly the avenue was a pandemonium of clashing blades, cursing warriors, and squealing thoats. In the first onslaught life blood was spilled upon both sides. Two of Gahan's men went down, and upon the enemies' side three riderless thoats attested at least a portion of their casualties.

Gahan was engaged with a fellow who appeared to have been selected to account for him only, since he rode straight for him and sought to cut him down without giving the slightest heed to several who slashed at him as he passed them. The Gatholian, practiced in the art of combating a mounted warrior from the ground, sought to reach the left side of the fellow's thoat a little to the rider's rear, the only position in which he would have any advantage over his antagonist, or rather the position that would most greatly reduce the advantage of the mounted man, and, similarly, the Manatorian strove to thwart his design. And so the guardsman wheeled and turned his vicious, angry mount while Gahan leaped in and out in an effort to reach the coveted vantage point, but always seeking some other opening in his foe's defense.

And while they jockeyed for position a rider swept swiftly past them. As he passed behind Gahan the latter heard a cry of alarm.

"Turan, they have me!" came to his ears in the voice of Tara of Helium.

A quick glance across his shoulder showed him the galloping thoatman in the act of dragging Tara to the withers of the beast, and then, with the fury of a demon, Gahan of Gathol leaped for his own man, dragged him from his mount and as he fell smote his head from his shoulders with a single cut of his keen sword. Scarce had the body touched the pavement when the Gatholian was upon the back of the dead warrior's mount, and galloping swiftly down the avenue after the diminishing figures of Tara and her abductor, the sounds of the fight waning in the distance as he pursued his quarry along the avenue that passes the palace of O-Tar and leads to The Gate of Enemies.

Gahan's mount, carrying but a single rider, gained upon that of the Manatorian, so that as they neared the palace Gahan was scarce a hundred yards behind, and now, to his consternation, he saw the fellow turn into the great entrance-way. For a moment only he halted by the guards and then he disappeared within. Gahan was almost upon him then, but evidently he had warned the guards, for they leaped out to intercept the Gatholian. But no! the fellow could not have known that he was pursued, since he had not seen Gahan seize a mount, nor would he have thought that pursuit would come so soon. If he had passed then, so could Gahan pass, for did he not wear the trappings of a Manato-

rian? The Gatholian thought quickly, and stopping his thoat called to the guardsmen to let him pass, "In the name of O-Tar!" They hesitated a moment.

"Aside!" cried Gahan. "Must the jeddak's messenger parley for the right to deliver his message?"

"To whom would you deliver it?" asked the padwar of the guard.

"Saw you not him who just entered?" cried Gahan, and without waiting for a reply urged his thoat straight past them into the palace, and while they were deliberating what was best to be done, it was too late to do anything — which is not unusual.

Along the marble corridors Gahan guided his thoat, and because he had gone that way before, rather than because he knew which way Tara had been taken, he followed the runways and passed through the chambers that led to the throne room of O-Tar. On the second level he met a slave.

"Which way went he who carried the woman before him?" he asked.

The slave pointed toward a nearby runway that led to the third level and Gahan dashed rapidly on in pursuit. At the same moment a thoatman, riding at a furious pace, approached the palace and halted his mount at the gate.

"Saw you aught of a warrior pursuing one who carried a woman before him on his thoat?" he shouted to the guard.

"He but just passed in," replied the padwar, "saying that he was O-Tar's messenger."

"He lied," cried the newcomer. "He was Turan, the slave, who stole the woman from the throne room two days since. Arouse the palace! He must be seized, and alive if possible. It is O-Tar's command."

Instantly warriors were dispatched to search for the Gatholian and warn the inmates of the palace to do likewise. Owing to the games there were comparatively few retainers in the great building, but those whom they found were immediately enlisted in the search, so that presently at least fifty warriors were seeking through the countless chambers and corridors of the palace of O-Tar.

As Gahan's thoat bore him to the third level the man glimpsed the hind quarters of another thoat disappearing at the turn of a corridor far ahead. Urging his own animal forward he raced swiftly in pursuit

Gahan of Gathol smote the man from his mount

and making the turn discovered only an empty corridor ahead. Along this he hurried to discover near its farther end a runway to the fourth level, which he followed upward. Here he saw that he had gained upon his quarry who was just turning through a doorway fifty yards ahead. As Gahan reached the opening he saw that the warrior had dismounted and was dragging Tara toward a small door on the opposite side of the chamber. At the same instant the clank of harness to his rear caused him to cast a glance behind where, along the corridor he had just traversed, he saw three warriors approaching on foot at a run. Leaping from his thoat Gahan sprang into the chamber where Tara was struggling to free herself from the grasp of her captor, slammed the door behind him, shot the great bolt into its seat, and drawing his sword crossed the room at a run to engage the Manatorian. The fellow, thus menaced, called aloud to Gahan to halt, at the same time thrusting Tara at arm's length and threatening her heart with the point of his short-sword.

"Stay!" he cried, "or the woman dies, for such is the command of O-Tar, rather than that she again fall into your hands."

Gahan stopped. But a few feet separated him from Tara and her captor, yet he was helpless to aid her. Slowly the warrior backed toward the open doorway behind him, dragging Tara with him. The girl struggled and fought, but the warrior was a powerful man and having seized her by the harness from behind was able to hold her in a position of helplessness.

"Save me, Turan!" she cried. Let them not drag me to a fate worse than death. Better that I die now while my eyes behold a brave friend than later, fighting alone among enemies in defense of my honor."

He took a step nearer. The warrior made a threatening gesture with his sword close to the soft, smooth skin of the princess, and Gahan halted.

"I cannot, Tara of Helium," he cried. "Think not ill of me that I am weak — that I cannot see you die. Too great is my love for you, daughter of Helium."

The Manatorian warrior, a derisive grin upon his lips, backed steadily away. He had almost reached the doorway when Gahan saw another warrior in the chamber toward which Tara was being borne — a fellow who moved silently, almost stealthily,

across the marble floor as he approached Tara's captor from behind. In his right hand he grasped a long-sword.

"Two to one," thought Gahan, and a grim smile touched his lips, for he had no doubt that once they had Tara safely in the adjoining chamber the two would set upon him. If he could not save her, he could at least die for her.

And then, suddenly, Gahan's eyes fastened with amazement upon the figure of the warrior behind the grinning fellow who held Tara and was forcing her to the doorway. He saw the newcomer step almost within arm's reach of the other. He saw him stop, an expression of malevolent hatred upon his features. He saw the great sword swing through the arc of a great circle, gathering swift and terrific momentum from its own weight backed by the brawn of the steel thews that guided it; he saw it pass through the feathered skull of the Manatorian, splitting his sardonic grin in twain, and open him to the middle of his breast bone.

As the dead hand relaxed its grasp upon Tara's wrist the girl leaped forward, without a backward glance, to Gahan's side. His left arm encircled her, nor did she draw away, as with ready sword the Gatholian awaited Fate's decree. Before them Tara's deliverer was wiping the blood from his sword upon the hair of his victim. He was evidently a Manatorian, his trappings those of the Jeddak's Guard, and so his act was inexplicable to Gahan and to Tara. Presently he sheathed his sword and approached them.

"When a man chooses to hide his identity behind an assumed name," he said, looking straight into Gahan's eyes, "whatever friend pierces the deception were no friend if he divulged the other's secret."

He paused as though awaiting a reply.

"Your integrity has perceived and you lips voiced an unalterable truth," replied Gahan, whose mind was filled with wonder if the implication could by any possibility be true — that this Manatorian had guessed his identity.

"We are thus agreed," continued the other, "and I may tell you that though I am here known as A-Sor, my real name is Tasor." He paused and watched Gahan's face intently for any sign of the effect of this knowledge and was rewarded with a quick, though guarded expression of recognition.

Tasor! Friend of his youth. The son of that great Gatholian noble who had given his life so gloriously, however futilely, in an attempt to defend Gahan's sire from the daggers of the assassins. Tasor an under-padwar in the guard of O-Tar, Jeddak of Manator! It was inconceivable — and yet it was he; there could be no doubt of it.

"Tasor," Gahan repeated aloud. "But it is no Manatorian name." The statement was half interrogatory, for Gahan's curiosity was aroused. He would know how his friend and loyal subject had become a Manatorian. Long years had passed since Tasor had disappeared as mysteriously as the Princess Haja and many other of Gahan's subjects. The Jed of Gathol had long supposed him dead.

"No," replied Tasor, "nor is it a Manatorian name. Come, while I search for a hiding place for you in some forgotten chamber in one of the untenanted portions of the palace, and as we go I will tell you briefly how Tasor the Gatholian became A-Sor the Manatorian.

"It befell that as I rode with a dozen of my warriors along the western border of Gathol searching for zitidars that had strayed from my herds, we were set upon and surrounded by a great company of Manatorians. They overpowered us, though not before half our number was slain and the balance helpless from wounds. And so I was brought a prisoner to Manataj, a distant city of Manator, and there sold into slavery. A woman bought me — a princess of Manataj whose wealth and position were unequaled in the city of her birth. She loved me and when her husband discovered her infatuation she beseeched me to slay him, and when I refused she hired another to do it. Then she married me; but none would have aught to do with her in Manataj, for they suspected her guilty knowledge of her husband's murder. And so we set out from Manataj for Manatos accompanied by a great caravan bearing all her worldly goods and jewels and precious metals, and on the way she caused the rumor to be spread that she and I had died. Then we came to Manator instead, she taking a new name and I the name A-Sor, that we might not be traced through our names. With her great wealth she bought me a post in The Jeddak's Guard and none knows that I am not a Manatorian, for she is dead. She was beautiful, but she was a devil."

"And you never sought to return to your native city?" asked Gahan.

"Never has the hope been absent from my heart, or my mind empty of a plan," replied Tasor. "I dream of it by day and by night, but always must I return to the same conclusion — that there can be but a single means for escape. I must wait until Fortune favors me with a place in a raiding party to Gathol. Then, once within the boundaries of my own country, they shall see me no more."

"Perhaps your opportunity lies already within your grasp," said Gahan, "has not your fealty to your own Jed been undermined by years of association with the men of Manator." The statement was half challenge.

"And my Jed stood before me now," cried Tasor, "and my avowal could be made without violating his confidence, I should cast my sword at his feet and beg the high privilege of dying for him as my sire died for his sire."

There could be no doubt of his sincerity nor any that he was cognizant of Gahan's identity. The Jed of Gathol smiled. "And if your Jed were here there is little doubt but that he would command you to devote your talents and your prowess to the rescue of the Princess Tara of Helium," he said meaningly. "And he possessed the knowledge I have gained during my captivity he would say to you, 'Go, Tasor, to the pit where A-Kor, son of Haja of Gathol, is confined and set him free and with him arouse the slaves from Gathol and march to The Gate of Enemies and offer your services to U-Thor of Manataj, who is wed to Haja of Gathol, and ask of him in return that he attack the palace of O-Tar and rescue Tara of Helium and when that thing is accomplished that he free the slaves of Gathol and furnish them with the arms and the means to return to their own country.' That, Tasor of Gathol, is what Gahan your Jed would demand of you."

"And that, Turan the slave, is what I shall bend my every effort to accomplish after I have found a safe refuge for Tara of Helium and her panthan," replied Tasor.

Gahan's glance carried to Tasor an intimation of his Jed's gratification and filled him with a chivalrous determination to do the thing required of him, or die, for he considered that he had received from the lips of his beloved ruler a commission that placed upon his shoulders a responsibility that encompassed not alone the life of Gahan and Tara but the welfare, perhaps the whole future, of Gathol. And so he hastened them onward through the musty corridors of the old palace where the dust of ages lay undisturbed upon the marble tiles. Now and again he tried a door until he found one that was unlocked. Opening it he ushered them into a chamber, heavy with dust. Crumbling silks and furs adorned the walls, with ancient weapons, and great paintings whose colors were toned by age to wondrous softness.

"This be as good as any place," he said. "No one comes here. Never have I been here before, so I know no more of the other chambers than you; but this one, at least, can I find again when I bring you food and drink. O-Mai the Cruel occupied this portion of the palace during his reign, five thousand years before O-Tar. In one of these apartments he was found dead, his face contorted in an expression of fear so horrible that it drove to madness those who looked upon it; yet there was no mark of violence upon him. Since then the quarters of O-Mai have been shunned for the legends have it that the ghosts of Corphals pursue the spirit of the wicked Jeddak nightly through these chambers, shrieking and moaning as they go. But," he added, as though to reassure himself as well as his companions, "such things may not be countenanced by the culture of Gathol or Helium."

Gahan laughed. "And if all who looked upon him were driven mad, who then was there to perform the last rites or prepare the body of the Jeddak for them?"

"There was none," replied Tasor. "Where they found him they left him and there to this very day his mouldering bones lie hid in some forgotten chamber of this forbidden suite."

Tasor left them then assuring them that he would seek the first opportunity to speak with A-Kor, and upon the following day he would bring them food and drink.[1]

After Tasor had gone Tara turned to Gahan and approaching laid a hand upon his arm. "So swiftly have events transpired since I recognized you beneath your disguise," she said, "that I have had no opportunity to assure you of my gratitude and the high esteem that your valor has won for

you in my consideration. Let me now acknowledge my indebtedness; and if promises be not vain from one whose life and liberty are in grave jeopardy, accept my assurance of the great reward that awaits you at the hand of my father in Helium."

"I desire no reward," he replied, "other than the happiness of knowing that the woman I love is happy."

For an instant the eyes of Tara of Helium blazed as she drew herself haughtily to full height, and then they softened and her attitude relaxed as she shook her head sadly.

"I have it not in my heart to reprimand you, Turan," she said, "however great your fault, for you have been an honorable and a loyal friend to Tara of Helium; but you must not say what my ears must not hear."

"You mean," he asked, "that the ears of a Princess must not listen to words of love from a panthan?"

"It is not that, Turan," she replied; "but rather that I may not in honor listen to words of love from another than him to whom I am betrothed — a fellow countryman, Djor Kantos."

"You mean, Tara of Helium," he cried, "that were it not for that you would — "

"Stop!" she commanded. "You have no right to assume aught else than my lips testify."

"The eyes are offtimes more eloquent than the lips, Tara," he replied; "and in yours I have read that which is neither hatred nor contempt for Turan the panthan, and my heart tells me that your lips bore false witness when they cried in anger: 'I hate you!'"

"I do not hate you, Turan, nor yet may I love you," said the girl, simply.

"When I broke my way out from the chamber of I-Gos I was indeed upon the verge of believing that you did hate me," he said, "for only hatred, it seemed to me, could account for the fact that you had gone without making an effort to liberate me; but presently both my heart and my judgment told me that Tara of Helium could not have deserted a companion in distress, and though I still am in ignorance of the facts I know that it was beyond your power to aid me."

"It was indeed," said the girl. "Scarce had I-Gos fallen at the bite of my dagger than I heard the approach of warriors. I ran

[1] Those who have read John Carter's description of the Green Martians in *A Princess of Mars* will recall that these strange people could exist for considerable periods of time without food or water, and to a lesser degree is the same true of all Martians.

then to hide until they had passed, thinking to return and liberate you; but in seeking to elude the party I had heard I ran full into the arms of another. They questioned me as to your whereabouts, and I told them that you had gone ahead and that I was following you and thus I led them from you."

"I knew," was Gahan's only comment, but his heart was glad with elation, as a lover's must be who has heard from the lips of his divinity an avowal of interest and loyalty, however little tinged by a suggestion of warmer regard it may be. To be abused, even, by the mistress of one's heart is better than to be ignored.

As the two conversed in the ill-lit chamber, the dim bulbs of which were encrusted with the accumulated dust of centuries, a bent and withered figure traversed slowly the gloomy corridors without, his weak and watery eyes peering through thick lenses at the signs of passage written upon the dusty floor.

Chapter XIX
THE MENACE OF THE DEAD

The night was still young when there came one to the entrance of the banquet hall where O-Tar of Manator dined with his chiefs, and brushing past the guards entered the great room with the insolence of a privileged character, as in truth he was. As he approached the head of the long board O-Tar took notice of him.

"Well, hoary one!" he cried. "What brings you out of your beloved and stinking burrow again this day. We thought that the sight of the multitude of living men at the games would drive you back to your corpses as quickly as you could go."

The cackling laugh of I-Gos acknowledged the royal sally. "Ey, ey, O-Tar," squeaked the ancient one, "I-Gos goes out not upon pleasure bound; but when one does ruthlessly desecrate the dead of I-Gos, vengeance must be had!"

"You refer to the act of the slave Turan?" demanded O-Tar.

"Turan, yes, and the slave Tara, who slipped beneath my hide a murderous blade. Another fraction of an inch, O-Tar, and I-Gos' ancient and wrinkled covering were even now in some apprentice tanner's hands, ey, ey!"

"But they have again eluded us," cried O-Tar. "Even in the palace of the great jeddak twice have they escaped the stupid

knaves I call The Jeddak's Guard." O-Tar had risen and was angrily emphasizing his words with heavy blows upon the table, dealt with a golden goblet.

"Ey, O-Tar, they elude thy guard but not the wise old calot, I-Gos."

"What mean you? Speak!" commanded O-Tar.

"I know where they are hid," said the ancient taxidermist. "In the dust of unused corridors their feet have betrayed them."

"You followed them? You have seen them?" demanded the jeddak.

"I followed them and I heard them speaking beyond a closed door," replied I-Gos; "but I did not see them."

"Where is that door?" cried O-Tar. "We will send at once and fetch them," he looked about the table as though to decide to whom he would entrust this duty. A dozen warrior chiefs arose and laid their hands upon their swords.

"To the chambers of O-Mai the Cruel I traced them," squeaked I-Gos. "There you will find them where the moaning Corphals pursue the shrieking ghost of O-Mai; ey!" and he turned his eyes from O-Tar toward the warriors who had arisen, only to discover that, to a man, they were hurriedly resuming their seats.

The cackling laughter of I-Gos broke derisively on the hush that had fallen on the room. The warriors looked sheepishly at the food upon their plates of gold. O-Tar snapped his fingers impatiently.

"Be there only cravens among the chiefs of Manator?" he cried. "Repeatedly have these presumptuous slaves flouted the majesty of your jeddak. Must I command one to go and fetch them?"

Slowly a chief arose and two others followed his example, though with ill concealed reluctance. "All, then, are not cowards," commented O-Tar. "The duty is distasteful. Therefore all three of you shall go, taking as many warriors as you wish."

"But do not ask for volunteers," interrupted I-Gos, "or you will go alone."

The three chiefs turned and left the banquet hall, walking slowly like doomed men to their fate.

Gahan and Tara remained in the chamber to which Tasor had led them, the man brushing away the dust from a deep and comfortable bench where they might rest in comparative comfort. He had found the ancient sleeping silks and furs too far gone to be of any service, crumbling to powder at a touch, thus removing any chance of making a comfortable bed for the girl, and so the two sat together, talking in low tones, of the adventures through which they already had passed and speculating upon the future; planning means of escape and hoping Tasor would not be long gone. They spoke of many things — of Hastor, and Helium, and Ptarth, and finally the conversation reminded Tara of Gathol.

"Yes," replied Turan.

"I met Gahan the Jed of Gathol at my father's palace," she said, "the very day before the storm snatched me from Helium — he was a presumptuous fellow, magnificently trapped in platinum and diamonds. Never in my life saw I so gorgeous a harness as his, and you must well know, Turan, that the splendor of all Barsoom passes through the court at Helium; but in my mind I could not see so resplendent a creature drawing that jeweled sword in mortal combat. I fear me that the Jed of Gathol, though a pretty picture of a man, is little else."

In the dim light Tara did not perceive the wry expression upon the half-averted face of her companion.

"You thought little then of the Jed of Gathol?" he asked.

"Then or now," she replied, and with a little laugh; "how it would pique his vanity to know, if he might, that a poor panthan had won a higher place in the regard of Tara of Helium," and she laid her fingers gently upon his knee.

He seized the fingers in his and carried them to his lips. "O, Tara of Helium," he cried. "Think you that I am a man of stone?" One arm slipped about her shoulders and drew the yielding body toward him.

"May my first ancestor forgive me my weakness," she cried, as her arms stole about his neck and she raised her panting lips to his. For long they clung there in love's first kiss and then she pushed him away, gently. "I love you, Turan," she half sobbed; "I love you so! It is my only poor excuse for having done this wrong to Djor Kantos, whom now I know I never loved, who knew not the meaning of love. And if you love me as you say, Turan, your love must protect me from greater dishonor, for I am but as clay in your hands."

Again he crushed her to him and then as suddenly released her, and rising, strode rapidly to and fro across the chamber as though he endeavored by violent exercise to master and subdue some evil spirit that had laid hold upon him. Ringing through his brain and heart and soul like some joyous paeon were those words that had so altered the world for Gahan of Gathol: "I love you, Turan; I love you so!" And it had come so suddenly. He had thought that she felt for him only gratitude for his loyalty and then, in an instant, her barriers were all down, she was no longer a princess; but instead a — his reflections were interrupted by a sound from beyond the closed door. His sandals of zitidar hide had given forth no sound upon the marble floor he strode, and as his rapid pacing carried him past the entrance to the chamber there came faintly from the distance of the long corridor the sound of metal on metal — the unmistakable herald of the approach of armed men.

For a moment Gahan listened intently, close to the door, until there could be no doubt but that a party of warriors was approaching. From what Tasor had told him he guessed correctly that they would be coming to this portion of the palace but for a single purpose — to search for Tara and himself — and it behooved him therefore to seek immediate means for eluding them. The chamber in which they were had other doorways beside that at which they had entered, and to one of these he must look for some safer hiding place. Crossing to Tara he acquainted her with his suspicion, leading her to one of the doors which they found unsecured. Beyond it lay a dimly-lighted chamber at the threshold of which they halted in consternation, drawing back quickly into the chamber they had just quitted, for their first glance revealed four warriors seated around a jetan board.

That their entrance had not been noted was attributed by Gahan to the absorption of the two players and their friends in the game. Quietly closing the door the fugitives moved silently to the next, which they found locked. There was now but another door which they had not tried, and this they approached quickly as they knew that the searching party must be close to the chamber. To their chagrin they found this avenue of escape barred.

Now indeed were they in a sorry plight, for should the searchers have information leading them to this room they were lost. Again leading Tara to the door behind which were the jetan players Gahan drew his sword and waited, listening. The sound of the party in the corridor came distinctly to their ears — they must be quite close, and doubtless they were coming in force. Beyond the door were but four warriors who might be readily surprised. There could, then, be but one choice and acting upon it Gahan quietly opened the door again, stepped through into the adjoining chamber, Tara's hand in his, and closed the door behind them. The four at the jetan board evidently failed to hear them. One player had either just made or was contemplating a move, for his fingers grasped a piece that still rested upon the board. The other three were watching his move. For an instant Gahan looked at them, playing jetan there in the dim light of this forgotten and forbidden chamber, and then a slow smile of understanding lighted his face.

"Come!" he said to Tara. "We have nothing to fear from these. For more than five thousand years they have sat thus, a moment to the handiwork of some ancient taxidermist."

As they approached more closely they saw that the lifelike figures were coated with dust, but that otherwise the skin was in as fine a state of preservation as the most recent of I-Go's groups, and then they heard the door of the chamber they had quitted open and knew that the searchers were close upon them. Across the room they saw the opening of what appeared to be a corridor and which investigation proved to be a short passageway, terminating in a chamber in the center of which was an ornate sleeping dais. This room, like the others, was but poorly lighted, time having dimmed the radiance of its bulbs and coated them with dust. A glance showed that it was hung with heavy goods and contained considerable massive furniture in addition to the sleeping platform, a second glance at which revealed what appeared to be the form of a man lying partially on the floor and partially on the dais. No doorways were visible other than that at which they had entered, though both knew that others might be concealed by the hangings.

Gahan, his curiosity aroused by the legends surrounding this portion of the palace, crossed to the dais to examine the figure that apparently had fallen from it, to find the dried and shrivelled corpse of a man lying upon his back on the floor with arms outstretched and fingers stiffly outspread. One of his feet was doubled partially beneath him, while the other was still entangled in the sleeping silks and furs upon the dais. After five thousand years the expression of the withered face and the eyeless sockets retained the aspect of horrid fear to such an extent, that Gahan knew that he was looking upon the body of O-Mai the Cruel.

Suddenly Tara, who stood close beside him, clutched his arm and pointed toward a far corner of the room. Gahan looked and looking felt the hairs upon his neck rising. He threw his left arm about the girl and with bared sword stood between her and the hangings that they watched, and then slowly Gahan of Gathol backed away, for in this grim and somber chamber, which no human foot had trod for five thousand years and to which no breath of wind might enter, the heavy hangings in the far corner had moved. Not gently had the moved as a draught might have moved them had there been a draught, but suddenly they had bulged out as though pushed against from behind. To the opposite corner backed Gahan until they stood with their backs against the hangings there, and then hearing the approach of their pursuers across the chamber beyond Gahan pushed Tara through the hangings and, following her, kept open with his left hand, which he had disengaged from the girl's grasp, a tiny opening through which he could view the apartment and the doorway upon the opposite side through which the pursuers would enter, if they came this far.

Behind the hangings there was a space of about three feet in width between them and the wall, making a passageway entirely around the room, broken only by the single entrance opposite them, this being a common arrangement especially in the sleeping apartments of the rich and powerful upon Barsoom. The purposes of this arrangement were several. The passageway afforded a station for guards in the same room with their master without intruding entirely upon his privacy; it concealed secret exits from the chamber; it permitted

the occupant of the room to hide eaves-
droppers and assassins for use against
enemies hat he might lure to his chamber.

The three chiefs with a dozen warriors
had had no difficulty in following the
tracks of the fugitives through the dust of
the corridors and chambers they had
traversed. To enter this portion of the
palace at all had required all the courage
they possessed, and now that they were
within the very chambers of O-Mai their
nerves were pitched to the highest key —
another turn and they would snap; for the
people of Manator are filled with weird
superstitions. As they entered the outer
chamber they moved slowly, with drawn
swords, no one seeming anxious to take
the lead, and the twelve warriors hanging
back in unconcealed and shameless terror,
while the three chiefs, spurred on by fear of
O-Tar and by pride, pressed together for
mutual encouragement as they slowly
crossed the dimly-lighted room.

Following the tracks of Gahan and Tara
they found that though each doorway had
been approached only one threshold had
been crossed and this door they gingerly
opened, revealing to their astonished gaze
the four warriors at the jetan table. For a
moment they were on the verge of flight, for
though they knew what they were, coming
as they did upon them in this mysterious
and haunted suite, they were as startled as
though they had beheld the very ghosts of
the departed. But they presently regained
their courage sufficiently to cross this
chamber too and enter the short passageway that led to the ancient sleeping apartment of O-Mai the Cruel. They did not
know that this awful chamber lay just before them, or it were doubtful that they
would have proceeded farther; but they
saw that those they sought had come this
way and so they followed, but within the
gloomy interior of the chamber they
halted, the three chiefs urging their followers, in low whispers, to close in behind
them, and there just within the entrance
they stood until, their eyes becoming accustomed to the dim light, one of them
pointed suddenly to the thing lying upon
the floor with one foot tangled in the
coverings of the dais.

"Look!" he gasped. "It is the corpse of
O-Mai! Ancestor of ancestors! we are in the
forbidden chamber." Simultaneously there
came from behind the hangings beyond

the grewsome dead a hollow moan followed
by a piercing scream, and the hangings
shook and bellied before their eyes.

With one accord, chieftains and warriors, they turned and bolted for the doorway; a narrow doorway, where they jammed, fighting and screaming in an effort to
escape. They threw away their swords and
clawed at one another to make a passage
for escape; those behind climbed upon the
shoulders of those in front; and some fell
and were trampled upon; but at last they all
got through, and, the swiftest first, they
bolted across the two intervening chambers to the outer corridor beyond, nor did
they halt their mad retreat before they
stumbled, weak and trembling, into the
banquet hall of O-Tar. At sight of them the
warriors who had remained with the jeddak leaped to their feet with drawn swords,
thinking that their fellows were pursued by
many enemies; but no one followed them
into the room, and the three chieftains
came and stood before O-Tar with bowed
heads and trembling knees.

"Well?" demanded the jeddak. "What
ails you? Speak!"

"O-Tar," cried one of them when at last
he could master his voice. "When have we
three failed you in battle or combat? Have
our swords been not always among the
foremost in defense of your safety and your
honor?"

"Have I denied this?" demanded O-Tar.

"Listen then, O Jeddak, and judge us
with leniency. We followed the two slaves to
the apartments of O-Mai the Cruel. We entered the accursed chambers and still we
did not falter. We came at last to that horrid
chamber no human eye had scanned before in fifty centuries and we looked upon
the dead face of O-Mai, lying as he has lain
for all this time. To the very death chamber
of O-Mai the Cruel we came and yet we were
ready to go farther; when suddenly there
broke upon our horrified ears the moans
and the shrieking that mark these
haunted chambers and the hangings
moved and rustled in the dead air. O-Tar, it
was more than human nerves could endure. We turned and fled. We threw away
our swords and fought with one another to
escape. With sorrow, but without shame, I
tell it, for there be no man in all Manator
that would not have done the same. If these
slaves be Corphals they are safe among
their fellow ghosts. If they be not Corphals,

then already are they dead in the chambers of O-Mai, and there may they rot for all of me, for I would not return to that accursed spot for the harness of a jeddak and the half of Barsoom for an empire. I have spoken.

O-Tar knitted his scowling brows. "Are all my chieftains cowards and cravens?" he demanded presently in sneering tones.

From among those who had not been of the searching party a chieftain arose and turned a scowling face upon O-Tar.

"The jeddak knows," he said, "that in the annals of Manator her jeddaks have ever been accounted the bravest of her warriors. Where my jeddak leads I will follow, nor may any jeddak call me a coward or a craven unless I refuse to go where he dares go. I have spoken."

After he had resumed his seat there was a painful silence, for all knew that the speaker had challenged the courage of O-Tar the Jeddak of Manator and all awaited the reply of their ruler. In every mind was the same thought — O-Tar must lead them at once to the chamber of O-Mai the Cruel, or accept forever the stigma of cowardice, and there could be no coward upon the throne of Manator. That they all knew and that O-Tar knew, as well.

But O-Tar hesitated. He looked about upon the faces of those around him at the banquet board; but he saw only the grim visages of relentless warriors. There was no trace of leniency in the face of any. And then his eye wandered to a small entrance at one side of the great chamber. An expression of relief expunged the scowl of anxiety from his features.

"Look!" he exclaimed. "See who has come!"

Chapter XX

THE CHARGE OF COWARDICE

Gahan, watching through the aperture between the hangings, saw the frantic flight of their pursuers. A grim smile rested upon his lips as he viewed the mad scramble for safety and saw them throw away their swords and fight with one another to be first from the chamber of fear, and when they were all gone he turned back toward Tara, the smile still upon his lips; but the smile died the instant that he turned, for he saw that Tara had disappeared.

"Tara!" he called in a loud voice, for he knew that there was no danger that their pursuers would return; but there was no response, unless it was a faint sound as of cackling laughter from afar. Hurriedly he searched the passageway behind the hangings finding several doors, one of which was ajar. Through this he entered the adjoining chamber which was lighted more brilliantly for the moment by the soft rays of hurtling Thuria taking her mad way through the heavens. Here he found the dust upon the floor disturbed, and the imprint of sandals. They had come this way — Tara and whatever the creature was that had stolen her.

But what could it have been? Gahan, a man of culture and high intelligence, held few if any superstitions. In common with nearly all races of Barsoom he clung, more or less inherently, to a certain exalted form of ancestor worship, though it was rather the memory or legends of the virtues and heroic deeds of his forebears that he deified rather than themselves. He never expected any tangible evidence of their existence after death; he did not believe that they had the power either for good or for evil other than the effect that their example while living might have had upon following generations; he did not believe therefore in the materialization of dead spirits. If there was a life hereafter he knew nothing of it, for he knew that science had demonstrated the existence of some material cause for every seemingly supernatural phenomenon of ancient religions and superstitions. Yet he was at a loss to know what power might have removed Tara so suddenly and mysteriously from his side in a chamber that had not known the presence of man for five thousand years.

In the darkness he could not see whether there were the imprints of other sandals than Tara's — only that the dust was disturbed — and when it led him into gloomy corridors he lost the trail altogether. A perfect labyrinth of passages and apartments were now revealed to him as he hurried on through the deserted quarters of O-Mai. Here was an ancient bath — doubtless that of the jeddak himself, and again he passed through a room in which a meal had been laid upon a table five thousand years before — the untasted breakfast of O-Mai, perhaps. There passed before his eyes in the brief moments that he traversed the chambers, a wealth of ornaments and jewels and precious metals that surprised even the Jed of Gathol whose harness was of diamonds and platinum and whose riches were the envy of a world. But a last his search of O-Mai's chambers ended in a small closet in the floor of which was the opening to a spiral runway leading straight down into Stygian darkness. The dust at the entrance of the closet had been freshly disturbed, and as this was the only possible indication that Gahan had of the direction taken by the abductor of Tara it seemed as well to follow on as to search elsewhere. So, without hesitation, he descended into the utter darkness below. Feeling with a foot before taking a forward step his descent was necessarily slow, but Gahan was a Barsoomian and so knew the pitfalls that might await the unwary in such dark, forbidden portions of a jeddak's palace.

He had descended for what he judged might be three full levels and was pausing, as he occasionally did, to listen, when he distinctly heard a peculiar shuffling, scraping sound approaching him from below. Whatever the thing was it was ascending the runway at a steady pace and would soon be near him. Gahan laid his hand upon the hilt of his sword and drew it slowly from its scabbard that he might make no noise that would apprise the creature of his presence. He wished that there might be even the slightest lessening of the darkness. If he could see but the outline of the thing that approached him he would feel that he had a fairer chance in the meeting; but he could see nothing, and then because he could see nothing the end of his scabbard struck the stone side of the runway, giving off a sound that the stillness and the narrow confines of the passage and the darkness seemed to magnify to a terrific clatter.

Instantly the shuffling sound of approach ceased. For a moment Gahan stood in silent waiting, then casting aside discretion he moved on again down the spiral. The thing, whatever it might be, gave forth no sound now by which Gahan might locate it. At any moment it might be upon him and so he kept his sword in readiness. Down, ever downward the steep spiral led. The darkness and the silence of the tomb surrounded him, yet somewhere ahead was something. He was not alone in that horrid place — another presence that he could not hear or see hovered before him — of that he was positive. Perhaps it was the thing that had stolen Tara. Perhaps Tara herself, still in the clutches of some nameless horror, was just ahead of him. He quickened his pace — it became almost a run at the thought of the danger that threatened the woman he loved, and then he collided with a wooden door that swung open to the impact. Before him was a lighted corridor. On either side were chambers. He had advanced but a short distance from the bottom of the spiral when he recognized that he was in the pits below the palace. A moment later he heard behind him the shuffling sound that had attracted his attention in the spiral runway. Wheeling about he saw the author of the sound emerging from a doorway he had just passed. It was Ghek the kaldane.

"Ghek!" exclaimed Gahan. "It was you in the runway? Have you seen Tara of Helium?"

"It was I in the spiral,"replied the kaldane; "but I have not seen Tara of Helium. I have been searching for her. Where is she?"

"I do not know," replied the Gatholian; "but we must find her and take her from this place."

"We may find her," said Ghek; "but I doubt our ability to take her away. It is not so easy to leave Manator as it is to enter it. I may come and go at will, through the ancient burrows of the ulsios; but you are too large for that and your lungs need more air than may be found in some of the deeper runways."

"But U-Thor!" exclaimed Gahan. "Have you heard aught of him or his intentions?"

"I have heard much," replied Ghek. "He camps at The Gate of Enemies. That spot he holds and his warriors lie just beyond The Gate; but he has not sufficient force to enter the city and take the palace. An hour since and you might have made your way to him; but now every avenue is strongly guarded since O-Tar learned that A-Kor had escaped to U-Thor."

"A-Kor has escaped and joined U-Thor!" exclaimed Gahan.

"But little more than an hour since. I was with him when a warrior came — a man whose name is Tasor — who brought a message from you. It was decided that Tasor should accompany A-Kor in an attempt to reach the camp of U-Thor, the great jed of Manatos, and exact from him the assurances you required. Then U-Thor was to return and take food to you and the Princess of Helium. I accompanied them. We won through easily and found U-Thor more than willing to respect your every wish, but when Tasor would have returned to you the way was blocked by the warriors of O-Tar. Then it was that I volunteered to come to you and report and find food and drink and then go forth among the Gatholian slaves of Manator and prepare them for their part in the plan that U-Thor and Tasor conceived."

"And what was this plan?"

"U-Thor has sent for reinforcements. To Manatos he has sent and to all the outlying districts that are his. It will take a month to collect and bring them hither and in the meantime the slaves within the city are to organize secretly, stealing and hiding arms against the day that the reinforcements arrive. When that day comes the forces of U-Thor will enter The Gate of Enemies and as the warriors of O-Tar rush to repulse them the slaves from Gathol will fall upon them from the rear with the majority of their numbers, while the balance will assault the palace. They hope thus to divert so many from The Gate that U-Thor will have little difficulty in forcing an entrance to the city."

"Perhaps they will succeed," commented Gahan; "but the warriors of O-Tar are many, and those who fight in defense of their homes and their jeddak have always an advantage. Ah, Ghek, would that we had the great warships of Gathol or of Helium to pour their merciless fire into the streets of Manator while U-Thor marched to the palace over the corpses of the slain." He paused, deep in thought, and then turned his gaze again upon the kaldane. "Heard you aught of the party that escaped with me from The Field of Jetan — of Floran, Val Dor, and the others? What of them?"

"Ten of these won through to U-Thor at The Gate of Enemies and were well received by him. Eight fell in the fighting upon the way. Val Dor and Floran live, I believe, for I am sure that I heard U-Thor address two warriors by these names."

"Good!" exclaimed Gahan. "Go then, through the burrows of the ulsios, to The Gate of Enemies and carry to Floran the message that I shall write in his own language. Come, while I write the message."

In a nearby room they found a bench and table and there Gahan sat and wrote in the strange, stenographic characters of Martian script a message to Floran of Gathol. "Why," he asked, when he had finished it, "did you search for Tara through the spiral runway where we nearly met?"

"Tasor told me where you were to be found, and as I have explored the greater part of the palace by means of the ulsio runways and the darker and less frequented passages I knew precisely where you were and how to reach you. This secret spiral ascends from the pits to the roof of the loftiest of the palace towers. It has secret openings at every level; but there is no living Manatorian, I believe, who knows of its existence. At least never have I met one within it and I have used it many times. Thrice have I been in the chamber where O-Mai lies, though I knew nothing of his identity or the story of his death until Tasor told it to us in the camp of U-Thor."

"You know the palace thoroughly then?" Gahan interrupted.

"Better than O-Tar himself or any of his servants."

"Good! And you would serve the Princess Tara, Ghek, you may serve her best by accompanying Floran and following his instructions. I will write them here at the close of my message to him, for the walls have ears, Ghek, while none but a Gatholian may read what I have writ to Floran. He will transmit it to you. Can I trust you?"

"I may never return to Bantoom," replied Ghek. "Therefore I have but two friends in all Barsoom. What better may I do than serve them faithfully? You may trust me, Gatholian, who with a woman of your kind has taught me that there be finer and nobler things than perfect mentality uninfluenced by the unreasoning tuitions of the heart. I go."

As O-Tar pointed to the little doorway all eyes turned in the direction he indicated and surprise was writ large upon the faces of the warriors when they recognized the two who had entered the banquet hall. There was I-Gos, and he dragged behind him one who was gagged and whose hands were fastened behind with a ribbon of tough silk. It was Tara the slave girl. I-Gos' cackling laughter rose above the silence of the room.

"Ey, ey!" he shrilled. "What the young warriors of O-Tar cannot do, old I-Gos does alone."

"Only a Corphal may capture a Corphal," growled one of the chiefs who had fled from the chambers of O-Mai.

I-Gos laughed. "Terror turned your heart to water," he replied; "and shame your tongue to libel. This be no Corphal, but only a woman of Helium; her companion a warrior who can match blades with the best of you and cut out your putrid hearts. Not so in the days of I-Gos' youth. Ah, then were there men in Manator. Well do I recall that day that I — "

"Peace, doddering fool!" commanded O-Tar. "Where is the man?"

"Where I found the woman — in the death chamber of O-Mai. Let your wise and brave chieftains go thither and fetch him. I am an old man, and could bring but one."

"You have done well, I-Gos," O-Tar hastened to assure him, for when he learned that Gahan might still be in the haunted chambers he wished to appease the wrath of I-Gos, knowing well the vitriolic tongue and temper of the ancient one. "You think she is no Corphal, then, I-Gos?" he asked, wishing to carry the subject from the man who was still at large.

"No more than you," replied the ancient taxidermist.

O-Tar looked long and searchingly at Tara of Helium. All the beauty that was hers seemed suddenly to be carried to every fibre of his consciousness. She was still garbed in the rich harness of a Black Princess of Jetan, and as O-Tar the Jeddak gazed upon her he realized that never before had his eyes rested upon a more perfect figure — a more beautiful face.

"She is no Corphal," he murmured to himself. "She is no Corphal and she is a princess — a princess of Helium, and, by the golden hair of the Holy Hekkador, she is beautiful. Take the gag from her mouth and release her hands," he commanded aloud. "Make room for the Princess Tara of Helium at the side of O-Tar of Manator. She shall dine as becomes a princess."

Slaves did as O-Tar bid and Tara of Helium stood with flashing eyes behind the chair that was offered her. "Sit!" commanded O-Tar.

The girl sank into the chair. "I sit as a prisoner," she said; "not as a guest at the board of my enemy, O-Tar of Manator."

O-Tar motioned his followers from the room. "I would speak alone with the Princess of Helium," he said. The company and the slaves withdrew and once more the Jeddak of Manator turned toward the girl. "O-Tar of Manator would be your friend," he said.

Tara of Helium sat with arms folded upon her small, firm breasts, her eyes flashing from behind narrowed lids, nor did she deign to answer his overture. O-Tar leaned closer to her. He noted the hostility of her bearing and he recalled his first encounter with her. She was a she-banth, but she was beautiful. She was by far the most desirable woman that O-Tar had ever looked upon and he was determined to possess her. He told her so.

"I could take you as my slave," he said to her; "but it pleases me to make you my wife. You shall be Jeddara of Manator. You shall have seven days in which to prepare for the great honor that O-Tar is conferring upon you, and at this hour of the seventh day you shall become an empress and the wife of O-Tar in the throne room of the jeddaks of Manator." He struck a gong that stood beside him upon the table and when a slave appeared he bade him recall the company. Slowly the chiefs filed in and took their places at the table. Their faces were grim and scowling, for there was still unanswered the question of their jeddak's courage. If O-Tar had hoped they would forget he had been mistaken in his men.

O-Tar arose. "In seven days," he announced, "there will be a great feast in honor of the new Jeddara of Manator," and he waved his hand toward Tara of Helium. "The ceremony will occur at the beginning of the seventh zode in the throne room. In the meantime the Princess of Helium will be cared for in the tower of the women's quarters of the palace. Conduct her thither, E-Thas, with a suitable guard of honor and see to it that slaves and eunuchs be placed at her disposal, who shall attend upon her all wants and guard her carefully from harm."

Now E-Thas knew that the real meaning concealed in these fine words was that he should conduct the prisoner under a strong guard to the women's quarters and confine her there in the tower for seven days, placing about her trustworthy guards who would prevent her escape or frustrate any attempted rescue.

As Tara was departing from the chamber with E-Thas and the guard, O-Tar leaned close to her ear and whispered: "Consider well during these seven days the high honor I have offered you, and — its sole alternative." As though she had not heard him the girl passed out of the banquet hall, her head high and her eyes straight to the front.

After Ghek had left him Gahan roamed the pits and the ancient corridors of the deserted portions of the palace seeking some clue to the whereabouts or the fate of Tara of Helium. He utilized the spiral runway in passing from level to level until he knew every foot of it from the pits to the summit of the high tower, and into what apartments it opened at the various levels as well as the ingenious and hidden mechanism that operated the locks of the cleverly concealed doors leading to it. For food he drew upon the stores he found in the pits and when he slept he lay upon the royal couch of O-Mai in the forbidden chamber, sharing the dais with the dead foot of the ancient jeddak.

In the palace about him seethed, all unknown to Gahan, a vast unrest. Warriors and chieftains pursued the duties of their vocations with dour faces, and little knots of them were collecting here and there and with frowns of anger discussing some subject that was uppermost in the minds of all. It was upon the fourth day following Tara's incarceration in the tower that E-Thas, the major-domo of the palace and one of O-Tar's creatures, came to his master upon some trivial errand. O-Tar was alone in one of the smaller chambers of his personal suite when the major-domo was announced, and after the matter upon which E-Thas had come was disposed of the jeddak signed him to remain.

"From the position of an obscure warrior I have elevated you, E-Thas, to the honors of a chief. Within the confines of the palace your word is second only to mine. You are not loved for this, E-Thas, and should another jeddak ascend the throne of Manator what would become of you, whose enemies are among the most powerful of Manator?"

"Speak not of it, O-Tar," begged E-Thas. "These last few days I have thought upon it much and I would forget it; but I have sought to appease the wrath of my worst enemies. I have been very kind and indulgent with them."

"You, too, read the voiceless message in the air?" demanded the jeddak.

E-Thas was palpably uneasy and he did not reply.

"Why did you not come to me with your apprehensions?" demanded O-Tar. "Be this loyalty?"

"I feared, O mighty jeddak!" replied E-Thas. "I feared that you would not understand and that you would be angry."

"What know you? Speak the whole truth!" commanded O-Tar.

"There is much unrest among the chieftains and the warriors," replied E-Thas. "Even those who were your friends fear the power of those who speak against you."

"What say they?" growled the jeddak.

"They say that you are afraid to enter the apartments of O-Mai in search of the slave Turan — oh, do not be angry with me, Jeddak; it is but what they say that I repeat. I, your loyal E-Thas, believe no such foul slander."

"No, no; why should I fear?" demanded O-Tar. "We do not know that he is there. Did not my chiefs go thither and see nothing of him?"

"But they say that *you* did not go," pursued E-Thas, "and that they will have none of a coward upon the throne of Manator."

"They said that treason?" O-Tar almost shouted.

"They said that and more, great jeddak," answered the major-domo. "They said that not only did you fear to enter the chambers of O-Mai, but that your feared the slave Turan, and they blame you for your treatment of A-Kor, whom they all believe to have been murdered at your command. They were fond of A-Kor and there are many now who say aloud that A-Kor would have made a wondrous jeddak."

"They dare?" screamed O-Tar. "They dare suggest the name of a slave's bastard for the throne of O-Tar!"

"He is your son, O-Tar," E-Thas reminded him, "nor is there a more beloved man in Manator — I but speak to you of facts which may not be ignored, and I dare do so because only when you realize the truth may you seek a cure for the ills that draw about your throne."

O-Tar had slumped down upon his bench — suddenly he looked shrunken and tired and old. "Cursed be the day," he cried, "that saw those three strangers enter the city of Manator. Would that U-Dor had been spared to me. He was strong — my enemies feared him; but he is gone — dead at the hands of that hateful slave, Turan; may the curse of Issus be upon him!"

"My jeddak, what shall we do?" begged E-Thas. "Cursing the slave will not solve your problems."

"But the great feast and the marriage is but three days off," plead O-Tar. "It shall be a great gala occasion. The warriors and the chiefs all know that — it is the custom. Upon that day gifts and honors shall be bestowed. Tell me, who are most bitter against me? I will send you among them and let it be known that I am planning rewards for their past services to the throne. We will make jeds of chiefs and chiefs of warriors, and grant them palaces and slaves. Eh, E-Thas?"

The other shook his head. "It will not do, O-Tar. They will have nothing of your gifts or honors. I have heard them say as much."

"What do they want?" demanded O-Tar.

"They want a jeddak as brave as the bravest," replied E-Thas, though his knees shook as he said it.

"They think I am a coward?" cried the jeddak.

"They say you are afraid to go to the apartments of O-Mai the Cruel."

For a long time O-Tar sat, his head sunk upon his breast, staring blankly at the floor.

"Tell them," he said at last in a hollow voice that sounded not at all like the voice of a great jeddak; "tell them that I will go to the chambers of O-Mai and search for Turan the slave."

Chapter XXI
A RISK FOR LOVE

"Ey, ey, he is a craven and he called me 'doddering fool'!" The speaker was I-Gos and he addressed a knot of chieftains in one of the chambers of the palace of O-Tar, Jeddak of Manator: "If A-Kor was alive there were a jeddak for us!"

"Who says that A-Kor is dead?" demanded one of the chiefs.

"Where is he then?" asked I-Gos. "Have not others disappeared whom O-Tar thought too well beloved for men so near

[1]About 1:00 A.M. Earth time.

the throne as they?"

The chief shook his head. "And I thought that, or knew it, rather; I'd join U-Thor at The Gate of Enemies."

"S-s-st," cautioned one; "here comes the licker of feet," and all eyes were turned upon the approaching E-Thas.

"Kaor, friends!" he exclaimed as he stopped among them, but his friendly greeting elicited naught but a few surly nods. "Have you heard the news?" he continued, unabashed by treatment to which he was becoming accustomed.

"What — has O-Tar seen an ulsio and fainted?" demanded I-Gos with broad sarcasm.

"Men have died for less than that, ancient one," E-Thas reminded him.

"I am safe," retorted I-Gos, "for I am not a brave and popular son of the jeddak of Manator."

This was indeed open treason, but E-Thas feigned not to hear it. He ignored I-Gos and turned to the others. "O-Tar goes to the chamber of O-Mai this night in search of Turan the slave," he said. "He sorrows that his warriors have not the courage for so mean a duty and that their jeddak is thus compelled to arrest a common slave," with which taunt E-Thas passed on to spread the word in other parts of the palace. As a matter of fact the latter part of his message was purely original with himself, and he took great delight in delivering it to the discomfiture of his enemies. As he was leaving the little group of men I-Gos called after him. "At what hour does O-Tar intend visiting the chambers of O-Mai?" he asked.

"Toward the end of the eighth zode[1]," replied the major-domo, and went his way.

"We shall see," stated I-Gos.

"What shall we see?" asked a warrior.

"We shall see whether O-Tar visits the chamber of O-Mai."

"How?"

"I shall be there myself and if I see him I will know that he has been there. If I don't see him I will know that he has not," explained the old taxidermist.

"Is there anything there to fill an honest man with fear?" asked a chieftain. "What have you seen?"

"It was not so much what I saw, though that was bad enough, as what I heard," said I-Gos.

"Tell us! What heard and saw you?"

"I saw the dead O-Mai," said I-Gos. The others shuddered.

"And you went not mad?" they asked.

"Am I mad?" retorted I-Gos.

"And you will go again?"

"Yes."

"Then indeed you are mad," cried one.

"You saw the dead O-Mai; but what heard you that was worse?" whispered another.

"I saw the dead O-Mai lying upon the floor of his sleeping chamber with one foot tangled in the sleeping silks and furs upon his couch. I heard horrid moans and frightful screams."

"And you are not afraid to go there again?" demanded several.

"The dead cannot harm me," said I-Gos. "He has lain thus for five thousand years. Nor can a sound harm me. I heard it once and live — I can hear it again. It came from almost at my side where I hid behind the hangings and watched the slave Turan before I snatched the woman away from him."

"I-Gos, you are a very brave man," said a chieftain.

"O-Tar called me 'doddering fool' and I would face worse dangers than lie in the forbidden chambers of O-Mai to know it if he does not visit the chamber of O-Mai. Then indeed shall O-Tar fall!"

The night came and the zodes dragged and the time approached when O-Tar, Jeddak of Manator, was to visit the chamber of O-Mai in search of the slave Turan. To us, who doubt the existence of malignant spirits, his fear may seem unbelievable, for he was a strong man, an excellent swordsman, and a warrior of great repute; but the fact remained that O-Tar of Manator was nervous with apprehension as he strode the corridors of his palace toward the deserted halls of O-Mai and when he stood at last with his hand upon the door that opened from the dusty corridor to the very apartments themselves he was almost paralyzed with terror. He had come alone for two very excellent reasons, the first of which was that thus none might note his terror-stricken state nor his defection should he fail at the last moment, and the other was that should he accomplish the thing alone or be able to make his chiefs believe that he had, the credit would be far greater than were he to be accompanied by warriors.

But though he had started alone he had become aware that he was being followed, and he knew that it was because his people had no faith in either his courage or his veracity. He did not believe that he would find the slave Turan. He did not very much want to find him, for though O-Tar was an excellent swordsman and a brave warrior in physical combat, he had seen how Turan had played with U-Dor and he had no stomach for a passage at arms with one whom he knew outclassed him.

And so O-Tar stood with his hand upon the door — afraid to enter; afraid not to. But at last his fear of his own warriors, watching behind him, grew greater than the fear of the unknown behind the ancient door and he pushed the heavy skeel aside and entered.

Silence and gloom and the dust of centuries lay heavy upon the chamber. From his warriors he knew the route that he must take to the horrid chamber of O-Mai and so he forced his unwilling feet across the room before him, across the room where the jetan players sat at their eternal game, and came to the short corridor that led into the room of O-Mai. His naked sword trembled in his grasp. He paused after each forward step to listen and when he was almost at the door of the ghost-haunted chamber, his heart stood still within his breast and the cold sweat broke from the clammy skin of his forehead, for from within there came to his affrighted ears the sound of muffled breathing. Then it was that O-Tar of Manator came near to fleeing from the nameless horror that he could not see, but that he knew lay waiting for him in that chamber just ahead. But again came the fear of the wrath and contempt of his warriors and his chiefs. They would degrade him and they would slay him into the bargain. There was no doubt of what his fate would be should he flee the apartments of O-Mai in terror. His only hope, therefore, lay in daring the unknown in preference to the known.

He moved forward. A few steps took him to the doorway. The chamber before him was darker than the corridor, so that he could but indistinctly make out the objects in the room. He saw a sleeping dais near the center, with a darker blotch of something lying on the marble floor beside it. He moved a step farther into the doorway and the scabbard of his sword scraped against the stone frame. To his horror he saw the sleeping silks and furs upon the central dais move. He saw a figure slowly arising to a sitting posture from the death bed of O-Mai the Cruel. His knees shook, but he gathered all his moral forces, and gripping his sword more tightly in his trembling fingers prepared to leap across the chamber upon the horrid apparition. He hesitated just a moment. He felt eyes upon him — ghoulish eyes that bored through the darkness into his withering heart — eyes that he could not see. He gathered himself for the rush — and then there broke from the thing upon the couch an awful shriek, and O-Tar sank senseless to the floor.

Gahan rose from the couch of O-Mai, smiling, only to swing quickly about with drawn sword as the shadow of a noise impinged upon his keen ears from the shadows behind him. Between the parted hangings he saw a bent and wrinkled figure. It was I-Gos.

"Sheathe your sword, Turan," said the old man. "You have naught to fear from I-Gos."

"What do you here?" demanded Gahan.

"I came to make sure that the great coward did not cheat us. Ey, and he called me 'doddering fool'; but look at him now! Stricken insensible by terror, but, ey, one might forgive him that who had heard your uncanny scream. It all but blasted my own courage. And it was you, then, who moaned and screamed when the chiefs came the day that I stole Tara from you?"

"It was you, then, old scoundrel?" demanded Gahan, moving threateningly toward I-Gos.

"Come, come!" expostulated the old man; "it was I, but then I was your enemy. I would not do it now. Conditions have changed."

"How have they changed? What has changed them?" asked Gahan.

"Then I did not fully realize the cowardice of my jeddak, or the bravery of you and the girl. I am an old man from another age and I love courage. At first I resented the girl's attack upon me, but later I came to see the bravery of it and it won my admiration, as have all her acts. She feared not O-Tar, she feared not me, she feared not all the warriors of Manator. And you! Blood of a million sires! but how you fight! I am sorry that I exposed you at The Fields of Je-

tan. I am sorry that I dragged the girl Tara back to O-Tar. I would make amends. I would be your friend. Here is my sword at your feet," and drawing his weapon I-Gos cast it to the floor in front of Gahan.

The Gatholian knew that scarce the most abandoned of knaves would repudiate this solemn pledge, and so he stooped, and picking up the old man's sword returned it to him, hilt first, in acceptance of his friendship.

"Where is the Princess Tara of Helium?" asked Gahan. "Is she safe?"

"She is confined in the tower of the women's quarters awaiting the ceremony that is to make her Jeddara of Manator," replied I-Gos.

"This thing dared think that Tara of Helium would mate with him?" growled Gahan. "I will make short work of him if he is not already dead from fright," and he stepped toward the fallen O-Tar to run his sword through the jeddak's heart.

"No!" cried I-Gos. "Slay him not and pray that he be not dead if you would save your princess."

"How is that?" asked Gahan.

"If word of O-Tar's death reached the quarters of the women the Princess Tara would be lost. They know O-Tar's intention of taking her to wife and making her Jeddara of Manator, so you may rest assured that they all hate her with the hate of jealous women. Only O-Tar's power protects her now from harm. Should O-Tar die they would turn her over to the warriors and the male slaves, for there would be none to avenge her."

Gahan sheathed his sword. "Your point is well taken; but what shall we do with him?"

"Leave him where he lies," counseled I-Gos. "He is not dead. When he revives he will return to his quarters with a fine tale of his bravery and there will be none to impugn his boasts — none but I-Gos. Come! he may revive at any moment and he must not find us here."

I-Gos crossed to the body of his jeddak, knelt beside it for an instant, and then returned past the couch to Gahan. The two quit the chamber of O-Mai and took their way toward the spiral runway. Here I-Gos led Gahan to a higher level and out upon the roof of that portion of the palace from where he pointed to a high tower quite close by. "There," he said, "lies the Princess of Helium, and quite safe she will be until the time of the ceremony."

"Safe, possibly, from other hands, but not from her own," said Gahan. "She will never become Jeddara of Manator — first will she destroy herself."

"She would do that?" asked I-Gos.

"She will, unless you can get word to her that I still live and that there is yet hope," replied Gahan.

"I cannot get word to her," said I-Gos. "The quarters of his women O-Tar guards with jealous hand. Here are his most trusted slaves and warriors, yet even so, thick among them are countless spies, so that no man knows which be which. No shadow falls within those chambers that is not marked by a hundred eyes."

Gahan stood gazing at the lighted windows of the high tower in the upper chambers of which Tara of Helium was confined. "I will find a way, I-Gos," he said.

"There is no way," replied the old man.

For some time they stood upon the roof beneath the brilliant stars and hurtling moons of dying Mars, laying their plans against the time that Tara of Helium should be brought from the high tower to the throne room of O-Tar. It was then, and then alone, argued I-Gos, that any hope of rescuing her might be entertained. Just how far he might trust the other Gahan did not know, and so he kept to himself the knowledge of the plan that he had forwarded to Floran and Val Dor by Ghek, but he assured the ancient taxidermist that if he were sincere in his oft-repeated declaration that O-Tar should be denounced and superseded he would have his opportunity on the night that the jeddak sought to wed the Heliumetic princess.

"Your time shall come then, I-Gos," Gahan assured the other, "and if you have any party that thinks as you do, prepare them for the eventuality that will succeed O-Tar's presumptuous attempt to wed the daughter of The Warlord. Where shall I see you again, and when? I go now to speak with Tara, Princess of Helium."

"I like your boldness," said I-Gos; "but it will avail you naught. You will not speak with Tara, Princess of Helium, though doubtless the blood of many Manatorians will drench the floors of the women's quarters before you are slain."

Gahan smiled. "I shall not be slain. Where and when shall we meet? But you

may find me in O-Mai's chamber at night. That seems the safest retreat in all Manator for an enemy of the jeddak in whose palace it lies. I go!"

"And may the spirits of your ancestors surround you," said I-Gos.

After the old man had left him Gahan made his way across the roof to the high tower, which appeared to have been constructed of concrete and afterward elaborately carved, its entire surface being covered with intricate designs cut deep into the stone-like material of which it was composed. Though wrought ages since, it was but little weather-worn owing to the aridity of the Martian atmosphere, the infrequency of rains, and the rarity of dust storms. To scale it, though, presented difficulties and danger that might have deterred the bravest of men — that would, doubtless, have deterred Gahan, had he not felt that the life of the woman he loved depended upon his accomplishing the hazardous feat.

Removing his sandals and laying aside all of his harness and weapons other than a single belt supporting a dagger, the Gatholian essayed the dangerous ascent. Clinging to the carvings with hands and feet he worked himself slowly aloft, avoiding the windows and keeping upon the shadowy side of the tower, away from the light of Thuria and Cluros. The tower rose some fifty feet above the roof of the adjacent part of the palace, comprising five levels or floors with windows looking in every direction. A few of the windows were balconied, and these more than the others he sought to avoid, although, it being now near the close of the ninth zode, there was little likelihood that many were awake within the tower.

His progress was noiseless and he came at last, undetected, to the windows of the upper level. These, like several of the others he had passed at lower levels, were heavily barred, so that there was no possibility of his gaining ingress to the apartment where Tara was confined. Darkness hid the interior behind the first window that he approached. The second opened upon a lighted chamber where he could see a guard sleeping at his post outside a door. Here also was the top of the runway leading to the next level below. Passing still farther around the tower Gahan approached another window, but now he clung to that side of the tower which ended in a court-yard a hundred feet below and in a short time the light of Thuria would reach him. He realized that he must hasten and he prayed that behind the window he now approached he would find Tara of Helium.

Coming to the opening he looked in upon a small chamber dimly lighted. In the center was a sleeping dais upon which a human form lay beneath silks and furs. A bare arm, protruding from the coverings, lay exposed against a black and yellow striped orluk skin — an arm of wondrous beauty about which was clasped an armlet that Gahan knew. No other creature was visible within the chamber, all of which was exposed to Gahan's view. Pressing his face to the bars the Gatholian whispered her dear name. The girl stirred, but did not awaken. Again he called, but this time louder. Tara sat up and looked about and at the same instant a huge eunuch leaped to his feet from where he had been lying on the floor close by that side of the dais far-thest from Gahan. Simultaneously the brilliant light of Thuria flashed full upon the window where Gahan clung silhouet-ting him plainly to the two within.

Both sprang to their feet. The eunuch drew his sword and leaped for the window where the helpless Gahan would have fall-en an easy victim to a single thrust of the murderous weapon the fellow bore, had not Tara of Helium leaped upon her guard dragging him back. At the same time she drew the slim dagger from its hiding place in her harness and even as the eunuch sought to hurl her aside its keen point found his heart. Without a sound he died and lunged forward to the floor. Then Tara ran to the window.

"Turan, my chief!" she cried. "What awful risk is this you take to seek me here, where even your brave heart is powerless to aid me."

"Be not so sure of that, heart of my heart," he replied. "While I bring but words to my love, they be the forerunner of deeds, I hope, that will give her back to me forever. I feared that you might destroy yourself, Tara of Helium, to escape the dishonor that O-Tar would do you, and so I came to give you new hope and to beg that you live for me through whatever may transpire, in the knowledge that there is yet a way and that if all goes well we shall be freed at last. Look for me in the throne room of O-Tar the

night that he would wed you. And now, how may we dispose of this fellow?" He pointed to the dead eunuch upon the floor.

"We need not concern ourselves about that," she replied. "None dares harm me for fear of the wrath of O-Tar — otherwise I should have been dead so soon as ever I en-tered this portion of the palace, for the women hate me. O-Tar alone may punish me, and what cares O-Tar for the life of a eunuch? No, fear not upon this score."

Their hands were clasped between the bars and now Gahan drew her nearer to him.

"One kiss," he said, "before I go, my princess," and the proud daughter of Dejah Thoris, Princess of Helium, and The Warlord of Barsoom whispered: "My chief-tain!" and pressed her lips to the lips of Tu-ran, the common panthan.

Chapter XXII

AT THE MOMENT OF MARRIAGE

The silence of the tomb lay heavy about him as O-Tar, Jeddak of Manator, opened his eyes in the chamber of O-Mai. Recollec-tion of the frightful apparition that had confronted him swept to his conscious-ness. He listened, but heard naught. Within the range of his vision there was nothing apparent that might cause alarm. Slowly he lifted his head and looked about. Upon the floor beside the couch lay the thing that had at first attracted his atten-tion and his eyes closed in terror as he rec-ognized it for what it was; but it moved not, nor spoke. O-Tar opened his eyes again and rose to his feet. He was trembling in every limb. There was nothing on the dais from which he had seen the *thing* arise.

O-Tar backed slowly from the room. At last he gained the outer corridor. It was empty. He did not know that it had emptied rapidly as the loud scream with which his own had mingled had broken upon the startled ears of the warriors who had been sent to spy upon him. He looked at the timepiece set in a massive bracelet upon his left forearm. The ninth zode was nearly half gone. O-Tar had lain for an hour un-conscious. He had spent an hour in the chamber of O-Mai and he was not dead! He had looked upon the face of his predecessor and was still sane! He shook himself and smiled. Rapidly he subdued his rebelli-ously shaking nerves, so that by the time he reached the tenanted portion of the

*Gahan looked in upon a small chamber
dimly lighted.*

palace 0e had gained control of himself. He walked with chin high and something of a swagger. To the banquet hall he went, knowing that his chiefs awaited him there and as he entered they arose and upon the faces of many were incredulity and amaze, for they had not thought to see O-Tar the jeddak again after what the spies had told them of the horrid sounds issuing from the chambers of O-Mai. Thankful was O-Tar that he had gone alone to that chamber of fright, for now no one could deny the tale that he should tell.

E-Thas rushed forward to greet him, for E-Thas had seen black looks directed toward him as the *tals* slipped by and his benefactor failed to return.

"O brave and glorious jeddak!" cried the major-domo. "We rejoice at your safe return and be of you the story of your adventure."

"It was naught," exclaimed O-Tar. "I searched the chambers carefully and waited in hiding for the return of the slave, Turan, if he were temporarily away; but he came not. He is not there and I doubt if he ever goes there. Few men would choose to remain long in such a dismal place."

"You were not attacked?" asked E-Thas. "You heard no screams, nor moans?"

"I heard hideous noises and saw phantom figures; but they fled before me so that never could I lay hold of one, and I looked upon the face of O-Mai and I am not mad. I even rested in the chamber beside his corpse."

In a far corner of the room a bent and wrinkled old man hid a smile behind a golden goblet of strong brew.

"Come! Let us drink!" cried O-Tar and reached for the dagger, the pommel of which he was accustomed to use to strike the gong which summoned slaves, but the dagger was not in its scabbard. O-Tar was puzzled. He knew that it had been there just before he entered the chamber of O-Mai, for he had carefully felt of all his weapons to make sure that none was missing. He seized instead a table utensil and struck the gong, and when the slaves came bade them bring the strongest brew for O-Tar and his chiefs. Before the dawn broke many were the expressions of admiration bellowed from drunken lips — admiration for the courage of their jeddak; but some there were who stilled looked glum.

Came at last the day that O-Tar would take the Princess Tara of Helium to wife.

For hours slaves prepared the unwilling bride. Seven perfumed baths occupied three long and weary hours, then her whole body was anointed with the oil of pimalia blossoms and massaged by the deft fingers of a slave from distant Dusar. Her harness, all new and wrought for the occasion, was of the white hide of the great white apes of Barsoom, hung heavily with platinum and diamonds — fairly encrusted with them. The glossy mass of her jet hair had been built into a coiffure of stately and becoming grandeur, into which diamond-headed pins were stuck until the whole scintillated as the stars in heaven upon a moonless night.

But it was a sullen and defiant bride that they led from the high tower toward the throne room of O-Tar. The corridors were filled with slaves and warriors, and the women of the palace and the city who had been commanded to attend the ceremony. All the power and pride, wealth and beauty of Manator were there.

Slowly Tara, surrounded by a heavy guard of honor, moved along the marble corridors filled with people. At the entrance to The Hall of Chiefs E-Thas, the major-domo, received her. The Hall was empty except for its ranks of dead chieftains upon their dead mounts. Through this long chamber E-Thas escorted her to the throne room which also was empty, the marriage ceremony in Manator differing from that of other countries of Barsoom. Here the bride would await the groom at the foot of the steps leading to the throne. The guests followed her in and took their places, leaving the central aisle from The Hall of Chiefs to the throne clear, for up this O-Tar would approach his bride alone after a short solitary communion with the dead behind closed doors in The Hall of Chiefs. It was the custom.

The guests had all filed through The Hall of Chiefs; the doors at both ends had been closed. Presently those at the lower end of the hall opened and O-Tar entered. His black harness was ornamented with rubies and gold; his face was covered by a grotesque mask of the precious metal in which two enormous rubies were set for eyes, though below them were narrow slits through which the wearer could see. His crown was a fillet supporting carved feathers of the same metal as the mask. To the least detail his regalia was that demanded of a royal bridegroom by the customs of Manator, and now in accordance with that same custom he came alone to The Hall of Chiefs to receive the blessings and the council of the great ones of Manator who had preceded him.

As the doors at the lower end of the Hall closed behind him O-Tar the Jeddak stood alone with the great dead. By the dictates of ages no mortal eye might look upon the scene enacted within that sacred chamber. As the mighty of Manator respected the traditions of Manator, let us, too, respect those traditions of a proud and sensitive people. Of what concern to us the happenings in that solemn chamber of the dead?

Five minutes passed. The bride stood silently at the foot of the throne. The guests spoke together in low whispers until the room was filled with the hum of many voices. At length the doors leading into The Hall of Chiefs swung open, and the resplendent bridegroom stood framed for a moment in the massive opening. A hush fell upon the wedding guests. With measured and impressive step the groom approached the bride. Tara felt the muscles of her heart contract with the apprehension that had been growing upon her as the coils of Fate settled more closely about her and no sign came from Turan. Where was he? What, indeed, could he accomplish now to save her? Surrounded by the power of O-Tar with never a friend among them, her position seemed at last without vestige of hope.

"I still live!" she whispered inwardly in a last brave attempt to combat the terrible hopelessness that was overwhelming her, but her fingers stole for reassurance to the slim blade that she had managed to transfer, undetected, from her old harness to the new. And now the groom was at her side and taking her hand was leading her up the steps to the throne, before which they halted and stood facing the gathering below. Came then, from the back of the room a procession headed by the high dignitary whose office it was to make these two man and wife, and directly behind him a richly-clad youth bearing a silken pillow on which lay the golden handcuffs connected by a short length of chain-of-gold with which the ceremony would be concluded when the dignitary clasped a handcuff about the wrist of each symbolizing their indissoluble union in the holy bonds of wedlock.

Would Turan's promised succor come too late? Tara listened to the long, monotonous intonation of the wedding service. She heard the virtues of O-Tar extolled and the beauties of the bride. The moment was approaching and still no sign of Turan. But what could he accomplish should he succeed in reaching the throne room, other than to die with her? There could be no hope of rescue.

The dignitary lifted the golden handcuffs from the pillow upon which they reposed. He blessed them and reached for Tara's wrist. The time had come! The thing could go no further, for alive or dead, by all the laws of Barsoom she would be the wife of O-Tar of Manator the instant the two were locked together. Even should rescue come then or later she could never dissolve those bonds and Turan would be lost to her as surely as though death separated them.

Her hand stole toward the hidden blade, but instantly the hand of the groom shot out and seized her wrist. He had guessed her intention. Through the slits in the grotesque mask she could see his eyes upon her and she guessed the sardonic smile that the mask hid. For a tense moment the two stood thus. The people below them kept breathless silence for the play before the throne had not passed unnoticed.

Dramatic as was the moment it was suddenly rendered trebly so by the noisy opening of the doors leading to The Hall of Chiefs. All eyes turned in the direction of the interruption to see another figure framed in the massive opening — a half-clad figure buckling the half-adjusted harness, hurridly in place — the figure of O-Tar, Jeddak of Manator.

"Stop!" he screamed, springing forward along the aisle toward the throne. "Seize the impostor!"

All eyes shot to the figure of the groom before the throne. They saw him raise his hand and snatch off the golden mask, and Tara of Helium in wide-eyed incredulity looked up into the face of Turan the panthan.

"Turan, the slave," they cried then. "Death to him! Death to him!"

"Wait!" shouted Turan, drawing his sword, as a dozen warriors leaped forward.

"Wait!" screamed another voice, old and cracked, as I-Gos, the ancient taxidermist, sprang from among the guests and reached the throne steps ahead of the foremost warriors.

At sight of the old man the warriors paused, for age is held in great veneration among the peoples of Barsoom, as is true, perhaps, of all peoples whose religion is based to any extent upon ancestor worship. But O-Tar gave no heed to him, leaping instead swiftly toward the throne. "Stop, coward!" cried I-Gos.

The people looked at the little old man in amazement. "Men of Manator," he cackled in his thin, shrill voice, "wouldst be ruled by a coward and a liar?"

"Down with him!" shouted O-Tar.

"Not until I have spoken," retorted I-Gos. "It is my right. If I fail my life is forfeit — that you all know and I know. I demand therefore to be heard. It is my right!"

"It is his right," echoed the voices of a score of warriors in various parts of the chamber.

"That O-Tar is a coward and a liar I can prove," continued I-Gos. "He said that he faced bravely the horrors of the chamber of O-Mai and saw nothing of the slave Turan. I was there, hiding behind the hangings, and I saw all that transpired. Turan had been hiding in the chamber and was even then lying upon the couch of O-Mai when O-Tar, trembling with fear, entered the room. Turan, disturbed, arose to a sitting position at the same time voicing a piercing shriek. O-Tar screamed and swooned."

"It is a lie!" cried O-Tar.

"It is *not* a lie and I can prove it," retorted I-Gos. "Didst notice the night that he returned from the chambers of O-Mai and was boasting of his exploit, that when he would summon slaves to bring wine he reached for his dagger to strike the gong with its pommel as is always his custom? Didst note that, any of you? And that he had no dagger? O-Tar, where is the dagger that you carried into the chamber of O-Mai? You do not know; but I know. While you lay in the swoon of terror I took it from your harness and hid it among the sleeping silks upon the couch of O-Mai. There it is even now, and if any doubt it let them go thither and there they will find it and know the cowardice of their jeddak."

"But what of this impostor?" demanded one. "Shall he stand with impunity upon the throne of Manator whilst we squabble about our ruler?"

"It is through his bravery that you have

learned the cowardice of O-Tar," replied I-Gos, "and through him you will be given a greater jeddak."

"We will choose our own jeddak. Seize and slay the slave!" There were cries of approval from all parts of the room. Gahan was listening intently, as though for some hoped-for sound. He saw the warriors approaching the dais, where he now stood with drawn sword and with one arm about Tara of Helium. He wondered if his plans had miscarried after all. If they had it would mean death for him, and he knew that Tara would take her life if he fell. Had he, then, served her so futilely after all his efforts?

Several warriors were urging the necessity for sending at once to the chamber of O-Mai to search for the dagger that would prove, if found, the cowardice of O-Tar. At last three consented to go. "You need not fear," I-Gos assured them. "There is naught there to harm you. I have been there often of late and Turan the slave has slept there for these many nights. The screams and moans that frightened you and O-Tar were voiced by Turan to drive you away from his hiding place." Shamefacedly the three left the apartment to search for O-Tar's dagger.

And now the others turned their attention once more to Gahan. They approached the throne with bared swords, but they came slowly for they had seen this slave upon the Field of Jetan and they knew the prowess of his arm. They had reached the foot of the steps when from far above there sounded a deep boom, and another, and another, and Turan smiled and breathed a sigh of relief. Perhaps, after all, it had not come too late. The warriors stopped and listened as did the others in the chamber. Now there broke upon their ears a loud rattle of musketry and it all came from above as though men were fighting upon the roofs of the palace.

"What is it?" they demanded, one of the other.

"A great storm has broken over Manator," said one.

"Mind not the storm until you have slain the creature who dares stand upon the throne of your jeddak," demanded O-Tar. "Seize him!"

Even as he ceased speaking the arras behind the throne parted and a warrior stepped forth upon the dais. An exclama-

"Turan, the Slave!" they cried. "Death to him!"

tion of surprise and dismay broke from the lips of the warriors of O-Tar. "U-Thor!" they cried. "What treason is this?"

"It is no treason," said U-Thor in his deep voice. "I bring you a new jeddak for all of Manator. No lying poltroon, but a courageous man whom you all love."

He stepped aside then and another emerged from the corridor hidden by the arras. It was A-Kor, and at sight of him there rose exclamations of surprise, of pleasure, and of anger, as the various factions recognized the *coup d'état* that had been arranged so cunningly. Behind A-Kor came other warriors until the dais was crowded with them — all men of Manator from the city of Manatos.

O-Tar was exhorting his warriors to attack, when a bloody and disheveled padwar burst into the chamber through a side entrance. "The city has fallen!" he cried aloud. "The hordes of Manatos pour through The Gate of Enemies. The slaves from Gathol have arisen and destroyed the palace guards. Great ships are landing warriors upon the palace roof and in the Fields of Jetan. The men of Helium and Gathol are marching through Manator. They cry aloud for the Princess of Helium and swear to leave Manator a blazing funeral pyre consuming the bodies of all our people. The skies are black with ships. They come in great processions from the east and from the south."

And then once more the doors from The Hall of Chiefs swung wide and the men of Manator turned to see another figure standing upon the threshold — a mighty figure of a man with white skin, and black hair, and gray eyes that glittered now like points of steel and behind him The Hall of Chiefs was filled with fighting men wearing the harness of far countries. Tara of Helium saw him and her heart leaped in exultation, for it was John Carter, Warlord of Barsoom, come at the head of a victorious host to the rescue of his daughter, and at his side was Djor Kantos to whom she had been betrothed.

The Warlord eyed the assemblage for a moment before he spoke. "Lay down your arms, men of Manator," he said. "I see my daughter and that she lives, and if no harm has befallen her no blood need be shed. Your city is filled with the fighting men of U-Thor, and those from Gathol and from Helium. The palace is in the hands of the slaves from Gathol, beside a thousand of my own warriors who fill the halls and chambers surrounding this room. The fate of your jeddak lies in your own hands. I have no wish to interfere. I come only for my daughter and to free the saves from Gathol. I have spoken!" and without waiting for a reply and as though the room had been filled with his own people rather than a hostile band he strode up the broad main aisle toward Tara of Helium.

The chiefs of Manator were stunned. They looked to O-Tar; but he could only gaze helplessly about him as the enemy entered from The Hall of Chiefs and circled the throne room until they had surrounded the entire company. And then a dwar of the army of Helium entered.

"We have captured three chiefs," he reported to The Warlord, "who beg that they be permitted to enter the throne room and report to their fellows some matter which they say will decide the fate of Manator."

"Fetch them," ordered The Warlord.

They came, heavily guarded, to the foot of the steps leading to the throne and there they stopped and the leader turned toward the others of Manator and raising high his right hand displayed a jeweled dagger. "We found it," he said, "even where I-Gos said that we would find it," and he looked menacingly upon O-Tar.

"A-Kor, Jeddak of Manator!" cried a voice, and the cry was taken up by a hundred hoarse-throated warriors.

"There can be but one jeddak in Manator," said the chief who held the dagger; his eyes still fixed upon the hapless O-Tar he crossed to where the latter stood and holding the dagger upon an outstretched palm proffered it to the discredited ruler. "There can be but one jeddak in Manator," he repeated meaningly.

O-Tar took the proffered blade and drawing himself to his full height plunged it to the guard into his breast, in that single act redeeming himself in the esteem of his people and winning an eternal place in The Hall of Chiefs.

As he fell all was silence in the great room, to be broken presently by the voice of U-Thor. "O-Tar is dead!" he cried. "Let A-Kor rule until the chiefs of all Manator may be summoned to choose a new jeddak. What is your answer?"

"Let A-Kor rule! A-Kor, Jeddak of Manator!" The cries filled the room and there was no dissenting voice.

A-Kor raised his sword for silence. "It is

the will of A-Kor," he said, "and that of the Great Jed of Manatos, and the commander of the fleet from Gathol, and of the illustrious John Carter, Warlord of Barsoom, that peace lie upon the city of Manator and so I decree that the men of Manator go forth and welcome the fighting men of these our allies as guests and friends and show them the wonders of our ancient city and the hospitality of Manator. I have spoken." And U-Thor and John Carter dismissed their warriors and bade them accept the hospitality of Manator. As the room emptied Djor Kantos reached the side of Tara of Helium. The girl's happiness at rescue had been blighted by sight of this man whom her virtuous heart told her she had wronged. She dreaded the ordeal that lay before her and the dishonor that she must admit before she could hope to be freed from the understanding that had for long existed between them. And now Djor Kantos approached and kneeling raised her fingers to his lips.

"Beautiful daughter of Helium," he said, "how may I tell you the thing that I must tell you — of the dishonor that I have all unwittingly done you? I can but throw myself upon your generosity for forgiveness; but if you demand it I can receive the dagger as honorably as did O-Tar."

"What do you mean?" asked Tara of Helium. "What are you talking about — why speak thus in riddles to one whose heart is already breaking?"

Her heart already breaking! The outlook was anything but promising, and the young padwar wished that he had died before ever he had had to speak the words he now must speak.

"Tara of Helium," he continued, "we all thought you dead. For a long year have you been gone from Helium. I mourned you truly and then, less than a moon since, I wed with Olvia Marthis." He stopped and looked at her with eyes that might have said: "Now, strike me dead!"

"Oh, foolish man!" cried Tara. "Nothing you could have done could have pleased me more. Djor Kantos, I could kiss you!"

"I do not think that Olvia Marthis would mind," he said, his face now wreathed with smiles. As they spoke a body of men had entered the throne room and approached the dais. They were tall men trapped in plain harness, absolutely without ornamentation. Just as their leader reached the dais Tara had turned to Gahan, motioning him to join them.

"Djor Kantos," she said, "I bring you Turan the panthan, whose loyalty and bravery have won my love."

John Carter and the leader of the new come warriors, who were standing near, looked quickly at the little group. The former smiled an inscrutable smile, the latter addressed the Princess of Helium. "'Turan the panthan!'" he cried. "Know you not, fair daughter of Helium, that this man you call panthan is Gahan, Jed of Gathol.

For just a moment Tara of Helium looked her surprise; and then she shrugged her beautiful shoulders as she turned her head to cast her eyes over one of them at Gahan of Gathol.

"Jed or panthan," she said; "what difference does it make what one's slave has been?" and she laughed roguishly into the smiling face of her lover.

His story finished, John Carter rose from the chair opposite me, stretching his giant frame like some great forest-bred lion.

"You must go?" I cried, for I hated to see him leave and it seemed that he had been with me but a moment.

"The sky is already red beyond those beautiful hills of yours," he replied, "and it will soon be day."

"Just one question before you go," I begged.

"Well?" he assented, good-naturedly.

"How was Gahan able to enter the throne room garbed in O-Tar's trappings?" I asked.

"It was simple — for Gahan of Gathol," replied The Warlord. "With the assistance of I-Gos he crept into The Hall of Chiefs before the ceremony, while the throne room and Hall of Chiefs were vacated to receive the bride. He came from the pits through the corridor that opened behind the arras at the rear of the throne, and passing into The Hall of Chiefs took his place upon the back of a riderless thoat, whose warrior was in I-Gos' repair room. When O-Tar entered and came near him Gahan fell upon him and struck him with the butt of a heavy spear. He thought that he had killed him and was surprised when O-Tar appeared to denounce him."

"And Ghek? What became of Ghek?" I insisted.

"After leading Val Dor and Floran to Tara's disabled flier, which they repaired, he accompanied them to Gathol, from where a message was sent to me in Helium.

He then led a large party including A-Kor and U-Thor from the roof, where our ships landed them, down a spiral runway into the palace and guided them to the throne room. We took him back to Helium with us, where he still lives, with his single rykor which we found all but starved to death in the pits of Manator. But come! No more questions now."

I accompanied him to the east arcade where the red dawn was glowing beyond the arches.

"Good-bye!" he said.

"I can scarce believe that it is really you," I exclaimed. "Tomorrow I will be sure that I have dreamed all this."

He laughed and drawing his sword scratched a rude cross upon the concrete of one of the arches.

"If you are in doubt tomorrow," he said, "come and see if you dreamed this."

A moment later he was gone.

JETAN, OR MARTIAN CHESS

For those who care for such things, and would like to try the game, I give the rules of Jetan as they were given my by John Carter. By writing the names and moves of the various pieces on bits of paper and pasting them on ordinary checkermen the game may be played quite as well as with the ornate pieces used upon Mars.

THE BOARD: Square board consisting of one hundred alternate black and orange squares.

THE PIECES: In order, as they stand upon the board in the first row, from left to right of each player.

WARRIOR: 2 feathers; 2 spaces straight in any direction or combination.

Padwar: 2 feathers; 2 spaces diagonal in any direction or combination.

Dwar: 3 feathers; 3 spaces straight in any direction or combination.

Flier: 3 bladed propellor; 3 spaces diagonal in any direction or combination; and may jump intervening pieces.

Chief: Diadem with ten jewels; 3 spaces in any direction; straight or diagonal or combination.

Princess: Diadem with one jewel; same as Chief, except may jump intervening pieces.

Flier: See above.

Dwar: See above.

Padwar: See above.

Warrior: See above.

And in the second row from left to right:

Thoat: Mounted warrior 2 feathers; 2 spaces, one straight and one diagonal in any direction.

Panthans (8 of them): 1 feather, 1 space, forward, side, or diagonal, but not backward.

Thoat: See above.

The game is played with twenty black pieces by one player and twenty orange by his opponent, and is presumed to have originally represented a battle between the Black race of the south and the Yellow race of the north. On Mars the board is usually arranged so that the Black pieces are played from the south and the Orange from the north.

The game is won when any piece is placed on same square with opponent's Princess, or a Chief takes a Chief.

The game is drawn when either Chief is taken by a piece other than the opposing Chief, or when both sides are reduced to three pieces, or less, of equal value and the game is not won in the ensuing ten moves, five apiece.

The Princess may not move onto a threatened square, nor may she take an opposing piece. She is entitled to one ten-space move at any time during the game. This move is called the escape.

Two pieces may not occupy the same square except in the final move of a game where the Princess is taken.

When a player, moving properly and in order, places one of this pieces upon a square occupied by an opponent piece, the opponent piece is considered to have been killed and is removed from the game.

The moves explained. Straight moves mean due north, south, east, or west; diagonal moves mean northeast, southeast, southwest, or northwest. A Dwar might move straight north three spaces, or north one space and east two spaces, or any similar combination of straight moves, so long as he did not cross the same square twice in a single move. This example explains combination moves.

The first move may be decided in any way that is agreeable to both players; after the first game the winner of the preceding game moves first if he chooses, or may instruct his opponent to make the first move.

Gambling: The Martians gamble at Jetan in several ways. Of course the outcome of the game indicates to whom the main stake belongs; but they also put a price upon the head of each piece, according to its value, and for each piece that a player loses he pays its value to his opponent.

THE MASTER MIND OF MARS

A LETTER

Helium, June 8th, 1925.

MY DEAR MR. BURROUGHS:

It was in the Fall of nineteen seventeen at an officers' training camp that I first became acquainted with John Carter, War Lord of Barsoom, through the pages of your novel "A Princess of Mars." The story made a profound impression upon me and while my better judgment assured me that it was but a highly imaginative piece of fiction, a suggestion of the verity of it pervaded my inner consciousness to such an extent that I found myself dreaming of Mars and John Carter, of Dejah Thoris, of Tars Tarkas and of Woola as they had been entities of my own experience rather than the figments of your imagination.

It is true that in those days of strenuous preparation there was little time for dreaming, yet there were brief moments before sleep claimed me at night and there were my dreams. Such dreams! Always of Mars, and during my waking hours at night my eyes always sought out the Red Planet when he was above the horizon and clung there seeking a solution of the seemingly unfathomable riddle he has presented to the Earthman for ages.

Perhaps the thing became an obsession. I know it clung to me all during my training camp days and at night, on the deck of the transport, I would lie on my back gazing up into the red eye of the god of battle—my god—and wishing that, like John Carter, I might be drawn across the great void to the haven of my desire.

And then came the hideous days and nights in the trenches—the rats, the vermin, the mud—with an occasional glorious break in the monotony when we were ordered over the top. I loved it then and I loved the bursting shells, the mad, wild chaos of the thundering guns, but the rats and the vermin and the mud—God! how I hated them. It sounds like boasting, I know, and I am sorry; but I wanted to write you just the truth about myself. I think you will understand. And it may account for much that happened afterward.

There came at last to me what had come to so many others upon those bloody fields. It came within the week that I had received my first promotion and my captaincy, of which I was greatly proud, though humbly so; realizing as I did my youth, the great responsibility that it placed upon me as well as the opportunities it offered, not only in service to my country but, in a personal way, to the men of my command. We had advanced a matter of two kilometers and with a small detachment I was holding a very advanced position when I received orders to fall back to the new line. That is the last that I remember until I regained consciousness after dark. A shell must have burst among us. What became of my men I never knew. It was cold and very dark when I awoke and at first, for an instant, I was quite comfortable—before I was fully conscious, I imagine—and then I commenced to feel pain. It grew until it seemed unbearable. It was in my legs. I reached down to feel of them, but my hand recoiled from what it found, and when I tried to move my legs I discovered that I was dead from the waist down. Then the moon came out from behind a cloud and I saw that I lay within a shell hole and that I was not alone—the dead were all about me.

It was a long time before I found the moral courage and the physical strength to draw myself up upon one elbow that I might view the havoc that had been done me. One look was enough, I sank back in an agony of mental and physical anguish—my legs had been blown away from midway between the hips and knees. For some reason I was not bleeding excessively, yet I know that I had lost a great deal of blood and that I was gradually losing enough to put me out of my misery in a short time if I were not soon found; and as I lay there on my back, tortured with pain, I prayed that they would not come in time, for I shrank more from the thought of going maimed through life than I shrank from the thought of death. Then my eyes suddenly focused upon the bright red eye of Mars and there surged through me a sudden wave of hope. I stretched out my arms toward Mars, I did not seem to question or to doubt for an instant as I prayed to the god of my vocation to reach forth and succor me. I knew that he would do it, my faith was complete, and yet so great was the mental effort that I made to throw off the hideous bonds of my mutilated flesh that I felt a momentary qualm of nausea and then a sharp click as of the snapping of a steel wire, and suddenly I stood naked upon two good legs looking down upon the bloody, distorted thing that had been I. Just for an instant did I stand thus before I turned my eyes aloft again to my star of destiny and with outstretched arms stand there in the cold of that French night—waiting.

Suddenly I felt myself drawn with the speed of thought through the trackless wastes of interplanetary space. There was an instant of extreme cold and utter darkness, then—

But the rest is in the manuscript that, with the aid of one greater than either of us, I have found the means to transmit to you with this letter. You and a few others of the chosen will believe in it—for the rest it matters not as yet. The time will come—but why tell you what you already know?

My salutations and my congratulations—the latter on your good fortune in having been chosen as the medium through which Earthmen shall become better acquainted with the manners and customs of Barsoom, against the time that they shall pass through space as easily as John Carter and visit the scenes that he has described to them through you, as have I.

Your sincere friend,

Ulysses Paxton,
*Late Captain, —th Inf.,
U.S. Army.*

Chapter I

THE HOUSE OF THE DEAD

I must have closed my eyes involuntarily during the transition for when I opened them I was lying flat on my back gazing up into up into a brilliant, sun-lit sky, while standing a few feet from me and looking down upon me with the most mystified expression was as strange a looking individual as my eyes ever had rested upon. He appeared to be quite an old man, for he was wrinkled and withered beyond description. His limbs were emaciated; his ribs showed distinctly beneath his shrunken

hide; his cranium was large and well developed, which, in conjunction with his wasted limbs and torso, lent him the appearance of top heaviness, as though he had a head beyond all proportion to his body, which was, I am sure, really not the case.

As he stared down upon me through enormous, many lensed spectacles I found the opportunity to examine him as minutely in return. He was, perhaps, five feet five in height, though doubtless he had been taller in youth, since he was somewhat bent; he was naked except for some rather plain and well worn leather harness which supported his weapons and pocket pouches, and one great ornament, a collar, jewel studded, that he wore around his scraggy neck—such a collar as a dowager empress of pork or real estate might barter her soul for, if she had one. His skin was red, his scant locks gray. As he looked at me his puzzled expression increased in intensity, he grasped his chin between the thumb and fingers of his left hand and slowly raising his right hand he scratched his head most deliberately. Then he spoke to me, but in a language I did not understand.

At his first words I sat up and shook my head. Then I looked about me. I was seated upon a crimson sward within a high walled enclosure, at least two, and possibly three, sides of which were formed by the outer walls of a structure that in some respects resembled more closely a feudal castle of Europe than any familiar form of architecture that comes to my mind. The facade presented to my view was ornately carved and of most irregular design, the roof line being so broken as to almost suggest a ruin, and yet the whole seemed harmonious and not without beauty. Within the enclosure grew a number of trees and shrubs, all weirdly strange and all, or almost all, profusely flowering. About them wound walks of colored pebbles among which scintillated what appeared to be rare and beautiful gems, so lovely were the strange, unearthly rays that leaped and played in the sunshine.

The old man spoke again, peremptorily this time, as though repeating a command that had been ignored, but again I shook my head. Then he lay a hand upon one of his two swords, but as he drew the weapon I leaped to my feet, with such remarkable results that I cannot even now say which of us was the more surprised. I must have sailed ten feet into the air and back about twenty feet from where I had been sitting; then I was sure that I was upon Mars (not that I had for one instant doubted it), for the effects of the lesser gravity, the color of the sward and the skin-hue of the red Martians I had seen described in the manuscripts of John Carter, those marvellous and as yet unappreciated contributions to the scientific literature of a world. There could be no doubt of it, I stood upon the soil of the Red Planet, I had come to the world of my dreams—to Barsoom.

So startled was the old man by my agility that he jumped a bit himself, though doubtless involuntarily, but, however, with certain results. His spectacles tumbled from his nose to the sward, and then it was that I discovered that the pitiful old wretch was practically blind when deprived of these artificial aids to vision, for he got to his knees and commenced to grope frantically for the lost glasses, as though his very life depended upon finding them in the instant. Possibly he thought that I might take advantage of his helplessness and slay him. Though the spectacles were enormous and lay within a couple of feet of him he could not find them, his hands, seemingly afflicted by that strange perversity that sometimes confounds our simplest acts, passing all about the lost object of their search, yet never once coming in contact with it.

As I stood watching his futile efforts and considering the advisability of restoring to him the means that would enable him more readily to find my heart with his sword point, I became aware that another had entered the enclosure. Looking toward the building I saw a large red-man running rapidly toward the little old man of the spectacles. The newcomer was quite naked, he carried a club in one hand, and there was upon his face such an expression as unquestionably boded ill for the helpless husk of humanity grovelling, mole-like, for its lost spectacles.

My first impulse was to remain neutral in an affair that it seemed could not possibly concern me and of which I had no slightest knowledge upon which to base a predilection toward either of the parties involved; but a second glance at the face of the club-bearer aroused a question as to

whether it might not concern me after all. There was that in the expression upon the man's face that betokened either an inherent savageness of disposition or a maniacal cast of mind which might turn his evidently murderous attentions upon me after he had dispatched his elderly victim, while, in outward appearance at least, the latter was a sane and relatively harmless individual. It is true that his move to draw his sword against me was not indicative of a friendly disposition toward me, but at least, if there were any choice, he seemed the lesser of two evils.

He was still groping for his spectacles and the naked man was almost upon him as I reached the decision to cast my lot upon the side of the old man. I was twenty feet away, naked and unarmed, but to cover the distance with my Earthly muscles required but an instant, and a naked sword lay by the old man's side where he had discarded it the better to search for his spectacles. So it was that I faced the attacker at the instant that he came within striking distance of his victim, and the blow which had been intended for another was aimed at me. I side-stepped it and then I learned that the greater agility of my Earthly muscles had its disadvantages as well as its advantages, for, indeed, I had to learn to walk at the very instant that I had to learn to fight with a new weapon against a maniac armed with a bludgeon, or at least, so I assumed him to be and I think that it is not strange that I should have done so, what with his frightful show of rage and the terrible expression upon his face.

As I stumbled about endeavoring to accustom myself to the new conditions, I found that instead of offering any serious opposition to my antagonist I was hard put to it to escape death at his hands, so often did I stumble and fall sprawling upon the scarlet sward; so that the duel from its inception became but a series of efforts, upon his part to reach and crush me with his great club, and upon mine to dodge and elude him. It was mortifying, but it is the truth. However, this did not last indefinitely, for soon I learned, and quickly too under the exigencies of the situation, to command my muscles, and then I stood my ground and when he aimed a blow at me, and I had dodged it, I touched him with my point and brought blood along with a savage roar of pain. He went more cautiously then, and taking advantage of the change I pressed him so that he fell back. The effect upon me was magical, giving me new confidence, so that I set upon him in good earnest, thrusting and cutting until I had him bleeding in a half dozen places, yet taking good care to avoid his mighty swings, any one of which would have felled an ox.

In my attempts to elude him in the beginning of the duel we had crossed the enclosure and were not fighting at a considerable distance from the point of our first meeting. It now happened that I stood facing toward that point at the moment that the old man regained his spectacles which he quickly adjusted to his eyes. Immediately he looked about until he discovered us, whereupon he commenced to yell excitedly at us at the same time running in our direction and drawing his short-sword as he ran. The red-man was pressing me hard, but I had gained almost complete control of myself, and fearing that I was soon to have two antagonists instead of one I set upon him with redoubled intensity. He missed me by the fraction of an inch, the wind in the wake of his bludgeon fanning my scalp, but he left an opening into which I stepped, running my sword fairly through his heart. At least I thought that I had pierced his heart, but I had forgotten what I had once read in one of John Carter's manuscripts to the effect that all the Martian internal organs are not disposed identically with those of Earthmen. However, the immediate results were quite as satisfactory as though I had found his heart, for the wound was sufficiently grievous to place him *hors de combat,* and at that instant the old gentleman arrived. He found me ready, but I had mistaken his intentions. He made no unfriendly gestures with his weapon, but seemed to be trying to convince me that he had no intention of harming me. He was very excited and apparently tremendously annoyed that I could not understand him, and perplexed, too. He hopped about screaming strange sentences at me that bore the tones of peremptory commands, rabid invective and impotent rage. But the fact that he had returned his sword to its scabbard had greater significance than all his jabbering, and when he ceased to yell at me and commenced to talk in a sort of pantomime I realized that he was making over-

tures of peace if not of friendship, so I lowered my point and bowed. It was all that I could think of to assure him that I had no immediate intention of spitting him.

He seemed satisfied and at once turned his attention to the fallen man. He examined his pulse and listened to his heart, then, nodding his head, he arose and taking a whistle from one of his pocket pouches sounded a single loud blast. There emerged immediately from one of the surrounding buildings a score of naked redmen who came running toward us. None was armed. To these he issued a few curt orders, whereupon they gathered the fallen one in their arms and bore him off. Then the old man started toward the building, motioning me to accompany him. There seemed nothing else for me to do but obey. Wherever I might be upon Mars, the chances were a million to one that I would be among enemies; and so I was as well off here as elsewhere and must depend upon my own resourcefulness, skill and agility to make my way upon the Red Planet.

The old man led me into a small chamber from which opened numerous doors, through one of which they were just bearing my antagonist. We followed into a large, brilliantly lighted chamber wherein there burst upon my astounded vision the most gruesome scene that I ever had beheld. Rows upon rows of tables arranged in parallel lines filled the room and with few exceptions each table bore a similar grisly burden, a partially dismembered or otherwise mutilated human corpse. Above each table was a shelf bearing containers of various sizes and shapes, while from the bottom of the shelf depended numerous surgical instruments, suggesting that my entrance upon Barsoom was to be through a gigantic medical college.

At a word from the old man, those who bore the Barsoomian I had wounded laid him upon an empty table and left the apartment. Whereupon my host, if so I may call him, for certainly he was not as yet my captor, motioned me forward. While he conversed in ordinary tones, he made two incisions in the body of my late antagonist; one, I imagine, in a large vein and one in an artery, to which he deftly attached the ends of two tubes, one of which was connected with an empty glass receptacle and the other with a similar receptacle filled with a colorless, transparent liquid resembling clear water. The connections made, the old gentleman pressed a button controlling a small motor, whereupon the victim's blood was pumped into the empty jar while the contents of the other was forced into the emptying veins and arteries.

The tones and gestures of the old man as he addressed me during this operation convinced me that he was explaining in detail the method and purpose of what was transpiring, but as I understood no word of all he said I was as much in the dark when, he had completed his discourse as I was before he started it, though what I had seen made it appear reasonable to believe that I was witnessing an ordinary Barsoomian embalming. Having removed the tubes the old man closed the openings he had made by covering them with bits of what appeared to be heavy adhesive tape and then motioned me to follow him. We went from room to room, in each of which were the same gruesome exhibits. At many of the bodies the old man paused to make a brief examination or to refer to what appeared to be a record of the case, that hung upon a hook at the head of each of the tables.

From the last of the chambers we visited upon the first floor my host led me up an inclined runway to the second floor where there were rooms similar to those below, but here the tables bore whole rather than mutilated bodies, all of which were patched in various places with adhesive tape. As we were passing among the bodies in one of these rooms a Barsoomian girl, whom I took to be a servant or slave, entered and addressed the old man, whereupon he signed me to follow him and together we descended another runway to the first floor of another building.

Here, in a large, gorgeously decorated and sumptuously furnished apartment an elderly red-woman awaited us. She appeared to be quite old and her face was terribly disfigured as by some injury. Her trappings were magnificent and she was attended by a score of women and armed warriors, suggesting that she was a person of some consequence, but the little old man treated her quite brusquely, as I could see, quite to the horror of her attendants.

Their conversation was lengthy and at the conclusion of it, at the direction of the woman, one of her male escort advanced and opening a pocket pouch at his side withdrew a handful of what appeared to me to be Martian coins. A quantity of these he counted out and handed to the little old man, who then beckoned the woman to follow him, a gesture which included me. Several of her women and guard started to accompany us, but these the old man waved back peremptorily; whereupon there ensued a heated discussion between the woman and one of her warriors on one side and the old man on the other, which terminated in his proffering the return of the woman's money with a disgusted air. This seemed to settle the argument, for she refused the coins, spoke briefly to her people and accompanied the old man and myself alone.

He led the way to the second floor and to a chamber which I had not previously visited. It closely resembled the others except that all the bodies therein were of young women, many of them of great beauty. Following closely at the heels of the old man the woman inspected the gruesome exhibit with painstaking care. Thrice she passed slowly among the tables examining their ghastly burdens. Each time she paused longest before a certain one which bore the figure of the most beautiful creature I had ever looked upon; then she returned the fourth time to it and stood looking long and earnestly into the dead face. For awhile she stood there talking with the old man, apparently asking innumerable questions, to which he returned quick, brusque replies, then she indicated the body with a gesture and nodded assent to the withered keeper of this ghastly exhibit.

Immediately the old fellow sounded a blast upon his whistle, summoning a number of servants to whom he issued brief instructions, after which he led us to another chamber, a smaller one in which were several empty tables similar to those upon which the corpses lay in adjoining rooms. Two female slaves of attendants were in this room and at a word from their master they removed the trappings from the old woman, unloosed her hair and helped her to one of the tables. Here she was thoroughly sprayed with what I presume was an antiseptic solution of some nature, carefully dried and removed to another table, at a distance of about twenty inches from which stood a second parallel table.

Now the door of the chamber swung open and two attendants appeared bearing the body of the beautiful girl we had seen in the adjoining room. This they deposited upon the table the old woman had just quitted and as she had been sprayed so was the corpse, after which it was transferred to the table beside that on which she lay. The little old man now made two incisions in the body of the old woman, just as he had in the body of the redman who had fallen to my sword; her blood was drawn from her veins and the clear liquid pumped into them, life left her and she lay upon the polished ersite slab that formed the table top, as much a corpse as the poor, beautiful, dead creature at her side.

The little, old man, who had removed the harness down to his waist and been thoroughly sprayed, now selected a sharp knife from among the instruments above the table and removed the old woman's scalp, following the hair line entirely around her head. In a similar manner he then removed the scalp from the corpse of the young woman, after which, by means of a tiny circular saw attached to the end of a flexible, revolving shaft he sawed through the skull of each, following the line exposed by the removal of the scalps. This and the balance of the marvellous operation was so skillfully performed as to baffle description. Suffice it to say that at the end of four hours he had transferred the brain of each woman to the brain pan of the other, deftly connected the severed nerves and ganglia, replaced the skulls and scalps and bound both heads securely with his peculiar adhesive tape, which was not only antiseptic and healing but anaesthetic, locally, as well.

He now reheated the blood that he had withdrawn from the body of the old woman, adding a few drops of some clear chemical solution, withdrew the liquid from the veins of the beautiful corpse, replacing it with the blood of the old woman and simultaneously administering a hypodermic injection.

During the entire operation he had not spoken a word. Now he issued a few instructions in his curt manner to his assistants, motioned me to follow him, and left the room. He led me to a distant part of the building or series of buildings that composed the whole, ushered me into a luxurious apartment, opened the door to a Barsoomian bath and left me in the hands of trained servants. Refreshed and rested I left the bath after an hour of relaxation to find harness and trappings awaiting me in the adjoining chamber. Though plain, they were of good material, but there were no weapons with them.

Naturally I had been thinking much upon the strange things I had witnessed since my advent upon Mars, but what puzzled me most lay in the seemingly inexplicable act of the old woman in paying my host what was evidently a considerable sum to murder her and transfer to the inside of her skull the brain of a corpse. Was it the outcome of some horrible religious fanaticism, or was there an explanation that my Earthly mind could not grasp?

I had reached no decision in the matter when I was summoned to follow a slave to another and near-by apartment where I found my host awaiting me before a table loaded with delicious foods, to which, it is needless to say, I did ample justice after my long fast and longer weeks of rough army fare.

During the meal my host attempted to converse with me, but, naturally, the effort was fruitless of results. He waxed quite excited at times and upon three distinct occasions laid his hand upon one of his swords when I failed to comprehend what he was saying to me, an action which resulted in a growing conviction upon my part that he was partially demented; but he evinced sufficient self-control in each instance to avert a catastrophe for one of us.

The meal over he sat for a long time in deep meditation, then a sudden resolution seemed to possess him. He turned suddenly upon me with a faint suggestion of a smile and dove headlong into what was to prove an intensive course of instruction in the Barsoomian language. It was long after dark before he permitted me to retire for the night, conducting me himself to a large apartment, the same in which I had found my new harness, where he pointed out a pile of rich sleeping silks and furs, bid me a Barsoomian good-night and left me, locking the door after him upon the outside, and leaving me to guess whether I were more guest or prisoner.

Chapter II

PREFERMENT

Three weeks passed rapidly. I had mastered enough of the Barsoomian tongue to enable me to converse with my host in a

*An attendant appeared bearing the body of the
beautiful girl.*

reasonably satisfactory manner, and I was also progressing slowly in the mastery of the written language of his nation, which is different, of course, from the written language of all other Barsoomian nations, though the spoken language of all is identical. In these three weeks I had learned much of the strange place in which I was half guest and half prisoner and of my remarkable host-jailer, Ras Thavas, the old surgeon of Toonol, whom I had accompanied almost constantly day after day until gradually there had unfolded before my astounded faculties an understanding of the purposes of the institution over which he ruled and in which he labored practically alone; for the slaves and attendants that served him were but hewers of wood and carriers of water. It was his brain alone and his skill that directed the sometimes beneficent, the sometimes malevolent, but always marvellous activities of his life's work.

Ras Thavas himself was as remarkable as the things he accomplished. He was never intentionally cruel; he was not, I am sure, intentionally wicked. He was guilty of the most diabolical cruelties and the basest of crimes; yet in the next moment he might perform a deed that if duplicated upon Earth would have raised him to the highest pinnacle of man's esteem. Though I know that I am safe in saying that he was never prompted to a cruel or criminal act by base motives, neither was he ever urged to a humanitarian one by high motives. He had a purely scientific mind entirely devoid of the cloying influences of sentiment, of which he possessed none. His was a practical mind, as evidenced by the enormous fees he demanded for his professional services; yet I know that he would not operate for money alone and I have seen him devote days to the study of a scientific problem the solution of which could add nothing to his wealth, while the quarters that he furnished his waiting clients were overflowing with wealthy patrons waiting to pour money into his coffers.

His treatment of me was based entirely upon scientific requirements. I offered a problem. I was either, quite evidently, not a Barsoomian at all, or I was of a species of which he had no knowledge. It therefore best suited the purposes of science that I be preserved and studied. I knew much about my own planet. It pleased Ras

Thavas' scientific mind to milk me of all I knew in the hope that he might derive some suggestion that would solve one of the Barsoomian scientific riddles that still baffle their savants; but he was compelled to admit that in this respect I was a total loss, not alone because I was densely ignorant upon practically all scientific subjects, but because the learned sciences on Earth have not advanced even to the swaddling-clothes stage as compared with the remarkable progress of corresponding activities on Mars. Yet he kept me by him, training me in many of the minor duties of his vast laboratory. I was entrusted with the formula of the "embalming fluid" and taught how to withdraw a subject's blood and replace it with this marvellous preservative that arrests decay without altering in the minutest detail the nerve or tissue structure of the body. I learned also the secret of the few drops of solution which, added to the rewarmed blood before it is returned to the veins of the subject, revitalized the latter and restores to normal and healthy activity each and every organ of the body.

He told me once why he had permitted me to learn these things that he had kept a secret from all others, and why he kept me with him at all times in preference to any of the numerous individuals of his own race that served him and me in lesser capacities both day and night.

"Vad Varo," he said, using the Barsoomian name that he had given me because he insisted that my own name was meaningless and impractical, "for many years I have needed an assistant, but heretofore I have never felt that I had discovered one who might work here for me wholeheartedly and disinterestedly without ever having reason to go elsewhere or to divulge my secrets to others. You, in all Barsoom, are unique—you have no other friend or acquaintance than myself. Were you to leave me you would find yourself in a world of enemies, for all are suspicious of a stranger. You would not survive a dozen dawns and you would be cold and hungry and miserable—a wretched outcast in a hostile world. Here you have every luxury that the mind of man can devise or the hand of man produce, and you are occupied with work of such engrossing interest that your every hour must be fruitful of unparalleled satisfaction. There is no selfish reason, therefore, why you should leave me and there is every reason why you should remain. I expect no loyalty other than that which may be prompted by egoism. You make an ideal assistant, not only for the reasons I have just given you, but because you are intelligent and quick witted, and now I have decided, after observing you carefully for a sufficient time, that you can serve me in yet another capacity—that of personal bodyguard.

"You may have noticed that I alone of all those connected with my laboratory am armed. This is unusual upon Barsoom, where people of all classes, and all ages and both sexes habitually go armed. But many of these people I could not trust armed as they would slay me; and were I to give arms to those whom I might trust, who knows but that the others would obtain possession of them and slay me, or even those whom I had trusted turn against me, for there is not one who might not wish to go forth from this place back among his own people—only you, Vad Varo, for there is no other place for you to go. So I have decided to give you weapons.

"You saved my life once. A similar opportunity might again present itself. I know that, being a reasoning and reasonable creature, you will not slay me, for you have nothing to gain and everything to lose by my death, which would leave you friendless and unprotected in a world of strangers where assassination is the order of society and natural death one of the rarest of phenomena. Here are your arms." He stepped to a cabinet which he unlocked, displaying an assortment of weapons, and selected for me a long-sword, a short-sword, a pistol and a dagger.

"You seem sure of my loyalty, Ras Thavas," I said.

He shrugged his shoulders. "I am only sure that I know perfectly where your interests lie—sentimentalists have words: love, loyalty, friendship, enmity, jealousy, hate, a thousand others; a waste of words—one word defines them all: self-interest. All men of intelligence realize this. They analyse an individual and by his predilections and his needs they classify him as friend or foe, leaving to the weak minded idiots who like to be deceived the drooling drivel of sentiment."

I smiled as I buckled my weapons to my harness, but I held my peace. Nothing could be gained by arguing with the man and, too, I felt quite sure that in any purely academic controversy I should get the worst of it; but many of the matters of which he had spoken had aroused my curiosity and one had reawakened in my mind a matter to which I had given considerable thought. While partially explained by some of his remarks I still wondered why the red-man from whom I had rescued him had seemed so venomously bent upon slaying him the day of my advent upon Barsoom, and so, as we sat chatting after our evening meal, I asked him.

"A sentimentalist," he said. "A sentimentalist of the most pronounced type. Why that fellow hated me with a venom absolutely unbelievable by any of the reactions of a trained, analytical mind such as mine; but having witnessed his reactions I become cognizant of a state of mind that I cannot of myself even imagine. Consider the facts. He was the victim of assassination—a young warrior in the prime of life, possessing a handsome face and a splendid physique. One of my agents paid his relatives a satisfactory sum for the corpse and brought it to me. It is thus that I obtain practically all of my material. I treated it in the manner with which you are familiar. For a year the body lay in the laboratory, there being no occasion during that time that I had use for it; but eventually a rich client came, a not overly prepossessing man of considerable years. He had fallen desperately in love with a young woman who was attended by many handsome suitors. My client had more money than any of them, more brains, more experience, but he lacked the one thing that each of the others had that always weighs heavily with the undeveloped, unreasoning, sentiment-ridden minds of young females—good looks.

"Now 378-J-493811-P had what my client lacked and could afford to purchase. Quickly we reached an agreement as to the price and I transferred the brain of my rich client to the head of 378-J-493811-P and my client went away and for all I know won the hand of the beautiful moron; and 378-J-483911-P might have rested on indefinitely upon his ersite slab until I needed him or a part of him in my work, had I not, merely by chance, selected him for resurgence because of an existing need for another male slave.

"Mind you now, the man had been murdered. He was dead. I bought and paid for the corpse and all there was in it. He might have lain dead forever upon one of my ersite slabs had I not breathed new life into his dead veins. Did he have the brains to view the transaction in a wise and dispassionate manner? He did not. His sentimental reactions caused him to reproach me because I had given him another body, though it seemed to me that, looking at the matter from a standpoint of sentiment, if one must, he should have considered me as a benefactor for having given him life again in a perfectly healthy, if somewhat used, body.

"He had spoken to me upon the subject several times, begging me to restore his body to him, a thing which, of course, as I explained to him, was utterly out of the question unless chance happened to bring to my laboratory the corpse of the client who had purchased his carcass—a contingency quite beyond the pale of possibility for one as wealthy as my client. The fellow even suggested that I permit him to go forth and assassinate my client, bringing the body back that I might reverse the operation and restore his body to his brain. When I refused to divulge the name of the present possessor of his body he grew sulky, but until the very hour of your arrival, when he attacked me, I did not suspect the depth of his hate complex.

"Sentiment is indeed a bar to all progress. We of Toonol are probably less subject to its vagaries than most other nations upon Barsoom, but yet most of my fellow countrymen are victims of it in varying degrees. It has its rewards and compensations, however. Without it we could preserve no stable form of government and the Phundahlians, or some other people, would overrun and conquer us; but enough of our lower classes have sentiment to a sufficient degree to give them loyalty to the Jeddak of Toonol and the upper classes are brainy enough to know that it is to their own best interests to keep him upon his throne.

"The Phundahlians, upon the other hand, are egregious sentimentalists, filled with crass stupidities and superstitions, slaves to every variety of brain withering conceit. Why the very fact that they keep the old termagant, Xaxa, on the throne brands them with their stupid idiocy. She is an ignorant, arrogant, selfish, stupid, cruel virago, yet the Phundahlians would fight and die for her because her father was Jeddak of Phundahl. She taxes them until they can scarce stagger beneath their burden, she misrules them, exploits them, betrays them, and they fall down and worship at her feet. Why? Because her father was Jeddak of Phundahl and his father before him and so on back into antiquity; because they are ruled by sentiment rather than reason; because their wicked rulers play upon this sentiment.

"She had nothing to recommend her to a sane person—not even beauty. You know, you saw her."

"I saw her?" I demanded.

"You assisted me the day that we gave her old brain a new casket—the day you arrived from what you call your Earth."

"She! That old woman was Jeddara of Phundahl?"

"That was Xaxa," he assured me.

"Why, you did not accord her the treatment that one of the Earth would suppose would be accorded a ruler, and so I had no idea that she was more than a rich old woman."

"I am Ras Thavas," said the old man. "Why should I incline the head to any other? In my world nothing counts but brain and in that respect, and without egotism, I may say that I acknowledge no superior."

"Then you are not without sentiment," I said, smiling. "You acknowledge pride in your intellect!"

"It is not pride," he said, patiently, for him, "it is merely a fact that I state. A fact that I should have not difficulty in proving. In all probability I have the most highly developed and perfectly functioning mind among all the learned men of my acquaintance, and reason indicates that this fact also suggests that I possess the most highly developed and perfectly functioning mind upon Barsoom. From what I know of Earth and from what I have seen of you, I am convinced that there is no mind upon your planet that may even faintly approximate in power that which I have developed during a thousand years of active study and research. Rasoom (Mercury) or Cosoom (Venus) may possibly support intelligences equal to or even greater than mine. While we have made some study of their thought waves, our instruments are not yet sufficiently developed to more than suggest that they are of extreme refinement, power and flexibility."

"And what of the girl whose body you gave to Jeddara?" I asked, irrelevantly, for my mind could not efface the memory of that sweet body that must, indeed, have possessed an equally sweet and fine brain.

"Merely a subject! Merely a subject!" he replied with a wave of his hand.

"What will become of her?" I insisted.

"What difference does it make?" he demanded. "I bought her with a batch of prisoners of war. I do not even recall from what country my agent obtained them, or from whence they originated. Such matters are of no import."

"She was alive when you bought her?" I demanded.

"Yes. Why?"

"You—er—ah—killed her, then?"

"Killed her! No; I preserved her. That was some ten years ago. Why should I permit her to grow old and wrinkled? She would no longer have the same value then, would she? No, I preserved her. When Xaxa bought her she was just as fresh and young as the day she arrived. I kept her a long time. Many women looked at her and wanted her face and figure, but it took a Jeddara to afford her. She brought the highest price that I have ever been paid.

"Yes, I kept her a long time, but I knew that some day she would bring my price. She was indeed beautiful and so sentiment has its uses—were it not for sentiment there would be no fools to support this work that I am doing, thus permitting me to carry on investigations of far greater merit. You would be surprised, I know, were I to tell you that I feel that I am almost upon the point of being able to reproduce rational human beings through the action upon certain chemical combinations of a group of rays probably entirely undiscovered by your scientists, if I am to judge by the paucity of your knowledge concerning such things."

"I would not be surprised," I assured him. "I would not be surprised by anything that you might accomplish."

Chapter III

VALLA DIA

I lay awake a long time that night thinking of 4296-E-2631-H, the beautiful girl whose perfect body had been stolen to furnish a gorgeous setting for the cruel brain of a tyrant. It seemed such a horrid crime that I could not rid my mind of it and I think that contemplation of it sowed the first seed of my hatred and loathing for Ras Thavas. I could not conjure a creature so utterly devoid of bowels of compassion as to even consider for a moment the frightful ravishing of that sweet and lovely body for even the holiest of purposes, much less one that could have been induced to do so for filthy pelf.

So much did I think upon the girl that night that her image was the first to impinge upon my returning consciousness at dawn, and after I had eaten, Ras Thavas not having appeared, I went directly to the storage room where the poor thing was. Here she lay, identified only by a small panel, bearing a number: 4296-E-2631-H. The body of an old woman with a disfigured face lay before me in the rigid immobility of death; yet that was not the figure that I saw, but instead, a vision of radiant loveliness whose imprisoned soul lay dormant beneath those graying locks.

The creature here with the face and form of Xaxa was not Xaxa at all, for all that made the other what she was had been transferred to this cold corpse. How frightful would be the awakening, should awakening ever come! I shuddered to think of the horror that must overwhelm the girl when first she realized the horrid crime that had been perpetrated upon her. Who was she? What story lay locked in that dead and silent brain? What loves must have been hers whose beauty was so great and upon whose fair face had lain the indelible imprint of graciousness! Would Ras Thavas ever arouse her from this happy semblance of death?—far happier than any quickening ever could be for her. I shrank from the thought of her awakening and yet I longed to hear her speak, to know that that brain lived again, to learn her name, to listen to the story of this gentle life that had been so rudely snatched from its proper environment and so cruelly bandied by the hand of Fate. And suppose she were awakened! Suppose she were awakened and that I—A hand was laid upon my shoulder and I turned to look into the face of Ras Thavas.

"You seem interested in this subject," he said.

"I was wondering," I replied, "what the reaction of this girl's brain would be were she to awaken to the discovery that she had become an old, disfigured woman."

He stroked, his chin and eyed me narrowly. "An interesting experiment," he mused. "I am gratified to discover that you are taking a scientific interest in the labors that I am carrying on. The psychological phases of my work I have, I must confess, rather neglected during the past hundred years or so, though I formerly gave them a great deal of attention. It would be interesting to observe and study several of these cases. This one, especially, might prove of value to you as an initial study, it being simple and regular. Later we will let you examine into a case where a man's brain has been transferred to a woman's skull, and a woman's brain to a man's. There are also the interesting cases where a portion of diseased or injured brain has been replaced by a portion of the brain from another subject; and, for experimental purposes alone, those human brains that have been transplanted to the craniums of beasts, and *vice versa*, offer tremendous opportunities for observation. I have in mind one case in which I transferred half the brain of an ape to the skull of a man, after having removed half of his brain, which I grafted upon the remaining part of the brain in the ape's skull. That was a matter of several years ago and I have often thought that I should like to recall these two subjects and note the results. I shall have to have a look at them—as I recall it they are in vault L-42-X, beneath building 4-J-21. We shall have to have a look at them some day soon—it has been years since I have been below. There must be some very interesting specimens there that have escaped my mind. But come! Let us recall 4296-E-2631-H."

"No!" I exclaimed, laying a hand upon his arm. "It would be horrible."

He turned a surprised look upon me and then a nasty, sneering smile curled his lips. "Maudlin, sentimental fool!" he cried. "Who dare say no to me?"

I laid a hand upon the hilt of my longsword and looked him steadily in the eye. "Ras Thavas," I said, "you are master in your own house; but while I am your guest treat me with courtesy."

He returned my look for a moment but his eyes wavered. "I was hasty," he said. "Let it pass." That, I let answer for an apology—really it was more than I had expected—but the event was not unfortunate. I think he treated me with far greater respect thereafter; but now he turned immediately to the slab bearing the mortal remains of 4296-E-2631-H.

"Prepare the subject the revivification," he said, "and make what study you can of all its reactions." With that he left the room.

I was now fairly adept at this work which I set about with some misgivings but with the assurance that I was doing right in obeying Ras Thavas while I remained a member of his entourage. The blood that had once flowed through the veins of the beautiful body that Ras Thavas had sold to Xaxa reposed in an hermetically sealed vessel upon the shelf above the corpse. As I had before done in other cases beneath the watchful eyes of the old surgeon I now díd for the first time alone. The blood heated, the incisions made, the tubes attached and the few drops of life-giving solution added to the blood, I was now ready to restore life to that delicate brain that had lain dead for ten years. As my finger rested upon the little button that actuated the motor that was to send the revivifying liquid into those dormant veins, I experienced such a sensation as I imagine no mortal man has ever felt.

I had become master of life and death, and yet at this moment that I stood there upon the point of resurrecting the dead I felt more like a murderer than a savior. I tried to view the procedure dispassionately through the cold eye of science, but I failed miserably. I could only see a stricken girl grieving for her lost beauties. With a muffled oath I turned away. I could not do it! And then, as though an outside force had seized upon me, my finger moved unerringly to the button and pressed it. I cannot explain it, unless upon the theory of dual mentality, which may explain many things. Perhaps my subjective mind directed the act. I do not know. Only I know that I did it, the motor started, the level of the blood in the container commenced gradually to lower.

Speel-bound, I stood watching. Presently the vessel was empty. I shut off the motor, removed the tubes, sealed the openings with tape. The red glow of life tinged the body, replacing the sallow, purplish hue of death. The breasts rose and fell regularly, the head turned slightly and the eyelids moved. A faint sigh issued from between the parting lips. For a long time there was no other sign of life, then, suddenly, the eyes opened. They were dull at first, but presently they commenced to fill with questioning wonderment. They rested on me and then passed on about that portion of the room that was visible from the position of the body. Then they came back to me and remained steadily fixed upon my countenance after having once surveyed me up and down. There was still the questioning in them, but there was no fear.

"Where am I?" she asked. The voice was that of an old woman—high and harsh. A startled expression filled her eyes. "What is the matter with me? What is wrong with my voice? What has happened?"

I laid a hand upon her forehead. "Don't bother about it now," I said, soothingly. "Wait until sometime when you are stronger. Then I will tell you."

She sat up. "I am strong," she said, and then her eyes swept her lower body and limbs and a look of utter horror crossed her face. "What has happened to me? In the name of my first ancestor, what has happened to me?"

The shrill, harsh voice grated upon me. It was the voice of Xaxa and Xaxa now must possess the sweet musical tones that alone would have harmonized with the beautiful face she had stolen. I tried to forget those strident notes and think only of the pulchritude of the envelope that had once graced the soul within this old and withered carcass.

She extended a hand and laid it gently upon mine. The act was beautiful, the movements graceful. The brain of the girl directed the muscles, but the old, rough vocal chords of Xaxa could give forth no sweeter notes. "Tell me, please!" she begged. There were tears in the old eyes, I'll venture for the first time in many years. "Tell me! You do not seem unkind."

And so I told her. She listened intently and when I was through she sighed. "After all," she said, "it is not so dreadful, now that I really know. It is better than being dead." That made me glad that I had pressed the button. She was glad to be alive, even draped in the hideous carcass of Xaxa. I told her as much.

"You were so beautiful," I told her.

"And now I am so ugly?" I made no answer.

"After all, what difference does it make?" she inquired presently. "This old body cannot change me, or make me different from what I have always been. The good in me remains and whatever of sweetness and kindness, and I can be happy to be alive and perhaps to do some good. I was terrified at first, because I did not know what had happened to me. I thought that maybe I had contracted some terrible disease that had so altered me—that horrified me; but now that I know—pouf! what of it?"

"You are wonderful," I said. "Most women would have gone mad with the horror and grief of it—to lose such wondrous beauty as was yours—and you do not care."

"Oh, yes, I care, my friend," she corrected me, "but I do not care enough to ruin my life in all other respects because of it, or to cast a shadow upon the lives of those around me. I have had my beauty and enjoyed it. It is not an unalloyed happiness I can assure you. Men killed one another because of it; two great nations went to war because of it; and perhaps my father lost his throne or his life—I do not know, for I was captured by the enemy while the war still raged. It may be raging yet and men dying because I was too beautiful. No one will fight for me now, though," she added, with a rueful smile.

"Do you know how long you have been here?" I asked.

"Yes," she replied. "It was day before yesterday that they brought me hither."

"It was ten years ago," I told her.

"Ten years! Impossible."

I pointed to the corpses around us. "You have lain like this for ten years," I explained. "There are subjects here who have lain thus for fifty, Ras Thavas tells me."

"Ten years! Ten years! What may not have happened in ten years! It is better thus. I should fear to go back now. I should not want to know that my father, my mother too, perhaps, were gone. It is better thus. Perhaps you will let me sleep again? May I not?"

"That remains with Ras Thavas," I replied; "but for a while I am to observe you."

"Observe me?"

"Study you—your reactions."

"Ah! and what good will that do?"

"It may do some good in the world."

"It may give this horrid Ras Thavas

some new ideas for his torture chamber—
some new scheme for coining money from
the suffering of his victims," she said, her
harsh voice saddened.

"Some of his works are good," I told her.
"The money he makes permits him to
maintain this wonderful establishment
where he constantly carries on countless
experiments. Many of his operations are
beneficent. Yesterday a warrior was
brought in whose arm was crushed beyond
repair. Ras Thavas gave him a new arm. A
demented child was brought. Ras Thavas
gave her a new brain. The arm and the
brain were taken from two who had met
violent deaths. Through Ras Thavas they
were permitted, after death, to give life and
happiness to others."

She thought for a moment. "I am content," she said. "I only hope that you will
always be the observer."

Presently Ras Thavas came and examined her. "A good subject," he said. He
looked at the chart where I had made a very
brief record following the other entries relative to the history of Case No. 4296-E-
2631-H. Of course this is, naturally, a
rather free translation of this particular
identification number. The Barsoomians
have no alphabet such as ours and their
numbering system is quite different. The
thirteen characters above were represented by four Toonolian characters, yet
the meaning was quite the same—they
represented, in contracted form, the case
number, the room, the table and the building.

"The subject will be quartered near you
where you may regularly observe it," continued Ras Thavas. "There is a chamber
adjoining yours. I will see that it is unlocked. Take the subject there. When not
under your observation, lock it in." *It* was
only another *case* to him.

I took the girl, if I may so call her, to her
quarters. On the way I asked her her name,
for it seemed to me an unnecessary dis-
courtesy always to address her and refer to
her as 4296-E-2631-H, and this I explained
to her.

"It is considerate of you to think of that,"
she said, "but really that is all that I am
here—just another subject for vivisection."

"You are more than that to me," I told
her. "You are friendless and helpless. I
want to be of service to you—to make your
lot easier if I can."

"Thank you again," she said. "My name
is Valla Dia, and yours?"

"Ras Thavas calls me Vad Varo," I told
her.

"But that is not your name?"

"My name is Ulysses Paxton."

"It is a strange name, unlike any that I
have ever heard, but you are unlike any
man I have ever seen—you do not seem
Barsoomian. Your color is unlike that of
any race."

"I am not of Barsoom, but from Earth,
the planet you sometimes call Jasoom.
That is why I differ in appearance from any
you have known before."

"Jasoom! There is another Jasoomian
here whose fame has reached to the remotest corners of Barsoom, but I never
have seen him."

"John Carter?" I asked.

"Yes, The Warlord. He was of Helium and
my people were not friendly with those of
Helium. I never could understand how he
came here. And now there is another from
Jasoom—how can it be? How did you cross
the great void?"

I shook my head. "I cannot even guess,"
I told her.

"Jasoom must be peopled with wonderful men," she said. It was a pretty compliment.

"As Barsoom is with beautiful women," I
replied.

She glanced down ruefully at her old and
wrinkled body.

"I have seen the real you," I said gently.

"I hate to think of my face," she said. "I
know it is a frightful thing."

"It is not you, remember that when you
see it and do not feel too badly."

"Is it as bad as that?" she asked.

I did not reply. "Never mind," she said
presently. "If I had not beauty of the soul, I
was not beautiful, no matter how perfect
my features may have been; but if I possessed beauty of soul then I should have it
now. So I can think beautiful thoughts and
perform beautiful deeds and that, I think,
is the real test of beauty, after all."

"And there is hope," I added, almost in a
whisper.

"Hope? No, there is no hope, if what you
mean to suggest is that I may some time regain my lost self. You have told me enough
to convince me that that can never be."

"We will not speak of it," I said; 'but we
may think of it and sometimes thinking a
great deal of a thing helps us to find a way

to get it, if we want it badly enough."

"I do not want to hope," she said, "for it will but mean disappointment for me. I shall be happy as I am. Hoping, I should always be unhappy."

I had ordered food for her and after it was brought Ras Thavas sent for me and I left her, locking the door of her chamber as the old surgeon had instructed. I found Ras Thavas in his office, a small room which adjoined a very large one in which were a score of clerks arranging and classifying reports from various departments of the great laboratory. He arose as I entered.

"Come with me, Vad Varo," he directed. "We will have a look at the two cases in L-42-X, the two of which I spoke."

"The man with half a simian brain and the ape with a half human brain?" I asked.

He nodded and preceded me toward the runway that led to the vaults beneath the building. As we decended, the corridors and passageways indicated long disuse. The floors were covered with an impalpable dust, long undisturbed; the tiny radium bulbs that faintly illuminated the subbarsoomian depths were likewise coated. As we proceeded, we passed many doorways on either side, each marked with its descriptive hieroglyphic. Several of the openings had been tightly sealed with masonry. What gruesome secrets were hid within? At last we came to L-42-X. Here the bodies were arranged on shelves, several rows of which almost completely filled the room from floor to ceiling, except for a rectangular space in the center of the chamber, which accommodated an ersite topped operating table with its array of surgical instruments, its motor and other laboratory equipment.

Ras Thavas searched out the subjects of his strange experiment and together we carried the human body to the table. While Ras Thavas attached the tubes I returned for the vessel of blood which reposed upon the same shelf with the corpse. The now familiar method of revivification was soon accomplished and presently we were watching the return of consciousness to the subject.

The man sat up and looked at us, then he cast a quick glance about the chamber; there was a savage light in his eyes as they returned to us. Slowly he backed from the table to the floor, keeping the former between us.

"We will not harm you," said Ras Thavas.

The man attempted to reply, but his words were unintelligible gibberish, then he shook his head and growled. Ras Thavas took a step toward him and the man dropped to all fours, his knuckles resting on the floor, and backed away, growling.

"Come!" cried Ras Thavas. "We will not harm you." Again he attempted to approach the subject, but the man only backed quickly away, growling more fiercely; and then suddenly he wheeled and climbed quickly to the top of the highest shelf, where he squatted upon a corpse and gibbered at us.

"We shall have to have help," said Ras Thavas and, going to the doorway, he blew a signal upon his whistle.

"What are you blowing that for?" demanded the man suddenly. "Who are you? What am I doing here? What has happened to me?"

"Come down," said Ras Thavas. "We are friends."

Slowly the man descended to the floor and came toward us, but he still moved with his knuckles to the pavement. He looked about at the corpses and a new light entered his eyes.

"I am hungry!" he cried. "I will eat!" and with that he seized the nearest corpse and dragged it to the floor.

"Stop! Stop!" cried Ras Thavas, leaping forward. "You will ruin the subject," but the man only backed away, dragging the corpse along the floor after him. It was then that the attendants came and with their help we subdued and bound the poor creature. Then Ras Thavas had the attendants bring the body of the ape and he told them to remain, as we might need them.

The subject was a large specimen of the Barsoomian white ape, one of the most savage and fearsome denizens of the Red Planet, and because of the creature's great strength and ferocity Ras Thavas took the precaution to see that it was securely bound before resurgence.

It was a colossal creature about ten or fifteen feet tall, standing erect, and had an intermediary set of arms or legs midway between its upper and lower limbs. The eyes were close together and nonprotruding; the ears were high set, while its snout and teeth were strikingly like those of our African gorilla.

With returning consciousness the creature eyed us questioningly. Several times it seemed to essay to speak, but only inarticulate sounds issued from its throat. Then it lay still for a period.

Ras Thavas spoke to it. "If you understand my words, nod your head." The creature nodded.

"Would you like to be freed of your bonds?" asked the surgeon.

Again the creature nodded an affirmative.

"I fear that you will attempt to injure us, or escape," said Ras Thavas.

The ape was apparently trying very hard to articulate and at last there issued from its lips a sound that could not be misunderstood. It was the single word no.

"You will not harm us or try to escape?" Ras Thavas repeated his question.

"No," said the ape, and this time the word was clearly enunciated.

"We shall see," said Ras Thavas. "But remember that with our weapons we may dispatch you quickly if you attack us."

The ape nodded, and then, very laboriously: "I will not harm you."

At a sign from Ras Thavas the attendants removed the bonds and the creature sat up. It stretched its limbs and slid easily to the floor, where it stood erect upon two feet, which was not surprising, since the white ape goes more often upon two feet than six; a fact of which I was not cognizant at the time, but which Ras Thavas explained to me latter in commenting upon the fact that the human subject had gone upon all fours, which, to Ras Thavas, indicated a reversion to type in the fractional ape-brain transplanted to the human skull.

Ras Thavas examined the subject at considerable length and then resumed his examination of the human subject which continued to evince more simian characteristics than human, though it spoke more easily than the ape, because, undoubtedly, of its more perfect vocal organs. It was only by exerting the closest attention that the diction of the ape became understandable at all.

"There is nothing remarkable about these subjects," said Ras Thavas, after devoting half a day to them. "They bear out what I had already determined years ago in the transplanting of entire brains; that the act of transplanting stimulates growth and activity of brain cells. You will note that in each subject the transplanted portions of the brains are more active—they, in a considerable measure, control. That is why we have the human subject displaying distinctly simian characteristics, while the ape behaves in a more human manner; though if longer and closer observation were desirable you would doubtless find that each reverted at times to his own nature—that is the ape would be more wholly an ape and the human more manlike—but it is not worth the time, of which I have already given too much to a rather unprofitable forenoon. I shall leave you now to restore the subjects to anesthesia while I return to the laboratories above. The attendants will remain here to assist you, if required."

The ape, who had been an interested listener, now stepped forward. "Oh, please, I pray you," it mumbled, "do not again condemn me to these horrid shelves. I recall the day that I was brought here securely bound, and though I have no recollection of what has transpired since I can but guess from the appearance of my own skin and that of these dusty corpses that I have lain here long. I beg that you will permit me to live and either restore me to my fellows or allow me to serve in some capacity in this establishment, of which I saw something between the time of my capture and the day that I was carried into this laboratory, bound and helpless, to one of your cold, ersite slabs."

Ras Thavas made a gesture of impatience. "Nonsense!" he cried. "You are better off here, where you can be preserved in the interests of science."

"Accede to his request," I begged, "and I will myself take over all responsibility for him while I profit by the study that he will afford me."

"Do as you are directed," snapped Ras Thavas as he quit the room.

I shrugged my shoulders. "There is nothing for it, then," I said.

"I might dispatch you all and escape," mused the ape, aloud, "but you would have helped me. I could not kill one who would have befriended me—yet I shrink from the thought of another death. How long have I lain here?"

I referred to the history of his case that had been brought and suspended at the head of the table. "Twelve years," I told him.

"And yet, why not?" he demanded of

*"The transplanted portions of the brain are more
active — that is why the ape behaves in a more
human manner."*

himself. "This man would slay me—why should I not slay him first."

"It would do you no good," I assured him, "for you could never escape. Instead you would be really killed, dying a death from which Ras Thavas would probably think it not worth while ever to recall you, while I, who might find the opportunity at some later date and who have the inclination, would be dead at your hands and thus incapable of saving you."

I had been speaking in a low voice, close to his ear, that the attendants might not overhear me. The ape listened intently.

"You will do as you suggest?" he asked.

"At the first opportunity that presents itself," I assured him.

"Very well," he said, "I will submit, trusting to you."

A half hour later both subjects had been returned to their shelves.

Chapter IV

THE COMPACT

Days ran into weeks, weeks into months, as day by day I labored at the side of Ras Thavas, and more and more the old surgeon took me into his confidence, more and more he imparted to me the secrets of his skill and his profession. Gradually he permitted me to perform more and more important functions in the actual practice of his vast laboratory. I started transferring limbs from one subject to another, then internal organs of the digestive tract. Then he intrusted to me a complete operation upon a paying client. I removed the kidneys from a rich old man, replacing them with healthy ones from a young subject. The following day I gave a stunted child new thyroid glands. A week later I transferred two hearts and then, at last, came the great day for me—unassisted, with Ras Thavas standing silently beside me, I took the brain of an old man and transplanted it within the cranium of a youth.

When I had done Ras Thavas laid a hand upon my shoulder. "I could not have done better myself," he said. He seemed much elated and I could not but wonder at this unusual demonstration of emotion upon his part, he who so prided himself upon his lack of emotionalism. I had often pondered the purpose which influenced Ras Thavas to devote so much time to my training, but

never had I hit upon any more satisfactory explanation than that he had need of assistance in his growing practice. Yet when I consulted the records, that were now open to me, I discovered that his practice was no greater than it had been for many years; and even had it been there was really no reason why he should have trained me in preference to one of his red-Martian assistants, his belief in my loyalty not being sufficient warrant, in my mind, for this preferment when he could, as well as not, have kept me for a bodyguard and trained one of his own kind to aid him in his surgical work.

But I was presently to learn that he had an excellent reason for what he was doing—Ras Thavas always had an excellent reason for whatever he did. One night after we had finished our evening meal he sat looking at me intently as he so often did, as though he would read my mind, which, by the way, he was totally unable to do, much to his surprise and chagrin; for unless a Martian is constantly upon the alert any other Martian can read clearly his every thought; but Ras Thavas was unable to read mine. He said that it was due to the fact that I was not a Barsoomian. Yet I could often read the minds of his assistants, when they were off their guard, though never had I read aught of Ras Thavas' thoughts, nor, I am sure, had any other read them. He kept his brain sealed like one of his own blood jars, nor was he ever for moment found with his barriers down.

He sat looking at me this evening for a long time, nor did it in the least embarrass me, so accustomed was I to his peculiarities. "Perhaps," he said presently, "one of the reasons that I trust you is due to the fact that I cannot ever, at any time, fathom your mind; so, if you harbor traitorous thoughts concerning me I do not know it, while the others, every one of them, reveal their inmost souls to my searching mind and in each one there is envy, jealously or hatred of me. Them, I know, I cannot trust. Therefore I must accept the risk and place all my dependence upon you, and my reason tells me that my choice is a wise one—I have told you upon what grounds it based my selection of you as my bodyguard. The same holds true in my selection of you for the thing I have in mind. You cannot harm me without harming yourself and no man will intentionally do that; nor is there any reason why you should feel any deep antagonism toward me.

"You are, of course, a sentimentalist and doubtless you look with horror upon many of the acts of a sane, rational, scientific mind; but you are also highly intelligent and can, therefore, appreciate better than another, even though you may not approve them, the motives that prompt me to do many of those things of which your sentimentality disapproves. I may have offended you, but I have never wronged you, nor have I wronged any creature for which you might have felt some of your so-called friendship or love. Are my premises incorrect, or my reasoning faulty?"

I assured him to the contrary.

"Very well! Now let me explain why I have gone to such pains to train you as no other human being, aside from myself, has ever been trained. I am not ready to use you yet, or rather you are not ready; but if you know my purpose you will realize the necessity for bending your every energy to the consummation of my purpose, and to that end you will strive even more diligently than you have to perfect yourself in the high, scientific art I am imparting to you.

"I am a very old man," he continued after a brief pause, "even as age goes upon Barsoom. I have lived more than a thousand years. I have passed the allotted natural span of life, but I am not through with my life's work—I have but barely started it. I must not die. Barsoom must not be robbed of this wondrous brain and skill of mine. I have long had in mind a plan to thwart death, but it required another with skill equal to mine—two such might live forever. I have selected you to be that other, for reasons that I already have explained—they are undefiled by sentimentalism. I did not choose you because I love you, or because I feel friendship for you, or because I think that you love me, or feel friendship toward me. I chose you because I knew that of all the inhabitants of a world you were the one least likely to fail me. You will understand now why I have not been able to choose carelessly.

"This plan that I have chosen is simplicity itself provided that I can count upon just two essential factors—skill and self-interested loyalty in an assistant. My body is about worn out. I must have a new one. My laboratory is filled with wonderful bodies, young and complete with potential strength and health. I have but to select

one of these and have my skilled assistant transfer my brain from this old carcass to the new one." He paused.

"I understand now, why you have trained me," I said. "It has puzzled me greatly."

"Thus and thus only may I continue my labors," he went on, "and thus may Barsoom be assured a continuance, practically indefinitely, of the benefits that my brain may bestow upon her children. I may live forever, provided I always have a skilled assistant, and I may assure myself of such by seeing to it that he never dies; when he wears out one organ, or his whole body, I can replace either from my great storehouse of perfect parts, and for me he can perform the same service. Thus we continue to live indefinitely; for the brain, I believe, is almost deathless, unless injured or attacked by disease.

"You are not ready as yet to be intrusted with this important ask. You must transfer many more brains and meet with and overcome the various irregularities and idiosyncrasies that constitute the never failing differences that render no two operations identical. When you gain sufficient proficiency I shall be the first to know it and then we shall lose no time in making Barsoom safe for posterity."

The old man was far from achieving hatred of himself. However, his plan was an excellent one, both for himself and for me. It assured us immortality—we might live forever and always with strong, healthy, young bodies. The outlook was alluring—and what a wonderful position it placed me in. If the old man could be assured of my loyalty because of self-interest, similarly might I depend upon his loyalty; for he could not afford to antagonize the one creature in the world who could assure him immortality, or withhold it from him. For the first time since I had entered his establishment I felt safe.

As soon as I had left him I went directly to Valla Dia's apartment, for I wanted to tell her this wonderful news. In the weeks that had passed since her resurrection I had seen much of her and in our daily intercourse there had been revealed to me little by little the wondrous beauties of her soul, until at last I no longer saw the hideous, disfigured face of Xaxa when I looked upon her, but the eyes of my heart penetrated deeper to the loveliness that lay within that sweet mind. She had become my confidant, as I was hers, and this association constituted the one great pleasure of my existence upon Barsoom.

Her congratulations, when I told her of what had come to me, were very sincere and lovely. She said that she hoped I would use this great power of mine to do good in the world. I assured her that I would and that among the first things that I should demand of Ras Thavas was that he should give Valla Dia a beautiful body; but she shook her head.

"No, my friend," she said, "if I may not have my own body this old one of Xaxa's is quite as good for me as another. Without my own body I should not care to return to my native country; while were Ras Thavas to give me the beautiful body of another, I should always be in danger of the covetousness of his clients, any one of whom might see and desire to purchase it, leaving to me her old husk, conceivably one quite terribly diseased or maimed. No, my friend, I am satisfied with the body of Xaxa, unless I may again possess my own, for Xaxa at least bequeathed me a tough and healthy envelope, however ugly it may be; and for what do looks count here? You, alone, are my friend—that I have your friendship is enough. You admire me for what I am, not for what I look like, so let us leave well enough alone."

"If you could regain your own body and return to your native country, you would like that?" I demanded.

"Oh, do not say it!" she cried. "The simple thought of it drives me mad with longing. I must not harbor so hopeless a dream that at best may only tantalize me into greater abhorrence of my lot."

"Do not say that it is hopeless," I urged. "Death, only, renders hope futile."

"You mean to be kind," she said, "but you are only hurting me. There can be no hope."

"May I hope for you, then?" I asked. "For I surely see a way; however slight a possibility for success it may have, still, it is a way."

She shook her head. "There is no way," she said, with finality. "No more will Duhor know me."

"Duhor?" I repeated. "Your—some one you care for very much?"

"I care for Duhor very much," she answered with a smile, "but Duhor is not someone—Duhor is my home, the country of my ancestors."

"How came you to leave Duhor?" I asked. "You have never told me, Valla Dia."

"It was because of the ruthlessness of Jal Had, Prince of Amhor," she replied. "Hereditary enemies were Duhor and Amhor; but Jal Had came disguised into the city of Duhor, having heard, they say, of the great beauty attributed to the only daughter of Kor San, Jeddak of Duhor; and when he had seen her he determined to possess her. Returning to Amhor he sent ambassadors to the court of Kor San to sue for the hand of the Princess of Duhor; but Kor San, who had no son, had determined to wed his daughter to one of his own Jeds, that the son of this union, with the blood of Kor San in his veins, might rule over the people of Duhor; and so the offer of Jal Had was declined.

"This so incensed the Amhorian that he equipped a great fleet and set forth to conquer Duhor and take by force that which he could not win by honorable methods. Duhor was, at that time, at war with Helium and all her forces were far afield in the south, with the exception of a small army that had been left behind to guard the city. Jal Had, therefore, could not have selected a more propitious time for an attack. Duhor fell, and while his troops were looting the fair city Jal Had, with a picked force, sacked the palace of the jeddak and searched for the princess; but the princess had no mind to go back with him as Princess of Amhor. From the moment that the vanguard of the Amhorian fleet was seen in the sky she had known, with the others of the city, the purpose for which they came and so she used her head to defeat that purpose.

"There was in her retinue a cosmetologist whose duty it was to preserve the lustrous beauty of the princess' hair and skin and prepare her for public audiences, for fetes and for the daily intercourse of the court. He was a master of his art; he could render the ugly pleasant to look upon, he could make the plain lovely, and he could make the lovely radiant. She called him quickly to her and commanded him to make the radiant ugly; and when he had done with her none might guess that she was the Princess of Duhor, so deftly had he wrought with his pigments and his tiny brushes.

"When Jal Had could not find the princess within the palace, and no amount of threat or torture could force a statement of her whereabouts from the loyal lips of her people, the Amhorian ordered that every woman within the palace be seized and taken to Amhor; there to be held as hostages until the princess of Duhor should be delivered to him in marriage. We were, therefore, all seized and placed upon an Amhorian war ship which was sent back to Amhor ahead of the balance of the fleet, which remained to complete the sacking of Duhor.

"When the ship, with its small convoy, had covered some four thousand of the five thousand haads that separate Duhor from Amhor, it was sighted by a fleet from Phundahl which immediately attacked. The convoying ships were destroyed or driven off and that which carried us was captured. We were taken to Phundahl where we were put upon the auction block and I fell to the bid of one of Ras Thavas' agents. The rest you know."

"And what became of the princess?" I asked.

"Perhaps she died—her party was separated in Phundahl—but death could not more definitely prevent her return to Duhor. The Princess of Duhor will never again see her native country."

"But you may!" I cried, for I had suddenly hit upon a plan. "Where is Duhor?"

"You are going there?" she asked, laughingly.

"Yes!"

"You are mad, my friend," she said. "Duhor lies a full seven thousand, eight hundred haads from Toonol, upon the opposite side of the snow clad Artolian Hills. You, a stranger and alone, could never reach it; for between lie the Toonolian Marshes, wild hordes, savage beasts and warlike cities. You would but die uselessly within the first dozen haads, even could you escape from the island upon which stands the laboratory of Ras Thavas; and what motive is there to prompt you to such a useless sacrifice?"

I could not tell her. I could not look upon that withered figure and into that hideous and disfigured face and say: "It is because I love you, Valla Dia." But that, alas, was my only reason. Gradually, as I had come to know her through the slow revealment of the wondrous beauty of her mind and soul, there had crept into my heart a knowledge of my love; and yet, explain it I cannot, I could not speak the words to that frightful old hag. I had seen the gorgeous mundane

tabernacle that had housed the equally gorgeous spirit of the real Valla Dia—*that* I could love; her heart and soul and mind I could love; but I could not love the body of Xaxa. I was torn, too, by other emotions, induced by a great doubt—could Valla Dia return my love. Habilitated in the corpse of Xaxa, with no other suitor, nay, with no other friend, she might, out of gratitude or through sheer loneliness, be attracted to me; but once again were she Valla Dia the beautiful and returned to the palace of her king, surrounded by the great nobles of Duhor, would she have either eyes or heart for a lone and friendless exile from another world? I doubted it—and yet that doubt did not deter me from my determination to carry out, as far as Fate would permit, the mad scheme that was revolving in my brain.

"You have not answered my question, Vad Varo," she interrupted my surging thoughts. "Why would you do this thing?"

"To right the wrong that has been done you, Valla Dia," I said.

She sighed. "Do not attempt it, please," she begged. "You would but rob me of my one friend, whose association is the only source of happiness remaining to me. I appreciate your generosity and your loyalty, even though I may not understand them; your unselfish desire to serve me at such suicidal risk touches me more deeply than I can reveal, adding still further to the debt I owe you; but you must not attempt it—you must not."

"If it troubles you, Valla Dia," I replied, "we will not speak of it again; but know always that it is never from my thoughts. Some day I shall find a way, even though the plan I now have fails me."

The days moved on and on, the gorgeous Martian nights, filled with her hurtling moons, followed one upon another. Ras Thavas spent more and more time in directing my work of brain transference. I had long since become an adept; and I realized that the time was rapidly approaching when Ras Thavas would feel that he could safely intrust to my hands and skill his life and future. He would be wholly within my power and he knew that I knew it. I could slay him; I could permit him to remain forever in the preserving grip of his own anesthetic; or I could play any trick upon him that I chose, even to giving him the body of a calot or a part of the brain of an ape; but he must take the chance and that I knew, for he was failing rapidly. Already almost stone blind, it was only the wonderful spectacles that he had himself invented that permitted him to see at all; long deaf, he used artificial means for hearing; and now his heart was showing symptoms of fatigue that he could no longer ignore.

One morning I was summoned to his sleeping apartment by a slave. I found the old surgeon lying, a shrunken, pitiful heap of withered skin and bones.

"We must hasten, Vad Varo," he said in a weak whisper. "My heart was like to have stopped a few tals ago. It was then that I sent for you." He pointed to a door leading from his chamber. "There," he said, "you will find the body I have chosen. There, in the private laboratory I long ago built for this very purpose, you will perform the greatest surgical operation that the universe has ever known, transferring its most perfect brain to the most beautiful and perfect body that ever has passed beneath these ancient eyes. You will find the head already prepared to receive my brain; the brain of the subject having been removed and destroyed—totally destroyed by fire. I could not possibly chance the existence of a brain desiring and scheming to regain its wondrous body. No, I destroyed it. Call slaves and have them bear my body to the ersite slab."

"That will not be necessary," I told him; and lifting his shrunken form in my arms as he had been an earthly babe, I carried him into the adjoining room where I found a perfectly lighted and appointed laboratory containing two operating tables, one of which was occupied by the body of a red-man. Upon the surface of the other, which was vacant, I laid Ras Thavas, then I turned to look at the new envelope he had chosen. Never, I believe, had I beheld so perfect a form, so handsome a face—Ras Thavas had indeed chosen well for himself. Then I turned back to the old surgeon. Deftly, as he had taught me, I made the two incisions and attached the tubes. My finger rested upon the button that would start the motor pumping his blood from his veins and his marvellous preservative-anesthetic into them. Then I spoke.

"Ras Thavas," I said, "you have long been training me to this end. I have labored assiduously to prepare myself that there might be no slightest cause for apprehension as to the outcome. You have, coinci-

dentally, taught me that one's every act should be prompted by self-interest only. You are satisfied, therefore, that I am not doing this for you because I love you, or because I feel any friendship for you; but you think that you have offered me enough in placing before me a similar opportunity for immortality.

"Regardless of your teaching I am afraid that I am still somewhat of a sentimentalist. I crave the redressing of wrongs. I crave friendship and love. The price you offer is not enough. Are you willing to pay more that this operation may be successfully concluded?"

He looked at me steadily for a long minute. "What do you want?" he asked. I could see that he was trembling with anger, but he did not raise his voice.

"Do you recall 4296-E-2631-H?" I inquired.

"The subject with the body of Xaxa? Yes, I recall the case. What of it?"

"I wish her body returned to her. That is the price you must pay for this operation."

He glared at me. "It is impossible. Xaxa has the body. Even if I cared to do so, I could never recover it. Proceed with the operation!"

"When you have promised me," I insisted.

"I cannot promise the impossible—I cannot obtain Xaxa. Ask me something else. I am not unwilling to grant any reasonable request."

"That is all I wish—just that; but I do not insist that you obtain the body. If I bring Xaxa here will you make the transfer?"

"It would mean war between Toonol and Phundahl," he fumed.

"That does not interest me," I said. "Quick! Reach a decision. In five tals I shall press this button. If you promise what I ask, you shall be restored with a new and beautiful body; if you refuse you shall lie here in the semblance of death forever."

"I promise," he said slowly, "that when you bring the body of Xaxa to me I will transfer to that body any brain that you select from among my subjects."

"Good!" I exclaimed, and pressed the button.

Chapter V
DANGER

Ras Thavas awakened from the anesthetic a new and gorgeous creature — a youth of such wondrous beauty that he seemed of heavenly rather than worldly origin; but in that beautiful head was the hard, cold, thousand-year-old brain of the master surgeon. As he opened his eyes he looked upon me coldly.

"You have done well," he said.

"What I have done, I have done for friendship—perhaps for love," I said, "so you can thank the sentimentalism you decry for the success of the transfer."

He made no reply.

"And now," I continued, "I shall look to you for the fulfillment of the promise you have made me."

"When you bring Xaxa's body I shall transfer to it the brain of any of my subjects you may select," he said, "but were I you, I would not risk my life in such an impossible venture—you cannot succeed. Select another body—there are many beautiful ones—and I will give it the brain of 4296-E-2631-H."

"None other than the body now owned by the Jeddara Xaxa will fulfill your promise to me," I said.

He shrugged and there was a cold smile upon his handsome lips. "Very well," he said, "fetch Xaxa. When do you start?"

"I am not yet ready. I will let you know when I am."

"Good and now begone—but wait! First go to the office and see what cases await us and if there be any that do not require my personal attention, and they fall within your skill and knowledge, attend to them yourself."

As I left him I noticed a crafty smile of satisfaction upon his lips. What had aroused that? I did not like it and as I walked away I tried to conjure what could possibly have passed through that wondrous brain to call forth at that particular instant so unpleasant a smile. As I passed through the doorway and into the corridor beyond I heard him summon his personal slave and body servant, Yamdor, a huge fellow whose loyalty he kept through the bestowal of lavish gifts and countless favors. So great was the fellow's power that all feared him, as a word to the master from the lips of Yamdor might easily send any of the numerous slaves or attendants to an ersite slab for eternity. It was rumored that he was the result of an unnatural experiment which had combined the brain of a woman with the body of a man, and there was much in his actions and mannerisms

to justify this general belief. His touch, when he worked about his master, was soft and light, his movements graceful, his ways gentle, but his mind was jealous, vindictive and unforgiving.

I believed that he did not like me, through jealousy of the authority I had attained in the establishment of Ras Thavas; for there was no questioning the fact that I was a lieutenant, while he was but a slave; yet he always accorded me the utmost respect. He was, however, merely a minor cog in the machinery of the great institution presided over by the sovereign mind of Ras Thavas, and as such I had given him little consideration; nor did I now as I bent my steps toward the office.

I had gone but a short distance when I recalled a matter of importance upon which it was necessary for me to obtain instructions from Ras Thavas immediately; and so I wheeled about and retraced my way toward his apartments, through the open doorway of which, as I approached, I heard the new voice of the master surgeon. Ras Thavas had always spoken in rather loud tones, whether as a vocal reflection of his naturally domineering and authoritative character, or because of his deafness, I do not know; and now, with the fresh young vocal chords of his new body, his words rang out clearly and distinctly in the corridor leading to his room.

"You will, therefore, Yamdor," he was saying, "go at once and, selecting two slaves in whose silence and discretion you may trust, take the subject from the apartments of Vad Varo and destroy it—let no vestige of body or brain remain. Immediately after, you will bring the two slaves to the laboratory F-30-L, permitting them to speak to no one, and I will consign them to silence and forgetfulness for eternity.

"Vad Varo will discover the absence of the subject and report the matter to me. During my investigation you will confess that you aided 4296-E-2631-H to escape, but that you have no idea where it intended going. I will sentence you to death as punishment, but at last, explaining how urgently I need your services and upon your solemn promise never to transgress again, I will defer punishment for the term of your continued good behavior. Do you thoroughly understand the entire plan?"

"Yes, master," replied Yamdor.

"Then depart at once and select the

slaves who are to assist you."

Quickly and silently I sped along the corridor until the first intersection permitted me to place myself out of sight of anyone coming from Ras Thavas' apartment; then I went directly to the chamber occupied by Valla Dia. Unlocking the door I threw it open and beckoned her to come out. "Quick! Valla Dia!" I cried. "No time is to be lost. In attempting to save you I have but brought destruction upon you. First we must find a hiding place for you, and that at once—afterward we can plan for the future."

The place that first occurred to me as affording adequate concealment was the half forgotten vaults in the pits beneath the laboratories, and toward these I hastened Valla Dia. As we proceeded I narrated all that had transpired, nor did she once reproach me; but, instead, expressed naught but gratitude for what she was pleased to designate as my unselfish friendship. That it had miscarried, she assured me, was no reflection upon me and she insisted that she would rather die in the knowledge that she possessed one such friend than to live on indefinitely, friendless.

We came at last to the chamber I sought—vault L-42-X, in building 4-J-21, where reposed the bodies of the ape and the man, each of which possessed half the brain of the other. Here I was forced to leave Valla Dia for the time, that I might hasten to the office and perform the duties imposed upon me by Ras Thavas, lest his suspicions be aroused when Yamdor reported that he had found her apartment vacant.

I reached the office without it being discovered by anyone who might report the fact to Ras Thavas that I had been a long time coming from his apartment. To my relief, I found there were no cases. Without appearing in any undue haste, I nevertheless soon found an excuse to depart and at once made my way toward my own quarters, moving in a leisurely and unconcerned manner and humming, as was my wont (a habit which greatly irritated Ras Thavas), snatches from some song that had been popular at the time that I quit Earth. In this instance it was "Oh, Frenchy."

I was thus engaged when I met Yamdor moving hurriedly along the corridor leading from my apartment, in company with two male slaves. I greeted him pleasantly, as was my custom, and he returned my greeting; but there was an expression of fear and suspicion in his eyes. I went at once to my quarters, opened the door leading to the chamber formerly occupied by Valla Dia and then hastened immediately to the apartment of Ras Thavas, where I found him conversing with Yamdor. I rushed in apparently breathless and simulating great excitement.

"Ras Thavas," I demanded, "what have you done with 4296-E-2631-H? She has disappeared; her apartment is empty; and as I was approaching it I met Yamdor and two other slaves coming from that direction." I turned then upon Yamdor and pointed an accusing finger at him. "Yamdor!" I cried. "What have you done with this woman?"

Both Ras Thavas and Yamdor seemed genuinely puzzled and I congratulated myself that I had thus readily thrown them off the track. The master surgeon declared that he would make an immediate investigation; and he at once ordered a thorough search of the grounds and of the island outside the enclosure. Yamdor denied any knowledge of the woman and I, at least, was aware of the sincerity of his protestations, but not so Ras Thavas. I could see a hint of suspicion in his eyes as he questioned his body servant; but evidently he could conjure no motive for any such treasonable action on the part of Yamdor as would have been represented by the abduction of the woman and the consequent gross disobedience of orders.

Ras Thavas' investigation revealed nothing. I think as it progressed that he became gradually more and more imbued with a growing suspicion that I might know more about the disappearance of Valla Dia than my attitude indicated, for I presently became aware of a delicately concealed espionage. Up to this time I had been able to smuggle food to Valla Dia every night, after Ras Thavas had retired to his quarters. Then, on one occasion, I suddenly became subsconsciously aware that I was being followed, and instead of going to the vaults I went to the office, where I added some observations to my report upon a case I had handled that day. Returning to my room I hummed a few bars from "Over There," that the suggestion of my unconcern might be accentuated. From the moment that I quit my quarters until I returned to them I was sure that eyes had been watching my every move. What was I to do? Valla Dia must have food, without it she would die; and were I to be followed to her hiding place while taking it to her, she would die; Ras Thavas would see to that.

Half the night I lay awake, racking my brains for some solution to the problem. There seemed only one way—I must elude the spies. If I could do this but one single time I could carry out the balance of a plan that had occurred to me, and which was, I thought, the only one feasible that might eventually lead to the resurrection of Valla Dia in her own body. The way was long, the risks great; but I was young, in love and utterly reckless of consequences in-so-far as they concerned me; it was Valla Dia's happiness alone that I could not risk too greatly, other than under dire stress. Well, the stress existed and I must risk that, even as I risked my life.

My plan was formulated and I lay awake upon my sleeping silks and furs in the darkness of my room, awaiting the time when I might put it into execution. My window, which was upon the third floor, overlooked the walled enclosure, upon the scarlet sward of which I had made my first bow to Barsoom. Across the open casement I had watched Cluros, the farther moon, take his slow deliberate way. He had already set. Behind him, Thuria, his elusive mistress, fled through the heavens. In five xats (about 15 minutes) she would set; and then for about three and three quarters Earth hours the heavens would be dark, except for the stars.

In the corridor, perhaps, lurked those watchful eyes. I prayed God that they might not be elsewhere as Thuria sank at last beneath the horizon and I swung to my window ledge, in my hand a long rope fabricated from braided strips torn from my sleeping silks while I had awaited the setting of the moons. One end I had fastened to a heavy sorapus bench which I had drawn close to the window. I dropped the free end of the rope and started my descent. My Earthly muscles, untried in such endeavors, I had not trusted to the task of carrying me to my window ledge in a single leap, when I should be returning. I felt that they would, but I did not know; and too much depended upon the success of my venture to risk any unnecessary chance of failure. And so I had prepared the rope.

Whether I was being observed I did not know. I must go on as though none were spying upon me. In less than four hours Thuria would return (just before the sudden Barsoomian dawn) and in the interval I must reach Valla Dia, persuade her of the necessity of my plan and carry out its details, returning to my chamber before Thuria could disclose me to any accidental observer. I carried my weapons with me and in my heart was unbending determination to slay whoever might cross my path and recognize me during the course of my errand, however innocent of evil intent against me he might be.

The night was quiet except for the usual distant sounds that I had heard ever since I had been here—sounds that I had interpreted as the cries of savage beasts. Once I had asked Ras Thavas about them, but he had been in ill humor and had ignored my question. I reached the ground quickly and without hesitation moved directly to the nearest entrance of the building, having previously searched out and determined upon the route I would follow to the vault. No one was visible and I was confident, when at last I reached the doorway, that I had come through undetected. Valla Dia was so happy to see me again that it almost brought the tears to my eyes.

"I thought that something had happened to you," she cried, "for I knew that you would not remain away so long of your own volition."

I told her of my conviction that I was being watched and that it would not be possible for me longer to bring food to her without incurring almost certain detection, which would spell immediate death for her.

"There is a single alternative," I said, "and that I dread even to suggest and would not were there any other way. You must be securely hidden for a long time, until Ras Thavas' suspicions have been allayed; for as long as he has me watched I cannot possibly carry out the plans I have formulated for your eventual release, the restoration of your own body and your return to Duhor."

"Your will shall be my law, Vad Varo."

I shook my head. "It will be harder for you than you imagine."

"What is the way?" she asked.

I pointed to the ersite topped table. "You

must pass again through that ordeal that I may hide you away in this vault until the time is ripe for the carrying out of my plans. Can you endure it?"

She smiled. "Why not?" she asked. "It is only sleep—if it lasts forever I shall be no wiser."

I was surprised that she did not shrink from the idea, but I was very glad since I knew that it was the only way that we had a chance for success. Without my help she disposed herself upon the ersite slab.

"I am ready, Vad Varo," she said, bravely; "but first promise me that you will take no risks in this mad venture. You cannot succeed. When I close my eyes I know that it will be for the last time if my resurrection depends upon the successful outcome of the maddest venture that ever man conceived; yet I am happy, because I know that it is inspired by the greatest friendship with which any mortal woman has ever been blessed."

As she talked I had been adjusting the tubes and now I stood beside her with my finger upon the starting button of the motor.

"Good-bye, Vad Varo," she whispered.

"Not good-bye, Valla Dia, but only a sweet sleep for what to you will be the briefest instant. You will seem but to close your eyes and open them again. As you see me now, I shall be standing here beside you as though I never had departed from you. As I am the last that you look upon tonight before you close your eyes, so shall I be the first that you shall look upon as you open them on that new and beautiful morning; but you shall not again look forth through the eyes of Xaxa, but from the limpid depths of your own beautiful orbs."

She smiled and shook her head. Two tears formed beneath her lids. I pressed her hand in mine and touched the button.

Chapter VI

SUSPICIONS

In-so-far as I could know I reached my apartment without detection. Hiding my rope where I was sure it would not be discovered, I sought my sleeping silks and furs and was soon asleep.

The following morning as I emerged from my quarters I caught a fleeting glimpse of a figure in a nearby corridor and

from then on for a long time I had further evidence that Ras Thavas suspicioned me. I went at once to his quarters, as had been my habit. He seemed restless, but he gave me no hint that he held any assurance that I had been responsible for the disappearance of Valla Dia, and I think that he was far from positive of it. It was simply that his judgment pointed to the fact that I was the only person who might have any reason for interfering in any way with this particular subject, and he was having me watched to either prove or disprove the truth of his reasonable suspicions. His restlessness he explained to me himself.

"I have often studied the reaction of others who have undergone brain transference," he said, "and so I am not wholly surprised at my own. Not only has my brain energy been stimulated, resulting in an increased production of nervous energy, but I also feel the effects of the young tissue and youthful blood of my new body. They are affecting my consciousness in a way that my experiments had vaguely indicated, but which I now see must be actually experienced to be fully understood. My thoughts, my inclinations, even my ambitions have been changed, or at least colored, by the transfer. It will take some time for me to find myself."

Though uninterested, I listened politely until he was through and then I changed the subject. "Have you located the missing woman?" I asked.

He shook his head, negatively.

"You must appreciate, Ras Thavas," I said, "that I fully realize that you must have known that the removal or destruction of that woman would entirely frustrate my entire plan. You are master here. Nothing that passes is without your knowledge."

"You mean that I am responsible for the disappearance of the woman?" he demanded.

"Certainly. It is obvious. I demand that she be restored."

He lost his temper. "Who are you to demand?" he shouted. "You are naught but a slave. Cease your impudence or I shall erase you—erase you. It will be as though you never had existed."

I laughed in his face. "Anger is the most futile attribute of the sentimentalist," I reminded him. "You will not erase me, for I alone stand between you and mortality."

"I can train another," he parried.

"But you could not trust him," I pointed out.

"But you bargained with me for my life when you had me in your power," he cried.

"For nothing that it would have harmed you to have granted willingly. I did not ask anything for myself. Be that as it may, you will trust me again. You will trust, for no other reason than that you will be forced to trust me. So why not win my gratitude and my loyalty by returning the woman to me and carrying out in spirit as well as in fact the terms of our agreement?"

He turned and looked steadily at me. "Vad Varo," he said, "I give you the word of honor of a Barsoomian noble that I know absolutely nothing concerning the whereabouts of 4296-E-2631-H."

"Perhaps Yamdor does," I persisted.

"Nor Yamdor. Of my knowledge no person in any way connected with me knows what became of it. I have spoken the truth."

Well, the conversation was not as profitless as it might appear, for I was sure that it had almost convinced Ras Thavas that I was equally as ignorant of the fate of Valla Dia as was he. That it had not wholly convinced him was evidenced by the fact that the espionage continued for a long time, a fact which determined me to use Ras Thavas' own methods in my own defense. I had had allotted to me a number of slaves and these I had won over by kindness and understanding until I knew that I had the full measure of their loyalty. They had no reason to love Ras Thavas and every reason to hate him; on the other hand they had no reason to hate me, and I saw to it that they had every reason to love me.

The result was that I had no difficulty in enlisting the services of a couple of them to spy upon Ras Thavas' spies, with the result that I was soon apprised that my suspicions were well founded—I was being constantly watched every minute that I was out of my apartments, but the spying did not come beyond my outer chamber walls. That was why I had been successful in reaching the vault in the manner that I had, the spies having assumed that I would leave my chamber only by its natural exit, had been content to guard that and permit my windows to go unwatched.

I think it was about two of our months that the spying continued and then my men reported that it seemed to have ceased entirely. All that time I was fretting at the delay, for I wanted to be about my plans which would have been absolutely impossible for me to carry out if I were being watched. I had spent the interval in studying the geography of the northeastern Barsoomian hemisphere where my activities were to be carried on, and also in scanning a great number of case histories and inspecting the subjects to which they referred; but at last, with the removal of the spies, it began to look as though I might soon commence to put my plans in active operation.

Ras Thavas had for some time permitted me considerable freedom in independent investigation and experiment, and this I determined to take advantage of in every possible way that might forward my plans for the resurrection of Valla Dia. My study of the histories of many of the cases had been with the possibility in mind of discovering subjects that might be of assistance to me in my venture. Among those that had occupied my careful attention were, quite naturally, the cases with which I had been most familiar, namely: 378-J-493811-P, the red-man from whose vicious attack I had saved Ras Thavas upon the day of my advent upon Mars; and he whose brain had been divided with an ape.

The former, 378-J-493811-P, had been a native of Phundahl—a young warrior attached to the court of Xaxa, Jeddara of Phundahl—and a victim of assassination. His body had been purchased by a Phundahlian noble for the purpose, as Ras Thavas had narrated, of winning the favor of a young beauty. I felt that I might possibly enlist his services, but that would depend upon the extent of his loyalty toward Xaxa, which I could only determine by reviving and questioning him.

He whose brain had been divided with an ape had originated in Ptarth, which lay at a considerable distance to the west of Phundahl and a little south and about an equal distance from Duhor, which lay north and a little west of it. An inhabitant of Ptarth, I reasoned, would know much of the entire country included in the triangle formed by Phundahl, Ptarth and Duhor; the strength and ferocity of the great ape would prove of value in crossing beast infested wastes; and I felt that I could hold forth sufficient promise to the human half of the great beast's brain, which really now dominated the creature, to win its support and loyalty. The third subject that I had tentatively selected had been a notorious Toonolian assassin, whose audacity, fearlessness and swordsmanship had won for him a reputation that had spread far beyond the boundaries of his country.

Ras Thavas, himself a Toonolian, had given me something of the history of this man whose grim calling is not without honor upon Barsoom, and which Gor Hajus had raised still higher in the esteem of his countrymen through the fact that he never struck down a woman or a good man and that he never struck from behind. His killings were always the results of fair fights in which the victim had every opportunity to defend himself and slay his attacker; and he was famous for his loyalty to his friends. In fact this very loyalty had been a contributing factor in his downfall which had brought him to one of Ras Thavas' ersite slabs some years since, for he had earned the enmity of Vobis Kan, Jeddak of Toonol, through his refusal to assassinate a man who once had befriended Gor Hajus in some slight degree; following which Vobis Kan conceived the suspicion that Gor Hajus had him marked for slaying. The result was inevitable: Gor Hajus was arrested and condemned to death; immediately following the execution of the sentence an agent of Ras Thavas had purchased the body.

These three, then, I had chosen to be my partners in my great adventure. It is true that I had not discussed the matter with any one of them, but my judgment assured me that I would have no difficulty in enlisting their services and loyalty in return for their total resurrection.

My first task lay in renewing the organs of 378-J-493811-P and of Gor Hajus which had been injured by the wounds that had layed them low; the former requiring a new lung and the latter a new heart, his executioner having run him through with a short-sword. I hesitated to ask Ras Thavas' permission to experiment on these subjects for fear of the possibility of arousing his suspicions, in which event he would probably have them destroyed; and so I was forced to accomplish my designs by subterfuge and stealth. To this end I made it a practice for weeks to carry my regular laboratory work far into the night, often requiring the service of various assistants that all might become accustomed to the sight of me at work at unusual hours. In my selection of these assistants I made it a point to choose two of the very spies that Ras Thavas had set to watching me. While it was true that they were no longer employed in this particular service, I had hopes that they would carry word of my activities to their master; and I was careful to see that they received from me the proper suggestions that would mold their report in language far from harmful to me. By the merest suggestion I carried to them the idea that I worked thus late purely for the love of the work itself and the tremendous interest in it that Ras Thavas had awakened within my mind. Some nights I worked with assistants and as often I did not, but always I was careful to assure myself that the following morning those in the office were made aware that I had labored far into the preceding night.

This groundwork carefully prepared, I had comparatively little fear of the results of actual discovery when I set to work upon the warrior of Phundahl and the assassin of Toonol. I chose the former first. His lung was badly injured where my blade had passed through it, but from the laboratory where were kept fractional bodies I brought a perfect lung, with which I replaced the one that I had ruined. The work occupied but half the night. So anxious was I to complete my task that I immediately opened up the breast of Gor Hajus, for whom I had selected an unusually strong and powerful heart, and by working rapidly I succeeded in completing the transference before dawn. Having known the nature of the wounds that had dispatched these two men, I had spent weeks in performing similar operations that I might perfect myself especially in this work; and having encountered no unusual pathological conditions in either subject, the work had progressed smoothly and with great rapidity. I had completed what I had feared would be the most difficult part of my task and now, having removed as far as possible all signs of the operation except the therapeutic tape which closed the incisions, I returned to my quarters for a few minutes of much needed rest, praying that Ras Thavas would not by any chance examine either of the subjects upon which I had been working; although I had fortified myself against such a contingency by entering full details of the operation upon the history card of each subject that, in the event of discovery, any suspicion of ulterior motives upon my part might be allayed by my play of open frankness.

I arose at the usual time and went at once to Ras Thavas' apartment, where I was met with a bomb shell that nearly wrecked my composure. He eyed me closely for a long minute before he spoke.

"You worked late last night. Vad Varo," he said.

"I often do," I replied, lightly; but my heart was heavy as a stone.

"And what might it have been that so occupied your interest?" he inquired.

I felt as a mouse with which the cat is playing. "I have been doing quite a little lung and heart transference of late," I replied, "and I became so engrossed with my work that I did not note the passage of time."

"I have known that you worked late at night. Do you think it wise?"

At that moment I felt that it had been very unwise, yet I assured him to the contrary.

"I was restless," he said. "I could not sleep and so I went to your quarters after midnight, but you were not there. I wanted someone with whom to talk, but your slaves knew only that you were not there—where you were they did not know—so I set out to search for you." My heart went into my sandals. "I guessed that you were in one of the laboratories, but though I visited several I did not find you." My heart arose with the lightness of a feather. "Since my own transference I have been cursed with restlessness and sleeplessness, so that I could almost wish for the return of my old corpse — the youth of my body harmonizes not with the antiquity of my brain. It is filled with latent urges and desires that comport illy with the serious subject matter of my mind."

"What your body needs," I said, "is exercise. It is young, strong, virile. Work it hard and it will let your brain rest at night."

"I know that you are right," he replied. "I have reached that same conclusion myself. In fact, not finding you, I walked in the gardens for an hour or more before returning to my quarters, and then I slept soundly. I shall walk every night when I cannot sleep, or I shall go into the laboratories and work as do you."

This news was most disquieting. Now I could never be sure but that Ras Thavas was wandering about at night and I had one more very important night's work to do, perhaps two. The only way that I could be sure of him was to be with him.

"Send for me when you are restless," I said, "and I will walk and work with you. You should not go about thus at night alone."

"Very well," he said, "I may do that occasionally."

I hoped that he would do it always, for then I would know that when he failed to send for me he was safe in his own quarters. Yet I saw that I must henceforth face the menace of detection; and knowing this I determined to hasten the completion of my plans and to risk everything on a single bold stroke.

That night I had no opportunity to put it into action as Ras Thavas sent for me early and informed me that we would walk in the gardens until he was tired. Now, as I needed a full night for what I had in mind and as Ras Thavas walked until midnight, I was compelled to forego everything for that evening, but the following morning I persuaded him to walk early on the pretext that I should like to go beyond the enclosure and see something of Barsoom beside the inside of his laboratories and his gardens. I had little confidence that he would grant my request, yet he did so. I am sure he never would have done it had he possessed his old body; but thus greatly had young blood changed Ras Thavas.

I had never been beyond the buildings, nor had I seen beyond, since there were no windows in the outside walls of any of the structures and upon the garden site the trees had grown to such a height that they obstructed all view beyond them. For a time we walked in another garden just inside the outer wall, and then I asked Ras Thavas if I might go even beyond this.

"No," he said. "It would not be safe."

"And why not?" I asked.

"I will show you and at the same time give you a much broader view of the outside world than you could obtain by merely passing through the gate. Come, follow me!"

He led me immediately to a lofty tower that rose at the corner of the largest building of the group that comprised his vast establishment. Within was a circular runway which led not only upward, but down as well. This we ascended, passing openings at each floor, until we came at last out upon its lofty summit. About me spread the first Barsoomian landscape of any extent upon which my eyes had yet rested during the long months that I had spent upon the Red Planet. For almost an Earthly year I had been immured within the grim walls of Ras Thavas' bloody laboratory, until, such creatures of habit are we, the weird life there had grown to seem quite natural and ordinary; but with this first glimpse of open country there surged up within me an urge for freedom, for space, for room to move about, such as I knew would not be long denied.

Directly beneath lay an irregular patch of rocky land elevated perhaps a dozen feet or more above the general level of the immediately surrounding country. Its extent was, at a rough guess, a hundred acres. Upon this stood the buildings and grounds, which were enclosed in a high wall. The tower upon which he stood was situated at about the center of the total area enclosed. Beyond the outer wall was a strip of rocky ground on which grew a sparse forest of fair sized trees interspersed with patches of a jungle growth, and beyond all, what appeared to be an oozy marsh through which were narrow water courses connecting occasional open water—little lakes, the largest of which could have comprised scarce two acres. This landscape extended as far as the eye could reach, broken by occasional islands similar to that upon which we were, and at a short distance by the skyline of a large city, whose towers and domes and minarets glistened and sparkled in the sun as though plated with shining metals and picked out with precious gems.

This, I knew, must be Toonol and all about us the Great Toonolian Marshes which extend nearly eighteen hundred earth miles east and west and in some places have a width of three hundred miles. Little is known about them in other portions of Barsoom as they are frequented by fierce beasts, afford no landing places for fliers and are commanded by Phundahl at their western end and Toonol at the east; inhospitable kingdoms that invite no intercourse with the outside world and maintain their independence alone by their inaccessibility and savage aloofness.

As my eyes returned to the island at our feet I saw a huge form emerge from one of the nearby patches of jungle a short distance beyond the outer wall. It was followed by a second and a third. Ras Thavas saw that the creatures had attracted my notice.

"There," he said, pointing to them, "are three of a number of similar reasons why it would not have been safe for us to venture outside the enclosure."

They were great white apes of Barsoom, creatures so savage that even that fierce Barsoomian lion, the banth, hesitates to cross their path.

"They serve two purposes," explained Ras Thavas. "They discourage those who might otherwise creep upon me by night from the city of Toonol, where I am not without many good enemies, and they prevent desertion upon the part of my slaves and assistants."

"But how do your clients reach you?" I asked. "How are your supplies brought in?"

He turned and pointed down toward the highest portion of the irregular roof of the building below us. Built upon it was a large, shed-like structure. "There," he said, "I keep three small ships. One of them goes every day to Toonol."

I was overcome with eagerness to know more about these ships, in which I thought I saw a much needed means of escape from the island; but I dared not question him for fear of arousing his suspicions.

As we turned to descend the tower runway I expressed interest in the structure which gave evidence of being far older than any of the surrounding buildings.

"This tower," said Ras Thavas, "was built some twenty-three thousand years ago by an ancestor of mine who was driven from Toonol by the reigning jeddak of the time. Here, and upon other islands, he gathered a considerable following, dominated the surrounding marshes and defended himself successfully for hundreds of years. While my family has been permitted to return to Toonol since, this has been their home; to which, one by one, have been added the various buildings which you see about the tower, each floor of which connects with the adjacent building from the roof to the lowest pits beneath the ground."

This information also interested me greatly since I thought that I saw where it too might have considerable bearing upon my plan of escape, and so, as we descended the runway, I encouraged Ras Thavas to discourse upon the construction of the tower, its relation to the other buildings and especially its accessibility from the pits. We walked again in the outer garden and by the time we returned to Ras Thavas' quarters it was almost dark and the master surgeon was considerably fatigued.

"I feel that I shall sleep well tonight," he said as I left him.

"I hope so, Ras Thavas," I replied.

Chapter VII

ESCAPE

It was usually about three hours after the evening meal, which was served immediately after dark, that the establishment quieted down definitely for the night. While I should have preferred waiting longer before undertaking that which I had in mind, I could not safely do so, since there was much to be accomplished before dawn. So it was that with the first indications that the occupants of the building in which my work was to be performed had retired for the night, I left my quarters and went directly to the laboratory, where, fortunately for my plans, the bodies of Gor Hajus, the assassin of Toonol, and 378-J-493811-P both reposed. It was the work of a few minutes to carry them to adjoining tables, where I quickly strapped them securely against the possibility that one or both of them might not be willing to agree to the proposition I was about to make them, and thus force me to anesthetize them again. At last the incisions were made, the tubes attached and the motors started. 378-J-483811-P, whom I shall hereafter call by his own name, Dar Tarus, was the first to open his eyes; but he had not regained full consciousness when Gor Hajus showed signs of life.

I waited until both appeared quite restored. Dar Tarus was eyeing me with growing recognition that brought a most venomous expression of hatred to his countenance. Gor Hajus was frankly puzzled. The last he remembered was the scene in the death chamber at the instant that his executioner had run a sword through his heart. It was I who broke the silence.

"In the first place," I said, "let me tell you where you are, if you do not already know."

"I know well enough were I am," growled Dar Tarus.

"Ah!" exclaimed Gor Hajus, whose eyes had been roaming about the chamber. "I can guess where I am. What Toonolian has not heard of Ras Thavas? So they sold my corpse to the old butcher, did they? And what now? Did I just arrive?"

"You have been here six years," I told him, "and you may stay here forever unless we three can reach an agreement within the next few minutes, and that goes for you too, Dar Tarus."

"Six years!" mused Gor Hajus. "Well, out with it, man. What do you want? If it is to slay Ras Thavas, no! He has saved me from utter destruction; but name me some other, preferably Vobis Kan, Jeddak of Toonol. Find me a blade and I will slay a hundred to regain life."

"I seek the life of none unless he stands in the way of the fulfilment of my desire in this matter that I have in hand. Listen! Ras Thavas had here a beautiful Duhorian girl. He sold her body to Xaxa, Jeddara of Phundahl, transplanting the girl's brain to the wrinkled and hideous body of the jeddara. It is my intention to regain the body, restore it to its own brain and return the girl to Duhor."

Gor Hajus grinned. "You have a large contract on your hands," he said, "but I can see that you are a man after my own heart and I am with you. It will give freedom and fighting, and all that I ask is a chance for one thrust at Vobis Kan."

"I promise you life," I replied; "but with the understanding that you serve me faithfully and none other, undertaking no business of your own, until mine has been carried to a successful conclusion."

"That means that I shall have to serve you for life," he replied, "for the thing you have undertaken you can never accomplish; but that is better than lying here on a cold ersite slab waiting for old Ras Thavas to come along and carve out my gizzard. I am yours! Let me up, that I may feel a good pair of legs under me again."

"And you?" I asked, turning to Dar Tarus as I released the bonds that held Gor Hajus. For the first time I now noticed that the ugly expression that I had first noted upon the face of Dar Tarus had given place to one of eagerness.

"Strike off my bonds!" he cried. "I will follow you to the ends of Barsoom and the way leads thus far to the fulfilment of your design; but it will not. It will lead to Phundahl and to the chamber of the wicked Xaxa, where, by the generosity of my ancestors, I may be given the opportunity to avenge the hideous wrong the creature did me. You could not have chosen one better fitted for your mission than Dar Tarus, one time soldier of the Jeddara's Guard, whom she had slain that in my former body one of her rotten nobles might woo the girl I loved."

A moment later the two men stood at my side, and without more delay I led them toward the runway that descended to the pits beneath the building. As we went, I described to them the creature I had chosen to be the fourth member of our strange party. Gor Hajus questioned the wisdon of my choice, saying that the ape would attract too much attention to us. Dar Tarus, however, believed that it might be helpful in many respects, since it was possible that we might be compelled to spend some time among the islands of the marshes which were often infested with these creatures; while, once in Phundahl, the ape might readily be used in the furtherance of our plans and would cause no considerable comment in a city where many of these beasts are held in captivity and often are seen performing for the edification of street crowds.

We went at once to the vault where the ape lay and where I had concealed the anesthetized body of Valla Dia. Here I revived the great anthropoid and to my great relief found that the human half of its brain still was dominant. Briefly I explained my plan as I had to the other two and won the hearty promise of his support upon my engaging to restore his brain to its rightful place upon the completion of our venture.

First we must get off the island, and I outlined two plans I had in mind. One was to steal one of Ras Thavas' three fliers and set out directly for Phundahl, and the other, in the event that the first did not seem feasible, was to secrete ourselves aboard one of them on the chance that we might either overpower the crew and take over the ship after we had left the island, or escape undetected upon its arrival in Toonol. Dar Tarus liked the first plan; the ape, whom we now called by the name belonging to the human half of his brain, Hovan Du, preferred the first alternative of the second plan; and Gor Hajus the second alternative.

Dar Tarus explained that as our principal objective was Phundahl, the quicker we got there the better. Hovan Du argued that by seizing the ship after it had left the island we would have longer time in which to make our escape before the ship was missed and pursuit instituted, than by seizing it now in the full knowledge that its absence would be discovered within a few hours. Gor Hajus thought that it would be better if we could come into Toonol secretly and there, through one of his friends, secure arms and a flier of our own. It would never do, he insisted, to attempt to go far without arms for himself and Dar Tarus, nor could we hope to reach Phundahl without being overhauled by pursuers; for we must plan on the hypothesis that Ras Thavas would immediately discover my absence; that he would at once investigate; that he would find Dar Tarus and Gor Hajus missing and thereupon lose no time in advising Vobis Kan, Jeddak of Toonol, that Gor Hajus the assassin was at large, whereupon the Jeddak's best ships would be sent in pursuit.

Gor Hajus' reasoning was sound and coupled with my recollection that Ras Thavas had told me that his three ships were slow, I could readily foresee that our liberty would be of short duration were we to steal one of the old surgeon's fliers.

As we discussed the matter we had made our way through the pits and I had found the exit to the tower. Silently we passed upward along the runway and out upon the roof. Both moons were winging low through the heavens and the scene was almost as light as day. If anyone was about discovery was certain. We hastened toward the hangar and were soon within it, where, for a moment at least, I breathed far more easily than I had beneath those two brilliant moons upon the exposed roof.

The fliers were peculiar looking contrivances, low, squat, with rounded bows and sterns and covered decks, their every line proclaiming them as cargo carriers built for anything but speed. One was much smaller than the other two and a second was evidently undergoing repairs. The third I entered and examined carefully. Gor Hajus was with me and pointed out several places where we might hide with little likelihood of discovery unless it were suspected that we might be aboard, and that of course constituted a very real danger; so much so that I had about decided to risk all aboard the small flier, which Gor Hajus assured me would be the fastest of the three, when Dar Tarus stuck his head into the ship and motioned me to come quickly.

"There is someone about," he said when I reached his side.

"Where?" I demanded.

"Come," he said, and led me to the rear of the hangar, which was flush with the wall of the building upon which it stood, and pointed through one of the windows into the inner garden where, to my consternation, I saw Ras Thavas walking slowly to and fro. For an instant I was sick with despair, for I knew that no ship could leave that roof unseen while anyone was abroad in the garden beneath, and Ras Thavas least of all people in the world; but suddenly a great light dawned upon me. I called the three close to me and explained my plan.

Instantly they grasped the possibilities in it and a moment later we had run the small flier out upon the roof and turned her nose toward the east, away from Toonol. Then Gor Hajus entered her, set the various controls as we had decided, opened the throttle, slipped back to the roof. The four of us hastened into the hangar and ran to the rear window where we saw the ship moving slowly and gracefully out over the garden and the head of Ras Thavas, whose ears must instantly have caught the faint purring of the motor, for he was looking up by the time we reached the window.

Instantly he hailed the ship and stepping back from the window that he might not see me I answered: "Good-bye, Ras Thavas! It is I, Vad Varo, going out into a strange world to see what it is like. I shall return. The spirits of your ancestors be with you until then." That was a phrase I had picked up from reading in Ras Thavas' library and I was quite proud of it.

"Come back at once," he shouted up in reply, "or you will be with the spirits of your own ancestors before another day is done."

I made no reply. The ship was now at such a distance that I feared my voice might no longer seem to come from it and that we should be discovered. Without more delay we concealed ourselves aboard

one of the remaining fliers, that upon which no work was being done, and there commenced as long and tiresome a period of waiting as I can recall ever having passed through.

I had at last given up any hope of the ship's being flown that day when I heard voices in the hangar, and presently the sound of footsteps aboard the flier. A moment later a few commands were given and almost immediately the ship moved slowly out into the open.

The four of us were crowded into a small compartment built into a tiny space between the forward and aft starboard buoyancy tanks. It was very dark and poorly ventilated, having evidently been designed as a storage closet to utilize otherwise waste space. We dared not converse for fear of attracting attention to our presence, and for the same reason we moved about as little as possible, since we had no means of knowing but that some member of the crew might be just beyond the thin door that separated us from the main cabin of the ship. Altogether we were most uncomfortable; but the distance to Toonol is not so great but that we might hope that our situation would soon be changed—at least if Toonol was to be the destination of the ship. Of this we soon had cheering hope. We had been out but a short time when, faintly, we heard a hail and then the motors were immediately shut down and the ship stopped.

"What ship?" we heard a voice demand, and from aboard our own came the reply:

"The Vosar, Tower of Thavas for Toonol." We heard a scraping as the other ship touched ours.

"We are coming aboard to search you in the name of Vobis Kan, Jeddak of Toonol. Make way!" shouted one from the other ship. Our cheer had been of short duration. We heard the shuffling of many feet and Gor Hajus whispered in my ear.

"What shall we do?" he asked.

I slipped my short-sword into his hand. "Fight!" I replied.

"Good, Vad Varo," he replied, and then I handed him my pistol and told him to pass it on to Dar Tarus. We heard the voices again, but nearer now.

"What ho!" cried one. "It is Bal Zak himself, my old friend Bal Zak!"

"None other," replied a deep voice. "And whom did you expect to find in command of the Vosar other than Bal Zak?"

"Who could know but that it might have been this Vad Varo himself, or even Gor Hajus," said the other, "and our orders are to search all ships."

"I would that they were here," replied Bal Zak, "for the reward is high. But how could they, when Ras Thavas himself with his own eyes saw them fly off in the Pinsar before dawn this day and disappear in the east?"

"Right you are, Bal Zak," agreed the other, "and it were a waste of time to search your ship. Come men! to our own!"

I could feel the muscles about my heart relax with the receding footfalls of Vobis Kan's warriors as they quitted the deck of the Vosar for their own ship, and my spirits rose with the renewed purring of our own motor as Ras Thavas' flier again got under way. Gor Hajus bent his lips close to my ear.

"The spirits of our ancestors smile upon us," he whispered. "It is night and the darkness will aid in covering our escape from the ship and the landing stage."

"What makes you think it is night?" I asked.

"Vobis Kan's ship was close by when it hailed and asked our name. By daylight it could have seen what ship we were."

He was right. We had been locked in that stuffy hole since before dawn, and while I had thought that it had been for a considerable time, I also had realized that the darkness and the inaction and the nervous strain would tend to make it seem much longer than it really had been; so that I would not have been greatly surprised had we made Toonol by daylight.

The distance from the Tower of Thavas to Toonol is inconsiderable, so that shortly after Vobis Kan's ship had spoken us we came to rest upon the landing stage at our destination. For a long time we waited, listening to the sounds of movement aboard the ship and wondering, upon my part at least, as to what the intentions of the captain might be. It was quite possible that Bal Zak might return to Thavas this same night, especially if he had come to Toonol to fetch a rich and powerful patient to the laboratories; but if he had come only for supplies he might well lie here until the morrow. This much I had learned from Gor Hajus, my own knowledge of the movements of the fliers of Ras Thavas being considerably less than nothing; for,

though I had been months a lieutenant of the master surgeon, I had learned only the day before of the existence of his small fleet, it being according to the policy of Ras Thavas to tell me nothing unless the telling of it coincided with and furthered his own plans.

Questions which I asked he always answered, if he reasoned that the effects would not be harmful to his own interests, but he volunteered nothing that he did not particularly wish me to know; and the fact that there were no windows in the outside walls of the buildings facing toward Toonol, that I had never before the previous day been upon the roof and that I never had seen a ship sail over the inner court toward the east all tended to explain my ignorance of the fleet and its customary operations.

We waited quietly until silence fell upon the ship, betokening either that the crew had retired for the night or that they had gone down into the city. Then, after a whispered consultation with Gor Hajus, we decided to make an attempt to leave the flier. It was our purpose to seek a hiding place within the tower of the landing stage from which we might investigate possible avenues of escape into the city, either at once or upon the morrow when we might more easily mix with the crowd that Gor Hajus said would certainly be in evidence from a few hours after sunrise.

Cautiously I opened the door of our closet and looked into the main cabin beyond. It lay in darkness. Silently we filed out. The silence of the tomb lay upon the flier, but from far below arose the subdued noises of the city. So far, so good! Then, without sound, without warning, a burst of brilliant light illuminated the interior of the cabin. I felt my fingers tighten upon my sword hilt as I glanced quickly about.

Directly opposite us, in the narrow doorway of a small cabin, stood a tall man whose handsome harness betokened the fact that he was no common warrior. In either hand he held a heavy Barsoomian pistol, into the muzzles of which we found ourselves staring.

Chapter VIII

HANDS UP!

In quiet tones he spoke the words of the Barsoomian equivalent of our earthly *hands up!* The shadow of a grim smile touched his lips, and as he saw us hesitate to obey his commands he spoke again.

"Do as I tell you and you will be well off. Keep perfect silence. A raised voice may spell your doom; a pistol shot most assuredly."

Gor Hajus raised his hands above his head and we others followed his example.

"I am Bal Zak," announced the stranger. My heart slumped.

"Then you had better commence firing," said Gor Hajus, "for you will not take us alive and we are four to one."

"Not so fast, Gor Hajus," admonished the captain of the Vosar, "until you learn what is in my mind."

"That, we already know for we heard you speak of the large reward that awaited the captor of Vad Varo and Gor Hajus," snapped the assassin of Toonol.

"Had I craved that reward so much I could have turned you over to the dwar of Vobis Kan's ship when he boarded us," said Bal Zak.

"You did not know we were aboard the Vosar," I reminded him.

"Ah, but I did."

Gor Hajus snorted his disbelief.

"How then," Bal Zak reminded us, "was I able to be ready upon this very spot when you emerged from your hiding place? Yes, I knew that you were aboard."

"But how?" demanded Dar Tarus.

"It is immaterial," replied Bal Zak, "but to satisfy your natural curiosity I will tell you that I have quarters in a small room in the Tower of Thavas, my windows overlook the roof and the hangar. My long life spent aboard fliers has made me very sensitive to every sound of a ship—motors changing their speed will awaken me in the dead of night, as quickly as will their starting or their stopping. I was awakened by the starting of the motors of the Pinsar; I saw three of you upon the roof and the fourth drop from the deck of the flier as she started and my judgment told me that the ship was being sent out unmanned for some reason of which I had no knowledge. It was too late for me to prevent the act and so I waited in silence to learn what would follow. I saw you hasten into the hangar and I heard Ras Thavas' hail and your reply, and then I saw you board the Vosar. Immediately I descended to the roof and ran noiselessly to the hangar, apprehending that you intended making away with this ship; but there was no one about the controls; and from a tiny port in the control room, through which one has a view of the main cabin, I saw you enter that closet. I was at once convinced that your only purpose was to stow away for Toonol and consequently, aside from keeping an eye upon your hiding place, I went about my business as usual."

"And you did not advise Ras Thavas?" I asked.

"I advised no one," he replied. "Years ago I learned to mind my own business, to see all, to hear all and to tell nothing unless it profited me to do so."

"But you said that the reward is high for our apprehension," Gor Hajus reminded him. "Would it not be profitable to collect it?"

"There are in the breasts of honorable men," replied Bal Zak, "forces that rise superior to the lust for gold, and while Toonolians are supposedly a people free from the withering influences of sentiment yet I for one am not totally unconscious of the demand of gratitude. Six years ago, Gor Hajus, you refused to assassinate my father, holding that he was a good man, worthy to live and one that had once befriended you slightly. Today, through his son, you reap your reward and in some measure are repaid for the punishment that was meted out to you by Vobis Kan because of your refusal to slay the sire of Bal Zak. I have sent my crew away that none aboard the Vosar but myself might have knowledge of your presence. Tell me your plans and command me in what way I may be of further service to you."

"We wish to reach the streets, unobserved," replied Gor Hajus. "Can you but help us in that we shall not put upon your shoulders further responsibility for our escape. You have our gratitude and in Toonol, I need not remind you, the gratitude of Gor Hajus is a possession that even the Jeddak has craved."

"Your problem is complicated," said Bal Zak, after a moment of thought, "by the personnel of your party. The ape would immediately attract attention and arouse suspicion. Knowing much of Ras Thavas' experiments I realized at once this morning, after watching him with you, that he had the brain of a man; but this very fact would attract to him and to you the closer attention of the masses."

"I do not need acquaint them with the fact," growled Hovan Du. "To them I need be but a captive ape. Are such unknown in Toonol?"

"Not entirely, though they are rare," replied Bal Zak. "But there is also the white skin of Vad Varo! Ras Thavas appears to have known nothing of the presence of the ape with you; but he full well knew of Vad Varo, and your description has been spread by every means at his command. You would be recognized immediately by the first Toonolian that lays eyes upon you, and then there is Gor Hajus. He has been as dead for six years, yet I venture there is scarce a Toonolian that broke the shell prior to ten years ago who does not know the face of Gor Hajus as well as he knows that of his own mother. The jeddak himself was not better known to the people of Toonol than Gor Hajus. That leaves but one who might possibly escape suspicion and detection in the streets of Toonol."

"If we could but obtain weapons for these others," I suggested, "we might even yet reach the house of Gor Hajus' friend."

"Fight your way through the city of Toonol?" demanded Bal Zak.

"If there is no other way we should have to," I replied.

"I admire the will," commented the commander of the Vosar, "but fear that the flesh is without sufficient strength. Wait! there is a way—perhaps. On the stage just below this there is a public depot where equilibrimotors are kept and rented. Could we find the means to obtain four of these there would be a chance, at least, for you to elude the air patrols and reach the house of Gor Hajus' friend; and I think I see a way to the accomplishment of that. The landing tower is closed for the night but there are several watchmen distributed through it at different levels. There is one at the equilibrimotor depot and, as I happen to know, he is a devotee of jetan. He would rather play jetan than attend to his duties as watchman. I often remain aboard the Vosar at night and occasionally he and I indulge in a game. I will ask him up tonight and while he is thus engaged you may go to the depot, help yourselves to equilibrimotors and pray to your ancestors that no air patrol suspicions you as you cross the city toward your destination. What think you of this plan, Gor Hajus?"

"It is splendid," replied the assassin. "And you, Vad Varo?"

"If I knew what an equilibrimotor is I might be in a better position to judge the merits of the plan," I replied. "However, I am satisfied to abide by the judgment of Gor Hajus. I can assure you, Bal Zak, of our great appreciation, and as Gor Hajus has put the stamp of his approval upon your plan I can only urge you to arrange that we may put it into effect with as little delay as possible."

"Good!" exclaimed Bal Zak. "Come with me and I will conceal you until I have lured the watchman to the jetan game within my cabin. After that your fate will be in your own hands."

We followed him from the ship onto the deck of the landing stage and close under the side of the Vosar opposite that from which the watchman must approach the ship and enter it. Then, bidding us good luck, Bal Zak departed.

From the summit of the landing tower I had my first view of a Martian city. Several hundred feet below me lay spread the broad, well lighted avenues of Toonol, many of which were crowded with people. Here and there, in this central district, a building was raised high upon its supporting, cylindrical metal shaft; while further out, where the residences predominated, the city took on the appearance of a colossal and grotesque forest. Among the larger palaces only an occasional suite of rooms was thus raised high above the level of the others, these being the sleeping apartments of the owners, their servants or their guests; but the smaller homes were raised in their entirety, a precaution necessitated by the constant activities of the followers of Gor Hajus' ancient profession that permitted no man to be free from the constant menace of assassination. Throughout the central district the sky was pierced by the lofty towers of several other landing stages; but, as I was later to learn, these were comparatively few in number. Toonol is in no sense a flying nation, supporting no such enormous fleets of merchant ships and vessels of war as, for example, the twin cities of Helium or the great capitol of Ptarth.

A peculiar feature of the street lighting of Toonol, and in fact the same condition applies to the lighting of other Barsoomian cities I have visited, I noted for the first time that night as I waited upon the landing stage for the return of Bal Zak with the watchman. The luminosity below me seemed confined directly to the area to be lighted; there was no diffusion of light upward or beyond the limits the lamps were designed to light. This was effected, I was told, by lamps designed upon principles resulting from ages of investigation of the properties of light waves and the laws governing them which permit Barsoomian scientists to confine and control light as we confine and control matter. The light waves leave the lamp, pass along a prescribed circuit and return to the lamp. There is no waste nor, strange this seemed to me, are there any dense shadows when lights are properly installed and adjusted; for the waves in passing around objects to return to the lamp, illuminate all sides of them.

The effect of this lighting from the great height of the tower was rather remarkable. The night was dark, there being no moons at that hour upon this night, and the effect was that obtained when sitting in a darkened auditorium and looking upon a brilliantly lighted stage. I was still intent upon watching the life and color beneath when we heard Bal Zak returning. That he had been successful in his mission was apparent from the fact that he was conversing with another.

Five minutes later we crept quietly from our hiding place and descended to the stage below where lay the equilibrimotor depot. As theft is practically unknown upon Barsoom, except for purposes entirely disassociated from a desire to obtain pecuniary profit through the thing stolen, no precautions are taken against theft. We therefore found the doors of the depot open and Gor Hajus and Dar Tarus quickly selected four equilibrimotors and adjusted them upon us. They consist of a broad belt, not unlike the life belt used aboard transoceanic liners upon Earth; these belts are filled with the eighth Barsoomian ray, or ray of propulsion, to a sufficient degree to just about equalize the pull of gravity and thus to maintain a person in equilibrium between that force and the opposite force exerted by the eighth ray. Permanently attached to the back of the belt is a small radium motor, the controls for which are upon the front of the belt. Rigidly attached to and projecting from each side of the upper rim of the belt is a strong, light wing with small hand levers for quickly altering its position.

Gor Hajus quickly explained the method of control, but I could apprehend that there might be embarrassment and trouble awaiting me before I mastered the art of flying in an equilibrimotor. He showed me how to tilt the wings downward in walking so that I would not leave the ground at every step, and thus he led me to the edge of the landing stage.

"We will rise here," he said, "and keeping in the darkness of the upper levels seek to reach the house of my friend without being detected. If we are pursued by air patrol we must separate; and later those who escape may gather just west of the city wall where you will find a small lake with a deserted tower upon its northern rim—this tower will be our rendezvous in event of trouble. Follow me!" He started his motor and rose gracefully into the air.

Hovan Du followed him and then it was my turn. I rose beautifully for about twenty feet, floating out over the city which lay hundreds of feet below, and then, quite suddenly, I turned upside down. I had done something wrong—I was quite positive of it. It was a most startling sensation, I can assure you, floating there with my head down, quite helpless; while below me lay the streets of a great city and no softer, I was sure, than the streets of Los Angeles of Paris. My motor was still going, and as I manipulated the controls which operated the wings I commenced to describe all sorts of strange loops and spirals and spins; and then Dar Tarus came to my rescue. First he told me to lie quietly and then directed the manipulation of each wing until I had gained an unright position. After that I did fairly well and was soon rising in the wake of Gor Hajus and Hovan Du.

I need not describe in detail the hour of flying, or rather floating, that ensued. Gor Hajus led us to a considerable altitude and there, through the darkness above the city, our slow motors drove us toward a district of magnificent homes surrounded by spacious grounds; and here, as we hovered over a large palace, we were suddenly startled by a sharp challenge coming from directly above us.

"Who flies by night?" a voice demanded.

"Friends of Mu Tel, Prince of the House of Kan," replied Gor Hajus quickly.

"Let me see your night flying permit and your flier's license," ordered the one above us, at the same time swooping suddenly to our level and giving me my first of a Martian policeman. He was equipped with a much swifter and handier equilibrimotor than ours. I think that was the first fact to impress us deeply, and it demonstrated the futility of flight; for he could have given us ten minutes start and overhauled each of us within another ten minutes, even though we had elected to fly in different directions. The fellow was a warrior rather than a policeman, though detailed to duty such as our earthly police officers perform; the city being patroled both day and night by the warriors of Vobis Kan's army.

He dropped now close to the assassin of Toonol, again demanding permit and license and at the same time flashing a light in the face of my comrade.

"By the sword of the jeddak!" he cried. "Fortune heaps her favors upon me. Who would have thought an hour since that it would be I who would collect the reward for the capture of Gor Hajus?"

"Any other fool might have thought it," returned Gor Hajus, "but he would have been as wrong as you," and as he spoke he struck with the short-sword I had loaned him.

The blow was broken by the wing of the warrior's equilibrimotor, which it demolished, yet it inflicted a severe wound in the fellow's shoulder. He tried to back off, but the damaged wing caused him only to wheel around erratically; and then he seized upon his whistle and attempted to blow a mighty blast that was cut short by another blow from Gor Hajus' sword that split the man's head open to the bridge of his nose.

"Quick!" cried the assassin. "We must drop into the gardens of Mu Tel, for that signal will bring a swarm of air patrols about our heads."

The others I saw falling rapidly toward the ground, but again I had trouble. Depress my wings as I would I moved only slightly downward and upon a path that, if continued, would have landed me at a considerable distance from the gardens of Mu Tel. I was approaching one of the elevated portions of the palace, what appeared to be a small suite that was raised upon its shining metal shaft far above the ground. From all directions I could hear the screaming whistles of the air patrols answering the last call of their comrade whose corpse floated just above me, a guide even in death to point the way for his fellows to search us out. They were sure to discover him and

then I would be in plain view of them and my fate sealed.

Perhaps I could find ingress to the apartments looming darkly near! There I might hide until the danger had passed, provided I could enter, undetected. I directed my course toward the structure; an open window took form through the darkness and then I collided with a fine wire netting—I had run into a protecting curtain that fends off assassins of the air from these high flung sleeping apartments. I felt that I was lost. If I could but reach the ground I might find concealment among the trees and shrubbery that I had seen vaguely outlined beneath me in the gardens of this Barsoomian prince; but I could not drop at a sufficient angle to bring me to ground within the garden, and when I tried to spiral down I turned over and started up again. I thought of ripping open my belt and letting the eighth ray escape; but in my unfamiliarity with this strange force I feared that such an act might precipitate me to the ground with too great violence, though I was determined to have recourse to it as a last alternative if nothing less drastic presented itself.

In my last attempt to spiral downward I rose rapidly feet foremost to a sudden and surprising collision with some object above me. As I frantically righted myself, fully expecting to be immediately seized by a member of the air patrol, I found myself face to face with the corpse of the warrior Gor Hajus had slain. The whistling of the air patrols sounded ever nearer—it could be only a question of seconds now before I was discovered—and with the stern necessity that confronted me, with death looking me in the face, there burst upon me a possible avenue of escape from my dilemma.

Seizing tightly with my left hand the harness of the dead Toonolian, I whipped out my dagger and slashed his buoyancy belt a dozen times. Instantly, as the rays escaped, his body started to drag me downward. Our descent was rapid, but not precipitate, and it was but a matter of seconds before we landed gently upon the scarlet sward of the gardens of Mu Tel, Prince of the House of Kan, close beside a clump of heavy shrubbery. Above me sounded the whistles of the circling patrols as I dragged the corpse of the warrior into the concealing depth of the foliage. Nor was

I an instant too soon for safety, as almost immediately the brilliant rays of a searchlight shot downward from the deck of a small patrol ship, illuminating the open spaces of the garden all about me. A hurried glance through the branches and the leaves of my sanctuary revealed nothing of my companions and I breathed a sigh of relief in the thought that they, too, had found concealment.

The light played for a short time about the gardens and then passed on, as did the sound of the patrol's whistles, as the search proceeded elsewhere; thus giving me the assurance that no suspicion was directed upon our hiding place.

Left in the darkness I appropriated such of the weapons of the dead warrior as I coveted, after having removed my equilibrimotor, which I was first minded to destroy, but which I finally decided to moor to one of the larger shrubs against the possibility that I might again have need for it; and now, secure in the conviction that the danger of discovery by the air patrol had passed, I left my concealment and started in search of my companions.

Keeping well in the shadows of the trees and shrubs I moved in the direction of the main building, which loomed darkly near at hand; for in this direction I believed Gor Hajus would lead the others as I knew that the palace of Mu Tel was to have been our destination. As I crept along, moving with utmost stealth, Thuria, the nearer moon, shot suddenly above the horizon, illuminating the night with her brilliant rays. I was close to the building's ornately carved wall at the moment; beside me was a narrow niche, its interior cast in deepest shadow by Thuria's brilliant rays; to my left was an open bit of lawn upon which, revealed in every detail of its terrifying presence, stood as fearsome a creature as my earthly eyes ever had rested upon. It was a beast about the size of a Shetland pony, with ten short legs and a terrifying head that bore some slight resemblance to that of a frog, except that the jaws were equipped with three rows of long, sharp tusks.

The thing had its nose in the air and was sniffing about, while its great pop eyes moved swiftly here and there, assuring me, beyond the shadow of a doubt, that it was searching for someone. I am not inclined to be egotistical, yet I could not avoid the conviction that it was searching for me. It was my first experience of a Martian watch dog; and as I sought concealment within the dark shadows of the niche behind me, at the very instant that the creature's eyes alighted upon me, and heard his growl and saw him charge straight toward me, I had a premonition that it might prove my last experience with one.

I drew my long-sword as I backed into the niche, but with a sense of the utter inadequacy of the unaccustomed weapon in the face of this three or four hundred pounds of ferocity incarnate. Slowly I backed away into the shadows as the creature bore down upon me and then, as it entered the niche, my back collided with a solid obstacle that put an end to further retreat.

Chapter IX

THE PALACE OF MU TEL

As the calot entered the niche I experienced, I believe, all of the reactions of the cornered rat, and I certainly know that I set myself to fight in that proverbial manner. The beast was almost upon me and I was metaphorically kicking myself for not having remained in the open where there were many tall trees when the support at my back suddenly gave way, a hand reached out of the darkness behind and seized my harness and I was drawn swiftly into inky blackness. A door slammed and the silhouette of the calot against the moonlit entrance to the niche was blotted out.

A gruff voice spoke in my ear. "Come with me!" it said. A hand found mine and thus I was led along through the darkness of what I soon discovered was a narrow corridor from the constantly recurring collisions I had first with one side of it and then with the other.

Ascending gradually, the corridor turned abruptly at right angles and I saw beyond my guide a dim luminosity that gradually increased until another turn brought us to the threshold of a brilliantly lighted chamber—a magnificent apartment, the gorgeous furnishings and decorations of which beggar the meager descriptive powers of my native tongue. Gold, ivory, precious stones, marvelous woods, resplendent fabrics, gorgeous furs and startling architecture combined to im-

It was my first experience with a Martian watch dog.

press upon my earthly vision such a picture as I had never even dreamed of dreaming; and in the center of this room, surrounded by a little group of Martians, were my three companions.

My guide conducted me toward the party, the members of which had turned toward us as we entered the chamber, and stopped before a tall Barsoomian, resplendent in jewel encrusted harness.

"Prince," he said, "I was scarce a tal too soon. In fact, as I opened the door to step out into the garden in search of him, as you directed, there he was upon the opposite side with one of the calots of the garden almost upon him."

"Good!" exclaimed he who had been addressed as prince, and then he turned to Gor Hajus. "This is he, my friend, of whom you told me?"

"This is Vad Varo, who claims to be from the planet Jasoom," replied Gor Hajus; "and this, Vad Varo, is Mu Tel, Prince of the House of Kan."

I bowed and the prince advanced and placed his right hand upon my left shoulder in true Barsoomian acknowledgment of an introduction; when I had done similarly, the ceremony was over. There was no silly pleased-to-meet-you, how-do-you-do? or it's-a-pleasure-I-assure-you.

At Mu Tel's request I narrated briefly what had befallen me between the time I had become separated from my companions and the moment that one of his officers had snatched me from impending disaster. Mu Tel gave instructions that all traces of the dead patrol be removed before dawn lest their discovery bring upon him the further suspicion of his uncle, Vobis Kan, Jeddak of Toonol, whom it seemed had long been jealous of his nephew's growing popularity and fearful that he harbored aspirations for the throne.

It was later in the evening, during one of those elaborate meals for which the princes of Barsoom are justly famous, when mellowed slightly by the rare vintages with which he delighted his guests, that Mu Tel discoursed with less restraint upon his imperial uncle.

"The nobles have long been tired of Vobis Kan," he said, "and the people are tiring of him—he is a conscienceless tyrant—but he is our hereditary ruler, and so they hesitate to change. We are a practical people, little influenced by sentiment;

yet there is enough to keep the masses loyal to their jeddak even after he has ceased to deserve their loyalty, while the fear of the wrath of the masses keeps the nobles loyal. There is also the natural suspicion that I, the next in line for succession, would make them no less tyrannical a jeddak than has Vobis Kan, while, having youth, I might be much more active in cruel and nefarious practices.

"For myself, I would not hesitate to destroy my uncle and seize his throne were I sure of the support of the army, for with the warriors of Vobis Kan at my back I might defy the balance of Toonol. It is because of this that I long since offered my friendship to Gor Hajus; not that he might slay my uncle, but that when I had slain him in fair fight Gor Hajus might win to me the loyalty of the jeddak's warriors, for great is the popularity of Gor Hajus among the soldiers, who ever look up to such a great fighter with reverence and devotion. I have offered Gor Hajus a high place in the affairs of Toonol should he cast his lot with me; but he tells me that he has first to fulfill his obligations to you, Vad Varo, and for the furtherance of your adventure he has asked me to give you what assistance I may. This I offer gladly, from purely practical motives, since your early success will hasten mine. Therefore I propose to place at your disposal a staunch flier that will carry you and your companions to Phundahl."

This offer I naturally accepted, after which we fell to discussing plans for our departure which we finally decided to attempt early the following night, at a time when neither of the moons would be in the heavens. After a brief discussion of equipment we were, at my request, permitted to retire since I had not slept for more than thirty-six hours and my companions for twenty-four.

Slaves conducted us to our sleeping apartments, which were luxuriously furnished, and arranged magnificent sleeping silks and furs for our comfort. After they had left us Gor Hajus touched a button and the room rose swiftly upon its metal shaft to a height of forty or fifty feet; the wire netting automatically dropped about us, and we were safe for the night.

The following morning, after our apartment had been lowered to its daylight level and before I was permitted to leave it, a slave was sent to me by Mu Tel with instructions to stain my entire body the beautiful copper-red of my Barsoomian friends; furnishing me with a disguise which I well knew to be highly essential to the success of my venture, since my white skin would have drawn unpleasant notice upon me in any city of Barsoom. Another slave brought harness and weapons for Gor Hajus, Dar Tarus and myself, and a collar and chain for Hovan Du, the ape-man. Our harness, while of heavy material and splendid workmanship, was quite plain, being free of all insignia either of rank or service—such harness as is customarily worn by the Barsoomian panthan, or soldier of fortune, at such times as he is not definitely in the service of any nation or individual. These panthans are virtually men without a country, being roving mercenaries ready to sell their swords to the highest bidder. Although they have no organization they are ruled by a severe code of ethics and while in the employ of a master are, almost without exception, loyal to him. They are generally supposed to be men who have flown from the wrath of their own jeddaks or the justice of their own courts, but there is among them a sprinkling of adventurous souls who have adopted their calling because of the thrills and excitement it offers. While they are well paid, they are also great gamblers and notorious spenders, with the result that they are almost always without funds and often reduced to strange expedients for the gaining of their livelihoods between engagements; a fact which gave great plausibility to our possession of a trained ape, which upon Mars would appear no more remarkable than would to us the possession of a monkey or parrot by an old salt just returned, from a long cruise, to one of our Earthly ports.

This day that I stayed in the palace of Mu Tel I spent much in the company of the prince, who found pleasure in questioning me concerning the customs, the politics, the civilization and the geography of Earth, with much of which, I was surprised to note, he seemed quite familiar; a fact which he explained was due to the marvellous development of Barsoomian astronomical instruments, wireless photography and wireless telephony; the last of which has been brought to such a state of perfection that many Barsoomian savants have succeeded in learning several Earthly languages, notably Urdu, English and Russian, and, a few, Chinese also. These have doubtless been the first languages to attract their attention because of the fact that they are spoken by great numbers of people over large areas of the world.

Mu Tel took me to a small auditorium in his palace that reminded me somewhat of private projection rooms on Earth. It had, I should say, a capacity of some two hundred persons and was built like a large camera obscura; the audience sitting within the instrument, their backs toward the lens and in front of them, filling one entire end of the room, a large ground glass upon which is thrown the image to be observed.

Mu Tel seated himself at a table upon which was a chart of the heavens. Just above the chart was a movable arm carrying a pointer. This pointer Mu Tel moved until it rested upon the planet Earth, then he switched off the light in the room and immediately there appeared upon the ground glass plate a view such as one might obtain from an aeroplane riding at an elevation of a thousand feet. There was something strangely familiar about the scene before me. It was of a desolate, wasted country. I saw shattered stumps whose orderly arrangement proclaimed that here once an orchard had blossomed and borne fruit. There were great, unsightly holes in the earth and over and across all a tangle of barbed wire. I asked Mu Tel how we might change the picture to another locality. He lighted a small radio bulb between us and I saw a globe there, a globe of Earth, and a small pointer fixed over it.

"The side of this globe now presented to you represents the face of the Earth turned toward us," explained Mu Tel. "You will note that the globe is slowly revolving. Place this pointer where you will upon the globe and that portion of Jasoom will be revealed for you."

I moved the pointer very slowly and the picture changed. A ruined village came into view. I saw some people moving among its ruins. They were not soldiers. A little further on I came upon trenches and dugouts—there were no soldiers here, either. I moved the pointer rapidly north and south along a vast line of trenches. Here and there in villages there were soldiers, but they were all French soldiers and never were they in the trenches. There were no

German soldiers and no fighting. The war was over, then! I moved the pointer to the Rhine and across. There were soldiers in Germany—French soldiers, English soldiers, American soldiers. We had won the war! I was glad, but it seemed very far away and quite unreal—as though no such world existed and no such peoples had ever fought—it was as though I were recalling through its illustrations a novel that I had read a long time since.

"You seem much interested in that war torn country," remarked Mu Tel.

"Yes," I explained, "I fought in that war. Perhaps I was killed. I do not know."

"And you won?" he asked.

"Yes, my people won," I replied. "We fought for a great principle and for the peace and happiness of a world. I hope that we did not fight in vain."

"If you mean that you hope that your principle will triumph because you fought and won, or that peace will come, your hopes are futile. War never brought peace—it but brings more and greater wars. War is Nature's natural state—it is folly to combat it. Peace should be considered only as a time for preparation for the principal business of man's existence. Were it not for constant warring of one form of life upon another, and even upon itself, the planets would be so overrun with life that it would smother itself out. We found upon Barsoom that long periods of peace brought plagues and terrible diseases that killed more than the wars killed and in a much more hideous and painful way. There is neither pleasure nor thrill nor reward of any sort to be gained by dying in bed of a loathesome disease. We must all die—let us therefore go out and die in a great and exciting game, and make room for the millions who are to follow us. We have tried it out upon Barsoom and we would not be without war."

Mu Tel told me much that day about the peculiar philosophy of Toonolians. They believe that no good deed was ever performed except for a selfish motive; they have no god and no religion; they believe, as do all educated Barsoomians, that man came originally from the Tree of Life, but unlike most of their fellows they do not believe that an omnipotent being created the Tree of Life. They hold that the only sin is failure—success, however achieved, is meritorius; and yet, paradoxical as it may seem, they never break their given word. Mu Tel explained that they overcame the baneful results of this degrading weakness—this sentimental bosh—by seldom, if ever, binding themselves to loyalty to another, and then only for a definitely prescribed period.

As I came to know them better, and especially Gor Hajus, I began to realize that much of their flaunted contempt of the finer sensibilities were specious. It is true that generations of inhibition had to some extent atrophied those characteristics of heart and soul which the noblest among us so highly esteem; that friendship's ties were lax and that blood kinship awakened no high sense of responsibility or love even between parents and children; yet Gor Hajus was essentially a man of sentiment, though he would doubtless have run through the heart any who had dared accuse him of it, thus perfectly proving the truth of the other's accusation. His pride in his reputation for integrity and loyalty proved him a man of heart as truly as did his jealousy of his reputation for heartlessness prove him a man of sentiment; and in all this he was but typical of the people of Toonol. They denied deity, and in the same breath worshipped the fetish of science that they had permitted to obsess them quite as harmfully as do religious fanatics accept the unreasoning rule of their imaginary gods; and so, with all their vaunted knowledge, they were unintelligent because unbalanced.

As the day drew to a close I became the more anxious to be away. Far to the west across desolate leagues of marsh lay Phundahl, and in Phundahl the beauteous body of the girl I loved and that I was sworn to restore to its rightful owner. The evening meal was over and Mu Tel himself had conducted us to a secret hangar in one of the towers of his palace. Here artisans had prepared a flier for us, having removed during the day all signs of its real ownership, even to slightly altering its lines; so that in the event of capture Mu Tel's name might in no way be connected with the expedition. Provisions were stored, including plenty of raw meat for Hovan Du, and, as the farther moon sank below the horizon and darkness fell, a panel of the tower wall, directly in front of the flier's nose, slid aside, Mu Tel wished us luck and the ship slipped silently out into the night. The flier, like many of her type, was without cockpit or cabin; a low, metal hand-rail surmounted her gunwale; heavy rings were set substantially in her deck and to these her crew was supposed to cling or attach themselves by means of their harness hooks provided for this and similar purposes; a low wind shield, with a rakish slant, afforded some protection from the wind; the motor and controls were all exposed, as all the space below decks was taken up by the buoyancy tanks. In this type everything is sacrificed to speed; there is no comfort aboard. When moving at high speed each member of the crew lies extended at full length upon the deck, each in his allotted place to give the necessary trim, and hangs on for dear life. These Toonolian crafts, however, are not overly fast, so I was told, being far outstripped in speed by the fliers of such nations as Helium and Ptarth who have for ages devoted themselves to the perfection of their navies; but this one was quite fast enough for our purposes, to the consummation of which it would be pitted against fliers of no higher rating, and it was certainly fast enough for me. In comparison with the slow moving Vosar, it seemed to shoot through the air like an arrow.

We wasted no time in strategy or stealth, but opened her wide as soon as we were in the clear, and directed her straight toward the west and Phundahl. Scarcely had we padded over the gardens of Mu Tel when we met with our first adventure. We shot by a solitary figure floating in the air and almost simultaneously there shrilled forth the warning whistle of an air patrol. A shot whistled above us harmlessly and we were gone; but within a few seconds I saw the rays of a searchlight shining down from above and moving searchingly to and fro through the air.

"A patrol boat!" shouted Gor Hajus in my ear. Hovan Du growled savagely and shook the chain upon his collar. We raced on, trusting to the big gods and the little gods and all our ancestors that that relentless eye of light would not find us out; but it did. Within a few seconds it fell full upon our deck from above and in front of us and there it clung as the patrol boat dropped rapidly toward us while it maintained a high rate of speed upon a course otherwise identical with ours. Then, to our consternation, the ship opened fire on us with ex-

plosive bullets. These projectiles contain a high explosive that is detonated by light rays when the opaque covering of the projectile is broken by impact with the target. It is therefore not at all necessary to make direct hit for a shot to be effective. If the projectile strikes the ground or the deck of a vessel or any solid substance near its target, it does considerable more damage when fired at a group of men than as though it struck but one of them, since it will then explode if its outer shell is broken and kill or wound several; while if it enters the body of an individual the light rays cannot reach it and it accomplishes no more than a non-explosive bullet. Moonlight is not powerful enough to detonate this explosive and so projectiles fired at night, unless touched by the powerful rays of searchlights, detonate at sunrise the following morning, making a battle field a most unsafe place at that time even though the contending forces are not longer there. Similarly they make the removal of unexploded projectiles from the bodies of the wounded a most ticklish operation which may well result in the instant death of both the patient and the surgeon.

Dar Tarus, at the controls, turned the nose of our flier upward directly toward the patrol boat and at the same time shouted to us to concentrate our fire upon her propellers. For my self, I could see little but the blinding eye of the searchlight, and at that I fired with the strange weapon to which I had received my first introduction but a few hours since when it was presented to me by Mu Tel. To me that all searching eye represented the greatest menace that confronted us, and could we blind it the patrol boat would have no great advantage over us. So I kept my rifle straight upon it, my finger on the button that controlled the fire, and prayed for a hit. Gor Hajus knelt at my side, his weapon spitting bullets at the patrol boat. Dar Tarus' hands were busy with the controls and Hovan Du squatted in the bow and growled.

Suddenly Dar Tarus voiced an exclamation of alarm. "The controls are hit!" he shouted. "We can't alter our course—the ship is useless." Almost the same instant the searchlight was extinguished—one of my bullets evidently having found it. We were quite close to the enemy now and heard their shout of anger. Our own craft, out of control, was running swiftly toward the other. It seemed that if there was not a collision we would pass directly beneath the keel of the air patrol. I asked Dar Tarus if our ship was beyond repair.

"We could repair it if we had time," he replied, "but it would take hours and while we were thus delayed the whole air patrol force of Toonol would be upon us."

"Then we must have another ship," I said.

Dar Tarus laughed. "You are right, Vad Varo," he replied, "but where shall we find it?"

I pointed to the patrol boat. "We shall not have to look far."

Dar Tarus shrugged his shoulders. "Why not!" he exclaimed. "It would be a glorious fight and a worthy death."

Gor Hajus slapped me on the shoulder. "To the death, my captain!" he cried.

Hovan Du shook his chain and roared.

The two ships were rapidly approaching one another. We had stopped firing now for fear that we might disable the craft we hoped to use for our escape; and for some reason the crew of the patrol ship had ceased firing at us—I never learned why. We were moving in a line that would bring us directly beneath the other ship. I determined to board her at all costs. I could see her keel boarding tackle slung beneath her, ready to be lowered to the deck of a quarry when once her grappling hooks had seized the prey. Doubtless they were already manning the latter, and as soon as we were beneath her the steel tentacles would reach down and seize us as her crew swarmed down the boarding tackle to our deck.

I called Hovan Du and he crept back to my side where I whispered my instructions in his ear. When I was done he nodded his head with a low growl. I cast off the harness hook that held me to the deck, and the ape and I moved to our bow after I had issued brief, whispered instructions to Gor Hajus and Dar Tarus. We were now almost directly beneath the enemy craft; I could see the grappling hooks being prepared for lowering. Our bow ran beneath the stern of the other ship and the moment was at hand for which I had been waiting. Now those upon the deck of the patrol boat could not see Hovan Du or me. The boarding tackle of the other ship swung fifteen feet above our heads; I whispered a word of command to the ape and simultaneously we crouched and sprang for the tackle. It

may sound like a mad chance—failure meant almost certain death—but I felt that if two of us could reach the deck of the patrol boat while her crew was busy with the grappling gear it would be well worth the risk.

Gor Hajus had assured me that there would not be more than six men aboard the patrol ship; that one would be at the controls and the others manning the grappling hooks. It would be a most propitious time to gain a footing on the enemy's deck.

Hovan Du and I made our leaps and Fortune smiled upon us, though the huge ape but barely reached the tackle with one outstretched hand, while my earthly muscles carried me easily to my goal. Together we made our way rapidly toward the bow of the patrol craft and without hesitation, and as previously arranged, he clambered quickly up the starboard side and I the port. If I were the more agile jumper Hovan Du far outclassed me in climbing, with the result that he reached the rail and was clambering over while my eyes were still below the level of the deck, which was, perhaps, a fortunate thing for me since, by chance, I had elected to gain the deck directly at a point where, unknown to me, one of the crew of the ship was engaged with the grappling hooks. Had his eyes not been attracted elsewhere by the shout of one of his fellows who was first to see Hovan Du's savage face rise above the gunwale, he could have dispatched me with a single blow before ever I could have set foot upon the deck.

The ape had also come up directly in front of a Toonolian warrior and this fellow had let out a yell of surprise and sought to draw his sword, but the ape, for all his great bulk, was too quick for him; and as my eyes topped the rail I saw the mighty anthropoid seize the unfortunate man by the harness, drag him to the side and hurl him to destruction far below. Instantly we were both over the rail and squarely on deck while the remaining members of the craft's crew, abandoning their stations, ran forward to overpower us. I think that the sight of the great, savage beast must have had a demoralizing effect upon them, for they hesitated, each seeming to be willing to accord his fellow the honor of first engaging us; but they did come on, though slowly. This hesitation I was delighted to see, for it accorded perfectly with the plan that I had worked out, which depended

*I saw the mighty anthropoid hurl him to
destruction far below.*

largely upon the success which might attend the efforts of Gor Hajus and Dar Tarus to reach the deck of the patrol when our craft had risen sufficiently close beneath the other to permit them to reach the boarding tackle, which we were utilizing with reverse English, as one might say.

Gor Hajus had cautioned me to dispatch the man at the controls as quickly as possible, since his very first act would be to injure them the instant that there appeared any possibility that we might be successful in our attempt to take his ship, and so I ran quickly toward him and before he could draw I cut him down. There were not four against us and we waited for them to advance that we might gain time for our fellows to reach the deck.

The four moved slowly forward and were almost within striking distance when I saw Gor Hajus' head appear above the stern rail, quickly followed by that of Dar Tarus.

"Look!" I cried to the enemy, "and surrender," and I pointed astern.

One of them turned to look and what he saw brought an exclamation of surprise to his lips. "It is Gor Hajus," he cried, and then, to me: "What is your purpose with us if we surrender?"

"We have no quarrel with you," I replied. "We but wish to leave Toonol and go our way in peace—we shall not harm you."

He turned to his fellows while, at a sign from me, my three companions stopped their advance and waited. For a few minutes the four warriors conversed in low tones, then he who had first spoken addressed me.

"There are few Toonolians," he said, "who would not be glad to serve Gor Hajus, whom we had thought long dead, but to surrender our ship to you would mean certain death for us when we reported our defeat at our headquarters. On the other hand were we to continue our defense most of us here upon the deck of this flier would be killed. If you can assure us that your plans are not aimed at the safety of Toonol I can make a suggestion that will afford an avenue of escape and safety for us all."

"We only wish to leave Toonol," I replied. "No harm can come to Toonol because of what I seek to accomplish."

"Good! and where do you wish to go?"

"That I may not tell you."

"You may trust us, if you accept my proposal," he assured me, "which is that we convey you to your destination, after which we can return to Toonol and report that we engaged you and that after a long running fight, in which two of our number were killed, you eluded us in the darkness and escaped."

"Can we trust these men?" I asked, addressing Gor Hajus, who assured me that we could, and thus the compact was entered into which saw us speeding rapidly toward Phundahl aboard one of Vobis Kan's own fliers.

Chapter X

PHUNDAHL

The following night the Toonolian crew set us down just inside the wall of the city of Phundahl, following the directions of Dar Tarus who was a native of the city, had been a warrior of the Jeddara's Guard and, prior to that, seen service in Phundahl's tiny navy. That he was familiar with every detail of Phundahl's defenses and her systems of patrols was evidenced by the fact that we landed without detection and that the Toonolian ship rose and departed apparently unnoticed.

Our landing place had been the roof of a low building within and against the city wall. From this roof Dar Tarus led us down an inclined runway to the street, which, at this point, was quite deserted. The street was narrow and dark, being flanked upon one side by the low buildings built against the city wall and upon the other by higher buildings, some of which were windowless and none showing any light. Dar Tarus explained that he had chosen this point for our entrance because it was a district of storage houses, and while a hive of industry during the day, was always deserted at night, not even a watchman being required owing to the almost total absence of thievery upon Barsoom.

By devious and roundabout ways he led us finally to a section of second rate shops, eating places and hotels such as are frequented by the common soldiers, artisans and slaves, where the only attention we attracted was due to the curiosity aroused by Hovan Du. As we had not eaten since leaving Mu Tel's palace, our first consideration was food. Mu Tel had furnished Gor Hajus with money, so that we had the means to gratify our wants. Our first stop was at a small shop where Gor Hajus purchased four or five pounds of thoat steak for Hovan Du, and then we repaired to an eating place of which Dar Tarus knew. At first the proprietor would not let us bring Hovan Du inside, but finally, after much argument, he permitted us to lock the great ape in an inner room where Hovan Du was forced to remain with his thoat meat while we sat at a table in the outer room.

I will say for Hovan Du that he played his role well, nor was there once when the proprietor of the place, or any of his patrons, or the considerable crowd that gathered to listen to the altercation, could have guessed that the body of the great, savage beast was animated by a human brain. It was really only when feeding or fighting that the simian half of Hovan Du's brain appeared to exercise any considerable influence upon him; yet there seemed little doubt that it always colored all his thoughts and actions to some extent, accounting for his habitual taciturnity and the quickness with which he was aroused to anger, as well as to the fact that he never smiled, nor appeared to appreciate in any degree the humor of a situation. He assured me, however, that the human half of his brain not only appreciated but greatly enjoyed the lighter episodes and occurrences of our adventure and the witty stories and anecdotes related by Gor Hajus, the Assassin, but that his simian anatomy had developed no muscles wherewith to evidence physical expression of his mental reactions.

We dined heartily, though upon rough and simple fare, but were glad to escape the prying curiosity of the garrulous and gossipy proprietor, who plied us with so many questions as to our past performances and future plans that Dar Tarus, who was our spokesman here, was hard put to it to quickly fabricate replies that would be always consistent. However, escape we did at last, and once again in the street, Dar Tarus set out to lead us to a public lodging house of which he knew. As we went we approached a great building of wondrous beauty in and out of which constant streams of people were pouring, and when we were before it Dar Tarus asked us to wait without as he must enter. When I asked him why, he told me that this was a temple of Tur, the god worshipped by the people of Phundahl.

"I have been away for a long time," he said, "and have had no opportunity to do honor to my god. I shall not keep you waiting long. Gor Hajus, will you loan me a few pieces of gold?"

In silence the Toonolian took a few pieces of money from one of his pocket pouches and handed them to Dar Tarus, but I could see that it was only with difficulty that he hid an expression of contempt, since the Toonolians are atheists.

I asked Dar Tarus if I might accompany him into the temple, which seemed to please him very much; and so we fell in with the stream approaching the broad entrance. Dar Tarus gave me two of the gold pieces that he had borrowed from Gor Hajus and told me to follow directly behind him and do whatever I saw him doing. Directly inside the main entrance, and spread entirely across it at intervals that permitted space for the worshippers to pass between them, was a line of priests, their entire bodies, including their heads and faces, covered by a mantle of white cloth. In front of each was a substantial stand upon which rested a cash drawer. As we approached one of these we handed him a piece of gold which he immediately changed into many pieces of lesser value, one of which we dropped into a box at his side; whereupon he made several passes with his hands above our heads, dipped one of his fingers into a bowl of dirty water which he rubbed upon the ends of our noses, mumbled a few words which I could not understand and turned to the next in line as we passed on into the interior of the great temple. Never have I seen such a gorgeous display of wealth and lavish ornamentation as confronted my eyes in this, the first of the temples of Tur that it was my fortune to behold.

The enormous floor was unbroken by a single pillar and arranged upon it at regular intervals were carven images resting upon gorgeous pedestals. Some of these images were of men and some of women and many of them were beautiful; and there were others of beasts and of strange, grotesque creatures and many of these were hideous indeed. The first we approached was that of a beautiful female figure; and about the pedestal of this lay a number of men and women prone upon the floor against which they bumped their heads seven times and then arose and dropped a piece of money into a receptacle provided for that purpose, moving on then to another figure. The next that Dar Tarus and I visited was that of a man with the body of a *silian*, about the pedestal of which was arranged a series of horizontal wooden bars in concentric circles. The bars were about five feet from the floor and hanging from them by their knees were a number of men and women repeating monotonously, over and over again, something that sounded to me like, *bibble-babble-blup.*

Dar Tarus and I swung to the bars like the others and mumbled the meaningless phrase for a minute or two, then we swung down, dropped a coin into the box, and moved on. I asked Dar Tarus what the words were that we had repeated and what they meant, but he said he did not know. I asked him if anyone knew, but he appeared shocked and said that such a question was sacrilegious and revealed a marked lack of faith. At the next figure we visited the people were all upon their hands and knees crawling madly in a circle about the pedestal. Seven times around they crawled and then they rose and put some money in a dish and went their ways. At another the people rolled about, saying, "Tur is Tur; Tur is Tur; Tur is Tur," and dropping money in a golden bowl when they were done.

"What god was that?" I whispered to Dar Tarus when we had quit this last figure, which had no head, but eyes, nose and mouth in the center of its belly.

"There is but one god," replied Dar Tarus, solemnly, "and he is Tur!"

"Was that Tur?" I inquired.

"Silence, man," whispered Dar Tarus. "They would tear you to pieces were they to hear such heresy."

"Oh, I beg your pardon," I exclaimed. "I did not mean to offend. I see now that that is merely one of your idols."

Dar Tarus clapped a hand over my mouth. "S-s-s-t!" he cautioned to silence. "We do not worship idols—there is but one god and he is Tur!"

"Well, what are these?" I insisted, with a sweep of a hand that embraced the several score images about which were gathered the thousands of worshippers.

"We must not ask," he assured me. "It is enough that we have faith that all the works of Tur are just and righteous. Come!

I shall soon be through and we may join our companions."

He led me next to the figure of a monstrosity with a mouth that ran entirely around its head. It had a long tail and the breasts of a woman. About this image were a great many people, each standing upon his head. They also were repeating, over and over, "Tur is Tur; Tur is Tur; Tur is Tur." When we had done this for a minute or two, during which I had a devil of a time maintaining my equilibrium, we arose, dropped a coin into the box by the pedestal and moved on.

"We may go now," said Dar Tarus. "I have done well in the sight of Tur."

"I notice," I remarked, "that the people repeated the same phrase before this figure that they did at the last—Tur is Tur."

"Oh, no," exclaimed Dar Tarus. "On the contrary they said just exactly the opposite from what they said at the other. At that they said, Tur is Tur; while at this they absolutely reversed it and said, Tur is Tur. Do you not see? They turned it right around backwards, which makes a very great difference."

"It sounded the same to me," I insisted.

"That is because you lack faith," he said sadly, and we passed out of the temple after depositing the rest of our money in a huge chest, of which there were many standing about almost filled with coins.

We found Gor Hajus and Hoven Du awaiting us impatiently, the center of a large and curious throng among which were many warriors in the metal of Xaxa, the Jeddara of Phundahl. They wanted to see Hoven Du perform, but Dar Tarus told them that he was tired and in an ugly mood.

"Tomorrow," he said, "when he is rested I shall bring him out upon the avenues to amuse you."

With difficulty we extricated ourselves, and passing into a quieter avenue, took a roundabout way to the lodging place, where Hovan Du was confined in a small chamber while Gor Hajus, Dar Tarus and I were conducted by slaves to a large sleeping apartment where sleeping silks and furs were arranged for us upon a low platform that encircled the room and was broken only at the single entrance to the chamber. Here were already sleeping a considerable number of men, while two armed slaves patrolled the aisle to guard the guests from assassins.

It was still early and some of the other lodgers were conversing in low whispers so I sought to engage Dar Tarus in conversation relative to his religion, about which I was curious.

"The mysteries of religions always fascinate me, Dar Tarus," I told him.

"Ah, but that is the beauty of the religion of Tur," he exclaimed, "it has no mysteries. It is simple, natural, scientific and every word and work of it is susceptible of proof through the pages of Turgan, the great book written by Tur himself.

"Tur's home is upon the sun. There, one hundred thousand years ago, he made Barsoom and tossed it out into space. Then he amused himself by creating man in various forms and two sexes; and later he fashioned animals to be food for man and each other, and caused vegetation and water to appear that man and the animals might live. Do you not see how simple and scientific it all is?"

But it was Gor Hajus who told me most about the religion of Tur one day when Dar Tarus was not about. He said that the Phundahlians maintained that Tur still created every living thing with his own hands. They denied vigorously that man possessed the power to reproduce his kind and taught their young that all such belief was vile; and always they hid every evidence of natural procreation, insisting to the death that even those things which they witnessed with their own eyes and experienced with their own bodies in the bringing forth of their young never transpired.

Turgan taught them that Barsoom is flat and they shut their minds to every proof to the contrary. They would not leave Phundahl far for fear of falling off the edge of the world; they would not permit the development of aeronautics because should one of their ships circumnavigate Barsoom it would be a wicked sacrilege in the eyes of Tur who made Barsoom flat.

They would not permit the use of telescopes, for Tur taught them that there was no other world than Barsoom and to look at another would be heresy; nor would they permit the teaching in their schools of any history of Barsoom that antedated the creation of Barsoom by Tur, though Barsoom has a well authenticated written history that reaches back more than one hundred

thousand years; nor would they permit any geography of Barsoom except that which appears in Turgan, nor any scientific researches along biological lines. Turgan is their only text book—if it is not in Turgan it is a wicked lie.

Much of all this and a great deal more I gathered from one source or another during my brief stay in Phundahl, whose people are, I believe, the least advanced in civilization of any of the red nations upon Barsoom. Giving, as they do, all their best thought to religious matters, they have become ignorant, bigoted and narrow, going as far to one extreme as the Toonolians do to the other.

However, I had not come to Phundahl to investigate her culture but to steal her queen, and that thought was uppermost in my mind when I awoke to a new day—my first in Phundahl. Following the morning meal we set out in the direction of the palace to reconnoiter, Dar Tarus leading us to a point from which he might easily direct us the balance of the way, as he did not dare accompany us to the immediate vicinity of the royal grounds for fear of recognition, the body he now possessed having formerly belonged to a well known noble.

It was arranged that Gor Hajus should act as spokesman and I as keeper of the ape. This arranged, we bade farewell to Dar Tarus and set forth, the three of us, along a broad and beautiful avenue that led directly to the palace gates. We had been planning and rehearsing the parts that we were to play and which we hoped would prove so successful that they would open the gates to us and win us to the presence of the Jeddara.

As we strolled with seeming unconcern along the avenue, I had ample opportunity to enjoy the novel and beautiful sights of this rich boulevard of palaces. The sun shone down upon vivid scarlet lawns, gorgeous flowered pimalia and a score of other rarely beautiful Barsoomian shrubs and trees, while the avenue itself was shaded by almost perfect specimens of the magnificent sorapus. The sleeping apartments of the buildings had all been lowered to their daytime level, and from a hundred balconies gorgeous silks and furs were airing in the sun. Slaves were briskly engaged with their duties about the grounds, while upon many a balcony women and children sat at their morning meal. Among the children we aroused considerable enthusiasm, or at least Hovan Du did, nor was he without interest to the adults. Some of them would have detained us for an exhibition, but we moved steadily on toward the palace, for nowhere else had we business or concern within the walls of Phundahl.

Around the palace gates was the usual crowd of loitering curiosity seekers; for after all human nature is much the same everywhere, whether skins be black or white, red or yellow or brown, upon Earth or upon Mars. The crowd before Xaxa's gates was largely made up of visitors from the islands of that part of the Great Toonolian Marshes which owes allegiance to Phundahl's queen, and like all provincials eager for a glimpse of royalty; though none the less to be interested by the antics of a simian, wherefore we had a ready made audience awaiting our arrival. Their natural fear of the great brute caused them to fall back a little at our approach so that we had a clear avenue to the very gates themselves, and there we halted while the crowds closed in behind, forming a half circle about us. Gor Hajus addressed them in a loud tone of voice that might be overheard by the warriors and their officers beyond the gates, for it was really them we had come to entertain, not the crowds in which we had not the slightest interest.

"Men and women of Phundahl," cried Gor Hajus, "behold two poor panthans, who, risking their lives, have captured and trained one of the most savage and ferocious and at the same time most intelligent specimens of the great white ape of Barsoom ever before seen in captivity and at great expense have brought it to Phundahl for your entertainment and edification. My friends, this wonderful ape is endowed with human intelligence; he understands every word that is spoken to him. With your kind attention, my friends, I will endeavor to demonstrate the remarkable intelligence that has entertained the crowned heads of Barsoom and mystified the minds of her most learned savants."

I thought Gor Hajus did pretty well as a bally-hoo artist. I had to smile as I listened, here upon Mars, to the familiar lines that I had taught him out of my Earthly experience of county fairs and amusement parks, so highly ludicrous they sounded falling from the lips of the Assassin of Toonol; but

they evidently interested his auditors and impressed them, too, for they craned their necks and stood in earnest eyed silence awaiting the performance of Hovan Du. Even better, several members of the Jeddara's Guard pricked up their ears and sauntered toward the gates; and among them was an officer.

Gor Hajus caused Hovan Du to lie down at word of command, to get up, to stand upon one foot, and to indicate the number of fingers that Gor Hajus held up by growling once for each finger, thus satisfying the audience that he could count; but these simple things were only by way of leading up to the more remarkable achievements which we hoped would win an audience before the Jeddara. Gor Hajus borrowed a set of harness and weapons from a man in the crowd and had Hovan Du don it and fence with him, and then indeed did we hear exclamations of amazement.

The warriors and the officer of Xaxa had drawn near the gates and were interested spectators, which was precisely what we wished, and now Gor Hajus was ready for the final, astounding revelation of Hovan Du's intelligence.

"These things that you have witnessed are as nothing," he cried. "Why this wonderful beast can even read and write. He was captured in a deserted city near Ptarth and can read and write the language of that country. Is there among you one who, by chance, comes from that distant country?"

A slave spoke up. "I am from Ptarth."

"Good!" said Gor Hajus. "Write some simple instructions and hand them to the ape. I will turn my back that you may know that I cannot assist him in any way."

The slave drew forth a tablet from a pocket pouch and wrote briefly. What he wrote he handed to Hovan Du. The ape read the message and without hesitation moved quickly to the gate and handed it to the officer standing upon the other side, the gate being constructed of wrought metal in fanciful designs that offered no obstruction to the view or to the passage of small articles. The officer took the message and examined it.

"What does it say?" he demanded of the slave that had penned it.

"It says," replied the latter: "Take this message to the officer who stands just within the gates."

There were exclamations of surprise

from all parts of the crowd and Hovan Du was compelled to repeat his performance several times with different messages which directed him to do various things, the officer always taking a great interest in the proceedings.

"It is marvellous," said he at last. "The Jeddara would be amused by the performance of this beast. Wait here, therefore, until I have sent word to her that she may, if she so desires, command your presence."

Nothing could have better suited us and so we waited with what patience we might for the messenger to return; and while we waited Hovan Du continued to mystify his audience with new proofs of his great intelligence.

Chapter XI

XAXA

The officer returned, the gates swung out and we were commanded to enter the courtyard of the palace of Xaxa, Jeddara of Phundahl. After that events transpired with great rapidity—surprising and totally unexpected events. We were led through an intricate maze of corridors and chambers until I became suspicious that we were purposely being confused, and convinced that whether such was the intention or not the fact remained that I could no more have retraced my steps to the outer courtyard than I could have flown without wings. We had planned that, in the event of gaining admission to the palace, we would carefully note whatever might be essential to a speedy escape; but when, in a whisper, I asked Gor Hajus if he could find his way out again he assured me that he was as confused as I.

The palace was in no sense remarkable nor particularly interesting, the work of the Phundahlian artists being heavy and oppressing and without indication of high imaginative genius. The scenes depicted were mostly of a religious nature illustrating passages from Turgan, the Phundahlian bible, and, for the most part, were a series of monotonous repetitions. There was one, which appeared again and again, depicting Turgan creating a round, flat Mars and hurling it into Space, that always reminded me of a culinary artist turning a flap jack in a Childs' window.

There were also numerous paintings of what appeared to be court scenes delineating members of the Phundahlian royal line in various activities; it was noticeable that the more recent ones in which Xaxa appeared had had the principal figure repainted so that there confronted me from time to time portraits, none too well done, of the beautiful face and figure of Valla Dia in the royal trappings of a jeddara. The effect of these upon me is not easy of description. They brought home to me the fact that I was approaching, and should presently be face to face with, the person of the woman to whom I had consecrated my love and my life, and yet in that same person I should be confronting one whom I loathed and would destroy.

We were halted at last before a great door and from the number of warriors and nobles congregated before it I was confident that we were soon to be ushered into the presence of the Jeddara. As we waited those assembled about us eyed us with, it seemed to me, more of hostility than curiosity and when the door swung open they accompanied us, with the exception of a few warriors, into the chamber beyond. The room was of medium size and at the farther side, behind a massive table, sat Xaxa. About her were grouped a number of heavily armed nobles. As I looked them over I wondered if among them was he for whom the body of Dar Tarus had been filched; for we had promised him that if conditions were favorable we would attempt to recover it.

Xaxa eyed us coldly as we were halted before her. "Let us see the beast perform," she commanded, and then suddenly: "What mean you by permitting strangers to enter my presence bearing arms?" she cried. "Sag Or, see that their weapons are removed!" and she turned to a handsome young warrior standing near her.

Sag Or! That was the name. Before me stood the noble for whom Dar Tarus had suffered the loss of his liberty, his body and his love. Gor Hajus had also recognized the name and Hovan Du, too; I could tell by the way they eyed the man as he advanced. Curtly he instructed us to hand our weapons to two warriors who advanced to receive them. Gor Hajus hesitated. I admit that I did not know what course to pursue. Everyone seemed hostile and yet that might be, and doubtless was, but a reflection of their attitude toward all strangers.

If we refused to disarm we were but three against a room full, if they chose to resort to force; or if they turned us out of the palace because of it we would be robbed of this seemingly god given opportunity to win to the very heart of Xaxa's palace and to her very presence, where we must eventually win before we could strike. Would such an opportunity ever be freely offered us again? I doubted it and felt that we had better assume a vague risk now than, by refusing their demand, definitely arm their suspicions. So I quietly removed my weapons and handed them to the warrior waiting to receive them; and following my example, Gor Hajus did likewise, though I can imagine with what poor grace.

Once again Xaxa signified that she would see Hovan Du perform. As Gor Hajus put him through his antics she watched listlessly; nor did anything that the ape did arouse the slightest flicker of interest among the entire group assembled about the Jeddara. As the thing dragged on I became obsessed with apprehensions that all was not right. It seemed to me that an effort was being made to detain us for some purpose—to gain time. I could not understand, for instance, why Xaxa required that we repeat several times the least interesting of the ape's performances. And all the time Xaxa sat playing with a long, slim dagger, and I saw that she watched me quite as much as she watched Hovan Du, while I found it difficult to keep my eyes averted from that perfect face, even though I knew that it was but a stolen mask behind which lurked the cruel mind of a tyrant and a murderess.

At last came an interruption to the performance. The door opened and a noble entered, who went directly to the Jeddara whom he addressed briefly and in a low tone. I saw that she asked him several questions and that she seemed vexed by his replies. Then she dismissed him with a curt gesture and turned toward us.

"Enough of this!" she cried. Her eyes rested upon mine and she pointed her slim dagger at me. "Where is the other?" she demanded.

"What other?" I inquired.

"There were three of you, beside the ape, nor I know nothing about the ape, nor where, nor how you acquired it; but I do know all about you, Vad Varo, and Gor Hajus, the Assassin of Toonol, and Dar

Tarus. Where is Dar Tarus?" her voice was low and musical and entirely beautiful—the voice of Valla Dia—but behind it I knew was the terrible personality of Xaxa, and I knew too that it would be hard to deceive her, for she must have received what information she had directly from Ras Thavas. It had been stupid of me not to foresee that Ras Thavas would immediately guess the purpose of my mission and warn Xaxa. I perceived instantly that it would be worse than useless to deny our identity, rather I must explain our presence—if I could.

"Where is Dar Tarus?" she repeated.

"How should I know?" I countered. "Dar Tarus has reasons to believe that he would not be safe in Phundahl and I imagine that he is not anxious that any one should know his whereabouts—myself included. He helped me to escape from the Island of Thavas, for which his liberty was to be his reward. He has not chosen to accompany me further upon my adventures."

Xaxa seemed momentarily disarmed that I did not deny my identity—evidently she had supposed that I would do so.

"You admit then," she said, "that you are Vad Varo, the assistant of Ras Thavas?"

"Have I ever sought to deny it?"

"You have disguised yourself as a redman of Barsoom."

"How could I travel in Barsoom otherwise, where every man's hand is against a stranger?"

"Any why would you travel in Barsoom?" Her eyes narrowed as she waited for my reply.

"As Ras Thavas has doubtless sent you word, I am from another world and I would see more of this one," I told her. "Is that strange?"

"And you come to Phundahl and seek to gain entrance to my presence and bring with you the notorious Assassin of Toonol that you may see more of Barsoom?"

"Gor Hajus may not return to Toonol," I explained, "and so he must seek service for his sword at some other court than that of Vobis Kan—in Phundahl perhaps, or if not here he must move on. I hope that he will decide to accompany me as I am a stranger in Barsoom, unaccustomed to the manners and ways of her people. I would fare ill without a guide and mentor."

"You shall fare ill," she cried. "You have seen all of Barsoom that you are destined to see—you have reached the end of your adventure. You think to deceive me, eh? You do not know, perhaps, that I have heard of your infatuation for Valla Dia or that I am fully conversant with the purpose of your visit to Phundahl." Her eyes left me and swept her nobles and her warriors. "To the pits with them!" she cried. "Later we shall choose the manner of their passing."

Instantly we were surrounded by a score of naked blades. There was no escape for Gor Hajus or me, but I thought that I saw an opportunity for Hovan Du to get away. I had had the possibility of such a contingency in mind from the first and always I had been on the lookout for an avenue of escape for one of us, and so the open windows at the right of the Jeddara had not gone unnoticed, nor the great trees growing in the courtyard beneath. Hovan Du was close beside me as Xaxa spoke.

"Go!" I whispered. "The windows are open. Go, and tell Dar Tarus what has happened to us," and then I fell back away from him and dragged Gor Hajus with me as though we would attempt to resist arrest; and while I thus distracted their attention from him Hovan Du turned toward an open window. He had taken but a few steps when a warrior attempted to halt him; with that the ferocious brain of the anthropoid seemed to seize dominion over the great creature. With a hideous growl he leaped with the agility of a cat upon the unfortunate Phundahlian, swung him high in giant hands and using his body as a flail tumbled his fellows to right and left as he cut a swath toward the open window nearest him.

Instantly pandemonium reigned in the apartment. The attention of all seemed centered upon the great ape and even those who had been confronting us turned to attack Hovan Du. And in the midst of the confusion I saw Xaxa step to some heavy hangings directly behind her desk, part them and disappear.

"Come!" I whispered to Gor Hajus. Apparently intent only upon watching the conflict between the ape and the warriors I moved forward with the fighters but always to the left toward the desk that Xaxa had just quitted. Hovan Du was giving a good account of himself. He had discarded his first victim and one by one had seized others as they came within range of his long arms and powerful hands, sometimes four at a time as he stood well braced upon two of his hand-like feet and fought with the other four. His shock of bristling hair stood erect upon his skull and his fierce eyes blazed with rage as, towering high above his antagonists, he fought for his life—the most feared of all the savage creatures of Barsoom. Perhaps his greatest advantage lay in the inherent fear of him that was a part of every man in that room who faced him, and it forwarded my quickly conceived plan, too, for it kept every eye turned upon Hovan Du, so that Gor Hajus and I were able to work our way to the rear of the desk. I think Hovan Du must have sensed my intention then, for he did the one thing best suited to attract every eye from us to him and, too, he gave me notice that the human half of his brain was still alert and watchful of our welfare.

Heretofore the Phundahlians must have looked upon him as a remarkable specimen of great ape, marvellously trained, but now, of a sudden, he paralyzed them with awe, for his roars and growls took the form of words and he spoke with the tongue of a human. He was near the window now. Several of the nobles were pushing bravely forward. Among them was Sag Or. Hoven Du reached forth and seized him, wrenching his weapons from him. "I go," he cried, "but let harm befall my friends and I shall return and tear the heart from Xaxa. Tell her that, from the Great Ape of Ptarth."

For an instant the warriors and the nobles stood transfixed with awe. Every eye was upon Hovan Du as he stood there with the struggling figure of Sag Or in his mighty grasp. Gor Hajus and I were forgotten. And then Hovan Du turned and leaped to the sill of the window and from there lightly to the branches of the nearest tree; and with him went Sag Or, the favorite of Xaxa, the Jeddara. At the same instant I drew Gor Hajus with me between the hangings in the rear of Xaxa's desk, and as they fell behind us we found ourselves in the narrow mouth of a dark corridor.

Without knowledge of where the passage led we could only follow it blindly, urged on by the necessity for discovering a hiding place or an avenue of escape from the palace before the pursuit, which we knew would be immediately instituted, overtook us. As our eyes became accustomed to the gloom, which was partially dispelled by a faint luminosity, we moved more rapidly and presently came to a narrow spiral runway which descended into a dark hole below the level of the corridor and also rose into equal darkness above.

"Which way?" I asked Gor Hajus.

"They will expect us to descend," he replied, "for in that direction lies the nearest avenue of escape."

"Then we will go up."

"Good!" he exclaimed. "All we seek now is a place to hide until night has fallen, for we may not escape by day."

We had scarcely started to ascend before we heard the first sound of pursuit—the clank of accouterments in the corridor beneath. Yet, even with this urge from behind, we were forced to move with great caution, for we knew not what lay before. At the next level there was a doorway, the door closed and locked, but there was no corridor, nor anywhere to hide, and so we continued on upward. The second level was identical with that just beneath, but at the third a single corridor ran straight off into darkness and at our right was a door, ajar. The sounds of pursuit were appreciably nearer now and the necessity for concealment seemed increasing as the square of their growing proportions until every other consideration was overwhelmed by it. Nor is this so strange when the purpose of my adventure is considered and that discovery now must assuredly spell defeat and blast forever the slender ray of hope that remained for the resurrection of Valla Dia in her own flesh.

There was scarce a moment of consideration. The corridor before us was shrouded in darkness—it might be naught but a blind alley. The door was close and ajar. I pushed it gently inward. An odor of heavy incense greeted our nostrils and through the small aperture we saw a portion of a large chamber garishly decorated. Directly before us, and almost wholly obstructing our view of the entire chamber, stood a colossal statue of a squatting man-like figure. Behind us we heard voices—our pursuers already were ascending the spiral—they would be upon us in a few seconds. I examined the door and discovered that it fastened with a spring lock. I looked again into the chamber and saw no one within the range of our vision, and then I motioned Gor Hajus to follow me and stepping into the room closed the door behind us. We had burned our bridges. As the door closed the lock engaged with a sharp, metallic click.

"What was that?" demanded a voice, originating, seemingly, at the far end of the chamber.

Gor Hajus looked at me and shrugged his shoulders in resignation (he must have been thinking what I was thinking—that with two avenues we had chosen the wrong one) but he smiled and there was no reproach in his eyes.

"It sounded from the direction of the Great Tur," replied a second voice.

"Perhaps someone is at the door," suggested the first speaker.

Gor Hajus and I were flattened against the back of the statue that we might postpone as long as possible our inevitable discovery should the speakers decide to investigate the origin of the noise that had attracted their suspicions. I was facing against the polished stone of the figure's back, my hands outspread upon it. Beneath my fingers were the carven bits of its ornamental harness—jutting protuberances that were costly gems set in these trappings of stone, and there were gorgeous inlays of gold filagree; but these things I had no eyes for now. We could hear the two conversing as they came nearer. Perhaps I was nervous. I do not know. I am sure I never shrank from an encounter when either duty or expediency called; but in this instance both demanded that we avoid conflict and remain undiscovered. However that may be, my fingers must have been moving nervously over the jeweled harness of the figure when I became vaguely, perhaps subconsciously, aware that one of the gems was loose in its setting. I do not recall that this made any impression upon my conscious mind, but I do know that it seemed to catch the attention of my wandering fingers and they must have paused to play with the loosened stone.

The voices seemed quite close now—it could be but a matter of seconds before we should be confronted by their owners. My muscles seemed to tense for the anticipated encounter and unconsciously I pressed heavily upon the loosened setting—whereat a portion of the figure's back gave noiselessly inward revealing to us the dimly lighted interior of the statue. We needed no further invitation; simultaneously we stepped across the threshold and in almost the same movement I turned and closed the panel gently behind us. I think that there was absolutely no sound connected with the entire transaction; and following it we remained in utter silence, motionless—scarce breathing. Our eyes became quickly accustomed to the dim interior which we discovered was lighted through numerous small orifices in the shell of the statue, which was entirely hollow, and through these same orifices every outside sound came clearly to our ears.

We had scarcely closed the opening when we heard the voices directly outside it and simultaneously there came a hammering on the door by which we had entered the apartment from the corridor. "Who seeks entrance to Xaxa's Temple?" demanded one of the voices within the room.

"'Tis I, dwar of the Jeddara's Guard," boomed a voice from without. "We are seeking two who came to assassinate Xaxa."

"Came they this way?"

"Think you, priest, that I should be seeking them here had they not?"

"How long since?"

"Scarce twenty tals since," replied the dwar.

"Then they are not here," the priest assured him, "for we have been here for a full zode* and no other has entered the temple during that time. Look quickly to Xaxa's apartments above and to the roof and the hangars, for if you followed them up the spiral there is no other where they might flee."

"Watch then the temple carefully until I return," shouted the warrior and we heard him and his men moving on up the spiral.

Now we heard the priests conversing as they moved slowly past the statue.

"What could have caused the noise that first attracted our attention?" asked one.

"Perhaps the fugitives tried the door," suggested the other.

"It must have been that, but they did not enter or we should have seen them when they emerged from behind the Great Tur, for we were facing him at the time, nor have once turned our eyes from this end of the temple."

"Then at least they are not within the temple."

"And where else they may be is no concern of ours."

"No, nor if they reached Xaxa's apartment, if they did not pass through the temple."

"Perhaps they did reach it."

"And they were assassins!"

"Worse things might befall Phundahl."

"Hush! the gods have ears."

"Of stone."

"But the ears of Xaxa are not of stone and they hear many things that are not intended for them."

"The old she-banth!"

"She is Jeddara and High Priestess."

"Yes, but——" the voices passed beyond the range of our ears at the far end of the temple, yet they had told me much—that Xaxa was feared and hated by the priesthood and that the priests themselves had none too much reverence for their deity, as evidenced by the remark of one that the gods have ears of stone. And they had told us other things, important things, when they conversed with the dwar of the Jeddara's Guard.

Gor Hajus and I now felt that we had fallen by chance upon a most ideal place of concealment, for the very guardians of the temple would swear that we were not, could not be, where we were. Already had they thrown the pursuers off our track.

Now, for the first time, we had an opportunity to examine our hiding place. The interior of the statue was hollow and far above us, perhaps forty feet, we could see the outside light shining through the mouth, ears and nostrils, just below which a circular platform could be discerned running around the inside of the neck. A ladder with flat rungs led upward from the base to the platform. Thick dust covered the floor on which we stood, and the extremity of our position suggested a careful examination of this dust, with the result that I was at once impressed by the evidence that it revealed; which indicated that we were the first to enter the statue for a long time, possibly for years, as the fine coating of almost impalpable dust that covered the floor was undisturbed. As I searched for this evidence my eyes fell upon something lying huddled close to the base of the ladder and approaching nearer I saw that it was a human skeleton, while a closer examination revealed that the skull was crushed and one arm and several ribs broken. About it lay, dust covered, the most gorgeous trappings I had ever seen. Its position at the foot of the ladder, as well as the crushed skull and broken bones, appeared quite conclusive evidence of the manner in which death had come—the man had fall-

*A tal is about one second, and a zode approximately two and one-half hours, Earth time.

en head foremost from the circular platform forty feet above, carrying with him to eternity, doubtless, the secret of the entrance to the interior of the Great Tur.

I suggested this to Gor Hajus who was examining the dead man's trappings and he agreed with me that such must have been the manner of his death.

"He was a high priest of Tur," whispered Gor Hajus, "and probably a member of the royal house—possibly a jeddak. He has been dead a long time."

"I am going up above," I said. "I will test the ladder. If it is safe, follow me up. I think we shall be able to see the interior of the temple through the mouth of Tur."

"Go carefully," Gor Hajus admonished. "The ladder is very old."

I went carefully, testing each rung before I trusted my weight to it, but I found the old sorapus wood of which it was constructed sound and as stanch as steel. How the high priest came to his death must always remain a mystery, for the ladder or the circular platform would have carried the weight of a hundred red-men.

From the platform I could see through the mouth of Tur. Below me was a large chamber along the sides of which were ranged other, though lesser, idols. They were even more grotesque than those I had seen in the temple in the city and their trappings were rich beyond the conception of man—Earthman—for the gems of Barsoom scintillate with rays unknown to us and of such gorgeous and blinding beauty as to transcend description. Directly in front of the Great Tur was an altar of palthon, a rare and beautiful stone, blood red, in which are traced in purest white Nature's most fanciful designs; the whole vastly enhanced by the wondrous polish which the stone takes beneath the hand of the craftsman.

Gor Hajus joined me and together we examined the interior of the temple. Tall windows lined two sides, letting in a flood of light. At the far end, opposite the Great Tur, were two enormous doors, closing the main entrance to the chamber, and here stood the two priests whom we had heard conversing. Otherwise the temple was deserted. Incense burned upon tiny altars before each of the minor idols, but whether any burned before the Great Tur we could not see.

Having satisfied our curiosity relative to the temple, we returned our attention to a further examination of the interior of Tur's huge head and were rewarded by the discovery of another ladder leading upward against the rear wall to a higher and smaller platform that evidently led to the eyes. It did not take me long to investigate and here I found a most comfortable chair set before a control that operated the eyes, so that they could be made to turn from side to side, or up or down, according to the whim of the operator; and here too was a speaking tube leading to the mouth. This again I must needs investigate and so I returned to the lower platform and there I discovered a device beneath the tongue of the idol, and this device, which was in the nature of an amplifier, was connected with the speaking tube from above. I could not repress a smile as I considered these silent witnesses to the perfidy of man and thought of the broken thing lying at the foot of the ladder. Tur, I could have sworn, had been silent for many years.

Together Gor Hajus and I returned to the higher platform and again I made a discovery—the eyes of Tur were veritable periscopes. By turning them we could see any portion of the temple and what we saw through the eyes was magnified. Nothing could escape the eyes of Tur and presently, when the priests began to talk again, we discovered that nothing could escape Tur's ears, for every slightest sound in the temple came clearly to us. What a valuable adjunct to high priesthood this Great Tur must have been in the days when that broken skeleton lying below us was a thing of blood and life!

Chapter XII

THE GREAT TUR

The day dragged wearily for Gor Hajus and me. We watched the various priests who came in pairs at intervals to relieve those who had preceded them, and we listened to their prattle, mostly idle gossip of court scandals. At times they spoke of us and we learned that Hovan Du had escaped with Sag Or, nor had they been located as yet, nor had Dar Tarus. The whole court was mystified by our seemingly miraculous disappearance. Three thousand people, the inmates and attaches of the palace, were constantly upon the lookout for us. Every part of the palace and the palace grounds had been searched and searched again. The pits had been explored more thoroughly than they had been explored within the memory of the oldest retainer, and it seemed that queer things had been unearthed there—things of which not even Xaxa dreamed; and the priests whispered that at least one great and powerful house would fall because of what a dwar of the Jeddara's Guard had discovered in a remote precinct of the pits.

As the sun dropped below the horizon and darkness came, the interior of the temple was illuminated by a soft white light, brilliantly but without the glare of Earthly artificial illumination. More priests came and many young girls, priestesses. They performed before the idols, chanting meaningless gibberish. Gradually the chamber filled with worshippers, nobles of the Jeddara's court with their women and their retainers, forming in two lines along either side of the temple before the lesser idols, leaving a wide aisle from the great entrance to the foot of the Great Tur and toward this aisle they all faced, waiting. For what were they waiting? Their eyes were turned expectantly toward the closed doors of the great entrance and Gor Hajus and I felt our eyes held there too, fascinated by the suggestion that they were about to open and reveal some stupendous spectacle.

And presently the doors did swing slowly open and all we saw was what appeared to be a great roll of carpet lying upon its side across the opening. Twenty slaves, naked but for their scant leather harness, stood behind the huge roll; and as the doors swung fully open they rolled the carpet inward to the very feet of the altar before the Great Tur, covering the wide aisle from the entranceway almost to the idol with a thick, soft rug of gold and white and blue. It was the most beautiful thing in the temple where all else was blatant, loud and garish, or hideous, or grotesque. And then the doors closed and again we waited; but not for long. Bugles sounded from without, the sound increasing as they neared the entrance. Once more the doors swung in. Across the entrance stood a double rank of gorgeously trapped nobles. Slowly they entered the temple and behind them came a splendid chariot drawn by two banths, the fierce Barsoomian lion, held in leash by slaves on either side. Upon the chariot was a litter and in the litter, reclining at ease,

lay Xaxa. As she entered the temple the people commenced to chant her praises in a monotonous sing-song. Chained to the chariot and following on foot was a red warrior and behind him a procession composed of fifty young men and an equal number of young girls.

Gor Hajus touched my arm. "The prisoner," he whispered, "do you recognize him?"

"Dar Tarus!" I exclaimed.

It was Dar Tarus—they had discovered his hiding place and arrested him, but what of Hovan Du? Had they taken him, also? If they had it must have been only after slaying him, for they never would have sought to capture the fierce beast, nor would he have brooked capture. I looked for Sag Or, but he was no where to be seen within the temple and this fact gave me hope that Hovan Du might be still at liberty.

The chariot was halted before the altar and Xaxa alighted; the lock that held Dar Tarus' chain to the vehicle was opened and the banths were led away by their attendants to one side of the temple behind the lesser idols. Then Dar Tarus was dragged roughly to the altar and thrown upon it and Xaxa, mounting the steps at its base, came close to his side and with hands outstretched above him looked up at the Great Tur towering above her. How beautiful she was! How richly trapped! Ah, Valla Dia! that your sweet form should be debased to the cruel purposes of the wicked mind that now animates you!"

Xaxa's eyes now rested upon the face of the Great Tur. "O, Tur, Father of Barsoom," she cried, "behold the offering we place before you, All-seeing, All-knowing, All-powerful One, and frown no more upon us in silence. For a hundred years you have not deigned to speak aloud to your faithful slaves; never since Hora San, the high priest, was taken away by you on that long gone night of mystery have you unsealed your lips to your people. Speak, Great Tur! Give us some sign, ere we plunge this dagger into the heart of our offering, that our works are pleasing in thine eyes. Tell us whither went the two who came here today to assassinate your high priestess; reveal to us the fate of Sag Or. Speak, Great Tur, ere I strike," and she raised her slim blade above the heart of Dar Tarus and looked straight upward into the eyes of Tur.

"Speak, Great Tur, ere I strike."

And then, as a bolt from the blue, I was struck by the great inspiration. My hand sought the lever controlling the eyes of Tur and I turned them until they completed a full circuit of the room and rested again upon Xaxa. The effect was magical. Never before had I seen a whole room full of people so absolutely stunned and awe struck as were these. As the eyes returned to Xaxa she seemed turned to stone and her copper skin to have taken on an ashen purple hue. Her dagger remained stiffly poised above the heart of Dar Tarus. Not for a hundred years had they seen the eyes of the Great Tur move. Then I placed the speaking tube to my lips and the voice of Tur rumbled through the chamber. As from one great throat a gasp arose from the crowded temple floor and the people fell upon their knees and buried their faces in their hands.

"Judgment is mine!" I cried. "Strike not lest ye be struck! To Tur is the sacrifice!"

I was silent then, attempting to plan how best to utilize the advantage I had gained. Fearfully, one by one, the bowed heads were raised and frightened eyes sought the face of Tur. I gave them another thrill by letting the god's eyes wander slowly over the upturned faces, and while I was doing this I had another inspiration, which I imparted to Gor Hajus in a low whisper. I could hear him chuckle as he started down the ladder to carry my new plan into effect. Again I had recourse to the speaking tube.

"The sacrifice is Tur's" I rumbled. "Tur will strike with his own hand. Extinguish the lights and let no one move under pain of instant death until Tur gives the word. Prostrate yourselves and bury your eyes in your palms, for whosoever sees shall be blinded when the spirit of Tur walks among his people."

Down they went again and one of the priests hurriedly extinguished the lights, leaving the temple in total darkness; and while Gor Hajus was engaged with his part of the performance I tried to cover any accidental noise he might make by keeping up a running fire of celestial revelation.

"Xaxa, the high priestess, asks what has become of the two whom she believed came to assassinate her. I, Tur, took them to myself. Vengeance is Tur's! And Sag Or I took, also. In the guise of a great ape I came and took Sag Or and none knew me; though even a fool might have guessed, for who is there ever heard a great ape speak with tongue of man unless he was animated by the spirit of Tur?"

I guess that convinced them, it being just the sort of logic suited to their religion, or it would have convinced them if they had not already been convinced. I wondered what might be passing in the mind of the doubting priest who had remarked that the gods had ears of stone.

Presently I heard a noise upon the ladder beneath me and a moment later someone climbed upon the circular landing.

"All's well," whispered the voice of Gor Hajus. "Dar Tarus is with me."

"Light the temple!" I commanded through the speaking tube. "Rise and look upon your altar."

The lights flashed on and the people rose, trembling, to their feet. Every eye was bent upon the altar and what they saw there seemed to crush them with terror. Some of the women screamed and fainted. It all impressed me with the belief that none of them had taken this god of theirs with any great amount of seriousness, and now when they were confronted with absolute proof of his miraculous powers they were swept completely off their feet. Where, a few moments before, they had seen a live sacrifice awaiting the knife of the high priestess they saw now only a dust covered human skull. I grant you that without an explanation it might have seemed a miracle to almost anyone so quickly had Gor Hajus run from the base of the idol with the skull of the dead high priest and returned again leading Dar Tarus with him. I had been a bit concerned as to what the attitude of Dar Tarus might be, who was no more conversant with the hoax than were the Phundahlians, but Gor Hajus had whispered "For Valla Dia" in his ear and he had understood and come quickly.

"The Great Tur," I now announced, "is angry with his people. For a long time they have denied him in their hearts even while they made open worship to him. The Great Tur is angry with Xaxa. Only through Xaxa may the people of Phundahl be saved from destruction, for the Great Tur is angry. Go then from the temple and the palace leaving no human being here other than Xaxa, the high priestess of Tur. Leave her here in solitude beside the altar. Tur would speak with her alone."

I could see Xaxa fairly shrivel in fright.

"Is the Jeddara Xaxa, High Priestess of the Great God Tur, afraid to meet her master?" I demanded. The woman's jaw trembled so that she could not reply. "Obey! or Xaxa and all her people shall be struck dead!" I fairly screamed at them.

Like cattle they turned and fled toward the entrance and Xaxa, her knees shaking so that she could scarce stand erect, staggered after them. A noble saw her and pushed her roughly back, but she shrieked and ran after him when he had left her. Then others dragged her to the foot of the altar and threw her roughly down and one menaced her with his sword, but at that I called aloud that no harm must befall the Jeddara if they did not wish the wrath of Tur to fall upon them all. They left her lying there and so weak from fright that she could not rise, and a moment later the temple was empty, but not until I had shouted after them to clear the whole palace within a quarter zode, for my plan required a free and unobstructed as well as unobserved field of action.

The last of them was scarce out of sight ere we three descended from the head of Tur and stepped out upon the temple floor behind the idol. Quickly I ran toward the altar, upon the other side of which Xaxa had dropped to the floor in a swoon. She still lay there and I gathered her into my arms and ran quickly back to the door in the wall behind the idol—the doorway through which Gor Hajus and I had entered the temple earlier in the day.

Preceded by Gor Hajus and followed by Dar Tarus, I ascended the runway toward the roof where the conversation of the priests had informed us were located the royal hangars. Had Hovan Du and Sag Or been with us my cup of happiness would have been full, for within a half a day what had seemed utter failure and defeat had been turned almost to assured success. At the landing were lay Xaxa's apartments we halted and looked within, for the long night voyage I contemplated would be cold and the body of Valla Dia must be kept warm with suitable robes even though it was inhabited by the spirit of Xaxa. Seeing no one we entered and soon found what we required. As I was adjusting a heavy robe of orluk about the Jeddara she regained consciousness. Instantly she recognized me and then Gor Hajus and finally Dar Tarus.

Mechanically she felt for her dagger, but it was not there, and when she saw my smile she paled with anger. At first she must have jumped to the conclusion that she had been the victim of a hoax, but presently a doubt seemed to enter her mind— she must have been recalling some of the things that had transpired within the temple of the Great Tur, and these, neither she nor any other mortal might explain.

"Who are you?" she demanded.

"I am Tur," I replied, brazenly.

"What is your purpose with me?"

"I am going to take you away from Phundahl," I replied.

"But I do not wish to go. You are not Tur. You are Vad Varo. I shall call for help and my guards will come and slay you."

"There is no one in the palace," I reminded her. "Did I, Tur, not send them away?"

"I shall not go with you," she announced firmly. "Rather would I die."

"You shall go with me, Xaxa," I replied, and though she fought and struggled we carried her from her apartment and up the spiral runway to the roof where, I prayed, I should find the hangars and the royal fliers; and as we stepped out into the fresh night air of Mars we did see the hangars before us, but we saw something else—a group of Phundahlian warriors of the Jeddara's Guard whom they had evidently failed to notify of the commands of Tur. At sight of them Xaxa cried aloud in relief.

"To me! To the Jeddara!" she cried. "Strike down these assassins and save me!"

There were three of them and there were three of us, but they were armed and between us we had but Xaxa's slender dagger. Gor Hajus carried that. Victory seemed turned to defeat as they rushed toward us; but it was Gor Hajus who gave them pause. He seized Xaxa and raised the blade, its point above her heart. "Halt!" he cried, "or I strike."

The warriors hesitated; Xaxa was silent, stricken with fear. Thus we stood in stalemate when, just beyond the three Phundahlian warriors, I saw a movement at the roof's edge. What was it? In the dim light I saw something that seemed a human head, and yet unhuman, rise slowly above the edge of the roof, and then, silently, a great form followed, and then I recognized it—Hovan Du, the great white ape.

"Tell them," I cried to Xaxa in a loud voice that Hovan Du might hear, "that I am Tur, for see, I come again in the semblance of a white ape!" and I pointed to Hovan Du. "I would not destroy these poor warriors. Let them lay down their weapons and go in peace."

The men turned, and seeing the great ape standing there behind them, materialized, it might have been, out of thin air, were shaken.

"Who is he, Jeddara?" demanded one of the men.

"It is Tur," replied Xaxa in a weak voice; "but save me from him! Save me from him!"

"Throw down your weapons and your harness and fly!" I commanded, "or Tur will strike you dead. Heard you not the people rushing from the palace at Tur's command? How think you we brought Xaxa hither with a lesser power than Tur's when all her palace was filled with her fighting men? Go, while yet you may in safety."

One of them unbuckled his harness and threw it with his weapons upon the roof, and as he started at a run for the spiral his companions followed his example. Then Hovan Du approached us.

"Well done, Vad Varo," he growled, "though I know not what it is all about."

"That you shall know later," I told him, "but now we must find a swift flier and be upon our way. Where is Sag Or? Does he still live?"

"I have him securely bound and safely hidden in one of the high towers of the palace," replied the ape. "It will be easy to get him when we have launched a flier."

Xaxa was eyeing us ragefully. "You are not Tur!" she cried. "The ape has exposed you."

"But too late to profit you in any way, Jeddara," I assured her. "Nor could you convince one of your people who stood in the temple this night that I am not Tur. Nor do you, yourself, know that I am not. The ways of Tur, the all-powerful, all-knowing, are beyond the conception of mortal man. To you, then Jeddara, I am Tur, and you will find me all-powerful enough for my purposes."

I think she was still perplexed as we found and dragged forth a flier, aboard which we placed her, and turned the craft's nose toward a lofty tower where Hovan Du told us lay Sag Or.

"I shall be glad to see myself again," said Dar Tarus, with a laugh.

"And you shall be yourself again, Dar Tarus," I told him, "as soon as ever we can come again to the pits of Ras Thavas."

"Would that I might be reunited with my sweet Kara Vasa," he sighed. "Then, Vad Varo, the last full measure of my gratitude would be yours."

"Where may we find her?"

"Alas, I do not know. It was while I was searching for her that I was apprehended by the agents of Xaxa. I had been to her father's palace only to learn that he had been assassinated and his property confiscated. The whereabouts of Kara Vasa they either did not know or would not divulge; but they held me there upon one pretext or another until a detachment of the Jeddara's Guard could come and arrest me."

"We shall have to make inquiries of Sag Or," I said.

We were now coming to a stop alongside a window of the tower Hovan Du had indicated, and he and Dar Tarus leaped to the sill and disappeared within. We were all armed now, having taken the weapons discarded by the three warriors at the hangars, and with a good flier beneath our feet and all our little company reunited, with Xaxa and Sag Or, whom they were now conducting aboard, we were indeed in high spirits.

As we got under way again, setting our nose toward the east, I asked Sag Or if he knew what had become of Kara Vasa, but he assured me, in surly tones, that he did not.

"Think again, Sag Or," I admonished him, "and think hard, for perhaps upon your answer your life depends."

"What chance have I for life?" he sneered, casting an ugly look toward Dar Tarus.

"You have every chance," I replied. "Your life lies in the hollow of my hand; and you serve me well it shall be yours, though in your own body and not in that belonging to Dar Tarus."

"You do not intend destroying me?"

"Neither you nor Xaxa," I answered. "Xaxa shall live on in her own body and you in yours."

"I do not wish to live in my own body," snapped the Jeddara.

Dar Tarus stood looking at Sag Or—looking at his own body like some disembodied soul—as weird a situation as I have ever encountered.

"Tell me, Sag Or," he said, "what has become of Kara Vasa. When my body has been restored to me and yours to you I shall hold no enmity against you if you have not harmed Kara Vasa and will tell me where she be."

"I cannot tell you, for I do not know. She was not harmed, but the day after you were assassinated she disappeared from Phundahl. We were positive that she was spirited away by her father, but from him we could learn nothing. Then he was assassinated," the man glanced at Xaxa, "and since, we have learned nothing. A slave told us that Kara Vasa, with some of her father's warriors, had embarked upon a flier and set out for Helium, where she purposed placing herself under the protection of the great War Lord of Barsoom; but of the truth of that we know nothing. This is the truth. I, Sag Or, have spoken!"

It was futile then to search Phundahl for Kara Vasa and so we held our course toward the east and the Tower of Thavas.

Chapter XIII

BACK TO THAVAS

All that night we sped beneath the hurtling moons of Mars, as strange a company as was ever foregathered upon any planet, I will swear. Two men, each possessing the body of the other, an old and wicked empress whose fair body belonged to a youthful damsel beloved by another of this company, a great white ape dominated by half the brain of a human being, and I, a creature of a distant planet, with Gor Hajus, the Assassin of Toonol, completed the mad roster.

I could scarce keep my eyes from the fair form and face of Xaxa, and it is well that I was thus fascinated for I caught her in the act of attempting to hurl herself overboard, so repugnant to her was the prospect of living again in her own old and hideous corpse. After that I kept her securely bound and fastened to the deck, though it hurt me to see the bonds upon those fair limbs.

Dar Tarus was almost equally fascinated by the contemplation of his own body, which he had not seen for many years.

"By my first ancestor," he ejaculated. "It must be that I was the least vain of fellows, for I give you my word I had no idea that I was so fair to look upon. I can say this now without seeming egotism, since I am speaking of Sag Or," and he laughed aloud at his little joke.

But the fact remained that the body and face of Dar Tarus were beautiful indeed, though there was a hint of steel in the eyes and the set of the jaw that betokened fighting blood. Little wonder, then, that Sag Or had coveted the body of this young warrior; for his own, which Dar Tarus now possessed, was marked by dissipation and age; nor that Dar Tarus yearned to come again into his own.

Just before dawn we dropped to one of the numerous small islands that dot the Great Toonolian Marshes and nosing the ship between the boles of great trees we came to rest upon the surface of the ground, half buried in the lush and gorgeous jungle grasses, well hidden from the sight of possible pursuers. Here Hovan Du found fruit and nuts for us which the simian section of his brain pronounced safe for human consumption, and instinct led him to a nearby spring from which there bubbled delicious water. We four were half famished and much fatigued, so that the food and water were most welcome to us; nor did Xaxa and Sag Or refuse them. Having eaten, three of us lay down upon the ship's deck to sleep, after securely chaining our prisoners, while the fourth stood watch. In this way, taking turns, we slept away most of the day and when night fell, rested and refreshed, we were ready to resume our flight.

Making a wide detour to the south we avoided Toonol and about two hours before dawn we sighted the high Tower of Thavas. I think we were all keyed up to the highest pitch of excitement, for there was not one aboard that flier but whose whole life would be seriously affected by the success or failure of our venture. As a first precaution we secured the hands of Xaxa and Sag Or behind their backs and placed gags in their mouths, lest they succeed in giving warning of our approach.

Cluros had long since set and Thuria was streaming toward the horizon as we stopped our motor and drifted without lights a mile or two south of the tower while we waited impatiently for Thuria to leave the heavens to darkness and the world to us. To the northwest the lights of Toonol shone plainly against the dark background of the sky, and there were lights too in some of the windows of the great laboratory of Ras Thavas, but the tower itself was dark from plinth to pinnacle.

And now the nearer moon dropped plummet-like beneath the horizon and left the scene to darkness and to us. Dar Tarus started the motor, the wonderful, silent motor of Barsoom, and we moved slowly, close to the ground, toward Ras Thavas' island, with no sound other than the gentle whirring of our propellor; nor could that have been heard scarce a hundred feet so slowly was it turning. Close off the island we came to a stop behind a cluster of giant trees and Hovan Du, going into the bow, uttered a few low growls. Then we stood waiting in silence, listening. There was a rustling in the dense undergrowth upon the shore. Again Hovan Dur voiced his low, grim call and this time there came an answer from the black shadows. Hovan Du spoke in the language of the great apes and the invisible creature replied.

For five minutes, during which time we were aware from the different voices that others had joined in the conversation from the shore, the apes conversed, and then Hovan Du turned to me.

"It is arranged," he said. "They will permit us to hide our ship beneath these trees and they will permit us to pass out again when we are ready and board her, nor will they harm us in any way. All they ask is that when we are through we shall leave the gate open that leads to the inner court."

"Do they understand that while an ape goes in with us none will return with us?" I asked.

"Yes; but they will not harm us."

"Why do they wish the gate left open?"

"Do not inquire too closely, Vad Varo," replied Hovan Du. "It should be enough that the great apes make it possible for you to restore Valla Dia's body to her brain and escape with her from this terrible place."

"It is enough," I replied. "When may we land?"

"At once. They will help us drag the ship beneath the trees and make her fast."

"But first we must top the wall to the inner court," I reminded him.

"Yes, true—I had forgotten that we cannot open the gate from this side."

He spoke again, then, to the apes, whom we had not yet seen; and then he told me that all was arranged and that he and Dar Tarus would return with the ship after landing us inside the wall.

Again we got under way and rising slowly above the outer wall dropped silently to the courtyard beyond. The night was unusually dark, clouds having followed Thuria and blotted out the stars after the moon had set. No one could have seen the ship at a distance of fifty feet, and we moved almost without noise. Quietly we lowered our prisoners over the side and Gor Hajus and I remained with them while Dar Tarus and Hovan Du rose again and piloted the ship back to its hiding place.

I moved at once to the gate and, unlatching it, waited. I heard nothing. Never, I think, have I endured such utter silence. There came no sound from the great pile rising behind me, nor any from the dark jungle beyond the wall. Dimly I could see the huddled forms of Gor Hajus, Xaxa and Sag Or beside me—otherwise I might have been alone in the darkness and immensity of space.

It seemed an eternity that I waited there before I heard a soft scratching on the panels of the heavy gate. I pushed it open and Dar Tarus and Hoven Du stepped silently within as I closed and relatched it. No one spoke. All had been carefully planned so that there was no need of speech. Dar Tarus and I led the way, Gor Hajus and Hovan Du brought up the rear with the prisoners. We moved directly to the entrance to the tower, found the runway and descended to the pits. Every fortune seemed with us. We met no one, we had no difficulty in finding the vault we sought, and once within we secured the door so that we had no fear of interruption—that was our first concern—and then I hastened to the spot where I had hidden Valla Dia behind the body of a large warrior, tucked far back against the wall in a dark corner. My heart stood still as I dragged aside the body of the warrior, for always had I feared that Ras Thavas, knowing my interest in her and guessing the purpose of my venture, would cause every chamber and pit to be searched and every body to be examined until he found her for whom he sought; but my fears had been baseless, for there lay the body of Xaxa, the old and wrinkled casket of the lovely brain of my beloved, where I had hidden it against this very night. Gently I lifted it out and bore it to one of the two ersite topped tables. Xaxa, standing there bound and gagged, looked on with eyes that shot hate and loathing at me and at that hideous body to which her brain was so soon to be restored.

As I lifted her to the adjoining slab she tried to wriggle from my grasp and hurl herself to the floor, but I held her and soon had strapped her securely in place. A moment later she was unconscious and the re-transference was well under way. Gor Hajus, Sag Or and Hovan Du were interested spectators, but to Dar Tarus, who stood ready to assist me, it was an old story, for he had worked in the laboratory and seen more than enough of similar operations. I will not bore you with a description of it—it was but a repetition of what I had done many times in preparation for this very event.

At last it was completed and my heart fairly stood still as I replaced the embalming fluid with Valla Dia's own life blood and saw the color mount to her cheeks and her rounded bosoms rise and fall to her gentle breathing. Then she opened her eyes and looked up into mine.

"What has happened, Vad Varo?" she asked. "Has something gone amiss that you have recalled me so soon, or did I not respond to the fluid?"

Her eyes wandered past me to the face of the others stand about. "What does it mean?" she asked. "Who are these?"

I raised her gently in my arms and pointed to the body of Xaxa lying deathlike on the ersite slab beside her. Valla Dia's eyes went wide. "It is done?" she cried, and clapped her hands to her face and felt of all her features and of the soft, delicate contours of her smooth neck; and yet she could scarce believe it and asked for a glass and I took one from Xaxa's pocket pouch and handed it to her. She looked long into it and the tears commenced to roll down her cheeks, and then she looked up at me through the mist of them and put her dear arms about my neck and drew my face down to hers. "My chieftain," she whispered—that was all. But it was enough. For those two words I had risked my life and faced unknown dangers, and gladly would I risk my life again for that same reward and always, forever.

Another night had fallen before I had completed the restoration of Dar Tarus and Hovan Du. Xaxa, and Sag Or and the great ape I left sleeping the death-like sleep of Ras Thavas's marvellous anesthetic. The great ape I had no intention of restoring, but the others I felt bound to return to Phundahl, though Dar Tarus, now resplendent in his own flesh and the gorgeous trappings of Sag Or, urged me not to inflict them again upon the long suffering Phundahlians.

"But I have given my word," I told him.

"Then they must be returned," he said.

"Though what I may do afterward is another matter," I added, for there had suddenly occurred to me a bold scheme.

I did not tell Dar Tarus what it was nor would I have had time, for at that very instant we heard someone without trying the door and then we heard voices and presently the door was tried again, this time with force. We made no noise, but just waited. I hoped that whoever it was would go away. The door was very strong and when they tried to force it they must soon have realized the futility of it because they quickly desisted and we heard their voices for only a short time thereafter and then they seemed to have gone away.

"We must leave," I said, "before they return."

Strapping the hands of Xaxa and Sag Or behind them and placing gags in their mouths I quickly restored them to life, nor ever did I see two less grateful. The looks they cast upon me might well have killed could looks do that, and with what disgust they viewed one another was writ plain in their eyes.

Cautiously unbolting the door I opened it very quietly, a naked sword in my right hand and Dar Tarus, Gor Hajus and Hovan Du ready with theirs at my shoulder, and as it swung back it revealed two standing in the corridor watching—two of Ras Thavas' slaves; and one of them was Yamdor, his body servant. At sight of us the fellow gave a loud cry of recognition and before I could leap through the doorway and prevent they had both turned and were flying up the corridor as fast as their feet would carry them.

Now there was no time to be lost—everything must be sacrificed to speed. Without thought of caution or silence we hastened through the pits toward the runway in the tower; and when we stepped into the inner court it was night again, but the farther moon was in the heavens and there were no clouds. The result was that we were instantly discovered by a sentry who gave the alarm as he ran forward to intercept us.

What was a sentry doing in the courtyard of Ras Thavas? I could not understand. And what were these? A dozen armed warriors were hurrying across the court on the heels of the sentry.

"Toonolians!" shouted Gor Hajus. "The warriors of Vobis Kan, Jeddak of Toonol!"

Breathlessly we raced for the gate. If we could but reach it first! But we were handicapped by our prisoners who held back the moment they discovered how they might embarrass us, and so it was that we all met in front of the gate. Dar Tarus and Gor Hajus and Hovan Du and I put Valla Dia and our prisoners behind us and fought the twenty warriors of Toonol with the odds of five to one against us; but we had more heart in the fight than they and perhaps that gave us an advantage, though I am sure that Gor Hajus was as ten men himself so terrible was the effect of his name alone upon the men of Toonol.

"Gor Hajus!" cried one, the first to recognize him.

"Yes, it is Gor Hajus," replied the assassin. "Prepare to meet your ancestors!" and he drove into them like a racing propeller, and I was upon his right and Hovan Du and Dar Tarus upon his left.

It was a pretty fight, but it must eventually have gone against us, so greatly were we outnumbered, had I not thought of the apes and the gate beside us. Working my way to it I threw it open and there upon the outside, attracted by the noise of the conflict, stood a full dozen of the great beasts. I called to Gor Hajus and the others to fall back beside the gate, and as the apes rushed in I pointed to the Toonolian warriors.

I think the apes were at a loss to know which were friends and which were foes, but the Toonolians apprised them by attacking them, while we stood aside with our points upon the ground. Just a moment we stood thus waiting. Then as the apes rushed among the Toonolian warriors, we slipped into the darkness of the jungle beyond the outer wall and sought our flier. Behind us we could hear the growls and the roars of the beasts mingled with the shouts and the curses of the men; and the sound still rose from the courtyard

as we clambered aboard the flier and pushed off into the night.

As soon as we felt that we were safely escaped from the Island of Thavas I removed the gags from the mouths of Xaxa and Sag Or and I can tell you that I immediately regretted it, for never in my life had I been subjected to such horrid abuse as poured from the wrinkled old lips of the Jeddara; and it was only when I started to gag her again that she promised to desist.

My plans were now well laid and they included a return to Phundahl since I could not start for Duhor with Valla Dia without provisions and fuel; nor could I obtain these elsewhere than in Phundahl since I felt that I held the key that would unlock the resources of the city to me; whereas all Toonol was in arms against us owing to Vobis Kan's fear of Gor Hajus.

So we retraced our way toward Phundahl as secretly as we had come, for I had no mind to be apprehended before we had gained entrance to the palace of Xaxa.

Again we rested over daylight upon the same island that had given us sanctuary two days before, and at dark we set out upon the last leg of our journey to Phundahl. If there had been pursuit we had seen naught of it; and that might easily be explained by the great extent of the uninhabited marshes across which we flew and the far southerly course that we followed close above the ground.

As we neared Phundahl I caused Xaxa and Sag Or to be again gagged, and further, I had their heads bandaged so that none might recognize them; and then we sailed straight over the city toward the palace, hoping that we would not be discovered and yet ready in the event that we should be.

But we came to the hangars on the roof apparently unseen and constantly I coached each upon the part he was to play. As we were settling slowly to the roof Dar Tarus, Hovan Du and Valla Dia quickly bound Gor Hajus and me and wrapped our heads in bandages, for we had seen below the figures of the hangar guard. Had we found the roof unguarded the binding of Gor Hajus and me had been unnecessary.

As we dropped nearer one of the guard hailed us. "What ship?" he cried.

"The royal flier of the Jeddara of Phundahl," replied Dar Tarus, "returning with Xaxa and Sag Or."

The warriors whispered among themselves as we dropped nearer and I must confess that I felt a bit nervous as to the outcome of our ruse; but they permitted us to land without a word and when they saw Valla Dia they saluted her after the manner of Barsoom, as, with the regal carriage of an empress, she descended from the deck of the flier.

"Carry the prisoners to my apartments!" she commanded, addressing the guard, and with the help of Hovan Du and Dar Tarus the four bound and muffled figures were carried from the flier down the spiral runway to the apartments of Xaxa, Jeddara of Phundahl. Here excited slaves hastened to do the bidding of the Jeddara. Word must have flown through the palace with the speed of light that Xaxa had returned, for almost immediately court functionaries began to arrive and be announced; but Valla Dia sent word that she would see no one for a while. Then she dismissed her slaves, and at my suggestion Dar Tarus investigated the apartments with a view to finding a safe hiding place for Gor Hajus, me, and the prisoners. This he soon found in a small antechamber directly off the main apartment of the royal suite; the bonds were removed from the assassin and myself and together we carried Xaxa and Sag Or into the room.

The entrance here was furnished with a heavy door over which there were hangings that completely hid it. I bade Hovan Du, who, like the rest of us, wore Phundahlian harness, stand guard before the hangings and let no one enter but members of our own party. Gor Hajus and I took up our positions just within the hangings through which we cut small holes that permitted us to see all that went on within the main chamber, for I was greatly concerned for Valla Dia's safety while she posed as Xaxa, whom I knew to be both feared and hated by her people and therefore always liable to assassination.

Valla Dia summoned the slaves and bade them admit the officials of the court, and as the doors opened fully a score of nobles entered. They appeared ill at ease and I could guess that they were recalling the episode in the temple when they had deserted their jeddara and even hurled her roughly at the feet of the Great Tur, but Valla Dia soon put them at their ease.

"I have summoned you," she said, "to hear the word of Tur. Tur would speak again to his people. Three days and three nights have I spent with Tur. His anger against Phundahl is great. He bids me summon all the higher nobles to the temple after the evening meal tonight, and all the priests, and the commanders and dwars of the Guard, and as many of the lesser nobles as be in the palace; and then shall the people of Phundahl hear the word and the law of Tur and all those who shall obey shall live and all those who shall not obey shall die; and woe be to him who, having been summoned, shall not be in the temple this night. I, Xaxa, Jeddara of Phundahl, have spoken! Go!"

They went and they seemed glad to go. Then Valla Dia summoned the odwar of the Guard, who would be in our world a general, and she told him to clear the palace of every living being from the temple level to the roof an hour before the evening meal, nor to permit any one to enter the temple or the levels above it until the hour appointed for the assembling in the temple to hear the word of Tur, excepting however those who might be in her own apartments, which were not to be entered upon pain of death. She made it all very clear and plain and the odwar understood and I think he trembled a trifle, for all were in great fear of the Jeddara Xaxa; and then he went away and the slaves were dismissed and we were alone.

Chapter XIV

JOHN CARTER

Half an hour before the evening meal we carried Xaxa and Sag Or down the spiral runway and placed them in the base of the Great Tur and Gor Hajus and I took our places on the upper platform behind the eyes and voice of the idol. Valla Dia, Dar Tarus and Hovan Du remained in the royal apartment. Our plans were well formulated. There was no one between the door at the rear of the Great Tur and the flier that lay ready on the roof in the event that we were forced to flee through any miscarriage of our mad scheme.

The minutes dragged slowly by and darkness fell. The time was approaching. We heard the doors of the temple open and beyond we saw the great corridor brilliantly lighted. It was empty for two priests who stood hesitating nervously in the doorway. Finally one of them mustered up sufficient courage to enter and switch on the lights.

More bravely now they advanced and prostrated themselves before the altar of the Great Tur. When they arose and looked up into the face of the idol I could not resist the temptation to turn those huge eyes until they had rolled completely about the interior of the chamber and rested again upon the priests; but I did not speak and I think the effect of the awful silence in the presence of the living god was more impressive than would words have been. The two priests simply collapsed. They slid to the floor and lay there trembling, moaning and supplicating Tur to have mercy on them, nor did they rise before the first of the worshippers arrived.

Thereafter the temple filled rapidly and I could see that the word of Tur had been well and thoroughly disseminated. They came as they had before; but there were more this time, and they ranged upon either side of the central aisle and there they waited, their eyes divided between the doorway and the god. About the time that I thought the next scene was about to be enacted I let Tur's eyes travel over the assemblage that they might be keyed to the proper pitch for what was to follow. They reacted precisely as had the priests, falling upon the floor and moaning and supplicating; and there they remained until the sounds of bugles announced the coming of the Jeddara. Then they rose unsteadily to their feet. The great doors swung open and there was the carpet and the slaves behind it. As they rolled it down toward the altar the bugles sounded louder and the head of the royal procession came into view. I had ordered it thus to permit of greater pageantry than was possible when the doors opened immediately upon the head of the procession. My plan permitted the audience to see the royal retinue advancing down the long corridor and the effect was splendid. First came the double rank of nobles and behind these the chariot drawn by the two banths, bearing the litter upon which reclined Valla Dia. Behind her walked Dar Tarus, but all within that room thought they were looking upon the Jeddara Xaxa and her favorite, Sag Or. Hovan Du walked behind Sag Or and following came the fifty young men and the fifty maidens.

The chariot halted before the altar and Valla Dia descended and knelt and the voices that had been chanting the praises of Xaxa were stilled as the beautiful creature extended her hands toward the Great Tur and looked up into his face.

"We are ready, Master!" she cried. "Speak! We await the word of Tur!"

A gasp arose from the kneeling assemblage, a gasp that ended in a sob. I felt that they were pretty well worked up and that everything ought to go off without a hitch. I placed the speaking tube to my lips.

"I am Tur!" I thundered and the people trembled. "I come to pass judgment on the men of Phundahl. As you receive my word so shall you prosper or so shall you perish. The sins of the people may be atoned by two who have sinned most in my sight." I let the eyes of Tur rove about over the audience and then brought them to rest upon Valla Dia. "Xaxa, are you ready to atone for your sins and for the sins of your people?"

Valla Dia bowed her beautiful head. "Thy will is law, Master!" she replied.

"And Sag Or," I continued, "you have sinned. Are you prepared to pay?"

"As Tur shall require," said Dar Tarus.

"Then it is my will," I boomed, "that Xaxa and Sag Or shall give back to those from whom they stole them, the beautiful bodies they now wear; that he from whom Sag Or took this body shall become Jeddak of Phundahl and High Priest of Tur; and that she from whom Xaxa stole her body shall be returned in pomp to her native country. I have spoken. Let any who would revolt against my word speak now or forever hold his peace."

There was no objection voiced. I had felt pretty certain that there would not be. I doubt if any god ever looked down upon a more subdued and chastened flock. As I had talked, Gor Hajus had descended to the base of the idol and removed the bonds from the feet and legs of Xaxa and Sag Or.

"Extinguish the lights!" I commanded. A trembling priest did my bidding.

Valla Dia and Dar Tarus were standing side by side before the altar when the lights went out. In the next minute they and Gor Hajus must have worked fast, for when I heard a low whistle from the interior of the idol's base, the prearranged signal that Gor Hajus had finished his work, and ordered the lights on again, there stood Xaxa and Sag Or where Valla Dia and Dar Tarus had been, and the latter were no where in sight. I think the dramatic effect of that transformation upon the people there was the most stupendous thing I have ever seen. There was no cord or gag upon either Xaxa or Sag Or, nothing to indicate that they had been brought hither by force—no one about who might have so brought them. The illusion was perfect—it was a gesture of omnipotence that simply staggered the intellect. But I wasn't through.

"You have heard Xaxa renounce her throne," I said, "and Sag Or submit to the judgment of Tur."

"I have not renounced my throne!" cried Xaxa. "It is all a—"

"Silence!" I thundered. "Prepare to greet the new jeddak, Dar Tarus of Phundahl!" I turned my eyes toward the great doors and the eyes of the assemblage followed mine. They swung open and there stood Dar Tarus, resplendent in the trappings of Hora San, the long dead jeddak and high priest, whose bones we had robbed in the base of the idol an hour earlier. How Dar Tarus had managed to make the change so quickly is beyond me, but he had done it and the effect was colossal. He looked every inch a jeddak as he moved with slow dignity up the wide aisle along the blue and gold and white carpet. Xaxa turned purple with rage "Imposter!" she shrieked. "Seize him! Kill him!" and she ran forward to meet him as though she would slay him with her bare hands.

"Take her away," said Dar Tarus in a quiet voice, and at that Xaxa fell foaming to the floor. She shrieked and gasped and then lay still—a wicked old woman dead of apoplexy. And when Sag Or saw her lying there he must have been the first to realize that she was dead and that there was now no one to protect him from the hatreds that are levelled always at the person of a ruler's favorite. He looked wildly about for an instant and then threw himself at the feet of Dar Tarus.

"You promised to protect me!" he cried.

"None shall harm you," replied Dar Tarus. "Go your way and live in peace." Then he turned his eyes upward toward the face of the Great Tur. "What is thy will, Master?" he cried. "Dar Tarus, thy servant, awaits thy commands!"

I permitted an impressive silence before I replied.

"Let the priests of Tur, the lesser nobles and a certain number of the Jeddak's Guard go forth into the city and spread the word of Tur among the people that they may know that Tur smiles again upon Phundahl and that they have a new jeddak who stands high in the favor of Tur. Let the higher nobles attend presently in the chambers that were Xaxa's and do honor to Valla Dia in whose perfect body their Jeddara once ruled them, and effect the necessary arrangements for her proper return to Duhor, her native city. There also will they find two who have served Tur well and these shall be accorded the hospitality and friendship of every Phundahlian—Gor Hajus of Toonol and Vad Varo of Jasoom. Go! and when the last has gone let the temple be darkened. I, Tur, have spoken!"

Valla Dia had gone directly to the apartments of the former jeddara and the moment that the lights were extinguished Gor Hajus and I joined her. She could not wait to hear the outcome of our ruse, and when I assured her that there had been no hitch the tears came to her eyes for very joy.

"You have accomplished the impossible, my chieftain," she murmured, "and already can I see the hills of Duhor and the towers of my native city. Ah, Vad Varo, I had not dreamed that life might again hold for me such happy prospects. I owe you life and more than life."

We were interrupted by the coming of Dar Tarus, and with him were Hovan Du and a number of the higher nobles. The latter received us pleasantly, though I think they were mystified as to just how we were linked with the service of their god; nor, I am sure, did one of them ever learn. They were frankly delighted to be rid of Xaxa; and while they could not understand Tur's purpose in elevating a former warrior of the Guard to the throne, yet they were content if it served to relieve them from the wrath of their god, now a very real and terrible god, since the miracles that had been performed in the temple. That Dar Tarus had been of a noble family relieved them of embarrassment, and I noted that they treated him with great respect. I was positive that they would continue to treat him so, for he was also high priest and for the first time in a hundred years he would bring to the Great Tur in the Royal Temple the voice of god, for Hovan Du had agreed to take service with Dar Tarus, and Gor Hajus as well, so that there would never be lacking a tongue wherewith Tur might speak. I foresaw great possibilities for the reign of Dar

Tarus, Jeddak of Phundahl.

At the meeting held in the apartments of Xaxa it was decided that Valla Dia should rest two days in Phundahl while a small fleet was preparing to transport her to Duhor. Dar Tarus assigned Xaxa's apartments for her use and gave her slaves from different cities to attend upon her, all of whom were to be freed and returned with Valla Dia to her native land.

It was almost dawn before we sought our sleeping silks and furs and the sun was high before we awoke. Gor Hajus and I breakfasted with Valla Dia, outside of whose door we had spread our beds that we might not leave her unprotected for a moment that it was not necessary. We had scarce finished our meal when a messenger came from Dar Tarus summoning us to the audience chamber, where we found some of the higher officers of the court gathered about the throne upon which Dar Tarus sat, looking every inch an emperor. He greeted us kindly, rising and descending from his dais to receive Valla Dia and escort her to one of the benches he had had placed beside the throne for her and for me.

"There is one," he said to me, "who has come to Phundahl over night and now begs audience of the jeddak—one whom I thought you might like to meet again," and he signed to one of his attendants to admit the petitioner; and when the doors at the opposite end of the room opened I saw Ras Thavas standing there. He did not recognize me or Valla Dia or Gor Hajus until he was almost at the foot of the throne, and when he did he looked puzzled and glanced again quickly at Dar Tarus.

"Ras Thavas of the Tower of Thavas, Toonol," announced an officer.

"What would Ras Thavas of the Jeddak of Phundahl?" asked Dar Tarus.

"I came seeking audience of Xaxa, replied Ras Thavas, "not knowing of her death or your accession until this very morning; but I see Sag Or upon Xaxa's throne and beside him one whom I thought was Xaxa, though they tell me Xaxa is dead, and another who was my assistant at Thavas and one who is the Assassin of Toonol, and I am confused, Jeddak, and do not know whether I be among friends or foes."

"Speak as though Xaxa still sat upon the throne of Phundahl," Dar Tarus told

him, "for though I am Dar Tarus, whom you wronged, and not Sag Or, yet need you have no fear in the court of Phundahl."

"Then let me tell you that Vobis Kan, Jeddak of Toonol, learning that Gor Hajus had escaped me, swore that I had set him free to assassinate him, and he sent warriors who took my island and would have imprisoned me had I not been warned in time to escape; and I came hither to Xaxa to beg her to send warriors to drive the men of Toonol from my island and restore it to me that I may carry on my scientific labors."

Dar Tarus turned to me. "Vad Varo, of all others you are most familiar with the work of Ras Thavas. Would you see him again restored to his island and his laboratory?"

"Only on condition that he devote his great skill to the amelioration of human suffering," I replied, "and no longer prostitute it to the foul purposes of greed and sin." This led to a discussion which lasted for hours, the results of which were of far reaching significance. Ras Thavas agreed to all that I required and Dar Tarus commissioned Gor Hajus to head an army against Toonol.

But these matters, while of vast interest to those most directly concerned, have no direct bearing upon the story of my adventures upon Barsoom, as I had no part in them, since upon the second day I boarded a flier with Valla Dia and, escorted by a Phundahlian fleet, set out toward Duhor. Dar Tarus accompanied us for a short distance. When the fleet was stopped at the shore of the great marsh he bade us farewell and was about to step to the deck of his own ship and return to Phundahl when a shout arose from the deck of one of the other ships and word was soon passed that a lookout had sighted what appeared to be a great fleet far to the southwest. Nor was it long before it became plainly visible to us all and equally plain that it was headed for Phundahl.

Dar Tarus told me then that as much as he regretted it, there seemed nothing to do but return at once to his capital with the entire fleet, since he could not spare a single ship or man if this proved an enemy fleet, nor could Valla Dia or I interpose any objection; and so we turned about and sped as rapidly as the slow ships of Phundahl permitted back toward the city.

The stranger fleet had sighted us at

about the same time that we had sighted it, and we saw it change its course and bear down upon us; and as it came nearer it fell into single file and prepared to encircle us. I was standing at Dar Tarus' side when the colors of the approaching fleet became distinguishable and we first learned that it was from Helium.

"Signal and ask if they come in peace," directed Dar Tarus.

"We seek word with Xaxa, Jeddara of Phundahl," came the reply. "The question of peace or war will be hers to decide."

"Tell them that Xaxa is dead and that I, Dar Tarus, Jeddak of Phundahl, will receive the commander of Helium's fleet in peace upon the deck of this ship, or that I will receive him in war with all my guns. I, Dar Tarus, have spoken!"

From the bow of a great ship of Helium there broke the flag of truce and when Dar Tarus' ship answered it in kind the other drew near and presently we could see the men of Helium upon her decks. Slowly the great flier came alongside our smaller ship and when the two had been made fast a party of officers boarded us. They were fine looking men, and at their head was one whom I recognized immediately though I never before had laid eyes upon him. I think he was the most impressive figure I have ever seen as he advanced slowly across the deck toward us—John Carter, Prince of Helium, Warlord of Barsoom.

"Dar Tarus," he said, "John Carter greets you and in peace, though it had been different, I think, had Xaxa still reigned."

"You came to war upon Xaxa?" asked Dar Tarus.

"We came to right a wrong," replied the Warlord. "But from what we know of Xaxa that could have been done only by force."

"What wrong has Phundahl done Helium?" demanded Dar Tarus.

"The wrong was against one of your own people—even against you in person."

"I do not understand," said Dar Tarus.

"There is one aboard my ship who may be able to explain to you, Dar Tarus," replied John Carter, with a smile. He turned and spoke to one of his aides in a whisper, and the man saluted and returned to the deck of his own ship. "You shall see with your own eyes, Dar Tarus." Suddenly his eyes narrowed. "This is indeed Dar Tarus who was a warrior of the Jeddara's Guard and supposedly assassinated by her command?"

"It is," replied Dar Tarus.

I must be certain," said the Warlord.

"There is no question about it, John Carter," I spoke up in English.

His eyes went wide, and when they fell upon me and he noted my lighter skin, from which the dye was wearing away, he stepped forward and held out his hand.

"A countryman?" he asked.

"Yes, an American," I replied.

"I was almost surprised," he said. "Yet why should I be? I have crossed—there is no reason why others should not. And you have accomplished it! You must come to Helium with me and tell me all about it."

Further conversation was interrupted by the return of the aide, who brought a young woman with him. At sight of her Dar Tarus uttered a cry of joy and sprang forward, and I did not need to be told that this was Kara Vasa.

There is little more to tell that might not bore you in telling—of how John Carter himself took Valla Dia and me to Duhor after attending the nuptials of Dar Tarus and Kara Vasa; and of the great surprise that awaited me in Duhor, where I learned for the first time that Kor San, Jeddak of Duhor, was the father of Valla Dia; and of the honors and the great riches that he heaped upon me when Valla Dia and I were wed.

John Carter was present at the wedding and we initiated upon Barsoom a good old American custom, for the Warlord acted as best man; and then he insisted that we follow that up with a honeymoon and bore us off to Helium, where I am writing this.

Even now it seems like a dream that I can look out of my window and see the scarlet and the yellow towers of the twin cities of Helium; that I have met, and see daily, Cathoris, Thuvia of Ptarth, Tara of Helium, Gahan of Gathol and that peerless creature, Dejah Thoris, Princess of Mars. Though to me, beautiful as she is, there is another even more beautiful—Valla Dia, Princess of Duhor—Mrs. Ulysses Paxton.

THE END